EARTH

EARTH

THE setting is La Beauce, rich wheat-growing plainland of France, on the eve of the 1870 war. The theme is the land, and the peasants' passion for it; their obsessing greed destroys all humanity in them. Fouan, a peasant-proprietor grown too old to farm, divides his property—like Lear, with no Cordelia—among his three children. He lives with each in turn, and is victimised by each —finally, horribly martyred by his youngest son. Interwoven with the Fouan story is that of Jean Macquart, decent artisan turned countryman, whose patient wooing of young Françoise Fouan involves him in the tragedy. Zola's story is realism at its starkest, redeemed by deep social significance and imaginative power.

EARTH

ÉMILE ZOLA

Preface by
ANGUS WILSON

ELEK BOOKS
GREAT JAMES STREET LONDON

Published 1954 by
Elek Books Limited
14 Great James Street
London, W.C.1
Copyright

2nd impression October 1954
3rd impression March 1955
4th impression September 1956
5th impression July 1958

Translated from the French by
ANN LINDSAY

Printed in Great Britain by
Clarke, Doble & Brendon Ltd
Oakfield Press, Plymouth

PREFACE

THE publication of Zola's *La Terre* in a good and complete English translation available to the general reading public is a literary event of first rate importance. There may be question about the exact place of Emile Zola among the great novelists of the nineteenth century; there can be no question about his being among them. *La Terre* is the culmination of his genius. It seems almost incredible that so tremendous a work, the final and overwhelming confluence of the two great nineteenth century rivers of romanticism and social realism, should have been withheld from the main body of English readers for nearly seventy years. The answer is at once very simple and very English. *La Terre* was the victim of one of those periodic and distasteful exhibitions of moral indignation which still unfortunately besmirch the good sense and rational decency of this country.

Since the publication of this new translation is a satisfactory if belated vindication of those, not least Zola himself, who were the victims of that unsavoury demonstration of Anglo Saxon self-righteousness, it may not be amiss to mention shortly the circumstances which attended the original attempt to publish *La Terre* in translation. The episode may perhaps illustrate the absurdities which inevitably attend the judgment of great works of art by an irrelevant censorship based upon an uninstructed and purely fragmentary reading of them. What makes the incident so instructive, perhaps, is the fact that the first reactions to *La Terre* in France and in England were largely the same, the results of those reactions so dismally different.

La Terre first appeared in serial form in France in 1886. Zola had already placed most of the idols of French *bourgeois* society under the strange magnifying glass of his personal vision. He had, like all great geniuses, a diseased vision which somehow saw a greater truth than all the healthy, ordinary people around him. Everything that came beneath his gaze was at once more detailed, more logical, blacker and fiercer than it appeared to other men. It was patently distorted and yet it was also monstrously and frighteningly true. Family life in the middle class world was not, of course, all adultery. The poor were not wholly sunk in a deadening round of drunkenness and fornication. Not all cocottes were like Nana possessed with greed for money, not all financiers swept along by insane schemes of

5

speculation like Aristide Saccard. Yet there was in all these pictures a truth that gave the lie to the rosy legends on which nineteenth century society fed its ease and self satisfaction. In turn, his books exposed the myths of the 'sanctity of the home', 'the happy thrift of the very poor', the 'good heartedness of tarts', and the 'integrity of finance'. Now with *La Terre* he hit and hit with all his force at the most cherished of all French *bourgeois* illusions—'the simple goodness of the peasants'. It was not surprising that there was a great outcry. Five younger and ambitious authors, almost certainly with the complicity of Zola's jealous contemporary lions Alphonse Dauder and Edmond de Goncourt, published a manifesto in the daily press against the new novel and hinted that Zola's preoccupation with sex was due to personal impotence. Even Anatole France, usually so admiring of Zola's work, condemned it roundly. Not a little of this outcry was due as Maupassant pointed out to Zola, to the serial method of publication which did not allow the work to be judged as a whole. It was just this piecemeal method that the English jury were to use in condemning the work two years later, but they had the whole book before them to read. Despite much indignation, however, *La Terre* was soon recognised in France as one of the master's most important novels. So dissimilar a writer as Mallarmé praised it highly. It was read by thousands and has continued to be so ever since.

Very different was the fate that attended the English translation which appeared in 1888. Published by the original and enterprising firm of Vizetelly, father and son, it was soon attacked by W. T. Stead, the watchdog of public morality, in the *Pall Mall Gazette*. The National Vigilance Association took up the cry. Although a motion was put forward in the House of Commons, the Government was unwilling to pursue the matter; a private prosecution, however, followed. Sir Edward Clarke had only to read the passage about the mating of the bull, for the horrified jury to request to hear no more. Vizetelly was fined £100 and *La Terre* in other than mangled form was removed from the gaze of almost all readers of the English language until 1954. Almost but not quite all, for in the last decade of the nineteenth century the Lutetian Society issued translations of Zola's major works for strictly limited circulation. Those critics, and there are still many cultivated people among them, who still regard Zola as a writer of dead social realism, of blue books in fictional form, should note that the translator of *La Terre* was the poet Ernest Dowson.

Enough, however, has been said by way of cautionary tale about the sensational views taken of *La Terre*. Zola was a sensualist and a puritan. It is not really surprising that so many Englishmen should have found such a combination so difficult to accept, for it is pre-eminently our national character, though it is seldom admitted so. What sort of a book was this novel which so deeply disturbed many of its readers?

La Terre, as its title implies, is the epic of land hunger and land lust. The Fouans, the peasant family in the plain of the Beauce around Chartres, live, think and love only in terms of the land they possess. For it they marry and cheat and murder, and in its back-breaking cultivation they are themselves worn down and destroyed. They crawl and labour over the plain like ants, and in a single night a hailstorm can make nonsense of all their self-denials and cruelties and dedication. With few exceptions, they are obstinate, cunning and brutal, yet there is not one, not even that most perfectly 'wicked' of nineteenth century fictional characters Buteau, who has not some strange quality of humanity, of potential 'goodness' that makes them the object of pity as well as of horror.

The plot of the book is a simple one—the Lear theme of a father who divides his inheritance and is hounded to death by his children for the small savings that his peasant cunning has urged him to keep upon his person. But the very simplicity of theme allowed Zola as in no other of his works to develop all his gifts to the full. In no other novel are there so many over-life-sized, utterly convincing characters; the Fouan father, dogged, suspicious, worn out by work, still occasionally bursting forth with a parody of his once terrible patriarchal rage, receiving from his children only the treatment he had given to his father, yet like all men not really believing it could happen to *him*; La Grande, his sister, the ninety year old woman with her stick and her look that alone secures obedience, far too hard and fierce to make her brother's mistake of believing in the mercy of her kin; Hyacinthe, the eldest son, called Jésus-Christ, the *Je m'en foutiste*, ex-soldier tramp, who alone cares more for what money can buy than for gold, hated by the village for his blas-phemous attitude to possession, yet somehow respected like a holy clown for his mockery of all that is sacred; Buteau, the youngest son, with so much that is easy-going and so much that more imag-inative turning eventually out of fear and distrust into the most brutal and insane of all the land worshippers—these are all master-pieces of horror. But, perhaps, the greatest triumph of all lies in

Françoise, the young heroine. From the moment in the first chapter when, at fourteen years, she helps the bull to mate, she remains, unlike any nineteenth century heroine, simple, dignified, gentle, yet never for one minute taken out of the context of the coarseness and lustfulness of her background.

There is, indeed, in this novel as in few of Zola's other works a blending of violence and lyricism that is masterly. The drama, the imagery, the evocation of atmospheres one expects to be good, for they were Zola's stock-in-trade, but in *La Terre* we find excellence in a quality not usually associated with his work. Dr. Hemmings in his recent excellent study has rightly emphasised the importance of humour in *La Terre*. In *L'Assomoir* he had already proved his powers in that irony of the grotesque more usually associated with Dickens or Flaubert. In *La Terre* his irony excels—the peasants gathered around listening to a reading of a Napoleonic propaganda leaflet about the nobility of peasant life and wondering where this Utopia exists—'*si tu as la paix du coeur*' say the pamphlets, '*ta fortune est faite*', '*l'argent seul est bon*', their hearts reply; the whole story of the *petit propriétaise* M. Charles with his wealth derived from the brothel in Chartres and his genteel, convent trained, bon-bon fed granddaughter only too ready to run the family business on more modern lines—these are Zola at his funniest. But there is another vein of humour in *La Terre* which I do not think can be found in any nineteenth century writer. Rabelaisian humour is often too self-conscious, too self-satisfiedly earthy to please, but the famous farting scene in which Jésus-Christ drives away the inspector from his hovel is as successful as it is unique.

The reputation of Zola so long at an ebb in England cannot but profit from this excellent translation of his greatest, his most 'Zolaesque' novel.

ANGUS WILSON

8

FIRST PART

I

THAT morning, Jean was in the fields, holding open with his left hand a blue canvas seedbag knotted round his waist; with his right he brought out a fistful of corn and scattered it broadcast with a single flick of the wrist, every three steps. As he swung rhythmically along, his heavy clogs sank in the rich soil and came away thickly-caked. And at each throw, through the ceaselessly flying golden grain, gleamed the two red stripes on the sleeve of the army jacket he was wearing out. He strode on in solitary grandeur; and a harrow slowly followed, burying the seeds. Two horses, whom the waggoner urged on with long regular whipcracks over the ears, were harnessed to the harrow.

The strip of land, scarcely an acre and a quarter in size, lay at the spot known as Les Cornailles, and was so insignificant that M. Hourdequin, proprietor of La Borderie, had not bothered to send down the drill, which anyway was busy elsewhere. Jean, travelling over the field due north, was directly facing towards the farm-buildings about a mile and a quarter away. At the end of the furrow, he raised his eyes and stared blankly, pausing to recover his breath.

In front were the low farm-walls, a brown patch of old slates, stranded on the edge of the plain of La Beauce which stretched as far as Chartres. Under the enormous sky, an overcast sky of late October, the ten leagues of arable land at this time of the year were broken into great ploughed squares of bare rich yellow earth alternating with green expanses of lucerne and clover—the whole scene, without a single hillock, without a single tree, blurring away and sinking down to a horizon-line as clear and rounded as at sea. Only towards the west a little wood fringed the sky with a reddish band. In the centre the road from Châteaudun to Orléans, white as chalk, ran straight on for four leagues, stringing out along its course the geometric progression of telegraph poles. And that was all, except for three or four wooden mills on log bases with unmoving sails. Villages formed little islands of stone, a steeple stuck up out of a dip in the earth some way off, with the church itself out of sight among the gentle undulations of this land of corn.

9

Jean turned round, and went swinging off again due south, holding the seedbag in his left hand and slashing out an unceasing scatter of grain from his right. Facing him, quite close, he had the narrow valley of the Aigre, which cut like a ditch across the plain; beyond it La Beauce stretched in its vastness right to Orléans. The only sign of meadows and shady spots was a row of tall poplars whose yellowish tips lifted up out of the hollow, just clearing its rim and looking like low bushes. Of the village of Rognes, built on the slope, only a few housetops were visible beside the church, which raised high its steeple of grey stone, the home of ancient families of crows. And eastward, past the valley of the Loir, where two leagues away nestled Cloyes, the canton's chief town, the distant hills of Le Perche were etched violet-tinged under the slate-grey light. Between Le Perche and La Beauce, on the very edge of La Beauce, in the area where the less fertile soil has won the name of Beauce the Lousy, stands the ancient Dunois, nowadays the District of Châteaudun. When Jean reached the field's end he stopped again, glanced down along the stream of the Aigre, glistening and rippling through the meadow-grasses and running alongside the Cloyes road which, that Saturday, was streaked with the tracks of peasants' carts on their way to market. Then he turned up and back.

And all the while, at the same pace with the same gesture, he went northward and then back southward, wrapped in the living dust-cloud of grain; while, behind him, the harrow, under the crack of the whip, buried the seeds with the same gentle, seemingly meditative movement. Constant rains had held up the autumn sowing; manuring had only been finished in August, and the plough-lands had long been ready, dug deep and cleared of clinging weeds, good for a fresh yield of corn after the clover and oats of the three-year crop rotation. And so the farmers were hurried on by fear of the frosts which threatened after the long rains. The weather had suddenly turned cold with sooty-coloured skies and not a breath of wind, with a drab level light spreading over the motionless sea of earth. On every side men were sowing. On the left, three hundred yards away, a second sower was at work; further along on the right, a third; and more and more, one opposite the other, were lost in the receding vista of flat fields. They showed up as little black silhouettes, mere strokes that dwindled till they faded out in the leagues of distance. Each man made the same gesture, the swing of broadcast grain, which seemed an enveloping wave of life. The plain itself took up the tremulous motion, right away into the drowned distance, where the scattered sowers disappeared from sight.

Jean was going down for the last time when he noticed a big red-and-white cow coming from Rognes. A young girl, scarcely more than a child, was leading it by a halter. The small peasant girl and the animal were following the path that bordered the valley at the plateau edge; and Jean had turned his back, gone up the field and completed his last furrow, when a noise of running, mingled with stifled cries, made him lift his head again at the moment of taking up his seedbag ready to leave. The cow was galloping head-long over a field of lucerne, with the exhausted girl behind her desperately trying to stop her. Afraid that there'd be an accident, he shouted, 'Hey there! Let go!'

The girl took no notice. She panted and abused the cow in tones of anger and fear. 'La Coliche! Stop it, will you? La Coliche! You dirty brute! You damned bitch!'

So far, running and jumping as well as her short legs would let her, she had managed to keep up. But now she tripped, fell once, got to her feet, and fell again a little further on. Then, as the beast grew more frenzied, she was dragged along and began screaming. Her body left a furrow through the lucerne.

'Let go, damn it all!' Jean kept shouting. 'Let go, I say!'

He was shouting mechanically in his fear; for he too was running, realising at last what was wrong: the halter was knotted round the girl's wrist, tightening with every fresh pull. Fortunately, cutting across a ploughed field, he arrived so abruptly in front of the cow that the stupid creature, terrified, stopped dead. He at once untied the halter and sat the girl up on the grass.

'Anything broken?'

But she hadn't even fainted. She rose to her feet, felt herself, calmly lifted her skirt up to her thighs, to have a look at her smarting knees, still so breathless that she couldn't speak.

'There, that's where it stings, there . . . All the same, I can move, there's nothing serious. Oh, I was so scared! I was getting cut to pieces on the road!'

And, examining her strained wrist, encircled with red, she wet it with her spit and put her lips hard against it; then, quite relieved and recovered, she added with a deep sigh, 'La Coliche isn't vicious, you know, but ever since this morning she's had us all on edge—she's on heat. I'm taking her to the bull at La Borderie.'

11

'La Borderie?' repeated Jean. 'That's fine. I'm going back there, so I'll go with you.'

He went on addressing her familiarly, treating her like a bit of a girl, she was so slight for all her fourteen years. And she, with her chin in the air, was gravely considering this big nutbrown lad with his cropped hair, full-faced with regular features, whose twenty-nine years made him an old man in her eyes.

'Ah, yes, I know you, you're Corporal, the carpenter who stayed on as farm-hand at Monsieur Hourdequin's.'

Hearing the nickname the peasants had given him, the young man smiled; and in his turn he looked at her, surprised to find her almost a woman with her small firm breasts, oval-faced with deep black eyes and full lips as fresh and rosy as ripening fruit. She was dressed in a grey skirt and a black woollen bodice, with a round cap on her head, and her skin was very brown, tanned and gilded by the sun.

'And you're Old Mouche's youngest girl,' he cried, 'I didn't recognise you. That so, isn't it? Your sister was Buteau's sweetheart last spring, when he was working with me at La Borderie.'

She replied simply, 'Yes, I'm Françoise. My sister Lise went round with cousin Buteau, and now she's six months gone. . . . He skipped off, he's down Orgères way now, at La Chamade farm.'

'That's it,' Jean agreed. 'I've seen them together.'

And they stood there silent a moment, face to face, he smiling at what he'd seen when he surprised the two lovers behind a rick, she still licking her bruised wrist as if the moisture of her lips soothed the smart away. Meanwhile, in a neighbouring field, the cow was quietly tearing up tufts of lucerne. The waggoner with the harrow had gone off by a roundabout way to the road. The cawing of the two crows wheeling round and round the church-steeple could be heard, and the three strokes of the Angelus clanged through the life-less air.

'What! Midday already!' exclaimed Jean. 'We'd better get a move on.'

Then, noticing La Coliche in the field, he said, 'Look, your cow's doing some damage. If anyone saw her . . . . Just wait, you old bitch, I'll give you lucerne.'

'No, let her alone,' Françoise interrupted him. 'That belongs to us, that plot. The trollop, she brought me down on my bottom in our own land. Our family owns the whole side as far as Rognes. We reach right from here to over there. The next lot belongs to Uncle Fouan. Then, beyond that, the land belongs to my aunt, La Grande.'

While she was pointing out the lots, she led the cow back to the pathway. And it was only then, as she once more held the halter in her hand, that she thought of thanking the young man.

'Anyway, I ought to be very grateful to you. And I do thank you, thank you from the bottom of my heart.'

They had begun walking, taking the narrow road that skirted the valley before losing itself in the fields. The last peal of the Angelus had just died away, and only the cawing of the crows was heard. And behind the cow, which tugged at the halter, the pair moved on without further conversation, sunk back into the silence of peasants who can tramp on together, league after league, without exchanging a word. They glanced at the drill drawn by horses, that passed close by on the right; the ploughman shouted 'Goodday!' and they answered 'Good-day', in the same solemn tone. Down the hill on their left, traps went driving in a continual line along the road to Cloyes; the market didn't open till one o'clock. They jolted heavily on their two wheels, looking like grasshoppers, so dwarfed by distance that only the white specks of the women's caps stood separately out.

'Uncle Fouan and Aunt Rose are down there, they're going to see the notary,' said Françoise, her eyes fixed on a vehicle the size of a nutshell, racing along about a mile away. She had a sailor's long sight, as is common among plains-folk trained to catch details and recognise man or beast in the tiny hurrying spot of a silhouette.

'Ah, yes, I heard about that,' Jean answered. 'So it's decided, eh? The old man is dividing his property up between his daughter and his two sons?'

'Yes, it's decided, they're all meeting to-day at Monsieur Baillehache's place.'

She kept her eyes on the speeding trap.

'As for the rest of us, we don't give a rap, none of us will get any fatter or thinner through it. . . . Except for that Buteau. My sister thinks he might marry her when he gets his share.'

Jean began laughing. 'That fellow Buteau! Used to be a friend of mine. He gets away with it, telling tales to the girls. But he can't do without them, though. He treats 'em rough if he can't get 'em by kindness.'

'He's a swine, that's all there is to it,' declared Françoise in a decided voice. 'It's not right to play such a dirty trick on your

13

cousin and leave her in the family way.' And then sharply, in a fit
of anger, she called, 'La Coliche! You wait, I'll make you skip.
There she is, at it again. She's crazy, she is, when she gets this way.'

With a furious jerk, she pulled the cow back. At this point the
road ceased skirting the plateau. The traps disappeared, and the
two of them went walking along flat ground, with nothing visible
right or left but an endless stretch of cultivated fields. Between the
ploughlands and the artificial meadows, the path went on dead flat,
without a single bush, to end at the farm which looked near enough
to be touched, yet kept receding under the ashen sky. The pair
relapsed into silence, never once opening their lips, as if overwhelmed by the contemplative gravity of La Beauce, so mournful
and so fecund.

On arrival they found that La Borderie's big square yard, closed
in on three sides by cowshed, sheepcotes and barns, was deserted.
But straightaway at the kitchen door appeared a young woman,
short in stature, with a bold attractive look.

'What's up, Jean—not eating this morning?'

'I'm just going to, Madame Jacqueline.'

Since the daughter of Cognet, road-mender of Rognes, who used
to be called La Cognette when she was dishwasher at the farm at
the age of twelve, had risen to the rank of her master's mistress, she
had turned despotic and insisted on being treated like a lady.

'Ah, it's you, Françoise,' she went on. 'Come for the bull. . . Well,
you'll have to wait. The cowman's at Cloyes with Monsieur Hourdequin. But he'll be back, he ought to be here now.' Then, as Jean
turned to enter the kitchen, she caught him round the waist, pressing herself up against him with a laughing air, without bothering
about being seen, greedy for love and not satisfied with the master.

Françoise, left alone, patiently waited, sitting on a stone bench
facing the manure pit which took up a third of the yard. Without
a thought in her head she watched a band of fowls pecking away
and warming their feet on the broad low bed of manure which was
steaming in the cool air with a thin bluish vapour. An hour and a
half later, when Jean came out again, finishing off a slice of bread
and butter, she hadn't stirred an inch. He sat down beside her, and
as the cow fidgetted, swinging her tail and lowing, he said at last,
'It's a nuisance the cowman isn't back.'

The young girl shrugged her shoulders. She wasn't in a hurry.
Then, after another silence, she remarked, 'So, Corporal, you're
called Jean, just Jean, eh?'

'Why, no. I'm Jean Macquart.'

'And you don't come from these parts?'

'No, I'm a Provençal, from Plassans, a town down south.'

She raised her eyes to study him, surprised that people could come from so far away.

'After Solférino,' he went on, 'eighteen months ago, I came back from Italy, discharged, and another soldier brought me along this way. Then, the way it worked out, my old trade of carpentering didn't suit me any longer, and one thing and another led me to stay on at the farm.'

'Ah,' she said simply, without taking her big black eyes from his face.

But at that moment La Coliche sent out a long despairing low of desire, and a hoarse snort replied from the cowshed, through the closed door.

'There now,' cried Jean. 'César, the old devil, heard her. Listen, he's talking away in there. Oh, he knows his business all right, you can't bring one of 'em into the yard without him knowing what he's wanted for. . . .' Then, interrupting himself, he went on, 'The cowman must have stayed with Monsieur Hourdequin. I'll bring out the bull for you, if you like. We could manage the job between us.'

'Oh, yes, that's a good idea,' said Françoise, rising.

As he opened the cowshed door, he asked her, 'Does your beast have to be tied up?'

'Tied up? Oh, no, it's not worth the trouble. She's quite ready. She won't budge.'

As the door opened, the thirty farm cows could be seen in two rows with a path along the middle separating them. Some were lying down in their litter, others were crunching the beets in their mangers; and one of the bulls, a black Friesian with white patches, stretched out his neck, in anticipation of his task, from the corner where he was tied.

As soon as he was loose, César came slowly out. But he suddenly stopped as if taken aback by the fresh air and daylight, and stayed a moment motionless, bracing himself on his legs, with his tail nervously flicking, his neck swollen, his muzzle outstretched to sniff. La Coliche, without moving, turned her large blank eyes towards him, lowing more gently. Then he came on, rubbed against her, laid his head on her rump with an abrupt rough pressure; his tongue was lolling out, and he pushed her tail aside with it and licked her down to the thighs. The cow, letting him have his way, still made no movement, except that her skin wrinkled all over with a quick quivering. Jean and Françoise watched with serious faces, their hands hanging loosely at their sides.

And when he was ready, César mounted La Coliche, in a sudden jump, with such heavy force that he shook the ground. She didn't give and he gripped her flanks with his forelegs. But she, a well-built creature from the Cotentin, was so tall and broad that he, of a smaller breed, couldn't manage. He knew what was wrong, tried to get further up, and failed.

'He's too small,' said Françoise.

'A bit,' replied Jean, 'doesn't matter, he'll get in all the same.'

She shook her head; and seeing that César was still fumbling about and getting exhausted, she made up her mind. 'No, he'll have to be helped. If he doesn't get properly in, it'll be sheer loss. She won't hold it.'

With a calm and watchful expression, as if undertaking an important task, she had drawn nearer. Her intense concentration deepened the black of her eyes and parted the red lips in her immobile face. There was nothing for it: she lifted her hand in a sweeping gesture, grasped the bull's member full in her hand and raised it up. And the bull, feeling himself on the edge of achievement, with vigour restored, went right in with a single lunge of his loins, deep. Then he withdrew. The job was done; the thrust of the dibble that buries the seed. Stolid, with the empressive fertility of earth which is sown with seed, the cow had absorbed the fecundating jet of the male without a stir. She had not even trembled at the shock. And he was already down, shaking the ground under him once more.

Françoise, after letting go, kept her arm lifted. But now at last she let it drop, and said, 'Well, that's that.'

'A good job,' Jean answered with an air of conviction, with the good worker's satisfaction at work well and speedily completed. He never thought of making one of the lewd jokes that the farm boys bandied about with the girls who brought their cows to be served by the bull. This bit of a girl seemed to find it all so simple and necessary that in all honesty there was nothing to laugh about. It was nature.

But during the last few moments Jacqueline had come out again on the doorstep, and with a characteristic gurgle, she cried out gaily, 'Ah, you're a handy girl for a tight corner. Got a lover that doesn't know his way about?'

16

Jean gave a roar of laughter and Françoise suddenly flushed a deep red. Embarrassed and trying to hide her confusion, while César went back of his own accord to the cowshed and La Coliche munched a stalk of oats sprouting from the manure pit, she searched through her pockets, at last got out her handkerchief and untied a knot at one corner, in which she had fastened the forty sous service-fee.

'There you are! There's the money,' she said. 'And good day to you.'

She set off with her cow, and Jean, who had slung his seedbag again, followed her, telling Jacqueline that he was off for the Poteau field according to M. Hourdequin's orders for the day.

'Right,' she replied. 'The harrow should be there.'

Then as the young fellow rejoined the peasant girl and they moved one behind the other down the narrow path, she shouted after them in her bawdy bantering tones, 'No danger of you getting lost together, is there? The girl can guide you if you miss your way.'

Behind them the farmyard grew deserted again. This time neither laughed. They walked slowly and the only noise was the clattering of their shoes on the stones. The young man could see only the nape of the girl's childlike neck over which fell little black curls from under the round cap. Then, after some fifty paces, 'She's not the one to chaff others about men,' said Françoise sedately. 'I could have said something back——' And, turning towards the young man and giving him a sly stare, 'It's true, isn't it, she plays tricks on Monsieur Hourdequin just as if they were married already? You know quite a lot about that, I suppose, eh?'

He was put out and assumed a stupid expression. 'Well, she does what she likes, it's her look-out.'

Françoise had turned her back and walked on. 'That's true enough. I was only joking, because you're more than old enough to be my father, and it doesn't matter anyway. . . . But you see, since Buteau played such a dirty trick on my sister, I've taken an oath to cut myself in four pieces before I let anyone get hold of me.'

Jean lowered his head, and they fell silent. The little Poteau field lay at the end of the path, halfway to Rognes. On reaching it, the young man stopped. The harrow was waiting and a sack of grain had been unloaded in a furrow. He filled his bag from it, saying, 'Good-bye, then.'

'Good-bye,' said Françoise. 'Thanks again.'

17

But he was struck with a sudden apprehension and straightened up again.

'I say, what if La Coliche starts again?' he called. 'Would you like me to see you home?'

Already some way off, she turned and raised her calm strong voice across the vast silence of the countryside. 'No, no. There's no need, no danger now. She's had a bellyfull.'

Jean, with seedbag tied around his waist, had begun to move down the patch of ploughed field, flinging out the grain with the same continuous movement of his arm. He lifted his eyes and watched Françoise grow smaller and smaller among the fields, all the smaller behind her lazy cow, who swayed her big body from side to side. As he turned up again, he ceased to see her, but as he came back, there she was again, even smaller, so slight indeed that she looked like a dandelion with her slender figure and white cap. Three times he saw her dwindling in this way; but when he glanced for her the fourth time, she must have turned down in front of the church.

Two o'clock struck, and still the sky was grey, heavy, frosty. It seemed as if shovelfuls of fine ash had buried the sun for long months, till springtime. Amid the dreariness a lighter patch glistened through the clouds, as if over there the sun were shining, somewhere, leagues away. It was against this pale ragged patch that the Rognes church-tower stood out, while the village sloped away, hidden in the unseen fold of the Aigre valley. But, over towards Chartres, northward, the level line of the horizon separated the clay-coloured uniformity of the vast heavens and the limitless expanse of La Beauce like a neat ink-stroke cutting across a monochrome sketch. Since the midday meal the number of sowers seemed to have grown. Now each strip of the little farmlands had its own sower. The men multiplied, swarmed like black toiling ants brought up out of the earth by some huge task, throwing themselves into a mighty under-taking gigantic in comparison with their tininess. And still, even in the furthest sower, the eye could make out the obstinate gesture which never varied: an insect stubbornness struggling with the immensity of the soil and ultimately victor over space and life.

Till nightfall Jean sowed. After the Poteau field came the Rigoles and the Quatre-Chemins. He went up and down the ploughlands with long regular steps; and the grain in his seedbag dwindled, the seeds behind him fertilised the earth.

II

MAITRE BAILLEHACHE, notary of Cloyes, lived on the left-hand side of the Rue Grouaise, on the way to Châteaudun, in a small white one-storey house; from a corner hung the solitary street-lamp that lit up the wide paved street, deserted during the week but loud and lively on Saturdays with the influx of peasants on their way to market. The two professional plates were visible from afar, shining against the chalky surface of the low buildings; behind the house, a narrow garden ran right down to the bank of the Loir.

On this particular Saturday, in the room to the right of the entrance hall, overlooking the street, the under-clerk, a pale puny lad of fifteen, had lifted one of the muslin curtains to watch the people passing. The other two clerks, an old man, pot-bellied and dirty, and a younger man, emaciated, ravaged with liver-trouble, were busy writing at a double desk of ebonised deal, the only piece of furniture in the room except for seven or eight chairs and a cast-iron stove which was never lighted until December, even if snow fell on All Saints' Day. The pigeon-holes covering the walls, the greenish cardboard boxes, broken at the corners and bursting with yellowed papers, fouled the atmosphere of the room with a smell of sour ink and dust-eaten papers.

Meanwhile, two peasants, a man and a woman, seated side by side, were waiting, patient and rigid, in respectful awe. The piles of papers, and particularly the gentlemen writing so fast, the pens crackling away together, put them in a meditative mood and set off trains of thought concerned with money and litigation. The woman, thirty-four years old, dark-haired, her pleasant face marred by a large nose, had folded her dried-up working-woman's hands over her black velvet-edged jacket; her sharp eyes pried into every corner, obviously dreaming of all the valuable securities nestling there; the man, five years older, sandy-haired and placid, dressed in black trousers and a long brand-new blue blouse, held his round felt hat on his knees; and not even the shadow of a thought animated his large earth-red face, clean-shaven, with big china-blue eyes staring into vacancy like those of a drowsy ox.

A door opened and Maître Baillehache, who had just lunched with his brother-in-law, the farmer Hourdequin, appeared; he was fresh-faced and high-coloured, despite his fifty-five years, with thick lips, drooping eyelids, and crow's-feet at the corners of his eyes which gave him a constantly laughing expression. He carried a double eye-glass and had an unconscious mannerism of continually plucking at his long grey side-whiskers.

'Ah! it's you, Delhomme!' he cried. 'So Old Fouan has decided on the division?'

The woman was the one to reply. 'That's right, Monsieur Baillehache. We're all to meet here and reach agreement, and get you to tell us how to do things.'

'Good, Fanny, good, we'll see. . . . It's hardly one o'clock yet, we must wait for the others.'

The notary chatted a moment longer, discussing the price of wheat, which had fallen during the past two months, and showing Delhomme the friendly respect due to a farmer who owned some fifty acres, a servant and three cows. Then he returned to his inner office.

The clerks, without raising their heads, had scratched away exaggeratedly with their pens; and now once again the Delhommes waited, unmoving. She was lucky, was Fanny, to have married a comfortably-off, honest suitor, without even being pregnant— especially as she couldn't hope for more than about seven or eight acres from Old Fouan. Her husband, for his part, never regretted the marriage, for he couldn't have found a more capable or hardworking housekeeper anywhere; indeed, he was so satisfied that he followed her lead in everything. A man of narrow outlook, he was yet so steady, so fair-dealing, that he was often asked to settle disputes at Rognes.

At that moment, the under-clerk, who was looking out into the street, stifled a titter behind his hand and whispered to the dirty, fat old man at his side, 'Jésus-Christ!'

Sharply, Fanny leaned towards her husband. 'Look here, leave me to manage things. I'm very fond of mama and papa, but I won't have them robbing us; and we must watch out against Buteau and that rascal Hyacinthe.'

She was talking about her two brothers, the elder of whom she had noticed passing the window. This was Hyacinthe, known all over the district as Jésus-Christ, an idler and a boozer who had been through the Algerian campaigns and then, on his release from the army, had taken to a hand-to-mouth existence, refusing any regular job and living by poaching and petty thieving, just as if he were still plundering a world made up of terrorised Bedouins.

He came in—a tall fellow, in all the sinewy pride of his forty

20

years, curly-haired, with pointed beard long and unkempt, and with the face of a ravaged Christ, a sodden Christ, a ravisher of girls, a highway robber. He had been in Cloyes since early morning, and was already drunk, his trousers spattered with mud, his shirt foully stained, his ragged cap pushed to the back of his head; he was smoking a halfpenny cigar, damp and dark, which stank out the room. Nevertheless, in the depths of his beautiful brimming eyes, there lurked a hint of unmalicious mockery, the mark of a jolly scoundrel's openheartedness.

'So the old people haven't turned up yet?' he asked.

And when the thin, jaundiced clerk answered with vehement head-shakings, he remained a moment staring at the wall, while his cigar smouldered away between his fingers. He had not even glanced at his sister and brother-in-law, who, in their turn, appeared not to have noticed his entrance. Then without another word he went out, preferring to wait in the street.

'Jésus-Christ! Jésus-Christ!' intoned the under-clerk, his nose flattened on the window-pane, tittering more and more as the nick-name revived memories of the amusing stories he had heard.

But, scarcely more than five minutes later, the Fouans arrived, two old folk with slow and cautious gait. The father, who must have been very vigorous in his youth, was now, at seventy, shrivelled and shrunken under the burden of such bitter toil, such a devouring passion for the earth, that his body sagged—as if returning to that earth so violently desired and possessed. Yet, apart from his legs, he was still hale and hearty, with little side-whiskers neatly trimmed like hare's-feet, with the long family-nose sharpening his thin face, and his leathery cheeks scored by deep wrinkles. In his shadow, not moving an inch outside it, was the mother, smaller than her husband but looking plumper, her stomach protruding with the first signs of dropsy, her face drab-coloured, pitted with two round eyes and a round mouth screwed up in an infinity of wrinkles like the mouth of a miser's purse. Stupid, degraded in her home to the level of a docile, hardworking animal, she had always trembled before her husband's despotic authority.

'So here you are at last!' cried Fanny as she stood up.

Delhomme also rose from his chair. And, behind the old people, Jésus-Christ came in again, slouching and silent. He pinched his cigar-butt to put it out, then stuffed the stinking end into his blouse-pocket.

21

'Well, here we are,' said Old Fouan. 'Only Buteau missing. .
Never on time, never like anyone else, blast him!'

'I saw him in the market-place,' Jésus-Christ stated in a voice
thick with brandy. 'He's on his way.'

Buteau, the younger son, twenty-seven years of age, owed his
nickname to his pigheadedness. He was always butting against a
brick wall, obstinately sticking to his own idea which never cor-
responded with anyone else's. Even as a boy, he hadn't got on with
his parents; and later, after drawing a lucky number in the conscription ballot, he had run away from home and hired himself out
first to the farm at La Borderie and then to the one at La Chamade.

Now, as the old man went grumbling on, he entered, lively and
cheerful. In him the large Fouan nose had been flattened, while the
lower part of the face, the jaw-bones, had been brought strongly
out, the jaw-bones of a carnivorous animal. His forehead receded,
the crown of his head was pointed, and in his laughing grey eyes
there was already a glint of cunning and violence. From his father
he inherited brutality of desire and tenacious possessiveness; from
his mother, narrow avarice. In every quarrel, when the two old
people poured reproaches on him, he would reply, 'Well, you
shouldn't have made me like that!'

'Look here, it's ten miles from La Chamade to Cloyes,' he interrupted the grumblings. 'And after all, I'm here as soon as you
were. . . Always trying to jump on me!'

Now they were all arguing. They shouted at the tops of their
piercing high-pitched voices, accustomed as they were to the open
air, and discussed their private affairs exactly as if they were at
home. The distracted clerks glanced askance at them, and at last
the notary was drawn by the noise to his office doorway.

'All here? Come in then, come in.'

His office looked on to the garden, the narrow strip of earth that
ran down to the Loir away in the distance; the line of leafless poplars along the bank was visible. As mantel-decoration, a black marble
clock stood packed between bundles of files; there was nothing else
in the room except the mahogany desk, a portfolio and some chairs.

M. Baillehache at once seated himself at the desk, looking like a
magistrate on the bench; the peasants, entering in single file, hesitated, glancing furtively around at the chairs, embarrassed at having
to decide where and how to sit.

'Come, come now, sit down!'

And so, pushed by the others, Fouan and Rose found themselves on two chairs at the front; Fanny and Delhomme sat side by side behind them; Buteau sat all alone in a corner against the wall; and only Hyacinthe remained standing by the window, blocking out the light with his broad shoulders. The notary called out familiarly and impatiently, 'Now do sit down, Jésus-Christ. . .' Finally he himself was obliged to broach the subject.

'Well, Father Fouan, so you have decided to divide your property between your two sons and your daughter while you are still alive?'

The old man did not reply. The others sat unmoving, and a profound silence filled the room. The notary, accustomed to such protracted procedure, himself gave no sign of haste. His business had been in the family for two hundred and fifty years; Baillehaches, father to son, had been in Cloyes all that time. They were of old Beauce stock, and had absorbed the ponderous thought-processes of their peasant clients, their sly circumspection which drew out the least of debates with lengthy pauses and irrelevant comment. He snapped open a pen-knife and started to trim his nails.

'Isn't that so? I believe you've made up your mind to it,' he repeated after a while, with his eyes fixed on the old man.

Fouan turned round and looked at everyone in the room before he spoke, searching for words, 'Yes, it's quite possible, Monsieur Baillehache. . . I mentioned it to you at harvest, and you told me to think it over. So I have thought it out all over again, and I see I must do it, no matter what.'

He set out his reasons in broken phrases, continually rambling off on digressions. And there was something left unsaid, something that was revealed in the emotion choked back in his throat: the endless grief, the heavy grudge, the rending of his whole body at this separation from his land—land so hotly coveted before his own father's death, and then cultivated with such avid tenacity and extended inch by inch at the cost of the most degrading avarice. Each little strip of earth represented starvation-months of bread and cheese, fireless winters, summers of toil in the scorching heat with no relief beyond a few mouthfuls of water. He had loved his land like a murderous woman for whom a man commits murder. Nothing else counted, neither wife, nor children, nor anything human: nothing but the earth! And now he was old, forced to yield his mistress to his sons, as his father, furious at his impotence, had yielded her to him.

'You see, Monsieur Baillehache, a man must be reasonable, my legs aren't what they used to be and my arms aren't much better,

23

and so the earth, curse it, suffers. . . I might have got along if there'd been some sort of understanding with my children. . .'

He shot a look at Buteau and Jésus-Christ. Neither man moved, staring into space as if a hundred miles from the conversation.

'But what can I do? Do you want me to take in someone off the street—a stranger who'll rob the house? No, servants nowadays cost a lot of money, they eat you out of house and home, day after day. And I'm at the end of my tether. Look, this year, out of my twenty-seven acres I've only had the strength to sow a quarter. Just enough to live on, wheat for us and fodder for the two cows. . . Ah, it breaks my heart to see all the good earth being wasted. Yes, I'd rather give it away than go on with such murder any more.'

His voice choked into silence and his hand moved in a broad movement of grief and resignation. Beside him, his wife, submissive, crushed by more than half a century of obedience and toil, listened to his words.

'The other day,' he went on, 'Rose was making cheese and she fell head-first in. And it all wears me out, even to take the trap to market. . . And then a man can't carry his land off when he goes. It's got to be left, left behind. . . And now we've worked enough, we want to die in peace. . . eh, Rose?'

'Aye, sure as God's looking down on us now,' sighed the old woman.

Silence fell again, a long silence. The notary finished trimming his nails and laid the pen-knife down on the desk as he spoke.

'Yes, you have excellent reasons. People are often obliged to settle on a deed of gift. . . I should add that in the case of families it means a saving of money, for inheritance taxes are heavier than the tax on transference of property.'

Buteau, for all his show of indifference, couldn't help exclaiming, 'That's really true then, Monsieur Baillehache?'

'Most certainly it is. You'll save some hundreds of francs.'

Everyone came to life, even Delhomme's face lighted up. It was settled, the whole thing was fixed, as long as it saved money.

'It remains for me to make the usual observations,' added the notary. 'Many good people disapprove of property being made over and regard it as a great danger to family bonds. . . Indeed, many deplorable examples could be cited where children have behaved very badly after their parents had given up all they possessed. . .'

The two sons and the daughter listened with mouths open, with fluttering eyelids and trembling cheeks.

'Let father keep everything, then, if he feels like that,' Fanny curtly interrupted, sensitive to the insinuation.

'We've always been dutiful children,' said Buteau.

'And we're not afraid of hard work,' put in Jésus-Christ.

With a gesture, M. Baillehache quietened them down.

'Let me finish, please. I know you are good children and honest workers; and in your case there is certainly no fear that the parents will be sorry for what they have done.'

There was no irony in his voice, he merely repeated the conciliatory phrases which five-and-twenty years of practice had brought roundly to his tongue. But the old woman, who didn't seem to be taking anything in, turned her suspicious eyes from her daughter to her two sons. She had raised them all without tenderness, with the frigid parsimony that blamed the children for eating into all her carefully hoarded stocks. She bore the youngest a grudge for leaving home just when he was at last beginning to earn his keep; she had never got on with her daughter, retreating beaten from the clash with one so like herself, a bold and energetic woman in whom the father's intelligence had turned into unyielding pride. Her eyes did not soften until they rested on the elder son, the vagabond who inherited nothing of her husband's or her own nature, a slip of bad stock come from no one knew where, and whom perhaps for that reason she forgave and preferred above the others.

Fouan also stared at his children, one after the other, with a sullen uneasiness arising from his fear as to what they would do with his property. The drunkard's laziness worried him less than the gloating covetousness of the other two. He shook his tremulous old head—what good did it do to fret? The thing had to be done!

'Now that the partition is decided on,' the notary continued, 'we must deal with the terms. Are you agreed on the allowance to be made?'

Immediately everyone relapsed into a motionless silence. The tanned faces were rigid, with the expressionless gravity of diplomats about to assess an empire. Then each threw a glance at the others, but still not a word was spoken. Once again the old father was the one to explain.

'No, Monsieur Baillehache, we haven't discussed anything, we waited till we were all together here. . . But it's quite simple, isn't it? I have nineteen *setiers*, or nine and a half hectares as they say nowadays. Well, if I rented it all out, that would be nine hundred and fifty francs at a hundred francs the hectare. . .'

Buteau, the least patient of them all, jerked round in his **chair.** "What! A hundred francs the hectare? Are you trying to do us down, dad?'

And the first argument started on the figures. There was a *setier* of vines—that, yes, that could be rented for fifty francs. But would you ever get such a price for the twelve *setiers* of ploughland, and what about the six *setiers* of meadowland, the fields near the banks of the Aigre, where the hay was almost worthless? The ploughland itself wasn't as good as all that, particularly at one end, the part at the edge of the plateau, for the arable layer thinned out towards the valley.

'Now, dad,' said Fanny reproachfully, 'you musn't be so mean to us.'

'It's all worth a hundred francs a hectare,' insisted the old man obstinately, slapping his thigh. 'I could let it out at a hundred the hectare if I wanted to. And what's it worth to you others then? Let's hear what you think it's worth!'

'Sixty francs a hectare,' said Buteau.

Fouan, quite beside himself, stuck to his price and launched into extravagant praise of his land—such good earth, it could grow corn all by itself. . . till Delhomme, who had so far kept mum, declared in his stolid, heavy voice, 'It's worth eighty francs, not a sou more, not a sou less.'

At once the old man calmed down.

'Right! let's say eighty francs. For my children I'm ready to make sacrifices.'

But Rose, pulling him by his sleeve, spoke a single word, which summed up her avarice, 'No!'

Jésus-Christ seemed indifferent. After his five years in Africa the land meant little to him. He had only one desire, to get his share and raise money on it. So he lounged in his chair with a jeering air of superiority.

'I said eighty,' shouted Fouan, 'and I mean eighty! I've always been a man of my word, I swear to God. . . Nine and a half hectares, let's see, that makes seven hundred and sixty francs, eight hundred in round figures. . . Well, the allowance will be eight hundred, that's fair!'

Buteau burst into raucous laughter, while Fanny protested by shaking her head, as if she were dumbfounded. And M. Baillehache, who had been staring out into the garden while the argument went on, dragged his attention back to his clients and appeared to be

26

listening as he mechanically tugged at his sidewhiskers, though he was almost asleep as a result of his excellent lunch.

This time the old man was right; what he offered was fair. But his children were now worked up, carried away by their anxiety to settle things at the lowest possible cost to themselves; they showed themselves at their worst, haggling and swearing, with all the double-dealing of peasants buying a pig.

'Eight hundred francs!' Buteau sneered. 'Seems you mean to live like gentlefolk? Eight hundred francs, you could feed four on that! Admit right off you just want to kill yourselves with overeating!'

Fouan did not lose his temper again. He found this haggling quite in order; he simply met the expected explosion, firing-up in his turn, but going straight on with the full list of his demands.

'And that's not all, mind! We keep the house and garden, of course, until we die. . . What's more, as we won't be getting anything from the crops and won't have the two cows any more, we want a cask of wine a year, and a hundred faggots, and eight quarts of milk a week as well as a dozen eggs and three cheeses.'

'O dad, dad!' moaned Fanny, grieved and incredulous. 'O dad!'

Buteau had passed beyond argument. He had jumped up and was now striding about with abrupt movements; he had even jammed his cap on his head, ready to walk out. Jésus-Christ had also got to his feet, uneasy at the thought that all this quarrelling would stop the sharing-out. Delhomme alone remained unmoved, with a finger against his nose in an attitude of deep thought and immense boredom.

Then M. Baillehache realised he must guide things forward a little. He shook off his drowsiness, and remarked with a yet more purposive twist of his whiskers, 'You know, my friends, that wine, faggots, cheeses and eggs are all customary. . .'

But he was interrupted by a torrent of harsh comments.

'Do we drink our wine ourselves? We sell it!'

'Not a bloody hand's turn, just sit by the fire while your children work their guts out!'

The notary, who had heard the same words from so many others, went calmly on.

'All that may be true. . . Sit down, Jésus-Christ, for heaven's sake! You've got all the daylight! And everyone's agreed, eh? You'll give the expected dues, otherwise people will be pointing at you. So we have only the figure of the allowance to discuss.'

Delhomme at last indicated that he wanted to speak. The others

27

had all resumed their seats, and he spoke slowly, in a hush of general attention.

'Well, I think what father's asking is fair. You might offer him eight hundred francs, because he could rent out his land for eight hundred. Only, we don't count that way, we don't. He isn't going to rent us his land, he's going to give it us, and the question is to know what he and mother need to live on. . . Not a sou more, but just what they need to live on.'

'Quite so,' agreed the lawyer, 'that is the normal basis on which we calculate.'

And another interminable quarrel broke out. The two old people's life was laid bare, pried into, argued over, item by item. Their bread was weighed, their vegetables, their meat; their clothing was estimated, linens and woollens measured down to the last details; even the small pleasures of age were examined—the father's two sous a day for tobacco, which, after lengthy recriminations, was fixed at one sou. When a man doesn't work, he must economise. And the old woman, couldn't she do without her black coffee? And what about their old dog, twelve years old, who was no good for anything and ate too much—he ought to have had a bullet in his skull long ago. When the calculations were finished, somebody started them all over again, looking for an item that could be cut: two shirts and six handkerchiefs a year, a centime out of the sum allocated for buying sugar. And trimming here and there, making the tiniest of economies, they drove the figure down to five hundred and fifty-odd francs—a figure which left the children restive and dissatisfied, for they had strenuously hoped to stop at the round figure of five hundred francs.

But Fanny was tired. She was not a bad soul, she had more kindness than the two men, her heart and skin not yet calloused by the bitter struggle for existence on the land. She wanted to finish the business and resigned herself to the concessions granted. Jésus-Christ, for his part, shrugged his shoulders, generous about money, even a little drunkenly sentimental, ready to make up the odd francs out of his share—though he would never have paid them, of course.

'All right,' said the daughter. 'Five hundred and fifty, eh?'

'Yes, yes,' cried Jésus-Christ. 'They ought to have a bit of comfort, poor old things.'

The mother looked at her elder son with a smile, while the father went on arguing with the younger. He had yielded step by step, battling against every reduction, obstinately sticking to certain figures. But, under his show of cold stubbornness, he felt a mounting rage, faced with the furious resolve of his own flesh-and-blood to grow fat on his carcass, to suck all his blood away while he was still alive. He forgot that in his day he had devoured his own father's body. His hands were trembling as he growled, 'Ah! bad stock! To think I raised them to snatch the bread out of my mouth! It makes me sick, it does! I'd rather rot in the earth. There's no way then of softening your hearts, you'll only give five hundred and fifty francs?'

He was giving in when his wife again pulled at his sleeve and whispered, 'No. . . No. . .'

'And that's not everything,' said Buteau after a moment's hesitation. 'What about your savings? If you've got some money—and you have, haven't you?—you surely don't mean to take ours?'

He stared straight at his father, having kept this point up his sleeve till the last moment. The old man went white.

'What money?' he asked.

'The money you've invested, of course, the money you hold bonds for.'

Buteau, who only suspected a hoard, wanted to make certain. One night he thought he had seen his father take a small roll of papers from behind the looking-glass. Next day, and for many days after, he had spied on the old man; but he hadn't caught him again and the hole remained empty.

Fouan's pallid face became suddenly suffused with blood as his pent-up anger burst out. He stood up and shouted with a gesture of fury.

'So you even go through all my pockets, do you? I haven't a sou, not even a farthing put by. You cost too much for that, you dirty buggers! But what has it got to do with you, anyway, aren't I master any more, aren't I your father?'

He seemed to grow taller as his authority re-awoke. For years everyone, wife and children, had quailed before him, before the harsh despotism of a peasant family's head. They were mistaken if they thought he was done for.

'O dad!' Buteau wanted to pass it off as a joke.

'Shut up, you, by God!' ranted the old man with his hand still raised, 'or I'll knock you flat!'

The younger son gaped and shrank down in his chair. He had

29

felt the wind of the blow and was caught up once more in his child-hood fears, lifting his elbow to shield himself.

'And you, Hyacinthe, take that grin off your face! And Fanny, lower your eyes. . . As sure as the sun's in the sky, I'll lead you all a dance yet, I will!'

He alone was on his feet, gesturing threateningly. The old woman trembled as if she feared a stray blow would somehow fall on her. The children neither stirred nor breathed, submissive, dominated.

'D'you hear then, I say the allowance is to be six hundred francs . . . Otherwise I'll sell my land and put the money in an annuity. Yes, I'll devour it all, and none of you will get so much as a radish after I'm gone. Yes or no, six hundred francs.'

'But, dad,' murmured Fanny, 'we'll give anything you ask.'

'Six hundred francs, that's fair,' added Delhomme.

'For my part,' stated Jésus-Christ, 'I agree with what's agreed.'

Buteau, bitterly gritting his teeth, seemed in his silence to yield. And Fouan still cowed them all, looking them over with the hard eyes of a master accustomed to obedience. Then, after a while, he sat down, saying, 'Well, that's right, we're agreed.'

M. Baillehache, unconcerned and again overcome with sleepiness had been waiting for the end of the quarrel. He re-opened his eyes, and tranquilly closed the consultation.

'You are all agreed then, so that's that. . . Now that I know the terms, I'll draw up the deed. On your side, get the surveying done, divide up the land, and tell the surveyor to send me a note marking the distribution of the strips. When you have drawn lots for them, we shall only have to write the number after each name and then sign.'

He had risen from his chair in dismissal. But they did not move at once, they hesitated and reflected. Had everything really been settled, hadn't they forgotten something? Had they made a mistake, and was there still time to put it right?

Three o'clock struck. They had been there almost two hours.

'Please go now,' the notary finally told them. 'There are others waiting.'

He precipitated their decision by pushing them into the next room, where other peasants, motionless and rigid in their chairs, were patiently waiting; the under-clerk was watching a dog-fight through the window, and the two other clerks were sullenly at work, with pens scratching over stamped papers.

Outside, the family remained standing a moment in the middle of the road.

'If you like,' said the father, 'the survey can be made the day after to-morrow, Monday.'

They all nodded in agreement, and went off down the Rue Grouaise in broken file, a few steps separating one from the other.

Then Old Fouan and Rose turned into the Rue du Temple towards the church, while Fanny and Delhomme went off by the Rue Grande. Buteau had come to a halt in Saint Lubin Square, trying to puzzle out whether or not his father had some hidden money. And Jésus-Christ, left alone, relighted the stub of his cigar and slouched into the *Jolly Ploughman*.

III

THE Fouans' house was the first in Rognes, on the road from Cloyes to Bazoches-le-Doyen, which ran through the village. On Monday, the old man was coming out of the house at seven o'clock, with the first light, to go to the meeting arranged outside the church, when in the doorway of the next house he noticed his sister, called La Grande, already up and about in spite of her eighty years.

These Fouans had been born and bred in the same place for centuries like persistent tenacious plants. In the old days they had been serfs to the Rognes-Bouquevals—of whom the only traces were some scattered buried stones of a ruined castle. They must have been freed under Philipe le Bel; and from that time they became landowners, with perhaps an acre or two of land bought from their ruined lord and paid for ten times over with their blood and sweat. The long struggle had begun, and had gone on four hundred years with a desperate passion that was passed down from father to son to hold and enlarge the property. Strips were lost, then bought back, the ridiculously small holding had its ownership continually in dispute and was passed on under such heavy inheritance taxes that it seemed almost to melt away; and yet pasture and arable expanded bit by bit through a property-lust which conquered by sheer tenacity. Generation after generation went under, the long lives of the men fattening the earth; but when the Revolution of 1789 legalised his rights, the Fouan of the day, Joseph-Casimir, possessed some twenty-six acres, wrested in the course of four centuries from the old manorial estates.

31

In '93 this Joseph-Casimir was twenty-seven years old; and the day when what remained of the old estates was declared national property and put up for sale in lots by auction, he longed to acquire a few more acres. The Rognes-Bouquevals, ruined and heavily in debt, had allowed the last tower of the castle to collapse and long ago abandoned the rents of La Borderie to their creditors, three-quarters of the land left lying fallow. There was one particular large field alongside Casimir's own strips which the peasant coveted with all the fierce desire of his breed. But the harvest had been poor, he had barely a hundred crowns saved up and hidden in an old jar behind the oven; moreover, even if it had crossed his mind that he might borrow from a money-lender in Cloyes, distrust and prudence held him back. The possession of a lord's land frightened him; who knew whether, later on, they might not snatch it back? And so, torn between desire and distrust, he had the bitter experience of seeing La Borderie bought up at the auctions at a fifth of its value, field by field, by a *bourgeois* of Châteaudun, Isidor Hourdequin, a former exciseman.

Joseph-Casimir Fouan in his old age divided his twenty-six acres between his elder daughter Marianne and his two sons, Louis and Michel—eight and a half acres each; his younger daughter, Laure, trained as a dressmaker, worked in Châteaudun and was indemnified in money. But marriage destroyed the equal shares. Marianne Fouan, called La Grande, married a neighbour, Antoine Péchard, who had about twenty-two acres; but Michel Fouan, called Mouche, got involved with a woman to whom her father was to leave no more than one and a half acres of vineyard. Louis Fouan, married to Rose Maliverne, heiress to fifteen acres, built up the twenty-three acres which he was, in his turn, about to divide up between his three children.

La Grande was respected and feared by the family, not for her age, but for her wealth. Still very straightbacked, tall, thin and tough, big-boned, she had the gaunt face of a bird of prey set on a long withered neck, which was suffused with blood. The family nose curved in her face to a terrible beak; she had round staring eyes, not a single hair surviving under the yellow scarf she always wore, and yet every tooth in her head—as well as jaws that could have crunched stones.

She never went out without her thorn-stick, which she kept lifted-up and used solely to lash out at beast and man. Left a young widow with a daughter, she threw the girl out of her house for rebelliously wanting to marry a poor man, Vincent Bouteroue. And even now, when the girl and her husband, dead from poverty, had left her a granddaughter and grandson, Palmyre and Hilarion, respectively thirty-two and twenty-four years old, she had refused forgiveness, and was letting them die of starvation, allowing no one to remind her of their existence. Since her husband's death, she personally supervised the cultivation of her fields; she had three cows, a pig and a servant, all fed from the common trough, and was obeyed by everyone in grovelling terror.

Fouan, seeing her at her door, went up as a courtesy. She was six years his elder and he regarded her hardness, her avarice, her obstinate possessiveness and hunger for life with the same respect and admiration as did the rest of the village.

'You see, La Grande, I wanted to let you know what's happening,' he said. 'I've made up my mind, I'm going along to make the division.'

She made no reply, but grasped her stick firmly and shook it.

'The other evening, I wanted to ask your advice again; but when I knocked nobody answered.'

Then she burst out in her sharp voice. 'You fool! You've had my advice! Only a lazy beast'd give up his property while he's still on his feet. I'd have bled to death, I would, I'd have said no under the knife. See others with what's your own, put yourself out of house and home for a pack of villainous children, no fear! No fear!'

'But when you can't plough any more,' Fouan objected, 'when the earth suffers. . .'

'Let it suffer! I'd go and watch the thistles growing every morning rather than give up a single yard!'

She drew herself up, looking like a savage old moulting vulture. Then, tapping him on the shoulder with her stick as if to impress her words on him more deeply, 'Listen, remember this. When you've nothing left and they've taken everything, your children will push you into the river, or you'll finish up with a beggar's staff, just like a tramp. Don't start knocking at my door then. I've warned you plain enough, and that's that. Like to know what I would do, eh? Like to know?'

He waited, the submissive younger brother; she went back in and slammed the door, shouting, 'That's what I'd do! Starve in the street!'

Fouan stayed a moment unmoving before the closed door. Then, with a shrug of resigned decision he climbed the path which led to the Place de l'Eglise. On that very spot stood the old family-

B 33

house of the Fouans, which his brother Michel, Called Mouche, had inherited; his own house, lower down the road, had come to him with his wife, Rose. Mouche, a widower for several years, lived here alone with his two daughters, Lise and Françoise, embittered and dogged by bad luck, still humiliated by his poor marriage, and accusing his brother and sister, after forty years, of having done him down when he was conscripted; he never stopped telling the tale about being left with the worst share at the bottom of the hat: a tale that seemed to have come true in the end, because he was so full of excuses and so little inclined to work that his portion lost half its value in his hands. Man makes the earth, as they say in La Beauce.

This particular morning, Mouche too was on his door-step, watching, when his brother turned the corner of the square. The division fascinated him by reviving old grudges, even though he had nothing to expect from it. But, to make a show of total indifference, he too turned his back and quickly shut the door.

Immediately afterwards, Fouan noticed Delhomme and Jésus-Christ waiting twenty yards apart from one another. He reached Delhomme and then Jésus-Christ came up. All three men, without a word, stared down the path running along the plateau edge.

'There he is,' said Jésus-Christ at last.

It was Grosbois, the land-surveyor, a peasant from the small neighbouring village of Magnolles. His knowledge of writing and reading had been his undoing. Called from Orgères to Beaugency for surveying, he left his wife in charge of his own land and picked up such drunken habits on his continual travels that he was now never sober. He was very fat, a lively fellow for all his fifty years, with a broad red face speckled over with violet pimples; and, in spite of the early hour he was already badly drunk, the result of a drinking bout held the night before among Montigny winegrowers to celebrate the division of an inheritance. But it didn't matter. The more drunk he was, the clearer his mind: never a mistake in measurement, never a false addition! Everyone listened to him and respected him, for he had the reputation of being extremely spiteful.

'Well? All here?' he said. 'Let's get to work!'

A child of some twelve years, dirty and dressed in rags, followed him, carrying the surveying-chain under one arm, the tripod and staff over one shoulder and swinging the square rule in its cracked old cardboard case from his remaining free hand.

They all started walking off without waiting for Buteau. They had just caught sight of him as he stood motionless, staring at a stretch of ploughland, the largest field in the inheritance, at the spot known as Les Cornailles. This field, about five acres in size, was the one which ran alongside the field where La Coliche had dragged Françoise a few days before. Buteau, feeling it unnecessary to walk any further, had stopped there, absorbed. When the others arrived, they saw him bend down, take up a handful of earth and let it run slowly through his fingers as if he were weighing and smelling it.

'Look here,' Grosbois spoke again, pulling a greasy little book out of his pocket, 'I've already made out a small plan of every strip of land, just as you asked me, Father Fouan. Now there's the job of dividing it all into three lots; and that, my children, we are going to carry out all together. . . Right? First, tell me what you want done.'

The light was growing, an icy wind chased endless flights of big clouds across the pale sky; and La Beauce, beaten down, lay stretched out in a mournful sadness. Yet not one of them seemed to notice this wind from the great space though it puffed out their blouses and threatened to snatch off their hats. The five men, dressed in their best because of the importance of the occasion, had nothing to say. There, by the edge of the field, in the heart of the limitless plain, they showed thoughtful and absorbed faces with the dreamy look of sailors who live alone under the wide sky. The flat fertile lands of La Beauce, easy to plough but demanding ceaseless effort, have made its men reserved and reflective, capable of passion only for the earth.

'Every piece must be divided into three,' Buteau finally spoke.

Grosbois shook his head and an argument started. He had been won over to progressive views through his connections with the big farmers, and sometimes went so far as to disagree with clients who were small property-owners, standing out against the parcelling-up of the land. Didn't labour and cartage become ruinous, with strips about as big as handkerchiefs? Could you call it farming at all in these allotments where nobody could improve crop-rotation or use machines? No, the only reasonable thing was to come to an agreement and not cut up a field as if it were a bit of cake, a murderous procedure! If one of them would be content with the arable land, the other could take over the pasture: in the end the lots could be equalised and the draw would then decide.

Buteau, still young enough to laugh easily, took him up on a

35

farcical note, 'And if I get the pasture, what'll I live on? Grass? No, no, I want a bit of everything, hay for the cow and the horse, wheat and vines for myself.'

Fouan nodded his head as he listened. They had always divided like that, from father to son; and purchases and marriage-settlements soon came along to widen the fields once more.

Rich in the possession of some fifty acres, Delhomme had broader ideas but showed himself agreeable; he had only come along as his wife's representative, to watch out for any cheating in the survey. As for Jésus-Christ, he had left the others and gone to chase some rising larks with a handful of pebbles. When one of the birds, breasting the wind, hung motionless for a few seconds with fluttering wings, he brought it down with brutal skill. Three in all fell to earth and he pushed them all bloody into his pockets.

'Get along, that's enough arguments, cut it all up into three!' cried Buteau gaily, addressing the surveyor familiarly; 'But not in six! You've got a look in your eyes this morning as if you could see both Chartres and Orléans at the same time!'

Grosbois, annoyed, drew himself up with much dignity.

'Young fellow, you just try getting as drunk as me and then see if you can open your eyes at all! Which of you clever fellows wants to take my place at the set-square?'

As no one dared to take up the challenge, he won his point and brusquely shouted to the boy, who stood in a stupor of admiration at Jésus-Christ's pebble-throwing. The square was already fixed in its stand and the staffs were being set up, when the method of dividing the field gave rise to another dispute. The surveyor, upheld by Fouan and Delhomme, wanted three strips running parallel to the valley of the Aigre, while Buteau demanded that the strips should run at right-angles to this valley, insisting that the arable layer thinned out more and more as it approached the slope. If the second way were chosen, everyone would have some of the bad end; if the first, then the third lot would be nothing but poor land. Fouan, however, got angry; he swore that the soil was equally good all over, and recalled that the previous partition between himself, Mouche and La Grande, had been carried out in the way he was arguing for; the proof was that the five acres belonging to Mouche would be adjacent to this third strip. Delhomme for his part made the decisive remark: even admitting that the strip might be not so good, its owner would profit when the day came for a road to be built along the edge of the field at this point.

'That's it!' cried Buteau, 'the famous road running direct from Rognes to Châteaudun, past La Borderie! Well, that's a road you'll wait a long time to see!'

Then as they took no notice for all his persistence, he protested with clenched teeth.

Even Jésus-Christ had now come up and they were all absorbed watching Grosbois trace out the lines of the division. They watched him with sharp eyes, as if they suspected him of scheming to give the benefit of a half-inch to one share or other. Three times Delhomme put his eye to the slit in the set-square to make quite sure that the thread cut the staff exactly. Jésus-Christ swore at the little bastard of an assistant for handling the chain awkwardly. But, above all, Buteau followed the whole business step by step, counting the feet with trembling lips and checking the calculations by his own system. And in his desire for possession, in his joy at getting a grip on the earth at last, his bitterness increased, a dumb rage at not cornering it all. Look how beautiful this field was, these five acres in a single holding. He had demanded the division so that nobody should have the whole field if he couldn't; and now the mangling of it drove him to despair.

Fouan, with arms dangling, watched his field cut up without a word.

'There we are,' said Grosbois. 'Check it as you like, you won't find a scrap of difference between the plots!'

Up on the plateau were still ten more acres of arable land, but these were already divided into a dozen strips, each one not much more than an acre in size. One parcel indeed was only about a rood; and when the surveyor sarcastically asked if he were to start cutting it up, the argument started again.

Buteau, with the gesture that was second-nature, had bent down, taken a handful of earth, and lifted it up to his face as if he meant to taste it. Then with a devout wrinkling of his nose, he seemed to pronounce it the best soil of all; and, letting the crumbs run gently through his fingers, he said that it would be all right if they left the strip to him; otherwise he demanded a division. Delhomme and Jésus-Christ, provoked, refused, and wanted a bit too. Yes, yes, a third of a rood each, it was only fair. So all the strips were divided and everyone was quite certain that neither of the others had anything he didn't have.

'On to the vineyard!' said Fouan.

But as they retraced their steps to the church, he glanced back at

37

the immense plain and his eyes came to rest on the distant barns of La Borderie. Then he cried out with inconsolable regret, alluding to the missed opportunity at the State auctions long ago:

'Ah! if father had only made up his mind, Grosbois, you'd have been measuring out everything from here to there.'

The two sons and the son-in-law turned abruptly and there was a fresh halt, a lingering look at the seven hundred and fifty acres of the farm spread out before them.

'Bah!' growled Buteau sullenly, starting to walk on, 'that does us a lot of good, that old affair! Doesn't it always work out that the *bourgeois* eat us up?'

Ten o'clock struck. They hastened their steps, for the wind had dropped and a large black cloud had just let fall a first shower. The few vineyards of Rognes lay beyond the church, on the hillside which ran down to the Aigre. Formerly the Castle stood at this spot, surrounded by its park; and it was only half a century ago that the peasants, encouraged by the success of the Montigny vineyards, near Cloyes, had taken the step of planting vines on this slope, because of its steepness and its southern aspect. The wine was thin, but agreeably keen, recalling the minor vintages of Orléans. In any case each villager owned merely a strip or two of vineyard; the richest, Delhomme, had seven acres or so; generally the countryside was given over to cereals and fodder crops.

They turned behind the church and skirted the ancient presbytery; then they threaded their way through the tightly packed vineslips, so trimmed as to resemble a chess-board. As they crossed some rocky ground, covered with bushes, a sharp voice, coming out of a hole, cried, 'Father, it's coming on to rain, I'm taking out the geese!'

This was La Trouille, Jésus-Christ's daughter, a ragamuffin of twelve, thin and prickly as a branch of holly, with matted fair hair. Her large mouth was twisted to the left and her green eyes stared so impudently that it was easy to mistake her for a boy. She was wearing in guise of a frock one of her father's old blouses pulled in at the waist by a piece of cord. And if everyone called her La Trouille (The Slut), though she was christened with the beautiful name of Olympe, the reason was that Jésus-Christ, who nagged at her from dawn to dusk, couldn't address her without adding, 'Just you wait! I'll give you what for, you dirty slut!'

He had fathered this wild girl on a tramp-woman whom he picked up on the edge of a ditch after a fair, and installed in his

38

den to the great scandal of Rognes. For nearly three years the household had squabbled and fought; then, one harvest evening, the woman departed as she had come, carried off by another man. The child, scarcely weaned, had grown up as tough as a weed; and from the time she could walk she had cooked for her father, whom she feared and adored. Her one passion was her geese. At first, she had only two, a gander and a goose, stolen as goslings from behind a farm hedge. Then, thanks to her motherly care, the flock multiplied, and she now had twenty birds, which she fed from the proceeds of her thefts.

When La Trouille appeared, with her cheeky goat-face, urging the geese forward with strokes of her switch, Jésus-Christ exploded.

'Here now, get back and look after the dinner, or watch out! And shut the house up, can't you, you dirty slut, in case there's robbers about!'

Buteau burst out laughing and even Delhomme and the others could not help joining in, so funny did they find the idea of Jésus-Christ being robbed. You only had to see the house, an old cellar with three walls, underground, a real fox's hide-out, among piles of fallen stones below a grove of old limetrees! It was all that remained of the Château; and when the poacher, after a quarrel with his father, fled to this rocky corner, which stood on common-land, he had to build up a fourth wall of dry stones to keep the weather out. Two spaces were left for window and door. Brambles had soon pushed over the stones and a huge rambling dog-rose hid the window. Throughout the district the place was known as The Château.

A new downpour began. Fortunately, the acre or so of vineyard was near by, and the division into three parts was done quickly with no further outbreaks of argument. It only remained to divide the eight acres of meadowland lower down on the edge of the Aigre; but at that moment the rain became so heavy and fell in such torrents that the surveyor, coming to the entry of a house, suggested they should go indoors.

'What about sheltering with Monsieur Charles for a bit?'

Fouan stopped irresolutely, full of respect for his brother-in-law and his sister, who, having made a fortune, lived in retirement in this *bourgeois* estate.

'No, no, they have lunch at midday,' he murmured. 'We'll disturb them.'

But M. Charles, who had come out to watch the downpour,

39

appeared at the end of the path, under the awning. Recognising them, he called out. 'Come in, come in now!'

Then, as they were dripping wet, he shouted to them to go round to the kitchen, where he would join them. He was a fine man of sixty-five, clean-shaven, with heavy eyelids over lack-lustre eyes and the solemn sallow face of a retired magistrate. He was dressed in a thick blue quilted jacket, fur-lined boots and a clerical skull-cap which he wore with the dignity of one whose life has been spent in handling delicate affairs with authority.

When Laure Fouan, then a dress-maker at Châteaudun, married Charles Badeuil, he owned a small café in the Rue Angoulême. Thence the ambitious young couple, eager for a quick fortune, had moved to Chartres. But in the early days nothing they touched succeeded, every gain dribbled away through their fingers; they tried in vain with another bar, a restaurant, even running a shop for dried fish; and they despaired of ever having a penny to put away when M. Charles, a man of enterprise, conceived the idea of buying one of the brothels in the Rue aux Juifs, which had fallen on bad days through unsatisfactory personnel and notorious dirtiness. At a glance, he had summed up the situation and measured the needs of Chartres, the gap to be filled in a large town lacking a respectable establishment whose standards of security and comfort were at the level required by modern progress. By the second year, then, Number Nineteen, redecorated, graced with curtains and mirrors, and supplied with a carefully chosen staff, became so very well known that the number of its women had to be increased to six. The army officers, the civil service, in fact the whole of local society came there and nowhere else. And this success was maintained, thanks to M. Charles's strong right arm and his firm paternal administration; while Madame Charles showed extraordinary activity, kept her eye on everything, obviated all waste and yet was shrewd enough to ignore when necessary the petty larcenies of rich clients.

In less than twenty-five years the Badeuils saved 300,000 francs; they then began to think of fulfilling their life's dream, an idyllic old age spent in the country, surrounded by trees, flowers and birds. What held them back for another two years was the inability to find a purchaser for Number Nineteen at the high price they set on it. Wasn't it heart-breaking that an establishment to which they had devoted the best years of their lives, and which was more remunerative than a farm, should have to pass into unknown hands, where it might possibly degenerate? Immediately on his arrival in Chartres, M. Charles had been presented with a daughter, Estelle, whom he sent to school with the nuns of The Visitation, at Châteaudun, while he took up residence in the Rue aux Juifs. It was a highly religious school with a rigid moral code, and he left the young girl there until she was eighteen to intensify her innocence, sending her far away in the holidays in complete ignorance as to the origin of his wealth. And he only took her away from school on the day he married her to a young man who worked in the excise-office, Hector Vaucogne, a handsome lad whose excellent qualities were marred by an extreme laziness. She was nearly thirty and had a daughter of seven, Elodie, when she finally learned the truth on being told that her father wished to give up his business; and she came in person to ask for an option on the establishment. Why should the business go out of the family, when it was so secure, so flourishing? Everything was arranged, the Vaucognes took over the house, and the Badeuils from the very first months had the fond satisfaction of knowing that their daughter, though brought up on quite contrary ideas, had proved a most capable mistress of the house, happily compensating for the weakness of their son-in-law, a man quite without any flair for administration. Five years ago, they had retired to Rognes where they took charge of their little granddaughter Elodie, who, in her turn, had been put into the convent at Châteaudun, with the Sisters of The Visitation, to be brought up religiously according to the strictest possible moral rule.

When M. Charles came into the kitchen, where a young servant-maid was beating up eggs with her eye on a pot of larks cooking in butter, all of them, even Old Fouan and Delhomme, removed their hats and appeared extremely flattered to shake his proffered hand.

'My goodness!' said Grosbois, making himself pleasant, 'what a delightful property you have here, Monsieur Charles. . . And to think you picked it up for a song. . . Yes, yes, you're a sharp one, aren't you?'

The other man preened himself.

'A piece of luck, a lucky find. We took a fancy to it. Besides, Madame Charles had made up her mind to end her days in the parts where she was born. . . You know, I always give in to the dictates of the heart.'

Roseblanche, as the property was named, was the 'folly' of a gentleman from Cloyes, who spent some fifty thousand francs on it, only to be struck down with apoplexy before the paint was dry.

The house, very trim, was situated half-way up the hill, surrounded by a garden of some seven acres that stretched down to the Aigre. In this isolated spot on the edge of the sombre Beauce, no purchaser could be found, and M. Charles got the place for twenty thousand francs. He blissfully satisfied all his hobbies there, fishing for trout and eels from the river, cultivating all varieties of roses and carnations with infinite care, and even keeping birds, a great aviary filled with every species of singing-bird found in the woods, tended by no hands but his own. The fond old couple ran through twelve thousand francs a year, in a perfect enjoyment which they regarded as the legitimate reward of thirty years of toil.

'That's so, eh?' added M. Charles. 'At least people know who we are, here.'

'Not a doubt people know you,' replied the surveyor. 'Your money talks for you.'

And all the others nodded.

'That's right, right enough.'

M. Charles told the servant to put out glasses, while he went down to the cellar himself to fetch two bottles of wine. All the men, their noses turned towards the stove where the larks were roasting, sniffed the good smell. And they drank gravely, rolling the wine over their tongues.

'Damn it, this isn't local wine, this isn't. . . Wonderful!'

'Have a few more drops. . . Your health!'

'Your health!'

As they put down their glasses, Mme Charles came in, a lady of sixty-two, very respectable in appearance, with plainly-done snow-white hair; she had the heavy face and large nose of the Fouans, but with a pinkish pallor, with the calm sweet face of an old nun who has spent her life in the shadow of the cloister. And her grand-daughter Elodie, on holiday for a few days in Rognes, followed her into the room, clinging tightly to her in the bewilderment of her gauche shyness. Debilitated by chlorosis, lanky for her twelve years, she had the soft flabby ugliness and thin colourless hair of impoverished blood and was so repressed by her education as an innocent maiden that she was almost imbecile.

'Hullo! You here?' said Mme Charles, shaking hands with her brother and her nephews, her gestures slow and dignified to mark the distance between them. Then, turning round, she took no more notice of the men. 'Come in, Monsieur Patoir. . . The animal is here.'

This was the vet from Cloyes, a small fat man, full-blooded and purple-faced, with a soldier's head and large moustachios. He had just arrived through the pouring rain in his muddy cab.

'The poor darling,' she went on, taking from the warm oven a basket which held a dying cat, 'the poor darling developed a trembling fit yesterday and so I wrote to you. Ah! he is not young, he's nearly fifteen. Yes, we had him ten years at Chartres; and last year my daughter had to get rid of him because he forgot himself in every corner of the shop.'

The term *shop* was used for Elodie's sake. She was always told that her parents had a sweet-shop where they were so busy they could never have her to stay there. And the peasants did not even smile; for the rumour was current in Rognes that 'even the Hourdequin farm isn't worth as much as M. Charles's shop.' With round eyes they stared at the pitiful old ginger cat, emaciated and mangy, the old cat who had purred in all the beds of the Rue aux Juifs, the much-caressed cat that had been stroked by the plump fingers of five or six generations of women. What a long time had he been pampered as the favourite cat, a familiar of the alcove and the private room, licking up remains of pomade, drinking the water out of toilet glasses, mute dreamer present at the goings-on, watching everything with the narrowed irises of his gold-encircled eyes!

'Monsieur Patoir, I beg and pray you,' Mme Charles ended, 'please cure him.'

The vet's eyes widened, his nose and mouth tightened, his whole hearty and brutal bulldog face was twisted; and he shouted out, 'What! You've dragged me all the way for this? I'll cure the wretch for you! Tie a string round its neck and chuck it in the river!'

Elodie burst into tears, Mme Charles choked with indignation.

'It stinks, this puss of yours! Do you want to keep such a horror and get cholera in the house? Chuck it in the river!'

Yet, faced with the old woman's anger, he finished up by sitting at the table, and grumblingly writing out a prescription.

'Well, if it amuses you to be infected. . . why should I worry as long as I'm paid? There! pour that down its gullet in spoonfuls every hour; and here is a mixture for two wash-outs, one to-night and one to-morrow morning.'

For the last few moments, M. Charles had been restless, distraught at seeing the larks burn, while the maid, tired of beating the omelette, stood idly by. He quickly handed the consultation-fee to Patoir and urged the others to put their drinks down.

43

'Time for lunch, eh? Well, till we meet again. It's stopped raining.'

They went regretfully out, and the vet, climbing into his rickety old trap continued muttering, 'A cat not worth the rope for swinging it into the water. . . . O well, when you've got the money!'

'Dirty money goes as easy as it comes,' laughed Jésus-Christ.

But the others, even Buteau who was pale with a sullen envy, protested and shook their heads; and Delhomme, the shrewd one, declared, 'Doesn't alter the fact that a man who's managed to put aside twelve thousand francs a year isn't an idler or a fool.'

The vet had whipped up his horse and the others went down towards the Aigre, over pathways now turned into rivers. They reached the eight-acre meadowland which had still to be divided, when the rain started again, with torrential violence. But this time they persisted obstinately, aching with hunger, wanting to get the matter done with. Only one dispute held them up, on the subject of the third lot, which had no trees, whereas a little grove had been divided between the other two claimants. Everything, however, seemed to have been worked out acceptably. The surveyor promised to send his papers to the lawyer who was to get the documents ready and it was agreed to defer the draw to the following Sunday, ten o'clock at the old father's house.

As they re-entered Rognes, Jésus-Christ suddenly swore aloud, 'You wait, you dirty slut, I'll give you what for!' On the edge of the grassy path La Trouille was walking her geese, without haste, under the roaring storm. At the end of the dripping but delighted flock the gander was strutting; and when he turned his great yellow beak to the right, all the other great yellow beaks swung the same way. But now the girl took fright and went lolloping off up-hill to prepare dinner, followed by the file of long necks stretched out behind the stretching neck of the gander.

IV

It happened that the following Sunday fell on the first of November, All Saints' Day. The clock was just striking nine when the Abbé Godard, priest of Bazoches-le-Doyen, in whose charge was the ancient parish of Rognes, appeared over the hillcrest that sloped down to the little bridge over the Aigre. Rognes, quite an important place in days gone by, but now reduced to a population of barely three hundred, had not had a priest for many years and showed itself so little anxious for one that the municipal council had lodged the local constable in the half-ruined presbytery.

So, every Sunday, the Abbé Godard walked the two miles between Bazoches-le-Doyen and Rognes. Short and fat, with a red neck so swollen that it tilted his head backwards, he forced himself to take this exercise for his health's sake. But this particular Sunday, realising he was late, he was dreadfully out of breath and his mouth gaped wide open in his flushed face, with its little snub nose and small grey eyes buried in fat. Under the livid sky threatening snow and in spite of the frost which had followed the week's rainstorms, he swung his three-cornered hat in his hand, walking with his thick mat of greying red hair uncovered.

The road descended sharply, and on the left bank of the Aigre, before the stone bridge was reached, there were only a few houses, a sort of suburb through which the Abbé tempestuously rushed. He did not spare one glance, up-stream or down-stream, at the slow-flowing crystal-clear river whose curves wound through the meadows and groves of willow and poplar.

On the right bank the village proper began, a double line of house-fronts edging the road, with other houses dotting the hillside haphazard; while just over the bridge stood the Town Hall and the school, an old lime-washed barn with an extra storey added on. For an instant the Abbé hesitated and poked his head inside the empty hall. Then he turned round and seemed to peer into the two taverns opposite: one of them, with a clean shop-front and fine show of bottles, had a small sign in yellow wood hung over it, inscribed in green letters—*Macqueron, Grocer*; the other, its door simply ornamented with a branch of holly, had *Lengaigne, Tobacconist* scrawled in black on roughly-plastered walls. The priest was just going to take a steep pathway between the two, a hard climb which led straight to the church-porch, but stopped on catching sight of an old peasant.

'Ah, there you are, Fouan, I'm in a great hurry, I wanted to come and see you. What can we do, eh? It's not right that your son Buteau should leave Lise in such a state. Why, her swollen belly hits you right in the eye! She is a Maid of the Virgin, it's a scandal, a scandal!'

The old man listened with an air of polite deference.

'Well, Monsieur le Curé, what do you want me to do if Buteau's

45

obstinate? After all the boy's got a good excuse, he's a bit young to marry on nothing.'

'But there's a child.'

'Yes, I know. Only, it isn't born yet, this child. You can never be sure. And anyhow it's no encouragement, a baby, when you haven't enough to buy a shirt for it.'

He made these comments with an air of wisdom, as an old man who knew life. Then in the same measured tones he added, 'Besides, something might be fixed up. Yes, I'm dividing my property, the lot will be drawn this morning, after Mass. When Buteau has his share, he'll see his way clear, I hope, to marry his cousin.'

'Good,' said the priest. 'That's all right then, I count on you, Father Fouan.'

But a bell-peal cut his remarks short and he asked apprehensively, 'That's the second bell, isn't it?'

'No, Monsieur le Curé, the third.'

'Heavens! That brute Bécu has rung without waiting for me again.' He swore and started hastily up the path. At the top he almost had a stroke, his breath wheezing out like wind from a bellows.

The bells went on ringing while the disturbed crows flew croaking round the top of the steeple, a slender fifteenth century spire which bore witness to the ancient importance of Rognes. In front of the wide-open door a group of peasants were waiting, among whom the freethinker Lengaigne, keeper of the wine-shop, was smoking away at his pipe; and further on, by the cemetery-wall, the mayor, Farmer Hourdequin, a fine-looking man with an energetic expression, chatted with his deputy, the grocer Macqueron. As the priest passed with greetings, they all followed him, except Lengaigne, who ostentatiously turned his back, sucking at his pipe.

Inside the church to the right of the porch, a man, hanging on to a rope, went on ringing the bell.

'That'll do, Bécu,' said the Abbé Godard, infuriated. 'I've told you a hundred times to wait for me before you give the third peal!'

The constable, who was also the bell-ringer, dropped down on his feet, aghast at his own disobedience. He was a small man of fifty, with the square head and tanned skin of an old soldier, with grey moustache and little beard, and a rigid neck that looked as if he were strangled by always wearing shirts too tight at the collar. Already half-drunk, he remained at attention, without daring to make excuses.

46

Moreover the priest was already crossing the nave, glancing quickly over the benches. There were few worshippers there. On the left, he as yet saw only Delhomme, attending in his capacity as municipal councillor. On the right, the women's side, there were at most a dozen: he recognised Coelina Macqueron, lean, wiry and insolent; Flore Lengainge, a fat motherly woman, fretful, mild and gentle; La Bécu, tall, swarthy and very dirty. But what put the finishing touch to his anger was the behaviour of the Maids of the Virgin in the front row. Françoise sat there between two of her friends—the Macquerons' daughter, Berthe, a pretty brunette brought up as a young lady at Cloyes, and Lengaigne's daughter, Suzanne, blonde, ugly and brazen, who was apprenticed as a dressmaker in Châteaudun. All three were laughing in a most unseemly manner. And beside them was poor Lise, fat and well-rounded, with a cheerful air, flaunting the scandal of her great belly right beneath the altar.

At last Abbé Godard reached the sacristy. There he encountered Delphin and Nénesse, who were pushing each other playfully about instead of preparing the wine-receptacles. The former, son of Bécu, aged eleven, was already tanned and solidly-built, loving the earth and playing truant from school to go ploughing; while Ernest, Delhomme's eldest, a thin, lazy, fair lad of the same age, always carried a mirror in his pocket.

'Hey there, you scamps,' cried the priest. 'D'you think you're in a stable?'

And he turned to a tall thin young man with a sparse yellow beard bristling on his pale face, who stood arranging some books on a cupboard-shelf. 'Really, Lequeu, you might keep them quiet when I'm not here.'

This fellow was the schoolmaster, a peasant's son who had imbibed with his education a hatred of his class. He was rough with his pupils, treated them like animals, and hid advanced ideas under his carefully correct behaviour towards the priest and the mayor. He sang well in the choir and even took care of the church-books; but he had defied custom by refusing point-blank to ring the bell, such a task being beneath the dignity of a free man.

'I'm not set to watch over the church,' he replied dryly. 'But if they were at school, I'd knock some sense into them!'

And as the Abbé, without replying, hurriedly put on the alb and stole, he went on, 'Low Mass, isn't it?'

47

'Of course, and a quick one too. I've got to be at Bazoches before ten-thirty for High Mass.'

Lequeu, who had taken out an old missal, closed the cupboard and went to lay the book on the altar.

'Hurry, hurry up,' repeated the priest, pushing Delphin and Nénesse.

Sweating and puffing, with the chalice in his hand, he went back into the church and started the Mass, served by the two boys with sly side-glances and giggles. The church was single-naved with rounded vault and oak wainscotting, falling to pieces because the municipal council obdurately refused money for maintenance: rain came in through broken tiles on the roof and there were great stains of damp-rot in the wood, while in the choir, shut behind a grille, the high fresco of the Holy Father adored by angels high up in the apse was cut in two by a greenish streak of damp.

When the priest turned towards the faithful with his arms wide open, he was somewhat soothed, seeing that more people had arrived the mayor, the deputy, the municipal councillors, Old Fouan and Clou the farrier, who played the trombone for sung Mass. With an air of dignity, Lequeu remained in the first row. Bécu, drunk though he was, stood stiff as a post at the back. And the benches were particularly full on the women's side. Fanny, Rose, La Grande, and many others as well had come, so that the Maidens of the Virgin had to squeeze up tight and were now on their best behaviour, with noses stuck in their prayer books. But what most pleased the curé was a glimpse of M. and Mme Charles with their grand-daughter Elodie, Monsieur in a black frock-coat, Madame in a dress of green silk, both of them serious and substantial, setting a good example.

All the same he hurried through the Mass, jumbled up the Latin phrases and raced through the ritual. For the sermon he did not go into the pulpit, but sat on a chair in the choir. There he stammered and stuttered, lost his train of thought and finally gave up trying to find it. Eloquence was his weak point, the words just would not come, he was full of *ahs!* and *ers!* and was never able to finish his sentences; which explained why the bishop had consigned him for twenty-five years to the oblivion of the small living of Bazoches-le-Doyen. The rest of the service was bounced through: at the elevation of the Host the bells ran like electric signals gone mad and he dismissed his congregation with an *'Ite, missa est'* like the crack of a whip.

The church was hardly empty before the Abbé re-appeared, his three-cornered hat rammed on back to front in his haste. Just inside the door a group of women was standing. Coelina, Flore, and La Bécu were all much offended at having been taken through the Mass at such a gallop. He despised them, did he? or why didn't he give them a better service on such an important festival day?

'See here, your reverence,' asked Coelina in her sharp voice, as she stopped him. 'Have you got a grudge against us? Why do you send us packing like so much trash?'

'Hey now,' he replied, 'my own people are waiting for me. I can't be at Bazoches and at Rognes at the same time. Get a priest of your own if you want a High Mass!'

This was the cause of endless disagreement between Rognes and the Abbé. The villagers demanded more consideration, while he held to the strict limit of his duty towards a village which refused to repair the church and which dismayed him by its perpetual scandals. He resumed his complaint, pointing at the Maids of the Virgin who were walking off together.

'And look, is it decent to celebrate divine service with all these young folk taking not the slightest notice of the Lord's Commandments?'

'You aren't talking about my daughter, I hope?' asked Coelina through clenched teeth.

'Nor of mine, of course?' added Flore.

That was the last straw.

'Whom the cap fits can wear it. The truth hits you in the eye. Just look at her all dressed up in white! I never have a procession here without at least one pregnant woman. No, no, you'd make even the good God lose his temper!'

He left them. La Bécu, who had said nothing, had the task of making peace between the two mothers, who in their excitement began casting their respective daughters into one another's teeth. But she set to work with such venomous insinuations that the quarrel grew worse. Berthe! Yes, you could easily see what she'd come to with her velvet bodice and her piano! And Suzanne! What a wonderful idea to send her to the dressmaking establishment at Châteaudun! She'd soon be ruined all right!

The Abbé Godard, free at last, was hurrying away when he found himself face to face with the Charleses. His face cleared and he smiled broadly, sweeping off his three-cornered hat. Monsieur majestically inclined his head while Madame made a beautiful

49

curtsey. But the priest was fated not to get away, for he had not quite reached the far side of the square when he was halted by a fresh encounter. This time it was a tall woman of about thirty, who looked a full fifty with her thinning hair, flat flabby face as yellow as bran; worn-out and broken by heavy work, she staggered along under a bundle of fire-wood.

'Palmyre,' he asked, 'why weren't you at Mass on All Saints' Day? It's very bad.'

She groaned, 'I'm sure it is, Monsieur le Curé, but what could I do? My brother's shivering, we're all freezing at home. I've been to pick this up along the hedgerows.'

'La Grande is still as hardhearted as ever?'

'I should say so. She'd die before throwing us a piece of bread or a faggot.'

In her piteous voice she went over the whole story again, how their grandmother had chased them out, how she had had to take refuge with her brother in an old abandoned stable. Poor Hilarion, with his bandy legs and his mouth twisted by harelip, was a gentle chap: in spite of his twenty-four years, such a simpleton that no one would give him work. And so she was killing herself with working for him in her passionate devotion, full of a mother's indomitable tenderness for the cripple.

As the Abbé listened, his fat sweaty face was transfigured with an exquisite kindliness, his angry eyes melted into an expression of gentle charity, his wide mouth drooped sorrowfully. This fierce grumbler, always liable to be carried away by storms of fury, was passionately devoted to the poor and gave them everything he had —money, linen, clothes. As a result there wasn't a priest in all La Beauce whose cassock was so rustily worn and so extensively darned.

He searched his pockets uneasily and slipped a five-franc piece into Palmyre's hand. 'Take that, but hide it, I haven't any for anyone else. I must speak to La Grande again about her hard heart.'

This time he escaped. Luckily, as he puffed and blew up the hill on the other side of the Aigre, the butcher from Bazoches-le-Doyen, who was going back home, gave him a lift in his cart; and he was carried off over the flat plain, jolted about with the jigging shape of his three-cornered hat outlined against the livid sky.

Meanwhile, the church square had emptied. Fouan and Rose had gone back down to their house, where they found Grosbois waiting. Shortly before ten Delhomme and Jésus-Christ also arrived; but they waited for Buteau in vain until midday. The scoundrel would

50

never keep an appointment to time; he had probably stopped on the way for a snack. Everyone wanted to go ahead without him; then the secret fear that they all felt for his hot-headedness made them decide to have a meal first and then draw the lots at about two o'clock. Grosbois, who accepted the Fouans' offer of a slice of bacon and a glass of wine, finished the bottle off, started a second and relapsed into his normal drunken state.

At two, still no sight of Buteau! Jésus-Christ, craving some of the booze that was making the whole village drowsy on this festival occasion, went strolling past Macqueron's place and tried to peer in. The ruse succeeded. For the door was thrown wide and Bécu came out with a shout. 'So here you are, you blasted scoundrel, just in time for me to buy you a noggin!'

He was still holding himself stiffly, more and more dignified the drunker he got. The fellow-feeling of old army-soaks, a hidden sympathy, drew him to the poacher; but he avoided recognising him when on duty with official armlet showing. Torn between duty and sentiment, he was always just on the point of catching him red-handed. Inside the tavern however, as soon as he was drunk, he treated him like a brother.

'What about a game of piquet, eh? Ah! by God! if the Bedouins bother us, we'll cut their ears off!'

They set themselves down at a table and noisily dealt out cards, while one quart of wine after another disappeared down their throats.

Macqueron, all humped up in a corner, twiddled his thumbs. Since he had begun making money by speculating in the lesser wines of Montigny, he had grown lazy, going off hunting or fishing, and generally acting the gentleman; but he remained dirty and roughly dressed, while his daughter Berthe flounced around him in silk. If his wife had heeded him, they'd have shut up the shop, grocery and tavern alike, for he was becoming vain, with secret ambitions, as yet unconscious. She however was a fiercely avaricious woman; and he, though himself refusing all business whatever, left her to go on filling up glasses of wine, just to annoy his neighbour Lengaigne who owned the tobacco shop and also sold drinks. The rivalry here was long-standing, steadily smouldering, and ready to burst into flame at any moment.

Still, they were sometimes at peace for weeks on end; and, as it happened, that morning Lengaigne came in with his son Victor, a tall awkward boy who was soon due to be conscripted. Lengaigne

51

himself was extremely tall, with hard eyes and a tiny owl's head set on broad bony shoulders. He busied himself on his land while his wife weighed out tobacco and visited the cellar. What gave him a certain importance was that he acted as village-barber and cut everyone's hair: a trade acquired while in the army. He did the cutting at his own place in the midst of all the customers, or at his clients' homes, just as they wished.

'How about your beard? Wasn't it to-day, friend?' he asked from the doorway.

'Good Lord, so it was! I asked you to come,' cried Macqueron. 'Carry on right away, please.'

He took an old shaving-basin down from its hook and fetched soap and warm water, while Lengaigne pulled a razor as big as a cutlass from his pocket and started sharpening it on a leather-strop fixed to the case. But a screeching protest came from behind the grocery counter.

'Goodness!' shouted Coelina, 'do you think you're going to make a mess all over the tables? I tell you I won't have *my* customers finding hairs in their glasses!'

She was making an attack on the cleanliness of the tavern next door where you ate more hair, she used to say, than you drank decent wine.

'You go on selling your salt and pepper and keep your mouth shut!' retorted Macqueron, annoyed at this affront before so many people.

Jésus-Christ and Bécu roared with laughter. One in the eye for the fine lady! They called for a fresh bottle, which she served in speechless fury. They shuffled the cards and threw them violently on the table as if they were hitting out at each other. Trump, trump and again trump!

Lengaigne had already lathered his client's face and was holding him by the nose when schoolmaster Lequeu pushed open the door.

'Evening, everyone!'

He remained standing without a word before the stove, warming his back, while young Victor, behind the players, was deeply absorbed in their play.

'By the way,' Macqueron went on, taking advantage of a moment's pause as Lengaigne wiped the soap off the razor on his shoulder, 'Just now before Mass, Monsieur Hourdequin spoke to me about the road again. It's got to be decided one way or another.'

This was the famous direct road from Rognes to Châteaudun,

which was to shorten the distance by about two leagues; for vehicles were now obliged to go through Cloyes. Naturally the farm was greatly interested in the new road; and the mayor counted strongly on his deputy to sway the municipal council. For Macqueron was also interested in a quick decision. The proposition was to link the road in question to the lower main road and so make it easier for vehicles to get to the church, which could at present be reached only by scrambling up goat-tracks. The projected route then followed the narrow pathway between the two taverns, widening it and lessening the incline; and the grocer's lands, which would give on to the road and become easy of access, would increase tenfold in value.

'Yes,' he went on, 'I hear that before giving us a grant, the government is waiting for us to vote something. That's right, isn't it? You're in on it, aren't you?'

Lengaigne, who was a municipal councillor, but had not even an inch of garden behind his house, replied, 'Sod it, I say! What's your road got to do with me?'

Starting on Macqueron's other cheek, he scraped away at the tough skin as if using a grater, and broke into abuse of the farm. Ah! these rich fellows to-day, they were worse than the nobles in the old days; yes, they got their hands on everything during the division of the land, they made laws only to suit themselves, they lived on the misery of the poor people. The others listened, embarrassed but secretly pleased at what he dared to put into words, the ineradicable unquenched hatred of the peasant for the big land-owner.

'It's a good thing we're among friends,' muttered Macqueron, glancing uneasily towards the schoolmaster. 'I'm for the government myself. And so is our deputy, Monsieur de Chédeville. He's a friend of the Emperor, so they say.'

Suddenly Lengaigne made a furious flourish with the razor.

'Another fine bugger, he is. A rich fellow like that, who owns more than two thousand acres up Orgères way, oughtn't he to make you a gift of your road instead of pinching pennies from the village? The dirty screw!'

But the grocer, now terrified, burst out in protest.

'No, no, he's an honest man and not at all stuck-up. Without him you'd never have got a tobacco licence. What'd you say if he took it away again?'

Sharply silenced, Lengaigne resumed work on the chin. He had

53

gone too far, he was enraged with himself: his wife was right when she said his ideas would get him into trouble. And then a row bubbled up between Bécu and Jésus-Christ. The former was a bad drunk, liable to turn nasty, while the latter on the contrary was a wild rascal when he was sober but became more and more genial with every glass and finished up in a state of mild benevolence like a tipsy apostle. And this contrast was accentuated by their radical difference of outlook: the poacher was a Republican, a Red as it was called, who boasted that in '48 at Cloyes he made the rich ladies dance for their lives; the constable, fiercely Bonapartist, adored the Emperor whom he claimed to know personally.

'I give you my oath! We shared some pickled herrings between us. And then he told me: 'Not a word, I'm the Emperor. . .' I recognised him because of his picture on the five-franc piece.'

'Maybe! He's a bastard all the same, he beats his wife and hasn't been a good son at all.'

'Shut up, damn you, or I'll smash your face in!'

The bottle that Bécu was brandishing had to be taken out of his hands, while Jésus-Christ, with tears in his eyes, waited in smiling resignation to be hit. Then, friends once more, they resumed their game. Trump, trump, and again trump!

Macqueron, worried at the schoolmaster's assumed indifference, at length asked him, 'And you, Monsieur Lequeu, what do you say about it all?'

Lequeu, warming his long pale hands on the stove-pipe, smiled the bitter smile of a superior man whose position compels silence.

'Don't ask me. It's no concern of mine.'

Macqueron plunged his face into a bowl of water, and then, while he was sniffling and drying himself, he said, 'Well, you listen to me, I want to do something. Yes, by God, if they vote for the road, I'll give my land for nothing!'

This statement stupefied the others. Jésus-Christ and Bécu, sozzled as they were, lifted their heads. A silence fell, and they all stared at Macqueron as if he had suddenly gone mad; and he, spurred on by the effect he had produced, though his hands trembled at the pledge he was giving, added, 'That'll mean at least half an acre. A man who goes back on his word is a swine! I've given you my oath.'

Lengaigne departed with his son Victor, exasperated and sickened at his neighbour's generosity: the land wouldn't cost him anything, he had thieved enough from everybody else! Macqueron himself, despite the cold, took up his rifle and went out to see if he could get the rabbit that he'd glimpsed the night before at the bottom of his vineyard. No one remained but Lequeu, who spent his Sundays in the tavern without a drink, and the two absorbed gamblers bent over their cards. Some hours drifted by, with a coming and going of other peasants.

Towards five o'clock, the door was roughly thrown open and Buteau appeared, followed by Jean. At the sight of Jésus-Christ he yelled, 'I'd have bet a franc! Don't you give a damn for the family? We're all waiting for you.'

But the drunkard, dribbling with laughter, retorted, 'Eh, you damned joker, it's me that's been waiting for you. You've kept us all hanging round ever since this morning.'

Buteau had stopped at La Borderie where Jacqueline, whom he had tumbled in the hay at the age of fifteen, had persuaded him to stay and eat buttered toast sopped in wine, with Jean. As Farmer Hourdequin had gone to lunch in Cloyes after Mass, the party had gone on till a late hour and the two young men had only just arrived in the village, sticking to one another.

Meanwhile Bécu was bawling out that he'd pay for the five litres of wine, and that the game must go on at the next session; while Jésus-Christ having pulled himself with difficulty out of his chair, followed his brother out, his eyes mistily mild.

'Wait here,' said Buteau to Jean, 'and in half an hour come and join me. Remember you're eating with us at father's place.'

At Fouan's house, when the two brothers came into the room, all the others were present. The father was standing with lowered head; the mother, sitting by the table in the middle of the room, was knitting mechanically. Opposite her was Grosbois, who had eaten and drunk himself half asleep and whose eyes were only just open, while, seated on two low chairs a little further away, Fanny and Delhomme patiently waited.

An odd sight in this smoky room, with its old cheap furnishings and its few utensils scratched with scouring, there lay on the table a sheet of white paper, an ink-well and a pen, beside the surveyor's hat—a huge rusty-black hat in which he had trudged about for the previous ten years, come rain or shine. Night was falling, the narrow window gave a last smudgy glimmer of light, in which the hat took on an extraordinary importance, with its flat edges and urnlike shape.

But Grosbois, always ready for business even when intoxicated, woke up and yawned, 'Here we all are then. . . I told you the document was ready. I called on Monsieur Baillehache yesterday, and he showed it to me. Only the lot-numbers after your names have been left blank. So we'll draw them now. Then the lawyer will only have to add them in, and you will be able to sign the papers at his office on Saturday.'

He shook himself and raised his voice.

'Now then, I'm going to get the slips ready.'

With a sudden movement the children came nearer, making no attempt to hide their distrust. They watched him closely, noting his slightest movement, as if he were a conjurer capable of juggling away the shares. First, with his fat fingers, the tremulous hands of an alcoholic, he cut the sheet of paper into three; then, on each slip he wrote a number—1, 2, 3—pressing hard and making the figures huge; and over his shoulder all eyes followed the pen while the father and mother nodded their heads, pleased to see there was no trickery possible. The slips were slowly folded up and thrown into the hat.

A solemn silence weighed on the room.

At the end of two long minutes Grosbois said, 'You must decide it now. Who'll begin?'

No one moved. The light faded, the hat seemed to grow larger and larger in the encroaching darkness.

'According to age, you agree to that?' the surveyor suggested. 'You're the one to start then, Jésus-Christ, you're the eldest.'

Jésus-Christ obligingly came forward; but he lost his balance and almost fell flat. He had thrust his fist into the hat with a violent effort, as if he were going to pull out a lump of rock. When he got a slip in his hand, he had to take it to the window.

'Two!' he shouted, obviously finding this number particularly funny, for he choked with laughter.

'Your turn, Fanny,' called Grosbois.

When Fanny had thrust her hand right in, she didn't hurry. She moved her fingers about, mixed the slips up, weighed one after the other.

'Choosing's not allowed,' said Buteau savagely. In his anxiety he found it hard to breath and had gone pale on hearing the number drawn by his brother.

'Oh! and why not?' she retorted. 'I'm not looking, I can feel them if I want to.'

'Get on,' murmured her father. 'They're both the same, there's no more weight in one than in the other.'

At last she decided and ran towards the window. 'One!'

'Well, Buteau gets number three,' Fouan went on. 'Draw it out, lad.'

In the increasing darkness they had not noticed how the younger son's face had changed. His voice broke with anger.

'Never!'

'What!'

'If you think I'll accept that, well I won't. The third strip, isn't it? The worst one! I've told you often enough I wanted it divided the other way. No, no, you're making a fool of me! Think I can't see through your game, eh? Shouldn't it have been the youngest who drew first? No, not on your life, I'm not drawing, it's all a cheat.'

The father and mother stared as he flung himself about, stamping his feet and banging his fists together.

'My poor boy, you're going mad,' said Rose.

'Ah, mother, I know you've never loved me. You'd rip the skin off my back to give to my brother. All of you, you'd take everything from me. . .'

Fouan interrupted him coldly. 'Enough of this foolery, stop it! Will you draw?'

'I want it done over again.'

But there was general protest. Jésus-Christ and Fanny grasped their bits of paper as if someone was trying to wrench them away. Delhomme declared that the draw had been honestly carried out. Grosbois, much offended, threatened to walk out if his good faith was called in question.

'All right then, I ask dad to add a thousand francs to my lot, a thousand francs from the money he's got hidden away.'

The old man stuttered, stupefied for a moment. Then he drew himself up and strode forward, terrible in his anger.

'What's that you're saying? You're still at it, are you? Wanting to get me murdered, you bad bugger! You can tear the house to pieces and you won't find a single copper. Take the slip, by God! or you'll get nothing!'

Buteau, his face rigid with obstinacy, did not flinch before his father's lifted fist.

'No!'

Awkward silence fell again. Now the huge hat was hostile, an

57

obstacle in all their ways, with its single slip of paper at the bottom, the slip that no one would touch. To get the business over, the surveyor finally advised the old man to draw it himself. And the old man gravely took it out and went to read it by the window as if he hadn't known what was on it.

'Three! You get the third strip, do you hear? The document is ready and you can be sure Monsieur Baillehache won't change anything. What's done can't be undone. And as you're sleeping here, I give you the night to think things over. There, that's done, let's hear no more about it.'

Buteau, hidden in the shadows, made no reply. The others gave their noisy approval, while the mother at last made up her mind to light a candle so that she could lay the table.

At that moment, Jean, who had come to join his friend, caught sight of two shadowy figures interlaced in the dark deserted road, spying on what was going on in the Fouan house. Snow-flakes were starting to flutter with the lightness of feathers across the slate-coloured sky.

'Oh, Monsieur Jean!' said a soft voice. 'How you frightened us!'

Then he recognised Françoise, cloaked, with her long face and full lips. She was clinging to her sister Lise with an arm round her waist. The two sisters were absorbed in one another and were always seen about like this, hanging round each other's necks. Lise, the taller, was a pleasant-looking girl, for all her large features and the obvious swelling of her whole plump body, and remained cheerful in spite of her mishap.

'Spying, eh?' he asked gaily.

'Go on!' she replied. 'I'm very interested in what's happening in there. . . Remains to be seen if it'll make up Buteau's mind.'

Françoise, with a gesture of tenderness, had put her other arm round her sister's swollen belly.

'He shan't get away with it, the swine. When he has the land, perhaps he'll want a better-off girl.'

Jean tried to cheer them up: the division must be completed and everything else could come out all right. Then, when he told them he was eating with the Fouans, Françoise added, 'Well, we'll see you later, we'll be at the wake.'

He watched them fade into the night. The snow was falling more now and their clothes, merged together, were furred with a fine white down.

58

At seven o'clock, after supper, the Fouans, together with Buteau and Jean, had gone into the cowshed, where lived the two cows that Rose was going to sell. The animals, tied up at the far end by the trough, warmed the shed with strong exhalations from their bodies and their straw; whereas the kitchen, with its two or three meagre logs of wood for the supper-fire, was already freezing cold in the early November frosts. During winter, the wake was always held in the cowshed with its hard trodden earthen floor, in snug warmth and comfort, and no preparations were needed except the bringing-in of a little round table and a dozen or so old chairs. Each neighbour in turn provided a candle. Huge shadows danced along the bare, black, dusty walls, wavering right up to the webs spun over the rafters. And the backs of the participants were warmed by the soft breath of the cows who lay ruminating.

La Grande arrived first, with some knitting. She took advantage of her great age and never brought a candle; so awe-inspiring was she that her brother never dared remind her of the custom. She immediately took the best place, pulled the candle near and kept it there on account of her bad eyesight. Against her chair she placed the stick which was never out of her reach. Twinkling specks of snow melted on the rough hairs that stuck up out of her vulturine bony head.

'Snowing?' asked Rose.

'Snowing,' she replied in her curt way.

She started to knit, sparing of words as usual, and screwed up her thin lips after throwing a piercing glance at Jean and Buteau.

The others appeared in turn. First, Fanny who had brought her son Nénesse for company as Delhomme never came to wakes, and, close behind her, Lise and Françoise who laughed boisterously as they shook the snow off. But when Lise saw Buteau, she blushed slightly. He looked at her undisturbed. 'Been keeping well, Lise, since last time?' 'Not bad, thanks.' 'Good, that's the way.'

Meanwhile Palmyre, had stealthily slipped in through the half-open door. She was creeping unobtrusively to a seat as far as possible from her grandmother, the terrible La Grande, when an uproar in the roadway made her start up. Furious stutterings were heard, screams, laughs and hoots.

'Ah, those naughty brats, they're after him again!' she cried.

With one leap she had the door open, and in a rush of courage, with the snarls of a lioness, she rescued her brother Hilarion from the teasing of La Trouille, Delphin and Nénesse. Nénesse had just come out to join the other two in yapping at the cripple's heels. Breathless, bewildered, Hilarion waddled in on his twisted legs. His harelip made him slobber and he mumbled without being able to explain his needs, looking worn-out though only twenty-four years old, and ugly as only a cretin can be. He had grown vicious, maddened at never being able to catch and belabour the young rascals who chased him on the roads. And this time again he was the one who had been hit by all the snowballs.

'He's a liar!' said La Trouille with an air of bland innocence. 'He bit my thumb, look!'

Hilarion at once tried to answer back but the words stuck and choked him. Palmyre calmed him down, wiped his face with her handkerchief and called him her darling.

'That's enough, d'you hear!' said Fouan at last. 'You there, you ought to be able to stop him following you. At least make him keep still in his seat. And you, you brats, shut up! or you'll be dragged home by the ears!'

But the cripple went on mumbling, wanting to prove himself in the right, till La Grande, whose eyes were spitting fire, seized her stick and struck the table so violently that everyone jumped. Palmyre and Hilarion shrank back in fright and stayed quiet.

The wake began. Around the solitary candle the women knitted, span, worked at sewing tasks without even watching their hands. The men, in the rear, smoked slowly with a few bare words now and then, while in a corner the children shoved and pinched each other with smothered laughter.

Occasionally a story was told: the one about the Black Pig, who kept guard over a treasure chest with a red key in his jaws, or the one about the beast of Orléans which had a man's face, bat's wings, hair right down to the ground, two horns and two tails (one for grabbing hold and one for killing)—this monster had eaten a traveller from Rouen, leaving nothing of the fellow but his boots and hat. At other times they would begin endless stories about wolves, those voracious wolves which, for centuries, had devastated La Beauce. In the old days when La Beauce, nowadays stripped bare, still had its groves and woods left over from the primeval forests, countless packs of starving wolves came marauding during the winter and attacked the flocks. Women and children were devoured, and the old people of the countryside remembered how during heavy bliz-

zards, wolves ventured right into the towns; at Cloyes they could
be heard howling in the Place Saint-Georges; at Rognes they snuffled
round the ill-fitting doors of stables and sheep-pens. Then familiar
anecdotes came thickly: about the miller, who, surprised by five
wolves, sent them all flying by striking a match; the little girl who
ran for over two leagues from a wolf bitch and who was eaten up
outside her own door when she fell down. More and more stories,
legends of werewolves, men changed into beasts, who jumped on
the shoulders of travellers in the dark and made them run till they
dropped.

But what froze the blood of the girls as they sat round the solitary
candle during the wake—what made them at the end of the evening scurry away, anxiously scanning the shadows—were the horror-
stories about the Warmers-up or *Chauffeurs*, the notorious gang of
Orgères, who still held the countryside in a state of panic. These
gangs were hundreds strong, made up of vagrants, beggars, deserters,
tricksters; men, women and children, whose lives were spent in
robbery, murder and debauchery. They were descendants of the
disciplined armed bands of the early brigands who took advantage
of the troubled days of the Revolution. They laid regular siege to
isolated houses, into which they burst like bombshells, using rams
to crash down the doors. As soon as night fell, they came like wolves
out of the Dourdan forest, the underbrush of La Conie, the wooded
recesses where they laired; and terror came with nightfall to the
farms of La Beauce from Etampes to Châteaudun, from Chartres
to Orléans. Among the legendary atrocities, that most frequently
remembered at Rognes was the pillaging of the Millouard farm,
only a few leagues distant, in the Orgères district. Beau-Françoise,
the famous leader, successor to Fleur-d'Epine, took with him that
night his lieutenant, Rouge d'Anneau, Grand-Dragon, Breton-le-cul-
sec, Longjumeau, Sans-Pouce, and fifty others, all with blackened
faces. First they drove the farm people into the cellar—the servants,
waggoners and shepherd—prodding them on with bayonets; then
they 'warmed up' the farmer, old Fousset whom they'd kept back.
When they had stretched his feet out over the embers in the fireplace, they set fire to his beard and all the hair on his body with
straw brands; then they turned back to his feet and gashed them
with a knife-point to let the flames penetrate more sharply. In the
end the old man agreed to tell them where his money was hidden,
so they released him and carried off considerable loot. Fousset, who
found strength to drag himself to a neighbouring house, did not

die till later. Invariably the story finished with the trial and execution of the gang of *Chauffeurs* at Chartres after their betrayal by Borgne-de-Jouy: a ghastly trial it was, that lasted eighteen months, and during it sixty-four prisoners died in prison of a plague caused by their own filth; a trial that sent one hundred and fifteen accused persons on to the Assize-Court, thirty-three condemned for contumacy. The jury had to deal with one thousand and eight hundred questions, and finally twenty-three sentences of death were pronounced. On the night of the execution, under the gallows red with blood, the hangmen of Chartres and Dreux came to blows over the division of the dead men's belongings.

Fouan, after telling about a murder committed near Janville, was once more narrating the appalling tale of the Millouard farm and had reached the petition written from prison by Rouge d'Anneau himself when the women were terrified by strange noises in the road—steps, knocks and curses. They listened with pallid faces, expecting a great gang to crash in like bombshells. But Buteau went courageously to open the door.

'Who's that?'

There stood Bécu and Jésus-Christ, who, after quarrelling with Macqueron, had left the wine-shop with cards and candle to finish their game elsewhere. They were so tipsy, and everyone else had been so alarmed, that one and all burst out laughing.

'Come in anyway, and behave yourselves,' said Rose, smiling at her burly scoundrel of a son. 'Your kids are here and you can take them home later.'

Jésus-Christ and Bécu sat down on the ground near the cows, set the candle between them, and carried on: Trump, trump, and trump again! But the conversation changed its course and turned on the boys of the district who were due to be conscripted, Victor Lengaigne and three others. The women became serious and grief slowed down their speech.

'It's no joke,' Rose spoke again, 'No, it's no joke for anyone.'

'Ah! war!' murmured Fouan. 'It's bad, bad. It's the death of growing crops. Yes, when the lads go, the best hands go with them, you can easily see it when the work starts; and when they come back, why, they've changed, they don't put their heart into ploughing. Better have cholera than war.'

Fanny stopped knitting. 'I don't want Nénesse to go,' she declared. 'Monsieur Baillehache explained a sort of system to us, something like a lottery. Several folk get together, each one puts a sum of money down and those who lose the draw are bought off.'

'Got to be rich for that,' said La Grande dryly.

But Bécu, between two tricks, had caught a word. 'War! that's the stuff! That's what makes you into a man. If you haven't been in war, you just can't know. That's the life—beat 'em up! . . Eh? down there, among the niggers. . .'

He winked his left eye, while Jésus-Christ laughed loudly and knowingly. Both men had been in African campaigns: the constable in the early days of the conquest, the other later on at the time of the last revolt. And so, in spite of the difference in period, they had common memories: Bedouins whose ears were cut off and threaded on strings, slippery-skinned Bedouin women pulled down behind the hedges and raped in every aperture of the body. Jésus-Christ above all had a story which always made the peasants shriek with laughter: about a vast ungainly woman, yellow as a lemon, whom they had forced to run around naked with a pipe stuck in her behind.

'Good Lord!' Bécu continued, addressing Fanny, 'do you want Nénesse to be a sissy? Just you watch me quick-step Delphin into the army!'

The children had stopped playing. Delphin raised his round solid small-boy's head, already redolent of earth. 'No!' he said firmly, with an obstinate look.

'Hey there! What did you say? I'll teach you what being brave is, you rotten Frenchman.'

'I don't want to go, I want to stay at home.'

The constable had his hand raised when Buteau stopped him.

'Leave the child alone. He's right. D'you think they need him? There's plenty of others. Why should we come into the world just to leave home, go and get smashed up because of a lot of flap-doodle that has nothing to do with us anyhow. I've never left our parts and I'm none the worse for it.'

In fact he had drawn a lucky number and was a proper stay-at-home, closely bound to the earth; he knew only Orléans and Chartres and had seen nothing beyond the flat horizon of La Beauce. And he seemed to draw pride from this, from the fact of his being rooted in his own soil, growing with the restricted but enduring energy of a tree. Now he had risen to his feet and the women were watching him.

'When they come back from service, they're so skinny,' Lise dared to murmur.

63

'And you, Corporal,' asked Rose, 'did you go far away?'

Jean was smoking away quietly like a thoughtful lad who preferred listening. He took his pipe slowly out of his mouth.

'Yes, pretty far. Not to the Crimea, though. I was due to go, but Sebastopol was taken. Still, later, I went to Italy. . .'

'And what's it like, Italy?'

The question seemed to surprise him. He hesitated, digging into his memories.

'Well now—in Italy—it's just like here. There's farming—and woods and rivers. It's the same all over.'

'And did you fight?'

'You bet I did. Of course.'

He had begun sucking at his pipe again, in no hurry to go on; and Françoise, who had raised her eyes, stayed open-mouthed, expecting a story. Indeed everyone was interested and La Grande herself gave another bang with her stick on the table to make Hilarion keep quiet. He had begun moaning after La Trouille invented the mild amusement of stealthily sticking a pin into his arm.

'At Solférino, it was terribly hot and yet it was raining. How it rained! I hadn't a dry stitch on me, the water was running down my back right into my shoes. Yes, I'm not telling a word of a lie when I say we were soaked!'

They all went on waiting, but he had nothing more to add. He'd told all he'd seen of battle. After a minute's silence, however, he went on in his matter-of-fact voice. 'Lord, war's not as hard as people think. It's a matter of luck, isn't it? You've got to do your duty. I left the army, it's true, because there were other things I liked better. But all the same it has its good points, supposing you're sick of your job and feel your blood boil when an invader comes trampling all over us here in France.'

'A dirty business all the same!' Old Fouan concluded, 'Everyone ought to defend his home, but that's all.'

Once again silence fell. It was very warm, a living damp warmth accentuated by the strong smell of the litter-straw. One of the two cows, which had got up, shat; and they heard the quiet pit-a-pat sound of the splashed dung. From the darkness of the rafters came down the melancholy rasp of a cricket, while along the walls the rapid fingers of the women with their busy knitting-needles cast shadows like giant scampering spiders amid the environing gloom.

Then Palmyre, having taken up the snuffers to trim the wick, snuffed the candle so low that she extinguished it. At once shouts

64

broke out, the girls laughed, the children drove the pin into Hilarion's buttock and the wake would have been broken up if the candle between Jésus-Christ and Bécu, who were drowsily bent over their cards, had not been there to re-light the other despite its long wick ballooning out at the top into a sort of red mushroom. Frightened by her own awkwardness, Palmyre trembled like a little girl afraid of being whipped.

'Now, who's going to give us some of this?' asked Fouan, 'to finish off the wake. Corporal, you ought to read print well.'

He had gone to fetch a little greasy book, one of the Bonapartist propaganda works with which the Empire had flooded the country-side. This one, which had turned up in the bag of a peddler, was a ferocious attack on the old régime, a dramatised history of the peasants before and after the Revolution, under the title: *The Misfortunes and The Triumph of Jacques Bonhomme*.

Jean took the book and straightaway, without waiting to be asked, began to read in the colourless stumbling voice of a school-boy without any idea of punctuation. The whole company listened devoutly.

First the booklet dealt with the freeborn Gauls reduced to slavery under the Romans, then conquered by the Franks who changed them from slaves into serfs in establishing feudalism. Then began the long martyrdom, the martyrdom of Jacques Bonhomme, the toiler on the land, exploited and worked to death over the centuries. While the townspeople rose in revolt, founded communes and won the rights of the *bourgeoisie*, the isolated peasant was dispossessed of everything, even his own body, and only managed to liberate himself much later, buying the right to be a free man with money. And what an illusory liberty was that won by the overwhelmed peasant, throttled with ruinous and bloody taxes, struggling against persistent challenges to his property rights, burdened with so many charges that he was left with little more than stones to eat! Then came a frightful account of the impositions that bore down the wretched man. Not that anyone could draw up the exact and com-plete list. The cursed things swarmed from all quarters, coming in the name of King, bishop and lord: three beasts of prey ravaging the same body. The King took quit-rent and poll-tax, the bishop took tithe, the lord laid tolls and fines on all sides and raised money out of everything. Nothing was left for the peasant; he owned neither earth nor water nor fire, nor even the air he breathed. He had to pay, pay, and keep on paying. He paid for being alive and he paid for dying. He paid for his contracts, his herds, his trade, his pleasures. He paid for turning the rain-water out of the ditches into his fields, he paid for the roadway-dust that his sheep stirred up in the great summer droughts. If he couldn't pay, he gave his body and his time, taxable and liable to forced-labour without limit, obliged to plough, harvest, reap, cultivate the vines, clean out the castle-ditches, make and maintain roads. And then there were the payments in kind; and the manor-dues, the mill, the oven, the wine-press, where a quarter of the harvests had to be left; and the exaction of watch and ward even after the demolition of the castle-keeps; and the exaction of domicile requisition tolls, of purveyance, which stripped the cottages, made every mattress and coverlet disappear, threw the inhabitant out of his own house, almost knocking down doors or windows when the man didn't scramble out quickly enough. But the most execrated imposition, the one which still rankled in the memory of every hamlet, was the hated salt-tax, the state-store of salt, with a salt-allowance (which still had to be bought from the King) fixed for every family—and an iniquitous system of collection which was so arbitrary that it stirred revolt and provoked bloodshed all over France.

'My father,' Fouan interrupted, 'was alive when salt was eighteen sous a pound. Ah, those times were hard.'

Jésus-Christ sniggered in his beard. He wanted to emphasise the more licentious rights, to which the little book was content to make modest allusion.

'And the right of the first-night, eh? Aha, the squire got his cut in the marriage-bed too, and the first cut at that——'

They shut him up. The women, even Lise with her great belly, were all blushing, while La Trouille and the two youngsters, with faces pressed to the ground, crammed their fists into their mouths to keep their laughter back. Hilarion listened gaping to every word as if he understood.

Jean went on. Now he had come to the law, the triple law of King, bishop and landlord, which racked the poor people sweating on the glebe lands. There was common law, statute law, and above all there was arbitrary whim, the most powerful law of all. There was no safeguard, no appeal; the sword was almighty. Even in the later centuries when protests were made in the name of equity, seats on the judiciary were bought up and justice was sold to the highest bidder. Still worse was the system of army recruiting, the blood-tax, which for a long time affected only the poor peasants.

They fled into the woods, were brought back in chains, beaten with musket-butts, pushed into army-service as though they were being flung into gaol. There was no promotion for them. A high-born younger son trafficked with a regiment as if it were a piece of merchandise he had paid for, gave the lesser commissions to the highest bidder, and drove the remainder of his human cattle to the slaughter. Finally came the hunting-rights, the rights over dove-cot and rabbit-warren, which even in our day, after their abolition, have left a ferment of hatred in peasant hearts. Hunting was the lord's hereditary mania, the ancient feudal prerogative which authorised him to hunt anywhere and imposed the death-penalty on a villein who had the audacity to hunt on his own land. It meant that all the wild creatures, all the wild birds, were caged under the wide sky for the pleasure of one man alone; it meant that the fields were divided among hunting-captaincies, and ravaged by wild beasts while the owners were forbidden to destroy even so much as a sparrow.

'That's only right,' murmured Bécu, who always said he'd shoot poachers like rabbits.

But Jésus-Christ had pricked up his ears at the mention of hunting; and now he gave a mocking whistle. The game belonged to the man able to bag it.

'O dear God!' was all Rose said, sighing deeply.

They all felt heavy at heart. The reading was depressing them, as though it were some grim ghost story. They did not always understand what they heard, and that made them doubly uneasy. Since such things had happened in the past, it might well be that they could happen again.

'Go on, Jacques Bonhomme,' Jean's flat schoolboy-voice resumed the tale, 'Give your sweat, give your blood, you are not at the end of your trials. . .'

The calvary of the peasant was unrolled. Suffering came to him from all quarters—from man, from nature, from himself. Under feudalism, when the nobles were out for plunder, he was hunted, tracked down, treated as part of the loot. Every private war between lord and lord ruined him when it did not kill him off: his cottage was burned down, his fields ravaged. Later came the great Companies, the direst scourge that ever laid waste our countryside, gangs of adventurers obeying the whims of anyone who paid them, now fighting for France, now against her, marking their passage by fire and sword, stripping the earth bare as they went. The towns could hold out because of their walls, but the villages were swept away in this frenzy of destruction which raged for years on end. There were whole centuries of bloodshed, when our rolling plainlands rang unceasingly with cries of agony—when women were violated, children crushed, men hanged. Then, when wars stopped, the King's tax-gatherers carried on the ceaseless torment of the poor; for the number and weight of the taxes was nothing compared with the fantastic and brutal system of levying them. Polltax and salt-tax were farmed out. Assessments were made at random and unjustly, exacted by armed troops who got the money in for the treasury as if they were dealing with war-levies. As a result hardly any of the proceeds ever reached the State Treasury. It was stolen on the way; it diminished with every pair of pillaging hands through which it passed. Then there was famine to take its toll. The idiotic tyranny of the law immobilised trade, held up the free market of produce, provoked every ten years or so the most appalling dearths, whenever the weather was too hot or too wet—and the sufferings were taken as punishments sent by God. A storm that flooded rivers, a rainless spring, the least excess of cloud or sunlight that upset the harvest, meant the death of thousands. Terrible agonies of famine were the consequence, a sharp general rise of prices, ghastly sufferings during which people browsed like cattle in the grass of the ditches, and inevitably when wars and droughts had done their worst, epidemics broke out, killing those whom the sword and hunger had spared. The contagion was ceaselessly reborn of ignorance and uncleanness, plague, the Black Death, levelling with its sickle the sorrowful wan folk of the countryside.

Then, when his sufferings grew unbearable, Jacques Bonhomme rose in revolt. Behind him lay centuries of fear and resignation, his shoulders had been hardened by blows, his heart was so broken that he did not realise his own degradation. He could be beaten for a long time, famished, robbed of all his possessions without being driven out of his shell of caution, out of the stupefaction in which he brooded confusedly over things that never rose directly into his mind. He could go on thus until one last injustice, one last pang made him suddenly leap at the throat of his masters like a tamed animal that had been maddened by over-beating. Again and again, century after century, the same desperate uprisings took place, the Jacquerie armed the ploughmen with forks and sickles when nothing remained to them but death. Once they were the Christian *Bagaudae* of Gaul, the *Pastoureaux* at the time of the Crusades, later the *Croquants* and the *Barefoot* falling on the nobles and the King's

68

soldiers. After four hundred years the Jacques' cry of anguish and wrath rings out again over the devastated fields and shakes the masters laired in their castles. What if these men, who are many, should grow enraged once more? What if they should finally claim their inheritance? The masters, as of old, are haunted by a vision of half-naked, ragged devils, mad with ferocity and lust, ruining and exterminating as they have themselves been ruined and exterminated, and in their turn raping other men's wives!

'Calm your fury, men of the fields,' Jean continued in his mild intent tones, 'for the hour of your triumph will soon ring out from the clock-towers of history. . .'

Buteau brusquely shrugged his shoulders. It was crazy to rebel! Crazy, only asking for gendarmes to pick you up! All of them, however, as the little book described their forefathers' uprisings, listened with lowered eyes, not venturing the slightest movement, gripped with distrust, even though they were at home. These were things one did not mention aloud; no one needed to ask what they thought about them in their hearts. Jésus-Christ attempted to interrupt, to shout how many necks he'd wring in the next revolt, and so Bécu fiercely denounced all Republicans as swine. Fouan had to call for silence solemnly, with the sad gravity of an old man who knew it all long ago, but wasn't going to say anything. La Grande, while the other women seemed to grow yet more absorbed in their knitting, spat out one sentence, 'What you have, you stick to!' —a comment with no apparent reference to the reading. Only Françoise, with her work fallen on to her knees, watched Corporal, amazed that he could go on reading so long without making mistakes. 'Ah, dear God, dear God,' Rose repeated, sighing still more deeply.

But the tone of the book changed, it became lyrical and eulogised the Revolution. That was when Jacques Bonhomme triumphed, in the apotheosis of '89. After the taking of the Bastille, while the peasants were burning the castles, the Night of August 4th legalised the conquests of centuries by recognising human liberty and civic equality. 'In one night the ploughman became the equal of the lord who, because he held parchment documents, used to drink the peasant's sweat and devour the fruits of his work.' Abolition of the status of serf, of all the privileges of the nobility and of the ecclesiastical and manorial courts of law; the re-purchase of ancient rights; equalisation of taxes; the right of all citizens to enter any civil or military office. And so the account went on. The evils of the

69

old life seemed to fade out one by one. It was the hosanna of a new golden age opening up before the ploughman; and one entire page flattered him servilely, calling him king and foster-father of the whole world. He alone mattered, everyone must bow to the holy plough! Then the horrors of '93 were stigmatised in fiery terms, and the book launched into an extravagant eulogy of Napoleon, the child of the Revolution, who had succeeded in 'raising it out of the mire of Licence, thereby ensuring the happiness of the Country-side.'

'That's true, every bit!' shouted Bécu as Jean was turning over the last page.

'Yes, it's true,' said Old Fouan. 'There were good times, all the same, in my youth. I myself who speak to you, I saw Napoleon once, in Chartres. I was twenty. We were free, we had land, it all seemed so good! I remember how my father one day said he sowed coppers and reaped crowns! Then came Louis XVIII, Charles X, Louis-Philippe. It was still good, we could eat, there was nothing to grumble about. And now to-day there's Napoleon III, and it still wasn't too bad, not till last year. Only. . .'

He wanted to stop there, but the words ran away with him.

'Only, what blasted good has it been to us, their liberty and equality?—to Rose and me? Has it made us any fatter after fifty years of bitter hard work?'

Then in a few slow and painful words he summed up the whole story without realising he was doing it: the earth so long cultivated for the lord of the manor by the lashed and stripped slave, a slave who owned nothing, not even his own skin; the earth, fertilised by his labours, passionately loved and desired in the warm intimacy of each hour of work, like somebody else's wife whom a man tends and embraces but cannot possess; the earth, after centuries of this torment of desire, won at last, conquered, become a man's chattel, his joy, the very spring of his life. And this age-old desire, with possession always out of reach, explained his love of his field, his passion for the earth, as much earth as possible, with rich soil that you can touch and weigh in the hollow of your hand. And yet how indifferent and ungrateful she was, this earth. You could love and adore her, but she showed no feeling and produced not one extra ear of grain. Too much rain rotted the seeds, hailstorms cut down the growing green wheat, a fierce wind beat down the stalks, two months of drought shrivelled up the corn-ears. And then there were devouring insects, killing frosts, cattle-diseases, leprosies of poisonous weeds spoiling the soil; anything could spell ruin, the battle had to be fought out every day, with mistakes liable to wreck your hopes and never a moment's relaxation. Aye, he hadn't spared himself, working with every sinew in his body, driven mad when he saw that his toil wasn't enough. He had exhausted his muscles, he had given himself every ounce to the earth; and the earth had just kept him alive. And now she was leaving him poor, unsatisfied, ashamed of his impotent old age; and she passed into the arms of another man, without a shred of pity for his poor old bones that soon would return to her.

'That's it! That's it!' the old man went on. 'When you're young, you work till you're ready to drop, and by the time you make both ends meet with a lot of trouble, you're old and you have to get out. Eh, Rose?'

The mother nodded her trembling head. Yes, good God, she had worked too, even harder than a man! Getting up before the others, making the meals, sweeping, scouring—her back broken by a thousand chores, the cows, the pig, the batch of bread—always the last in bed! She had to be strong or she'd be killed by it. And her only recompense was to have stayed the course: she had got nothing out of it but wrinkles, fortunate if after pinching and scraping, going to bed in the dark and making do with bread and water there was enough to keep them from dying of hunger in their last days.

'All the same,' Fouan went on, 'we mustn't complain. I've been told there are places where the earth makes you live a dog's life. In Le Perche, for instance, it's all flints. La Beauce is still in good heart, she only asks that you keep hard at it without stopping. But she's not what she was. She's certainly getting less fertile. The fields where we used to harvest seven quarters only give five now. And prices have been going down this last year, they say corn is coming from where the savages live. There's something starting to go wrong—a crisis, they call it. Will hard times never end? Take this universal suffrage, it doesn't put any meat in the stew, does it? The land-tax pulls us down and they're always taking our children for wars. And as for their revolutions, they can keep them, six of one and half a dozen of the other, and still the peasant stays a peasant.'

Jean, a methodical man, was waiting to finish his reading. As soon as a pause came he quietly read on, 'Happy ploughman, don't leave the country for the town where you have to buy everything, milk, meat and vegetables; where you'll spend over and above what is necessary because the opportunity's always there. In your village,

71

haven't you air and sun, healthy work, honest pleasures? Country life cannot be equalled, you have real happiness, far from gilded mansions; and the proof is that the town workers come to enjoy themselves in the country, and even the *bourgeois* have only one dream, to retire near you, to pick flowers, eat fruit off trees, frolic on the green. Tell yourself, Jacques Bonhomme, that money is an illusion. If you have a heart at peace, you have wealth.'

His voice had changed, he was trying to restrain the emotion of a big soft-hearted fellow brought up in a town, and moved deep in his soul by the notion of pastoral bliss. The others remained gloomy, the women bending over their needles, the men sunk into themselves with closed faces. Was the book jeering at them? Money was the sole good and they were crushed by poverty. Then as if the silence, heavy with suffering and rancour, disturbed him, the young man hazarded a sage remark.

'All the same, it might perhaps be better if there was education. If we were wretched in days gone by, it was because we didn't know anything. To-day we know something, and it certainly isn't as bad as it was. So we ought to have some thorough teaching— proper agricultural colleges. . .'

Fouan, the old man clinging to the old ways, interrupted savagely, 'Shut your trap, you and your science! The more you know, the worse you do things. Haven't I told you that fifty years ago the earth gave a bigger yield! It only annoys her to be teased and bothered. She never gives what she doesn't want to, the old bitch! And hasn't Monsieur Hourdequin thrown away a pile of money as tall as himself, by meddling with all these new-fangled inventions . . . No, no, that's all stupid, the peasant stays a peasant!'

Ten o'clock struck, and Old Fouan's declaration brought the wake to an end with the finality of an axe blow. Rose went to get the pot of chestnuts left in the warm embers of the kitchen fire, the customary treat on All Saints' Eve. She even brought back two litres of white wine to complete the festival. From that moment everyone forgot the stories, jollity increased, and nails and teeth were busy tearing the steaming boiled chestnuts out of their husks. La Grande had immediately swept her share into her pocket because she was the slowest eater. Bécu and Jésus-Christ swallowed their lot without skinning them, tossing them to the back of their mouths; while Palmyre, grown bold, cleaned hers extremely carefully, then stuffed them into Hilarion as if he were a chicken. As for the children, they played at 'sausage-making': La Trouille split the skin with her tooth then pressed it so as to force out a thin strip which Delphin and Nénesse promptly licked. As the trick was such a success, Lise and Françoise decided to follow suit. The candle was snuffed for the last time, glasses clinked to the good fellowship of the company. The heat had intensified, a reddish steam rose from the liquid dung of the litter, the cricket sang more loudly out of the huge moving shadows of the rafters; and to bring the cows into the treat they were given the husks, which they munched with a steady sound, coarse and subdued.

At half-past ten people started to go home. First Fanny took Nénesse away. Then Jésus-Christ and Bécu went out quarrelling, their tipsiness revived by the shock of the cold air. And La Trouille and Delphin could be heard holding up their respective fathers, pushing them along and pulling them back on to the road like mulish beasts which refuse to recognise the way to the stable. With every swing of the door an icy breath came in off the snow-blanched road. But La Grande was in no hurry as she tied her handkerchief round her neck and drew on her mittens. Not one glance did she cast at Palmyre and Hilarion, who slouched off in dismay, shivering in their rags. But at last she went off to her own house nearby and slammed the door behind her with a heavy thud. Only Françoise and Lise remained.

'Corporal,' asked Fouan, 'you'll see them home as you go back to the farm, won't you? It's on your way.'

Jean nodded in agreement while the two girls were covering their heads with their kerchiefs.

Buteau, who had got to his feet, was walking from end to end of the cowshed with hardened face and uneasy brooding step. He had not spoken a word since the reading, as if completely absorbed by what the book had said, all those stories of the laborious conquest of the earth. Why couldn't he have the whole estate? The idea of division had become intolerable to him. And there were other things too, confused things which whirled inside his thick skull, anger, pride, the determination not to go back on what he had said, the exasperated desire of the male who wants a thing and doesn't want it, afraid of finding himself fooled. Abruptly he made a decision.

'I'm going to bed, good-bye.'

'What's that—good-bye?'

'Yes, I'm going back to La Chamade before dawn. Good-bye, I won't see you again.'

His father and mother stood side by side, facing him.

'And what about your land?' asked Fouan. 'Do you accept it?'

Buteau walked to the door, then turned round.

'No.'

The old peasant shook all over. He straightened up and let go in one last flash of his old authority.

'Right you are, you're a bad son. I am going to give your share to your brother and sister, I'll rent it out to them, and when I die, I will arrange for them to keep it. You'll get nothing, out you go!'

Buteau did not wince, set in his rigid attitude. Then Rose in her turn tried to soften him. 'But we love you as much as the others, you fool. You're cutting off your own nose to spite your face. Take your share.'

'No!' And he went out, going up to bed.

Outside, Lise and Françoise, still disturbed by this scene, walked a few steps in silence. They again put their arms round one another, their forms melted together, black against the azure of the snow. But Jean, as he followed in silence, presently heard them weeping. He tried to comfort them.

'Come now, he'll think it over and accept to-morrow.'

'Ah, you don't know him,' cried Lise. 'He'd rather be chopped into bits than give in. No, no, it's the end!' Then in a voice of desperation she added, 'What shall I do with his child?'

'You can't stop it coming now anyway,' murmured Françoise.

They couldn't help laughing at that. But the girls were too depressed, they began to cry again.

When Jean had left them at their door, he went on his way across the plain. The snow had ceased, the sky was light and clear again, pricked with stars, a wide frosty sky from which fell a blue light, limpid as crystal; and La Beauce stretched away into infinity, all white, flat and motionless as a sea of ice. Not a breath of wind came from the far horizon. Jean could hear nothing but the thump of his heavy boots on the hard soil. The utter stillness of extreme cold reigned all around. All that he had read was seething in his head and there was an ache behind his ears; he took off his cap to cool himself, trying to make his mind a blank. The thought of the pregnant girl and her sister also worried him. His heavy boots went on ringing against the ground. A single shooting star slid out and silently furrowed the sky with a flight of flame.

Over there, the farm of La Borderie was fading out, seen as a mere tiny hump in the white carpet; and as Jean turned into the cross-pathway he remembered the field he had sown here a few days before. He looked to his left and recognised the place beneath its shroud of snow. The layer was thin, of the lightness and purity of ermine, outlining the tips of the furrows, hinting at the earth's benumbed limbs. How deep the seeds must be sleeping! How profoundly at rest within those icy flanks until that warm morning when the spring sun would reawaken them to life!

SECOND PART

I

It was four o'clock and dawn was just breaking, the rosy dawn of early May. Under the paling sky the buildings of La Borderie were still asleep, half-shadowed, three long buildings round three sides of the huge square yard, the sheep pen at the far end, the haylofts on the right, the cowshed, stable and house on the left. Closing the fourth side, the wide gate was fastened-to, locked with an iron bar. On the manure-heap a big yellow cockerel, all alone, was sounding reveille with his piercing trumpet call. A second cock replied, then a third. The call was repeated from farm to farm, from one end of La Beauce to the other.

That night, as on practically every night, Hourdequin had gone to Jacqueline in her bedroom, the small servant's-room which he had let her embellish with flowered wall-paper, cambric curtains and mahogany furniture. In spite of her growing hold over him, she had been sharply refused every time she tried to share the room where his dead wife had slept—the marriage-chamber which he kept inviolate as a last mark of respect. Jacqueline was very hurt, understanding that she would never be the real mistress until she occupied the old oak bed with the red cotton hangings.

At the first rays of day, she woke up and went on lying on her back with eyes wide open, while the farmer still snored at her side. Her dark eyes showed dreamy as she lay in the exciting warmth of the bed; a shudder stirred her slender naked body. For a while she hesitated; then she made up her mind, gently climbed over her master with her shift tucked up, so light and nimble that he felt nothing. Noiselessly, her hands feverish with her sudden desire, she pulled on her petticoat; but she knocked a chair and he in turn opened his eyes.

'Hullo, getting dressed? Where are you off to?'

'I'm worried about the bread, I'm going to have a look.'

Hourdequin drifted back to sleep, mumbling his surprise at the excuse, his drowsy brain went on dully arguing about it. What an idea! the bread didn't need her at this time of day. And he leaped awake, stabbed by a keen suspicion. Finding her gone, bemused, he looked slowly round this servant's-room and saw his slippers, his pipe, his razor. The slut was after one of the men again! In the two minutes needed to get himself under control again, his whole life flashed through his mind.

His father, Isidor Hourdequin, was the descendant of an old peasant family of Cloyes, raised to middle-class statue and manners in the sixeteenth century. They had all held posts in the salt-tax revenue offices: one had been a storehouse-keeper, another had been controller at Châteaudun, and Isidor, orphaned in youth, possessed some sixty thousand francs when, at twenty-six, deprived of his situation by the Revolution, he conceived the idea of making his fortune out of the thefts of the Republican brigands who were putting all national property up for sale. He knew the country extremely well, he sniffed around, calculated things out, and for thirty thousand francs (hardly a fifth of their real value) bought the three hundred and seventy acres of La Borderie, all that remained of the ancient domain of the Rognes-Bouquevals. Not one peasant had dared to risk his money; only the *bourgeois*, the lawyers and the financiers, got any benefit out of the revolutionary measures. In any case, it was a simple piece of speculation, for Isidor was not interested in burdening himself with a farm, but counted on re-selling it at his own price as soon as order was restored, and thereby recouping himself five times what he had paid. But the Directory arrived and the depreciation of land-values went on: he was unable to sell with the dreamed-of profit. His land held him fast and he became its prisoner, till at last in his obstinacy, refusing to let an inch of it go, he got the idea of working it himself, hoping to win a fortune after all. About this time he married a neighbouring farmer's daughter who herself had a hundred and twenty acres, so that he now owned five hundred. And thus the townsman whose line had broken away from its peasant origins for three centuries, went back to farming—but this time to farming on a large scale; to the class of big land-owners which had replaced the ancient all-powerful feudal lords.

Alexandre Hourdequin, his only son, was born in 1804. He had started studying, with deplorable results, at the Châteaudun College; but the land strongly attracted him, he wanted to come back to help his father, and so yet another of his father's dreams was wrecked. Isidor, finding wealth slow in coming, would have liked to sell everything up and send his son into one of the liberal professions. The young man was twenty-seven when he became master of La Borderie on his father's death. He was interested in new methods. His chief aim in marrying was to find, not land, but money, because according to him the poor development of the property was due to insufficient capital expenditure; and he found the desired dowry, fifty thousand francs, in the hands of a sister of Lawyer Baillehache, a mature maiden, five years his elder, extremely ugly, but sweet-tempered. Then began a long struggle between him and his five hundred acres. At first he was cautious, but little by little he became reckless through disappointments; the struggle went on unslackening every season, every day, and, without enriching him, allowed him to live the life of a sensual full-blooded man, determined to gratify his every appetite. The last few years, things had gone from bad to worse. His wife had borne him two children: a boy, who hated farming and had just been made an army captain, after Solférino, and a charming, delicate daughter, the one person he really loved, and heiress to La Borderie since his ungrateful son had become a soldier of fortune. First, in mid-summer, he lost his wife; and the following autumn his daughter died. The blow was shattering. The captain did not turn up more than once a year and the father found himself suddenly alone, his future a blank without the spur of working for a family. But even if the wound bled inwardly, he remained apparently intact, violent and despotic. Faced with peasants who sneered at his machines, who hoped for the ruin of a *bourgeois* bold enough to dabble in their trade, he grew obstinate. What else could he do, anyhow? He was more and more closely imprisoned by his land. Work piled up and the capital he had sunk tied him up more tightly every day. There was no possible way-out unless by some catastrophe.

Hourdequin, broad shouldered, with a large ruddy face, retained nothing of middle-class refinements other than his small hands, and had always been tyrannically male towards his women servants. Even when his wife was alive, every single one of them had had him in her bed—embraced without thought, without consequences, as a matter-of-course. The daughters of poor peasants who are apprenticed to dressmakers sometimes escape; but all who become farm-servants are used at will by the men, labourers and master alike. Mme Hourdequin was still alive when Jacqueline was brought to La Borderie as an act of charity: old Cognet, a drunkard, used to beat her unmercifully, she was so scraggy and worn-out that her bones stuck out through her skin and showed through her rags and tatters. Moreover, she was thought so ugly that the children shouted after her. She looked fifteen at most, though she was almost eighteen. She helped the kitchen-maid and was given the most menial jobs—the washing-up, the yard-sweeping, cleaning of the livestock—which put the finishing touch to her squalid appearance. Still, after the death of Hourdequin's wife, she seemed to smarten up a bit. All the farm labourers turned her over in the hay; not one man came to the farm without enjoying her; and one day when she was accompanying the master to the cellars, he, previously uninterested, decided to try out the ugly slattern: but she defended herself furiously, scratched him and bit him till he was forced to let her go. From that moment her fortune was made. She resisted him for six months, then gave herself bit by bit. From the yard she was raised to the kitchen, as servant proper; next, she engaged a girl to help her, then, grown quite the lady, she had a maid of her own. And now the slattern of bygone days had grown into a girl with extremely dark hair, delicate pretty features and firm breasts, and a body strong and resilient though deceptively slight. She became an extravagant coquette, drenched herself with perfume without being able to cover up her persisting dirtiness. The people of Rognes and the neighbouring farmers were none the less amazed at the affair: was it possible that a wealthy man could be caught by such a slut, a wench who wasn't good-looking or even well-padded! In short, of La Cognette, old Cognet's daughter, the old boozer who'd been breaking stones on the road for twenty years. What a fine father-in-law! What a notable tart! And the peasants did not even realise that this whore was their vengeance, the revenge of the village on the farm, of the poor peasant of the parish against the jumped-up *bourgeois* become a rich landowner. Hourdequin, at the critical age of fifty-five, became infatuated. He was physically snared and hungered for Jacqueline as a starving man for bread and water. When she wanted to be pleasant, she rubbed all round him like a cat, and set to work on him with an unscrupulous and shameless lewdness. For one hour of this sort he was ready to humiliate himself, plead with her to stay, even after quarrels and tortured moments of determination when he threatened to kick her out of the house.

Only the evening before, he had hit her after a scene when she made an attempt to sleep in the bed where his wife died; and all night she had refused to give herself, hitting out at him as soon as he approached her. For though she enjoyed herself regularly with

80

all the farm servants, she rationed the master, sharpening his desire with abstinence to increase her power. And so that morning, in the damp room, in the tumbled bed where he could still feel her warmth, he was once more seized with fury and lust. For long he had suspected her continual unfaithfulness. He leaped from bed and shouted out, 'Ah, you bitch, if I catch you at it!'

He dressed in haste and went downstairs.

Jacqueline had slipped through the silent house, still dim with the first faint rays of dawn. As she crossed the yard, she shrank back at the sight of the old shepherd, Soulas, already about. But her desire was so strong that she went on: it couldn't be helped! She avoided the stable with its fifteen horses where the four waggoners slept and made for the loft at the end where Jean had his bed—some straw, a blanket, not even any sheets. Embracing him as he slept, she closed his mouth with a kiss, trembling and breathless, and whispered softly: 'It's me, you big fool. Don't be frightened . . . but quick, quick. Let's hurry.'

But he was alarmed. He didn't want her there, in his own bed, for fear of being caught. The ladder to the hayloft was near, so they climbed up, leaving the trap door open, and flung themselves into the hay. 'Oh, you big fool, you big fool,' Jacqueline went on saying, transported, in the throbbing voice that he felt coming up warmly out of her bowels.

Jean Macquart had been at the farm for nearly two years. On leaving the army he had found himself at Bazoches-le-Doyen with a friend, a carpenter like himself, and he had got a job with his mate's father, a small artisan in the village, who employed two or three workers. But he lost heart for the work. The seven years of military service had spoiled his skill and made him restless; he was so fed up with saw and plane that he no longer seemed the same man. Before, at Plassans, he used to work hard at carpentering, without any turn for book-learning, just knowing how to read, write and count, yet very thoughtful, very industrious, resolved to make himself independent and get away from his terrible family. Old Macquart kept him as much under control as if he'd been a daughter, snatched his girls from under his nose, and turned up every Saturday at the workshop door to rob him of his wages. And so, when beatings and overwork had killed off his mother he followed the example of his sister Gervaise who had run off to Paris with a lover: he decamped in his turn to escape having to keep his fraud of a father. And now he could not recognise himself, not that he too had become lázy, but because his army service had widened his outlook. Politics, for instance, which he used to find boring, now fascinated him and made him brood over equality and fraternity. He had been affected too by the habits of killing time, the dull and indolent sentry duties, the sleepy life of the barracks, the stop-at-nothing brutalities of war. And so the tools would slip from his hands and he dreamed of his Italian campaigns. A deep need of rest seized him, a desire to lie down and forget everything with his face buried in the grass.

One morning his master sent him to La Borderie to carry out repairs. The job involved a good month's work—rooms to floor, doors and windows to be strengthened all over the place. He was happy and made the work drag on for six weeks. In the meantime the master died and his son, who had married, went to set himself up in his wife's home district. Jean stayed on at La Borderie where there was always some rotten wood to replace, and paid for his keep by his daily work; then with the coming of harvest he lent a hand and stayed another six weeks. The farmer, seeing him so attracted to the land, ended by taking him on completely. In less than a year the ex-artisan became a first-rate farm worker, driving, ploughing, sowing, reaping, in that peace of the country where he hoped at last to satisfy his need for tranquillity. He was finished with sawing and planing! He seemed born for fieldwork, with his sober slow ways, his liking for orderly labour, his ox-like temperament inherited from his mother. At first he was delighted and revelled in country charms which peasants never notice—an attitude springing from odd sentimental books he read, from ideas of simplicity, virtue and perfect bliss such as are set out in little moral tales for children.

To tell the truth, he had another reason for staying on happily at the farm. At the time when he was mending the doors, La Cognette used to come and sprawl amid the wood shavings. She was the one who had done the seducing, infatuated by the sturdy limbs of the big fellow whose heavy regular features announced him to be reliably male. He let her have her way, then carried on with the affair for fear of being thought a fool, tormented as well by a need for the vicious wench who knew how to excite a man. At heart his innate honesty didn't like the whole thing. It was bad to go with the mistress of M. Hourdequin, to whom he was grateful. Naturally he found excuses for his behaviour: she wasn't the master's wife, she was only his gutter-piece; and as she betrayed him in every hole and corner, he might as well have the pleasure of her as leave her to the others. But these excuses did not stop his uneasiness from growing as he saw the farmer get more and more obsessed. The thing was sure to end nastily.

Amid the hay Jean and Jacqueline were holding their breath when the man, whose ear was cocked for danger, heard the ladder creaking. With one leap he was on his feet; and risking death, he let himself drop down the hole used for sending the hay down. Hourdequin's head appeared that very moment on the other side, level with the trapdoor. The farmer glimpsed in one glance the shadow of the fugitive man and the belly of the woman still sprawling with legs apart. His spasm of rage was so acute that he never thought of descending to find out who the man was, but with a blow capable of felling a bullock, he struck Jacqueline back again as she was struggling to her knees. 'You whore!'

She screamed, denying the evidence with an angry cry: 'It's not true!'

He had to hold himself back from driving his heel into the belly he had seen, the outstretched nakedness of a bitch on heat. 'I saw you. Tell the truth, or I'll finish you off!'

'No, no, no, it's not true.'

Then, when she managed to get to her feet and pull her skirt down, she became insolent, provocative, determined to exercise her full power.

'Anyway what's it to do with you? Am I your wife? You don't want me to sleep in your bed, so I'm free to sleep where I please.'

She gave her cooing laugh as if in mocking lubricity. 'Get along, shift out of my way and let me down. . . I'll go away to-night.'

'This moment!'

'No, to-night. Give yourself time to think twice.'

He remained there quivering, lost to all self-control, not knowing on whom to vent his anger. Though he already hadn't the courage to throw her out of doors immediately, how joyously would he have kicked the fellow out! But how to find him now? He had come straight up to the hayloft, drawn on by the open doors, without looking at the beds; and when he came down, the four waggoners from the stable were getting dressed, as also Jean in his corner. Which of the five? One was as likely as another—maybe she'd been taking them in relays. Still, he hoped the man would betray himself. He gave his orders for the morning, sent no one out to the fields and did not go out himself. Instead, he prowled around the farm

83

with clenched fists, looking furtively round with a keen desire to knock someone down.

After the seven o'clock breakfast, his angry supervision had the whole household on edge. At La Borderie there were five drivers for the five ploughs, three threshers, two cowmen or yardmen, a shepherd and a little swineherd, twelve servants in all, without counting the maidservant. He started on the servant in the kitchen because she hadn't hung up the baking-shovels again. Then he roamed around the barns, the oat-barn and then the wheat-barn. The latter was a huge spacious building, tall as a church, with doors fifteen feet high; and there he picked a quarrel with the two threshers, whose flails, he said, were cutting up the straw too much. Thence he went through the cowshed, furious to find the thirty cows in good condition, the pathway down the middle well-washed, and the troughs clean. He had no excuse for abusing the two cowmen until outside he glanced at the water-cisterns for which they were also responsible and noticed a pipe blocked by sparrows' nests. As in every farm in La Beauce, the rainwater from the roofs was zealously caught in a complicated system of gutters. He shouted at the men, demanding if they meant to let the sparrows do him in with drought. But it was on the drivers that the storm burst. Though the fifteen horses in the stable had fresh litter, he began vociferating that it was disgusting to leave them in such filthy conditions. Then, ashamed of his injustice and more exasperated than ever, in the course of overhauling every corner of the buildings he went into the four barns where the tools were stacked. To his delight he saw there a plough with broken shafts. He let himself go. Were these five buggers having a good joke smashing up his stock? He sacked all five on the spot. Yes! all five, so that there'd be no favouritism about it! As he cursed them, his fiery eyes tried to probe right inside them, watching out for a sudden whitening, a twitch, which would give his betrayer away. But not one of them budged and he left them with a wild gesture of despair.

As he went to complete his round by looking in at the sheepfold, he had the idea of cross-questioning Soulas, the shepherd. This sixty-five-year-old man had been at the farm for half a century without saving a penny; everything had been consumed by his wife, a boozy whore, whom he'd had the joy of burying at long last. He was haunted by the fear that his age might soon mean his dismissal. Maybe the master would help him; but who could tell whether masters mightn't die first? They never gave you anything for tobacco and liquor. Besides, he had made an enemy of Jacqueline, whom he hated with all the jealousy of an old retainer, revolted by the rapid rise of an upstart. When she gave him orders nowadays, the thought that he had seen her in tatters working in the dungheap exasperated him unbearably. She would certainly have had him dismissed if she had felt herself strong enough, and that made him cautious, he wanted to keep his job, and avoided all conflict, even though he felt sure of the master's protection.

The sheep-fold, at the end of the yard, took up the whole building. It was a tall structure twenty yards long where the eight hundred sheep of the farm were only separated from each other by hurdles. On one side were the ewes in various groups; on the other, the lambs; and at the end, the rams. The rams who were to be sold were castrated at two months, while the females were retained to renew the herd of breeders; only the oldest ones were disposed of once a year. The rams served the young ewes at fixed dates, dishleys crossed with merinos, superb creatures with a gentle stupid look, heavy-headed, with great rounded noses like sensual men. When you entered the sheep-fold, you encountered a strong suffocating smell, the ammoniacal exhalation from the litter, old straw covered up by fresh and changed only once in three months. Along the walls were racks by which the mangers were raised to keep above the level of the thickening dung. A certain amount of fresh air, however, came in through large windows; and the ceiling of the hayloft was made of movable planks, which could be taken away piecemeal as the fodder store decreased. Folk held, in any case, that this living heat, the soft and hot fermenting litter, was needed to bring the sheep up well.

Hourdequin, as he passed one of the doors, caught sight of Jacqueline slipping out through another. She too had thought of Soulas, uneasily certain that she'd been spied on when with Jean; but the old man's face remained inexpressive, showing no signs of understanding why she was being so amiable, so unlike her usual self. The sight of the young woman going out of the sheep-fold, which she never visited, increased the farmer's uncertainty.

'Well, Soulas,' he asked, 'anything to report this morning?'

The shepherd, very tall and lean, with a long face scored by wrinkles as if hacked out of a knotted oak with a bill-hook, replied slowly, 'No, Monsieur Hourdequin, nothing at all, except that the shearers are coming and will soon be on the job.'

The master chatted for a moment to take away the effect of

questioning him. The sheep, who were fed indoors from the first frosts of All Saints, would be going out about the middle of May, as soon as they could be taken to the clover fields. The cows were only led out to pasture after the harvest. The dry Beauce plain, lacking in natural pasture, still produced good meat; and it was only ingrained custom and laziness which held back the breeding of fat cattle. Even with pigs, a farm fattened only five or six for its own food supplies.

With his fevered hand Hourdequin stroked the ewes who had come running up with raised heads and soft bright eyes; while the mass of lambs imprisoned further on pushed bleating against the hurdles.

'So, Soulas, you haven't seen anything this morning?' he asked again, looking the man straight in the eyes.

The old man had seen, but why should he talk? His late wife, the bitch and drunkard, had taught him the wickedness of women and the stupidity of men. Perhaps La Cognette, even when betrayed, would come out on top, and then it'd be on his head the trouble would fall, they'd want to get rid of an awkward witness.

'Nothing, nothing at all!' he repeated with blank eyes and impassive face.

When Hourdequin went back across the yard, he noticed that Jacqueline had stayed there, nervously straining her ears, fearful of what was being said in the sheep-fold. She was pretending to be busy with the poultry, the six hundred birds, chickens, ducks, pigeons, all flying about, chattering, and scratching on the dung-heap, making a tremendous racket. The little swineherd upset a bucket of water he was carrying to the pigs and she relieved her nerves slightly by slapping him over the ear. But one glance at the farmer reassured her: he didn't know anything, the old man had kept his mouth shut. Her insolence at once gained a new lease of life.

And so, at dinner-time, she showed a provocative gaiety. As heavy work hadn't yet started, there were only four meals; bread and milk at seven, sopped toast at noon, bread and cheese at four, soup and fat bacon at night. Meals were taken in the kitchen, a huge room with a long table flanked by benches. Modernity was represented only by the cast-iron stove which occupied a corner of the enormous hearth-place. At the end gaped the black mouth of the oven; and along the smoke-darkened walls glistened saucepans and old-fashioned utensils hung in strict rows. As the kitchenmaid, a fat ugly girl, had baked that morning, a good smell of hot bread rose from the open bread-pan.

'So your stomach's corked up to-day, is it?' Jacqueline boldly asked Hourdequin as he entered last.

Since the death of his wife and daughter, he had taken to eating with the servants so as not to be left alone. It was just like bygone days: he sat at one end while the mistress-servant sat at the other. There were fourteen round the table; the maid served them.

The farmer sat down without replying and La Cognette said she must see to the meal. It consisted of slices of grilled bread broken into the soup-tureen, then sprinkled with wine, sweetened with *ripopée*, the old Beauce term for treacle. She asked for another spoonful, pretending she wanted to spoil the men, and told jokes which made them roar with laughter. Every sentence had a double meaning playing on the fact that she was leaving that night: you met, you parted, and the one who was left behind would be sorry he hadn't dipped his finger in the sauce just once more. The shepherd ate with his usual face, while the silent master also seemed not to understand. Jean, to avoid giving himself away, had to laugh with the others, despite his uneasiness; for he didn't much like his own behaviour in the business.

After dinner, Hourdequin gave his orders for the afternoon. There were only a few small jobs to be finished outside: oats to be rolled, the ploughing-over of the fallow lands to be finished while the lucerne and the clover weren't ready for cutting. So he kept back two men, Jean and another, to clear out the hayloft. He himself was exhausted now; his ears buzzed in the reaction from his fit of rage and he began wretchedly wandering about, not knowing what to do to cover up his misery. The shearers had settled themselves under one of the barn-roofs, in a corner of the yard; and he took up his stand in front of them, watching.

There were five of them, lean and sallow-faced, squatting on the ground with their big steel shears gleaming. The shepherd was bringing up the ewes, with their four feet tied together so that they looked like skin-bottles and laid them down in rows on the beaten-earth floor of the outhouse, where they could only just move their heads, bleating. As soon as one of the shearers seized an ewe, she quietened down, relaxed, fluffed out with the thick growth of wool, which grease and dust crusted over with a hard black film. Then, under the quick-moving edge of the shears, the beast emerged from the fleece like a hand naked out of a dark glove, all pink and clean in the golden snow-lining of the inner wool. Held tight between the knees of a big gaunt fellow, a dam was laid on her back with her thighs wide apart and her head pulled right back; she spread out her belly, which had the hidden whiteness, the sensitive tense skin of someone being undressed. The shearers got three sous a sheep, and a good worker could shear twenty a day.

Hourdequin, absorbed, reflected that wool had fallen to eight sous the pound; this lot must be sold quickly before it dried out and lost its weight. The year before, bleeding of the spleen had decimated the flocks of La Beauce. Everything was going from bad to worse; there was nothing but ruin ahead; the earth was impoverished and the price of grain went on falling from month to month. And, overwhelmed by his farming worries again, he felt stifled in the yard. Leaving the farm, he went off to have a look round the fields. His quarrels with La Cognette always finished this way: after raging and clenching his fists, he weakened under the pressure of a grief that could only be solaced by the sight of his wheat and his oats rolling their greenness on into infinity.

Ah, how he had come to love this earth of his! His passion lacked the avaricious harshness of the peasants; it was a matter of sentiment, almost of the intellect. He felt the earth was the mother of all, the mother who had given him life and sustenance and to whom he would return. At first, when he was a youngster brought up on the land, his hatred of college, his longing to burn his books, had sprung merely from the accustomed freedom of his life, his splendid gallops over the ploughed fields, his ecstatic enjoyment of a fresh-air life amid the four winds of the plains. Later on, when he had taken his father's place, he had loved the land like a lover; his love had ripened as if he had taken the earth in marriage, to make her conceive. And his tenderness grew deeper and deeper as he gave her his time, his money, his entire life, as one gives such things to a good and fertile wife, forgiving her caprices and even her infidelities. He broke out at times, when she turned mean— when, through an excess of drought or damp, she rotted the seeds and yielded up no harvests. Then, doubts had been born and he had come to accuse himself of impotence or clumsiness: he was the one to blame if she hadn't conceived. Since that time he had turned to the quest for new methods; he had grasped at every innovation. He regretted having been a waster at college, and not having followed the courses at one of the agricultural schools which he and his father had so scorned. How many futile attempts lay behind him—experiments that went wrong, machines wrecked by his labourers, chemical fertilisers adulterated by dealers. He had poured his whole fortune into the earth and yet La Borderie brought him hardly enough to eat while he waited for the agricultural crisis to engulf him. No matter, he'd remain the prisoner of his earth, he'd bury his bones in her after holding her as wife up to the very end.

That day, as soon as he was out in the open, he remembered his son, the captain. If only they'd carried on together, what fine work they might have done! But he dismissed the memory of the fool who preferred to trail a sword. He had no child left, he would die alone. Then he thought of his neighbours, especially the Coquarts, landowners who worked their farm at Saint-Juste themselves, father, mother, three sons, and two daughters; they were hardly any better off than he was. At La Chamade, the farmer Robiquet, come to the end of his lease, wasn't bothering to manure any longer; he was letting the property go to rack and ruin. That's how it was— on the down-grade everywhere; kill yourself with work and give up useless grumbling. Still, gradually he felt a lulling comfort invade his spirit out of the broad green fields that he was walking round. Light April showers had given a good start-off to the crops. The red clover charmed him and he forgot everything else. Then as he cut across the ploughed field to inspect the work of the two plough-men, the earth stuck to his boots. He felt its richness and fertility as if it wanted to grasp him, to hold him there fast; once more she unreservedly accepted him, restoring the virility of his young days, with all its strength and joy. Could any woman take her place? What did all the Cognettes matter, the whole two-a-penny lot of them? Plates that anyone ate out of: you took them as they came, as long as they were fairly clean! Such an excellent palliative of his debased need for the slut succeeded in cheering him up. He walked on for three hours and exchanged jokes with a girl—servant to those very Coquarts—who was coming back from Cloyes, riding a donkey with her skirt pulled up from her legs.

When he returned to La Borderie, he found Jacqueline in the yard saying good-bye to the farm cats. There was always a troop of them, twelve, fifteen, twenty, no one knew exactly how many; for the mothers used to litter in hidden corners among the hay and re-appear with five or six kittens miaowing after them. Next Jacqueline went over to the kennels where the shepherd's two dogs, Emperor and Massacre, were kept; but they loathed her and growled. In spite of these farewells to the animals, supper went on as usual. The master ate and chatted as if nothing had happened. And so, as the day drew to its close, there was no question of anyone leaving. Everyone went to bed, and darkness enveloped the hushed farm.

That night Jacqueline slept in the late Mme Hourdequin's room. It was the farm's show-room, with its great bed in an alcove hung with red. There was a wardrobe, a round table, an armchair of Voltaire style and on top of a mahogany desk the prize-medals, won by the farmer at agricultural meetings, shone inside their glass cases. When La Cognette, in her shift, climbed into the marriage-bed, she threw herself down flat with arms and thighs open as if she wanted to take hold of the whole thing; and she laughed her throaty dove-laugh.

Next morning, when she tried to catch Jean round the neck, he shoved her off. If the affair were turning serious, it was definitely not right and he wasn't going to have any more of it.

II

A few days later Jean was coming back on foot in the evening from Cloyes, when, a couple of miles from Rognes, he was struck by the strange way a peasant cart was travelling ahead of him. It seemed empty: there was no one on the driver's seat, and the horse, given its head, was ambling back to its stable along the road it obviously knew very well. The young man soon caught it up. Stopping it, he hoisted himself up to look into the vehicle; a man was lying at the bottom, a fat stumpy man of about sixty, who had fallen over backwards and whose face was so flushed that it seemed to be turning black.

Jean in his surprise cried out aloud. 'What a sight—is he asleep or drunk? Lord! it's old Mouche, father of those two down there! It looks—O Lord! I believe he's croaked! Well I never—what a business!'

But, though laid out by an apoplectic fit, Mouche was still breathing in short laboured gasps. Jean straightened him out and lifted up his head, then got on to the driving seat, whipped up the horse and drove the dying man home at a gallop, afraid that he might yet slip through his fingers.

As he turned into the Place de l'Eglise, he noticed Françoise standing in front of the door. The sight of the young fellow driving the family cart dumbfounded her. 'What's going on here?' she demanded. 'Your father's taken bad.' 'Where is he?' 'There, look!'

She climbed on to the wheel and looked over. For a second she stayed aghast without seeming to take it in, staring at the deeply flushed face of which one side was contorted as if it had been pulled violently upwards. Night was falling; a great tawny cloud yellowed the sky and lit up the dying man with a fiery glow.

Then all at once she burst out sobbing, jumped down and ran inside to warn her sister. 'Lise, Lise! O, my God!'

Left alone, Jean hesitated. But he couldn't very well leave the old man at the bottom of the cart. The house-door was three steps below ground on the side facing the square; to get down that dark hole would not be easy. Then he remembered how, on the side facing the road, to the left, another door opened level on the yard. The yard itself was fair-sized, surrounded by an evergreen hedge; a muddy pond took up half the space and two-thirds of an acre of fruit and vegetable garden filled one end. So he loosed the horse, which slouched off by itself and halted in front of the stable near the shed with the two cows.

Françoise and Lise ran up crying and moaning. Lise, confined four months previously, had been caught as she was suckling the baby; in her consternation she still held him in her arms and he was howling along with the others. Françoise climbed back on a wheel while Lise scrambled up on the other side, and their lamentations grew piercingly shrill, while old Mouche, at the bottom, went on wheezing in painful gasps.

'Dad, say something, won't you? What's the matter, tell us. What in God's name is the matter? It's your head, is it, and that's why you can't say anything? Dad, dad, speak to us, answer us.'

'Come down, we'd better get him out of the cart,' Jean sensibly interrupted them.

They gave him no help, they merely shrieked more loudly. Luckily a neighbour, La Frimat, was attracted by the noise and at last came along. She was a tall bony dried-up old woman, who had been looking after her paralysed husband for two years, and who kept him alive by ploughing their plot of an acre or so with her own hands, plodding away like a beast of burden. She showed no excitement, but took the situation as a matter of course, and lent a hand as if she were a man. Jean now grasped Mouche by the shoulders and tugged until La Frimat could reach the legs. Then they carried the old man into the house.

'Where are we to put him?' asked La Frimat.

The two girls, who followed, had lost their heads and could not decide. Their father used to sleep in a little room upstairs, partitioned off from the attic; but it was hardly possible to lug him up there. Downstairs, besides the kitchen, there was the big room with two beds, which he had given up to his daughters. In the kitchen it was pitch dark, and the young man and the old woman waited there with straining arms, not daring to move on for fear of stumbling against a piece of furniture.

'Hurry, decide on something!'

Françoise at last lit a candle. And at the same moment La Bécu, the constable's wife, came in. No doubt she had scented the disaster, warned by that secret agency which in an instant flashes news from one end of a village to the other.

'Hey, what's up with the poor old chap? O, I see, the blood has started going the wrong way round in his body. Quick, get him sitting up on a chair.'

But La Frimat thought otherwise. Did you sit a man down when he couldn't hold himself up? The best thing was to stretch him out on his back on one of his daughters' beds. And so the discussion wrangled on until Fanny came in with Nénesse: she had heard the news while she was buying vermicelli at Macqueron's, and hastened to look in, upset on her cousin's behalf. 'Yes, maybe he ought to sit on a chair,' she declared, 'so that his blood can run back.'

So Mouche was huddled on to a chair by the table on which the candle was burning. His chin fell forward on his chest, his arms and legs hung loose. His left eye was open, pulled up by the contortion of that side of the face, and the corner of his twisted mouth whistled more loudly than ever. The others fell silent. Death was pervading the damp room with its floor of beaten earth, its stained walls, its great black chimney-piece.

Jean still waited, feeling awkward, while the two girls and the three women, with hands hanging loosely, stared at the old man.

'I'm ready to go and find the doctor,' the young man offered.

La Bécu nodded her head but none of the others took any notice. If it turned out not to be serious, why spend money on calling the doctor? And if it really was the end, what was there that the doctor could do?

'What would help is woundwort,' La Frimat put in.

'I've got some camphorated spirits,' whispered Fanny.

'That's good, too,' stated La Bécu.

Lise and Françoise, now completely stupefied, listened and did nothing at all, the one nursing her little son Jules, the other holding out all the while a glass of water which her father ignored. Fanny, however, saw their state and bundled Nénesse out as he stared fascinated at the contorted face of the dying man.

'You run home and ask for the little bottle of camphorated spirits in the cupboard—on the left. D'you hear? In the cupboard on the left. And call at Grandfather Fouan's and at your great-aunt's, La Grande. Tell them Uncle Mouche is taken bad. Run, run quick.'

The youngster went bounding off and the women resumed their discussion of the case. La Bécu knew a gentleman who'd been saved by having his soles tickled for three hours. La Frimat, remembering there was some lime-tea left over from the two-pennorth she'd bought last winter for her husband, went to fetch it; and she was coming back with the little bag and Lise was lighting the fire after handing the baby to Françoise, when Nénesse reappeared.

'Grandfather Fouan was asleep. La Grande only said if Uncle Mouche hadn't drunk so much, he wouldn't be in such a bad way.'

Fanny had taken the bottle and was scrutinising it. 'Idiot!' she cried, 'I told you on the left. You've brought the Eau de Cologne.'

'That's good too,' repeated La Bécu.

They made the old man take a cup of lime-tea by forcing a spoon between his clenched teeth. Then they massaged his head with Eau de Cologne. And yet he got no better; it was most disheartening. His face had grown darker and they had to prop him up on to his chair because he kept slipping down and threatening to fall flat on the floor.

'Oh,' whispered Nénesse, going back to the doorway, 'it's going to rain like I don't know what. The sky's a very funny colour.'

'Yes,' said Jean, 'I saw an ugly storm-cloud coming up.'

And, as if he'd been led back to his first idea, he added, 'Never mind, I'll still go and fetch the doctor if you like.'

Lise and Françoise looked anxiously at one another. At last the latter made up her mind, with the generosity of youth, 'Yes, yes, Corporal, go to Cloyes for Monsieur Finct. Nobody shall say we didn't do all we ought.'

In the bustle the horse had not even been unharnessed, and Jean only had to jump into the trap. The others heard the clank of iron and the quick rattling of the wheels. Then La Frimat thought of the priest. But the others, with a gesture, gave her to understand that they had taken enough trouble already; and when Nénesse offered to walk the two miles to Bazoches-le-Doyen, his mother got angry:

as if she'd let him go chasing about on such a threatening night, under that awful rust-coloured sky! Besides, as the old man couldn't hear or speak, you might just as well knock up the priest for a mile-stone.

Ten o'clock struck from the cuckoo-clock of painted wood. Everyone was astounded. To think that they'd been there two hours, without getting a single thing done! And yet not one of them thought of leaving; they were spellbound by the sight and wanted to see things through to the end. A ten-pound loaf was on the bread board with a knife. First the girls, desperately hungry in spite of their anguish, mechanically cut themselves slices and ate them dry without noticing; then the three women followed their example. The loaf dwindled. One or other was cutting or chewing all the while. They had not lit a second candle or even bothered to snuff the one that was burning; and the scene was a gloomy one in that poor peasant's kitchen, dark and scantily-furnished, with the deathrattle coming from the body bunched up by the table.

All of a sudden, half an hour after Jean's departure, Mouche doubled up and slid down flat on the floor. He was no longer breathing, he was dead.

'What did I say? But you would go and fetch the doctor!' said La Bécu bitterly.

Françoise and Lise burst into tears again. Impulsively they flung their arms round one another in their loving sisterly tenderness. And they repeated over and over in broken sentences, 'My God, only us two left. It's the end, only the two of us left. What's going to become of us, O my God?'

But the dead man could not be left on the floor. La Frimat and La Bécu lost no time in doing what was indispensable. As they dared not carry the body, they pulled the mattress off one of the beds, carried it over and stretched Mouche out on it, covering him up to his chin with a blanket. Meanwhile, Fanny lit the candles in two other candlesticks and set them on the floor in place of wax tapers, left and right of the head. That would do for the moment: except that the left eye, though shut three times by someone's thumb, promptly opened again and seemed to watch them all from out of the misshapen and blackened face which contrasted so sharply with the whiteness of the sheet.

Lise finally put Jules to bed and the wake started. Twice Fanny and La Bécu said they were going, as La Frimat offered to spend the night with the young girls. But they did not go, they went on talking in low voices, now and then glancing at the dead body; while Nénesse, who had got hold of the Eau de Cologne, was using it all up by pouring it over his hands and hair.

Midnight struck. La Bécu raised her voice. 'And Monsieur Finet, where on earth is he? He gives people lots of time to die, I must say. More than two hours to fetch him from Cloyes!'

The door on to the yard had been left open and a strong gust blew in, putting out the candles to right and left of the corpse. Everyone was scared; and as they relit the candles, the storm-wind rose again, wilder than ever, while a drawn-out howling burst in swelling volume out of the black spaces of the countryside. It sounded just like the gallop of an approaching host of invaders, what with the crack of branches, the moaning of devastated fields. The women, who had run to the threshold, saw a coppery cloud rush in mad eddies over the livid heavens. Then abruptly came a crackle like musketry and a shower of pellets crashed down, stinging and bouncing at their feet.

A cry of despair and desolation escaped their lips: 'Hail! hail!'

Dazed, horrified and pallid under the scourge, they stood watching. The storm lasted barely ten minutes. There was no thunder; but great bluish lightnings seemed to dart continuously along the earth in broad phosphorescent furrows; and the night became less black, the hailstones lit it up with innumerable pale streaks as if a cascade of shattered glass were falling. The noise grew deafening, like a volley of grapeshot or a train clanging endlessly at full speed over an iron bridge. The wind blew dementedly and the slanting hailstones slashed everything down, piled up and hid the earth under a layer of white.

'Hail, O God! What a disaster! Just look, as big as hen's eggs.'

They did not dare venture into the yard to pick them up. The fury of the hurricane increased till all the window-panes were broken; and the hailstones were driven with such force that one smashed a jug and others rolled in as far as the dead man's mattress.

'It'd take less than five to a pound,' said La Bécu, weighing some in her hand.

Fanny and La Frimat made despairing gestures. 'Everything's smashed up, it's a shambles.'

At last it was ended. They heard the disastrous roar rapidly lessening in the distance and a death-like silence fell. The sky, in the rear of the cloud, had turned inky-black. A thin close rain poured noiselessly down. Nothing could be seen on the ground but the thick shroud of hailstones, a glimmering sheet which seemed to emit its own light, a glow as of millions of tiny night-lights stretching on and on.

Nénesse, rushing out of doors, came back carrying an irregular and jagged lump of ice as big as his own fist; and La Frimat couldn't stay still any longer, she simply had to go and see for herself.

'I'm going to get my lantern, I must find out the damage.'

Fanny controlled herself for a few more minutes and went on with her lamentations. O what a dreadful business! The wreckage there'd be among the vegetables and fruit trees! The wheat, oats and barley were none of them high enough to have suffered much. But the vines, the vines! From the doorway, she kept peering into the heavy impenetrable darkness, trembling in a fever of uncertainty, trying to estimate the destruction, exaggerating it, imagining she saw the shattered countryside bleeding from all its many wounds.

'Well, my dears,' she said at length, 'I'm borrowing your lantern, I'll just run over to our vineyard.'

She lit one of the two lanterns and disappeared with Nénesse.

La Bécu, who owned no land, didn't really give a damn. She sighed deeply and called on the heavens but only because she was always moaning and groaning. Curiosity, however, took her repeatedly to the door, and a lively interest kept her rooted there when she noticed the village pinpointed with lights. Through a gap in the yard, between the stable and an outhouse, she could see straight across the whole of Rognes. The hailstones had obviously woken the peasants, and everyone was seized by the same impatience to run and see his fields, too anxious to wait for daylight. So the lanterns came out one by one, grew in number, floated and flitted about. And La Bécu, knowing where each house lay, managed to name every lantern.

'Look, there's light in La Grande's, and there's someone coming out of Fouan's, and over there the Macquerons are out, and Lengaigne too. O God, the poor people, it breaks your heart. . . Ah, I must go.'

Lise and Françoise remained alone with their father's body. The rain still streamed down and little gusts of damp air swept over the floor, making the candles waver. They should have closed the door but neither of them thought of it; they were enthralled and excited by the drama out-of-doors despite the grief come on their house. Wasn't it enough to have death at home? The good God was smashing everything up, you couldn't even be sure if there'd be a bite of bread left.

'Poor dad,' whispered Françoise, 'how upset he'd have been! Just as well he can't see it.'

Then, as her sister picked up the second lantern, she asked, 'Where are you going?'

'I'm thinking of the peas and beans. I'll be back in a minute.'

Under the downpour Lise crossed the yard and went into the vegetable garden. Françoise was left all alone with the dead man. She remained in the doorway, excitedly watching the lantern moving to and fro. She thought she could hear cries and weeping. Her heart was wrung. 'What is it? Eh?' she shouted. 'What's happened?'

There was no reply. The lantern rushed faster from side to side as if gone crazy. 'The beans are down, are they? And the peas, are they damaged? O God, and the fruit and the lettuces?'

A cry of distress, clearly audible, made up her mind for her. She gathered up her skirts and ran through the rain to join her sister. And the dead man, deserted, was left in the empty kitchen, stiff beneath the coverlet, between the two smokily dripping candles. The left eye, obstinately open, stared at the old ceiling joists.

The storm had wrought havoc in the region and cries of despair rang out as the extent of the damage was revealed by the flickering light of the lanterns. Lise and Françoise walked about holding out their lantern which so streamed with rain as to yield scarcely a glimmer; they held it close to the beds, and confusedly, in the tiny circle of light, made out beans and peas beaten to the ground, lettuces slashed and sliced till not a single leaf was eatable. But above all the trees had suffered: the twigs, the fruits were cut as if by knives. Even the battered trunks were oozing their sap through holes in the bark. And further on, among the vines, things were worse. The lanterns swung, jumped, swayed amid the groans and curses of the villagers. The vine-stocks were scythed down and the blossom-clusters strewed the ground, mixed with splinters of wood and broken branches. Not only was the year's harvest ruined; the stems, stripped bare, would decay and die. No one felt the rain. A dog was howling at the sky and the women burst into tears as if they stood by an open grave. Macqueron and Lengaigne, competitors though they were, passed backwards and forwards on one another's properties, sharing lanterns and crying out together on God as each fresh glimpse of the desolation, briefly and luridly illuminated, appeared and then was swallowed up behind them by

D

the dark. Although no longer a landowner, Old Fouan wanted to see everything, and as he looked he grew indignant. Gradually they were all swept away on a wave of anger: was it possible to lose the fruits of a whole year's work in a quarter of an hour? What had they done to be punished like this? There was no security, no justice; nothing but senseless scourges, capricious acts that wrecked their whole world. Suddenly La Grande, mad with rage, collected some stones and threw them up to pierce the sky shrouded from sight. She screamed, 'Hey, you Goddamned swine! Can't you bloody well leave us in peace?'

On the mattress in the kitchen, the abandoned Mouche was still staring at the ceiling with his one fixed eye when two vehicles stopped outside the door. Jean was at last bringing M. Finet after waiting three hours for him at his house; he had come back in the cart, while the doctor had driven in his gig.

Finet, who was tall and thin, with a face jaundiced by stillborn ambitions, pushed roughly in. At heart he loathed his peasant patients whom he blamed for his own mediocrity. 'What! no one here?' he called. 'He's better then?' He caught sight of the corpse. 'No, too late. I told you so, I didn't want to come. It's always the same story, they only call me in when they're dead.'

The pointless disturbance in the middle of the night irritated him; and as Lise and Françoise returned to the house at that moment, he became properly infuriated, learning that they'd waited two hours before calling him in. 'You can lay his death at your own door! I've never seen such stupidity—Eau de Cologne and lime-tea for an apoplectic fit! And on top of it all, nobody in attendance. Not much chance of his being saved, eh?'

'O sir,' stammered Lise through her tears, 'it was because of the hail.'

M. Finet grew interested and quietened down. What! had there been a hailstorm? Through living among peasants he had come to share their emotions. Jean had also come in and both men exclaimed in astonishment. They hadn't met a single hailstone all the way from Cloyes. Some places untouched, others laid waste, and only a mile or two between them! What bad luck to be on the wrong side! Then Fanny brought the lantern back, followed by La Bécu and La Frimat: and all three women burst out in tearful complaints, interminably piling up every detail of the horrors they had seen. The doctor gravely summed up, 'It's a calamity, a great calamity. It's the greatest calamity that could come to country-people.'

A heavy sound, a kind of bubbling, interrupted him. It came from the dead man who lay forgotten between the two candles. Everyone fell silent and the women crossed themselves.

III

A MONTH went by. Old Fouan had been appointed guardian to Françoise, who was entering her fifteenth year; and he persuaded her and her sister Lise, who was ten years older, to lease their fields, with the exception of one corner of meadowland, to their cousin Delhomme, so that the land might be properly tended and cultivated. Now that the two girls lived alone, without a man in the house, they would have had to employ a servant—and that would have been a crushing expense because of the rising cost of labour. And Delhomme, who was simply doing them a service, undertook to terminate the arrangement as soon as the marriage of either girl made a division of their inheritance necessary.

Lise and Françoise also handed over their horse to their cousin as it was no longer of any use to them. But they kept the two cows, La Coliche and Blanchette, as well as the donkey, Gédéon. They also kept their vegetable patch, which the elder sister undertook to tend while the younger cared for the animals. Indeed there was still plenty of work involved; but they weren't weaklings, thanks be to God, and they'd manage to pull through.

The first weeks were hard going. They had to repair the damage done by the hail, dig the garden and replant vegetables; and that was when Jean felt impelled to give them a hand. A bond had been created between them since he brought home their dying father. The day after the burial he came to ask how they were. After that he often dropped in for a chat, gradually becoming a welcome and obliging visitor, until at last one afternoon he took the spade from Lise's hands to finish trenching one of the beds. From then on, accepted as a friend, he gave them all his free time after finishing at the farm. He became one of the household, part of the old Fouan house built by an ancestor three centuries earlier and honoured with a sort of family-worship. When Mouche had been alive, complaining that he had drawn the worst number in the division and accusing his sister and brother of having swindled him, they retorted, 'But the house! What about the house?'

It was a poor little dilapidated house, subsiding, cracked and insecure, patched all over with odd planks and bits of plaster. It must have been originally constructed of rubble and mud; later, two walls had been rebuilt in mortar; finally, about the beginning of the century, the thatch had been reluctantly replaced by a roof of small slates, now flaking away. In this way the house had lasted and still held together, sunk down three feet, as all houses were set in times gone by—no doubt to make them warmer. It was inconvenient during bad storms when water flooded in; and you could sweep the beaten earth-floor of the submerged room all day, but some mud always clung about in the corners. Still the house after all was shrewdly situated, its back turned north towards the immense plain of La Beauce whence came the terrible winter winds; on this side, in the kitchen, there was only a narrow dormer-window, barricaded by a shutter, at ground level; while on the other side, facing south, were the door and windows. It was like a fisherman's hovel at the ocean edge, with not even a slit giving on to the waves. The fierce Beauce storms had banged on it till it leaned forward; it sagged over like one of those hobbling old women who cannot stand up straight.

Soon Jean knew every little corner in it. He helped to clean out the dead man's room, a cramped closet cut away from the loft by a simple partition of boards and furnished with nothing but an old chest filled with straw, serving as a bed, a chair and a table. Downstairs he never went beyond the kitchen and avoided following the two sisters into their own room, where, as the door was always swinging, he could see the alcove with its two beds, the big walnut wardrobe, and the splendid carved round table, no doubt a relic carried off from the castle long ago. There was another room behind, but it was so damp that the father had preferred to sleep upstairs: the family were even averse from storing potatoes there because they immediately sprouted. Their life was spent in the kitchen, in the huge room thick with smoke, where for three centuries generations of Fouans had succeeded one another. It was redolent of the endless toil, the meagre fare, the unslackening efforts of a family which, worked to death, just managed to avoid starvation, but was never a penny the richer in December than in January. A door opened directly into the cowshed so that cows and family lived together; and when the door was shut, the animals could still be watched over through a slab of glass plastered into the wall. Next came the stable where Gédéon now lived on his own, then a shed and a woodhouse; one section led into another so that there was never any need to go out of doors. Outside, the rain ran into the pond which gave water for the beasts and the garden. For drinking water they had to go every morning to the well down in the village road.

Jean felt happy there without asking himself what attracted him. Lise, plump and merry, always gave him a warm welcome. Yet she was already looking faded at twenty-five and had become quite plain, particularly since her confinement. But she had big strong arms, she worked with such zest, bustling about, shouting and laughing, that she was a sight for sore eyes. Jean treated her as a woman, never spoke familiarly to her, while he still thought of fifteen-year-old Françoise as a child, and talked to her as such. The latter's good looks were still unspoiled by open air and long toil; she retained her long pretty face with narrow obstinate forehead, dark secretive eyes, thick lips, shadowed by an early down; and even though everyone considered her a child, she was all the same a woman and it wouldn't take too close a tickle, as her sister used to say, to get her with child. Lise had brought her up after their mother's death: that was the cause of their great fondness for one another—a fondness shown actively and boisterously by the elder girl, passionately and yet restrainedly by the younger.

Françoise, small as she was, had the reputation of being very strong-willed. Injustice infuriated her. When she said, 'That's mine and that's yours,' she would have died rather than retract. And, leaving everything else aside, she adored Lise because she believed such adoration her due. Generally she showed herself sensible, very well-behaved, without malice, tormented only by her precocious physical development, which made her slack, rather greedy and lazy. One day she too began to speak familiarly with Jean as an older and kindly friend, who played with her, sometimes teased her, and used to tell lies on purpose, defending injustices, to enjoy the fun of seeing her speechless with indignation.

One Sunday, on a June day of extreme heat, Lise was at work in the kitchen-garden weeding the pea-rows. She had laid Jules down under a plum-tree where he went fast asleep; and the sun burned straight down on her back. She was breathing hard as she bent over to tear out some weeds, when a voice came from over the hedge.

'What's this? No rest, not even on Sunday!'

She recognised the voice and stood upright, with her reddened arms and flushed face, laughing in spite of everything.

'Well, the work doesn't do itself on Sunday any more than on weekdays!'

It was Jean. He walked along the hedge and came in by the yard.

'You leave that. I'll show you how to knock off that little job.'

But she refused. She'd soon be finished; and anyhow, if she wasn't doing one thing, she'd be doing something else. A body couldn't just sit about! Although she got up at four o'clock and sat sewing by candle-light every evening, she still never came to an end of her work.

Not wanting to cross her, Jean stretched out in the plum-tree's shade, taking care not to sit on Jules. He watched her as she bent down again with her buttocks uppermost, pulling down her skirt as it worked up and bared her stout legs; while, with bosom close to the earth, she kept her arms busy, unafraid of the rush of blood that swelled her throat out.

'You're lucky,' he said, 'to be so solidly built.'

She showed some pride at his words and gave a complacent laugh. He laughed too, sincerely admiring her and finding her as strong and decent as a lad. No wayward desire disturbed him as he watched her raised buttocks and her firm calves—a woman on all fours, sweating and smelling like a bitch on heat. He was simply thinking that anyone with such limbs couldn't half get through some work! You could be sure that in a home a woman of such build would be as good as her man.

An association of ideas must have dominated his mind, for thoughtlessly he blurted out a piece of news he'd meant to keep to himself: 'I saw Buteau the day before yesterday.'

Lise slowly stood up to her full height. But she had no time to question him. Françoise, who had recognised his voice, came from her dairy at the far end of the cowshed, her bared arms white with milk, and burst out, 'You saw him. . . the swine!'

Her antagonism had grown stronger. Nowadays the very sound of her cousin's name stirred up one of her fits of righteous indignation as if she had a personal injury to revenge.

'Of course he's a swine,' stated Lise calmly, 'but it doesn't do any good to say so at this time of day.' She was standing with arms akimbo now and asked seriously, 'And what's he got to say for himself?'

'Nothing at all, nothing of course,' replied Jean, embarrassed and annoyed at having let his tongue run away with him. 'We talked about his own affairs, because his father's telling everyone he's

102

going to disinherit him; and he says he's got plenty of time, the old man'll live for years and he doesn't give a damn anyway.'

'Does he know Jésus-Christ and Fanny have signed the deed in any case? That they've taken over their shares?'

'Yes, he knows that and also he knows Old Fouan's fixed with his son-in-law Delhomme for the share that he, Buteau, wouldn't take. And he knows that Monsieur Baillehache was furious about it, and swore never to let lots be drawn again until he's seen the papers signed. And, O yes, he knows it's all finished and done with.'

'Ah! and he's saying nothing?'

'Not a thing.'

Without a word Lise bent down again, moved about weeding for a moment, showing nothing of herself but the spreading curves of her behind; then she turned her head and added, without raising her head, 'D'you want to know something, Corporal? Well, that's that, and I can keep Jules all on my own account.'

Jean who had been keeping her hopes up till now, added. 'Yes indeed, I think you're right.'

And he glanced at Jules, whom he had forgotten. The infant, wrapped in swaddling-clothes, still dozed, his small unmoving face full in the sun. That was the snag, the baby! Otherwise why shouldn't he marry Lise now she was free? The idea struck him then and there, suddenly, as he watched her at work. Perhaps he loved her, perhaps it was the pleasure of seeing her that drew him to the house. All the same he was taken aback, never having desired her, never having played with her as he played, for instance, with Françoise. And at that moment he raised his head and saw Françoise, standing erect and stiff with anger in the sunlight, her eyes so ablaze with passion, so odd-looking that he was diverted from his unsettling discovery.

But a trumpet blast, a peculiar tara-ta-ta was heard; and Lise, leaving her peas, cried out, 'There's Lambourdieu! I want him to bring me a hood.'

On the other side of the hedge, in the roadway, appeared a short little man, trumpeting and walking in front of a big long vehicle drawn by a grey horse. It was Lambourdieu, a substantial shop-keeper from Cloyes, who had gradually added millinery, odds and ends, cotton goods, shoe-making, even ironmongery to his novelty trade—an entire bazaar which he trundled around from village to village within a radius of some five to six leagues. The peasants had ended by buying everything from him, from pots and pans to wedding clothes. His vehicle was made to open out and let down, displaying rows of drawers and all the trappings of a real shop.

When he had taken the order for the hood, he went on, 'While you're waiting, wouldn't you like to buy a fine scarf?'

He pulled some red scarves with gold patterns out of a box and made them glitter in the sunlight. 'What d'you think of them? Three francs, it's giving them away! Five francs a pair.'

Lise and Françoise took the scarves over the hawthorn hedge where Jule's nappies were spread out to dry; they fingered them and longed to buy. But they were sensible girls, they didn't need the things, so why spend the money? They were just handing the scarves back when Jean suddenly decided he wanted to marry Lise, baby and all. So, to bring things to the point, he called out to her, 'No, no, keep it, I want to give it to you! I'll be hurt if you don't Just to show we're good friends, of course.'

He had said nothing to Françoise. She was still holding out her scarf to the dealer; and as he looked her way, he felt a sudden pang. Surely her cheek paled and her lips quivered with disappointment. 'Keep yours too, you silly. I insist, keep it. None of that pigheadedness of yours now!'

He wouldn't take no, though the two sisters gaily resisted for a while. Lambourdieu had already stretched his hand over the hedge for the five francs. He pocketed the coins and went off, while in his rear the straining horse got the vehicle started. The raucous fanfare died away in the windings of the road.

Jean had come to a sudden decision to put the question to Lise. But an accident held him up. The stable door must have been carelessly fastened; for unexpectedly they saw the donkey, Gédéon, in the middle of the kitchen-garden cheerfully crunching some carrot tops. Now the donkey, big, vigorous, reddish, with a grey cross over the spine, was given to practical jokes, as crafty as they're made. He lifted latches with his mouth and went poking about for bread in the kitchen; and by the way he wagged his long ears when scolded for his misdeeds, it was obvious that he understood. As soon as he saw their eyes on him, he assumed an indifferent negligent air; then, as they shouted and waved, he ran off. But instead of going back to the yard, he trotted down the track right to the bottom of the garden. Then a real chase started; and when Françoise finally caught him, he hunched himself up, tensing his neck and legs, to make himself heavy and more difficult to move. Nothing worked, kicks or coaxings. Jean had to help, pushing from behind

104

with all his masculine strength; for since he had been in the charge of two women, Gédéon had developed the liveliest contempt for them. Jules, woken up by the noise, was howling. The opportunity was lost, the young man had to leave without having spoken out that day.

A week went by and a deep shyness came over him. He now did not dare to make a move. Not that he felt the project a bad one: on the contrary, after thinking it over, he'd come to see its advantages yet more clearly. Both parties stood to gain. If he owned nothing, the girl was encumbered with her baby: that put them on a level. He was making no sordid calculations: no, he was putting the case for her happiness as much as for his own. Then again, marriage, by making him leave the farm, would rid him of Jacqueline, to whom he had succumbed again out of sheer weakness of the flesh. So his mind was settled and he merely waited for an opportunity of declaring himself, trying to think out the right words; for even regimental life had left him a bit of a coward with women.

At last one day he slipped away from the farm at four o'clock, resolved to speak out. The hour was that when Françoise took her cows to pasture for the evening; and he had chosen it so as to be alone with Lise. But he came at once upon a demoralising obstacle. La Frimat, acting the kindly neighbour, had installed herself to help the young woman boil the linen in the kitchen. The evening before, the two sisters had soaked the dirty things; and since morning, the ash-water, scented with orris root, had been boiling in a cauldron slung on a hook over a good fire of poplar-wood. Lise, with bare arms and tucked-up shirt, was dipping a yellow earthen pot into the water and pouring it over the linen that filled the wash-tub: the coverlets at the bottom, then the dusters and underclothes, and on top another lot of sheets. La Frimat was not much help; but she chatted away, contenting herself with lifting the pail from under the tub where it stood to catch the drips and emptying it back into the cauldron every five minutes or so.

Jean waited patiently, hoping that she would go. But she stayed on, talking of her poor husband, the paralytic, who could now move only one hand. A terrible affliction it was. They'd never been rich; but when he'd been able to work, he had rented land which he turned to good account, while now it was all she could do to cultivate the one small plot that was their own. And she worked like a slave. As they had no animals, she collected the droppings in the road for manure; she looked after her salad stock, her haricot

105

beans, and peas, plant by plant; watered everything, even her three plum-trees and her two apricots; and ended by wringing a considerable profit from her plot. Every Saturday she went to Cloyes market, doubled up under the weight of two enormous baskets; and besides that there were heavy vegetables taken in a neighbour's trap. She rarely came home with less than two or perhaps three five-franc pieces, especially in the fruit season. But her unending complaint was the lack of manure: she never had enough with all the road-droppings or the sweepings from her few rabbit-hutches and the hen-coops. She had come at length to storing her own and her husband's excrement, using the despised human dung which even country-people find disgusting. Everyone knew about her practice and made fun of it by calling her Mother Caca, a nickname which did her a lot of harm in the market. *Bourgeois* families refused to buy her magnificent carrots and cabbages, turning away from her stall with qualms of revulsion. Mild-tempered though she was, she violently resented such an attitude.

'Look, tell me, you there, Corporal, is it reasonable? Aren't we allowed to use everything the good God drops into our hand? As if the animal dung's any nicer! No, it's all jealousy. They've got it in for me at Rognes because I grow bigger vegetables. Tell me, Corporal, do you for one think it's disgusting?'

Jean answered in embarrassment, 'Well, it's not what I call savoury. We're not used to it. Maybe it's only a way of thinking.'

His frankness made the old woman miserable. She was not a gossip, but she couldn't hold back her bitterness. 'All right, they've turned you against me already. Ah! if you only knew how wicked they are, if you only suspected what they say about you!'

And she began to relate all the tittle-tattle of Rognes about the young man. First, everyone had hated him because he was an artisan, sawing and planing instead of ploughing the earth. Then, when he had turned to the plough, he was accused of coming to steal the bread out of the mouths of others, in a country that wasn't his own. Did anyone know where he came from? Hadn't he committed some crime in his home-place so that he didn't dare go back? Then they spied on his relations with La Cognette and remarked that one fine night the pair would give old Hourdequin some broth to put him properly to sleep so they could rob him.

'The dirty dogs!' muttered Jean, pale with anger.

Lise, who was drawing a jugful of boiling lye from the cauldron, started to laugh at the mention of La Cognette; for she sometimes used to tease Jean about her.

'Well, as I've begun, perhaps I'd better finish,' went on La Frimat. 'There's no end to the awful things they say since you've been coming here. Last week, wasn't it, you made a present to these two, silk scarves, and they were seen wearing them at Mass on Sunday. It's wicked, but they swear you take the brace of them to bed.'

The time had come. Trembling but resolute, Jean stood up and said, 'Listen, mother, I'm going to answer in front of you. I don't mind you being here. Yes, I'm going to ask Lise if she'd like me to marry her. D'you hear, Lise? I am asking you, and if you say yes, you'll make me as happy as can be.'

At that moment Lise was emptying her bowl into the wash-tub. She did not hurry; she finished carefully pouring the water over the linen; then with her arms bare and damp with steam, she became grave and looked straight at him.

'So you're serious?'

'I'm serious all right.'

She showed no surprise. It was natural. Only she said neither yes nor no; she obviously had something disquieting on her mind.

'You mustn't refuse because of La Cognette,' he started again. 'As for her——'

She stopped him with a gesture; she knew very well that the goings-on at the farm had no importance at all.

'And of course it's a fact that all I bring you is what I stand up in, while you own this house and some land.'

Again she waved her hand as if to say that in her position, with a child, she too considered that one thing cancelled out another.

'No, no, it isn't that at all,' she said at length. 'But you see, there's Buteau. . .'

'He's refused!'

'I know, and there's no question of sentiment—he's behaved too badly. . . But all the same we must consult him.'

Jean thought it carefully over. Then, sensibly, he agreed. 'Just as you like. It's right enough because of the child.'

And La Frimat, also grave, who was emptying the bowl of drips back into the cauldron, felt herself called on to give the seal of her approval to the proceedings—rather taking the side of Jean, a decent chap all right, not headstrong or harsh at all—when they heard Françoise returning with the two cows.

'I say, Lise,' she called, 'come and see. La Coliche has hurt her foot.'

They all went out; and when Lise saw the animal limping, with her left forefoot bruised and bleeding, she let fly in an outburst of temper—one of her surly outbursts which had often fallen on her sister when small and in which she was herself in the wrong.

'Careless again, eh? You snoozed off in the grass like the time before.'

'I didn't, really I didn't. I can't make out what she did. I tied her to the stake and perhaps she caught her foot in the rope.'

'Hold your tongue, liar! You'll have my cow dying on me one day, you know you will.'

Françoise's dark eyes glittered. Pale, she stammered indignantly, 'Your cow, your cow! You might at least say our cow.'

'What! your cow? A bit of a girl like you with a cow!'

'Yes, half of everything here is mine, I've a right to take half and smash it up if I feel like it.'

Face to face, the two sisters stared at each other, threatening and hostile. In all their long friendship this was the first grievous quarrel, under the whip-lash of Mine and Thine; Lise angry at the younger girl's rebellion, Françoise obstinate and furious because of her unjust treatment. The elder gave way and went back into the kitchen so as not to slap the other. And when Françoise, after putting the cows into the shed, reappeared and went to the bread-bin to cut herself a slice of bread, there was a dead silence.

Lise however had calmed down. She felt irritated now at the sight of her tense sulky sister. She spoke first, wanting to end the quarrel with a piece of unexpected news.

'What do you think? Jean wants me to marry him, he proposed.'

Françoise, who was eating standing up in front of the window, remained indifferent and didn't even look round.

'What's that got to do with me?'

'He'll be your brother-in-law and I wanted to know if you like him.'

Françoise shrugged her shoulders. 'Like him? What does it matter? Him or Buteau, as long as it's not me that has to sleep with him! All the same, if you want to know what I think, I don't call it decent.'

She went outside to finish her bread in the yard.

To throw off his discomfort, Jean tried to laugh as at a spoiled child's fancies; while La Frimat declared that when she was a girl, a wench like that would have been whipped till the blood ran. As for Lise, she stayed awhile musing gravely, again absorbed in her washing. Then she decided.

'Well, we'll leave it at that, Corporal. I don't say no to you, I don't say yes. Haymaking's here and I'll see my people and ask them. Then I'll know where I stand. And so we'll decide something. All right?'

'All right.'

He held out his hand and shook the hand she offered. From head to foot her body, steeped in warm steam, exhaled a proper housewifely smell—the smell of wood-ash scented with orris-root.

IV

For two days now Jean had been driving the mowing-machine over the few acres of meadowland belonging to La Borderie near the banks of the Aigre. From dawn to dusk the regular clatter of the blades had sounded; and that morning he was nearing the end. The last swathes were falling in rows behind the wheels, leaving a carpet of slender soft-green stalks. As the farm had no tedding-machine, he had been told to engage two tedders, Palmyre, who was wearing herself out with toil, and Françoise, who had taken on the engagement as a whim, for the work amused her. Both women came to the field at five, and with long forks spread out the heaps of half-dried grass which had been stooked at sunset the day before as protection from the night-dews. The sun had risen in a burning clear sky with a refreshing breeze. Perfect weather for making good hay.

After breakfast, when Jean came back with his haymakers, the hay on the first mown acre was finished. He fingered it and found it dry and brittle.

'Here now,' he cried, 'we'll turn it once more and this evening we'll begin to stack it.'

Françoise, in a grey linen dress, had knotted a blue kerchief over her head, with one edge falling over her neck and two corners hanging loosely on her cheeks, shading her face from the blazing sun. With a swing of the fork, she took up the grass, threw it into the wind, and sent it flying like golden dust. From the fluttering stalks came a strong penetrating scent, the scent of cut grasses, of wilted flowers. She was very hot as she moved on through this continual grass-shower, which delighted her.

'Ah! my child,' said Palmyre in her doleful voice, 'it's easy to see you're young. You'll feel it in your arms to-morrow.'

They were not alone. All Rognes was out mowing and forking in the fields around. Delhomme had been out since before dawn. The dew-soaked grass is tender to cut, like spongy bread; but it grows tougher as it is warmed by the sun. At this time of day they could easily hear its resistant whistling under the scythe that circled round and back in Delhomme's strong bare arms. Nearer, right beside the farm's meadow, were two strips, one Macqueron's, the other Lengaigne's. In the first, Berthe, dressed in a fashionable flounced gown with straw hat on her head, had come out with the haymakers just for amusement; but, soon tired, she stood still, leaning on her fork in the shade of a willow.

In the other field, Victor, mowing for his father, had just sat down and, with his anvil held between his knees, was beating on his scythe. For the last five minutes, in the great throbbing silence of the air, no sound had been heard but this regular tapping, the tiny quick blows of hammer on steel. At that moment Françoise came up to Berthe.

'Hey, had enough?'

'Just about, beginning to get tired. When one's not used to it!'

They chatted, talked about Suzanne, Victor's sister, whom the Lengaignes had sent to a dressmaking establishment in Châteaudun and who after six months had run away to Chartres to live a fast life. The rumour was that she had gone off with a notary's clerk; and all the girls in Rognes whispered together about it, dreaming up the details. To live a fast life meant orgies of raspberry syrup and Seltzer, amid a stampede of men, dozens at a time lying with you, one after the other, in the back room of a wine-shop.

'Yes, my dear, that's what it's like. Ah! she's going it!'

Françoise, so much younger, stared in stupefication. 'What a funny way to enjoy yourself!' she said finally. 'But, if she doesn't come back, the Lengaignes are going to be left all alone, because Victor's due for the army.'

Berthe, who took her father's side in the quarrel, shrugged her shoulders. Lengaigne didn't care a bit! His only regret was that the girl hadn't stayed at home to draw custom to the shop by being seduced under the counter. Hadn't an uncle of hers, an old fellow of forty, already had her before she went off to Châteaudun, one day when they were cleaning carrots together? Lowering her voice,

Berthe described in detail exactly how it happened. Françoise, bent double, laughed till she choked: it all seemed so ridiculous.

'O Lord! how stupid to get up to such tricks!'

She resumed work and moved off, lifting forkfuls of grass and shaking them in the sunlight. The constant sound of the hammer tapping on the steel continued. And a few minutes later she approached the young man as he sat on the ground, and spoke to him.

'So you're going off soldiering?'

'Not till October. I've plenty of time, no hurry.'

She struggled against the wish to question him about his sister, then asked in spite of herself.

'Is it true what they say about Suzanne being in Chartres?'

He replied indifferently, 'Seems so. Well, if she likes it. . .'

All at once he straightened up, seeing Lequeu the schoolmaster in the distance, looking as if he'd come that way by chance, on a stroll. 'Hullo! there's somebody after the Macqueron girl. What did I say? He's stopped, he's pushing his face into her hair. Get along with you, you ugly muggins, sniff at her if you like, you'll get no more than smell of her.'

Françoise had begun laughing again, and Victor took up the family feud, ranting on about Berthe. No doubt the schoolmaster wasn't worth much, a bully who caned the children, a sly chap who hid his opinions from everyone, he was quite capable of making up to a girl so as to get his hands on her father's cash. But Berthe herself wasn't anything to write home about in spite of her put-on airs of a town-bred young lady. Yes, it was no use her wearing such billowing skirts and velvet bodices, padding her bottom with bits of cloth: what was underneath was no better for it all. Quite the opposite; she knew more than was good for her, she'd learned lots more by being brought up at the Cloyes school than by staying home to watch the cows. Not much fear of that girl getting stuck with a baby: she preferred to wreck her health by playing about on her own.

'What d'you mean?' asked Françoise, who didn't understand a word.

He waved his hand. She became serious and commented without embarrassment. 'You mean she's always blurting out dirty things and rubbing herself against you?'

Victor had begun hammering again. He was laughing through the noise and talking between each blow.

'And then, you know, Baldy. . .'

'Eh?'

'Berthe, of course! Baldy, that's the name the boys give her because she hadn't got any!'

'Got any what?'

'Hairs. She's just like a small girl all over, as smooth as your palm.'

'Get along with you, you liar.'

'But I'm telling you!'

'Have you seen it?'

'No, not me—but others have.'

'Who are the others?'

'Oh, boys who told some boys I know, on their oath.'

'And where did they see it? How?'

'Dammit, the way you see when you stick your nose into something—when you peep through a crack. How do I know? Say they haven't slept with her; still there's times when you pull up your skirts, isn't there?'

'So they've been spying on her?'

'Anyway, what's it matter? Seems she looks beastly, horrid when she's naked! Just like the ugliest of those horrible little featherless tits in the nest opening their beaks, ugh, ugly, ugly enough to make you spew.'

Françoise, all of a sudden, was shaken with a new fit of mirth; she was so amused by the picture of the featherless tit. And she couldn't calm down or start haymaking again until she saw her sister Lise coming down the road to the field. Lise went up to Jean and explained that she was off to see her uncle about Buteau. This step had been arranged three days earlier, and she promised to come back the same way to tell him what came out. When she went on her way, Victor was still hammering; Françoise, Palmyre and the other women, under the dazzling light of the wide clear sky, tossed the hay again and yet again; while Lequeu, very obliging, gave Berthe a lesson, pointing the prong, lifting and lowering it as stiffly as a soldier at drill. In the distance the mowers advanced without a pause, with the same rhythmical movement, their bodies swinging from the hips, the scythe endlessly thrown forward and drawn back. For an instant Delhomme stopped, stood upright, towering over the others. He pulled his hone from the pouch hung at his waist, a cow-horn filled with water, and sharpened his scythe with long rapid strokes. Then he bent again and the sharpened steel could be heard biting through the meadow with a shriller whistle.

Lise had arrived at the Fouan house. At first she thought there was no one at home, the building looked so dead. Rose had got rid of her two cows and the old man had just sold his horse, so they had neither animals nor work left, nothing living and moving in the emptiness of the out-houses and the yard. But the door opened under her hand; and she went into the dark silent room—closed away from all the merrymaking outside—and saw Old Fouan on his feet just finishing off a piece of bread and cheese, while his wife sat idly watching him.

'Good-day, aunt. Things going well?'

'Of course,' replied the old woman, her face lighting up with pleasure at this visit. 'Now we're gentlefolk we do nothing but enjoy ourselves from morning to night.'

Lise wanted to be agreeable to her uncle as well. 'Your appetite keeps up, from what I can see.'

'Oh,' he replied, 'it's not that I'm hungry. Only, eating a slice of bread now and then gives you something to do. It helps the time to pass.'

He looked so depressed that Rose started off again enthusiastically explaining how happy they were at not having to work any longer. They'd earned it right enough, and not a day too soon— the right to sit back living on their income and watching the others slave away. Getting up late, twiddling their thumbs, not bothering whether it's hot or cold, without a care in the world, ah! it was a great change, like finding themselves in paradise, really. The old man, roused in turn to an even greater excitement, praised their conditions yet more strongly. And under the forced joy, under the hectic words, was felt the heavy boredom, the cruel idleness that had racked the two old souls ever since their arms, suddenly deprived of motion, had ceased to function from disuse, like worn-out machinery thrown on the scrapheap.

At last Lise dared to touch on the reason for her visit.

'Uncle, I was told you saw Buteau the other day.'

'Buteau's a dirty bugger!' shouted Fouan, suddenly infuriated, without giving her time to finish. 'D'you think that if he hadn't been as obstinate as a red-haired donkey, I'd have had such trouble with Fanny?'

He had meant to hide this first clash between him and his children; but the bitterness he felt was too keen. In handing over Buteau's share to Delhomme, he had intended to exact a rent of eighty francs a hectare, while Delhomme expected to pay only a double

113

allowance, two hundred francs for his own share and two hundred for the other. A fair enough arrangement, and the old man was all the angrier for being in the wrong.

'What trouble?' asked Lise. 'Aren't the Delhommes paying you?'

'O yes,' replied Rose. 'Every three months, at exactly midday, the money's put down on the table. Only, there's ways of paying, isn't there? and father's got his feelings, he'd like at least a little consideration. Fanny comes in looking as though she was paying the bailiff, like we were robbing her.'

'That's right,' added the old man, 'they pay and that's all. Well, it's not enough for me. I want some respect as well. Does money settle everything that's due, eh? We're just people they owe money to, now, nothing more. And yet we're wrong to grumble about that. If only they all paid!'

He stopped and an embarrassed silence fell. The mother's heart was wrung by the reference to Jésus-Christ, who hadn't given them a single sou, who mortgaged his share bit by bit and then drank up the proceeds. If only she could defend the scoundrel, the apple of her eye! She trembled at the exposure of yet another sore and hastily took up her husband.

'Don't fret yourself away over such stupid things. As we're so happy, what are you upsetting yourself about? Enough's as good as a feast!'

She had never stood up to him before like this. He stared at her.

'You talk too much, old woman. I'm ready to be happy, but they mustn't drive me too far.'

She shrank back into herself, hunched up and idle in her chair, and he finished his bread, rolling the last mouthful round his teeth to make the pleasure last longer. The dreary room slumbered on.

'Well, then,' Lise managed to resume, 'I wanted to know what Buteau means to do about me and his child. I haven't pestered him much but it's time things were fixed one way or another.'

The two old people didn't breathe a word. She questioned the father directly. 'You saw him, he must have had something to say about me. What was it?'

'Nothing, he didn't open his mouth about it. And there's nothing to say anyway, I tell you! The priest is always on at me about it, as if anything can be done as long as the fellow refuses to take his share of the land!'

Lise, in great perplexity, considered a moment. 'You think he may take it one day?'

'It's still possible.'

'And d'you think he'll marry me?'

'There's a chance he might.'

'So you advise me to wait?'

'Well! that's up to you. Everyone acts the way he feels.'

She was silent, reluctant to mention Jean's proposal and not knowing how to get a definite answer. Then she made a last effort.

'You see, I'm sick of not knowing what to expect after waiting so long. I must have a yes or a no. Uncle, please go and ask Buteau, I beg you!'

Fouan shrugged his shoulders. 'In the first place I'll never speak to the bugger again. And then, my girl, what a nitwit you are! Why make such an obstinate chap say no, when you know he'll then keep on saying it ever after? Leave him free to say yes one day if it suits him.'

'That's right,' Rose chimed in, simply, once more her man's echo.

Lise failed to get anything more definite out of them. She said good-bye and closed the door behind her. The room returned to its torpor and once again the house, from outside, looked empty.

In the fields near the Aigre, Jean and the two haymakers had begun on the first stack. Françoise was building it up. Standing in the middle of a heap of grass, she took the loads of hay forked up by the young man and Palmyre and spread them round her in a circle. Bit by bit the stack grew bigger and taller with the girl still in the middle. As soon as the wall around her reached her knees, she put the trusses under her feet in the hollow where she stood. The rick began to take shape. Already she was six feet up in the air. Palmyre and Jean now had to stretch up with their forks; and the work went on amid screams of laughter in the exhilaration of the open air, the shouted jokes, the pleasant scent of hay. In particular Françoise was having the time of her life on the growing heap which now buried her to her thighs. Her kerchief slipped from her hair, her head was bare in the sun and her loose hair was stuck full of bits of straw. Her bare arms dug into the heap and every truss thrown from below sent a shower of straw over her. She sank out of sight, pretending to be sucked down in the whirls and eddies.

'O Lord, something's pricking me.'

'Where?'

'Under my skirt, up here.'

115

'It's a spider. Watch out—keep your legs tight together.'

And there was louder laughter, a torrent of smutty jokes that made them rock.

Delhomme, in the distance, began to worry and raised his head a moment without interrupting the swing and withdrawal of his scythe. Ah, that girl, a lot of work she was doing, playing about like that! Nowadays girls were spoiled, they only worked for fun. And he went on with his work, laying the swathes low with yet faster strokes and leaving a wide wake behind him. The sun was almost on the horizon and the haymakers cleared more and more of the fields. Victor, no longer hammering his blade, seemed in no particular hurry; and when La Trouille passed with her geese, he slyly dodged away, slipping off to join her under a thick row of willows on the river-bank.

'Good,' cried Jean, 'he's got another tool to set now. The lady knife-grinder's there waiting ready for him.'

Françoise burst out laughing again at this allusion. 'He's too old for her.'

'Too old! Listen then if they're not grinding away together.'

With a skilful whistle he imitated the sound of a stone biting into the edge of a blade so well that Palmyre had to hold her stomach as if she was racked with colic. 'What's the matter with this fellow Jean to-day?' she gasped. 'He's so funny!'

The forkfuls of hay were thrown higher and higher as the stack rose. They all joked now about Lequeu and Berthe, who had finally sat down. Quite likely Baldy was being tickled with a straw at a decent distance; and after all, the schoolmaster might warm up the oven, but he wasn't the one who'd get his teeth into the pastry.

'Isn't he filthy-minded!' repeated Palmyre, who, unused to laughing, kept choking.

Jean began teasing her. 'Don't tell me you're thirty-two and never lifted the figleaf to see what's under.'

'Me? Never!'

'What! No lad's ever turned you over! You've never had a lover!'

'Not one!'

She had gone quite pallid and serious, with her long wretched face, withered and stunned by toil and with eyes like the eyes of a kindly old bitch, deep and bright with devotion. Perhaps she was musing over her sad life, friendless and loveless, single—a beast-of-burden existence, whipped back to the stable every night half-dead with exhaustion. She stopped work and stood there with her hands

116

on her fork and her eyes staring into the distant countryside which she had never even seen.

There was a silence. Françoise was still, listening on the stack-top, while Jean, also taking a breather, continued his backchat, hesitating to say what was on the tip of his tongue. Then he made up his mind and blurted it out: 'It's a lie then what they say, that you sleep with your brother?'

Palmyre's white face was suffused with a hot flush which made her look young again. She stammered, surprised and angry, unable to find the denial she wanted.

'Oh, the devils! If you believe that. . .'

Françoise and Jean, once again rowdily mirthful, talked at one and the same time, drove her hard and wore her down. Why! in the ruined stable where she and her brother slept there was hardly room to move without falling over one another. Their straw mattresses lay touching on the ground; naturally they got into the wrong one in the dark!

'Come on, it's true, admit it's true! Anyway, everybody knows it's true.'

Palmyre stood there erect, cornered, and then flared up in her misery. 'What if it's true, what the devil has it got to do with you? The poor fellow hasn't got so much pleasure out of life. I'm his sister, I might as well be his wife, seeing how all the girls turn him down.'

Tears rolled down her cheeks at this confession, in the anguish of her motherly love for the cripple which carried her as far as incest. After working to bring him food, in the evening she could at least give him what everyone else refused, a treat that didn't cost a thing. And in the depths of their earth-bound darkened minds, these two unloved and loveless outcasts would have been quite unable to say how it happened—a spontaneous contact without conscious consent; the man tormented and brutish, the woman passive and boundlessly willing, then the two of them yielding to the pleasure of increased warmth, huddling together in the hovel where their teeth chattered with the cold.

'She's right. What's it got to do with us?' Jean remarked in his kindly way, touched to see her so upset. 'It's their own business, they're not doing any harm to anyone else.'

Besides, another incident caught their interest. Jésus-Christ had just come down from the Castle, the old cellar in the bushes halfway up the hill where he lived; and from further up the road he was shouting for La Trouille at the top of his voice, swearing, bawling out that his slut of a daughter had gone off two hours ago without a thought for his evening meal.

'Your daughter,' Jean shouted to him, 'has gone under the willows to have a look up at the moon with Victor.'

Jésus-Christ lifted his fists to the sky. 'The cursed whore'll disgrace me. I'll go and get my whip out.'

And he rushed back up the hill. He owned a huge horse-whip which he hung on the left side of the door ready for these occasions. But La Trouille must have heard him. From under the leaves came a long rustling, the noise of someone running off; and two minutes later Victor reappeared, nonchalantly strolling. He examined his scythe and after a while started working again. When Jean shouted an inquiry whether he had colic, he replied, 'That's it.'

The stack was almost finished. It stood twelve feet high, solid, rounded in shape like a bee-hive. Palmyre threw up the last trusses with her long thin arms, and Françoise, standing on the point top, seemed magnified against the pale sky, in the wild brilliance of the setting sun. She was quite breathless, tense with her exertions and soaked with sweat; her hair stuck to her skin and she was so rumpled that her bodice had come open over her small firm breasts and her skirt with hooks torn-off was slipping down over her hips.

'O Lord, how high it is. I'm getting giddy.'

She gave a shuddering laugh and hesitated. Scared of the descent, she put her foot out, then drew it quickly back.

'It's too high. Go and fetch a ladder.'

'You silly fool,' said Jean, 'sit down and let yourself slide.'

'No, no, I'm frightened, I can't.'

Then there were shouts, exhortations, crude jokes. 'Not on your belly, that'll make it swell! On your bottom, unless you've got chilblains there!' Jean, below, felt himself excited as he looked up at the girl and watched her legs. Gradually he became exasperated at seeing her so high, out of his reach; and without realising it, he was mastered by the male desire to pull her down and hold her fast in his arms.

'But I tell you you won't break anything! Roll down, I'll catch you in my arms.'

'No, I can't.'

He stood in front of the stack, held his arms wide, and offered his chest so that she could throw herself on it. And when at last she closed her eyes and took the plunge, she skidded so quickly down

118

the slippery slope of the hay that she knocked him down and straddled over him with his ribs between her thighs. Sprawled on the ground with her skirts blown up, she spluttered breathlessly with laughter and assurances that she wasn't hurt. But with the smell of her burning sweating flesh against his face, he had gripped her tight. The sharp feminine smell mingled with the vivid scent of beaten hay in the open air intoxicated him and stiffened every muscle in his body in a sudden harsh fury of desire. Then still another feeling awoke, an unrealised passion for this youngster; he was abruptly gripped by a tenderness of flesh and spirit, which, born long past, had grown with their play, their hearty merriment and had now matured in this yearning to take her then and there, in the grass.

'Jean, stop it, you'll break my bones.'

She was still laughing, thinking it was all a game. He caught Palmyre's round eyes staring at him, started and stood up, trembling all over, with the bewildered air of a drunkard suddenly sobered by the sight of a gaping chasm at his feet. Good God! then it wasn't Lise he wanted, it was this young creature! The thought of Lise's flesh against his own had never once made his heart beat faster; yet he felt faint at the mere thought of kissing Françoise. Now he knew why he had enjoyed so much going to see the two sisters and helping them out. But the girl was so young! He felt ashamed and hopeless.

At that moment Lise was on her way home from the Fouans. On the road she had been reflecting. She'd prefer Buteau, since after all he was the father of her child. The old people were right, why rush things? The day that Buteau said no, there'd still be Jean to say yes.

She came up to Jean and said without hesitation, 'No reply, uncle doesn't know anything. Let's wait.'

Still distraught and trembling, Jean stared at her without comprehension. Then he remembered: marriage, the baby, Buteau's permission, the whole plan that only two hours ago he had thought so advantageous for both Lise and himself. He hurried to reply. 'Yes, yes, let's wait, that's best.'

Night was coming down, one star already glittered deep in the violet sky. Nothing could be distinguished in the growing twilight except the shadowy contours of the first stacks, which bulged up out of the flat stretch of meadowland. But the smells of the hot earth poured out more and more strongly into the calm air, and every noise travelled far, echoing on and on with a musical limpidity,

Men's and women's voices, laughter dying away, the snorting of a beast, the clank of a tool; while obstinately, in one corner of the pasture, the mowers went still on without a pause and the broad regular whizzing of the scythes still rose up although the work itself was now lost to sight.

V

Two years had gone by in the busy monotony of the country-side; and Rognes had lived through the fated cycle of the seasons, the unending round of things, the same labours and the same slumbers.

Lower down the road, at the corner of the school, stood a fountain fed by a spring. From it all the women drew their drinking-water, since their houses had only ponds used for cattle and gardens. At six in the evening the fountain became the district newspaper; the most trivial of events found an echo there, gossip raged tire-lessly over the families who had meat for dinner that day, over so-and-so's daughter, expecting since Candlemas. For two years the same scandals had circulated with the seasons, always renewed and yet never new—babies begotten before they should have been, men who got drunk, women who were beaten, unceasing toil for un-ceasing hardship. So many things had happened and yet nothing had happened.

The Fouans, whose property-division had caused intense excite-ment, went rubbing along in so humdrum a way that they were forgotten. Things had remained as they were. Buteau was still obstinate and wouldn't marry Mouche's elder girl who was bringing up his kid. Nothing had changed either with Jean whom they'd accused of sleeping with Lise. Maybe he never went to bed with her after all; but then why was he always at the two sisters' house? It looked suspicious. But the hour spent at the fountain would have been very dull some days but for the rivalry between Coelina Mac-queron and Flore Lengaigne, which was stirred up by La Bécu while she pretended to make peace. Then the calm was shattered by two tremendous and startling events—the forthcoming elections and the matter of the famous road from Rognes to Châteaudun, which gave rise to a terrific blast of scandal-mongering. The brimming pitchers stood in rows but the women would not leave. On Saturday evening there was nearly a brawl.

As it happened, the very next day M. de Chédeville, outgoing deputy, was lunching at La Borderie with Hourdequin. He was on his electoral tour and was humouring the farmer whose influence over the peasants of the district was considerable, even though he felt sure of re-election thanks to his official backing. He had once been to Compiègne and now the whole countryside had called him 'the Emperor's Friend'. Nothing more was needed. He was nominated as if he spent every night in the Tuileries. This M. de Chédeville, an old rake who had been a leader of fashion under Louis-Philippe, kept Orléanist sympathies tucked away in his innermost soul. He had thrown all his money away on women and now owned nothing but a farm at La Chamade, over towards Orgères, where he never set foot except at election times. He was upset by the falling value of farm property, and had moreover formed, late in life, the project of rebuilding his fortunes by public life. Tall, still elegant, with corseted waist and dyed hair, he led a reformed life, though his eye still kindled at the passing flutter of a petticoat-fringe; and he let it be known that he was preparing important speeches on agricultural questions.

The night before, Hourdequin had had a bitter quarrel with Jacqueline who wanted to attend the luncheon-party.

'Your deputy, your deputy! D'you think I'll eat him? So you're ashamed of me, are you!'

But he held his ground and only two places were laid. She sulked in spite of M. de Chédeville's gallantries. As soon as he saw her, he grasped the situation and kept turning his eyes all the while towards the kitchen where in her dignified huff she had gone to shut herself up.

The luncheon was drawing to its close: an omelette, followed by a trout fresh from the Aigre, and roast pigeons.

'The thing that is ruining us,' said M. de Chédeville, 'is the Emperor's craze for commercial freedom. Admittedly, things went well after the treaties of 1861 and people talked of a miracle. But to-day we are feeling the full consequence. You can see how prices are falling. I'm all for tariffs. We must protect ourselves against foreigners.'

Hourdequin, leaning back in his chair and forgetting the food, talked slowly, with vacant eyes.

'Wheat, which sells at fifty-two francs the quarter costs forty-six to produce. If it goes any lower, it means ruin. And they say that America is increasing her cereal exports every year. We are threatened with a proper glut of the market. What'll become of us then? Listen! I've always stood for progress, for science, for liberty. Well, my belief's shaken, on my word! Yes, indeed, we can't starve to death. Let's have Protection!'

He returned to his pigeon-wing and went on, 'You know that our opponent, M. Rochefontaine, the owner of the building works at Châteaudun, is an enthusiastic Free-trader?'

They chatted for a bit about this industrialist who employed some twelve hundred workers, a big chap with much intelligence and energy, not to mention wealth. He was always ready to serve the Empire but had been so hurt at failure to win the prefect's support that he'd insisted on putting up as an independent candidate. He had no chance at all; the country electors treated him like a public enemy from the moment he showed himself opposed to the ruling powers.

'Good heavens!' said M. de Chédeville, 'all he wants is cheaper bread so that he won't have to pay his workers so much.'

The farmer, who was just going to pour a glass of claret, put the bottle back on the table. 'That's the worst of it,' he cried, 'on one hand here are we, the country-folk, who want a good price for our grain. On the other hand there's the industrialist driving the price down so as to lower wages. It's war to the knife, and how will it all end up, tell me that?'

This, indeed, was the burning problem of the day, the antagonism rending the social fabric. It was a question that went far beyond the meagre intelligence of the old rake, who merely shook his head and made an evasive gesture.

Hourdequin filled his glass and emptied it at one gulp. 'There's no way out of it. If the countryman sells his wheat at a good price, the worker will die of hunger. If the worker eats, the peasant will starve. So what's the way out? I just don't know. It's dog eat dog.'

Then, with elbows planted on the table, he launched out and his feelings ran furiously away with him. His voice took on a particular ironic intonation from the secret contempt he felt for this absentee landlord, who knew nothing about the land from which he drew his livelihood.

'You asked me for facts to put into your speeches. Well, here you are! First, it's your own fault if La Chamade is losing money. Robiquet, the farmer you've installed there, has given up trying; his lease is running out and he suspects you of wanting to increase his rent. We never set eyes on you; people have no respect for you and so they rob you. It's bound to happen. And there's an even simpler reason for your ruin: the fact that we are all being ruined, La Beauce is worked out, yes, the rich Beauce plain, our nurse, our mother!'

He explained further. In his youth, for example, Le Perche, on the other side of the Loir, had been a poor country, sparsely cultivated, with almost no grain crops, and its people hired themselves out at harvest in Cloyes or Châteaudun or Bonneval. To-day, owing to the constant rise in the price of labour, Le Perche was the place that prospered; it would soon leave La Beauce well in the rear. Moreover, it was doing well out of stock-breeding; the markets of Mondoubleau, Saint-Calais and Couralain were supplying the plain-lands with horses, cattle and pigs. La Beauce herself was only kept going by her sheep. Two years before, when the bloody spleen had decimated the flocks, the region had gone through a dreadful crisis, and if the plague had lasted any longer, it would have been utterly ruined.

Then he turned to his own struggles, his own history—a thirty years' war with the earth, from which he had emerged poorer than he began. He had never had enough capital; he had been unable to bring on certain fields as he wanted to. Marling was the only cheap process and he was the only one who'd ever taken it up. It was the same with manures. The farmers used only farm-manure, which was inadequate; and all the neighbours laughed at him for trying out chemical fertilisers which were, anyway, often of such bad quality as to put the mockers in the right. In spite of his ideas about crop rotation, he had had to fall in with the local custom, three-fold rotation without a fallow period, ever since the spread of artificial pasture and the cultivation of hoed plants. One machine only, the threshing-machine, was beginning to win acceptance. Such was the paralysing effect of routine, deadly and inevitable; and if he himself, a progressive who used his brains, had let himself be affected by it, what could the small landowners expect, hardheaded fellows, dead set against new ideas? A peasant would die of hunger rather than pick up a handful of earth and take it to be analysed by a chemist, who could tell him what it lacked or had in excess, the manuring it required, the crops best adapted to it. Through the centuries the peasant had taken the earth without ever dreaming of putting anything back, recognising no manure save what came from his two cows and his horse, and greedily hoarding their dung. Everything else was left to chance. Seeds were thrown into any

123

kind of soil, where they germinated by pure chance; and if they didn't germinate, the heavens were blamed. On the day when the peasant learned his lesson and decided on rational scientific husbandry, production could be doubled. But till that day, ignorant and obstinate, without a farthing's worth of progress to his name, he'd go on murdering the earth. And that was why La Beauce, one-time granary of France, La Beauce, a waterless plain-land with nothing but her crops, was dying of gradual exhaustion, tired of being bled white to afford nourishment to such a race of idiots.

'Everything's buggered up!' he cried crudely. 'Yes, our children will live to see it—the murder of the earth. Do you know, our peasants used to save up their sous to buy a strip of that land they'd coveted year after year, but now they're buying stocks and shares—Spanish, Portuguese, even Mexican? They won't risk ten francs even to improve their little plots! Their confidence is gone. The old men go round and round in their grooves like broken-down hacks; the girls and lads dream of nothing but an escape from their cows, they want to scrape the mud off their shoes and slip away to the towns. But the worst part of it is that education—you know, that famous education which was going to save the situation—in fact encourages the exodus, the depopulation of the countryside. It gives children a ridiculous conceit and a taste for sham comfort. Take Rognes now. There they have a teacher, a man called Lequeu, a chap who skipped off from the plough; he's filled with hatred of the earth which he only just escaped having to toil over. Well, how do you think he's going to reconcile his pupils to their lot when day in and day out he treats them like a pack of savages, and sends them back to the paternal dungheap with all the contempt of his book-learning? The remedy, my God, the one certain remedy is to have a different sort of school—practical teaching, graded courses in agriculture. There, Monsieur le Deputé, there is one concrete point I can give you. Insist on it. Schools like that may save things, if it's not too late.'

M. de Chédeville, bored and uncomfortable under this heavy torrent of information, hastened to reply, 'Doubtless, doubtless.'

The maid who was bringing in the dessert, a cream cheese and fruit, left the door to the kitchen wide ajar; and he glimpsed Jacqueline's pretty profile, leaned forward, winked and fidgetted about to catch the delightful young woman's attention. Then he spoke up again, in the fluting tones of an old dandy, 'But you've left out the small-holders.'

124

He set out the current ideas: the small landowners, created in '89, encouraged by the Code, called upon to regenerate agriculture; in effect, every man a landowner, dedicating all his energies of mind and body to the task of cultivating his own little strip.

'Please spare me that!' cried Hourdequin. 'Firstly, the small landowners existed before '89, almost as numerous, relatively, as now. Secondly, there's a lot to be said on the subject of strip-farming, both for and against.'

Again, with his elbows on the table, he went into details while eating cherries and spitting the stones out. In La Beauce almost eighty per cent of the men on the land were the small farmers who inherited less than fifty acres. For some time past almost all the day-labourers, the men who worked on the farms, had been buying strips of land, bits and pieces from the broken-up estates, and cultivating them in their spare time. That was excellent, of course, for the farmworker was henceforth firmly attached to the land. Another point in favour of small land-holdings was that it developed men who were worthier, more independent, more knowledgeable. Finally, it produced proportionately better crops, in quantity and quality alike, since the owner put his whole heart into the work. On the other hand, what drawbacks there were! Firstly, what superiority the system had was due to excessive toil—parents and children killing themselves with work. Then, strip-farming multiplied the problems of transport, wore out the roads, pushed up the cost of production, not to mention the time it wasted. It was impossible to use machines on the small-holdings, and there was also the disadvantage of the three-yearly rotation, which scientific methods would certainly proscribe; for it was unreasonable to ask for two cereals to follow one another, wheat and then oats. In short, strip-farming carried to an extreme seemed so likely to become a danger that after fostering it by law just after the Revolution—for fear of a new growth of big estates—the State had now come round to making land-transfers easier by lessening the charges.

'Mark my words,' he went on, 'there is a struggle, a sharpening struggle, between large and small landownership. Some men, like myself, are for big estates, as seeming more in line with science and progress, with the extended use of machines, and with the movement of big capital. There are others, however, who believe only in personal enterprise and cry up the small owners, dreaming of some kind of miniature agriculture, everyone producing his own manure and cultivating his quarter-acre, choosing his crops one by one.

125

giving them the land they need, and giving each plant individual attention, under cloches. Which method will win the day? Damned if I know! What I do know, and only too well, as I told you, is that each year the big farms of this area are being ruined and broken up, falling into the hands of gangs of swindlers, and small landowners are certainly gaining ground. There is a very curious instance I know, at Rognes, an old woman who wrings a good living, even a few comforts, for herself and her man out of less than an acre. People have given her the nickname Mother Caca, because she doesn't shrink from using her own and her husband's chamber pots in her vegetable plot, the Chinese method, so they say. But that is merely gardening. I can't see cereals growing in beds like turnips; and if in order to get sufficient to live on the peasant is forced to grow a bit of everything, what will happen to the people of La Beauce, who have one crop, wheat, when the district is cut up like a chess-board? Well, the man who manages to survive will see what the future brings, large-scale or small-scale. . .'

He broke off and shouted, 'That coffee—is it coming to-day?'

Then he lit his pipe and rounded off his picture. 'Unless we kill them both off straight away—and that's what we're busy doing now. Get it into your head, Monsieur le Deputé, farming is in its death throes and will die unless help comes. It's carrying everything on its back: taxes, foreign competition, the continual rise in wages, the shift of capital to industry and the Stock Exchange. Of course, there are plenty of generous promises, everybody flings them about, the prefects, the ministers, the Emperor. And then the dust-clouds rise on the roads and nothing arrives. Do you want the exact truth? To-day the farmer who holds on is wasting either his own money or other people's. I've got a few sous in reserve, I'm all right. Yet I know men who are borrowing at six per cent when their land yields only three per cent. That's certain bankruptcy. A peasant who borrows is finished, he'll have to pay down to his last shirt. A week or so ago, they threw out one of my neighbours. Man, wife and four children were pushed out into the street after the lawyers had impounded his live-stock, his land and his house. Yet for years and years they have been promising us farming credits at reasonable interest. Yes, we'll believe it when we see it! All this disheartens even the good workers, they begin to think twice before getting their wives with children. Lord, another mouth to feed, another starveling to rue the day he was born! When there isn't food to go round, men don't get children, and the nation goes down!'

M. de Chédeville, much relieved, risked an uneasy smile, murmuring, 'You don't look on the bright side of things.'

'True, there are days when I feel like letting everything slide,' Hourdequin gaily replied. 'Remember, these troubles have been going on for thirty years! I can't think why I've stuck to it, I ought to have sold up the farm and gone in for something else. Habit, of course, and then the hope that things would change, and then, why not confess it, this bitchy earth, once she gets a hold on you, won't let you go. See there! On that sideboard—perhaps it's stupid, but I feel better when I look at it.'

Stretching out his hand, he pointed to a silver cup protected from flies by a muslin cloth, first prize in an agricultural show. Such shows, where he came out on top, acted as a spur to his vanity and were one of the causes of his pertinacity.

In spite of the obvious weariness of his guest, he took his time over coffee; he was pouring a third cognac into his cup when, drawing out his watch, he jumped to his feet. 'Damnation! two o'clock, and I've got a meeting of the municipal council! Yes, it's about a road. We are definitely willing to pay half the cost, but we want to get a State subsidy for the other half.'

M. de Chédeville had risen from his chair, happy to be released. 'Now look here, I can do you a good turn, I can get you your subsidy. As you are in a hurry would you like me to take you to Rognes in my carriage?'

'Splendid!'

And Hourdequin went out to get the carriage harnessed as it had been left in the yard. When he came back, he found the deputy was no longer in the room and at last ran him down in the kitchen. The deputy had pushed open the door and was standing there smiling at the ecstatic Jacqueline, complimenting her at such close quarters that their faces were almost touching. With easy intuition, they had summed one another up and said everything there was to say with one unequivocal glance.

When M. de Chédeville got up again into his carriage, La Cognette held Hourdequin back a moment to whisper in his ear, 'Eh, he's nicer than you and doesn't think I'm only fit to be hidden away, he doesn't.'

On the road, while the carriage rolled along between the cornfields, the farmer came back to the subject of the earth, his ceaseless obsession. He now produced manuscript reports, facts and figures, for he had kept records over several years. In the whole of La

127

Beauce there were not more than two or three people who did as much; and the small landowners and peasants shrugged their shoulders at an idea that they couldn't comprehend at all. Still, only full accounts could clarify the position by indicating which products were profitable and which a loss; in addition they showed cost price against selling price. In Hourdequin's calculations every servant, every animal, every crop, even every tool, was given its own page, in debit and credit columns, so lucidly that at any moment he could check the result of his operations, his profit and his loss.

'At least,' he commented with his loud laugh, 'I know exactly how my ruination is proceeding.'

But he suddenly stopped talking and swore through clenched teeth. For the last few minutes, as the carriage rolled on, he had been trying to make out what was happening a little further along the road. Although it was Sunday he had sent a newly-bought hay-making machine to cut some ripe lucerne which had to be dealt with promptly. And the farm labourer, not recognising his master in the unfamiliar carriage, unsuspectingly went on jeering at the machine with three peasants whom he had stopped on the way.

'Look,' he was saying, 'look at the clumsy contraption! It bruises the grass and infects it. Honest! three sheep have already died.'

The peasants were sneering, examining the machine as if it were a ridiculous evil beast. One of them declared, 'All these things are inventions of the devil to get poor people down. What'll our wives do if they aren't wanted for haymaking?'

'Oh that! The masters care bugger-all for that!' replied the labourer, giving the machine a kick. 'Gee up, you old carcass!'

Hourdequin had heard the remarks. He leaned furiously out of the carriage and shouted, 'Back to the farm you go, Zéphyrin, and get paid off!'

The labourer stood gaping while the three peasants went off with loud shouts of insulting laughter and jeers.

'There!' said Hourdequin, dropping back on the seat. 'Now you've seen it. You'd think our up-to-date machines burned their fingers. They treat me as a *bourgeois*; they work less on my farm than elsewhere, on the pretext that I can afford to pay better; and they're encouraged by my neighbours, the other farmers, who accuse me of teaching the country people to work badly and rage about the way they'll soon be able to find nobody to work for them like the workers in the good old days.'

The carriage was entering Rognes by the Bazoches-le-Doyen

road when the deputy noticed the Abbé Godard coming out of Macqueron's, where he had lunched after Mass. His election worries revived and he asked, 'How's the religious feeling in our country parishes?'

'Oh, the usual show, but nothing beneath,' Hourdequin carelessly answered.

He stopped the driver in front of Macqueron's, where the proprietor stood in the doorway with the Abbé; and he introduced the deputy-mayor, who was dressed in a shabby stained coat. But Coelina, very trim in her print dress, ran up, pushing forward her daughter Berthe, the pride of the family, dressed like a young lady in a silk dress with mauve stripes.

Meanwhile the village, which had appeared deserted, as if everyone had been sent to sleep by the lovely Sunday weather, was waking up under the shock of this extraordinary visit. The peasants emerged one by one and the children ventured out, clinging to their mothers' skirts. At Lengaigne's particularly there was much coming-and-going. The master himself craned out of the window with his razor in his hand, while his wife Flore stopped weighing out two-penn'orth of tobacco to flatten her face against the windowpane— man and wife alike envious and angry that the gentlemen had got down at their rival's door. Gradually people came up and groups gathered. The entire village of Rognes was now buzzing with the important event.

'Monsieur le Deputé,' Macqueron was repeating, his face red with embarrassment, 'this is indeed an honour. . .'

But M. de Chédeville wasn't listening. He was charmed by the pretty looks of Berthe, whose clear blue-circled eyes stared impudently back at him. Her mother was telling the deputy her age and the school she'd been to, and the girl herself, curtseying and smiling, invited the gentlemen to condescend to come in.

'Of course, my dear child,' he cried.

Meanwhile, the Abbé Godard, who had buttonholed Hourdequin, besought him once again to persuade the municipal council to vote funds so that Rognes might at long last have its own priest. Every six months he brought up the subject and set out his reasons: the strain he felt and his constant embroilment with the villagers, not to mention the inadequacy of the services.

'Don't refuse me!' he added quickly, seeing the landowner make an evasive gesture. 'Do bring the matter up again, I'll wait to hear the decision.'

Then just as M. de Chédeville was going to follow Berthe into the house, he rushed forward and stopped him in his good-humoured persistent way.

'Excuse me, Monsieur le Deputé. The poor church here is in such a state. I'd like to show it to you, you must get it repaired for me. No one listens to me any more. Do come, I beg you.'

Very annoyed, the old rake was resisting, when Hourdequin, learning from Macqueron that several of the municipal councillors had been waiting for him at the Town Hall for half an hour, said in his offhand way, 'That's right, go and see the church. You'll kill time till I'm done and then you can take me home.'

M. de Chédeville had to follow the Abbé. The crowd had swollen and a large section of it came trailing after him. People were getting bolder and one and all were thinking up requests to put to him.

When Hourdequin and Macqueron had gone up to the mayor's room opposite, they found there three councillors: Delhomme and two others. The huge white-washed room had no furniture beyond the long whitewood table and twelve straw-bottomed chairs; between the two windows, which opened on the road, was fixed a cupboard in which the archives were kept mixed up with odd administrative documents; and, around the walls on the shelves were piled up canvas fire-buckets: a rich citizen's gift which they did not know where to store and which remained a cumbrous nuisance, since the village had no fire-engine.

'Gentlemen,' said Hourdequin politely, 'I beg your pardon, I had M. de Chédeville to lunch.'

No one moved a muscle; it was impossible to say whether or not they accepted this excuse. They had looked out of the window and seen the deputy arrive, they were deeply interested in the coming election; but that was no reason for a rash statement.

'Damn it all!' said the farmer, 'if we're only five, we haven't a quorum.'

Fortunately Lengaigne came in. At first he had resolved not to go to the council, as the question of the road did not concern him; he even hoped that his absence would thwart the vote. But the arrival of M. de Chédeville began arousing his curiosity and he decided to go up and find out what was on. 'Good, we're six, so we can take decisions,' cried the mayor.

Lequeu, who acted as secretary, appeared with a haughty sullen air, the minute book under his arm, so that nothing now held up the opening of the session. But Delhomme had started talking in a low voice to his neighbour Clou, the farrier, a tall dry saturnine man. As the others began to listen, they promptly stopped. All the same a name had been overheard, that of the independent candidate, M. Rochefontaine; and so all of them, after preliminary soundings, fell with a word, a laugh, a mere grimace, on this candidate whom nobody knew anything about. They all stood for law and order, for keeping things as they were, for obedience to the authorities who kept the market stable. Did this gentleman think himself stronger than the Government? Could he swing the price of grain up to eighty-eighty francs the quarter? He was a cool customer, sending out prospectuses and promising more butter than bread, with no support from anyone or anything. They ended by treating him as an adventurer, a low rogue who was stirring up the villages and trying to steal their votes as he'd certainly steal their pence. Hourdequin could have explained that M. Rochefontaine, a Free Trader, was essentially following the same line of policy as the Emperor, but he deliberately allowed Macqueron to spread himself in his Bonapartist zeal, while Delhomme made his points in a narrow common-sense way and Lengaigne, gagged by his position as treasurer, grumbled out his vague Republican notions in a corner. Though M. de Chédeville's name wasn't mentioned, every remark related to him and worked out as a sort of kowtowing before him in his rôle of official candidate.

'Come along, gentlemen,' said the mayor at last, 'suppose we start.'

He was seated at the table in his presidential chair, which was larger than the others and boasted arms. Only the deputy-mayor sat beside him. The four councillors remained, two standing, two leaning on a window-sill.

But Lequeu had handed the mayor a sheet of paper, and after whispering in his ear walked out with a dignified step.

'Gentlemen,' said Hourdequin, 'I have a letter here from the schoolmaster.'

He read it out—a plea for increase of salary, thirty francs more a year, in return for time and trouble taken. Every face darkened. They were all tight-fisted with the public money, as if each member had to meet charges out of his own pocket, especially school costs. There was not even any discussion; the request was flatly turned down.

'Right. We'll tell him to wait. This young man is liable to get ahead of himself. Now let's get on to the question of the road.'

131

'Excuse me, Monsieur le Maire,' Macqueron interrupted, 'first I'd like to say something about the priest. . .'

Hourdequin was taken aback and then realised why Abbé Godard had lunched with the store-keeper. What scheme was pricking him on to come out like this? Anyway his proposals met with the same treatment as the schoolmaster's. He might have saved his breath when he suggested they were rich enough to support a priest of their own, that it was not exactly dignified to put up with the leavings of Bazoches-le-Doyen. The others all shrugged their shoulders and asked if the Mass would be any the better for it. No, of course it wouldn't! The vicarage would have to be repaired; a priest of their own would cost far too much; and a half an hour of the other priest on Sundays was enough, surely.

The mayor, offended at his deputy's presumption, shut the discussion down. 'There is nothing to discuss. The council has already decided. And now for our road: we must reach a decision. Delhomme, be good enough to call in Monsieur Lequeu. Does the creature think we are going to debate his letter until nightfall?'

Lequeu, who was waiting on the stairway, came in with grave face; and as he was not informed of the fate of his request, he remained tense, uneasy, oppressed by unspoken abuse. What a foul breed these peasants were! He had to fetch the road-plan out of the cupboard and unfold it on the table-top.

The councillors knew the plan by heart. It had been on their hands for years. Yet they all came pressing up, elbow to elbow, and once again brooded over it. The mayor enumerated the advantages for Rognes: a gentler approach allowing carriages to drive right up to the church; the saving of two leagues on the Rognes-Châteaudun road, which at present swerved aside through Cloyes; the shortening by two miles or so of the length of highway that the community would have to keep in good condition, since their Blanville neighbours had already voted for the remaining section—that as far as the junction with the Châteaudun-Orléans road. They all listened with eyes fast on the paper and never opened their mouths. The main reason for the long delay in carrying the project through had been the question of indemnities. Everyone saw the chance of a fortune and was anxious to get the road running through one of his own fields so that he could sell his land to the Commune at a hundred francs a perch. And if his land wasn't touched at any point, why should he vote for someone else's enrichment? A gentler slope, a shortened road! Why, let the horse pull a bit harder—that would do.

Hourdequin had no need to make them talk to find out what they thought. His own support for the road derived from the fact that it passed in front of his farm and cut into several of his fields. Macqueron and Delhomme, whose land also would be affected, pressed equally hard for a vote. That made three. But neither Clou nor the other councillor had any interest in the road; and as for Lengaigne, he was violently opposed to the project, having nothing to gain by it and being fiercely jealous that his rival the deputy-mayor should reap some advantage. If Clou and the other man, a dark horse, voted against, the count would be three against three. Hourdequin became uneasy. Then at last discussion began.

'What's the use of it? What's the use?' Lengaigne kept on repeating. 'There's already a road! It's just a scheme to spend money, taking it out of Jean's pocket and putting it into Pierre's. And then, you there, you promised to give your land free.'

This was a cunning thrust at Macqueron. But the deputy-mayor, who bitterly regretted his fit of generosity, gave the lie direct.

'Me? I didn't promise anything! Who told you that?'

'Who? Why, in God's name, you did—and in front of witnesses. Yes, Monsieur Lequeu was there, he can confirm it. Wasn't that so, Monsieur Lequeu?'

The schoolmaster, still smarting under the delay in answering his request, made a gesture of rough disdain. What had their dirty intrigues to do with him!

'All right then,' went on Lengaigne, 'if there's no honour left here, we might as well go off and live in the woods! No, I wash my hands of your road. It's plain robbery!'

Seeing things were going wrong, the mayor hastened to intervene.

'All that's nothing but gossip. We mustn't get involved in personal wrangles. It's the public interest, the common interest, that should guide us.'

'That's right,' agreed Delhomme sagely. 'The new road will give good service to the whole community. But there's one thing we must know. The prefect has always told us: "Vote a sum of money, then we'll see what the Government can do for you". But suppose it does nothing, why waste time voting?'

Hourdequin decided the moment had come for him to divulge the great news he had been keeping back.

'On that point, gentlemen, I can tell you that Monsieur le Chédeville undertakes to obtain a subsidy from the Government covering half the outlay. You know he's a friend of the Emperor. He has only to talk to him about us, over coffee.'

Lengaigne himself was overwhelmed. Every face assumed a beatific smile, as if the holy sacrament was passing. The deputy's reelection was fully assured: the Emperor's friend was the man for them, the man who was at the fountainhead of office and money, the man who was known, honourable, powerful, the master! Nothing happened, however, except some head-noddings. The points were obvious: why put them in words?

Yet Hourdequin was still worried about the attitude of the silent Clou. He stood up and glanced out of the window; and catching sight of the constable he ordered him to find Father Loiseau and bring him along, dead or alive. Loiseau was a deaf old peasant, Macqueron's uncle, and the grocer had had him nominated as council member; but he never attended meetings because he said they gave him bad headaches. His son worked at La Borderie and he was completely devoted to the mayor. And so, as soon as he appeared in a scared state, Hourdequin merely shouted in his ear that the matter of the road had come up. Everyone was already writing awkwardly in his ballot paper, with nose close to the paper and elbows stuck out wide so that no one else could read what he wrote. Then they went on to vote about the half of the outlay, in a small whitewood box just like a poor-box in a church. The majority was splendid, six for and only one against—Lengaigne. The rascal Clou had voted right. And the session was over, after everyone had signed the minute-book, which the schoolmaster had prepared beforehand, with a blank space left for the result of the vote. Then they all stumped heavily out without a good-bye or a handshake, drifting off down the staircase.

'O, I forgot,' said Hourdequin to Lequeu who was still waiting, 'your request for an increase is turned down. The council considers we are already spending too much on the school.'

'The bunch of beasts!' cried the young man, livid with rage, as soon as he was alone. 'Go and live in your pigsties, then!'

The session had lasted two hours, and Hourdequin found M. de Chédeville again in front of the Town Hall, only just returned from his tour of the village. To begin with, the priest had not let him off a single dilapidation of the church: the ruined roof, the smashed windows, the bare walls. Then, as he finally escaped from the sacristy, which needed a new coat of paint, the villagers, with their timidity quite evaporated, began debating who should take him round. Each one had a claim to put forward, a favour to win. One dragged him to the common pond, which was no longer cleaned out through lack of money; another pointed out the exact position on the banks of the Aigre where he wanted a covered wash-house; a third demanded the widening of the road in front of his house so that his cart could turn round; until finally an old woman who, after pushing the deputy into her house, showed him her swollen legs and asked if he knew some remedy in Paris. Bewildered and breathless, he smiled, acted the good fellow, and promised everything. A good fellow all right, and not stand-offish with poor folk!

'Well, shall we go?' asked Hourdequin. 'I'm expected at the farm.'

But just then Coelina and her daughter Berthe ran to their door, pleading with M. de Chédeville to come in for one moment; and the deputy would have liked nothing better, a respite at last, as he looked again with pleasure into the bright pretty dissipated eyes of the young girl.

'No, no,' the landowner went on, 'we haven't time, another day.'

He hurried the dazed deputy to the carriage; while in reply to the patiently-waiting priest he remarked that the council had deferred judgment on the parish question. The driver whipped up his horse and the carriage rolled away through the friendly delighted village. The priest, left alone in his vexation, started off on his two-mile walk from Rognes to Bazoches-le-Doyen.

A fortnight later, M. de Chédeville was elected by a huge majority; and before the end of August, he had fulfilled his promise. A subsidy was granted to the community for the opening of the new road. Work immediately started.

On the evening of the first pickaxe-swing, Coelina, thin and swarthy, stood by the well listening to the lanky La Bécu who, with her hands clasped under her apron, prattled on without pause. For the past week, the gossip at the spring had been revolutionised by the tremendous matter of the road: no one talked of anything but the indemnities to be paid to some lucky people and the vicious rage of the others. Every day La Bécu gave Coelina the latest news of what Flore Lengaigne was saying; not to fan their hatred, of course; no, on the contrary, to help them to understand each other, because that was the best way to bring them into harmony. The women stood around, arms akimbo; their filled jugs stood forgotten at their feet.

'And then she said how there was an arrangement between your husband the deputy and the mayor, just a way of getting a rake-off from the land sold. Yes, and she said that your husband was two-faced.'

At that moment Flore came out of her house with her pitcher in her hand. As she approached, fat and flabby, Coelina let go at once a volley of foul words. With her fists on her hips, a virtuous shrew, she told her what she was, in fine style, throwing her trollop of a daughter in her face and accusing Flore herself of never denying the customers anything they wanted. Flore, in her down-at-heel slippers, could only keep on whimpering: 'O what a slut! O what a slut!'

La Bécu threw herself in between and did her best to force them to kiss and be friends; which all but made them try to tear each other's hair out. Then she flung out another piece of news. 'I say, that reminds me, you know the Mouche girls are to get five hundred francs.'

'I can't credit it!'

At once the quarrel was forgotten and they all drew together among the scattered jugs. Not a shred of doubt, the road, at Les Cornailles up there, passed alongside the sisters' field and would cut off five hundred yards: at a franc a yard that piled up to five hundred francs; and the land bordering the road would gain in value as well. It was a fine bit of luck.

'So it turns out,' said Flore, 'that Lise is now a proper match, even with her kid. That big lout Corporal knew a good thing after all when he stuck to her.'

'Unless,' added Coelina, 'Buteau comes back into the picture. His strip is also worth a lot now this road's come.'

La Bécu turned round, then nudged them.

'Ssh! be quiet!'

Lise was coming up merrily swinging her jug. And the queue by the fountain began moving once more.

VI

BLANCHETTE had grown too fat and would not calve again; so Lise and Françoise decided to visit Cloyes market that Saturday and buy another cow. Jean offered to drive them there in one of the farm-carts. He had the afternoon free; and his master, having heard

the rumours of a coming marriage between the lad and the elder
Mouche girl, had given him permission to take the cart. And indeed
the marriage was decided upon. At least, Jean had promised to see
Buteau the following week and put the question to him. One man
or the other must have Lise: it was time to settle the matter.

They started off about one o'clock, Jean in front with Lise, Françoise by herself on the back bench. From time to time Jean turned
round and smiled at Françoise, feeling her knees press warmly
against his loins. It was a great pity that she was fifteen years
younger than he; and although, after much reflection and delay,
he had resigned himself to marrying the elder, he had been ultimately moved, no doubt, by the thought of living near the younger
sister as a relative. Besides, folk just drift along with no conscious
idea of why they do this or that, except that a decision was once
taken long ago.

As they entered Cloyes, Jean put the brake on and started the
horse down the steep hill beside the cemetery. As he came to the
cross-roads between the Rue Grande and the Rue Grouais, meaning
to put up at the *Jolly Ploughman*, he suddenly pointed to a man
walking away from them down the latter street.

'Hey, that looks like Buteau.'

'It's him,' declared Lise. 'I suppose he's on his way to Monsieur
Baillehache's. Is he going to take over his share of land?'

Jean cracked his whip and laughed. 'You can never tell, he's so
sly.'

Buteau was acting as if he hadn't seen them, though he had in
fact recognised them from a distance. He walked on with bent back;
and Lise and Jean, as they watched him pass from sight were silently
thinking that everything was now to be cleared up. In the *Jolly
Ploughman* yard, Françoise, who had not spoken a word, jumped
down first, over one of the wheels. The yard was already full of
unharnessed vehicles resting on their shafts, while a buzz of activity
stirred the old buildings of the inn.

'Ready to go?' asked Jean as he returned from stabling the horse.

'Of course, straightaway.'

Nevertheless, instead of making directly for the cattle-market
through the Rue du Tempe to the Place Saint-Georges, the man and
the two girls dawdled in front of the vegetable and fruit stalls
lining the streets and loitered down the whole length of the Rue
Grande. Jean wore a silk cap and a long blue blouse with black
cloth trousers; the girls too were in their Sunday best with hair

137

pulled back under little round bonnets. They wore identical dresses, a bodice of dark woollen material over an iron-grey skirt, brightened by a wide cotton apron with narrow pink stripes. They did not link arms but walked in single file with arms swinging, amid the jostling crowd. There was a crush of servants and middle class ladies, all round the squatting peasants who, arriving with one or two baskets, simply put them down on the ground and opened them. They recognised La Frimat with her swollen wrists, who had a bit of everything in her two overflowing baskets—lettuces, beans, plums, even three live rabbits. By her side an old man had just poured out a barrowload of potatoes, which he was selling by the bushel. Two women, mother and daughter—the latter a well-known whore called Norine—had spread out on a rickety table cod, salted and smoked herrings, the scrapings from barrel-bottoms with a strong brine odour that caught at the throat. As for the Rue Grande, so quiet during the week despite its fine shops—its chemist, its jewellers, above all its Paris Novelties, Lambourdieu's emporium—it wasn't nearly wide enough on Saturdays. The shops were packed and the roadway obstructed by the encroachments of traders.

Lise and Françoise, followed by Jean, shoved through to the poultry market in the Rue Baudone. The farms had sent huge open-work baskets in which cocks were crowing or frightened ducks thrusting their necks out through the holes. Plucked chickens lay dead in boxes, ranged in deep layers. Then there were the peasant women, each one carrying her four or five pounds of butter, some dozens of eggs, cheeses—large and dry, small and rich, wine-moistened and ash-grey. Several women had brought braces of chickens corded by their feet. The women haggled and the arrival of a large supply of eggs drew a crowd in front of the inn *Au Rendez-vous des Poulaillers*. Among the men discharging the eggs they noticed Palmyre. Every Saturday, when there was no work at Rognes, she hired herself out at Cloyes, carrying loads enough to crack her spine.

'There's a woman who works for her living!' Jean remarked.

The crowd was thickening. More traps were coming in by the Mondoubleau road, trotting slowly one after another over the bridge. To right and left, the Loir flowed along its gentle bends, level with the meadows; the left bank was bordered by town gardens with lilacs and laburnums dipping their branches down into the water. Further upstream stood a tanner's mill with its deep tick-tacking sound, and a huge grain-mill, an enormous building whitened by the steady cloud of flour blown out through the roof-ventilators.

'Well,' Jean repeated, 'shall we go on?'

'Yes, yes, of course.'

They went back through the Rue Grande, stopping in the Place Saint-Lubin opposite the Town Hall, where the corn market was held. Lengaigne, who had brought four sacks, stood there with his hands in his pockets. In the middle of a group of silent peasants, who kept their eyes on the ground, Hourdequin was holding forth and angrily gesturing. They had hoped for a rise in prices; but even the price of eighteen francs was unstable and they were afraid there might even be another drop of twenty-five centimes. Macqueron passed with his daughter Berthe on his arm; he was dressed in a shabby overcoat, while she wore a muslin dress with a bunch of roses and lily-of-the-valley in her hat.

As Lise and Françoise turned through the Rue du Temple and passed the Saint-Georges church where the hawkers set up their stalls with haberdashery, ironmongery and lengths of cloth, they exclaimed, 'There's Aunt Rose!'

And indeed there was old Rose Fouan. Fanny, who had come in place of Delhomme to deliver some oats had brought her mother along for an outing. Both women were waiting stockstill in front of the whizzing wheel of the knife-grinder to whom the old woman had handed her scissors. He had ground them for the last thirty years.

'Good gracious, it's you two!'

Fanny turned round and noticed Jean, then added, 'So you're out for a walk, are you?'

But when they heard that the girls were going to buy a cow to replace Blanchette, they grew interested and, as the oats had been handed over, they accompanied them. Jean, crowded out, walked behind the four women who went along in a widely-spaced line, four abreast; and in this way they entered the Place Saint-Georges.

The square was very wide and extended beyond the apse of the church which dominated it with its old stone clock-tower. Tufted lindens grew all round it. Two sides were cut off by chains riveted to stone posts, the other two had long wooden railings to which animals were tethered. On this side of the square, near the gardens, the grass grew and it was just like a meadow; while on the opposite side, skirted by two roads and bordered with wine-shops—the *Saint-Georges, A la Racine, Aux bons Moissonneurs*—the ground was trodden, hardened, whitened with dust which eddied to and fro in the wind.

Lise and Françoise, followed by the others, had some difficulty in crossing the middle of the square where the main crowd had gathered. Among the mass of blouses, a confused jumble of all shades of blue (ranging from the hard blue of new linen to the pale blue of shirts faded by a couple of dozen boilings) all that could be seen of them was the little white bonnets bobbing along. A few ladies walked about under the glistening silk of their parasols. There was much laughter and shouting, merging into a great living murmur now and again broken by the neigh of a horse or the lowing of a cow. Then a donkey came in with a desperate bray.

'This way,' said Lise over her shoulder.

The horses were at the end, tied to the bar, with bare quivering coats and no harness but a rope knotted at neck and tail. To the left the cows were almost all loose, merely held by the hands of the vendors, who walked them up and down to show them off better. Groups of passers-by stopped and stared; and here there was no laughter and only a few terse words.

Without any delay the four women paused meditatively before a black and white cow, a Cotentine, offered for sale by a man and his wife. The woman, swarthy and stubborn-faced, stood in front holding the beast; the man kept in the background, motionless and inscrutable. A detailed and solemn inspection went on for about five minutes; but the women did not exchange a single word or glance. Then they moved on to give the same consideration to another cow twenty paces away. This one, a huge all-black beast, was being put up for sale by a young girl, almost a child, looking very pretty as she stood with her hazel switch. Then followed seven or eight halts, just as long, just as silent, till the line of animals for sale had been studied from end to end. After that the four women went back to the first cow and again became absorbed.

Only, this time it was a more serious matter. They stood in a straight line, piercing the cow through and through with their keen fixed eyes. Not a word was spoken by the woman offering the cow either; she turned away as if she hadn't seen them come back and stand there in a row.

Then Fanny leaned forward and whispered something to Lise. Old Rose and Françoise also exchanged a low comment. Then they all fell back into unstirring silence and the inspection continued.

'How much?' suddenly asked Lise.

140

'Four hundred francs,' replied the peasant woman.

The women pretended to retreat in dismay; and as they looked for Jean, they were surprised to find him close behind with Buteau, the two men chatting away like old friends. Buteau had come from La Chamade to buy a young pig and was now haggling. The pigs, in a portable pen attached to the back of the cart which had brought them along, were biting one another and squealing loud enough to deafen the bystanders.

'Will you take twenty francs?' Buteau asked the vendor.

'No, thirty.'

'All right, go to bed with your litter.'

With a cheerful, light-hearted air, he turned towards the women, smiling unconstrainedly at his mother, his sister and his two cousins as if he had left them only the day before. The women also were not a whit put out and seemed to have forgotten the two years of quarrelling and backbiting. Only his mother, who had been told about the first encounter in the Rue Grouaise, watched him out of her wrinkled eyes, trying to learn from his face why he had been to the lawyer. But there was nothing to be read there; and neither side raised the subject.

'What's this, cousin,' he went on, 'buying a cow? Jean told me. Well, listen, there's one that way, the best value in the market, a real beast.'

And he pointed to the black and white Cotentine.

'Forty pistoles, no thanks,' muttered Françoise.

'Forty pistoles for you, my little darling!' he said, poking her in the back by way of being jocular.

But she got angry and slapped him back in sharp resentment.

'Leave me alone, will you? I don't muck about with men.'

He grew still more playful and turned to Lise who had remained serious and looked rather pale.

'And you, would you like me to come in on this? I bet I'll get her for three hundred francs. Will you bet five francs?'

'All right, I'm ready. If you'd like to try.'

Rose and Fanny nodded agreement. They knew the fellow was a ferocious haggler, an inveterate and shameless liar, a swindler who sold things at three times their value and picked up everything for himself for a song. So the women let him go forward with Jean while they went to wait further back where they wouldn't appear to have any connection with him.

The crowd thickened round the cattle. The idlers left the swelter-

141

ing centre of the square and moved over to the avenues. There was a continual coming and going, with the blue blouses darkening in the shadows of the lime-trees and the swaying bunches of the leaves throwing green shadows over the tanned faces. However, there was no buying yet. Though the market had been open for an hour not a single sale had been registered. Customers were so far considering things and nerving themselves up. But above the heads of the crowd an uproar echoed along the warm wind. It came from two horses tied side by side, who reared and bit at each other with frantic neighings and with their hooves rattling on the pavement. There was a panic and some women ran for safety. But calm was restored by a volley of fierce whip-cracks like rifle-fire; and into the space cleared by the scare, a flock of pigeons flew down and hurried about pecking the oats out of the dung.

'Well, ma, what'll you sell her for, eh?' Buteau asked the peasant woman.

The woman, who had noted the arrangement being made, calmly repeated, 'Forty pistoles.'

At first he took the thing as a joke, began making fun and asked the man who still stood mutely in the background, 'Say, old fellow, is your old lady thrown in too at that price?'

But amid his banterings he closely examined the cow and found that she would definitely turn out a good milker. She had a lean head, slight horns and big eyes, a good-sized belly lined with large veins, somewhat slender limbs, and with thin high-set tail. He bent down, tested the length of the udders and the elasticity of the squarely-set and well-pierced dugs. Then, leaning with one hand on the animal, he got down to the haggling, mechanically rubbing the bones of the rump.

'Forty pistoles, eh? It's ridiculous. Will you take thirty?'

His hand made certain of the strength and good formation of the bones. It slipped down and ran over the thighs to the spot where the bare skin, of a fine saffron colour, promised abundant milk. 'Thirty pistoles, it's a deal.'

'No, forty,' replied the peasant woman.

He turned away, then came back. She decided to talk. 'She's a good cow, come on now, not a fault in her. She'll be two years old on Trinity Sunday and she'll calve in a fortnight's time. She's certainly what you're after.'

'Thirty pistoles,' he repeated.

Then, as he was going away, she glanced quickly at her husband

and shouted, 'Wait! I can't hang about all day—call it thirty-five and it's done.'

He stopped short and began to run down the cow. She wasn't well-built, she was weak in the loins, she was in short a creature that had had an ailing life and would have to be kept for a couple of years at a loss. Then he asserted that she was lame, which wasn't true. He lied for lying's sake, in obvious bad faith, hoping to irritate the woman into losing her head. But she shrugged her shoulders.

'Thirty pistoles.'

'No, thirty-five.'

She let him walk off. He rejoined the women and told them that his bait was taking; now he must go and haggle over another cow. So the group settled itself in front of the big black cow held by the pretty young girl. Here the price asked for was exactly three hundred francs. Buteau pretended to find that sum not at all excessive, and went into raptures over the animal, then brusquely turned back to the first one. 'It's fixed then, I must take my money elsewhere?'

'Of course, if you find you can. But you can't, you know. What you need is to screw up your courage, you do.' And leaning down to take a handful of udder, the woman went on, 'Just look how lovely that is!'

He would not agree and repeated, 'Thirty pistoles.'

'No, thirty-five.'

The deal seemed definitely off. Buteau took Jean's arm, to show clearly that he was dismissing the whole thing. The women joined them in great anxiety, for they thought the cow well worth three hundred and fifty frances. Françoise in particular, who liked the animal, spoke of accepting the price. But Buteau got angry: did they think he was going to be robbed like that? And he stuck it out for a good hour, despite the perturbation of the girls, who trembled every time another buyer went near the cow. He himself never went quite out of sight of it. He was certain that he was on the right tack, a man had to have steady nerves. Nobody was likely to rush in and throw their money away; the girls would soon see if anyone was fool enough to pay more than three hundred francs for the cow. And in fact the money was still not showing up though the market was near to closing-time.

On the road the horses were now being tried out. One, all white, was trotting round, urged on by guttural cries from a man holding the rope and running fast alongside; Patoir, the fat, red-faced veterinary, stood watching beside the buyer at the corner of the square, both hands in his pockets, giving his advice in a loud voice. The inns buzzed with a constant stream of drinkers going in, coming out, going back, carrying on the interminable market-day bargainings. The peak moment of bustle and noise had come, and no one could hear himself speak. A calf, separated from its mother, lowed incessantly; black griffon terriers and big yellow water-spaniels ran yelping out of the crush with trodden paws; sometimes, in sudden lulls, you could only hear the flight of crows, disturbed by the tumult, wheeling and croaking round the steeple. And, stronger even than the hot animal-smell, came the powerful stink of burning horn, a nuisance from the neighbouring farriery where the peasants were taking advantage of their visit to the market to get their animals shod.

'Well? Three hundred francs!' repeated the tireless Buteau, returning to the peasant woman.

'No, three hundred and fifty.'

Then, as another buyer stood there, also haggling, he seized the cow's jaws and forced them open to inspect the teeth. Then he let go, grimacing. At this moment the animal started to drop dung, the turds falling softly; he watched them fall and made a worse grimace than before. The buyer, a big sallow chap, was much impressed and went off.

'I'm not interested now,' said Buteau. 'Her blood's gone curdled.'

This time the woman made the mistake of losing her temper: the very thing that Buteau was trying for. When she began abusing him, he retorted with a flood of filth. People gathered round laughing. Behind the woman, her husband still stood unstirring. But at last he touched her elbow and she abruptly shouted, 'Will you take her for thirty-two pistoles?'

'No, thirty.'

He went off again and she called him back in a strangled voice, 'All right then, you damned bastard, take her! But, hell! If I had to go through it again, I'd give you a bloody punch in the face first!'

She was beside herself, trembling with fury. He laughed raucously and threw in some lewd jokes, offering to sleep with her to equal things out.

Lise came up at once. She drew the peasant woman to one side and paid out the three hundred francs behind a tree. Françoise was already holding the cow, which didn't want to budge—Jean

144

had to push her from behind. The party had now been hanging about for two hours, but Rose and Fanny were silently and tirelessly awaiting the outcome. Then at last, as they were preparing to go, Buteau couldn't be found. But they came on him again hobnobbing with the pig-dealer. He had just got his pig for twenty francs. When he paid, he first counted the money inside his pocket, brought out the exact sum and recounted it in his half-closed fist. Then there was a tremendous hullabaloo when he tried to shove the pig into a sack he had brought tucked in his shirt. The rotten cloth tore and the animal's hooves and snout came through. But Buteau slung it over his shoulder as it was and carried it off squirming with hideous grunts and squeals.

'I say, Lise, what about my five francs?' he called. 'I won.'

She didn't think for a moment that he'd take them and she gave them to him as a joke. But he took them without demur and whisked them into his pocket. Then the whole party moved slowly off towards the *Jolly Ploughman*.

The market was closing. Money glinted in the sunlight and rang on the wine-shop tables. At the last minute all the deals were hastily clinched. In the corner of the square there remained only a few unsold animals. Slowly the crowd had ebbed back towards the Rue Grande where the fruit and vegetable sellers were clearing up the pavement and going off home with empty baskets. Similarly in the Place de la Volaille nothing remained but straw and feathers. Already traps were being driven off; people were fixing harnesses in the inn-yards or untying horses from pavement rings. From every odd corner wheels were rumbling off and blue blouses puffed out in the wind as the carts jolted over the pavements.

Lengaigne, who had taken advantage of his journey to buy a scythe, trotted past on his little black horse. Macqueron and his daughter Berthe still lingered in the shops. La Frimat walked home on foot, as heavily loaded as on arrival; for she took her baskets home full of dung gathered on the road. Amid the gilt decorations of the chemist's shop in the Rue Grande, the exhausted Palmyre stood patiently waiting while they prepared a medicine for her brother, who had been ill for the past week: some foul drug which would consume one franc of the two she had worked so hard to get. But what quickened the sauntering steps of the two Mouche girls and their companions was the sight of Jésus-Christ, rolling drunk and taking up the whole breadth of the road. They supposed that he must have managed that day to borrow money on the security of his last bit of land. He was laughing away to himself and jingling the francs in his capacious pockets.

When they arrived at the *Jolly Ploughman* at last, Buteau said straightforwardly with a cheerful look, 'Going now? Listen, Lise, what about you and your sister staying and having something to eat here?'

She was taken by surprise; and as she turned towards Jean, Buteau added, 'Jean can stay too. That's how I'd like it.'

Rose and Fanny exchanged a look. The fellow had something up his sleeve for sure. His face, as usual, told them nothing. No matter! it wasn't for them to stand in the way of things.

'Good then,' said Fanny, 'you stay. I'll get home with mother. They're waiting for us.'

Françoise, who had stuck fast to the cow all the while, stated dryly, 'I'm going too.' And she persisted. She didn't like it at the inn, she wanted to get the cow home straightaway. They had to give in, she became so irritable. As soon as the cart was harnessed, the cow was attached behind and the three women climbed in.

At the last moment, Rose, who had expected an avowal from her son, got up courage to ask him, 'Any message for your father?'

'No, nothing,' replied Buteau.

She looked straight into his eyes and persisted. 'There's no change then?'

'If there is you'll know it all in good time.'

Fanny flicked the horse which set slowly off while the cow in the rear let herself be dragged along stretching out her neck. Lise was left on her own between Buteau and Jean.

At six o'clock the three of them sat down at table in a room of the inn that opened into the café. Buteau, with no indication whether he was treating them or not, went into the kitchen to order an omelette and a rabbit. In his absence Lise urged Jean to explain things, to get the position straightened out and save himself a journey.

But they finished their omelette and had begun the rabbit stew, and still the embarrassed young fellow had not managed to broach the subject. In any case the other fellow did not seem to be bothered about the matter. He ate heartily, laughed with his mouth wide open, and nudged the knees of both the others under the table, as friendly as could be. Then the talk turned to more serious themes and got on to Rognes and the new road; and although not a single mention was made of the indemnity of five hundred francs,

146

or the increased value of the strips, the thought of these developments was present under all they said. Buteau resumed his joking and clinked glasses; but the look in his grey eyes clearly showed that he was forming an idea of good business. He was thinking of the third strip with its enhanced value, of the former mistress who could become a bride now that her field, beside his own, had almost doubled its market price.

'Good Lord,' he cried, 'aren't we going to have any coffee?'

'Three coffees,' Jean ordered.

An hour went by in tippling. The brandy bottle was emptied, and still no declaration came from Buteau. He advanced, then drew back, spun things out at length as if he were still haggling for the cow. He had made up his mind; but he had to examine the question from all sides just the same. Suddenly he turned to Lise and said to her, 'Why didn't you bring the child?'

She began to laugh, understanding that now the matter was settled; and she gave him a playful tap, merely replying with a happy and indulgent smile, 'Ah, what a rascal he is!'

That was all. He laughed too. The marriage was settled. Jean, who had previously been very embarrassed, joined in their pleasure with a look of relief on his face. At last he even spoke right out. 'Y'know, it's just as well you've come back, I was going to step into your shoes.'

'Yes, they told me that. But I wasn't worried. You wouldn't do it without tipping me off, I suppose.'

'Of course not! Specially as it's better to be you because of the child. That's what we always said, isn't it, Lise?'

'Always, it's the honest truth.'

The faces of all three softened tenderly. They felt very warm towards each other, particularly Jean, who was without jealousy and who felt surprised at being an accomplice in the marriage. He called for beer when Buteau shouted, 'Good Lord, they must have something else to drink.' With their elbows on the table and Lise between them, they were now chatting about the recent rains that had stamped the corn down.

But in the café-room next door, Jésus-Christ, seated with an old peasant as drunk as himself, was making an appalling din. As a matter of fact none of the customers who sat in their shirt-sleeves, drinking, smoking and spitting under the reddish light of the lamps, could speak under a shout; but Jésus-Christ's voice, brassy and shattering, dominated everyone else's. He was playing *chouine* and

147

a dispute had broken out between him and his companion over the last deal of the cards. The old peasant, who calmly and obstinately stuck to his winnings, seemed to be in the wrong. The row went on and on. Jésus-Christ, furious, set up such tremendous roaring that the *patron* intervened. He then got up and went round from table to table with drunken persistence, showing his cards and asking the other drinkers if he wasn't right. He bored everyone stiff. And he began to roar again as he turned back to the old man who, immovable in his unrighteous gains, sat tranquilly accepting all the insults. 'Coward! Slacker! Come out here where I can get at you!'

Then suddenly he sat down opposite his partner and coolly remarked, 'I know a game. . . but y'must bet, eh? Want to?'

He brought out a handful of five-franc pieces, fifteen or twenty, and placed them in a single pile before him.

'This is the idea. You do what I've done.'

The old man, interested, produced his purse without a word and put out an equal pile.

'Now, I take one from your pile—watch!'

He grabbed a coin, placed it gravely on his tongue like a communion wafer and then, with a wiggle of his adam's apple, swallowed it.

'Your turn now, take one of mine. The one who eats the most keeps the lot. That's the game.'

With staring eyes, the old man agreed; with some difficulty he got the first coin down. But Jésus-Christ, while continually shouting that there was no need to hurry, wolfed the coins as if they were plums. At the fifth there was a murmur in the café and a circle formed round them, agog with admiration. Ah! the dirty dog, what a throat he must have, sticking money down his gizzard like that! The old man swallowed the fourth coin, then fell over backwards, black in the face, and choking with a rattling noise. For ᴀ moment everyone thought he was dead. Jésus-Christ stood up, with a scoffing grin, not in the least upset: he had ten coins down in his belly and so he'd make a clear gain of thirty francs.

Buteau was uneasy, afraid of being compromised if the old man did not recover, and he got up from the table. As he went on staring vacantly at the wall without mentioning the bill, Jean paid the account, even though Buteau had invited them. Buteau's happiness brimmed over. In the yard, after harnessing the horses, he took his friend by the shoulders.

'Y'know, I expect you to come. The wedding will be in three

weeks' time. I've been to the lawyer, I've signed the papers. Every-thing will be ready.'

Then he pushed Lise up into the trap. 'Come on, up! I'll take you back. I'm going through Rognes, it isn't much longer for me.'

Jean returned on his own in his cart. He found it all quite natural and just followed the others. Cloyes was asleep, relapsing into its deadly torpor, lighted by the yellow stars of the street lamps; and instead of the babel of the market there was no sound but the belated stumbling steps of a drunken peasant. Then the road stretched out into the darkness ahead. But at last he again caught sight of the other vehicle, the one that was taking the couple home. Things were better that way, just as they should be. He whistled heartily, refreshed by the night air, feeling free and very lighthearted.

VII

ONCE again harvest time had come round, with a burning blue sky that breezes kept refreshing; and the marriage was fixed for Midsummer Day, which fell that year on a Saturday.

The Fouans had strongly advised Buteau to give the first invita-tion to La Grande, the eldest of the family. She insisted on being treated with respect as if she were a rich and awe-inspiring queen. And so, one evening, Buteau and Lise, dressed in their best, went along to ask her to attend the wedding ceremony and the supper to be held at the bride's house.

They found La Grande knitting, alone in her kitchen. Without a pause in the play of her needles she stared fixedly and left the pair to explain themselves and to repeat the same phrases three times over. Finally in her sharp voice she commented, 'The wed-ding, eh? Indeed I won't come. What would I do at a wedding? It's all right for those with nothing better to do.'

They had seen her parchment-coloured face flush slightly at the thought of the jollification which wouldn't cost her a penny; and they were sure she'd accept. But custom demanded that she should take a lot of urging.

'Aunt, but you must, we can't do without you.'

'No, I won't, it's nothing to do with me. D'you think I've got time or clothes for it? Money—always something to spend money on. Folk get along without going to a wedding.'

They had to repeat the invitation ten times and she finished by saying with a growl, 'Very well, as I can't get out of it, I'll come. But I wouldn't put myself out for anybody but you.'

Then as they still lingered, she went through a fierce struggle; for tradition demanded the offering of a glass of wine on such occasions. She brought herself to the point and went down to the cellar, though she had a bottle broached in the kitchen. She kept some dregs of bad wine down below for such occasions, stuff she could not drink because it was so sour—she had a name for it, 'Cousin-chaser'. She filled two glasses and watched her nephew and niece with unblinking eyes; they were obliged to swallow the stuff without pulling faces so as not to offend her. Their throats were raw as they left her.

That same evening the pair went along to Roseblanche, the Charles's house. But there they found themselves plunged into a tragic scene.

M. Charles was in the garden, very perturbed. He had doubtless had a very great shock just as he started to trim a climbing rose; for he was still holding his clippers in his hand and the ladder still stood against the wall. He mastered himself, however, and invited them into the drawing-room where Elodie was doing her embroidery with a maidenly air.

'Ah! you are to be married next week. Very good, my dear children. But we can't be with you. Madame Charles is at Chartres and will be there for a fortnight.'

He lifted his heavy eyebrows and cast a glance at the young girl.

'Yes, yes, when the great fairs are on, things are very busy and Madame Charles goes over to give a helping hand to her daughter. You know, business is business, and some days there is such a crowd of customers in the little shop. Even though Estelle is in full charge now, her mother can help her a lot, especially as our son-in-law Vaucogne hardly does a hand's turn. And then Madame Charles is always delighted to see the house again. It's natural enough. We've left thirty years of our life there and that means something!'

He waxed sentimental; his eyes grew wet and misty as he gazed vacantly into the past. And indeed, in her smug and refined retreat, so pleasantly endowed with flowers and birds and sunlight, his wife often felt homesick for the little house in the Rue aux Juifs. She had only to close her eyes to find herself back in old Chartres, where it sprawled on the hill slope, from the Cathedral Square down to the banks of the Eure. She imagined herself slipping through the Rue de la Pie and the Rue Porte-Cendreuse; then in the Rue des Ecuyers she followed the shortest route and passed down the Tertre du Pied-Plat; and on the last step, at the corner of the Rue aux Juifs and the Rue de la Panche-aux-Carpes, she caught sight of the white façade of number nineteen with its perpetually-drawn green blinds. The two streets were of a slum-type. For thirty years she had looked out at their dirty hovels and wretched people, at the gutter in the middle running with foul water. But then, how many weeks and even months she had lived there in the shadowy rooms without once going outside her own door! She was still proud of the couches and mirrors in the drawing-room, the bed-linen and the mahogany furniture of the bedrooms, all so luxurious, chaste yet comfortable—their own creation, their own work, the source of their property. A melancholy faintness came upon her when she recalled certain intimate corners, the persistent perfume of the washing-water, that peculiar smell of the entire house, which clung to her skin like a regret. She looked forward to the busy seasons and went off happy and enlivened after getting two warm kisses from her granddaughter, which she promised to deliver to the child's mother that very evening in the sweet-shop.

'Oh! what a nuisance, it's very annoying,' Buteau repeated over and over again, much annoyed at the idea of not having the Charleses at the wedding. 'Couldn't our cousin write to ask aunt to come back?'

Elodie, who was now nearly fifteen, lifted her puffy greenish face. Her hair was thin and her anæmic blood seemed to get poorer than ever in the fresh air of the country.

'O no,' she whispered, 'grandmother told me definitely that she'd not be able to get away from the sweets for at least two weeks. She said she'll bring me back a bagful if I'm good.'

She referred to a pious fraud. From every journey she was brought back a bag of sweets which she believed her parents had made in their shop.

'Well then,' proposed Lise at last, 'come without her, uncle, come with the child.'

But M. Charles was no longer listening; his agitation had returned. He went to the window and appeared to be watching out for someone, obviously trying to suppress a burst of fury. Then, unable to contain himself any longer, he dismissed the child shortly: 'Go out and play for a while, my dear.'

When she had gone, accustomed to being sent out when grown-ups discussed something, he planted himself in the middle of the room and folded his arms, looking like a retired magistrate with his respectable flabby sallow face which was trembling with indignation.

'Would you believe it? Have you ever seen anything so abominable? I was pruning the roses, on the top rung of the ladder, leaning over the wall without thinking, and what did I see? Honorine, yes, my maid Honorine with a man, on top of one another with their legs in the air, busy with their dirty tricks. Ah! the swine, the swine, at the foot of my garden-wall!'

He choked and began stamping up and down with noble gestures of denunciation. 'I'm just waiting to throw her out, the slut, the wretched creature! We can't keep one of them. They all get pregnant. At the end of six months, regularly, they're impossible in a decent house with their big bellies. And this one I've caught in the very act, wallowing in it. Definitely it's the end of the world, there's no limit to debauchery nowadays.'

Buteau and Lise, astounded, joined in his indignation out of respect for him. 'Indeed, it's not right, no, not at all right.'

But again he stopped before them. 'Just suppose Elodie had climbed that ladder and seen them! She's so innocent, she knows nothing, we watch over her very thoughts. Heavens, it makes me shudder! What a mercy Madame Charles isn't here!'

Just at that moment, as he glanced out of the window, he saw the child drawn by an impulse of curiosity to set her foot on the first ladder-rung. He rushed forward and cried out in a voice that couldn't have been more hoarse with anguish if he had seen her at the edge of an abyss.

'Elodie! Elodie! come down, come away from there, for the love of God!'

His legs gave way and he fell into a chair, continuing his laments on servant-girls' lack of morals. Hadn't he once found one of them beside the hen-house showing the little girl what the backside of a chicken was like! It was trouble enough to shield her from all the gross ways of the peasants and the shameless behaviour of animals: and he felt like giving up when he found immorality constantly breaking out in his own household.

'Here she is, coming in now,' he said suddenly. 'Now you'll see.'

He rang and remained seated to receive Honorine; the effort he had to make to recover a dignified calm made him look severe.

'Miss, pack up your box and leave at once. I'll pay you a week's wages in place of notice.'

The maid, a pitiful, skinny little thing, with a frightened shame-faced expression, tried to explain and stammered out some excuses.

'It's no good, the best I can do for you is to refrain from reporting you to the authorities for indecent behaviour.'

Then she revolted. 'Oh, so it's because we neglected to come to you and pay for it!'

He rose, drew himself to his full height and dismissed her with a majestic gesture, pointing to the door. Then, when she had departed, he gave coarse vent to his relief. 'The idea of a harlot like that bringing shame on my house!'

'O yes, that's what she is, all over,' Buteau and Lise servilely agreed. And Buteau went on, 'You'll come then, uncle, you and the little girl?'

M. Charles was still shaken. In a sudden anxiety he went to look at himself in the mirror, but turned back satisfied.

'Where? Ah, yes, to your marriage. I thoroughly approve, my dear young people, of your getting married. You can count on me, I'll be there; but I don't promise to bring the child. You know, at a wedding, people loosen up. . . That trollop—you saw how I threw her out! I can't stand being annoyed by women! Well, good-bye, and rely on me.'

The Delhommes, to whom Buteau and Lise next went, accepted the invitation after the traditional refusals and pleas. Jésus-Christ was the only member of the family not yet invited. But, honestly, he was becoming insufferable, on bad terms with everybody, playing the most disgusting tricks and disgracing the family. They decided to leave him out, though they shuddered to imagine what abomination he might think up in revenge.

Rognes was all agog, impatiently looking forward to the considerable event of this long-deferred marriage. Hourdequin, the mayor, agreed at some inconvenience to officiate at the Town Hall, but had to excuse himself from attending the evening banquet as he was obliged to spend the night in Chartres for a lawsuit. Still, he promised that Madame Jacqueline would come as they were kind enough to include her in the invitation. They had thought for a moment of inviting the Abbé Godard, so as to have some respectable people present. Only, as soon as it was mentioned, the priest lost his temper at the ceremony being fixed for Midsummer Day. That day he had a High Mass, an endowed service at Bazoches-le-Doyen: how did they expect him to be at Rognes in the morning? The women, Lise, Rose and Fanny, retorted by turning obstinate;

they made no further mention of an invitation and he ended by giving way. But he came at noon in such a towering fury and rattled through the Mass so irritably that they were deeply hurt.

After much discussion they had resolved on a quiet family wedding because of the bride's position with a little son now almost three years old. Still, they went to order a fruit-pie and dessert from a pastrycook at Cloyes, deciding to spend recklessly and show that they could throw money around when it was called for. There'd be, just as at the wedding of the eldest girl of the Coquarts (farmers at Saint-Juste), a tiered wedding-cake, two custards, four plates of sweets, and some small cakes. At the house there'd be soup, pork sausages, four fried chickens, four rabbits in a stew, some roast beef and veal. All this for some fifteen people—they weren't yet sure of the exact number. If there was any food left over, it could be eaten next day.

The sky, slightly overcast in the morning, had cleared and the day drew to a warm and limpid close. The table was set in the middle of the huge kitchen facing the fireplace and the range where the meats were roasting and the sauces bubbling. The fires gave out such heat that the two windows and the door were left wide open and the good penetrating smell of the new-mown hay was blown in.

Fanny and Rose had been helping the two Mouche girls since the day before. At three in the afternoon there had been great excitement when the pastrycook's cart was seen and all the village women rushed to their doors. The pie was laid on the table at once to see how it looked; and at the same moment La Grande arrived, long before the proper time. She sat down, holding her stick between her knees and never once took her sharp eyes off the food. Surely it was wrong to spend so much money! She hadn't had a bite since morning so as to be ready to stuff herself in the evening.

The men—Buteau, Jean the best-man, Old Fouan, Delhomme and his son Nénesse—were all dressed in black trousers and frock-coats, with high silk hats permanently stuck on their heads; they were playing pitch-and-toss in the yard. M. Charles arrived alone, having taken Elodie back to her school in Châteaudun the night before; and, without joining in, he watched the game with interest, making judicious comments.

But at six o'clock, when everything was ready, Jacqueline had still not arrived. The women let down their skirts, which they had pinned up to keep unsoiled while cooking. Lise was in blue, Françoise in pink, out-of-date dresses of harsh-coloured silks which

Lambourdieu had sold them at over twice their value, passing them off as the last word in Paris fashion. Rose Fouan had dug out the dress of purple poplin which she had paraded at every wedding in the district for the past forty years; and Fanny, in green, was wearing all her jewels, her chain watch, a brooch, rings, and earrings. Every minute one of the women went into the road and ran up to the corner of the church to see if the lady of the farm was coming. The meats were burnt; the soup, which had unfortunately been served, was getting cold. Then at last a cry was raised: 'There she is! There she is!'

The carriage came into view and then Jacqueline jumped lightly down. She looked delightful, having had the good taste to set off her charms in a simple white cretonne dress with red pin-spots; and she wore no jewels on her bare skin, except some brilliants in her ears, a present from Hourdequin which had set all the neighbouring farms buzzing. But everyone was surprised that, after the labourer who had brought her had stabled the carriage, she didn't send him home. The fellow was Tron, a fair-skinned, red-haired giant with a child-like expression. He came from Le Perche and had been at La Borderie for about a fortnight as yard-boy.

'Tron is staying, you know,' she said lightly. 'He'll take me home later.'

The folk of La Beauce don't like those of Le Perche, accusing them of being dishonest and sly. Now everyone exchanged glances: so here was La Cognette's new lover, this great lout. But Buteau, who had been very agreeable and playful all day, replied, 'Of course he'll stay. If he's with you, that's good enough.'

Lise asked them all to begin and they sat down to table with a lot of pushing and shouting. They were three chairs short, so someone ran to find two stools with straw-seats and balanced a plank across them. The spoons were already clattering on the bottom of the soup-plates. The soup was cold and covered with specks of congealing fat. No one cared about that and Old Fouan remarked that it would be warmed up again in their bellies, which sent everyone into fits of laughter. From then on, the scene was one of sheer wolfing and guzzling: the chickens, the rabbits, the roasts came up and disappeared in quick succession amid a hideous grinding of jaws. Frugal in their own homes, they nearly burst with overeating in other people's houses. La Grande refused to speak at all, so as to be able to get more in; she went steadily on remorselessly chewing and it was terrifying to see how much her flat dried-up eighty-

155

year-old body could engulf without the slightest sign of enlargement. For the look of the thing, Françoise and Fanny had been set the serving, so that the bride would not have to move from table; but Lise couldn't keep still and left her chair time and time again, rolling up her sleeves, intently pouring out sauces or taking a roast off the spit. Anyway, everybody was soon helping to serve; there was always someone on his or her feet, cutting bread or grabbing at a fresh dish. Buteau, in charge of the wine, couldn't cope with the demand. He had decided to put out a cask on tap to save himself the time and trouble of corking and uncorking bottles; but he had no time to eat and Jean had to take turns with him in keeping the jugs filled. Delhomme, solidly seated in his chair, declared in his sagacious way that plenty of liquor was essential to keep the gullet clear. When the fruit-pie was brought in, the size of a cartwheel, there was a stir. The forcemeat balls made a great impression and M. Charles carried politeness to an extreme by swearing that he hadn't seen such a pie even in Chartres. Suddenly, Old Fouan, on top of his form, made another joke.

'I say, if you stuck that on your bum, it would cure the cracks and chappings.'

Everyone split their sides, especially Jacqueline who laughed till she cried. She spluttered and tried to go one better, but couldn't be heard through her laughter.

The bridal couple sat facing one another, Buteau between his mother and La Grande, Lise between Old Fouan and M. Charles; and the other guests were seated according to their preferences— Jacqueline beside Tron who watched her all the while with his mild stupid eyes, Jean near Françoise, only separated by little Jules whom both of them had promised to look after. But when the fruit-pie arrived, a fierce bout of indigestion overcame the small boy and the bride had to take him away to bed. So Jean and Françoise finished the meal side by side. Françoise was very restless; her face was red from the heat of the fire and she trembled with exhaustion despite all her excitement. Jean, eager to help her, wanted to do the running about; but she would not let him and was particularly taken up with Buteau, who, always keen on teasing people when in a good temper, had been tormenting her since the supper began. He kept pinching her as she passed, and she furiously hit back at him; then again, under some pretext or another, as if fascinated, she would get up again for another pinch and slap. She complained that her hips were bruised blue.

'Stop where you are then!' Jean repeated.

'O no,' she cried, 'he mustn't think he's my man too because he's Lise's.'

As night drew on, six candles were lit. The party had been eating for three hours, and finally, at ten o'clock, attacked the dessert. From this moment they began drinking coffee, not one or two cups, but bowl-fulls, all the time. The jokes grew wilder. Coffee gave stamina, yes, and was the very thing for men inclined to too much sleep. So, every time one of the married guests gulped a mouthful, there were shouts of laughter.

'You've good reason to drink it!' said Fanny to Delhomme, shaken out of her usual reserve and laughing uproariously.

He flushed, and to excuse himself, sedately explained that he was working too hard. Nénesse laughed from ear to ear amid explosive yells and thigh-slappings provoked by this conjugal revelation. The lad had anyway eaten so much that he looked ready to burst. He disappeared and wasn't found again till everyone was leaving, asleep with the two cows.

La Grande held out the longest. At midnight she fell upon the tartlets in mute anguish at being unable to finish them. The bowls had been cleared of cream, the crumbs of cake swept up. And in the abandon of increasing tipsiness bodices were unhooked and trouser buttons undone; the company kept moving about, chatting in little groups around the table which was greasy with sauce-spots and stained with wine. Songs were started but never got under way; only old Rose, with a maudlin expression, went on bumbling a smutty song she remembered from her youth of long ago, marking the rhythm with her shaky head. There were not enough for dancing, and anyway the men preferred to stick to the brandy-bottles and smoke their pipes, tapping them out on the tablecloth. In a corner Fanny and Delhomme in front of Jean and Tron reckoned to a sou what the financial position and expectations of the married couple would be. They went on doggedly till every square inch of land was valued; the two of them knew what every Rognes family possessed, even what had been paid for household linen. At the other end of the room Jacqueline had captured M. Charles and was staring at him with a winning smile, her pretty perverse eyes glistening with curiosity. She was asking him questions.

'Well, is Chartres an amusing place? Can you have a good time there?'

He responded with a long eulogy of the town-sights: the line of boulevards planted with ancient trees which made a shady belt all round Chartres. In the lower section, especially along the banks of the River Eure, the boulevards were very cool in summer. Then there was the cathedral. He discoursed about it at length, acting the well-educated man with a deep respect for religion. Yes, one of the most beautiful monuments to be seen anywhere, but too large for this age of failing belief—almost empty, standing at the centre of its deserted square, which only the footsteps of pious women crossed on weekdays. He had himself felt the desolation of the huge place when one Sunday he had gone in casually during vespers. You shivered inside with cold, you couldn't see anything because of the stained-glass and you had to wait till your eyes were accustomed to the darkness before you made out two knots of schoolgirls lost in space like a handful of ants, singing in thin piping voices under the dome. Ah, indeed it was heartbreaking to see people abandoning the church for the cabaret!

Jacqueline was astonished at this tirade, but continued to stare at him with her set smile. Then she murmured, 'But, tell me, the Chartres women. . .'

He understood, grew very grave, but still unbosomed himself under the influence of the general intoxication. Jacqueline, rosy, shaken by continual gigglings, pressed up against him as if to enter into that mystery of hurrying crowding men night after night. But she didn't hear what she expected. He described what hard work the profession was; for he always turned melancholy and paternal in his cups. But he brightened up when she told him that she had once gone for fun to see the brothel in Châteaudun at the corner of the Rue Davignon and the Rue Loiseau, a broken-down little house with drawn blinds almost falling to pieces. At the back there was an untidy garden with a big silvered ball of glass reflecting the house; in front of the upper dormer-window, turned into a dove-cot, the birds flew around cooing in the sunlight. On that day children had been playing on the doorstep and you could hear the orders coming over the wall of the cavalry-barracks next door. He interrupted her angrily. Yes, yes, he knew the place, two disgusting broken-down women and not even any mirrors downstairs. Hovels like that were what gave a bad name to the trade.

'But what can you expect in a mere sub-prefecture?' he said at last, calming down and assuming the tolerant philosophical outlook of a superior man.

It was now one o'clock in the morning and people began talking of bed. As the newly-weds had already had a baby, there wasn't much point, was there? in making a fuss about putting them under a single sheet. The same went for the customary jokes—what point in unbolting the bedstead, putting into the bed scratchy hairs or toys that squeaked when pressed, and such things? It would have been like offering mustard after the meat was eaten.

The best thing would be to drink one more glass and then say good night.

At that moment Lise and Fanny screamed. Through the open window some excrement had been thrown, a lump of filth picked up at the foot of the hedge; and the two women's frocks were ruined, spattered from top to bottom. Who was the dirty swine who'd done it? The company ran out and peered about the square, the road, and behind the wall. Nobody. But they all agreed that Jésus-Christ had had his revenge for not being invited.

The Fouans and the Delhommes went off and so did M. Charles. La Grande toured the table once more to see if she could find anything left; then she took herself off after telling Jean that the Buteau pair would die without a stick to their name. While the others stumbled about drunkenly on the cobbles, she walked off with firm heavy steps. Gradually the tapping of her stick died away.

When Tron had harnessed the trap for Mme Jacqueline, she turned round with her foot on the step, 'Are you coming back with us, Jean? You're not, are you?'

The lad, who was getting ready to mount, changed his mind, glad to leave her to the other chap. He watched her huddling up against the big body of her new lover and couldn't help grinning after the carriage had gone. He would walk back, he decided. But first he went to sit down for a moment on the stone bench in the yard beside Françoise, who, overcome with heat and exhaustion, had sat herself down there waiting for everyone to go. The Buteaus were already in their room and she had promised to lock up before going to bed herself.

'Ah, how nice it is here,' she sighed, after five long minutes of silence.

Silence fell again, a deep pervasive hush. The deliciously fresh night was sprinkled with stars and the scent of hay was breathed out and rose up so strongly from the Aigre fields that it sweetened the air like the smell of wildflowers.

'Yes, it is good,' Jean repeated at last. 'It makes you feel peaceful.

She made no reply and he saw that she was asleep. She slid down

159

lower and leaned against his shoulder. He stayed there for another hour, with a whirl of confused thoughts in his head. Brutish thoughts stirred him, then faded. She was too young. He felt that if he waited, she alone would get older, she'd come nearer to his age.

'I say, Françoise, bedtime. We'll take cold.'

She woke up with a start.

'Gracious! You're right, we'd be better in bed. See you soon, Jean.'

'See you soon, Françoise.'

THIRD PART

I

AND SO at long last Buteau had hold of his share, the ardently coveted bit of earth which he had refused for over two and a half years in a rage of mingled desire, bitterness and obstinacy. He himself didn't know now why he had been so bullheaded. His heart had been burning to sign the deed; yet he had feared a trick and could not console himself for failing to gain the whole inheritance, the whole nineteen acres, now mutilated and scattered. But since he had accepted his share, he felt his passionate longing assuaged in the brutal joy of possession—a joy that was doubled by the thought that his sister and brother had been swindled, his land being so much more valuable now that the new road ran alongside. He never met them now without bursting into sly laughter, winking as if to say, 'All the same I've done them in the eye!'

And that wasn't all. He had another triumph in his marriage, long-deferred though it was, for Lise brought him five acres which ran beside his own. For the thought of the division which must ultimately be made by the two sisters never occurred to him; or at least he set it so far into the future that he hoped before then to strike on some way of evading the issue. He owned, including Françoise's share, eight acres of ploughland, eight of pasture, and about five of vineyard; and he was determined to keep them all, he'd rather cut off his hand than lose an inch. Above all, he meant never to let go of the land by the road at Les Cornailles, which now made up a field of six acres. Neither his sister nor his brother had anything like it, and he talked about it, gloating, his cheeks puffed out with pride.

A year went by, and that first year of possession was sheer bliss for Buteau. In all his time as a hired labourer he never ploughed so deep, the earth he now turned was his earth, he wanted to penetrate right in, fertilise it in the very bowels. Each evening he came home exhausted, with the ploughshare gleaming silver. In March he harrowed his wheat, in April his oats, unstinting in his care and giving every ounce of his strength. When the strips had no need of more work, he still went to look at them like a lover. He walked round, bent down and with his habitual gesture took up a fistful of earth, a rich clod which he loved to crumble and let run through his fingers, supremely happy when he felt it neither too dry nor too humid and smelt in it the good smell of growing bread.

La Beauce spread out her greenery before him from November to July, from the moment when the green tips first sprouted to the moment when the tall stalks turned golden. He wanted the great plain under his eyes even when he was still in the house. He had taken down the bars of the kitchen window, the one at the back which looked out over La Beauce; and he would stand there staring over the ten leagues of plain, a huge expanse, that stretched out quite bare under the dome of the sky. Not a single tree, nothing except the telegraph poles on the Châteaudun-Orléans road running in one long straight line till they faded in the distance. First, in the big squares of brown soil, low on the earth there appeared a greenish shade, barely visible. Then, the tender green deepened into carpets of green velvet almost uniform in hue. Then the stalks grew and thickened, and each plant took on its own tinge, so that the watcher could tell at a distance the yellow-green of the wheat, the blue-green of the oats, the grey-green of the barley, the strips stretching indefinitely in every direction with red patches of clover gleaming between. Now was the time when La Beauce was lovely in her youth, clad in the spring, smooth and fresh to the eye in her universal growth. The stalks grew stronger and she became the sea, a sea of corn, rolling, deep, limitless. On mornings of fine weather a fleeting rose mist swathed her. As the sun rose in the limpid air, a breeze blew in big steady puffs, furrowing the fields with a swell that started from the horizon, lengthened and then ebbed away at the outer edge. The hues fluttered and paled, and moiré-lights of old gold rippled through the wheat, the oats were brushed with bluish tints and the trembling rye turned up violet reflections. Endlessly one wave succeeded another, the ceaseless swell went on under the wind from the great spaces. When evening came, the distant buildings, brightly lit up, looked like white sails and church steeples rose up like masts out of dips in the earth. The air turned cold, the deep shadows increased the cool sensation of a murmurous open sea. A distant wood faded from sight like the lost outline of a continent.

In bad weather also Buteau watched La Beauce spread flat below him, as the fisherman stares out over the maddened sea from his cliff-top, while the storm-winds are taking the bread out of his mouth. He saw a violent tempest, a black cloud turning the plain to a livid leaden hue, red lightnings sparkling on the grass-tips amid crashes of thunder. He saw a waterspout come up from a distance of six leagues, first a thin tawny cloud twisted like rope, then a howling mass rushing on with monstrous speed and leaving in its wake a vast wreckage of crops, a furrow two miles wide, with everything in it trampled down, smashed, slashed to pieces. His own fields had not suffered and he commiserated his neighbours' disaster with secret delight. As the wheat grew, his pleasure increased. Already the grey clump of one village had disappeared behind the mounting tips of the green crops. Now there were only the buildings of La Borderie; then they were submerged in their turn. A mill with outspread wings remained all alone like a castaway. Everywhere was corn, an invading sea of corn, overflowing, covering the earth with its green immensity.

'Ah, by God!' he said every evening as he sat down to table, 'if the summer isn't too dry, we'll have bread enough and to spare.'

In the Buteau house everything had now fallen into place. The married couple had taken the big room downstairs and Françoise made do with the little room above, where old Mouche used to sleep. This room had been scoured out and furnished with a folding bed, an old chest of drawers, a table and two chairs. Françoise tended the cows and lived her life just as before. And yet, inside the peace, a source of discord lay quiescent—the question of land division between the two sisters, which had been left on one side up to the present. After the marriage of the older girl, Old Fouan, who was guardian to Françoise, had wanted the division to be made, to avoid later trouble. But Buteau had protested. What was the good? Françoise was too young, she didn't need her land. Was there any change? Didn't she still live with her sister as before? She got her food and her clothes, she couldn't grumble, could she? Of course she couldn't. Faced with these arguments, the old man shook his head. You never knew what might happen; the best thing was to get everything properly fixed. And the girl herself pressed, she wanted to have her share settled—though she was quite ready then to leave it in her brother-in-law's care. But Buteau won the day by his jolly bluntness, his playful obstinacy. The matter was dropped. He talked expansively everywhere on the joy of living as they did friends, in a happy family.

'What's needed is goodwill—that's everything in my view.'

Indeed for the first ten months there was no quarrelling between the sisters, no conflict in the household. But then slowly things

163

began to go wrong. It all began with bouts of bad temper. There were fits of sulking, exploding in hard words; and underneath, the ferment of *mine* and *thine* went on with its ravages, steadily corroding all affection.

It was obvious that Lise and Françoise no longer loved one another as deeply as before. No one ever met them nowadays with their arms round one another, sharing a shawl as they sauntered about in the dusk. They had drawn apart, and a coldness stiffened their relations. Since there'd been a man in the house, Françoise felt that her sister was being taken away from her. She who had previously shared everything with Lise, did not share this man; and so he had become the alien, the barrier that kept her out of the heart where she had dwelt. She would go out of the room without kissing her sister when Buteau kissed her, offended, as if someone had drunk out of her cup. On questions of ownership she still thought as she had done when a child, with a passionate intensity: 'That's mine and that's yours.' And now that her sister belonged to someone else, she let her go, but she wanted her own share in things, half the land and half the house.

Behind her anger there was something else, something she herself could not have explained. Up to that time, in the chill of their father's widowhood, there had been no love-making in the house and Françoise had felt no disturbing influences. And now here was a man living there, starkly male, a fellow with the habit of tumbling girls in ditches, whose larkings with Lise shook the partitions and whose panting breath sounded through cracks in the panelling. She knew all there was to know, had learnt it all from animals, and she felt disgusted and irritated. In the daytime she preferred to go out, leaving the couple to play their filthy games on their own. At night, if they began giggling as they rose from the evening meal, she cried out for them to wait at least until she had done the washing-up. And then she rushed to her room slamming the doors and muttering abuse through clenched teeth. 'Beasts, beasts. . .' In spite of all her efforts she always thought she could hear what was going on below. With her head pressed deep in her pillow and the coverlet drawn up to her eyes, she burned feverishly; her hearing and sight were obsessed by hallucinations, and she was tortured by the rebellious ferment of adolescence.

The worst of all was that Buteau, seeing what was on her mind, teased her about it as a joke. . . Well? what was the fuss? What would she say when her turn came? Lise too laughed at her, seeing

164

nothing wrong in it. And then Buteau explained his ideas on the subject. The good God had provided this pleasure for everybody and it didn't cost a penny; so it was right to treat oneself to it as much as one could, soak oneself in it—but no children, not a single brat more! You always got too many before you were married, out of carelessness. That's how Jules came, though he was a confounded surprise all the same, which had to be put up with. But when a man was married, he turned serious, he'd rather have himself cut like a tomcat than start another one. No, thanks! bring another mouth into the house when food already melted away so fast! So he had to keep his senses about him and watch himself with his wife; she was so ready, the bitch, she might take everything in at one wallop, he said, adding with a laugh that he ploughed hard without sowing seed. Wheat, yes, wheat, as much as the swollen belly of the earth could give; but kids, no, that was finished for good!

With all these endless details, all this mating which she seemed to touch and feel, Françoise's restlessness grew. People said her character was changing and indeed she had inexplicable fast-changing moods, gay and then sad, then sulky and morose. Every morning she gave Buteau a black look as he crossed the kitchen half-stripped and shameless. Quarrels broke out between the sisters over trifles, over a smashed cup. Wasn't the cup Françoise's too, or at least half of it? Couldn't she break half of everything if she liked? These questions of ownership gave rise to sharper arguments and left bitter feelings for several days afterwards.

Buteau himself at this time gave way to fearful tempers. The earth was suffering from extreme drought; not a drop of rain had fallen for six weeks. He would come into the house with fists clenched, sickened by watching the spoiled crops, the stunted rye, the meagre oats, the wheat shrivelled up before the ears had formed. He became physically ill, like the corn itself; his stomach contracted, his limbs were knotted with cramp and he grew shrunken and parched up with worry and rage. So one morning for the first time he clashed with Françoise himself. It was hot, and after washing himself at the well he left his shirt out loose and his trousers un-buttoned. As he sat down to eat, Françoise, who was serving, came up for a moment behind him. Then at last she burst out with darkly-flushed face.

'Put your shirt in, it's disgusting.'

He was already in a bad temper and flared up. 'In God's name, can't you stop picking me to pieces? Don't look if it upsets you. Something here you'd like to feel, eh, you little slut—you're always on about it.'

She flushed even redder and stammered, and Lise made the mistake of adding, 'He's right, you're getting us fed up. Go away if you won't let us do as we like in our own home.'

'All right! I'll go away!' cried Françoise in a fury and she went out slamming the door.

But the next day Buteau was happy and jolly again, quite ready to make it up. In the night the sky had become overcast and for twelve hours a light, warm, penetrating rain had fallen, one of those summer rains which give new life to the country; he had opened the window over the plain and had stood there from dawn watching the pouring water, beaming, his hands in his pockets, crying over and over again 'Now we're *bourgeois*—the good God is on our side. Ah, heavens alive, this is the life! Not a stroke to do, it's better than working your fingers to the bone with nothing to show for it.'

Slow, gentle, interminable, the rain pattered down; and he heard La Beauce drinking, the thirsting riverless and springless plain changing under his eyes. A vast murmur seethed all around, a universal gurgle, full of well-being. Everything absorbed the rain, soaked it in, everything bloomed again under the downpour. The wheat regained its young health, firm and upright, carrying high the ears which would swell enormously, bursting with meal. And Buteau himself, like the earth, like the corn, drank in through every pore, relaxed, refreshed, healed—returning to stand in front of the window and shout, 'Go on, go on then. It's franc pieces falling!'

Suddenly he heard the door open, turned round and was surprised to see Old Fouan. 'Eh, it's father. Been out hunting frogs?'

The old man, after a struggle with a huge blue umbrella, came in, leaving his sabots on the doorstep. 'Fine bit of watering,' he said simply. 'It was needed.'

Over the past year, since the division of land had been finally settled, signed and registered, he had had only one occupation—to go out and look at his old fields. He was always to be seen prowling round, watching them, grave or gay according to the state of the crops, grumbling about his children because things were done differently, because it was all their fault if things weren't going well. The rain made him years younger.

'So,' went on Buteau, 'you've dropped in to see us in passing?'

Françoise, who had been silent up to then, came forward and said dryly, 'No, I asked uncle to come.'

Lise, who was standing at the table podding peas stopped her work and waited with her arms hanging loosely, her face suddenly hard. Buteau, whose fists had closed tight, put on a smiling face again, determined not to lose his temper.

'Yes,' the old man said slowly, 'the girl told me yesterday. You see now I was right in wanting to put things in order straight away. Let everyone have his or her share: you can't fall out then. On the contrary, it prevents quarrels. And now it's high time to settle matters. It's her right, isn't it? She ought to know what's coming to her. Otherwise I wouldn't be doing my duty. And so we'll settle a day and go all together to Monsieur Baillehache.'

But Lise couldn't restrain herself. 'Why didn't she put the police on us? You'd think we were robbing her, heavens above! Do I talk about her outside, do I? Do I tell people what a stinking thing she is, we can't touch her without getting bitten!'

Françoise was going to reply in the same strain when Buteau, who had playfully caught her from behind, cried out, 'What's all this nonsense? We tread on one another's toes, but we're good friends, aren't we? A pretty state of affairs if two sisters can't agree.'

The girl shook herself free with a violent wrench and the quarrel was going to break out again when Buteau gave a joyful shout. He saw the door again opening.

'Jean! Soaked to the skin! A proper drowned rat!'

Jean had run over from the farm as he often did. He had just thrown a sack over his shoulders for protection, and he was wet right through, dripping and steaming, but good-naturedly laughing at his state. While he shook himself, Buteau returned to the window and brightened up more and more as he watched the persistent rain.

'Down it comes, down it comes, it's a blessing. Honest, it's a real lark, so much rain.'

Then, turning back, 'You've just come in time, you have. These two were at one another. Françoise wants us to divide up so she can go off.'

'What? That kid!' cried Jean in astonishment.

His desire had become a fierce hidden passion, and he knew no other happiness but meeting her in this house where he was accepted as a friend. He would have already asked for her hand twenty times if he hadn't felt himself much too old for her. There hadn't been

167

any use in waiting; they were still separated by fifteen years. Nobody seemed to think it possible he could want her as his wife, not Françoise herself or her sister or even her brother-in-law. That was why Buteau welcomed him so warmly, with no fear of anything developing.

'Kid! ah, that's just the right word,' he said with a fatherly shrug of his shoulders.

But Françoise, standing tensely, her eyes on the ground, persisted, 'I want my share.'

'It'd be best,' murmured Old Fouan.

Then Jean took her gently by the wrist and drew her against his knees; and he kept her like that, his hands trembling at the touch of her skin, and talked to her in his kindly voice which shook as he begged her to stay. Where would she go? To strangers, to domestic service in Cloyes or Châteaudun? Wasn't she better off in this house where she had grown up, among people who loved her? She listened and softened in her turn; even if she never dreamed of him as a lover, she usually did not resist his suggestions, mainly out of a liking for him but also partly through fear. He was such a serious person.

'I want my share,' she repeated, weakening, 'only, I don't say I'll go away.'

'Idiot!' Buteau intervened. 'Why worry about your share if you're staying here? Everything is yours, as much as it's mine or your sister's. What do you want the half for? It's ridiculous. Listen. The day you get married we'll share out.'

Jean's eyes, fixed on her, flickered as if his heart had stopped beating. 'D'you hear? The day you marry.'

She didn't reply, she was too dejected. 'And now, my little Françoise, kiss your sister. It's better like that.'

Lise, the plump young wife with her chattering merriment, hadn't yet lost all her better feelings. She cried when Françoise clasped her round the neck. Buteau, delighted at having once more delayed things, shouted that, by God, they'd have a drink. He brought out five glasses, opened one bottle, then went for a second. The tanned face of Old Fouan had reddened while he explained that he was only doing his duty. They all drank, women as well as men, to each other's health and to the health of the company.

'It's good, this wine,' cried Buteau slamming down his glass, 'but say what you like, it's not as good as the rain. Look at it, it's still falling, falling, falling! Ah, it's precious!'

All of them gathered at the windows, glowed in a kind of religious ecstasy while they watched the warm soft rain endlessly falling, as if they could see the tall green corn spring up under the blessed water.

II

ONE day that summer, old Rose, who had suffered from faintness and whose legs were getting very weak, sent for her niece Palmyre to come and clean the house out. Old Fouan was away as usual wandering round the fields; and while the wretched girl was on her knees, drenched and scrubbing till she was exhausted, the old woman followed her about, step by step, chewing together over the same old cud of gossip.

First they discussed Palmyre's misfortunes, for her brother Hilarion had now taken to beating her. Yes, the idiot cripple had turned vicious; and as he had no idea of his own strength, with fists strong enough to smash stones, she was always afraid of being killed when he hit her. But she wouldn't let others intervene, sent them all packing, and managed to quieten the creature with the infinite tenderness she felt for him. The week before there had been a scandal that still echoed through Rognes: the scrimmage had been so furious that the neighbours had run in and found the brother treating her in an abominable way.

'Tell me, girl,' asked Rose, trying to worm out some revelation, 'Was he trying to force you, the beast?'

Palmyre left off scrubbing to squat in her sopping rags, and flew into a rage without answering the question. 'What's it got to do with them? Why do they have to come and spy on us? We don't rob anybody.'

'But good gracious,' the old woman went on, 'if you sleep together as they say, it's very wicked.'

For a moment the unfortunate woman remained mute, her face taut with suffering and her eyes staring fixedly into the distance; then she bent over her scrubbing again, and spoke with a jerk of her scraggy arms between each stammered sentence. 'How do we know it's wicked? The priest sent for me and told me we'd go to hell. But not my poor darling anyway. He's a natural, Monsieur le Curé, I said, with no more sense than a baby three weeks old; and he'd have been dead long ago if I hadn't cared for him, and he hasn't had any happiness from being what he is! As for me, that's my own business. The day he strangles me, in one of his fits that come over him nowadays, I'll soon find out if the good God's going to pardon me.'

Rose, who had known the truth for a long time, saw that she wouldn't get any fresh details out of Palmyre and concluded with a wise air, 'Well, if things go one way, they can't go another. But whichever way you look at it, you've not made much of a life for yourself, my girl.'

And she lamented that people had their troubles, the world over. Look what miseries she and her husband endured after generously giving up everything for their children's sake. Once launched on this theme—her unending source of complaints—she didn't know how to stop.

'My God! you come down so low that you can do without even respect. If children are swine, well, there it is, they're swine. But if only they'd pay the rent. . .'

She explained for the hundredth time that only Delhomme brought his fifty francs a quarter on the dot. Buteau was always late and kept on trying to pay small sums on account. This time he was ten days overdue and she was still waiting; he'd promised to come this evening and pay up. As for Jésus-Christ, well, that was simple, he never gave them anything, they'd never even seen the colour of his money. That very morning he'd had the nerve to send La Trouille, who'd started snivelling and asked for a loan of five francs —she wanted to make some broth for her father who was ill! Ah, they all knew his disease—the bottomless sink under his nose! So the young slut had been given a warm reception and ordered to tell her father that if he didn't bring his fifty francs that same evening, like his brother Buteau, they'd put the bailiff on him.

'Just to frighten him; the poor boy isn't bad at heart in spite of everything,' added Rose, whose preference for her elder son was already blunting her anger.

As dusk thickened, Fouan came home to supper and at table she started all over again as he sat eating with lowered head, unanswering. Was it possible, in God's name, that from the six hundred francs allowance they'd only had two hundred from Delhomme, a mere hundred from Buteau and nothing whatever from Jésus-Christ, making in all just half of what was due! And the scoundrels had signed at the lawyer's, it was all down in black and white, under legal control. But a lot they cared for the law!

Palmyre, who was just finishing off wiping the kitchen tiles in the gloom, replied to each complaint with an identical phrase, like a refrain of misery. 'Aye, sure enough, we've all got our troubles, and they break us in the end.'

Rose was finally deciding to light up when La Grande came in with her knitting. In these long days there were no wakes; but to save the cost of a single candle-end, she had taken to coming and spending the day's last hours with her brother before groping her way to bed in the dark. She settled herself down at once while Palmyre, who still had the pots and pans to scour, made no further sound, paralysed by her grandmother's presence.

'If you need some hot water, my girl,' said Rose, 'get another faggot.'

She restrained herself for a moment and attempted to change the subject. In front of La Grande, the Fouans tried not to complain, knowing that she was delighted when they moaned about being stripped of their property. But Rose's rage was too strong for her.

'Go on, put the whole bundle on— if you can call it a bundle. Twigs of dead wood, odds and ends from the hedgerows! I really believe Fanny must have scraped out her woodshed before sending us such rotten scraps.'

Fouan, still sitting at the table with a full glass of wine before him, broke the silence in which he seemed to want to enclose himself. 'Haven't you finished yet? It's trash and we know it. But what the devil can I say about this vile vinegary stuff that Delhomme gives me for wine?'

He lifted the glass and held it against the candle. 'Eh? what can he have put into it? It isn't even the rinsings from the barrel. And he's the honest one, he is! The two others would let us die of thirst, wouldn't even go and fetch us a bottle of water from the river.'

At last he decided to drink the wine off at one gulp. But as soon as he'd got it down, he spat violently. 'Ugh! poison! Maybe it's just the stuff to polish me off quick!'

From that moment Fouan and Rose uncontrollably gave vent to all their bitterness. Their cankered hearts found relief as, each in turn, they poured out the stored-up grief in a litany of recriminations. Take the ten litres of milk each week: to begin with, they only got six; and then, even if it didn't go through the hands of the priest, it was still true Christian milk, well baptised with water.

The eggs were the same: they must have been specially ordered from the hens, you wouldn't find such tiny ones if you foraged

171

through the whole of Cloyes market. They were really peculiar eggs and given with such bad grace that they always had time to get addled on the way. As for the cheese, oh, what cheese! Rose was twisted with colic every time she ate any. She ran to fetch a sample and insisted on Palmyre tasting it. Well, wasn't it horrible? Didn't it cry out for redress? They must put flour in it, maybe even plaster. But Fouan was now off grumbling about being reduced to a sou of tobacco a day; and Rose at once began sadly recalling the black coffee she'd been forced to give up. Then they joined in accusing the children of their helpless old dog's death; for the night before they had decided to drown him as he cost too much nowadays.

'I gave them all I had,' cried the old man, 'and the buggers don't care a fig for me. It'll be the death of us, we get so worked-up, living in such misery!'

At last they stopped. La Grande, whose lips had remained tightly closed, looked first at one, then at the other, out of her round vulturine eyes.

'Serve you right,' she said.

But just at that moment Buteau came in. Palmyre, who had finished her task, took advantage of the opening of the door to escape with the fifteen sous Rose had slipped into her hand. And Buteau, in the middle of the room, stood motionless, warily silent, with the peasant's characteristic unwillingness to be the first to speak. Two minutes went by. The old man was obliged to broach the subject. 'Well, you've decided, thank goodness. You've made us wait ten days.'

The son rocked to and fro on his heels. 'A man does what he can. Every man knows best how his own bread's baked.'

'Maybe, but at this rate, if there's no change, you'll eat your bread but we two'll starve. You signed and you ought to pay up on the right day and hour.'

Seeing his father grow angry, Buteau started joking. 'I say, if I'm too late, I'll go away again. Anyway aren't you glad that I'm at least paying? There are some people who don't.'

This allusion to Jésus-Christ made Rose uneasy and she found the courage to tug at her husband's coat. He repressed an irritated gesture and went on, 'All right, give me your fifty francs, I've got the receipt ready.'

Buteau slowly fumbled in his pockets. He had scowled at La Grande and seemed put out by her presence. She now stopped knitting and stared with fixed pupils, keen to see the glint of money.

172

The parents had also drawn near, intently watching their son's hand. So, under the scrutiny of three pairs of eyes, he reluctantly drew out the first coin, a five-franc piece.

'One,' he said, placing it on the table.

The others followed, each more slowly than the last. He went on counting out aloud with a weakening voice. After the fifth coin he halted and had to search hard to find the next, then called in a firm strong voice, 'Six!'

The Fouans waited, but that was the end.

'Only six?' said the old man at last. 'You owe ten. Are you laughing at us up your sleeve? Last quarter you paid forty, this time it's thirty!'

Buteau at once began whining. Everything was going wrong! The wheat prices had fallen, the oats were pitiful. And his horse had had a swollen belly, he'd had to get the vet twice. In fact he was facing ruin; he didn't know how to make ends meet.

'That's nothing to do with me,' Fouan went on furiously. 'Put down your fifty francs or I'll have the law on you.'

Still, he quietened down as he thought of accepting the six coins on account; he said he'd alter the receipt.

'All right, give me the other twenty francs next week. I'll put that on the paper.'

But with a sweep of his hand Buteau removed the coins from the table. 'No, no, none of that! I want things settled. Leave the receipt as it is or I'm off. You've got a hope! I'm not going to pinch and scrape and still be in your debt!'

A terrible wrangle began. Both father and son stuck to their points, repeating the same words over and over again. The father was exasperated at not having pocketed the money straightaway, the son held the coins tight in his fist, determined not to hand them over again without a receipt in full. Once again the old woman had to tug at her husband's coat and once again he surrendered.

'You damned thief, there's your receipt then! I ought to have slapped you in the face with it. Give me the money.'

The coins passed from fist to fist; and Buteau, having successfully played his game, began laughing. He went off, happy, satisfied, wishing everybody a very good night. Fouan had sat down at the table, looking exhausted. Then La Grande, before taking up her knitting again, shrugged her shoulders and spat two furious words, 'Bloody fool!'

There was a silence. Then the door opened again and Jésus-

Christ came in. La Trouille had informed him that his brother was paying that night, and he had watched out for him on the road. When he saw him emerge from the house, he entered in his turn. His gentle expression was simply due to a hangover from a drunken bout of the previous night. On the very threshold he noted at once the six five-franc pieces that Fouan had carelessly put back down on the table.

'Oh, it's Hyacinthe,' cried Rose, happy to see him.

'Yes, it's me. Hope you're all well.'

And he came in, with eyes that never left the white coins that gleamed like moons in the candlelight. The old father turned his head, followed his son's gaze, and caught sight of the money with a twinge of anxiety. Quickly he put a plate over the coins, but too late!

'Bloody fool,' he thought, annoyed at his own negligence. 'La Grande is right.'

Then he exclaimed fiercely, 'Just as well you've come to pay us, because as true as this candle gives us light, I was going to put the bailiff on to you to-morrow.'

'Yes, La Trouille told me,' groaned Jésus-Christ very humbly, 'and I dragged myself over, because surely you can't want me dead. Pay you, good God, what with? I haven't anything to eat. We've sold everything, I'm not pulling your leg, come and see for yourselves if you think I am. There aren't any blankets on the bed, no furniture, no nothing. And on top of it all I'm sick.'

A sneer of disbelief interrupted him, but he went on unheeding, 'Perhaps I don't look sick, but that doesn't mean that I haven't got something wrong in my guts. I can't stop coughing and I feel I'm done for. If we only had some broth! But when you can't get any broth, you turn up your toes, eh, don't you? Too true, you do. You know I'd pay you if I'd any money to my name. Tell me where to get it and I'll give you some, and put something on the fire to cook. It's a fortnight since I saw a bit of meat.'

Rose was beginning to feel sorry while Fouan grew angrier.

'Your money's all gone down your gullet, you useless loafer— well, that's too bad for you! Such lovely land, that's been in the family years and years and you've mortgaged it! Yes, for months on end you and your loose piece of a girl have had a roaring time; and if you've run through everything, you can starve!'

Jésus-Christ hesitated no longer, he burst into sobs.

'You're no father, the things you say. You can't be human if you chuck your son out. I'm too kindhearted, it's my ruin. If you didn't have any money—but you've got some, so how can you refuse your son a bit of kindness? I'll go and beg somewhere else and that'll be a fine thing, won't it, eh?'

At each phrase, between sobs, he peered sideways at the plate and the old man trembled. Then, pretending to choke, he let out deafening yells as if his throat was being cut.

Rose, disturbed and won over by his sobs, clasped her hands to plead with Fouan, 'Look, husband. . .'

But the old man, struggling hard and still refusing, interrupted her. 'No, no, he doesn't care a damn for us. Won't you shut up, you beast? What's the point of such howling? The neighbours will come in, you're making us all ill.'

The drunkard promptly redoubled his shrieks. He bawled, 'I haven't told you—the bailiff's coming in to-morrow. Yes, for a note I signed with Lambourdieu. I'm a swine, I'm a disgrace to you, I'd better end it all. Yes, swine that I am, there's nothing left but to swallow enough of the Aigre to quench my thirst for good. And all I need is thirty francs.'

Fouan, driven to his limit and beaten by the uproar, trembled at the mention of thirty francs. He took the plate away. What was the use? The bugger had seen the coins, he could count them through the china.

'You want the lot, is that reasonable, in God's name? Look here, you're driving us crazy—take half and get out and don't let me set eyes on you again!'

Jésus-Christ, recovering instantly, reflected a moment, and said, 'Fifteen francs, no, it's not enough, I can't manage with that. Make it twenty and I'll go.'

Then, when he had the four five-franc coins safe in his hand, he made them all laugh by describing how he had played a joke on Bécu. He'd fixed what looked like bottom-lines in the reserved section of the Aigre in such a way that the constable had fallen into the water on trying to pull them out. And he finally went off at length after inviting himself to a glass of the foul wine, denouncing Delhomme as a dirty dog for daring to give his father such poison.

'He's a good sort, all the same,' said Rose when the door had closed behind him.

La Grande, who had got to her feet, was folding up her knitting, preparing to go home. She glared fixedly at her sister-in-law, then at her brother; and she too went out after screaming in a long-repressed fury, 'Not one sou, you bloody fools, never ask me for a single sou! Never! Never!'

Outside she met Buteau on his way back from Macqueron's where he had been surprised to meet Jésus-Christ in the best of spirits with a jingling pocket. He had suspected something of what had happened.

'It's quite true, that great clod's carried off your money. He's off to wash his mouth out all right! And what a fool he'll think you are.'

Buteau, beside himself, beat with both fists on the Fouan door. If they hadn't opened, he would have crashed it down. The two old people were already getting ready for bed; his mother had taken off her bonnet and her dress, and stood in her petticoat with her grey hair falling over her forehead. When they finally brought themselves to open the door again, he flung himself between them, crying out in a strangled voice, 'My money! My money!'

They were terrified and backed away, dazed, unable to grasp his meaning.

'D'you think I'm going to dig myself an early grave, all for that lousy brother of mine? He's to live in idleness, eh, while I wear myself to a shadow to keep him. I won't, see? I won't!'

Fouan tried to deny things but his son interrupted callously, 'Eh, what? So you're lying now! I tell you he's got my money. I smelt it, I heard it jingling in his pocket, the bastard! The money that I sweated for, my money that he's going to booze away. If it isn't true, show me the coins. That's it, if you've still got them, bring them out. I'll know the coins, every single one of them. Come on, bring them out.'

He shouted the same phrase twenty times over, whipping up his anger. He went as far as beating on the table, demanding the coins, there, immediately, swearing that he wasn't going to reclaim them, he only wanted the sight of them. Then as the old couple trembled and stammered, he roared out, 'He's got them, that's clear! God strike me down if I ever bring you another sou! We'd bleed ourselves white for you, but not to keep that stinking scoundrel going. I'd rather cut off my arms!'

At last the old father too burst out angrily, 'That's enough, shut up! What business is it of yours what we do? It's mine, that money, I can do what I like with it.'

'What's that?' replied Buteau, advancing on him, livid, clenching his fists. 'So you want me to give everything up. Well, I say it's rotten, yes, rotten to drag pence out of your children when you've certainly got enough to live on. Oh, it's no use shaking your head—you've got a hoard stuck away somewhere here, I know.'

Startled, the old man denied the charge. His voice cracked and his arms hung weakly; there was no shred of his old authority left to throw his son out.

'No, no, there isn't a farthing. Will you get out now?'

'Let me look! Let me look!' Buteau repeated and began opening drawers and tapping the walls.

Then Rose, aghast, scared of a tussle between father and son, clung to the latter, moaning, 'Cruel boy, d'you want to kill us?'

He turned abruptly on her, grasped her by her wrists and yelled right into her face, with no consideration for her poor grey, worn and weary head, 'You, it's all your fault! You gave the money to Hyacinthe. You've never loved me, you're an old bitch!'

He pushed her away so roughly that she staggered and slid fainting down against the wall, till she sat on the floor. Then she gave a muffled cry. For an instant he looked at her as she crouched there like a bundle of rags; then he went out dementedly and slammed the door, cursing all the while, 'God damn God damn God damn God. . .'

Next day Rose was unable to get out of bed. Doctor Finet was called in and came back three times without being able to ease her at all. On the third visit he found her in her death-throes. Taking Fouan on one side, he asked him as a favour to be permitted to write out the death certificate on the spot and leave it with him. This expedient which he often used in his dealings with distant hamlets would save him a journey. Nevertheless she lasted out for another thirty-six hours. The doctor, questioned, had answered that the cause of death was old age and hard work; you couldn't expect to go on living when the body was used up. But in Rognes the true story was known and everyone said 'her blood curdled'. A large crowd attended the funeral, where Buteau and the rest of the family conducted themselves very dutifully.

When the grave was filled in at the cemetery, Old Fouan went back alone to the house where they had lived and suffered together for fifty years. He munched a bit of bread and cheese without sitting down. Then he wandered round the empty buildings and

177

gardens, not knowing what jobs would help him to bury his grief. As he could find nothing left to do, he went out and climbed on the plateau towards his old fields, to see if the wheat was springing.

III

FOR a whole year, Fouan lived in this way, silent in the deserted house. He was always to be found there roaming about, coming and going with trembling hands and doing nothing. He stayed for hours in front of the mouldering troughs in the cowshed, then turned and stood stockstill in front of the empty barn as if rooted there by some deep day-dream. He worked a little in the garden, but he was growing feeble and bent even nearer the earth which seemed calling him back; and twice he had been picked up where he lay with his face buried in his lettuces.

Since the twenty francs had been given to Jésus-Christ, Delhomme was the only one who paid the allowance. Buteau stuck obstinately to his oath that he wouldn't give another sou, declaring he would rather be summoned than see his money slip into his degraded brother's pocket. Jésus-Christ still managed now and then to drag some loans out of his father, whom he broke down with his hysterical weeping-fits.

Then Delhomme, seeing how the old man was going to pieces, badgered and sick with loneliness, had the idea of taking him into his own house. Why didn't he sell the old place and come and live with his daughter? He'd want for nothing and the two hundred francs of the allowance wouldn't have to be paid. Next day, Buteau, who'd got wind of the offer, rushed along and put the same proposition, with a great display of filial devotion. Money to throw away? No! but when it was a question of his father being left on his own, the old man could move in, he could eat and sleep in comfort. At bottom, Buteau must have had the idea that his sister was only trying to entice the old man so as to get her hands on the supposed hoard. But even he, after sniffing in vain, had begun to doubt the money's existence. He was torn two ways, offering his house for shelter out of pride, quite confident that the old man would refuse, yet tormented at the thought of his accepting the hospitality of the Delhommes. In any case Fouan showed extreme repugnance, almost terror, at both offers. No, never! Better eat dry bread in one's own house than baked meats in another's; it was less bitter. He had lived in the old place and he'd die there.

So things went on until mid-July, the day of Saint Henri, the patron saint of Rognes. An itinerant canvas dance-tent was usually set up for a ball on the banks of the Aigre; and on the roadside, opposite the town hall, were three booths—a shooting-gallery, a huxter's stall selling something of everything, down to ribbons, and a place for playing turnabout, at which sticks of barley-sugar could be won. That day M. Baillehache happened to be lunching at La Borderie, and he took the opportunity of calling for a chat with Delhomme, who asked the notary to accompany him to Fouan's to help in persuading the old man to see reason. Since Rose's death the notary also had advised Fouan to sell the useless house, now much too big for him. It was worth at least 3,000 francs, and the notary even offered to take charge of the money and pay out an allowance in small sums according to the old man's humble needs.

They found him in his usual confusion, shambling about at random in a state of stupor. He was staring at a heap of wood which he wanted to saw up but was too weak to tackle. That morning his poor hands were shaking more than usual; for the evening before he had undergone a merciless assault from Jésus-Christ, who, to screw out twenty francs for the next day's fair, had brought all his resources into play, yelling insanely, dragging himself along the ground, threatening to stab himself in the heart, brandishing a blade which he had carefully brought along in his sleeve. Old Fouan had given the twenty francs, as he immediately admitted to the notary with an air of anguish.

'Tell me, would you do any different? I can't go on, I can't go on.'

So M. Baillehache took advantage of the moment. 'You can't remain like this, you'll be skinned alive. At your age it isn't sensible to live alone; if you don't want to be devoured, listen to your daughter, sell this place and go and live with her.'

'Ah, so you too advise it?' muttered Fouan. He shot a glance sideways at Delhomme. The latter was affecting to stand outside the conversation; but when he saw the old man's look of distrust, he spoke out.

'You know, father, I've not spoken because you may think I hope to get something out of taking you into my house. But damn it, it'll only mean a lot of upset. Only, don't you see, it annoys me to see you getting into such a mess when you could be living at your ease.'

'All right, then,' replied the old man, 'but the matter needs a bit

179

more thinking over. As soon as I make up my mind, I'll be sure and let you know.'

Neither his son-in-law nor the notary could get anything more out of him. He complained of being rushed off his feet; his frittered-away authority showed the ghost of itself in the obstinacy of old age, even at the cost of his own betterment. Apart from a vague terror of being left without a house after suffering so deeply from the loss of his land, he said no because everybody wanted him to say yes. The bastards must be hoping to make something out of the plan. He'd say yes when he felt like it.

The evening before, Jésus-Christ in his excitement had been weak enough to show La Trouille his four five-franc pieces. Then he went to sleep with the coins clasped tight in his fist; last time the wench had pinched one from under his pillow, taking advantage of his drunken condition on coming home to swear that he must have lost it outside. When he awoke, he got a fright at finding that the coins had slipped out of his grasp in sleep; but he found them all again, lying warm under his buttocks, and he was shaken with a tremendous joy; his mouth already watered at the thought of spending them at Lengaigne's. It was the village festival—down with the swine who got home with a sou left in his pockets! All the morning La Trouille tried vainly to wheedle a coin from him—one, just a little tiny one, she said. He thrust her away and didn't even say thank you for the omelette made with stolen eggs that she prepared for him. No! it wasn't enough to love your father; money is made for men. So in an outrageous temper she put on her blue poplin dress, a present left over from their days of plenty, saying that she too was going out for a bit of fun. But she was scarcely twenty yards from the door when she turned round and shouted, 'Father, father, look!'

She raised her hand and revealed a fine five-franc piece held by her finger-tips and shining like a sun.

He thought she had pinched it from him and his face grew pallid as he searched his pockets. But his twenty francs were safely stowed away. The slut must have sold some of her geese; and the trick struck him as so funny that he gave a paternal chuckle and let her go.

Jésus-Christ was strict on one point alone: morals. And it was this which some half an hour later sent him into a violent fury. He was leaving in his turn, fastening the door, when a peasant, dressed in his best, hailed him from the road below:

180

'Jésus-Christ! Ho, there, Jésus-Christ!'

'What?'

'Your daughter's flat on her back.'

'Well, why not?'

'With a lad on top.'

'Where are they?'

'Over there in the ditch, at the corner of Guillaume's field.'

Jésus-Christ brandished his furious fists at the heavens.

'Right, thanks. I'll get the whip out. The dirty trollop disgracing me, eh!'

He turned back into his house and took down from behind the door on the left a long horse-whip which he kept for such occasions; and off he went with the whip under his arm, crouching as he slipped along the hedges as though after game, wanting to surprise the couple in the act.

But when he came round the bend in the road, Nénesse, who was acting the look-out on a heap of stones, noticed him. Delphin was the one who was with La Trouille. The pair were indeed taking turns, one watching while the other got down to business.

'Look out!' cried Nénesse. 'Jésus-Christ coming.'

He had seen the whip and scampered off over the fields like a hare.

In the grassy ditch La Trouille with a single heave threw Delphin off. What a blasted nuisance her father was! But she still had enough presence of mind to hand the lad her five-franc piece.

'Hide that in your shirt and give it back after. Quick, skedaddle, damn you!'

Jésus-Christ came tempestuously up, shaking the ground with his heavy tread and cracking his big whip with a noise like rifle-shots.

'Ah, you bitch, you whore, I'll make you skip!'

He was so enraged when he recognised the constable's son, that he missed him and the boy scuttled off through the brambles on all fours. The girl, caught with her skirt still round her waist, was in no position to deny anything. A slash that wealed her thighs sent her scrambling up and out of the ditch. Then the chase began.

'Take that, you slut! Perhaps that'll stop you up!'

La Trouille said nothing, accustomed to such races, but leapt off like a goat. Her father's usual tactics were to drive her back to the house, corner her and shut her up. So she tried to get away towards the open ground, hoping to tire him out. And this time she all but succeeded through a chance encounter. For the last few minutes

M. Charles, who was taking Elodie to the fair, had been brought to a standstill in the middle of the road. He and the young girl had seen everything; Elodie staring in bewilderment and wide-eyed innocence, her father flushed with shame and bursting with respectable indignation. The worst of it was that La Trouille in her brazenness, noticing him there, tried to claim his protection. He thrust her away; but the whip was now swinging close at hand, and to avoid its strokes she dodged round her uncle and cousin while her father swearing and cursing, named all her misdeeds with coarse precision, himself too dodging about and lashing wildly with all the strength of his arms. M. Charles, unable to break through this abominable ring-a-rosy, stood aghast and confounded, and could think of no course except to push Elodie's face into his waistcoat. In fact he lost his head to such a degree that he too used gutter-language.

'Leave us alone, you filthy slut! Why am I buggered up with such a family in this whorehouse of a village!'

Dislodged at last, La Trouille felt herself lost. A slash of the whip caught her under the armpits and she spun round like a top; a second slash knocked her down and tore out a patch of hair. Thenceforth, driven on to the homeward road, she thought only of regaining her burrow as quickly as possible. She hopped over hedges, jumped the ditches and cut across the vineyards without fear of impaling herself on the stakes. But her little legs were giving out and the whip went on showering blows on her rounded shoulders, on her yet-quivering loins, her whole precocious body. Not that she bothered about the blows; she had come to think it funny to be tickled so hard. With a burst of nervous laughter she streaked at length into the house and took refuge in a corner where the long whip could no longer reach her.

'Hand over your five francs,' said her father. 'As a punishment.'

She swore she had lost them as she ran; but he guffawed incredulously and searched her all over. When he found nothing, he grew angry again.

'Damnation! you gave them to your boy friend! You bloody fool! You're the one that gives them their fun and then you pay them for it!'

He went off in a transport of rage, shutting her in and shouting that she'd be left there all alone till next day, as he didn't mean to come home that night.

As soon as he had gone, La Trouille examined her body all over and found no more than two or three weals. So she tidied her hair and straightened her dress. Then she calmly picked the lock with the ease of long practice and scampered off without even bothering to close the door again. If any robbers ventured in, they'd be nicely done in the eye themselves! She knew where to find Nénesse and Delphin, down in a little grove on the banks of the Aigre. And there they were, waiting for her. This time it was Nénesse's turn, Nénesse had three francs, Delphin had six sous. Delphin returned her money and she magnanimously decided that they'd spend the whole sum together. They went back to the fair and she made them shoot for macaroons, after buying a huge red satin bow which she stuck in her hair.

Meanwhile Jésus-Christ had come to Lengaigne's. There he met Bécu with his official badge polished up and attached to a new blouse, and he noisily abused the constable.

'Hey there, you! You've a fine way of going on your rounds! Know where I found your Delphin?'

'Where?'

'On top of my daughter. I'm going to write to the prefect and have you booted out. Your son's a swine, and you're a swine yourself too.'

Bécu flared up at once. 'Your daughter! I've never seen her yet without her legs stuck up. So she's seduced Delphin, has she? Damn me if I don't set the police on her!'

'Just you try, you blackguard!'

The two men were yelling into each other's faces. Then abruptly the tension snapped and their rage fell away.

'We'd better sort it out,' said Jésus-Christ. 'Come and have a drink.'

'I'm flat broke,' said Bécu.

The other gaily pulled out his first five-franc coin, flipped it in the air, and then stuck it in his eye.

'What about this? Let's crack it, you old joker. Come on in, my boy. It's my treat, you've paid often enough before.'

They went into Lengaigne's, chuckling happily and giving each other fond slaps on the back. That year Lengaigne had had an idea. The owner of the travelling dance-hall had refused to return with his booth, annoyed at failing to clear expenses last time; so the innkeeper had daringly turned his barn into a dance-hall. This barn, next door to the inn, had a big waggon-doorway opening on the road; Lengaigne had even cut another door in the partition-wall so that barn and tavern now gave into one another. The whole village was patronising his establishment, and his rival Macqueron in the empty tavern over the road was simmering with rage.

'Two quarts at once, one each!' bawled Jésus-Christ.

Flore, confused and beaming at such a crush of customers, was dealing with the order when Jésus-Christ noticed that he had interrupted Lengaigne in reading aloud from a letter in the midst of a group of peasants. Questioned, the innkeeper replied importantly that the letter was from his son Victor, now on military service.

'Ho, that rascal!' said Bécu, interested. 'What's he got to say? Start all over again.'

So Lengaigne began again from the beginning.

'My dear Parents, this is only to let you know we have been at Lille in Flanders for a month all but seven days. The country wouldn't be bad but for the price of wine. We've got to pay as much as sixteen sous a quart. . .'

In all the four pages of laboured handwriting hardly anything else was said. The same detail cropped up monotonously in phrases which grew longer and longer. But all the listeners exclaimed every time the price of wine was cited. So there were countries like that, pity the poor soldiers! Then, right at the end of the letter there emerged an attempt at cadging, a request for twelve francs to replace a pair of mislaid shoes.

'Ah, the rascal!' repeated Bécu. 'There's a lad for you now, damn it.'

After the first two quarts Jésus-Christ ordered another two—wine that cost twenty sous a bottle. He paid on the nail, for show, rapping his money on the table; and everyone in the tavern was flabbergasted. Then, when the first five-franc piece had been drunk up, he drew out a second one, screwed it into his eye, and shouted that there was lots more where it had come from. In this way the afternoon drifted on; drinkers came in and went out; and the tide of drunkenness rose higher. These men, so grave and reserved all the week of work, were now bellowing, banging with their fists, furiously spitting about. A tall lean fellow decided to have a shave, and Lengaigne without more ado sat him down among the others and scraped away so roughly that the razor rasped on his bristly cheeks as if on a scalded pig. A second man sat down to be shaved and the sport grew riotous. All tongues were loudly wagging with jeers at Macqueron, who didn't dare show his face any longer. Wasn't he himself, the fool of a deputy-mayor, to blame for the travelling dance-booth not turning up? Something could have been fixed.

But of course he preferred voting for roads that would treble the value of his land. The allusion let lose a storm of laughter. And fat Flore, for whom this day was to remain a triumphal memory, bustled to the door to have a good insulting laugh every time she glimpsed Coelina's face, green with envy, at the window-pane opposite.

'Cigars, Madame Lengaigne!' roared Jésus-Christ. 'Don't consider the cost!'

With the falling of night the lamps were lit and La Bécu came in looking for her husband. But he was engrossed in a terrific game of cards.

'Are you coming? It's long past eight. You can't do without eating.'

He glared at her with all a drunkard's majesty.

'You know what to go and do with yourself.'

Then Jésus-Christ let himself go. 'Madame Bécu, sit down, it's my invitation. What d'you say? We'll have a snack, just the three of us. Hear that, Madame Flore? Bring all the best you've got—ham, rabbit, dessert. And don't worry yourself. Just look here. Just a moment!'

He pretended to search himself all over for a long time. Then he suddenly snatched out his third coin and held it up.

'Cuckoo! What-ho, there it is!'

Everybody writhed with laughter and one fat man almost suffocated himself. Jésus-Christ was a one, you couldn't beat him! Some of the drinkers carried the joke on by prodding him here and there, from top to toe, as if he had coins stuck conveniently in his carcasss to be whisked out at need.

'I say, La Bécu,' he repeated at least a dozen times as they ate, 'if Bécu doesn't object, we'll sleep together. What about it?'

She was unwashed, not having known, she remarked, that she'd be staying out at the festival; and she giggled, a swarthy pole-cat of a woman, wiry and rusty as an old needle, while her entertainer lost no time in grabbing hold of her bare thighs under the table. The husband, dead-drunk, slobbered and spluttered with laughter as he mumbled that the piece could take on more than two and still ask for more.

Ten o'clock struck and the dancing began. Through the communicating door the four lamps, hung from the rafters by iron wire, could be seen brilliantly alight. Clou the farrier had come with his trombone, and the nephew of a rope-maker from Bazoches-le-

Doyen, who played the violin, was there as well. No entry-fee was charged, but every dance cost two sous. The beaten-earth floor of barn had recently been sprinkled to keep the dust down. As soon as the instruments stopped playing, there came sharp regular cracks from the shooting-gallery outside. The roadway, generally deep in shadow, was bathed in light from the lamps of the other two booths; the stall of gewgaws glistened with bits of gilt, and the turn-about was bedizened with mirrors and swathed with red curtains like a chapel.

'Hallo! There's my girlie!' cried Jésus-Christ, with misty eyes.

Yes, it was La Trouille, just entering the dance-booth with Delphin and Nénesse at her tail; and her father didn't seem in the least astonished, though he had left her shut up at home. Besides the gaudy red bow in her hair, she now flaunted a weighty necklace of imitation coral (made of beads of sealing-wax) blood-red against her brown skin. All three youngsters, bored with roaming about in front of the booths, were sticky and crammed with a surfeit of sweetmeats. Delphin, only happy in the open air, was wearing a blouse, while his head, round and shaggy as a little savage's, was bare. Nénesse, already yearning for town-finery, had on a suit bought at Lambourdieu's, a tight ready-made suit manufactured by the cheapest of Paris clothiers; and he wore a round felt hat to express his hatred and contempt of his native village.

'Hullo girlie!' called Jésus-Christ. 'Girlie, come and have a sip with me. Don't you like it, eh?'

He made her drink from his glass, while La Bécu asked Delphin sharply, 'What have you done with your cap?'

'Lost it.'

'Lost it? Come here and be slapped.'

But Bécu intervened, chuckling smugly at the thought of his son's precocious love-making. 'Leave him alone, he's too big now. Well, you guttersnipes, so you've been up to tricks together? You little terrors, naughty little blighters.'

'Run off and play,' Jésus-Christ dismissed them paternally. 'And behave yourselves.'

'They're drunk as swine,' said Nénesse disgustedly, as the trio returned to the dance-room.

La Trouille laughed. 'You're right there! I was counting on it. They're so much nicer when they're boozed-up.'

The dance was livening up. All other sounds were blotted out by the wild blasts of Clou's trombone, which completely covered up

186

the faint trilling of the little violin. The beaten-earth, abundantly moistened, was turning muddy under the heavy boots; and soon, from all the swinging petticoats, from the bodices and jackets that grew damp under the armpits with spreading sweat-stains, arose a strong goatish smell accentuated by the acrid smoke wisping from the lamps. A commotion arose when, between two quadrilles, Berthe, Macqueron's daughter, made her entry in a foulard dress, just like those worn by the tax-collector's young ladies at Cloyes on Saint Lubin's Day. Had her parents really given her permission to come? Or had she dodged out when they weren't looking? Everyone noticed that she danced the whole time with a wheelwright's son whom her father had forbidden her to meet on account of a family quarrel. Jokes went the rounds. Maybe she was bored now with ruining her health all on her own.

Jésus-Christ, despite his sodden state, had been for a while watching the unpleasant Lequeu who stood in the communicating doorway with his eyes on Berthe as she hopped around in her admirer's arms; and at last Jésus-Christ had to speak.

'Say, Monsieur Lequeu, aren't you dancing with your sweetheart?'

'Who's my sweetheart?' asked the schoolmaster, his face pale with resentment.

'The pretty poached-eyes over there of course.'

Lequeu, furious at being caught out, turned his back and stood without moving, resorting to his customary prudent pose of disdainful, supercilious silence. And as Lengaigne came past, Jésus-Christ hooked him. Hey! he'd given him what for, the ink-piddler! Thought the rich girls were for him, did he? Not that Berthe's such a catch, bald all over except on her head! Now thoroughly lit up, he swore to the fact as if he'd verified it himself. Besides, everybody knew it, from Cloyes to Châteaudun all the lads made a joke of it. Not a single hair, honest! As bare as the parson's nose! The others, astounded before such a phenomenon, craned their necks to look at Berthe and made faint grimaces of revulsion whenever the dance brought her near, a whirl of white amid her flying skirts.

'You old swindler,' Jésus-Christ went on, addressing Lengaigne as an old pal. 'Your girl's not like that, she's got what's needed.'

Lengaigne responded in conceited tones, 'Obviously.'

Suzanne was now in Paris, in the smart set, the story went. Lengaigne, remaining discreet, mentioned a good situation she'd found. But the peasants were still thronging in, and when a farmer asked him for news of Victor, he brought out the letter again. 'My dear Parents, this is to tell you we are now at Lille in Flanders. . .' Everybody listened, even those who had heard it all five or six times before. They gathered round and remarked: it couldn't really cost sixteen sous the quart? Yes, sixteen sous the quart!

'Awful place it must be,' repeated Bécu.

At this moment Jean arrived. He went first to look around the dance-room as if in search of someone. Then he came back disappointed and disturbed. For two months he had not dared go so often to the Buteau household; he sensed a coolness in Buteau almost amounting to hostility. He must have failed to hide his feelings towards Françoise, the deepening affection which at the moment fevered him; and his comrade had noticed it. It must have displeased Buteau, upsetting his plans.

'Good evening,' said Jean, approaching a table where Fouan and Delhomme were consuming a bottle of beer.

'Take a seat, Corporal,' said Delhomme politely.

Jean accepted the invitation, clinked glasses and remarked, 'Odd that Buteau isn't here.'

'Here he is, the very man,' cried Fouan.

Indeed Buteau was coming in, but alone. He walked slowly round the tavern shaking hands; then, reaching the table where his father and his brother-in-law were seated, he remained standing there, refusing to sit down or take a glass.

'So Lise and Françoise don't dance?' asked Jean at last in a shaky voice.

Buteau looked straight at him with his small merciless eyes. 'Françoise is in bed; it's the best place for young folk.'

But an uproar nearby cut them short and drew their attention. Jésus-Christ was brawling with Flore. He was demanding a bottle of rum to make a punch and she was refusing to fetch it.

'No, not another drop, you're drunk enough.'

'What's she nattering about? D'you think I won't pay, you old stinker? Look, all I've got to do is blow my nose, see!'

He held his fourth coin hidden in his palm, pinched his nose between two fingers, blew hard, and pretended to draw the money out of his nostrils. He then went round lifting the coin up like a monstrance.

'That's the kind of snot I blow out when I've got a cold!'

The applause shook the walls. Flore, defeated, brought him a bottle of rum and some sugar. After that he called for a salad-bowl.

The rascal had attracted the attention of the whole room as he stirred the punch with his elbows sticking out; his red face was illuminated by the flames which intensified the heat of a room already thick with the fug of lamps and pipes. But Buteau, exasperated by the sight of the money, suddenly burst out, 'You great swine, aren't you ashamed to booze away the money you stole from father?'

The other started larking. 'What's that you say, my young brother? Is it your empty belly making you blurt out such nonsense?'

'You're a dirty bastard, I say, you'll finish in clink. And first of all you killed our mother with misery. . .'

The boozer plunged his spoon into the bowl and stirred up a tempest of flames, rolling about with merriment. 'That's right, go on, go on. Sure enough it was me—if it wasn't you.'

'And what's more, wasters of your kind don't deserve to have corn grown for them. To think of our land, yes, the land that our old people toiled so hard to leave us—and you've gone and mortgaged it, handed it over to strangers! You low scoundrel, what have you done with the land?'

Suddenly Jésus-Christ was roused. He let his punch go out and he leaned back solidly in his chair, noting that all the drinkers were now quietly listening, ready to judge between the two brothers.

'The land,' he bawled. 'The land doesn't give a damn! You're her slave. She takes your happiness away, your strength, your very life, you idiot. She doesn't even fill your pockets. Look at me, I despise her, I cross my arms and just give her a kick now and then, and I'm my own boss, I wet my gullet when I will. But you, you're a bloody simpleton.'

The peasants laughed again, while Buteau, taken aback by the force of the attack, could only mutter, 'Good-for-nothing! A botcher who never does a stroke of work and then boasts about it.'

'The land, it's all humbug!' Jésus-Christ went on, now thoroughly worked-up. 'You want your brains tested if you still believe in humbug of that sort. Does it even exist, this land of yours? She's mine, she's yours, she's nobody's. Wasn't she the old man's? And didn't he have to slice her up and share her out? And you, won't you have to do the same for your kids? So what? She goes, she comes, swells out, shrinks again, most of all she keeps shrinking. Here you

189

are, a fine gent with your eight acres, but father had twenty. Well, I've had enough of it. My share was too small, so I blued it. And what's more, I like solid investments, and the land, mark my words, young fellow, land's flimsy! I wouldn't risk a sou on it. It stinks of some damned disaster that's going to sweep you all away. Bankruptcy! You're a pack of boneheads.'

A deadly hush stole over the inn-room. Now no one laughed. The uneasy faces of the peasants were all turned towards the lanky devil who, in his tipsiness, was belching out all his grotesquely confused opinions—ideas picked up as an Algerian campaigner, as a lounger at street-corners, as a tavern-politician. What had come uppermost in him was the man of '48, the humanitarian Communist who still knelt at the altar of '89.

'Liberty, equality, fraternity!' he yelled. 'We've got to get back to the Revolution. The *bourgeois* cheated us in the land-division, they stole everything, and by God, we'll force them to hand it back. Isn't one man worth as much as another? Is it right, for instance, that the blighter at La Borderie should hold so much land while I've got nothing? I want my rights, I want my share. Everybody'll get his share!'

Bécu, far too drunk to speak up on the side of authority, nodded approval without understanding a word. But he had a glimmer of sense left and insisted on some limitation. 'That's right, that's right, but the king's the king and what's mine isn't yours.'

A mutter of assent ran round the room and Buteau took his revenge. 'Don't listen to him, he's only fit for killing-off!'

Another round of laughter answered him. Jésus-Christ lost his self-control, stood up, and angrily shook his fists.

'Just you wait till the next time. Yes, I'll have something to tell you, you damned coward! You talk big now because the mayor's on your side, and the deputy and that tuppenny-ha'penny councillor. Right, you lick his boots, you're fool enough to think that he's on top of things and ready to help you sell your corn. Well, I've nothing to sell and I don't give a tinker's curse for you, the mayor, the deputy, or the police! To-morrow it'll be us that come out on top and that doesn't mean only me, it means all the poor buggers who've had enough of starving to death. Yes, and you too— you, I say—when you're tired of feeding the *bourgeois* without even a crust for yourselves! Landowners will be wiped out, we'll break their jaws and the earth'll belong to those who take her. D'you hear, lad? I'll take this earth of yours and shit on it!'

190

'You come and try it! I'll shoot you like a dog!' screamed Buteau, so carried away with anger that he rushed out and slammed the door behind him.

Lequeu, after listening with a poker-face, had gone off, reluctant to compromise his official position any longer. Fouan and Delhomme kept their noses in their glasses and didn't breath a word; they felt ashamed and knew that any intervention of theirs would only make the drunkard shout more vehemently. At the neighbouring tables the peasants were at last becoming wrathful. What, so their property wasn't their own? Someone was going to take it away? So they growled, preparing to leap with their fists at the advocate of 'Shares for all' and throw him out. But at that moment Jean rose to his feet. He had kept his eyes fixed on Jésus-Christ and hadn't missed one single word, his face grave as if he were trying to sort out the element of truth from the many remarks which repelled him.

'Jésus-Christ,' he said quietly, 'you'd better shut up. It's not the kind of thing to talk about; and if you should happen to be in the right, you're being very foolish, for you're putting every one against you.'

These sensible words from the coolheaded fellow quietened Jésus-Christ down in an instant. He slopped back on to his chair, announcing that he didn't give a damn after all. And he began playing about once more. He kissed La Bécu, whose husband was asleep, flat out on the table; he finished off the punch, drinking out of the salad-bowl. Laughter had started again in the smoke-filled room.

At the other end of the barn the dance never ceased. Clou was still drowning the squeaky tune of the little fiddle with the thunders of his trombone accompaniment. Sweat trickled down everybody's face and added its acrid smell to the stink of lamp-smoke. La Trouille, twirling round now in the arms of Nénesse, now of Delphin, was distinguishable only by her red bow. Berthe too was still there, faithful to her admirer and dancing with him alone. In one corner were some young men whom she had jilted and who were sniggering at her. Sure, if that big boob could put up with the thing she was, she was right enough in gripping him fast; for there were lots of others round who, despite her money, would have insisted on a proper growth in the necessary place before marrying her.

'Let's go to bed,' said Fouan to Jean and Delhomme.

Outside, after Jean had said good night, the old man strolled on in silence, seeming deep in thought over the things he had just heard; then suddenly, as if those things made up his mind for him, he turned to his son-in-law.

'I'll sell the shanty and come and live with you. That's settled. Good-bye!'

Slowly he went on home alone. His heart was heavy, his feet slithered on the dark road, a dreadful sense of loss made him stumble like a drunken man. As things were, he had no land and soon he wouldn't have a house. He felt as if people were already sawing down the old beams and removing the tiles from over his head. Now he had not a single stone to shelter him; he'd wander over the countryside like a beggar without resting, night and day; and when it rained, the chilly rain, the endless rain would drench him through and through.

IV

THE bright August sun had been going up the sky since five o'clock and La Beauce spread out her ripe grain under the fiery vault. Since the summer showers, the green expanse, ceaselessly growing, had gradually turned yellow. Now it was a white-gold sea, on fire, seeming to reflect the glow of the air, a sea undulating its flame-surge at the slightest breeze. Nothing but corn, without a single house or tree in sight, a limitless stretch of corn! At moments in the heat a leaden calm lay slumbrous on the ears and a smell of fecundity wreathed and reeked out of the earth. The time of labour was come, the swollen seed could be felt bursting from the general summer-womb, in warm heavy grains. And there was a growing disquiet in the face of the plain and its mighty harvest; could man with his tiny insect form, a mere speck in the immensity, ever cope with the task?

At La Borderie, Hourdequin, having dealt with his barley, had turned to the wheat. Last year, his reaping-machine had failed to function; discouraged by the opposition of his workmen and even beginning himself to doubt the value of machinery, he had had to safeguard things by hiring a team of reapers from Ascension Day. As was customary, he had hired them from Le Perche, at Mondoubleau: the foreman, a tall lanky fellow, six more reapers and six gatherers, four women and two girls. They had been brought to Cloyes by cart and there the farm-wagon picked them up. They all slept in the sheep-cot, as it was unused at this time of year, girls, women

192

and men, all half-naked in the intense heat, huddled anyhow in the straw.

This was the time of year when Jacqueline was most hard-worked. The look of dawn or sunset decided what sort of work was to follow. The workers shook themselves up at three in the morning and dropped back on their straw at ten at night. And Jacqueline had always to be the first up, to prepare a meal for four o'clock, as well as being the last abed after serving the heavy nine o'clock meal of bacon, beef and cabbage. Between these two meals came three others, bread and cheese for breakfast, soup at midday, bread and milk-sops in the afternoon. So there were five considerable meals in all, washed down with cider and wine, for reapers, who work hard, are exacting people. But she laughed at it all as if the rush stimulated her. She had sinews of steel, with the litheness of a cat; her resistance to fatigue was all the more surprising as she was wearing out that great lump of a cowman, Tron, with her demands, insatiable for his huge soft body. She had him quite tamed to her will; she kept taking him off into the barns, into the hay-loft, even into the sheep-cot now that the shepherd whose watchful eye she had feared was sleeping out in the open with his sheep. But it was night-time above all, with its tumult of male junketing, that somehow made her more sinuous and glowing than ever, brimming over with energy. Hourdequin saw nothing, heard nothing. He was deep in his harvest fever, dominated by the great event, the yearly crisis of his passion for the earth. Within, he felt only the trembling possession, his head burned, his heart beat wildly, his flesh shuddered as he watched the ripe ears falling.

This year the nights were so stifling that sometimes Jean could not stay pent in the loft where he slept near the stable. He went and stretched himself out, with his clothes on, on the yard ground. And it wasn't only the unbearable living warmth of the horses and the exhalations from the litter which forced him out: it was sleeplessness too, the persistent image of Françoise. He could think of nothing but her coming to him to be clasped, to be utterly possessed. Now that Jacqueline, otherwise engaged, left him in peace, his affection for the girl had changed into a torment of desire. Again and again, as he lay agonised in a half-doze, he swore that he'd go and take her the next day; but when he got up and put his head in a bucket of cold water, the thought disgusted him. He was too old for her. But the pang returned with darkness. When the reapers arrived, he recognised among them a woman who had married a

G   193

reaper and whom he had tumbled in the hay two years before, when she was still a young girl. One night his torment was so keen that he slipped into the sheep-cot and tugged at her feet as she lay between her snoring open-mouthed husband and brother. She yielded without a struggle. No word was spoken as they grappled in the burning dark on the beaten earth which, in spite of a raking, still kept so sharp a stench of ammonia left by the wintering sheep that it brought tears to the eyes. Throughout the three weeks of reaping, he returned every night to this woman.

From the second week in August the work went ahead. The reapers had begun on the northern fields, working down to those along the Aigre. The vast expanse fell sheaf by sheaf; every scythe-swing bit into it and cleared a rounded space. The slight creatures, dwarfed by the enormous labour, emerged from it victorious. In their rear, as they moved slowly on in line, the shaven ground showed up with its bristly stubble over which the gatherers bent double. Now was the season when the huge melancholy solitude of La Beauce woke most fully into happy activity, thronged and enlivened with a continual coming-and-going of men, carts and horses. As far as the eyes could see, teams were advancing with the same oblique movement, the same swing of the arms: some so close that the whistling of their scythes could be heard, others thinned into black streaks like ants, right on to the edge of the sky. On all sides gaps were opening as though the plain were a piece of cloth wearing away all over into holes. Strip by strip under the ant-like activity, La Beauce was losing her luxurious cloak, her special summer-toilette, and was left suddenly desolate and bare.

In the last days of the harvest the heat was overwhelming, particularly on the day when Jean was carting sheaves from near the Buteau field to one of the farm fields where a large stack, twenty-four foot high, comprising some three thousand sheaves, was to be built up. The stubble was cracking with drought, and the wheat which was still uncut stood motionless in the scorching air. Indeed the wheat seemed itself to be bursting into flame in the quivering sunlight. Not a single bough shed coolness: only the stumpy shadows that the workers cast on the earth. Since morning Jean had been sweating under the fiery sky, loading and unloading his wagon without a word, merely glancing, as he passed, towards the field where Françoise, bending low, followed behind Buteau with his scythe.

Buteau had been obliged to hire Palmyre as a help. Françoise wasn't enough on her own and he couldn't count on Lise who was now eight months gone. Her pregnancy exasperated him. After all the precautions he had taken, how did this blasted child come about? He bullied his wife, accusing her of having got caught on purpose, and moaned for hours as if some poor beggar or stray dog had sneaked in to eat him out of house and home; and now at the end of eight months he couldn't even look at Lise's belly without abusing her. That damned thing of yours! Got no more sense than a goose, the ruination of the place! That morning she had come to help gather the sheaves; but he had packed her off, infuriated by her heavy cumbrous movements. She was to come back at four in the afternoon, however, with the afternoon snack.

'Good Lord,' said Buteau, determined to finish off the field, 'my back's fairly baked and my tongue's like a bit of dry kindling.'

He straightened himself and stood up, his feet sockless in his heavy boots, dressed only in a shirt and canvas trousers. His open shirt hung half out of the trousers exposing his hairy flesh, damp with sweat, right down to the navel.

'Can't get on without another drink.'

He went to fetch a quart bottle of cider, which he had put under the shade of his jacket. Then after gulping down a couple of mouthfuls of the tepid drink, he remembered the girl.

'Aren't you thirsty?'

'I am.'

Françoise took the bottle and drank deep without repugnance; and as she leaned backwards with her loins curved and her breasts rounding out the thin stuff of her dress, he watched her. She too was dripping with sweat, with her print dress half undone and her unhooked bodice revealing a rim of white flesh. Under the blue kerchief covering her head and neck, the eyes looked huge in her expressionless face, glowing with heat.

Without another word Buteau went back to work, swinging his hips and cutting a swathe with every sweep. The scraping swish of the scythe echoed in time with his steps; and Françoise, once more stooping, came in his wake with her sickle in her right hand, which she used to bring up the armfuls of corn out of the thistles. At every third step she left a sheaf, regularly spaced, in line with those behind. Whenever Buteau straightened up long enough to wipe his brow with the back of his hand and noticed her too far behind, with raised buttocks and her head close to the ground, in the posture of a ready bitch, his tongue seemed to grow drier than ever and

195

he shouted in a hoarse voice, 'Hey, you slacker! What are you doing with yourself there?'

In the neighbouring field, where the gathered sheaves had been drying out for three days, Palmyre was binding the sheaves. Buteau didn't bother to keep his eye on her; for, contrary to custom, he had put her on a piece-rate, so much for a hundred sheaves, on the plea that she was old, used-up, and he'd lose money if he paid her a franc and a half per day like the young women. She had even had to plead for the piece-rate, as he had made up his mind to take her on only if he could do her down; which he did with the resigned expression of a Christian engaged in charity. The wretched woman picked up three or four sheaves—all that her shrivelled arms could hold—then, with a prepared twist she tightly knotted the sheaf. The work, which was so exhausting as to be normally kept for men, was wearing her out. Her breasts were crushed with the continual heavy pressure, her arms were aching, strained with lifting the solid bundles and wrenching at the straw-twists. In the morning she had brought along a bottle, and every hour or so she went to refill it at a foul and stagnant pond nearby. Then she gulped the water down in spite of the diarrhœa which had been tearing her inside out since the hot weather began, in a general breakdown of her health from over-work.

The blue of the sky had waned away; the heavens were an arch of white-hot metal and burning coals seemed falling from the sun, now fiercer than ever. The oppressive hour of the midday siesta had come. Delhomme and his team had been busy nearby stacking sheaves (four below, one on top as a roof); but already they had all gone from sight, stretched out in a dip of the ground. Old Fouan remained standing a moment longer—he had sold his house a fortnight earlier and was now living with his son-in-law—but he too was forced to lie down and dropped out of sight. Nothing was left to show up on the burning stubble-ground against the blank horizon, but the bony silhouette of La Grande, who was examining a lofty rick begun by her labourers among a litter of lesser ones half-demolished. She looked like a tree toughened by the years, with nothing left to fear from the sun, bolt upright without a drop of sweat on her skin, ferociously indignant at all the dozers.

'Hell, my skin's cracking!' said Buteau.

He turned towards Françoise. 'Let's sleep, eh?'

He looked round for a scrap of shade, but in vain. The sun was beating straight down on all sides, and there wasn't the shelter of

196

a single bush anywhere. At last he noticed at the end of the field, in a kind of little ditch, a brownish streak of shadow thrown by the yet-standing wheat.

'Hey, Palmyre!' he shouted, 'you coming too?'

Some fifty paces off, she replied in a smothered voice that reached them like a whisper, 'No, no, no time.'

She was the only one left working on all the burning plain. If she didn't take her thirty sous home at the day's end, Hilarion would thrash her; for besides wearing her down with his brutish appetites, he now stole all her money to get drunk on brandy. But her last reserve of strength was going. Her flat body, planed like a plank with hard work, cracked almost to breaking-point with each new sheaf that she caught up and tied. With her ashen face, worn as an old coin, she looked sixty instead of thirty-five; and she was letting the blazing sun drink up her life's blood as she made her last desperate struggles, those of a beast-of-burden on the edge of sinking down to die.

Buteau and Françoise lay side by side. They were steaming with sweat now that they no longer moved about, and they lay there silent with closed eyes, instantly weighed down by a leaden sleep. They slept on for an hour; and the sweat still ran off their limbs in the heavy furnace-like heat. When Françoise opened her eyes, she saw Buteau turned over on his side and watching her with an ugly look. She let her eyelids fall back and pretended to relapse into sleep. Without a word from him, she felt that he wanted her since he'd seen her rounding out into a proper woman. The thought enraged her. Would the swine dare, after the way she heard him letting himself go nightly with her sister? His rutting stallion-manner had never annoyed her so much before. Would he dare? She waited for his advances, desirous without knowing it, resolved that if he laid a finger on her she'd strangle him.

Suddenly, as her eyelids closed, Buteau grabbed her.

'Swine, you swine!' she stammered, pushing him off.

'O, you fool, come on. I tell you they're all asleep, no one'll see.'

At that moment Palmyre's wan face of anguish showed up above the corn. She had heard the sound and turned. But she didn't count, any more than a cow lifting up her muzzle. And indeed she returned indifferently to her sheaves. Once again the creaking of her hip-bones was heard each time she made an effort.

'You fool, why not have a bit, Lise won't know.'

At the mention of her sister, Françoise, who was weakening into surrender, stiffened herself again. And from that moment she resisted, beating Buteau with her fists and kicking out wildly with the naked legs from which he had managed to pull up her skirt waist-high. Was he hers, this fellow? Did he think she'd take someone else's leavings?

'Go and get my sister, you swine. Poke her if she likes it. Give her a baby every night!'

Under the shower of blows Buteau was growing angry. Thinking she was only afraid of what might result, he muttered, 'You damn fool, I promise you I'll withdraw, I won't put you in the family way.'

She managed to kick him between the legs and he had to let her go; but his shove was so rough that she stifled a cry of pain.

The tussle was ended only just in time. When Buteau got to his feet, he saw Lise on her way back with the bundle of food. He went to meet her and stopped her for a moment to give Françoise time to pull her skirts down. The thought that she might give him away made him regret that he hadn't knocked her out with a good kick. But she said nothing; she sat down in the midst of the sheaves with a stubborn insolent air. When he began scything again, she still sat there doing nothing, like a lady.

'What's happened?' asked Lise, who was lying down on the ground too, tired after her walk. 'Aren't you going to work?'

'No, I've had enough of it,' she replied savagely.

Buteau, afraid to stir her up, started on his wife. What the hell was she doing there, stretched out like a sow, warming her belly in the sun? Just the thing, eh, a fine pumpkin for ripening. She began to laugh at his turn of phrase with all her old coarse gaiety: maybe it was true that the heat would ripen the baby and make it grow. She spread her big belly wide under the fiery sky until it looked like a great round sprout, sprung from the fecund earth. But he didn't laugh. He brutally made her get up and insisted on her lending a hand. Clumsy with the burden dragging at her loins, she was forced to kneel and pick up the stalks with a sideways movement, puffiing and misshapen, her belly hung well over on one side.

'As you're loafing,' she said to her sister, 'at least go home and get a meal ready.'

Françoise went off without replying. The heat was still oppressive, but La Beauce had once more come to life. The little black specks of the teams reappeared, swarming indefinitely on. Delhomme was putting the finishing touches to his ricks with the

198

help of his two labourers; La Grande was watching her stack rise, leaning on her stick and quite ready to swing it across the face of anyone who slacked. Fouan went over to have a look, returned to stare at his son-in-law's work, then wandered ponderously about, an old man full of memories and regrets. And Françoise, still rather dazed from her shock, was moving along the new road when some-one called out, 'Over here—come on!'

It was Jean, half-hidden behind the sheaves which he'd been carting from the neighbouring fields since morning. He had just unloaded his cart and the two horses stood waiting motionless in the sunlight. The big stack wouldn't be started till next morning and he had simply left the sheaves in three heaps which stood like the three walls of a little room, a deep and secret lair of straw.

'Come on, it's only me.'

Françoise mechanically obeyed his call. She did not even think of looking back. If she had turned her head, she'd have seen Buteau straightening up, surprised at seeing her turn from the road.

Jean began by joking, 'You're getting proud, are you, going by without a hullo for your friends!'

'Why,' she replied, 'you were hiding, nobody could see you.'

He went on complaining about the cool welcome that he now always got at the Buteau house. But she couldn't take in what he was saying, and remained silent, only putting in a word now and then. Of her own accord she had let herself drop on the straw that lined the nook, as though knocked-out with fatigue. One thing alone pervaded her mind and still shivered in her flesh, palpable and keen: that man's assault at the edge of the field over there, his hot hands which she still felt clutching her thighs, his smell persisting in her nostrils, his advances which she still awaited, breathless, in an agony of repressed desire. She closed her eyes and felt herself choking.

Jean stopped talking. As he watched her lying defenceless on her back, his blood beat strongly in his veins. He hadn't planned the meeting and he tried to hold back, still thinking it shameful to take advantage of this child. But the loud thumping of his heart stupified him; he had longed so much for her. The image of possess-ing her gripped and maddened him, as it had in his nights of fever. He lay down beside her, satisfying himself first with one of her hands, then taking both her hands and crushing them between his own without even daring to lift them to his lips. She didn't pull away, she opened her faraway eyes with their heavy lids and looked at him, unsmiling, without a blush, her face tense with strain. And this mute almost sorrowful look was what suddenly made him brutal. He pushed under her skirts and grasped her thighs, just as the other man had done.

'No, no,' she stammered. 'Please, no, it's dirty. . .'

But she didn't fight. She only gave one cry of pain. It seemed to her that the earth was falling away under her; and in her giddiness she couldn't think clearly. Had the other man come back? She felt the same rough hands, the same acrid smell, drawn out by hard work in the sun. Her confusion was so great in the flickering darkness of her tight closed eyes that she let out some stammered words without thought.

'Please, no kid. . . withdraw. . .'

He jerked away. The human seed, diverted and lost, spurted into the ripe corn, on to the earth which never denies her body, gaping to take in all and any seed, eternally fecund.

Françoise opened her eyes again, wordless, unmoving, bewildered. What? it was all over and she had got no pleasure out of it! She felt only a sense of loss. And the other man came back into her mind, in the unconscious regret of her unsatisfied desire. She was angry with Jean, lying there by her side. Why had she yielded? She couldn't love anyone so much older. He remained as motionless as she did, upset at what had happened. After a while, he made a discontented gesture and sought for something to say, but couldn't find it. More ill at ease than ever, he tried to kiss her; but she drew back, she didn't want him to touch her again.

'I must go,' he whispered. 'You stay here.'

She didn't reply but stared distractedly into the sky.

'Don't you agree? Wait five minutes so they won't see you come out with me.'

At last she brought herself to open her mouth. 'Right, go away.'

That was all. He cracked his whip, swore at his horses and went off beside his cart, with dragging steps and bent head.

Meantime Buteau was wondering why Françoise had disappeared behind the sheaves; and when he saw Jean's departure, he began to suspect. Without saying anything to Lise he started off bending down warily like a hunter. Then with a leap he landed right in the middle of the nook, at the bottom. Françoise was still lying there, enveloped in her dull stupor, gazing vaguely upwards with her legs still bared. There was no hope of denying things and she didn't try.

200

'You stinking whore, so that's the bastard you lie with, and all I get is a kick in the crutch. Well, we'll soon see about that.'

He had already got hold of her. She could clearly tell by his congested face that he wanted to seize the chance. And why shouldn't he have his turn now that the other fellow had been at her? But as soon as she felt his hot hands again, she was filled with the old revulsion. In his presence she no longer regretted him, she didn't want him, quite unaware of the inconsistencies of her impulse, but feeling a rancorous and jealous protest tauten her whole being.

'Let me go, you swine! I'll bite you.'

Again he had to let her go. But he spluttered with rage, tormented that she had taken her pleasure with another man.

'I had a notion you were mucking about together! I should have kicked him out long ago. You dungheap trollop, what do you mean by letting such a skunk do your business for you?'

He poured out a flood of filth, using every abominable word possible, and described her behaviour with a crudity that stripped her shamefully naked. She, as furious as he was, stiff and whitefaced, put on a show of calm and replied to his foul tirade with a few curt words.

'What's it to do with you? Can't I do as I like?'

'All right, I'll throw you out of the house! Yes, as soon as we get back. I'll tell Lise how I caught you, with your shift over your head, and you can go and bang away at your fun somewhere else.'

He was now pushing her before him towards the field where his wife was waiting.

'Tell Lise then. I'll go off on my own if I like.'

'If you like! We'll see about that! With a boot up your backside!'

As a short cut he was driving her across Les Cornailles, the field hitherto held in common by her sister and herself, the field he had always put off dividing. And suddenly he was seized with consternation; a painful thought leapt to his mind. In a flash he realised that if he threw her out, the field would be cut in two, she'd take one half away and perhaps hand it over to her lover. The thought turned him cold and blotted out his baulked lust. No, it'd be stupid to lose everything because a girl had left him high and dry for once. He could have a tumble in the hay any day; but when a man's got his hands on a piece of earth, the thing is to hang on to it.

He said nothing more but slowed down his pace, confusedly wondering how he could withdraw his threats before they reached his wife. At last he found a way out.

201

'I don't like trouble-makers. I'm only annoyed because you seem so turned against me. Besides, I don't want to upset my wife, in her state. . .'

She fancied that he too was afraid of being betrayed to Lise.

'You can be sure of one thing. If you talk, so will I.'

'Oh, I'm not afraid of that,' he retorted, cool and composed. 'I'll say you're lying out of revenge because I caught you.' Then, as there wasn't much time left, he wound up quickly. 'Right then, it'll all stay between the pair of us. We'll have to talk it over some other time.'

Lise, however, was beginning to feel surprised. She couldn't understand why Françoise was coming back in such a way with Buteau. So he spun the yarn that the lazybones had gone to sulk behind the haystack over there. Then suddenly a harsh scream interrupted him and put the matter out of mind.

'What was that? Who screamed?'

It was a fearful scream, a long howling sigh, like the death-gasp of an animal having its throat cut. It rose up and ebbed away under the merciless glare of the sun.

'Eh, what is it? Sounds like a horse that's broken its legs!'

They turned round and saw Palmyre still on her feet in the next stubble-field among the trusses of wheat. She was clasping a last sheaf to her flat breast with her weakening arms and was trying to bind it. But she let out a second scream of agony, even more piercing than the first, a cry of ghastly suffering; and letting everything drop she spun round and toppled over among the corn, struck down by the sun that had been beating on her for the last twelve hours.

Lise and Françoise hurried over, while Buteau followed more slowly; all the workers from the surrounding fields were coming over as well—the Delhommes, Old Fouan, drawn from his aimless wandering, and La Grande, scattering the stones with the point of her stick.

'What's wrong?'

'Palmyre's had a fit.'

'I saw her fall from right over there.'

'O God!'

The crowd of them stood round watching, afraid to approach too near, gripped by the mysterious fear with which disease strikes the peasantry. She was stretched out with face turned up and her arms extended as if she were crucified on that earth which had worn her out so quickly with hard work and which was now killing her off. Some blood-vessel must have burst, for a red stream was trickling from her mouth. But she was dying more from exhaustion, broken by toil that would have crushed a beast of burden. She lay in the stubble, a withered shrunken thing, a fleshless and sexless rag of womanhood, breathing out her last faint gasp amid the plenteous yield of the harvest.

La Grande, her grandmother, who had renounced her and who never spoke to her, walked forward at last.

'I think she's really dead.'

She prodded her with her stick. The body, with its eyes staring vacantly into the brilliant light, did not move. The stream of blood was drying on the chin. The grandmother, bending lower, added, 'Yes, she's dead, no doubt of it. And better dead than living to be a burden on others.'

They all stood aghast and motionless. Dared they touch her without going to fetch the mayor? At first they talked in low murmurs; then they began to raise their voices to make themselves heard.

'I'm going to fetch my ladder from the stack over there,' Delhomme said after a while. 'It'll make a stretcher. You must never leave a corpse on the earth, it brings bad luck.'

But when he returned with the ladder and they wanted to take some sheaves as a bed for the corpse, Buteau objected.

'You'll get your corn back!'

'I should hope so!'

Lise, somewhat ashamed at such miserliness, added two bundles as a pillow, and Palmyre's body was laid on top, while Françoise, in a kind of dream, dazed by this death which had come at the same moment as her first experience with a man, could not take her eyes off the corpse. She felt wretched and, above all, astonished that the thing could ever have been a woman. She remained with Old Fouan to watch until the removal of the body; and the old man was as silent as she was, though he looked as if he thought the dead were the ones to be envied.

As the sun was setting and putting an end to work, two men came to carry the stretcher away. The weight was not a great one and there was scarcely need to change bearers. Still, other men walked with them and there was quite a procession. They cut across the fields to avoid the bend in the road. On the sheaves the body was stiffening, and some corn-ears, hanging down behind the head, swung to and fro at each jolt in the measured pace of the bearers.

Now there remained nothing in the sky but the day's accumulated heat—a reddish heat that weighted the blue air. On the horizon, on the further side of the Loir valley, the sun, blurred in a haze, now spread over La Beauce a layer of yellow rays level with the earth. Everything was turned yellow, golden in the lovely harvest evening. The corn that still stood was plumed with rosy fires; the stubble lifted tips of glistening red; and in every direction, on and on, jutting up out of the golden sea, the stacks seemed to grow grotesquely large, islands of sparkling flame on one side while on the other they were dark, with lengthening shadows that stretched on into the lost distances of the plain. A deep quiet held the world, broken only by the song of a lark high up in the air. Not one of the group of tired harvesters spoke as they followed the corpse with heads lowered in resignation like a flock of sheep. The only sound was the faint creaking of the ladder under the swaying body of the dead woman borne back through the ripe corn.

That evening Hourdequin paid off his harvesters who had completed the work for which they had been hired. The men received one hundred and twenty francs, the women sixty, for a month's work. The season had been a good one: not too much corn blown down to jag the scythes, and not a single storm during the reaping. And so the cheers were loud when the foreman at the head of his team presented the harvest-home sheaf, the plaited cross of eared stalks, to Jacqueline, whom they treated as mistress of the household. The *ripane*, the traditional feast at harvest-end, was very jolly. The feasters ate three legs of mutton and five rabbits, and drank so hard and so late that everyone tumbled abed quite drunk. Jacqueline, herself tipsy, all but let herself be caught by Hourdequin as she clasped Tron in her arms. In a stupor, Jean had gone to throw himself on the straw in his loft-corner. Despite his exhaustion he could not sleep, for the image of Françoise had returned to torment him. He was surprised, almost angered; for he had had so little enjoyment with the girl after so many nights of longing. He had felt so empty afterwards that he swore to leave her alone for the future. And yet here he was, no sooner in bed than the image of her rose up before him and he wanted her again in a fury of sensual reminiscence. The act of possession revived in his mind again, an act in which he had had no pleasure and which yet in its smallest details now passionately stirred him. How was he to see the girl again? Where was he to embrace her again to-morrow, the days after that, all the days of his life? A rustling sound startled him and a woman came sliding down at his side; it was the gatherer from Le Perche, astonished that he hadn't come to her for this last night. First he pushed her away; then he held her crushed in his embraces. And the woman he held was Françoise, whom he wanted to hold like this, close to him, close, till their senses left them.

At that very moment, Françoise had woken with a start and risen from bed to open the dormer-window of her room for a breath of fresh air. She had been dreaming of a scrimmage of dogs at the door downstairs. As soon as the night air revived her, her head was again filled with the image of the two men, the one wanting her and the other who had possessed her. That was as far as her mind could go. The image merely revolved in her mind without any judgment or decision on her part. But something at length caught her ear. It wasn't a dream then, there was a dog howling in the distance, near the banks of the Aigre. Then she remembered: it was Hilarion who had been howling since dusk beside the corpse of Palmyre. People had tried to get him away, but he had clung tight and bitten their hands, refusing to leave the remains of his sister, his wife, his all-in-life; and his howling went on and on through the night.

Françoise listened for a long time, shuddering.

V

'I ONLY hope that La Coliche won't calve at the same time as me!' Lise repeated every morning.

Dragging about with her huge belly, Lise stood musing with an air of disquiet before the cow, whose belly also was enlarged to a remarkable size. Never had a beast swollen out to such an extent; the cow looked like a big barrel balanced on spindle-shanks. The nine months fell exactly on Saint Fiacre's Day, for Françoise had carefully noted down the date she had led La Coliche to the bull. Lise, unfortunately, was not sure on her side—to within a few days, anyhow. Still, it would be somewhere round Saint Fiacre's Day, perhaps a day earlier, perhaps a day later. She repeated anxiously, 'If only La Coliche doesn't calve at the same time as me! That'd be a business all right. Ah, good Lord, we'd be in a mess!'

La Coliche, who had been with them ten years, was very spoilt. She had ended by becoming one of the family. In the winter the Buteaus snuggled close to her, with no heating in the place beyond the warm exhalations from her flanks; and she in her turn showed much affection for them all, especially for Françoise. She'd lick her with her rough tongue till the blood came, or take her skirt between her teeth to pull her close and have her all to herself. And as her time drew near, she was more pampered than ever—warm mashes, little outings at the most pleasant times of the day, hourly attentions. All this care was not simply an expression of love; it was also based on the fact that she represented five hundred francs in cash, besides the milk, butter and cheeses in produce; quite a fortune, which they'd lose if they lost her.

A fortnight had passed since the harvest. Françoise had carried on with her daily duties in the household as if nothing had happened between her and Buteau. He seemed to have forgotten and she was anxious to banish memories that upset her. Jean, whom she had seen and warned, had not come back. He took to watching for her at hedge-corners, pleading with her to slip out and meet him at dusk in ditches which he carefully detailed. But she refused in panic and hid her revulsion under a show of extreme caution. Later, she told him, when there was less need of her at home. One evening when he came on her as she was hurrying to Macqueron's for some sugar, she obstinately refused to go with him behind the church and chattered to him the whole time about La Coliche, whose bones were beginning to crack and whose behind was opening out—clear signs which made him comment that her time couldn't now be far off.

And, sure enough, precisely on the eve of Saint Fiacre's Day, Lise was taken with severe pains after supper as she was visiting the cowshed with her sister to inspect the cow who, with legs pushed apart by the swelling of her womb, was also lowing mildly as the pangs took her.

'What did I tell you?' Lise complained furiously. 'Now we're in a mess!'

Bending low, she held her own womb tightly in her arms, squeezing it harshly as a punishment. She scolded and talked to it. Hell! Couldn't it leave her in peace? It could wait and be damned! She felt she was being stung by flies on the flanks; pains were wrenching at her loins, moving downwards as far as her knees. She refused to lie down; she walked about repeating that she wanted to make the nuisance go back till she was ready.

At ten o'clock, after little Jules had been put to bed, Buteau, annoyed that nothing had yet happened, decided to retire too. He left Lise and Françoise, and they stayed on stubbornly in the cowshed

206

beside La Coliche, whose pangs seemed to grow worse. Both girls were becoming uneasy: there was hardly any change even though the labour seemed over as far as the bones were concerned. The passage was open, why didn't the calf come out? They stroked the animal, encouraged her, and fetched her dainties—sugar, which she refused, her head lowered and her croup agitated with sharp spasms. At midnight, Lise who up to that moment had been twisting with pain, experienced a sudden relief. What she had been feeling was in fact a false alarm, with sporadic pains; but she was convinced that she had sent the baby back into her womb, just as she might have controlled her bowels. She and her sister sat up all night with La Coliche, attending to her and applying fomentations of hot rags to her flesh; while Rougette, the other cow, bought in Cloyes market, astonished by the candle-light watched all their activities with her large, bluish drowsy eyes.

At dawn, Françoise, seeing that there were no results whatever, decided to run and fetch their neighbour La Frimat. The latter had a big name for her lore and had helped so many cows that people gladly had recourse to her in difficult cases, to avoid calling in the vet. As soon as she entered, she grimaced.

'She doesn't look too good,' she murmured. 'How long's she been like this?'

'Twelve hours.'

The old woman continued to walk round the beast, sticking her nose in everywhere, giving little jerks of her chin and making wry faces that worried the two girls.

'All the same,' she concluded, 'here comes the water-bag. We'd better wait and see.'

And so the whole morning was spent in watching the water-bag forming, the bag which is swollen and pushed out by the water. They studied it, measured it and discussed it: a bag just like any other, even though it stretched out more and more and grew too big. Then at nine o'clock the labour ceased again and the bag hung stationary, pitiful, swinging regularly with the convulsive shudders of the cow, whose condition was obviously worsening.

When Buteau came back from the fields for breakfast, he was frightened too and talked of going to fetch Patoir, though the thought of the fee made him wince.

'A vet!' said La Frimat tartly, 'to slaughter her, eh? Old Saucisse's went and died on him, right under his nose. Now look here, I'll cut the bag and have a look for the calf.'

Françoise intervened. 'Monsieur Patoir says the water-bag should not be cut. He says it helps, the water in it.'

La Frimat shrugged her shoulders in irritation. He was an ass, that Patoir. She slit the bag open with a pair of scissors. The water shot out like a mill-race and everyone jumped back too late, spattered all over. For a moment La Coliche's breath was less laboured and the old woman smiled in triumph. She had rubbed butter over her right hand and reached inside, trying to find the calf's position. As she unhurriedly rummaged around, Lise and Françoise watched her fearfully with blinking eyes. Buteau too, who had not gone back to the fields, waited breathless and stockstill.

'I can feel the feet,' she muttered, 'but not the head. There's something wrong when you can't find the head.'

She had to take her hand out. La Coliche, shaken by a violent spasm, pressed so hard that the feet came into view. That was always the case; the Buteaus sighed with relief. They felt they already had a portion of the calf in their possession now that the feet were protruding; and from that moment they were obsessed by one idea—to pull it out, to have it all at once, as if they were afraid it would retreat and never come out again.

'Better not rush her,' said La Frimat sagely, 'it'll come out by itself in good time.'

Françoise agreed. But Buteau became restless, touching the calf's feet every other minute, getting angry that they didn't come further out. Suddenly he picked up a rope and tied a firm knot with the help of his wife who was trembling as much as he was; and as La Bécu came in just at that moment, following her sharp nose, they all pulled together, clinging to the rope; first Buteau, then La Frimat, La Bécu, Françoise and Lise at the end crouching with her big belly.

'Ho, pull!' shouted Buteau, 'all together. . . O, the bitch, it hasn't shifted an inch, it's stuck in there. . . Heave, ho! Come on, you bastard!'

The women, panting and sweating, joined in the shout, 'Heave ho! Come on, you bastard!'

Then there was a mishap. The rope, old and half-rotted, broke. They all fell over backwards in the litter, shouting and cursing.

'It's all right, no harm done!' cried Lise, who had rolled over against the wall. They hurried to help her up.

As soon as she was on her feet she fainted. She had to sit down. Fifteen minutes later she was holding her stomach; the pains were starting off as on the evening before, sharp and regular. And she thought she had pushed the baby back! What rotten luck all the same, why couldn't the cow hurry up? Now she was taken with pains again she might easily catch up with the beast! You couldn't escape fate, it was written down that the two should calve together. Lise sighed heavily, and a quarrel broke out between her and her husband. In the name of God, why had she pulled? What cause had she to go and meddle with someone else's inside? Her job was to empty her own first! She retorted with insults, in the midst of her throes: You swine! Stinker! If he hadn't tinkered about with her inside, it wouldn't now be such a nuisance!

'Here now,' La Frimat intervened, 'this is all talk, it doesn't help a bit.'

And La Bécu added, 'It's a relief all the same.'

Fortunately they had sent little Jules to the Delhommes, to get him out of the way. It was three in the afternoon and they waited till seven. Nothing happened and the house became utter hell. Here was Lise obstinately sitting on an old chair, writhing and groaning; and there was La Coliche lowing, shivering and sweating, and getting worse every minute. The other cow, Rougette, was scared and added her lowing cries. Françoise was distracted, and Buteau, swearing and bawling, wanted to try another pull. Two neighbours were called in; and six persons pulled, enough to uproot an oak, with a new rope that wouldn't snap. But La Coliche staggered and fell on her side, and lay stretched out on the straw, pitiably panting.

'Bugger it, it won't come out,' declared Buteau in a fury. 'And now the blasted cow is going to die on us too!'

Françoise clasped her hands in an entreaty. 'O, go and fetch Monsieur Patoir. Never mind what it costs, call him in.'

Buteau's face darkened. Then, after a last struggle with himself, he went out without a word to get the cart.

La Frimat had demonstratively washed her hands of the cow as soon as they talked again of the vet; but now she began to fuss about Lise. She was an expert also in confinements; all the village-women had been through her hands. She was disquieted and did not hide her worries from La Bécu, who called Buteau away from harnessing the horse.

'Look, your wife's pretty bad. What about bringing the doctor along at the same time?'

He stood speechless with staring wide eyes. What, a second

creature wanting to be cossetted? Did the whole world think they could pile costs on his shoulders?

'No, no,' cried Lise, between two contractions. 'I'll manage. We can't throw money out of the window like that.'

Buteau hastily whipped up the horse and the cart was whisked away into the dusk that thickened over the road to Cloyes.

When Patoir finally arrived two hours later, things were just the same. La Coliche lay groaning on her side, and Lise, writhing like a worm, had half slid off her chair. This state of things had now persisted for twenty-four hours.

'Which am I called in for, hey?' asked the vet, who was a jolly sort of fellow. Then he addressed Lise familiarly, 'You there, fatty, if I haven't been brought for you, be so good as to go and dump yourself in bed. That's what you need.'

She made no reply and stayed where she was. He was already examining the cow.

'Damnation, she's in a bloody awful state, this beast of yours. You always come for me too late. And you've been pulling, I can see. Admit it! You'd rather split her in two than wait, you clumsy devils!'

They all listened with a hang-dog look, their heads respectfully and despondently bent; all but La Frimat, who scornfully tightened her lips. He took off his cloak, turned up his sleeves, pushed the calf's feet back after slipping a thread round them so as to be able to find them again; then he plunged his right hand in.

'Exactly,' he said, 'just as I thought. The head is bent back to the left, you could have pulled till to-morrow morning and it'd never have come out. I tell you, my children, your calf is done for. I have no wish to get my fingers cut on his teeth trying to turn him round. Anyway, I'd never get him out and I'd wreck the mother.'

Françoise burst into tears. 'Monsieur Patoir, I beg and pray you, save our cow. Poor Coliche, she loves me. . .'

And Lise, turning pale at a sudden spasm, and Buteau himself, who was so healthy that he had no feeling for other people's pain, both lamented and melted, with the same beseeching cry.

'Save our cow, our old cow who's given us such good milk for years and years. Save her, Monsieur Patoir. . .'

'Well, get this clear first, I'll have to cut up the calf.'

'Blast the calf! Save our cow, Monsieur Patoir, save the cow.'

The veterinary, who had brought a large blue apron, borrowed a pair of canvas trousers; then he stripped himself behind Rougette,

210

slipped the trousers on and tied the apron round his waist. When he came out in this scanty costume, with his amiable bull-dog face and his solid thickset figure, La Coliche raised her muzzle and paused in her moaning, no doubt from astonishment. But no one even smiled, so intensely did they suffer the strain.

'Get some candles.'

He arranged four candles on the ground, then lay flat on his stomach behind the cow, which was now too weak to rise. For an instant he lay unmoving with his head between the beast's legs. Then he decided to pull at the thread and again bring out the feet, which he attentively examined. Close at hand he had set a long thin box, and he was lifting himself on one elbow to get a scalpel from it, when a hoarse groan startled him and made him sit right up.

'What, still there, are you, fatty! I thought it wasn't the cow making such a row.'

Lise, gripped in her final pangs, was straining away with her thighs moving apart.

'In God's name, go and get your business over in your own room and leave me to do mine here! You put me off, you get on my nerves, really you do, when I hear you straining there behind me. Think a moment, is there any sense in it? O, take her away, you others.'

La Frimat and La Bécu decided to take Lise by each arm and lead her to her room. She let them have their way, lacking the strength to resist. But as they went through the kitchen, where one lonely candle was burning, she demanded that all the doors should be left open, feeling that she then wouldn't be so cut off. La Frimat had already prepared the bed of labour according to country custom —a simple sheet spread in the middle of the room on a truss of straw and three chairs set upside down. Lise squatted down and stretched herself out with her back against one chair and a leg against each of the others. She had not even taken off her clothes, her feet in her down-at-heel shoes pressed hard, her blue stockings reached up to her knees; and her petticoat, pulled up over her breasts, exposed her monstrous belly and her plump white thighs, extremely white and so spread-out that one seemed to see right up inside her to her heart.

Buteau and Françoise had remained in the cowshed to light Patoir. Each of them was squatting down with outstretched candle, while the veterinary, again laid flat on his stomach, used the scalpel to cut a section round the left ham. He loosened the skin, then pulled at the calf's shoulder, which came away in his hand. Françoise, pallid and faint, dropped her candle and ran off with a scream, 'My poor old Coliche, I can't look on!'

Patoir lost his temper, all the more because he had to get up and stamp out the fire started by Françoise's candle as it fell into the straw. 'Who does the wench think she is? Got the fine feeling of a lady, eh? She'd smoke us out as if we were bacon.'

Françoise went on running till she flung herself down in a chair in the room where her sister lay in labour. Lise's wide-opened loins aroused no emotion in her; after what she had just seen the scene here was something natural and normal. She waved her hand in dismissal of her memories of living flesh being cut away; and stammered out an account of what they were doing to the cow.

'It's bound to get in a mess,' said Lise abruptly. 'I must get back there.' And in spite of her pains, she tried to get up from the three chairs. But La Frimat and La Bécu angrily held her down.

'Hey, keep still there, will you? What's got into you?'

And La Frimat added, 'Good, your water's breaking too.'

And indeed the water spurted out and was at once absorbed by the straw under the sheet. The final spasms began. The naked belly pressed now of its own accord and swelled as if about to burst, while the blue-stockinged legs drew up and opened again in unconscious movement like a diving frog.

'Look here,' La Bécu went on, 'To keep you quiet, I'll go down myself and bring you the news of what happens.'

After that La Bécu did nothing but run to and fro between the room and the cowshed—until, to spare herself too much movement, she took to shouting the news up from the middle of the kitchen. The veterinary went on with his dismemberment in the litter-straw soaked with blood and mucilage, a difficult and dirty job from which he emerged filthy from head to foot.

'All going well, Lise,' shouted La Bécu. 'Keep on pushing. We've got the other shoulder now. And now he's pulling the head out. He's got it, O, what a head! And now he's done it—one good wrench and the body's come out in a lump.'

Lise greeted each phase of the operation with a deep-felt sigh; and no one knew if she was grieving for herself or for the calf. Then without warning Buteau brought in the calf's head for her to see. They all exclaimed, 'O, what a beautiful calf!'

Lise did not halt her labour, pressing even harder, her muscles tense and her thighs swelling; but now she seemed gripped by an inconsolable anguish.

'My God, what bad luck. Such a beautiful calf, my God! What bad luck, such a beautiful calf, a real beauty, no one ever saw a finer specimen.'

Françoise too was sorrowing; and everyone's laments took on such an aggressive tone, were so full of hostile undertones, that Patoir was offended. He ran along, but stopped at the door out of respect for the scene.

'Now look here, I warned you. You pleaded with me to save your cow. I know you, you blighters! Don't you go round telling everyone that I killed your calf.'

'Of course not, of course not!' muttered Buteau, returning with him to the cowshed. 'All the same, it was you cut him up.'

On the ground, pressed against her three chairs, Lise was caught up by a kind of billowing shudder, which ran down her hips under the skin and ended below the thighs in a steady pressing-open of her flesh. Françoise, who in her desolation had so far taken no notice, was suddenly aghast as she stood before her sister, looking down on her foreshortened nakedness which was reduced to the lifted angle of the knees on either side of the stomach-mound caverned by a round hole. What she saw was so unexpected, so disfigured, so huge, that she wasn't upset. She could never have imagined anything like it, the yawning hole like a broached barrel or the wide-open window of the loft through which the hay's thrown down, with ivy tufted blackly around. Then when she noticed that another rounded shape, smaller than the stomach, the baby's head, pressed out and retreated with each spasm, in a continual game of hide-and-seek, she was gripped by such a violent desire to laugh that if she hadn't coughed she'd have gained a name for heartlessness.

'Just a speck more patience,' said La Frimat, 'it'll come soon.'

She was on her knees between the legs watching for the child, ready to receive it. But the baby was having a game with them, as La Bécu put it; once, even, it went so far back you'd have thought it was off back home. Then, and then only, Françoise tore herself away from the fascination of the big oven-mouth that seemed gaping at her; and immediately embarrassed, she went to take her sister's hand, full of sympathy as soon as she had turned away her eyes.

'My poor Lise, it must be awful.'

'Yes, yes, and nobody's sorry for me. If only people were sorry. O, Lord, there it starts again, it's never going to come out!'

The whole thing might have gone on a good while longer; but cries were heard from the cowshed. Patoir, surprised to see La Coliche still quivering and lowing, had suspected the presence of a second calf; and indeed, when he plunged in his hand again, he pulled a calf out, this time without the slightest difficulty—as easy as pulling a handkerchief out of his pocket. The delight of the jolly fat man was so great that he forgot all decency and ran into the room of Lise's confinement with the calf in his arms. Buteau, in high spirits, came after him. Patoir cried out:

'Well, fatty, you wanted one—so here it is!'

He rolled about laughing, naked under his apron, with arms, face and entire body plastered with dung, while the calf, still glistening wet, with its top-heavy bewildered head, looked as if it was tipsy.

In the midst of the acclamations Lise was seized with uncontrollable endless screams of laughter.

'O, how funny he looks! O, it's too bad to make me laugh at such a time. It hurts, I'm splitting. Stop, stop! Don't make me laugh any more, I've had enough!'

The laughs swelled up the depths of her big bosom and down into her belly, where they stirred up a tempestuous agitation. She was blown out with the tumult, and the baby's head resumed its to-and-fro game, like a cannon-ball about to come hurtling out.

The last touch was added when the vet, putting the calf down at his feet, tried to wipe the sweat off his forehead with the back of his hand. He streaked himself with dung and everyone became helpless again; the woman in labour was suffocating, gasping out cries like those of a hen laying an egg.

'It's killing me, stop! You blasted fool, you'll make me bust with laughing. O my God, my God, I'm done for.'

The gaping hole grew rounder until it seemed that La Frimat, all this while on her knees, would disappear into it; and suddenly, as if shot from a cannon moulded in a woman's shape, the baby appeared, red all over, with extremities weak and wan. The only sound was a gurgle like that of a huge bottle being emptied. Then the baby mewed, and the other, shaking like an empty leather bottle, laughed harder than ever. Cries at one end and screams of laughter at the other! Buteau was slapping his thigh, La Bécu holding her sides, Patoir bellowing in his deep voice, while Françoise herself, with her hand caught tight in her sister's last spasm, finally let her repressed laughter out. She couldn't blot from her mind what she'd seen, a proper cathedral where the husband could have got all of himself inside.

'A girl,' said La Frimat.

'No, no,' said Lise, 'I don't want a girl. I want a boy.'

'Right you are, I'll put it back, my pretty one, and you can produce a boy to-morrow.'

That set them off again, laughing yet louder. They almost made themselves sick with laughter. Then, as the calf was still there in front of her, the mother, calming down at last, regretfully remarked, 'The other one was such a fine one. All the same, we should have had two.'

Patoir went off after seeing two quarts of sugared wine administered to La Coliche. In the bedroom La Frimat undressed Lise and put her to bed, while La Bécu, helped by Françoise, removed the straw and swept the room out. In ten minutes everything was tidied up and there wasn't a sign of a confinement save for the continual mewing of the baby which was being washed in warm water. But when she'd been swaddled and laid in her cradle, she gradually grew quiet; and the mother, now quite knocked-out, fell asleep like a log and lay with her face congested and almost black between the thick brownish sheets.

At eleven o'clock when the two neighbours had left, Françoise told Buteau he had better go up into the hayloft to sleep. She had laid a mattress on the floor and meant to spend the night there so as not to leave her sister alone. He ignored her words and mutely finished his pipe. A profound silence came over the room and only the heavy breathing of the sleeping Lise could be heard. Then, as Françoise was kneeling on her mattress at the very foot of the bed, in a dark corner, Buteau, still without a word, came up suddenly behind her and laid her flat. She turned her head and instantly grasped the situation from the look on his drawn flushed face. He was at it again, he hadn't dropped his plan to have her; and his desire must have been devilishly strong if he wanted her like that, at his wife's very side, just after events which were hardly pretty. She pushed him away and sent him sprawling. A dumb panting struggle went on.

Derisively, he muttered in a choking voice, 'Come on, what the hell does it matter? I'm up to dealing with the two of you.'

He knew her well, he knew she wouldn't cry out. And she fought

215

on without a word, too proud to call her sister, unwilling to let anyone interfere in her affairs, not even such an affair as this. He was
throttling her and she felt her resistance weaken.

'It'd be fine—we're living together and so we'd always be near
one another.'

Then it was all he could do to hold back a cry of pain. She had
silently dug her nails into his neck; he grew furious and brought
Jean up.

'Do you think you'll marry him, that blackguard of yours? Never,
as long as you're under age.'

This time, just as he was violating her by sheer brute strength
under her skirt, she kicked him so hard between the legs that he
howled. With a leap he was on his feet, scared, with eyes turned
towards the bed. His wife was still asleep, still breathing tranquilly;
but he went off with a ferocious threatening gesture.

When Françoise was stretched out on the mattress in the deep
peace of the room, she lay awake with her eyes open. She didn't
want him, she'd never let him have his way, not even if she herself
wanted it. And she wondered, for the idea of marrying Jean had
never before occurred to her.

VI

For the past two days Jean had been working in the Hourdequin
fields near Rognes; the farmer had installed there a steam-threshing
machine hired from a Châteaudun engineer who covered the area
from Bonneval to Cloyes. The young man carried the sheaves from
the ricks all round in his two-horse waggon, then fetched the grain
back to the farm; while the machine, puffing away from morning
to night, sent golden dust billowing into the sunlight and filled the
countryside with a vast, incessant snorting.

Jean, sick with longing, was turning over and over schemes for
getting hold of Françoise again. It was a good month since he had
clasped her in his arms on that very spot, among the wheat now
being threshed; and ever since, she had kept timidly evading him.
He began to despair of ever getting a fresh start and yet to re-
possess her had become a mounting desire, a passion of his whole
being. As he drove his horses along, he asked himself why he
shouldn't go openly to the Buteaus and ask for her hand in marriage.
There was nothing of an open and settled break between himself

and them. He still gave them a good-day as he passed. So as soon as the idea of marriage had occurred to him as the only way of having the girl again, he persuaded himself that it was his duty, that he'd be acting dirtily if he didn't marry her.

Still, when next morning he came back to his machine, he lost his nerve. He'd never have risked the step if he hadn't seen Buteau and Françoise leaving together for the fields. He began thinking that Lise had always been inclined to favour him and that he'd be less nervous with her; so he slipped off for a few moments, putting his horses in his comrade's charge.

'Why, it's Jean!' said Lise, who was sturdily bustling about again after her confinement. 'We haven't seen you for ever so long. What's up?'

He made excuses. Then, hurriedly, with the curtness of shy people, he blurted things out; and at first she might have been forgiven for thinking that he was making her a declaration; for he reminded her that he had loved her and would gladly have had her for his wife. But he went on without a pause, 'And that's why I'd marry Françoise all the same, if I had the chance.'

She stared at him with such surprise that he began stammering, 'O, I know it's not as simple as all that. I only wanted to have a word with you about it.'

'Gracious!' she replied at last, 'it's a bit of a shock, as it never entered my mind because you're so much older. Well, first we must find out what Françoise thinks.'

He had come determined to tell her everything, hoping thus to precipitate matters. But at the last moment a scruple kept him silent. If Françoise hadn't confided in her sister, if no one knew what had happened, what right had he to make it public? He lost heart and felt ashamed because of his thirty-three years.

'Of course,' he muttered, 'she must be asked, there mustn't be any compulsion.'

Lise, however, as her astonishment passed, regarded him with an air of delight; she was clearly not at all displeased by the proposition. She even became very amiable.

'We'll do just as she chooses, Jean. I'm not of Buteau's mind, he thinks she's too young. She's almost eighteen and she could take on two husbands as easy as one. And then, it's all very well for two sisters to be fond of one another, of course, but now that she's a woman, I'd rather have a servant to carry out my orders. If she

217

says yes, you marry her. You're a good sort and it's often the old cocks who're the best.'

She was giving away what she felt deep down, the slow estrangement that had been irresistibly widening between herself and her young sister. Their hostility was aggravated by small daily quarrels; a secret ferment of jealousy and hatred had been working under the surface ever since a man had come into the house with his will and his lust.

The happy Jean gave her a hearty kiss on each cheek, and she added, 'It so happens we're christening the baby; we've invited the family along to supper this evening. You come along too and put your request to Old Fouan who's the girl's guardian, that is, if Françoise will have you.'

'Agreed!' he cried. 'To-night then!'

He strode rapidly back to his horses and drove them hard all day long, making his whip whistle and crack like gunshots on the morning of a fête.

The Buteaus were indeed having their child christened after several delays. First, Lise had insisted on holding things up until she was quite recovered, as she wanted to play her part in the feasting. Then, gripped by an ambitious hope, she had obstinately insisted on having the Charleses as godparents; and as they had condescendingly accepted, the ceremony had to be postponed on account of Mme Charles, who had just gone to Chartres to give her daughter a helping hand—the September fair was in full blast and the house in the Rue aux Juifs was always packed. Otherwise, as Lise had told Jean, it was to be a simple family affair: Fouan, La Grande, the Delhommes, besides the godparents.

But, at the very last, considerable problems had arisen through the Abbé Godard, who was in a sort of continual feud with Rognes. He had forced himself to bear his grievances with patience—the four miles to walk to every Mass, the vexatious demands made by the irreligious village—as long as he cherished a hope of the municipal council eventually giving themselves the luxury of a priest of their own. But now his long-suffering had worn out; he could deceive himself no longer. The council put off the repairs to the parsonage year after year; Mayor Hourdequin stigmatised the expenses as already too heavy; and only Macqueron, the assessor, flattered the priest in pursuance of some unknown ambitious projects. Consequently the Abbé, no longer having any reason to play for safety with Rognes, treated the village cavalierly and only gave it the strictest minimum of divine service, refusing to indulge them with extra prayers, extra tapers, or incense. He was always embroiled with the village-women. In June indeed there had been an open clash about first communion. Five children, two girls and three boys, had been attending catechism after Sunday Mass; and to save himself from having to return yet again to confess them, he insisted on their coming to him at Bazoches-le-Doyen. The first revolt of the women was stirred up. No thank you! Three-quarters of a league each way! Who could tell what mightn't happen with boys and girls running about loose together? Next, the storm broke in full violence at his point-blank refusal to celebrate the ceremony at Rognes with sung Mass and all the rest of it. He intended to hold the celebration in his own parish and the five children were free to join him there if they so wished. For an entire fortnight the women chattered with rage round the fountain. What, he baptised them all, married them, buried them in their own village, and now he wouldn't give them a proper communion! But he stuck out, said low Mass and dismissed the five communicants without even the consolation of a flower or an *oremus*; he even bullied the women when, vexed almost to tears at such a mean ritual, they pleaded with him to sing vespers. Not a bit of it! He gave them their exact dues. They could have had high Mass, vespers, everything they wanted, at Bazoches, if their mulish tricks hadn't made them rebels against God Himself! After this altercation a total break between the Abbé Godard and Rognes seemed imminent and the slightest collision was certain to lead to catastrophe.

When Lise went to see the priest about the baby's christening, he suggested fixing it for Sunday after Mass; but she begged him to come to Rognes on Tuesday at two in the afternoon as the god-mother was only coming back from Chartres on the morning of that day; in the end he gave way, but bade them be punctual, for he was resolved, he exclaimed, not to wait a second.

On Tuesday, precisely at two o'clock, the Abbé Godard arrived at the church, puffing after his journey and wet from a sudden shower. Nobody else had arrived. Only Hilarion was in the nave-entrance, busy clearing up a corner of the baptistery which was piled high with a years-old litter of cracked old flag-stones. Since his sister's death, the cripple lived on public charity, and the priest, who now and again slipped odd francs in the wretch's palm, had thought of giving him the clearance-job which had been decided on scores of times but always put off. For a few moments he was preoccupied in watching the work; then he was shaken with his first burst of wrath.

'Hey, are they making fun of me? It's already ten past two.'

As he glanced across the square towards the Buteaus' house, silent and sleepy-looking, he noticed the rural policeman waiting under the porch and pulling at his pipe.

'Ring the bells, Bécu!' he shouted. 'That'll fetch them, the slow-coaches!'

Bécu, drunk as ever, grasped the bell-rope and hung on to it. The priest went to put on his surplice. He had drawn up the entry in the register on Sunday and he counted on performing the ceremony by himself without the aid of the choir-boys, who drove him to distraction. When everything was ready he again grew impatient. Ten more minutes passed and the bell went on ringing persistently and exasperatingly through the deep silence of the deserted village.

'What on earth are they doing? Do they have to be dragged by their ears?'

At last he saw La Grande coming out of the Buteau house. She walked along with the air of some evil old queen, as straight and dry as a thistle for all her eight-five years. The family were in the throes of an appalling worry; all the guests had turned up except the godmother, for whom they had waited in vain since morning; and M. Charles, quite dumbfounded, remarked over and over again that it was quite inexplicable; he'd received a letter the evening before, Madame Charles had perhaps been delayed at Cloyes and she'd arrive at any moment. Lise was anxious, knowing that the priest was not very fond of being kept waiting, and at last she had the idea of sending La Grande over to keep him in a good temper.

'What's going on?' he called out before she came up. 'Is the christening to-day or to-morrow? Maybe you think God Almighty's got nothing better to do than obey your whims.'

'In a moment, your reverence, in a moment,' replied the old woman, imperturbably calm.

Hilarion was bringing out the last pieces of flag-stones. He went by, hugging a huge lump of stone against his stomach and swaying on his twisted legs but without a single lurch, firmly based as a rock, with muscles strong enough to cart an ox. He was dribbling through his harelip, but not one drop of sweat moistened his tough skin.

The Abbé Godard, infuriated by La Grande's impassive air, immediately attacked her: 'Look here, La Grande, as I've got you here, is it charitable, when you've plenty of money, to let your only grandson beg on the highway?'

She retorted harshly, 'His mother wouldn't do as I said, the child's nothing to me.'

'Well, I've warned you often enough, and I tell you again, you'll go to hell if you're so stony-hearted. The other day without the alms I gave him he'd have starved to death, and to-day I had to invent an odd job for him.'

At the word hell La Grande gave a thin smile. As she used to say, she knew all about it, hell was here on earth for the poor. But the sight of Hilarion carrying the stones exercised her mind far more than the priest's threats. She was surprised; she'd never have thought him so strong, what with his legs crumpled and bent like coat-sleeves.

'If it's work he wants,' she went on at last, 'I daresay there's something we can find him to do.'

'His place is with you. Take him, La Grande.'

'We'll see. Let him come along to-morrow.'

Hilarion, who had understood, began trembling so badly that he almost crushed his feet as he dropped the last slab outside. And as he slunk off he squinted furtively at his grandmother with the look of a beaten, scared and submissive animal.

Another half-hour dragged by Bécu, tired of ringing, had returned to his pipe outside. And La Grande stood there, mute and imperturbable, as if her presence alone was a sufficient mark of respect for the priest; while the latter, with mounting irritation, was running every few moments to the church-door and casting a baleful glance across the empty square towards the Buteau house.

'Why aren't you ringing the bell, Bécu?' he suddenly yelled. 'If they're not here in three minutes, I'm off!'

Then as the bell pealed out madly once more, making the aged ravens flock cawing out, the Buteaus and their guests were seen emerging one after another and crossing the square. Lise was in consternation, as the godmother had still not arrived; so they'd decided to walk slowly over to the church, giving her as much time as possible to turn up. But when they were still a hundred yards away, the Abbé began all at once hustling them along.

'Come on, now, are you trying to play a joke on me? I put myself out to suit you and all my thanks is to be kept waiting an hour! Hurry up now, hurry!'

He pushed them towards the baptistery, the mother with the

new-born child in her arms, the father, grandfather Fouan, uncle
Delhomme, aunt Fanny, and even M. Charles, a very dignified god-
father in his black frock-coat.

'Your reverence,' said Buteau, with an exaggeratedly humble
tone which masked a sly snigger of disrespect, 'if you'd only be
good enough to hang on a little bit longer.'

'What for?'

'Why, for the godmother, your reverence.'

The Abbé Godard flushed so darkly that he seemed near an
apoplectic fit. He stuttered out in a choked voice, 'Choose someone
else!'

They glanced around at one another. Delhomme and Fanny
shook their heads, and Old Fouan declared, 'It can't be done. It'd
be bad manners.'

'A thousand pardons, your reverence,' said M. Charles, who felt
that it was up to him as a well-bred person to explain matters. 'It's
our fault and yet it isn't. My wife wrote to say she'd definitely be
back this morning. She's in Chartres.'

The Abbé Godard started, and then, losing control, he threw
restraint to the winds.

'In Chartres! What, in Chartres! I'm sorry you're mixed up in
all this, Monsieur Charles. But it can't go on, I won't put up with
it a moment longer. . .'

And he burst out: 'No one here bothers how much he insults God
in my person. Every time I come to Rognes I receive a fresh blow.
Well, I've threatened you often enough, but to-day I'm leaving you
and never coming back. Tell that to your mayor; if you want a
priest find one and pay him. I'll speak to the bishop, I'll tell him
the sort of people you are, and I'm quite sure he'll approve my
step. Yes, we'll soon see who'll be penalised. You'll all live without
a priest, like beasts.'

They all listened to him, with curiosity but with the blank indifference of practical people who in their hearts no longer feared
his God of wrath and chastisement. What was the use of quaking
and prostrating themselves to buy a pardon when the very idea of
the devil made them smile nowadays and they had ceased believing
that wind, hail and thunder were directed by an avenging Lord?
The whole thing was a complete waste of time; there was much
more point in keeping on the right side of the Government police,
who were the people with the power.

Under the deferential show of gravity the Abbé saw that Buteau

222

was sniggering, La Grande scornful, and even Delhomme and Fouan were quite unmoved; the evasive indifference of their faces completed the rupture.

'I know quite well that your cows have more religion than you have,' he said. 'Good-bye, you can dip your barbarian child in the pond and baptise it.'

He rushed away to tear off his surplice, came back through the church and departed in such a whirl of wrath that the christening party, left in the lurch, had not even a chance to get a word in edgeways, but stood gaping and round-eyed.

The worst of it all was that at this very moment, as the Abbé was hurrying off down Macqueron's new road, they saw a carriage coming along the highway, with Madame Charles and Elodie in it. The lady explained that she had stopped at Châteaudun to give her little granddaughter a kiss, and that she'd been granted permission to bring the child home on a two days' holiday. She expressed the utmost regret for the delay and hadn't even driven to Rose Blanche to leave her trunk.

'We must catch the priest,' said Lise. 'Only dogs are left unchristened.'

Buteau chased off and in his turn was heard galloping down Macqueron's street. But the Abbé had had a good start. The father crossed the bridge and climbed the slope before he caught a glimpse of the priest turning the corner at the hilltop-turn of the road.

'Your reverence, your reverence!'

At last the priest turned and waited.

'What is it?'

'The godmother's arrived. You can't refuse a christening.'

For an instant the Abbé made no move. Then at the same furious pace he started back down the hill behind the peasant; and so, without another word passing between them, they re-entered the church. The ceremony was performed at breakneck speed. The priest abbreviated the Credo of the godparents, anointed the child, applied the salt and sprinkled the water—all in a fierce rush. Before they knew where they were he'd come to the signing of the register.

'Your reverence,' said Mme Charles, 'I've a box of sweetmeats for you, but it's still in my trunk.'

He nodded his thanks and went off, after turning back and repeating, 'Good-bye then. Good-bye this time.'

The Buteaus and their guests, breathless after such a hustle, watched him disappear round the corner of the square with his

223

black cassock flying. The whole village was out in the fields except for three urchins whose mouths watered for some sweets. Amid the deep silence only the ceaseless snorting of the steam-thresher could be heard in the distance.

As soon as the guests once more reached the Buteaus' house, where the carriage stood outside with the trunk, they all agreed to have a drop of something and then separate till supper-time. It was only four o'clock, and what on earth could they have done together until seven o'clock? Then, after the glasses and the two quart bottles of wine were laid out on the table, Mme Charles absolutely insisted on having her trunk brought in and on giving out her presents on the spot. She opened the trunk and took out a baby's dress and cap—somewhat belated in their bestowal—and then six boxes of sweetmeats, which she handed to the mother.

'Do they come from mama's sweetshop?' asked Elodie, who was watching.

For a moment Mme Charles was embarrassed. Then she calmly answered, 'No, my darling, your mother doesn't keep this kind.'

And turning towards Lise, she went on, 'Look, I thought of some linen for you too. There's nothing comes in so useful in a household as old linen. I asked my daughter and turned out all her cupboards.'

At the word linen the whole family gathered round: Françoise, La Grande, the Delhommes, even Old Fouan. Making a circle round the trunk, they watched the old lady unpack a large assortment of rags, boiled clean and white but emitting despite everything an ineradicable musk smell. First came some fine linen sheets, all in tatters, then women's chemises, torn up with the lace obviously ripped off.

Mme Charles unfolded them all, shook them out and explained, 'Of course, the sheets aren't new. They've been quite five years in use; and in that time, what with friction and rubbing, they get worn. Look here, there's a big hole in the middle of each, but the edges are still good and lots of things can be made up out of them.'

They all closely inspected the sheets and fingered them with nods of approval, especially the women. La Grande and Fanny were tight-lipped with suppressed envy. Buteau was laughing to himself, tormented by smutty jokes which he kept back for the sake of propriety; while Fouan and Delhomme, both extremely serious, showed their respect for linen. Linen was real wealth, second only to land.

'As for the chemises,' Mme Charles went on, unfolding them in their turn, 'look, they're hardly worn at all. Of course there are plenty of tears in them, they've been through a bad time; and they can't be mended—that'd make thick seams and wouldn't be very smart. So she prefers to throw them away for old linen. But they'll come in handy enough for you, Lise.'

'I'll wear them,' cried the peasant woman. 'It doesn't bother me to wear a mended chemise.'

'Me too,' said Buteau with a sly wink. 'I'd be very pleased if you'd make me some handkerchiefs out of them.'

This time they all giggled in undisguised merriment. Elodie, who had intently watched every single sheet and chemise, cried out, 'O, what a funny smell, how strong it is. Was all that linen mama's?'

Mme Charles did not hesitate a moment. 'Of course, my darling. I mean it's linen used by her shop-girls. Lots of shop-girls are needed in business, I can tell you.'

As soon as Lise had packed everything away in her wardrobe with Françoise's aid, they all clinked glasses at last and drank to the health of the baby whom the godmother had christened Laure, after herself. Then they forgot themselves for a moment and chatted; and M. Charles, seated on the trunk, was heard to question Mme Charles without even waiting to get her on his own, so great was his impatience to learn how things were going down there. He was still deeply interested, his thoughts kept turning back to the house that he had built up so energetically in his youth and now so sorely missed! The news was not good. True enough, their daughter Estelle had a good hand and head; but their son-in-law Vaucogne, that lazybones, didn't give her any decent support. He spent the whole day smoking and let everything get soiled and broken. The bedroom curtains were stained, the mirror in the small red drawing-room was cracked, all the water-jugs and basins were chipped, and he never did the least thing about it. Only a strong man's active arm could exact respect for furniture and furnishings! At every fresh detail of damage M. Charles gave a deep sigh, lifted and dropped his arms, and grew paler. One last grievance, whispered in a lower voice, finished him off.

'On top of it all, he goes upstairs with the woman in No. 5, a big fat one. . .'

'What are you saying?'

'Oh, I'm sure of it. I've seen them with my own eyes.'

M. Charles, who was shaking, clenched his fists in a twinge of

H   225

sharpened indignation. 'The wretch! Tiring out his employees and spoiling his own goods. That beats everything!'

Mme Charles signed him to be quiet, for Elodie was coming back from the yard where she had gone to look at the hens. A last quart bottle was drained, the trunk was lifted back into the cart, and the Charleses followed on foot as far as their house. All the others also went off to give a look round their own homes while they waited for the feast.

As soon as he was left alone, Buteau, unwilling to waste an afternoon, removed his jacket and set to work threshing in the paved corner of the yard; he needed a fresh sack of corn. But he grew tired of threshing alone and wanted the rhythm of the two flails beating one against the other to warm him up; so he called Françoise, who often helped him in this work with her strong loins and arms as firm-set as a lad's. Despite the slowness and wearisomeness of this primitive method of threshing, he had always refused to buy a machine, saying, like all the small landowners, that he preferred to thresh as much as he needed from day to day.

'Hey, Françoise, are you coming?'

Lise, busy over a veal stew with carrots, had put her sister to supervise a loin of roast pork; and she wanted to prevent the girl from going out. But Buteau, not in the best of tempers, threatened to thrash the pair of them.

'You cursed women, I'll smash your saucepans over your heads! What's the use of sweating for our bread when you'd fry the whole house and gobble it down with strangers!'

Françoise had already slipped on a workaday-dress to save her best frock from being spoilt; and she had to go out. In the yard she picked up a flail with long handle and cornelwood flap, fastened together with leather buckles. It was her own, polished by use, and bound tightly with string to prevent slipping. Grasping it in both hands, she swung it up over her head and brought it down on the sheaf so that the flap struck smartly with its full length. Without a pause she went on lifting the flail up high, turning it as if on a hinge and then bringing it down again, with the mechanical rhythmical swing of a blacksmith; while Buteau, facing her, swung in the same way, between her swings. Soon they warmed up to the work. The rhythm quickened and nothing could now be seen but the flying wooden flaps rebounding in turn and whirling behind their heads like birds tied by the feet.

After ten minutes Buteau gave a low cry. The flails stopped and he turned the sheaf over. Then the flails began afresh. After another ten minutes, he once more called for a halt and laid the sheaf open. It had to pass six times under the flails before the grain was completely separated from the ears and he could tie the straw up. Sheaf followed sheaf, and for two hours nothing was heard in the house but the regular tap-tap of the flails—while louder still, from the distance, came the prolonged snort of the steam-thresher.

Françoise's cheeks were now flushed, her wrists were swollen, and her whole body was burning; she seemed to give off a kind of fire-wave which quivered visibly in the air. She was breathing heavily through parted lips. Wisps of straw were clinging to the loose locks of her hair. And with each stroke, as she raised the flail, her right knee stretched out her skirt and her hips and breasts expanded, straining the cotton; the naked shape of her sturdily-built girl's body was roughly revealed in a single long contour. A button flew off her bodice. Buteau saw the rim of white flesh below the sunburn across her neck, a bulge of flesh which kept showing up at each swing of the arm in the powerful play of her shoulder-muscles. He seemed to grow excited more than ever at the sight; and the flails went on beating, the grain leaped and fell like hail under the panting tap-tap of the two threshers.

At a quarter to seven, as dusk was falling, Fouan and the Delhommes presented themselves.

'We must finish this,' Buteau shouted at them, without pausing. 'Keep it up, Françoise.'

She did not hesitate; she struck still harder in the excitement of the work and the clatter. And they were still at it when Jean in his turn arrived, having obtained permission to dine out. He felt a rush of jealousy and stood watching as though he had surprised them together, mated in this fiery work, striking one after the other in exact time and running with sweat, so overheated and disarranged that it looked more as if they were making love than threshing corn. Perhaps Françoise, who was letting herself go so wholeheartedly, had the same feeling; she suddenly stopped short in embarrassment. Then Buteau turned round and stood stockstill for an instant in surprise and anger.

Lise was just strolling out to greet Fouan and the Delhommes. Now she came down with them and exclaimed in her cheerful way, 'Gracious, I forgot to mention it. I saw him the other morning and asked him to look in to-night.'

Her husband's inflamed face glowered so ferociously that she added, by way of excusing herself, 'I've a notion, Father Fouan, that he has something to ask you.'

'To ask me?' said the old man.

Jean flushed and stammered, very much put out that the matter should be broached in such a way, so hastily, with everybody present. And anyhow Buteau interrupted him furiously; the smiling glance which his wife threw at Françoise had been enough to make everything clear to him.

'Trying to make us a laughing-stock? She's not for the likes of you, you ugly cuckoo!'

This brutal reception restored courage to Jean. He turned his back and addressed the old man.

'This is how it is, Father Fouan, it's all quite simple. You're Françoise's guardian, so it's you I must ask if I can have her, isn't that so? If she'll have me, I'd be very glad to have her. I'm asking her hand in marriage.'

Françoise, who was still holding her flail, dropped it in amazement. She ought to have expected it; but she'd never have thought that Jean would dare ask for her in such a way, all at once. Why hadn't he spoken to her first? She was flustered and couldn't tell whether her tremor came from hope or fear. Still vibrating from her work, with her bosom rising and falling inside her opened bodice, she stood there between the two men, flushed with such a rush of blood that they could feel the radiation from where they stood.

Buteau did not give Fouan time to reply. He went on with rising fury, 'What, you've got a nerve! An old man of thirty-three marrying a kid of eighteen! Only fifteen years between them! Isn't it disgusting? You expect a chicken, eh, you with that dirty hide of yours!'

Jean was beginning to lose his temper. 'What's it got to do with you if she likes me and I like her!'

He turned towards Françoise, so that she could declare herself. But she stood there startled and tense, without seeming to understand. She couldn't say no and she didn't say yes. Buteau was glaring at her so murderously that the yes stuck in her throat. If she got married he'd lose her and lose the land as well. The sudden realisation gave the last touch to his rage.

'Look here, dad! and you too, Delhomme, aren't you disgusted? Giving this child to this old brute who doesn't even come from these parts. God knows where he comes from, after roving round

228

here, there and everywhere? A carpenter who was a failure and turned peasant to cover up some dirty business, sure enough.'

All his hatred of the town worker burst out.

'And what then? If I like her and she likes me!' repeated Jean, who was holding himself in and who had vowed that out of decency he'd let her be the first to tell their story. 'Come on, Françoise, say something.'

'That's right,' cried Lise, carried away by the wish to see her sister married and out of the way, 'what have you got to do with it, Buteau, if they agree? She doesn't need your consent and it's only out of good nature that she hasn't told you to mind your own business. You're turning into a damned nuisance!'

Buteau saw that the thing would be agreed on if the girl spoke up. What he dreaded was that the marriage would be considered the right thing if Françoise's affair with Jean was known. At that moment La Grande came into the yard, followed by the Charleses who were returning with Elodie. He beckoned them near, not yet knowing what he was going to say. Then he had it, and with swollen face he bawled out, shaking his fists at his wife and his sister-in-law, 'The god-damned cows! Yes, both of them, cows, whores! Would you like to know something? I sleep with them both! That's why they think they can bugger about with me! Yes, both of them, I tell you, the trollops!'

The Charleses received this volley of words full in their gaping faces. Mme Charles rushed forward as if to shield the listening Elodie with her body; then, pushing the child towards the vegetable garden, she screeched at the top of her voice, 'Come and see the lettuces, come and see the cabbages. O what beautiful cabbages!'

Buteau carried on, inventing details and describing how when one had had her share it was the other one's turn to get her bellyfull; and he set everything out in the crudest terms, venting a flood of filth in unutterably vicious words. Lise, in sheer astonishment at this sudden outburst, simply shrugged her shoulders, repeating, 'He's mad, it's the only explanation, he's gone mad.'

'Tell him he's lying!' Jean cried out to Françoise.

'Of course he's lying,' said the young girl calmly.

'O, so I'm lying?' retorted Buteau. 'O, and isn't it true that you asked for it at harvest-time in the hay? But now I'll give you what-for, the two of you, bitches that you are!'

This crazily bold stroke paralysed and stupefied Jean. Was it possible now for him to recount how he'd taken Françoise? He felt

229

it would be a dirty trick to do so, especially as she wouldn't help him out. Meanwhile the others, the Delhommes, Fouan, La Grande, all kept their mouths tight shut. They didn't seem surprised, they evidently thought that if the rascal did sleep with both the girls, he could do what he liked with them. When a man has his rights, he asserts them. From that moment Buteau felt he had won, in his undisputed strength of possession. He turned on Jean.

'And you, you stinker, take care you don't come and try to mess up my household again! And as a start, bugger off at once. Eh, you won't? Just you wait then, just you wait. . .'

He picked up his flail and swung the flap round. Jean only just had time to pick up the other flail, Françoise's, to defend himself. The others shouted and some of them tried to intervene; but the pair were so terrible that everyone recoiled. The long handles could strike several yards and the yard was soon left clear. The two fighters remained alone in the middle, some distance apart, widening the circles of their whirling sticks. They uttered no words more, but kept their teeth clenched. No sound was heard but the cracks of the wooden flaps at each stroke.

Buteau had struck first; and Jean, still stooping, would have had his head split open if he hadn't leapt backwards. He immediately stiffened his muscles, raised his flail and brought it cracking down just as if he were a thresher beating the grain. But the other man was also striking; the two flaps clashed and bent back on their straps like wounded birds in a wild flurry. Three times the same clash was repeated. Nothing could be seen but the sticks twisting and whistling through the air at the end of the long handles, only just averted in time from splitting the threatened skulls.

Delhomme and Fouan, all the same, were rushing forward, when the women uttered a shriek. Buteau had treacherously whipped his flail along the ground and, though the force of the blow was fortunately weakened, the flap had caught Jean's legs and tripped him up in the straw. Scrambling up again, Jean brandished his flail in a fury which his pain increased tenfold. The flap flew round in a wide circle and came down on the right when his adversary was expecting it from the left. A fraction of an inch closer and Buteau's skull would have been cracked open. Only his ear, however, was grazed. The slanting blow fell with its full force on his arm, which was sharply broken. The bone snapped with a noise like breaking glass.

'Murderer!' screamed Buteau. 'He's killed me!'

230

Jean, with haggard face and blood-suffused eyes, let his flail drop. He stared at them all for an instant, as if at a loss before the sudden twist of events; then he limped off with a fierce gesture of despair.

As he turned the corner of the house on his way towards the plain, he caught sight of La Trouille, who had been watching the battle over the garden hedge. She was still laughing to herself, having come along to prowl about the christening party to which neither her father nor herself had been invited. How Jésus-Christ would roar with laughter when he heard about the little family fête and his brother's broken limb! She went on wriggling as if someone was tickling her, and nearly tumbled over on her back, so intense was her delight.

'O, Corporal, what a whack!' she cried. 'The bone went crick-crack! O, it was funny!'

He gave no reply, but slowed down in dejection. And she followed him, whistling along the geese that she had brought as a good excuse for halting to listen behind walls. He returned mechanically to the steam-thresher, which was still chuffing away as the long day ended. He felt that he was done-for, that he'd never see the Buteaus again, that they'd never give him Françoise. How stupid it all was! Ten minutes had been enough to spoil everything—an unsought quarrel, an unlucky blow, at the very moment when his hopes had been so high. And now never again, never! The snorting of the machine echoed through the dusk like a great moan of misery.

Another clash rounded off the day. La Trouille's geese, as they were being led home, found themselves at the turn of the crossroads, confronted with old Saucisse's geese on their unguided way down to the village. The opposing ganders of each flock pulled up short, rested on one leg and turned their great yellow beaks towards one another; and all the beaks of either flock moved at the same moment on the same side. For a second the two flocks stood stone-still—like an armed reconnaissance, two patrols exchanging the password. Then one gander, with round and satisfied eyes, proceeded straight ahead while the other gander moved on to the left; each troop filed off behind its leader, going about its own affairs with the same waddling march.

FOURTH PART

I

AFTER May with its shearing and its sale of lambs, Soulas the shepherd had led the La Borderie sheep out of the farm. The flock amounted to nearly four hundred head as he herded it along with the aid of only the young swineherd Auguste and his two fierce dogs, Emperor and Massacre. Till August the flock grazed in the fallowlands, among clover and lucerne, or in the wasteland that bordered the roads; and barely three weeks had gone by since he turned them into the stubble-fields, as soon as harvest was over, in the last fiery days of September.

Now was the terrible season of the year. La Beauce was stripped and desolate; her naked fields lay without a speck of green. The scorching summer heat and the total lack of water had dried the soil till it cracked. All plant life withered away; nothing was left save the blots of dead grass and the hard bristles of the stubble, the strips indefinitely stretching on through the ravaged melancholy emptiness of the plain, as if a great fire had swept from one horizon to the other. A yellowish glow still seemed emitted by the soil, a dubious light, a livid gleam like storm-fires: everything showed yellow, a horribly dismal yellow, the baked earth, the bristly cut stalks, the country-roads rutted and disfigured by wheels. At the slightest puff of wind great dust-clouds arose, covering the banks and hedges ashily; and the blue sky, the brilliant sun over the scene of desolation, only added to its gloom.

That day there was a high wind, coming up in hot sudden gusts that brought heavy scudding clouds; and when the sun broke through, its rays were like red-hot irons biting into the skin. Since morning Soulas had been waiting for water from the farm for himself and his animals, as the stubble-field where he happened to be lay north of Rognes, well removed from any ponds. In the grazing space, between movable hurdles which were held fast by cross-staves stuck in the earth, the sheep, lying on their bellies, were breathing in short painful gasps; while the two dogs, stretched at full length outside the pens were also panting with lolling tongues. The shepherd, to secure a bit of shade, was sitting close against a

233

little hut raised on two wheels—a narrow box which served him as bed, wardrobe and pantry—and which he shoved along whenever he changed the grazing area. But at noon, as the sun was beating straight down, he rose and peered into the distance to find out if Auguste was coming back from the farm where he'd been sent to discover why the water-barrel hadn't turned up.

At last the little swineheard reappeared, 'They're on the way,' he shouted. 'There weren't any horses this morning.'

'You mutton-headed bastard, haven't you brought us a bottle of water?'

'No, I didn't think. I've had a drink, myself.'

Soulas hit out with his closed fist, which the boy dodged with a jump. The shepherd cursed but decided to eat without a drink, although he was nearly choking with thirst. Auguste, on his orders, warily fetched out of the hut some eight-days-old bread, some old walnuts and a dry cheese; and the pair of them began to eat. The dogs came to squat before them with keen bright eyes and had a crust thrown their way from time to time, so hard that they crunched it between their teeth as if it were a bone. For all his seventy years the shepherd managed as well with his gums as the boy with his teeth. His body was still straight when he stood up, as tough and knotty as a thornwood staff. The years had merely added more furrows to his face, like an old tree-trunk beneath the mat of his faded hair, now the colour of earth. The little swineherd didn't succeed in escaping his punishment—a whack which sent him sprawling into the hut as he was stowing away the remnants of the bread-and-cheese, forgetting to watch out.

'There, you damned son-of-a-bitch! Drink that while we're waiting.'

There was no sign of any relief before two o'clock came. The heat had increased and was unbearable whenever the wind suddenly dropped. After a calm, however, the wind again whipped up tiny whirlwinds of powdery soil like a kind of blinding stifling smoke that dreadfully intensified the tortures of thirst.

The shepherd waited on with his stoical, uncomplaining patience and at last let out a growl of satisfaction.

'Thank heaven, and not a bit too soon.'

Two carts had just shown up, hardly larger than a man's fist on the skyline of the plain. In the first cart, which Jean was driving, Soulas had distinguished a water barrel; while the second, driven by Tron, was loaded up with sacks of corn for a mill whose tall wooden frame stood out some five hundred yards distant. The second cart polted to a stop in the roadway and Tron accompanied Jean across the stubble-field to the grazing ground, on the excuse of helping with the barrel, but in fact for the chance of stopping work and chatting for a moment.

'What's the idea? D'you want us to die of the pip?' shouted the shepherd.

The sheep too had scented the water. They scrambled up in a rush, jostling against the hurdles, craning their heads out and plaintively bleating.

'Wait now, wait!' replied Jean. 'Here's what you need for a booze-up.'

The trough was quickly set into position and filled through a wooden spout. Some of the water spilled over, but the two dogs saw it wasn't wasted, lapping it up like mad, while the shepherd and the little swineherd, unable to wait, drank greedily out of the very trough. The whole flock huddled up, and no sound was to be heard but the trickle of the reviving water and the gurgle of the busy throats—men and animals all happily splashing and drenching themselves.

'And now,' said Soulas, restored to cheerfulness, 'I'd be glad if you'd give me a hand in shifting the pens.'

Jean and Tron agreed. The hurdles were continually shifted over the far-spreading stubble-fields, never halting more than two or three days in the same spot, staying just long enough for the sheep to crop any odd vegetation. The system had the extra advantage of manuring the earth, strip after strip. While the shepherd, helped by his two dogs, kept the sheep together, the two men and the boy pulled up the stakes and moved the hurdles some fifty yards further along; and once again they marked out a huge square into which the animals of their own accord rushed for shelter even before it was fully enclosed.

Despite his great age Soulas was already pushing the hut towards the new grazing ground. Then, glancing at Jean, he remarked, 'What's wrong with this fellow? Looks as if he was carrying the hearse of God Almighty.'

The young man sadly shook his head; he had been miserable ever since he felt sure that Françoise was lost, so the old man added, 'I smell a wench here, for sure. The cursed whores, they all ought to have their necks twisted.'

The gigantic Tron, with his simple handsome face, began laughing, 'The only man who says that is the man who's past it.'

'Past it, past it,' repeated the shepherd contemptuously. 'How can you tell? Have I ever had a try with you? As for you, my lad, there's one person you know well enough with whom it's safer to be past it—or you'll strike trouble for sure.'

The labourer blushed to his ears at this reference to his affair with Mme Jacqueline. Soulas had caught the pair one morning in the barn behind some sacks of oats. In his hatred for the ex-scullery-maid who treated her old companions so badly, he had finally decided to open his master's eyes; but no sooner had he begun than the farmer gave him such a fierce look that he had fallen silent again, resolved to hold his tongue unless La Cognette gave him no alternative by getting him dismissed. As a result the two of them lived in a state of war: he dreaded that he'd be turned adrift like a decrepit old beast-of-burden, and she held her hand till she felt strong enough to insist on Hourdequin dismissing the shepherd, to whom he was much attached. In all La Beauce there wasn't a shepherd as skilled at grazing a flock: he damaged nothing and wasted nothing, and his sheep cropped each field from one end to the other without leaving a single blade of grass.

The old man was gripped by the longing to talk which sometimes forces lonely folk to unburden their hearts. He went on, 'Now, take my bitch of a wife: if she hadn't drunk away all my brass as fast as I earned it, so that she killed herself in the end, I'd have bunked away from the farm so as not to see such beastly goings-on. Or take Cognette: she's one that's done more work with her bottom than with her hand, and it's her person, not her deserts, that have got her where she is now! Just think of the master letting her sleep in his dead wife's bed and even going so far as to eat alone with her as if she was his lawful wife! He ought to look out for her, she'll boot us all out as soon as she can, and the master too into the bargain! She's just a slut that's wallowed with every sort of swine!'

Tron's fists clenched tighter at each additional phrase. He was capable of surly rages which became frightening because of his giant strength. 'That's enough!' he bawled. 'If you were still a man I'd have knocked you down before now. She's got more decency in her little finger than you have in all your old carcass.'

Soulas merely sneered and shrugged his shoulders at the threat. He who never laughed gave an abrupt grating laugh, like the creak of a long-disused pulley.

'You fool you, you big booby. You're as stupid as she's crafty! O yes, she's got it under glass for you, that maidenhead of hers, eh? Why, I tell you the whole countryside has passed through her legs. I move about a lot, I've only got to use my eyes, and without trying I can't help seeing girls being put in the family way. But as for her, I can't count the times I've seen her poked. See here, she was hardly fourteen when old Mathias, a hunchback who's dead now, had her in the stable. Later on, when she was kneading dough one day, I saw her pushed down over the trough with Guillaume on her—the swincherd who's gone into the army. And every labourer who's ever come to the district has had her, any old way, on hay or sacks or the bare ground. And anyway there's no need to strain your eyes. If you want to talk the matter over, you've got the very chap there I saw once all out in the hayloft threading her needle.'

He guffawed again; and his sidelong look highly embarrassed Jean, who had been silently hunched up ever since Jacqueline's name was mentioned.

'No one had better try to touch her now!' growled Tron, shaken with the rage of a dog whose bone is being snatched away. 'I'll put him off his food, I will!'

Soulas stared a moment, surprised at his burst of animal jealousy. Then he relapsed into his normal incommunicative calm and concluded dryly, 'Well, it's your own business, lad.'

After Tron had gone back to the cart that he was driving to the mill, Jean remained a few more minutes with the shepherd, helping the old man to hammer down some of the stakes; and Soulas, seeing him so reserved and morose, at last began talking again.

'I hope it isn't La Cognette getting you down?'

The young fellow shook his head vigorously.

'So it's some other wench? Who is it then? I don't remember seeing you with anyone.'

Jean looked at old Soulas, considering that sometimes old people could give good advice on such matters. And he longed to unburden himself. So he brought out the whole story, how he had had Françoise and how he was in despair about ever having her again after his brawl with Buteau. At one time he had even been afraid of Buteau taking him to law on account of his broken arm, which still prevented him from doing any work though it was more than half re-knitted. But Buteau had probably thought it was always a bad job to let the law stick its nose into one's private concerns.

'You've given Françoise a tumble, then?' asked the shepherd.

237

'Once, yes.'

The old man reflected gravely, then pronounced judgment. 'You must go and tell Fouan about it. Perhaps he'll give her to you.'

Jean was astonished; he had never thought of so obvious a procedure. As soon as the new grazing ground was fixed up, he went off with the resolution of calling on Old Fouan that very evening. And as he faded into the distance in the back of his empty cart, Soulas resumed his everlasting watch with his thin upright figure cutting the flat expanse of the plain with a greyish stroke. The little swineherd was stretched out between the two dogs in the shade of the hut. The wind had suddenly fallen and the storm-clouds had rolled away eastward; the air was still extremely hot and the sun blazed in the sheer azure of the heavens.

That evening Jean left work an hour earlier than usual and went to Delhomme's to see Old Fouan before supper. As he walked down the hillside, he saw the two Delhommes in their vineyard stripping the leaves to expose the clusters to the light. The moon's last quarter had brought heavy rains and the grapes were ripening badly, so it was necessary to get all possible profit out of the last days of sun. As the old man wasn't there with the Delhommes, Jean hastened his pace, hoping for a chat with him alone, which he much preferred. The Delhomme house was at the far end of Rognes, over the bridge, a small farmhouse recently enlarged by some new barns and out-houses; the three sets of buildings were grouped irregularly, enclosing a fairly large yard, which was swept out every morning, and seemed to have even its manure-heaps laid out by rule.

'Good-day, Father Fouan!' Jean shouted from the road in rather unsteady tones.

The old man was sitting in the yard with a stick between his legs and his head bent. However, at a second shout, he lifted his eyes and after a moment recognised the speaker.

'Ah, it's you, Corporal. Coming to visit us?'

His greeting was so natural, so devoid of malice, that the young man went into the yard. But at first he did not dare raise the subject on his mind. His courage failed him at the thought of blurting out anyhow the tale of his tumble with Françoise. The two men chatted about the lovely weather and the good it'd do the grapes. Another week of sunshine and the wine would be fine. Then the young man put himself out to please the old man.

'You are a real gent, there isn't a landowner in the district as lucky as you are.'

'Yes, indeed.'

'And look at your children. Anyone'd have to go a long way to find better!'

'Yes, yes, but everyone has his own ways of doing things, you know.'

The old man's mood grew gloomier. Since he had lived with the Delhommes, Buteau had ceased paying any allowance, saying that he didn't want his sister to fatten herself on his money. Jésus-Christ had never given him a penny, and as for Delhomme, now that he was feeding and lodging the old man, he too had stopped all payments. But it wasn't the lack of pocket-money which worried the old man; for he received from M. Baillehache five hundred francs a year, exactly twelve francs fifty a month, the interest on the proceeds of the sale of his house. With that he was quite able to buy himself his little luxuries, a daily two-penn'orth of tobacco, a drop of brandy at Lengaigne's, a cup of coffee at Macqueron's—for Fanny, a very thrifty housekeeper, never produced coffee or brandy from her cupboard unless someone was ill. But in spite of this, even though he had enough money for any entertainments he wanted outside and though he went short of nothing in his daughter's house, the old man felt on edge there and seemed to live in perpetual peevishness.

'Ah yes, indeed,' Jean replied, unintentionally putting his finger on the open wound, 'when you live in someone else's house, you're not in your own home.'

'That's it, that's it, exactly!' repeated Fouan in a grumbling voice. Then he rose to his feet as if seized by a need to assert himself.

'Let's have a glass together. Perhaps I've the right to offer a glass of wine to a friend!'

But on the threshold he succumbed to fear. 'Wipe your feet, Corporal. You see, they make such a fuss about keeping the place tidy.'

Jean entered awkwardly, longing to make a clean breast of things before the Delhommes came in again. He was surprised by the neatness of the kitchen. The pans were gleaming, not a speck of dust dulled the furniture, the floor-boards were worn down with constant scrubbing. It was all as clean and cold as if nobody lived there. Near the fire damped-down with cinders, yesterday's cabbage-soup stood warming.

'Your health!' cried the old man, who had taken two glasses and a half-empty bottle from the sideboard.

His hand trembled a little as he drained his glass, out of fear at the step he had taken. He put the glass down with the air of a man who had dared all a man can dare, and suddenly exclaimed, 'Would you believe it, Fanny hasn't spoken to me since the day before yesterday, because I spat! Think of it! Doesn't everybody spit? Of course I spit when I want to spit. No, better clear out than be so nagged at!'

He poured himself another glass, delighted at finding someone ready to heed his complaints, and unburdened himself without letting Jean get a word in edgeways. The tale was wholly about trivial pricks, the wrath of an old man whose faults weren't tolerated, who was straitjacketed into habits other than those to which he was used. But serious ill-treatment or cruel impositions would not have afflicted him more. A comment repeated in too sharp a tone hit him as hard as a blow; and his daughter made matters worse by her extreme touchiness, the typical suspicious vanity of the honest peasant-woman, quick to take offence and harbour resentment at the slightest misunderstood word. Relations between father and daughter were becoming daily more and more strained. She who once, before the division of the property, had certainly been the best of his children, was now getting shrewish and was almost persecuting the poor old man; she kept following him about with her duster and broom, and found fault with everything he did as well as everything he didn't do. There was nothing much you could pick on, yet every moment was a torment which brought him in the end to tears in odd corners.

'You must make allowances,' Jean repeated after every complaint. 'With patience you can always get things cleared up.'

But Fouan, who had just lighted a candle, was carried away by his excitement. 'No, no, I've had enough of it. If only I'd known what I'd find here! I'd better have died the day I sold my house. What's more, they're very much mistaken if they think they can keep me here. I'd rather go and break stones on the road.'

He choked and had to sit down. Jean took advantage of the pause to put a word in at last.

'Look here, Father Fouan, I wanted to see you about that business, you know what. It's made me very sorry, but I had to defend myself, didn't I, when the other fellow attacked me? And what happened doesn't change the fact that I'd come to an agreement with Françoise. But now there's only you who can settle things. If you'd go to the Buteaus' house, you could explain how things are.

240

The old man had become serious. He wagged his chin and seemed hard put to it for a reply. Then the return of the Delhommes saved him the trouble. They did not seemed surprised to find Jean in their house and gave him their usual warm welcome. But Fanny at once caught sight of the bottle and two glasses on the table. She took them away and went to fetch a rag. Then she made her first remark to her father for forty-eight hours—in dry tones and without looking him in the face. 'Father, you know I won't have this sort of thing.'

Fouan stood up, trembling with anger at being rebuked before a stranger. 'What next? In the name of God, can't I even offer a glass of wine to a friend? Lock it up then, that precious wine of yours! I'll drink water.'

Fanny in her turn was upset, deeply vexed at such an accusation of meanness. She paled as she retorted. 'You can drink the house up and bust yourself if you like. But I won't have my table marked with the bottoms of your sticky glasses, just like an inn.'

Tears sprang to the old man's eyes. He had the last word.

'It'd be better with a little less cleaning-up and a little more feeling, my girl.'

Then, while she energetically wiped the table, he went and stood in front of the window, watching the dark night fall, and trying to hold down the misery that kept breaking out in shudders.

Delhomme had avoided a share in the incident, but his silence obviously supported his wife's firm and sensible attitude. He now would not let Jean go without another round of wine, which he poured into glasses brought by Fanny on plates. She began to defend her conduct calmly in a low voice.

'You've no idea what a trouble these old people are! They're full of whims and bad ways, and they'd rather die than put themselves right. The one in question isn't too bad, he isn't strong enough. But all the same I'd rather look after four cows than one old man.'

Jean and Delhomme nodded approvingly at her. But she was interrupted by the sudden entrance of Nénesse, dressed up in town-fashion in fancy coat and trousers bought ready-made at Lambourdieu's, with a small hat of hard felt on his head. He strutted about with an equivocal girlish air, with his blue eyes and pretty rounded face, his slender neck and shaven nape. He had always had a horror of the soil and was off next day to Chartres to take up a job in a restaurant where public dances were given. For a long time his parents had stood out against his abandonment of the land; but at

241

last his mother, coaxed over to his side, had persuaded his father to agree. And so, since morning, he had been on a farewell spree with his village pals.

For a moment he looked put out at finding a stranger in the room; then he plucked up courage, 'I say, mother, I'm going to treat them to a dinner at Macqueron's. I'll need some cash.'

Fanny gave him a hard look and her mouth opened to frame a refusal. But she was so vain that Jean's presence restrained her. Of course their son could spend twenty francs without beggaring them! So she retired from the room, stiff and silent.

'You've got someone with you, haven't you?' Delhomme asked his son.

He had caught sight of a shadow in the doorway. He came closer and recognised the boy who had stayed outside.

'O, it's Delphin. Come in, come in, my lad!'

Delphin ventured into the room, saluting those present and apologising. He wore a short coat and a blue blouse, as well as his big work-boots. He had no tie and his neck and his skin were already tanned from work in the open air.

'Well,' continued Delhomme, who thought very highly of the lad, 'are you going off to Chartres too, one of these days?'

Delphin opened his eyes very wide; then he violently exclaimed, 'Good God, no! I'd give up the ghost in a town!'

The father threw a sidelong glance at his son while Delphin came to his friend's rescue.

'It's all right for Nénesse to go there, he can dress up and play the cornet.'

Delhomme smiled, for his son's talent on the cornet filled him with pride. Fanny now returned with a handful of two-franc coins and slowly counted them out into Nénesse's palm. The coins were quite white from having been stuck away under a heap of wheat. She never trusted her money to her wardrobe; she hid it away in small sums in odd lairs all over the house, in corn, coal, sand; in consequence, whenever she paid any monies out the coins varied in colour—sometimes white, sometimes black or yellow.

'That'll just about do,' said Nénesse by way of thanks. 'Coming, Delphin?'

The two youngsters rushed off and their laughter was heard dying away in the distance.

Jean emptied his glass. He had noticed that Old Fouan, who had not turned round once during this scene, had left the window and gone out into the yard. He took his leave and came on the old man standing outside in the midst of the dark.

'Now, Father Fouan, will you go to the Buteaus and get Françoise for me? You're the master, you've only got to say the word.'

The old man, lost in the shadows, repeated in a jerky voice, 'I can't, I can't do it.'

Then he let loose his pent-up feelings. He was finished with the Delhommes, he would go away to-morrow morning to live with Buteau, who had offered to take him in. Even if his son beat him, it'd hurt less than being killed off by his daughter's pinpricks.

Exasperated at this new obstacle, Jean at last spoke out. 'I must tell you, Father Fouan, Françoise and I have lain together.'

The old peasant simply exclaimed, 'Ah!' Then, after a moment's reflection, 'Is the girl pregnant?'

Jean was certain that she couldn't be because he'd withdrawn; but he replied, 'You never know.'

'Then there's nothing to do but wait. If she's pregnant, we'll see.'

At that moment Fanny appeared in the doorway to call her father in for his soup. But he turned and shouted back.

'You can stuff your soup up your backside. I'm going to bed.'

And he went up to bed with an empty stomach, out of bitterness.

Jean walked slowly away from the farm in such torments of disappointment that he found himself on the plateau again without knowing how he got there. The night, with a dark blue sky riddled with stars, was close and hot. In the stifling air you could feel a new storm approaching from the distance where the reflections of lightning glittered to the east. As Jean raised his head he caught sight of hundreds of phosphorescent eyes shining like candles and turned towards his footfalls. It was the sheep in the pen alongside which he was passing. He heard the slow voice of old Soulas.

'And how did it go, lad?'

The dogs, sprawled on the ground, had not moved; they had scented a man from the farm. The little swineherd, driven from the hut by the heat, was asleep in a furrow. The shepherd stood solitary on the stripped plain, now drowned in darkness.

'Well, lad, is it settled?'

Without even stopping, Jean replied, 'He said that if the girl is pregnant, he'll see.'

He had already passed the pen when old Soulas's response reached him, sounding solemnly in the huge silence.

'That's fair, you must wait.'

Jean continued on his way. La Beauce stretched out all around him, crushed under a leaden slumber. The mute desolation could almost be felt, in the scorched stubble and the parched baked soil, in the smell of burning and the song of the crickets which rang like the crackling of embers among ashes. Nothing but the shadowy humps of ricks rose out of the melancholy bareness of the plain. Every twenty seconds or so, flashes of lightning streaked a violet furrow, swift and mournful, low on the horizon.

II

NEXT morning Fouan settled in with the Buteaus. The removal put nobody out. The old man had only a couple of bundles of clothes which he insisted on carrying himself in two journeys. The Delhommes tried in vain to extract an explanation. He went off without a word.

At Buteau's house he was given the big room on the ground floor behind the kitchen. It had never been used for anything except to store potatoes and beets for the cows. Its worst feature was that the only light came through a small window six or seven feet above ground, which made the place as gloomy as a cellar. And the bare beaten earthen floor, the piles of vegetables, the rubbish pushed into the corners, kept the room so damp that moisture trickled in yellow streaks down the walls' bare plaster. Besides, everything was left as it was, only one corner was cleared to make way for an iron bed, and a chair and a table of deal. The old man seemed delighted.

So Buteau had his triumph. Since Fouan had been with the Delhommes, he had been furious with jealousy; for he knew very well what was being said in Rognes: of course the Delhommes had no trouble in looking after their father, while the Buteaus, after all, didn't have a penny to spare. And so, in the first days, he forced a lot of food on the old man to fatten him up and prove that nobody starved in his house. Then, there were the five hundred francs coming in from the sale of the house, which the old man would be sure to leave to the person who looked after him. Moreover, Delhomme, no longer burdened with the old man, would doubtless begin to pay his part of the annual allowance, two hundred francs; and in fact he did so. Buteau was counting on this two hundred francs. He had calculated everything and flattered himself that he'd get the credit of being a dutiful son without spending a penny

of his own, while nursing the prospect of reaping a later reward—
to say nothing of the secret hoard which he still suspected the old
man of owning, though he could never be quite sure about it.

The move was a perfect honeymoon for Old Fouan. He was
fêted and shown round to the neighbours—didn't he look well set-
up? Could anyone say he was wasting away? The children, Laure
and Jules, were always scrambling all over him, keeping him busy
and gratifying him. But he was particularly happy at being permitted to indulge his old man's whims, to behave as he pleased in
the larger tolerance of the house. Though a careful and tidy house-
wife, Lise wasn't as finicky and touchy as Fanny. He could spit
anywhere, come and go as he wished, eat all the while if he felt
like it, according to the peasant's custom of never passing a loaf
without cutting off a thick slice, at the mercy of work-hours as he
is. Three months passed easily in this fashion, and December had
come. The terrible frosts froze the water in the jug at the foot of
his bed; but he made no complaints. Thaws brought the moisture
running down the walls like heavy rain, but he found it all quite
natural, it was the way he had always lived. As long as he had his
tobacco and coffee, and wasn't badgered, he said, he wouldn't call
the King his uncle.

Things began to go wrong, however, one morning when everyone thought he'd gone out and he went back into his room to fetch
his pipe. He found Buteau there trying to get Françoise down on
the potatoes. The girl, who was resisting dumbly and strenuously,
got up and left the room after taking the beets she had come to fetch
for her cows; and the old man, left facing his son, grew angry.

'You filthy swine, making a pass at the girl with your wife almost
at your elbow. And she didn't want you, I could see how she lashed
out with her legs.'

Buteau, still red-faced and short of breath, took the criticism
badly. 'Must you poke your nose into everything? Shut your blinkers
and put a lock on your mouth, or it'll be the worse for you.'

Since Lise's confinement and the fight with Jean, Buteau had
been once more hotly pursuing Françoise. He had waited till his
arm was strong, and now he pounced on her all over the house,
sure that if he once had her, she'd let him thereafter do as he liked
with her. What better way of preventing the marriage and keeping
hold of both girl and land? His two passions were fused, his resolute
determination not to let go anything he'd got hold of, his tenacious
possession of the land, his rabid lust sharpened by resistance. His

245

wife was getting enormously fat, a mountain of flesh, and she was still suckling Laure, who always seemed to be attached to one of her nipples; while his sister-in-law had the good smell of young flesh and her breasts were as supple and firm as the udders of a young heifer. Not that he wanted to turn up his nose at either woman; he could do with the brace—one soft of flesh and the other unyielding, each delectable in her own way. He was a cock quite capable of settling two hens and he dreamed of a pasha's life, petted, caressed and glutted with enjoyment. Why couldn't he marry the two of them, if they'd consent? That would be the best way of binding them all together in kindness and avoiding the division of the land, which affected him as painfully as the threat of a limb's amputation.

Henceforth, in the stable, in the kitchen, wherever they were left alone for a moment, the sudden attack and the defence as sudden went on. Buteau threw himself on Françoise and she repulsed him. The same short abortive struggle repeated itself. His hand went up under her skirt and clutched at her bare body, grabbing a handful of skin and hair, just as if she were a beast he was trying to mount. She, with teeth clenched and darkened eyes, forced him to let go by punching him hard right between the legs. No words were ever spoken, the only sound was the harsh breathing, a sort of stifled panting, the deadened sound of scuffling. He repressed a cry of pain while she pulled down her clothes and went limping away, her genitals pummeled and bruised, still feeling as if his five fingers were being jabbed into her. The struggle went on when Lise was near or even in the same room with her back turned as she arranged linen in the cupboard. It was as if his wife's presence excited him, assured of the girl's proud obstinate silence.

But quarrels had broken out since Old Fouan caught him among the potatoes. He had bluntly told Lise everything so that she should stop her husband from carrying on; and Lise, after yelling at the old man to mind his own business, had violently attacked her sister. It was her own fault if she led men on! All men were so many swine, and so she had only to expect what she got! That evening, however, she made such a scene with Buteau that she came out of their room next morning with her eyes blackened and bunged up, having got into the way of his fist during the argument. After that there was constant bickering between the three of them. There were always at least two trying to bite each other's heads off, husband

246

and wife, or sister-in-law and husband, or sister and sister, apart from the times when all three snapped at one another simultaneously.

Then it was that the deeply-hidden simmering hatred between Lise and Françoise became increasingly bitter. Their previous close affection turned into a seemingly inexplicable rancour, which made them clash from morning to night. At bottom the sole cause was this man, Buteau, who acted like a poisonous leaven. Françoise would have yielded long ago in the excited state set up by his assaults if her will had not reacted against the wish to succumb whenever he touched her. She inflicted harsh suffering on herself by an obstinate adhesion to her simple idea of what was right: to abandon nothing of herself and not to take anything of another's. Her anger sprang from the jealousy she felt towards her sister for having this man as her own. Françoise herself would have died rather than share him with anyone else. When he chased her with his clothes loose and his belly exposed, she spat furiously on his male nakedness and sent him back to his wife with her spit on him. She thus felt repressed desire eased, as if she were spitting in her sister's face, in her suffering contempt for the pleasure she couldn't share. Lise herself felt no jealousy; she had been quite certain that Buteau was merely bragging when he asserted the two girls were at his disposal. Not that she believed him incapable of the trick; but she was convinced that her sister was too proud to yield. The only grudge she had against Françoise was the way her refusal turned the house into a hell on earth. The larger she grew, the more she settled down in her fat, satisfied with life and merry with a rapacious egoism that gathered up all surrounding enjoyment. How could anyone go on brawling so madly, spoiling life for themselves and everyone else, when they had everything they needed for happiness! O that bitch of a girl! Her cursed character was what caused all the troubles.

Every evening as she went to bed she cried out to Buteau, 'She may be my sister, but if she doesn't stop annoying me, I'll have her thrown out!'

But that was an argument Buteau always failed to hear.

'What an idea, everyone'd blame us. To hell with you females! I swear I'll soak you both in the pond till you learn how to live quietly together!'

Two months went by in this way, and Lise, harassed and distrait, could have sugared her coffee twice, as she used to say, without finding it any the sweeter. She guessed when her sister had repulsed yet another of her husband's assaults because of his vicious temper; she now lived in continual dread of his failures, feeling anxious whenever she saw him sneak up behind Françoise's skirts, knowing that he would come back vilely irritated, smash everything in his way and make the whole household miserable. These days were a torture and she couldn't forgive the confoundedly obstinate girl for not doing something to make family-life run more smoothly.

One day a disastrous point was reached. Buteau had gone down to the cellar with Françoise to draw some cider and he came up in such a mess and such ungovernable anger that on the slightest pretext, just because his soup was too hot, he smashed his plate against the wall and rushed out after knocking Lise down with a blow that might have killed an ox.

Weeping and bleeding, she struggled to her feet with her cheek swelling out, and fell on her sister. 'You trollop! Go to bed with him and get it over! I've had enough of it and I'll run off if you go on being so obstinate, just to get me beaten!'

Françoise listened, whitefaced and horror-stricken.

'As true as God hears me, I'd prefer it! Perhaps he'd leave us in peace then!'

She collapsed into a chair, weeping and gasping; her whole fat body seemed to be melting and betrayed her collapse, her sole desire to be happy, even at the cost of sharing her husband. As long as she kept her half, she'd be none the worse off. People were stupid: married life wasn't at all like a loaf of bread which got smaller with every slice you had. Couldn't they come to some arrangement, draw close to one another so as to have harmony, and live like a proper family?

Choking with disgust, Françoise could only cry out angrily, 'You're filthier than he is!'

She too ran from the room, to sob her heart out in the cowshed where La Coliche watched her out of her great sad eyes. What embittered her was not so much the thing itself, but the way she had to accept it and surrender herself for the sake of peace in the house. If the man had been hers, she'd never had given up an inch of him—not that much! Her resentment against her sister turned into contempt, and she swore to let herself be flayed alive rather than yield now.

From that day forward her life became even harder to bear. She was turned into the house-drudge, the beast-of-burden that anyone can maltreat. She was reduced to the level of a slavey, burdened with all the heaviest chores, continually snarled at, jostled, beaten. Lise would not allow her a moment's rest, but forced her to rise before dawn and kept her up so late at night that the poor girl often dropped asleep without having enough strength left to undress. Buteau slyly tortured her with little familiarities, slapping her on the bottom, pinching her thighs, all kinds of brutal caresses that left her bleeding, with tears blurring her eyes, but still obdurately dumb. Buteau grinned; he found a certain satisfaction in seeing her almost swoon in the effort to suppress a scream at the shock of pain. Her body was bruised all over, striped with scratches and contusions. In her sister's presence, above all, she forced herself to check her trembling; she wanted to deny what was going on, as if to prove it wasn't true after all that those male fingers kept on rummaging her flesh. Sometimes, however, she was no complete mistress of her reactions and replied with a swinging blow. Then followed an open scrimmage: Buteau thrashed her, while Lise, under a show of separating them, belaboured them both with her heavy sabots. Little Laure and her brother Jules yelled at the tops of their voices. All the neighbouring dogs burst out barking, and the neighbours took to pitying Françoise. Poor child, she must have plenty of grit to stay in such a hell's-kitchen!

Her position, indeed was the wonder of Rognes. Why didn't she run away? The knowing ones shook their heads. She wasn't yet of age, she had to wait another eighteen months; to run away now and put herself in the wrong without being able to take her property with her—hell! she was right in thinking twice! If only her guardian, Old Fouan, had stood up for her. But he himself no longer felt quite on a holiday in his son's house. The fear of getting splashed with the mud held him aloof. And anyhow Françoise forbade him to interfere in her affairs, with the wild recklessness and pride of a girl who trusts nobody but herself.

Nowadays all the quarrels ended with the same insults. 'Bugger off then, bugger off!'

'Yes, that's just what you're hoping for, I was a fool before; I wanted to get away. Now you can murder me, but I'll stay. I'm waiting for my share, I want my land and the house, and I'll get them, yes, I'll have every stick and stone!'

In the first months Buteau's great fear had been that Françoise was pregnant by Jean. Since he had surprised them together in the corn, he had counted every day and watched her out of the corner of his eye, anxiously scanning her belly; for the advent of a child would have spoiled everything and made her marriage a necessity. She was not worried; she knew she couldn't be with child. But when she noticed his interest in her waist-line, she had a lot of fun in sticking her stomach out to make him think she was growing fatter. And when he grasped her now, she could feel him prodding her there, assessing her size with his gross fingers. She ended by saying defiantly, 'Yes, there's somebody in there! He's getting bigger!'

One morning she went so far as to fold up some towels and wrap them round her waist. But that almost led to murder in the evening. She was seized with panic at the fiendish glint in his eyes and realised that if she had really been carrying a baby, the brute would certainly have found some way of striking her so as to bring on an abortion. She stopped her jokes and let her stomach go flat again. But even so she once caught him in her room searching through her soiled linen so as to be quite sure.

'Why don't you get yourself one!' he said to her with a leer.

And she replied, pale and furious, 'If I don't, it's because I don't want to.'

That was true. She steadily persisted in refusing Jean. Buteau crowed none the less noisily in his triumph. And he began to insult the girl's lover. A proper weakling he must be, not worth spitting on. Why, he must be rotten to the core if he couldn't plant a kid! He might break people's arms by underhand tricks; but he hadn't got what it needs to stuff a girl with child! From this time onwards he pestered Françoise with remarks of this kind, and commenting on the leak in her copper-bottom.

When Jean heard what Buteau was saying about him, he threatened to go and break his jaw. He went on hovering round Françoise with pleas for her surrender, then everyone would see whether he could get a child, and a hefty one at that! His desire for her was now intensified by anger. But she always found some new excuse, in the revulsion she felt at the thought of starting things off again, with this fellow. She did not dislike him, she simply had no desire for him; and she must have been really devoid of desire for him since she still resisted when she fell into his arms behind a hedge, still flushed and angry from one of Buteau's assaults. O, the filthy swine! In a state of permanent excitement, she talked of nothing but the swine he was, till she suddenly cooled down as Jean tried to profit by her heat and take her. No, no, she cried out, she'd be ashamed to do it! One day, cornered, she told him that he must wait—till the night when they were married. This was the first time

250

she had committed herself; she had always previously avoided a definite reply when he asked her to be his wife. After that, it was taken as settled that he would marry her when she came of age, as soon as she controlled her property and was in a position to demand a settling of accounts. Jean was much impressed by this reasonable attitude; he counselled her to be patient and ceased to torment her except at those moments when he was carried away by an impulse to enjoy things while he had the chance. Françoise, relaxed and soothed by the vagueness of a surrender set so far in the future, simply took hold of his two hands to make him behave himself and looked at him with her pretty pleading eyes—the eyes of a sensitive woman who didn't want to risk having a child by anyone but her husband.

Though Buteau was now sure that she was not pregnant, he felt a fresh fear: that she might become pregnant if she went with Jean again. He still mistrusted the fellow and was very perturbed when the whole village told him how Jean had vowed to stuff Françoise up to the eyes, as no girl had ever been stuffed before. So he spied on her from morning to night, making her toil every minute of the day and keeping her close at hand under threat of a whipping, like a beast-of-burden that one fears to leave alone for a moment. She was then subject to a new kind of torture: she could sense her brother-in-law or her sister always at her rear, she couldn't even slip out to the manure-heap to relieve herself without being watched. At night she was locked in her room. One evening, after a quarrel, she even found a padlock on the shutter of her little window. But as she still managed to get away at moments, there were awful scenes on her return, interminable questions and sometimes even examinations, when the husband pinioned her by the shoulders while his wife half-undressed her to have a look. This treatment brought her nearer to Jean and she began to make appointments, delighted at thwarting her jailers. She might even have let Jean have his way if she'd felt Buteau and Lise were still spying on her. At all events, she definitely committed herself. She swore to him by all that she held most sacred that Buteau had lied in claiming that he slept with both sisters; he had only said it to make himself out the cock of the castle and to force into being a state of affairs which just didn't exist. Jean had been previously tormented with uncertainty, accepting Buteau's claim as possible and natural enough; but now he showed much relief. On parting they kissed like two good friends; and from that moment the girl treated Jean as her confidant and adviser, trying to see him at the least opportunity and undertaking nothing without his approval. He never touched her now, but treated her like a comrade with the same interests as his own.

Every time that she now ran to join him behind a wall, their conversation followed the same lines. She excitedly tore open her bodice or lifted her skirt. 'Look! that swine's pinched me again!'

Jean inspected the bruises and remained quite calm and impersonal.

'He'll have to pay for that; you ought to show it to the women who live near. Above all, don't try to revenge yourself. The courts will act for us when we're in a position to take legal action.'

'And my sister's hand in glove with him, really! Only yesterday, when he leapt on me, didn't she just stand watching instead of throwing a bucket of cold water over him from behind!'

'Your sister'll have plenty of trouble from the bastard yet. All that's to the good. If you don't want him, he can't force you, that's certain; and what does the rest matter? If we keep together, he's done for.'

Although Old Fouan tried to keep out of the whole thing, he was continually drawn into the uproars. No matter how he held his mouth shut, they dragged him in. If he walked out, on his return he always found the household upside down and his appearance was often the one thing needed to set the sparks flying again. So far he had not himself directly suffered; but now privations began; his food was doled out and his little luxuries withdrawn. He was no longer stuffed with food as in the early days; every time he cut himself a rather thick slice of bread, he came in for a round of abuse. What a bottomless pit he'd got for a belly! So the less a man did, the more he crammed himself, eh? He was spied on and his pockets emptied every quarter when he went to Cloyes to fetch his interest from M. Baillehache. Françoise went so far as to steal odd coppers from her sister in order to buy him tobacco; for she too was left without any money for herself. Further, since breaking a pane in the window, the old man was very uncomfortable in the damp room where he slept; the hole had merely been stuffed with straw to save the expense of a new pane of glass. O, children were monsters, without exception! He grumbled from morning to night and bitterly regretted having left the Delhommes, broken-hearted to find himself fallen from bad to worse. But he hid his feelings, only betraying them by involuntary outcries; for he knew that

Fanny had gone round saying, 'Dad will soon be on his knees begging us to take him back!' That settled things: the words lay across his life like a bar of iron that nothing could break. He'd rather die of hunger and rage with the Buteaus than humiliate himself in front of the Delhommes.

Then one day as he was walking back from Cloyes after receiving his money from the lawyer, he sat down to rest in a ditch. Jésus-Christ, who was on the prowl around the neighbourhood poking into rabbit-warrens, noticed the old man deeply absorbed as he busily counted a number of five-franc pieces in his handkerchief. Immediately crouching down and moving up along the slope, he noiselessly made his way till he was above his father. Lying in his vantage-point, he was surprised to see the old man carefully knotting up a large sum of money, perhaps as much as eighty francs. His eyes glistened and his wolfish teeth were bared in a silent grin. The image of the secret hoard immediately re-awoke in his mind. The old man obviously had secret investments and took advantage of the quarterly visits to M. Baillehache to collect his dividends. Jésus-Christ's first thought was to put on a tearful act and extort twenty francs. Then, as that seemed a bit paltry, a much bolder project took shape in his head, so he slid away as quietly as he had come, supple as a snake. As a result, Fouan, now upon the road once more, had not the slightest suspicion when he met his son a hundred yards or so further ahead; the fellow just happened, it seemed, to be making his way to Rognes. They sauntered along together, chatting. The father began grumbling bitterly about the Buteaus, heartless beasts, who were starving him to death; and the son, with his kind heart and his eyes full of tears, offered to rescue the old man from such wretches by taking him into his own place. Why not? He wouldn't be bored there, in his house they had fun from morning till night. La Trouille cooked for two, so she could cook for three. A damned good cook when she had the wherewithal!

Taken aback by the offer and vaguely feeling there was a flaw somewhere, Fouan refused. No, no, he was too old to flit about and change his way of living one year after another.

'All right, father, but I make my offer in all good faith and perhaps you'll think it over. Now you know there's no fear of ever being without a roof over your head. Come to the Château as soon as you're fed up with those dirty skunks.'

Then Jésus-Christ went off, perplexed and intrigued, wondering what the old man was doing with the income which he undeniably had. A lump of money like that coming in four times a year must add up to at least three hundred francs. If the old man didn't spend it, he must be hoarding it. The problem was to find the hiding-place. A tremendous treasure, obviously.

That day, a mild damp day of November, when Old Fouan reached the house, Buteau demanded the thirty-seven francs fifty centimes which he received every quarter from the proceeds of the sale of the house. It had been agreed that the old man should hand over the sum as well as the two hundred francs allowance from Delhomme. But this time, however, one of the five-franc pieces had got mixed in with the ones he knotted in his handkerchief; and when he turned out his pockets and found only thirty-two francs fifty, his son broke out in a fury, called him a dirty thief, and accused him of squandering the missing francs in drink and abominations. Dumbfounded, the old man clutched his handkerchief tightly in blind fear that it would be examined, stammered out his explanations, and swore by all he held holy that he must have lost the coin while blowing his nose. Once again the house was topsy-turvy till nightfall.

What had put Buteau in such a beastly temper was a glimpse he caught of Jean and Françoise scurrying behind a wall as he brought his harrow home. The girl, who had gone out on the pretext of getting grass for her cows, had not come back for fear of the scene which would greet her. Night was already falling, and every other minute Buteau went angrily out into the yard and even on to the road to see if the bitch was at last slinking back from her man. He swore at the top of his voice and poured out a torrent of obscenities without noticing Old Fouan, who was seated on the stone bench, cooling down after the quarrel and enjoying the soft warm air which made that sunny November like a spring month.

A pair of clogs came clattering up the slope and Françoise appeared bent forward under the weight of a huge bundle of grass, tied up in an old cloth. She was panting and sweating, half hidden under the burden.

'Your cursed tart!' shouted Buteau. 'So you think you can make a sucker of me, letting that fellow of yours turn you over for hours on end when there's jobs to be done at home.'

He knocked her over on the heap of grass, which had fallen down, and threw himself on top of her just as Lise in her turn emerged from the house to bawl at the girl.

'You bitch, too lazy to wipe yourself, just come here and get my boot up your backside! Haven't you any shame left?'

But Buteau had already got hold of the girl under her skirt. His outbreaks of rage always turned into sudden fits of lust. As he went on fumbling at her on the grass, he growled, in a smothered voice, his face empurpled and swollen with blood.

'You damned whore, now it's my turn inside! God's thunderbolt can fall, but I'm going up after the other fellow!'

A furious struggle began. Old Fouan could hardly distinguish the shapes in the darkness; but he certainly saw Lise stand there watching without the least attempt to interfere, while her husband, sprawling there and shoved from one side to the other, kept on pushing away in vain, and got his satisfaction as best he could, no matter where.

When it was finished, Françoise, with one last heave of her body, managed to tear herself free, breathless and stammering.

'Swine, swine, swine! You couldn't do it—you did just nothing. I don't care a damn for that! You'll never get what you want, never!'

She had the triumph. She picked up a handful of grass and wiped down her leg; her body trembled all over as if she herself felt some satisfaction in her successfully sustained refusal. With taunting bravado she flung the handful of grass down at her sister's feet.

'Here, this is yours. It's not your fault if I give it back to you!'

Lise was just silencing her with a slap on the mouth when Old Fouan left his bench and intervened, brandishing his stick, revolted at what he had seen.

'You filthy brutes, the two of you! Can't you leave the girl alone? There's been more than enough of this!'

Lights were showing in the neighbouring houses as people began to grow uneasy at the murderous noise. Buteau hurriedly drove his father and the girl into the kitchen where the light from a solitary candle showed Laure and Jules hiding terrified in a corner. Lise also came in, struck dumb by the old man's appearance out of the shadows. He turned to her and went on, 'You're too vile and too beastly. You were watching all the while, I saw you.'

Then Buteau, with all his might, smashed his fist down on the edge of the table.

'Silence! It's finished with. I'll do for the first who says another word.'

'And if I want to say some more, eh?' asked Fouan in a quivering voice. 'Will you do for me?'

'You as much as anyone else. You make me sick!'

Françoise bravely came between the two men.

'I beg you not to get mixed up in this, uncle. You've seen how well I can look after myself.'

But the old man pushed her aside. 'Leave me alone, it's nothing to do with you now. It's my affair.'

Lifting his stick, he went on, 'So you'll do me in, will you, you murderer! We'll see then. Perhaps I'll teach you a lesson.'

Buteau swiftly snatched the stick from him and threw it under the wardrobe. Then, sneering, with a vicious glint in his eyes, he planted himself right before Fouan and thrust his nose into the old man's face as he spoke.

'You can damn well give me a bit of peace. If you think I'm going to put up with your fancy ways, you're wrong! Just look at me and remember my name.'

Face to face, they stood silent for a moment, glaring ferociously: each was trying to cow the other with his glance. The son, since the division of the property, had grown bigger and stood squarely on his feet; his jaws seemed to protrude even further out of his bull-dog face with its narrow, retreating brow. On the other hand, the father, broken by his sixty years of hard work, had kept on shrinking; his stoop was worse; and he preserved none of his former features intact except his immense nose.

'Your name,' repeated Fouan. 'I know it only too well, I got you.'

Buteau guffawed. 'Well, you shouldn't have got me. But you said the right thing. Everyone's turn comes in time. I'm your own flesh and blood, and I don't like being played with. Now once again, leave me in peace or it'll be the worse for you!'

'For yourself, you mean. I never spoke to my father like that!'

'That's a bit stiff. You'd have murdered your father if he hadn't died first.'

'You stinking swine, that's a lie! And by God, you'll swallow your words this very minute!'

For the second time Françoise tried to intervene. Lise herself also made an effort; for she was desperately afraid of the new turn of things. But the two men thrust the women aside in their determined confrontation, breathing furiously into one another's faces, as the father's fierce despotic will clashed with his son's, inherited from him.

Fouan was attempting to regain his old authority as the all-powerful family-head; he wanted to get on top of things. For over half a century in days when he still held the property and the power with it, the family had trembled before him: wife, children and animals.

'Admit you've lied, you stinking swine, admit you've lied, or I'll make you jump to it, sure as that candle is giving us light!'

His threatening hand was raised with the gesture which once upon a time had made the whole family sink to the ground.

'Admit you're a liar!'

Buteau in his youth had lifted his elbow to shield himself at the mere wind of a blow and his teeth had chattered; now he merely shrugged his shoulders with an air of insolent contempt.

'Do you think you can scare me! That sort of thing was all right when you were the master.'

'I'm still the master. I'm your father.'

'Go on with you, you old joker, you're nothing at all. D'you mean that you still refuse to leave me in peace, eh?'

Seeing the old man's tremulous hand come down to deal a blow, he caught it in mid-air and held it, crushing it in his rough grasp.

'Blasted pigheaded fool that you are! Have we got to have a hell of a row before it enters your thick skull that nobody cares a damn for you now! What are you good for? You cost money to keep, that's all. When you've had your day and passed your land over, your job's to swallow your soup and leave other people in peace.'

He shook his father to stress the words; then, with a final shake, he flung him, trembling and staggering backwards, into a chair near the window. And Old Fouan remained there, half choking for a moment, beaten and humiliated by the final death of his old authority. He was at the end of his tether. He counted for nothing since he had given up his property.

Profound silence held the room. Everyone stood motionless with loose hands. The children hardly dared breathe for fear of being slapped. Then work began again as if nothing had happened.

'What about the grass?' asked Lise. 'Is it going to be left out in the yard?'

'I'll go and put it under cover,' replied Françoise.

After she came back, they had supper; then the incorrigible Buteau thrust his hand into her open bodice after a flea which she said was biting her. She accepted his behaviour without any show of anger and even joked about it.

'No, no, it's somewhere where you'd get bitten.'

Fouan had not budged. He sat stiff and speechless in his dark corner. Two large tears went on rolling down his cheeks. He was remembering the evening when he had broken with the Delhommes; and to-night everything was happening all over again—the same humiliation at no longer being the master, the same fury which prevented him from joining in the meal. They had called him three times, but he refused to eat his helping. Suddenly he rose and went off to his bedroom. Next morning, as soon as it was light, he left the Buteaus and went to settle down with Jésus-Christ.

III

JÉSUS-CHRIST was a very windy fellow. Continual explosions blew through the house and livened things up. Damn it all, no one could ever be bored in that rascal's house, for he never let fly without blurting out some joke or other as well. He despised timid little squeaks, smothered between the cheeks, squirting out uneasily and ashamedly. He never emitted anything but frank detonations, substantial and ample as cannon-shots. Whenever he raised his leg and settled himself with a comfortable and tactical motion, he called his daughter in tones of urgent command, with a grave expression on his face:

'La Trouille, hurry, for God's sake!'

She rushed up and the blast went off pointblank with such a vibrating energy that she gave a jump.

'Run after it. Get hold of it between your teeth and see if there's any knots in it!'

At other times, as soon as she reached him he would give her his hand. 'Pull hard, draggle-tail! Make it go off with a bang!'

Then when the explosion occurred with the roar and splurge of a tightly-jammed charge, 'Ah, that was a hard one, thanks all the same.'

At other times again, he raised an imaginary gun to his shoulder and took a long and careful sight; then after the shot was fired, he shouted, 'Find it out now, retrieve it, you lazy bitch!'

La Trouille choked and fell over on her backside with laughter. The joke never palled; in fact it was funnier every time. It made no difference that she knew the game inside-out and awaited the thunderous blast that was to round it off, he always transported her with the vivid comedy of his rowdy act. O, what a joker she had for a father! Sometimes he talked of a lodger who never paid his rent and whom he had to throw out; sometimes he turned round with a grimace of surprise and bowed gravely as if the table had bidden him good morning; sometimes he had a whole posy of explosions, one for M. le Curé, one for M. le Maire, and another for the ladies. The fellow's belly, you'd have almost thought was a musical box from which he could extract any sound he liked; so much so that in the *Jolly Ploughman* at Cloyes they used to bet him: 'It's one on me if you let off six'; and he discharged six broadsides and won an overwhelming victory. He had gained quite a name with his knack and La Trouille was extremely proud of it. As soon as he stuck out his behind, she began laughing and wriggling in anticipation; and she was unflagging in her admiration for his prowess, gripped by the mingled fear and affection he inspired in her.

On the very evening when Old Fouan moved into the Château, as people called the old cellar where the poacher had buried himself, at the very first meal served by the girl, who stood behind her father and grandfather like a respectful servant, the jollifications were launched with loud eruptions. The old man had contributed five francs, and a tempting smell rose from the kidney-beans and the veal and onions which the young girl was an adept at cooking in a mouth-watering way. As she brought in the beans she almost dropped the dish in her fits of helpless laughter, Jésus-Christ, before sitting down, let off three regular reports, full-blast.

'Gun-salute for the feast! Now we can set to.'

Then, bracing himself, he achieved a fourth, unique, tremendous and insulting.

'That's for those rotten Buteaus. Hope it'll choke them!'

Old Fouan, who had been very downcast since his arrival, let out a sudden chuckle. He nodded his head in approval. The ceremony put him at his ease, for he too had been famous in his time as a joker. In his house the children had been brought up to ignore the paternal bombardment going on all round. He leaned his elbows on the table and allowed a wave of relaxation to engulf him as he sat opposite that tall rascal of a Jésus-Christ who gazed at him with moist eyes and an air of childlike scoundrelly joviality.

'By God, dad, we're going to put up our feet and enjoy ourselves! You'll see my scheme. Trust me, I'll pull you up out of the bog. When you're eating dust along with the moles, how will you be any better off for having denied yourself a tit-bit up here?'

Uprooted from his life-long sobriety, and craving for forgetful-

259

ness, Old Fouan found himself replying, 'Aye, it's better to stuff everything into yourself than leave a scrap for others. Your health, my boy!'

La Trouille brought on the veal and onions. There was a moment's silence. Jésus-Christ, not wanting to let the conversation languish, let out a prolonged blast which went through the straw of his chair with the whining modulations of a human cry. He immediately turned to his daughter and solemnly enquired, 'What was that you said?'

She couldn't answer, she had to sit down and hold her sides. But what finished her off, after the veal and cheese, was the final relaxation of father and son when they began smoking and drinking the brandy set out on the table. Their mouths were sticky and their brains fuddled; all attempts at talking had ended.

Slowly Jésus-Christ tilted to one side, thundered, then looked at the door and shouted, 'Come in!'

Old Fouan took up the challenge. He had been feeling out of things for some time now. He regained something of his youth, lifted a buttock, and thundered in turn, replying, 'Here I come!'

The two men slapped each other's hands, slobbering and laughing cheek to cheek. They were enjoying themselves. The scene was altogether too magnificent for La Trouille, who had collapsed on the floor. So shaken was she with wild screams of laughter that she too let off an explosion—but a tiny one, soft and musical, like the thin note of a fife in comparison with the deep organ-notes of the two men.

Indignant and disgusted, Jésus-Christ rose and extended his arm in a gesture of tragic authority.

'Out of here, you filthy sow! Out of here, you stinkpot! By God, I'll teach you to show respect for your father and grandfather.'

He had never allowed her such a familiarity. The sport was reserved for grown-ups. He waved his hand in the air, pretending to be asphyxiated by the little flute-puff—his own, he said, only smelt of gunpowder. Then, as the culprit, very red in the face and agitated at her lapse, denied the act and struggled against dismissal he ejected her with a single shove.

'You dirty lump, go out and shake your skirt! And don't return for an hour, not till you've been properly aired.'

From that day began a life with no cares and with plenty of fun. The old man was put into the girl's room, one of the compartments made by cutting the old cellar in two with a wooden partition; the girl quite happily moved into a hole in the rock at the far end of the cellar. The local legend went that this hole led into immense underground caves blocked by landslides. The worst thing about this fox-hole of a Château was that it was getting more deeply buried every winter during the heavy rains which rushed down the steep slope of the hill, carrying earth and pebbles along. Even the old ruin would have been swept away, with its ancient foundations and rough repairs, if the lime-trees, planted over it centuries ago had not held things together with their weighty roots. However, when spring came round, the place was a retreat of delightful freshness, a little grotto lying hidden under a tangle of briars and hawthorns. The sweet-briar that climbed all over the window was starred with rosy flowers, and the door itself was curtained with wild honeysuckle, which had to be lifted like a curtain before one could enter.

Certainly not on every evening did La Trouille have beans and veal and onions to cook. Such a meal was served only when the old man had been induced to part with a five-franc piece. Jésus-Christ, without actually being tactful, never used force on the old man; but he played on his greed and his paternal feelings to get money out of him. They lived well in the first days of every month as soon as Fouan got his sixteen francs allowance from the Delhommes; and there were uproarious celebrations every quarter when the notary handed over his thirty-seven francs fifty dividend. At first, Fouan used to pay out in fifty centime coins, sticking to his old parsimonious habits and trying to spin his money out; but step by step he put himself under the thumb of his great scoundrel of a son, who flattered him and coaxed him with outrageous yarns, sometimes reducing him to tears, till he handed over two or three francs. He had taken to stuffing himself with food, saying you might as well enjoy what you were eating since it would all be eaten sooner or later. However, in justice to Jésus-Christ it must be admitted that he shared everything with the old fellow, and if he robbed him he also kept him amused. At first, when his belly was satisfied with fat living, he forgot all about the hoard and made no attempt to pry it out. His father was free to do as he liked as long as he paid for the junketing. It was only during the second half of the month, when the old man's pockets were empty, that he began to dream about the secret whereabouts of the money he had glimpsed: there it was and not a sou of it could be got at. He grumbled at La Trouille, who served nothing but potato cakes without butter; and as he pulled his belt in, he thought how stupid it was to go short for the sake of putting money in a hole. Some day he'd certainly have to dig it up and have a fling!

Still, even after lean days, as he stretched out his great hulking limbs, he struggled against irritations and was as jolly and hilarious as if he'd just made an excellent meal, restoring merriment by a cannonade of heavy artillery.

'That's for the turnips, La Trouille, that one! And that's for the butter, by God!'

Fouan wasn't much distressed even during the hard-put days at the end of the month. Father and daughter then scoured the countryside to keep the stockpot full; and the old man, drawn in, ended by playing his part as well. The first time he saw La Trouille bringing back a chicken she had fished up over a wall with a string, he angrily told her off. But the second time, when one morning she hid in a tree and dangled a meat-baited hook in the middle of a troop of ducks on a stroll, he couldn't stop laughing. One of the ducks suddenly darted forward and swallowed the whole contraption, meat, hook and thread; then it disappeared, jerked up aloft, before it could utter a single quack. Hardly the most honourable way of replenishing the larder; but the creatures who live in the open belong to those who can catch them, and provided you don't steal money, good God! you're honest enough. Thenceforth the old man grew absorbed in the marauding feats of the young tomboy. At times she carried out incredible coups, such as stealing a sack of potatoes and getting the owner to help her carry it, milking the cows at pasture into a bottle, or sinking the washerwomen's bundles to the bottom of the Aigre by loading them with stones and then going back at night to dive in and bring them up again. She was always to be seen on the roads, with her geese as the ready excuse for wandering round the countryside. Scouting for her chance, she sat on the edge of a ditch for hours with the air of a drowsy goosegirl concerned only with tending her flock. She even made use of her geese as watch-dogs; the gander hissed a warning at the untimely approach of someone who might surprise her at her work. She was now eighteen years old, and yet was scarcely larger than she had been at twelve; still as slight and supple as a hazel-branch, with her goat-like head, her green squinting eyes, her large mouth twisted to the left. Under her father's old blouses her small childish breasts had hardened without rounding out. She was a proper tomboy with no feeling for anything but her geese. She had no interest in men; but that did not prevent her, when she got larking about

262

with some urchin or other, from ending up on her back—just as a matter of course, because lads were made like that and it was so unimportant, anyway. She was lucky to be left to rapscallions of her own age; it would have been revolting if adult men, who found her unattractive, hadn't left her alone. In the words of her grandfather, who had been amused and then won over by her, apart from the fact that she stole too much and didn't care much for respectability, she was quite a jolly girl and less spoiled than might have been expected.

But what Fouan delighted in most of all was to accompany Jésus-Christ on his rambles and prowls across the fields. Every peasant, however law-abiding, is at heart a poacher; the old man was fascinated by the setting of snares, the laying of lines and all the devices of the primitive hunter used in this war of wits—a ceaseless battle waged against gamekeeper and policeman. As soon as the laced hats and the yellow belts of the police were seen emerging from a lane and threading their way across the corn-fields, the father and son, stretched out on the side of a bank, made a show of deep sleep; then the son quickly crawled on all fours along the ditch to lift his traps, while the father, with his honest aged face, kept an attentive eye on the receding belts and hats. The Aigre was full of splendid trout which could be sold for forty or fifty sous apiece to a dealer in Châteaudun; the drawback was that they were so crafty the poachers had to lie flat on their stomachs watching them for hours. They often pushed on as far as the Loir for the fine eels to be got from the muddy bed. For the days when his lines brought nothing in, Jésus-Christ had worked out a very handy method of catching fish, which was simply to clear the fish-preserves of the riverside gentry in the dark. But fishing was only a passing entertainment; his real passion was the hunting of game. He ravaged the countryside for miles around and no creature was too insignificant for his bag. He snared quail as well as partridges, starlings as well as larks. He rarely used a gun, for the report carried too far over flat country. Not a single covey of partridge rose from the clover or the lucerne without his knowledge, and he could tell exactly when and where the young birds, heavy with sleep and drenched with dew, could be easily caught by hand. He had perfected a way of setting limed twigs for larks and quails, and the stones he threw always reached their mark in the dense flight of starlings which the high autumn winds seemed to fetch along. For twenty years he had been exterminating the game of the district and now there was scarcely a rabbit to be glimpsed among the undergrowth on the banks of the Aigre, to the extreme annoyance of the huntsmen. Only the hares escaped him. They were anyhow few and far between, and such as there were went running safe over the open country where it was dangerous to follow. Ah, the few hares of La Borderie haunted his dreams and he even risked prison to knock one over now and again with a shot from his gun. When Fouan saw him take the gun he never went with him. It was crazy; he would certainly be nabbed some day.

And of course it happened. Farmer Hourdequin, enraged at the slaughter of his game, had issued Bécu the most stringent instructions; and the constable, perturbed at never having caught a single poacher, began to spend his nights in a haystack and keep systematic watch. One morning, at the blink of daybreak, a gunshot slashed right across his face and woke him up with a start. Jésus-Christ, who had been on the look-out behind the stack, had just killed a hare at almost point-blank range.

'So it's you, in God's name!' cried the rural constable, grabbing the gun which the poacher had leaned against the stack while picking up the hare. 'Ah, you dog, I ought to have guessed.'

At the inn they were boon companions; but in the fields it was dangerous for them to meet. One man was always on the point of arresting the second, who in his turn was worked up to wring the other's neck.

'What if it is? I shit on you! Give back my gun.'

Bécu was already sorry about his capture. Normally, as soon as he saw Jésus-Christ on his left, he turned of his own accord to the right. What was the good of making trouble with a friend? But this time he simply couldn't shut his eyes; his duty lay clear before him. And anyway a man caught red-handed ought at least to be polite.

'Your gun, you bastard! I'm keeping it and I'm going to take it to the mayor's office. Now don't you move and don't try any tricks, or I'll let you have the other barrel in your guts!'

Jésus-Christ, disarmed and furious, wavered on the edge of an assault. Then when he saw Bécu starting off towards the village, he followed him, with the hare still dangling from his hand. The two men covered a couple of miles without a word, now and then glaring ferociously at one another. Every moment a fight to the death seemed on the point of breaking out; and yet with each step they both were regretting more keenly the course of events. What a damned unlucky meeting!

264

As they passed behind the church, just a couple of paces from the Château, the poacher made a last effort.

'Look here, don't act the fool, old chap. Come and have a drink in my place.'

'No, I must make a report,' stubbornly replied the constable.

And he wouldn't be shifted, an old soldier who stuck strictly to the letter of his orders. However, after a while, he stopped and said, as the poacher grasped his arm to lead him down, 'If you've got paper and ink, we might. It doesn't matter a curse whether we get the report done at your house or anywhere else as long as it's drawn up.'

When Bécu reached Jésus-Christ's abode, the sun was just rising. Fouan, who was already smoking his pipe in the doorway, guessed what had happened and became very uneasy; the more so as it became clear that his worst suspicions were correct. Ink and an old rusty pen were dug out, and the constable, with his elbows sprawled wide over the table, began scowling and racking his brains for the right official phrases. Meanwhile La Trouille, at a word from her father, had produced three glasses and a quart of wine; and at the fifth line, Bécu, tired out and completely at sea in the complicated recital of facts, accepted a tumblerful. Then the atmosphere slowly but steadily grew less tense. A second bottle appeared, then a third. Two hours later, the three men were chatting in roaring friendly voices with their heads close together. They were blind-drunk and had completely forgotten the morning's episode.

'You damned cuckold!' shouted Jésus-Christ. 'You know I sleep with your wife.'

This was quite true. Since the day of the festival, he had tumbled La Bécu in any odd corner, treating her like an old piece who needed no respectful preliminaries. But Bécu, who was vicious in his drink, lost his temper. If he put up with things when he was sober, they got under his skin when he was drunk. He brandished an empty bottle, bawling, 'You God-damned swine!'

The bottle smashed against the wall, just missing Jésus-Christ, who sat there drooling with his blissful tipsy smile. To soothe the cuckold, they decided not to break up the party, but to eat the hare without delay. Whenever La Trouille cooked a jugged hare, the appetising smell was wafted to the far end of Rognes. They had a fine feast that lasted all day. They were all still at table sucking the bones as night came down. Two candles were lighted and still they sat on. Fouan dug out a couple of two-franc pieces and sent the girl off to buy a quart of brandy. Everyone else was asleep in the village, but they went on tippling. And Jésus-Christ, whose hand kept on groping round after a light for his pipe, came across the unfinished report which lay on a corner of the table blotched with wine and gravy.

'Ah yes, this must be finished!' he managed to get out, his belly shaking with drunken laughter.

He stared at the paper, trying to think up some practical joke, some trick to express his utter contempt for the report and the law. Suddenly he lifted one leg, slid the paper under his bottom with the writing upwards, and blurted on to it—a thick, heavy explosion, the sort that he used to say came from a thickly-loaded mortar.

'There, it's signed, stamped and sealed!'

Everyone, even Bécu, laughed uproariously. There wasn't a dull moment at the Château that night.

About this time Jésus-Christ made a friend. As he went to earth one evening in a ditch to avoid the police, he found it already occupied by another fellow also anxious to escape attention. They struck up a conversation. The other dodger was a pleasant chap, Leroi, known as Canon, a working carpenter who had left Paris about two years before after some upsetting little incidents, and who now preferred to live in the countryside, skipping from village to village, working a week here and a week there, and applying for a job at one farm or another when his employers got rid of him. At the present moment, jobs were scarce and he had taken to begging on the road, living on stolen vegetables and fruits, and glad enough to be allowed to doss down in a hay-rick. At a matter of fact, his looks were not exactly calculated to inspire confidence. His clothes were ragged; he himself was ugly and dirty, branded with all the signs of a life of hardship and vice; and at the sight of his thin pallid face with its scanty matted beard, the women banged their doors shut. Even worse was the horrible way he talked. He spoke of cutting the throats of the rich and going some fine day on a spree till he bust, with other men's wives and other men's wines. He dropped these threats in an ominous voice, clenching his fists and pouring out revolutionary phrases picked up in the slums of Paris—demands for social restitution couched in inflammatory language, which bewildered and terrified the peasants in their wild flow. For the past two years the farming folk had grown accustomed to seeing him loom up at dusk and ask for a corner in the straw where he might sleep; and when he sat down beside the fire, he curdled everyone's blood with his frightening words. Then next day he disappeared, only to turn up again a week later, at the same cheerless hour of dusk, with the same prophecies of ruin and death. As a result, he was now refused shelter everywhere, such were the terror and anger that followed in the wake of the sinister figure prowling round the countryside.

Jésus-Christ and Canon were straightaway on the best of terms. 'Ah, by God!' the former cried. 'How wrong I was in '48 not to cut every throat in Cloyes! Come along, old fellow, we must have a drink together.'

He took Canon to the Château and made him sleep there that night, overcome with ever greater respect and admiration the more he listened to his words. He looked up to Canon as a superior person who knew what he was talking about and who had plans for remaking the social order in one fell swoop. Two days later Canon went away. Then after two weeks he came back, disappearing again at daybreak. From that time onwards he frequently dropped into the Château, eating and sleeping as though he were at home, swearing each time he came that the rich would be swept away before three months were out. One night when the father was out poaching, he tried to seduce the daughter; but La Trouille, furious and flushed with shame, scratched and bit him so severely that he had to let her go. What did he take her for, the old beast? He told her she was a stupid muff.

Fouan didn't like Canon much more than the girl did. He described him as a loafer who wanted to smash things up and who'd end on the scaffold. When the wretch was in the house, the old man went into a sulk and preferred to go and smoke his pipe outside. Besides, a fresh trouble had cropped up to spoil things. He no longer celebrated so wholeheartedly with his son since a sharp disagreement had made bad blood between them. Jésus-Christ had previously sold his land, bit by bit, only to his brother Buteau and his brother-in-law Delhomme; and Fouan had always given the necessary signature without a word, content as long as the land remained in the family. But a problem had arisen about the last field, upon which the poacher had borrowed money. The mortgagee, who had not received a sou of the agreed interest, was threatening to put the field up for auction. M. Baillehache was consulted and had advised the immediate sale of the land; otherwise they'd be ruined by law-costs. But unfortunately Buteau and Delhomme were refusing to buy, enraged at the way the old man was letting himself be stripped by his rascally eldest son, and determined to give him no aid whatever as long as he lived in the Château. And now the field was to be sold by order of the authorities; writs and stamped documents were passing to and fro. It was the first piece of earth lost to the family. The old man was kept awake all night by the thought. That land, so long and ardently coveted by his father and his grandfather, that land so hardly won—that land possessed and guarded as jealously as one's own wife! To see it being consumed piecemeal by lawsuits, depreciating, passing into a stranger's hand, one of the neighbours' for half its real value! He shuddered with rage and was so broken-hearted that he sobbed like a child. O, what a swine was Jésus-Christ!

There were terrible scenes between father and son. The latter never said a word, but let the old man exhaust himself in reproaches and groanings, standing tragically erect and howling out his suffering.

'Aye, you're a murderer, you might as well take a knife, yes, and slice a piece of flesh off me. Such a fine field, there isn't a better one anywhere! Anything will grow in that field, you've only got to breathe on it! What a spineless miserable wretch you must be not to give up the ghost rather than let it pass to a stranger. God! to a stranger! The very thought makes me go faint all over. You've got no guts, you damned boozer. And all the trouble comes from your drinking the earth up, you damned useless good-timer, you scoundrel, you swine!'

Then, when the old man choked with rage and was collapsing with exhaustion, the son calmly answered.

'Really there's no sense, old chap, in tormenting yourself like this. You can whack me as much as you like if it relieves you; but you're not much of a philosopher, are you? And so what? You can't eat earth. If someone put a plate of earth in front of you, you'd pull a funny face. I borrowed on my land because that's my way; I like a crop of five-franc pieces. And then they'll sell it. But after all they sold my namesake, Jesus Christ. If we get a few crowns out of it all, we'll drink 'em up, and that's true wisdom all right. In God's name, time enough when you're dead to stick to a length of earth!'

On one point, however, father and son were fully agreed, and that was in hatred of Vimeux the bailiff, a shabby little fellow who was given the duties which his colleague at Cloyes shrank from carrying out and who had ventured to visit the Château with a formal notification of judgment. Vimeux was a fag-end of a man, extremely dirty: a red nose and a pair of bleary eyes peeping out of a tangle of yellow whiskers. He was always dressed like a gentleman, with top hat, frock-coat and black trousers; but each item of clothing was badly worn and stained. He was famous in the canton for the terrible beating-up he got from the peasants whenever he came out on his own to present writs or the like against them in some area remote from aid. Tales were widely told of sticks snapped across his shoulders, duckings in cow-ponds, a two-mile race with a pitch-fork held at his back to stimulate speed, by a mother and daughter after they'd pulled his trousers down.

When Vimeux called, Jésus-Christ was coming in with his gun; Old Fouan, smoking his pipe as he sat on a tree-trunk, growled to his son, 'See the disgrace you're bringing on our heads, you rogue!'

'Wait till you see!' the poacher muttered between his teeth.

Vimeux, noticing him and his gun, stopped some thirty paces off; the whole of his lamentable, black, dirty and correctly-attired person quaked with fear.

'Monsieur Jésus-Christ,' he said in a small shrill voice, 'I am here on the matter you know about. I'll put this down there. Good evening.'

He planted the official document on a stone and was rapidly retreating when the other shouted out.

'You damned ink-pisser, do you want me to teach you manners? Just you have the politeness to bring me that paper.'

And as the miserable creature stood rooted to the ground, terrified out of his wits and not daring to move forward or backwards, he took aim at him.

'I'll send you a bit of lead if you don't hurry. Come on, pick up your paper and bring it over here. Nearer, nearer, still nearer, you bloody coward, or I'll fire!'

Frozen pale with terror, the bailiff tottered on his short legs. He looked imploringly at Fouan. But the old man went on calmly smoking his pipe, withdrawn in his vehement hatred of the legal charges and the man who personified them in the eyes of the peasantry.

'Ah, there we are at last, it's not so bad. Give me your paper. No, not with the tips of your fingers as if you didn't want to part with it. Politely, for God's sake, and show some goodwill. There! that's the proper way, thanks.'

Vimeux, paralysed by the mockery of the towering scoundrel,

269

blinked as he awaited the threatening joke, the punch or blow which he felt sure was coming.

'Now you can turn round.'

He understood, refused to move, tensed his buttocks.

'Turn round, or I'll come and turn you myself.'

Vimeux saw that he'd have to submit. He turned sadly round and presented to view his poor little bottom as thin as a starving cat's. The poacher sprang forward vigorously and planted the toe of his boot just in the right spot with such force that the little man went flat on his face fully four yards away. He rose painfully to his feet and bolted in abject terror as he heard a further shout.

'Look out, I'm going to fire!'

Jésus-Christ's gun was at his shoulder. But he contented himself with raising his leg—and bang! he released a blurt with such a resounding crack that Vimeux, terrified at the detonation, once again fell flat. This time his black hat fell off and rolled away among the stones. He ran after it, snatched it up, then went dodging off faster than before. Behind him the shots continued—bang! bang! bang! without a pause: a perfect fusillade accompanied by shouts of laughter which completed his bewilderment. Bounding down the slope like a grasshopper, he was already a hundred yards distant, but Jésus-Christ's cannonade still echoed through the valley. Indeed the whole countryside reverberated and there was one last formidable blast as the bailiff, who from the distance now looked about the size of an ant, disappeared into Rognes. La Trouille, who had run out at the uproar, lay on the ground holding her stomach and clucking like a hen. Old Fouan had taken his pipe from his mouth so as to laugh more heartily. Ah, that devil of a Jésus-Christ, what a good-for-nothing, and yet what a funny chap when he liked.

The next week, however, the old man had to reach a decision about giving his signature in permission for the sale of the land. M. Baillehache had found a purchaser and it seemed wisest to follow his advice. It was settled that father and son should go to Cloyes on the third Saturday of September, on the eve of Saint Lubin's Day, one of the town's two festivals. The old man, who had the dividends on his hidden investments since July to collect, relied on taking advantage of the journey to give his son the slip during the festivities. They were to go and return on Shanks's pony.

As the pair were standing in front of the closed barrier at the level-crossing just outside Cloyes, they were joined by Buteau and Lise, who had driven up in their cart. At once a quarrel broke out between the two brothers, who hurled insults at one another until the barrier was lifted; and even when Buteau was carried off down the hill beyond by his horse, he still turned back, with his blouse puffed out by the wind, and shouted words of the kind better left unsaid.

'Go along with you, you shirker, I'm keeping your father!' roared Jésus-Christ, with all the force of his lungs, making a speaking-trumpet with his two hands.

In M. Baillehache's office in the Rue Grouaise, Fouan went through a very painful moment; all the more so as the office was chock-full with clients who had also taken advantage of the market-day, and he had to wait for two long hours. The situation kept reminding him of that Saturday when he had come here to decide on the division of property. Now it was obvious he'd have done better that day if he'd gone and hanged himself. When the lawyer finally received them and the time came for signing, the old man took out his spectacles and wiped them; but his watering eyes misted the lens and his hand trembled so much that they had to place his fingers on the right spot, where he then scrawled his name in a series of blots. The effort cost him so much that he was left sweating, dazed, shivering, staring round like a man after an operation, who has had his leg amputated and who still looks about for it. M. Baillehache delivered Jésus-Christ a severe lecture and showed the two men out, while expounding his ideas on the law. The life-time division of property was immoral, he insisted, and would one day certainly be declared illegal, otherwise it would override the whole system of inheritance.

Outside, in the Rue Grande, just at the entrance to the *Jolly Ploughman*, Fouan slipped away from Jésus-Christ in the middle of the tumultuous crowd. His son, however, with a quiet grin, helped him in his getaway, for he guessed what the old man's business was. And in effect Fouan made straight for the Rue Beaudonnière where M. Hardy, the tax-collector, lived in a bright little house with courtyards and garden. M. Hardy was a fat, red-faced jolly man with a well-combed black beard. He was greatly feared by the peasants who accused him of confusing and diddling them with his jargon. He received his clients in a narrow office, a room cut into two by a low railing, he staying on one side and his visitors on the other. Often he had a dozen or so visitors in the office all standing jammed together in a crowd. At this particular moment there was only Buteau, who had just come in.

Buteau could never make up his mind to pay his taxes straight down in a lump. When he received the demand-note in March, he was bad-tempered for a week. He denounced the land-tax, the poll-tax, the property-tax, the tax on doors and windows; but his fiercest wrath was turned on the extra centimes which, according to him, piled up every year. Then he waited till he was served with a free summons. That gained him a week. Next he paid a twelfth of the tax monthly when he went to market; and every month the same torture began all over again. He felt quite ill on the day before paying and took his money along as reluctantly as if he were taking his neck to the gallows. That damned government: it was just a way of taking everybody's money.

'So here you are!' exclaimed M. Hardy cheerfully. 'Just as well you've come, I was about to put you to the expense of a summons.'

'That'd've been the last straw,' grumbled Buteau. 'But I'm letting you know that I refuse to pay the extra six francs on the property-tax. I won't—it's daylight robbery!'

The tax-collector began to laugh.

'Whoa, every month the same refrain! I've already explained that your income must have been increased by the sowing of crops on the old pasture-field along the Aigre. We've got grounds for our figures, O yes we have!'

Buteau fought hard. So his income was increasing, was it? Yes, just like the field itself which used to be a couple of acres; but now the river had changed its course and bitten a great slice of earth out, and yet he was still forced to pay on the two acres, was that justice? M. Hardy coolly replied that he was not concerned with survey questions and that any tax changed would have to depend on changes in the survey. Under the pretext of explaining things, he dazed Buteau with statistics and technical phrases, not one of which could the listener comprehend. Then he ended with a sly smile, 'Anyhow, I don't give a damn—don't pay if you don't want to. My job is simply to set the bailiff on you.'

Scared and perplexed, Buteau swallowed his anger. When you're on the weaker side, you have to give way. All that happened was that his long-inherited hate was intensified by the fear he felt—his hate of the obscure and complicated authority which he felt weighing him down—the bureaucracy, the courts, the *bourgeoisie* who did no work, as he used to complain. Reluctantly he drew out his purse. His thick fingers trembled. He had received a large number of coppers in the market and he fingered every coin before placing it down in front of him. Three times he recounted the sum, paying

272

it all in coppers; and the sight of the great pile that he had to surrender gave him an additional heart-pang. With grieving eyes, he
stood watching the tax collector put the money away in the safe,
and at that moment Old Fouan came in.

The old man had not recognised his son from the back and was
filled with consternation when he turned round.

'How are you, Monsieur Hardy?' he stammered. 'I was just
passing and thought I would drop in to say good morning. It isn't
often we see one another these days.'

Buteau wasn't taken in for a moment. He said good-bye and
went out as if pressed for time; but five minutes later he pushed his
way in, saying he'd forgotten about some information he wanted—
just as the tax-collector was paying over the dividend due for the
quarter, seventy-five francs all in five-franc pieces. Buteau's eyes
glittered; but he refrained from looking at his father. He pretended
not to have seen the old man throw his handkerchief over the coins,
then fish them up as if he were using a cast-net, and stuff them
down into the bottom of his pocket. This time the two men left
together, Fouan was very upset and kept giving suspicious glances
sideways, while Buteau, in expansive mood, had suddenly resumed
his old affectionate tones. He wouldn't let the old man go, insisted
on taking him home in the cart and went along with him to the
Jolly Ploughman.

There they found Jésus-Christ with little Sabot from Brinqueville,
a vinedresser, another notorious joker, who, like his companion, had
enough wind to keep a windmill turning. Now, on meeting, they
had wagered ten quarts as to which of them could blow out the
larger number of candles. Excited and shouting with laughter, their
friends had retired with them into a back room. There a circle was
formed. One competitor was placed on the right and the other on
the left, with trousers down and bottom stuck out. The champions
then proceeded with putting out the candle again and again with a
single blast. At the moment the position was that Sabot had just
blown out his tenth; while Jésus-Christ, having once failed to produce enough wind, had scored only nine. He was extremely perturbed, since his reputation was at stake. Courage! was Rognes to
be beaten by Brinqueville? He blew as never forge-bellows had
blown. Nine! Ten! Eleven! Twelve! The drummer from Cloyes
who was re-lighting the candle, was himself almost blown over.
Sabot had painfully extinguished his tenth, and was now empty and
deflated, as Jésus-Christ in his triumph let off two more, shouting

to the drummer to set them on fire as a final touch of finesse. The drummer struck a light, and the gas burned yellow, with a level yellow flame the colour of gold, which floated up like the sun in its glory.

'By God! what a marvel he is. What guts! Pin the medal on his chest.'

The crowd of friends bellowed and laughed till they almost cracked their jaws. Admiration and envy sounded in their laughter for it certainly needed a man of solid build to carry so much wind and let it off just when he pleased. The next two hours were taken up in consuming the ten quarts and all the time no one talked of anything but the exploit.

As Jésus-Christ was fastening up his trousers again, Buteau gave him a friendly slap across the buttocks. Peace seemed restored by a victory which redounded so much to the family's credit. Lively as in the old days, Fouan told a story of his youth, of the time when the Cossacks were in La Beauce. Yes, a Cossack had gone to sleep on the banks of the Aigre with his mouth open and Fouan had let go full in his face so that the man was buried right up to his hair. The market was closing and they all went off home well-soaked.

So it came about that Buteau took both Fouan and Jésus-Christ home in his cart. Lise, who'd had a few words whispered in her ear by her husband, was on her best behaviour. The Buteaus no longer insulted Fouan, rather they fussed over him. But the elder son, who was sobering up, began to do some hard thinking. If the younger son was so amiable, the dog must have discovered the secret payments at the tax-collector's. But hold on—if he, rogue as he was, had so far had the decency to refrain from plundering the hoard, he wasn't going to be such a fool as to let it be returned to the other fellow's place. He determined to get the matter properly settled, tactfully and without any loss of temper, now that the family was on good terms again.

When they reached Rognes and the old man asked to be set down, both sons sprang out and rivalled each other in their show of respect and affection.

'Lean on me, father.'

'Give me your hand, father.'

They took hold of him and assisted him out of the cart. The old man, held between the two, stood startled, stricken to the heart by a conviction that his secret was known. His last doubt was dispelled.

'What's the matter with you both? Why are you so loving all of a sudden?'

Their respect was what terrified him. He'd have preferred their usual disrespectful selves. Just his damned luck! What miseries lay ahead for him now that they knew about his nest-egg! Deeply depressed, he returned to the Château.

It happened that Canon, who had not been round for the last two months, was seated on a stone waiting for Jésus-Christ. As soon as he saw him, he called out, 'I say, your girl's in Pouillard's wood with a man on top of her.'

The father seemed shattered by rage; blood rushed to his face. 'The damned bitch, disgracing me!'

He plucked down the big carter's whip from behind the door and went racing along the rocky slope towards the little wood. But La Trouille's geese kept watch like good watch-dogs whenever she was having a tumble. The gander immediately scented the father's approach and darted forward followed by the whole flock. With beating wings and outstretched neck, he broke into a prolonged threatening shrill hiss, while the geese, forming up into a battle-line, also thrust out their necks and held their great yellow beaks ready to snap. The whip cracked and a scurrying sound was heard under the bushes. La Trouille had taken the warning and slipped away.

Jésus-Christ, on hanging the whip up again, seemed overcome with a profoundly philosophical melancholy. Perhaps the unsubdued lewdness of his daughter made him full of pity for human passions, or perhaps it was simply reaction from the glory of his victory at Cloyes. He shook his head, the shaggy head of a thieving and drunken Christ.

'Bah!' he said to Canon. 'Want to know something? All that isn't worth a fart!'

And, easing up his buttock, he sent one ringing over the darkening valley, powerful and contemptuous, as if he wished to smash the earth.

IV

It was now early in October. The vintage season was about to begin, a wonderful week of tippling when families which usually were at daggers drawn became reconciled over a pot of new wine. For a whole week Rognes stank of grapes. Everyone swallowed so many that behind every hedge the women pulled up their petticoats and the men let down their trousers; pairs of lovers, their faces stained with juice, kissed each other full on the mouth among the vines. It was always rounded off with the men getting drunk and the girls getting pregnant.

On the morning after their return from Cloyes, Jésus-Christ began to search for the secret hoard. As the old man surely didn't carry the deed and his money about, he must have stuck them away in some hole. But although La Trouille helped him and they turned the house upside down, they found nothing, in spite of all their cunning and their nimble thieves'-fingers. But in the following week as the poacher by sheer chance took down from a shelf an old cracked pot which was no longer in use, he found in it, under some lentils, a bundle of papers carefully wrapped in a piece of gum-covered canvas from the crown of a hat. But as for the coins, there wasn't a single one. The money must be hidden somewhere else, and a sizeable pile it ought to be by now, as the old man hadn't spent anything for five years. The papers definitely represented three hundred francs a year in five per cent bonds. As Jésus-Christ counted and studied the script, he disturbed another piece of paper, stamped and covered with large handwriting. As he read it he was thunderstruck. Good God! So that was where the money was going!

It was almost unbelievable. Two weeks after dividing his property at the lawyer's office, Fouan had fallen sick from his perturbation at no longer owning anything, not even a handful of corn. He felt that he couldn't go on living like that; he'd soon have his very skin stripped off. Then it was that he had committed the folly, a folly like that of an old man in love, who spends his last pence in secretly sneaking back to the whore who deceived him. Fouan, for all the shrewdness of his early days, had allowed himself to become entangled by one of his friends, old Saucisse! The frantic ache for land must have got right into the marrow of his bones, as it does in all old peasants who have spent their lives making the earth conceive; he was so thoroughly possessed that he had signed an agreement with old Saucisse to pay him fifteen sous every day of life that he lived, and in exchange old Saucisse was to bequeath him at death an acre and a half of land. To make such an agreement at the age of seventy-six when Saucisse was ten years younger! The fact was that Saucisse had had the craftiness to take to his bed at the time; he coughed so loudly and seemed so near the edge of death that Fouan's wits were blunted by his hopes. He thought

276

himself the craftier man of the two and hurried to conclude the agreement. The whole thing went to prove that when a man has a fire in his tail, for a woman or a field, it's wiser to share a bed than sign an agreement; for the payment of the fifteen sous daily had been going on for five years, and the more Old Fouan paid, the more desperately he burned for the earth, the more he longed for it. Only think: he'd cut himself free from all his long years of toil; he had nothing to do but await a peaceful death while watching others work themselves to the bone for the ungrateful earth; and yet he had gone back to her so that she should finish him off! No, there's not much wisdom in men, young or old.

For a moment Jésus-Christ thought of stealing all he'd found, deed and securities. But his heart failed him. Such a theft would mean flight. It wasn't like taking money: you just swiped that and sat back waiting for more to be coined. He angrily replaced the papers under the lentils at the bottom of the pot; but his exasperation soon became so unbearable that he could not keep his mouth shut. The next day all Rognes knew about the Saucisse agreement, the fifteen sous a day for a piece of inferior land, which was certainly not worth three thousand francs. In five years Saucisse had received nearly fourteen hundred francs; and if he lived another five years, he'd both have the money and keep his field. Everyone poked fun at Old Fouan. All the same, he, whom everyone had ignored after he'd stripped himself to the skin, was once again nodded to and greeted since he was now known to have an income and own land.

His family in particular was turned upside down by the news. Fanny had been very chilly towards her father, offended at his departure to live with his worthless elder son instead of returning to her house; but she now brought him linen—some of Delhomme's old shirts. He, however, would not relent, and alluding to the words which still left a sting in his heart, 'Father'll come and beg us on his knees to take him back!' he met her with the greeting, 'So it's you who've come on your knees to get me back!' This cut her to the quick, and on arriving back home, she wept with shame and rage, in her proud peasant sensitivity which could be wounded by a look. Honest, hard-working, well-off, she had nevertheless quarrelled with almost everybody in the district. And Delhomme now had to promise to pay the allowance over to the old man; for Fanny swore she could never speak another word to him.

As for Buteau, he astonished everyone by turning up at the

277

Château one day, coming, so he said, to pay his father a little visit. Jésus-Christ sneered, brought out the brandy, and bade them all clink glasses. But his mockery turned to amazement when he saw his brother take out ten franc pieces and set them in a line on the table. 'Father, we must settle accounts,' Buteau said. 'Here's your last quarter's allowance.'

The damned cheat! He hadn't given his father a sou for years; he could only be trying to trick him into something when he once again showed him the colour of his money. But as soon as the old man's hand moved out for the allowance, Buteau thrust it aside and swept up the coins again.

'Hey, that's only to show you I've got the money! I'm going to keep it for you. Now you'll know where it is.'

Jésus-Christ began to see daylight and grew angry.

'Look here, you just want to lure father away!'

But Buteau made a joke of the whole thing. 'You're jealous? What if I take father one week, and you take him the next? Wouldn't that be the natural thing? Suppose you cut yourself in two, dad? Here's your health meanwhile!'

As he was leaving, he invited them to come along next day and take part in the vintaging. They'd be able to gorge themselves with grapes, as much as their stomachs could hold. Indeed he made himself so pleasant that the other two decided he was a shocking rascal, but none the less a very entertaining fellow, as long as you didn't trust him an inch. They went some way along the road with him, for the pleasure of his company.

Just as they reached the bottom of the hillside, they met M. and Mme Charles walking back to Roseblanche with Elodie after a stroll along the Aigre. All three were in mourning for Mme Estelle, as the girl's mother was called. She had died in July of overwork. Every time the grandmother came back from Chartres she talked of how her daughter was killing herself, working so hard to keep up the good name of the establishment in the Rue aux Juifs, with less and less help from her useless husband. M. Charles had been deeply moved by the funeral. He had not dared to take Elodie, to whom the news had been broken only after her mother had been buried three days. How his heart beat when, for the first time for years, he had seen No. 19 again, the house at the corner of the Rue de la Planche-aux-Carpes, with its yellow-washed façade and its closed green shutters, the house which had been his life's work, hung now with black drapery, the little door thrown open and the passageway blocked with the coffin standing between four tapers. He had been deeply touched by the way in which the whole neighbourhood shared his grief. The ceremony passed off really very well. When the coffin was brought out on to the pavement, all the women of the neighbourhood had crossed themselves. The funeral cortège moved to the church amid general mourning. The five women of the house were present in sombre clothes, looking most respectable, as was widely remarked that evening in Chartres. One of them even wept at the graveside. Indeed, from this aspect, M. Charles had every reason for satisfaction. But how he had suffered next day when he talked with his son-in-law Vaucogne and went all over the house! It was already shabbier; he could feel the lack of a strong male hand in control, and he noticed many laxities which he would never have permitted in his own time. He observed with approval however that the decorous behaviour of the five women at the funeral had created such a favourable impression that the establishment remained working all the week at full pressure. When he left No. 19, disturbed in spirit, he didn't hesitate to inform Hector that with poor Estelle no longer there to steer the business, it was up to him to reform himself and put his shoulder to the wheel if he didn't want to fritter away his daughter's fortune.

Buteau at once included the Charles family in his invitation to join in the vine harvest. But they declined because of their mourning. Their faces were gloomy and their movements deliberate. On being pressed, they gave in only to the extent of agreeing to taste the new wine.

'Just to distract this poor little girl of ours,' said Mme Charles. 'She's had so little to amuse her here since we took her away from school. But what choice did we have? She can't stay at school for ever.'

Elodie was listening with downcast eyes, blushing for no reason at all. She had grown very tall and thin, pale as a lily lurking in the shadows.

'And what are you going to do with this big girl?' asked Buteau.

The girl blushed more deeply while her grandmother replied, 'Heavens, we hardly know. She'll decide for herself; we leave her quite free.'

But Fouan had taken M. Charles aside and was asking him with great interest, 'Business going well?'

M. Charles shrugged his shoulders and his face grew depressed. 'Bah, only this morning I spoke with someone from Chartres. That's why we're so upset. The house is going downhill. The management is so bad that there's brawling in the corridors and some clients don't even pay any more!'

He folded his arms, took a deep breath and unburdened himself of the latest news which had been weighing on him since the morning, news which he simply hadn't been able to take in properly

'Would you believe it, the wretch has now begun going out to a café! A café! And there's one in his own house!'

'Must be off his head!' firmly exclaimed Jésus-Christ, who was listening.

They stopped talking. Mme Charles and Elodie were approaching Buteau. All three were discussing the dead woman and the girl was saying how sad she was at not having been able to kiss her poor mama good-bye. She added in her innocent way, 'But it seems she was taken ill so suddenly, and they were all so busy in the sweet-shop. . .'

'Yes, making sweets for a christening party,' Mme Charles hastily interjected, winking as she turned her head towards the others.

But not one of them even smiled. They all wagged their chins in expression of sympathy. And the young girl, looking down at a ring on her finger, kissed it with tears in her eyes.

'This is all I have of hers. Grandmother took it from her finger to give to me. She wore it for twenty years and I mean to keep it on all my life.'

It was an old wedding ring, of common heavy make, and now so worn that nearly all its turnings had gone. Obviously the hand on which it had worn so thin had never baulked at any kind of work, but had always been on the go, in the wash-tub, making beds, polishing, cleaning, dusting, rummaging into every corner. There was indeed such a story wound around the ring, it had left specks of its gold in so many vanished scenes, that the men stared at it with dilated nostrils and could not speak.

'When you've worn it away as much as your mother did,' said M. Charles, choking with a burst of grief, 'you'll have truly earned a rest. If that ring could speak, it could teach you that money's earned by hard work and orderly ways.'

Elodie was once more holding the ring to her lips as she went.

'You know, I want you to use this ring,' went on Mme Charles, 'when you get married.'

But at that last word, at the mere mention of marriage, the weeping young girl was so deeply shocked and confused that she

280

threw herself wildly on her grandmother's bosom and hid her face. The old lady smilingly soothed her.

'Now, now, you mustn't be ashamed, my little pussycat. You must get used to the idea; there's nothing dreadful about it. You know I wouldn't mention anything wrong in front of you. Your cousin Buteau asked just now what we were going to do with you —well, we'll start by marrying you. O, really now, look up, don't chafe your face like that against my shawl. You'll inflame your cheeks.'

Then she added in a low tone, with an air of profound complacency, 'Isn't she well-bred? She doesn't know a thing.'

'Ah, if we hadn't this angel to comfort us,' M. Charles concluded, 'we'd really give way to our grief—because of what I've told you. On top of it all, my roses and pinks have done badly this year, and I've no idea what is going on in my aviary, all my birds are off colour. Only fishing gives me a little consolation: yesterday I caught a three-pound trout. You see, one must make an effort to enjoy oneself when one's in the country; that's why one's there.'

They took their leave, M. and Mme Charles repeating their promise to come and taste the new wine. Fouan, Buteau and Jésus-Christ walked on a few paces in silence, then the old man uttered their thoughts.

'Whoever marries that girl with the house will be a lucky young fellow.'

The Rognes drummer had given a roll on his drum to proclaim the opening of the vine harvest; and on Monday morning the whole countryside was in a flutter. Every dwelling had its vines and that day there wasn't a family that failed to turn up on the hillside running down to the Aigre. But what stirred up the excitement most was the fact that on the evening before, at nightfall, the new priest—the village had at last made up its mind to this luxury—had been set down outside the church. It had been so dark that no one could make him out distinctly. But the tongues didn't wag any the less—and the more so as the whole circumstance had something rather odd about it.

After his quarrel with the village of Rognes, the Abbé Godard had for months refused to set foot again in the place. He baptised, confessed and married those who went to him in Bazoches-le-Doyen. If anyone had died in Rognes, they would no doubt have withered away waiting for him; but this point was never settled, for no one presumed to die during the great controversy. He had declared to the Bishop that he'd rather be deprived of his living than conduct God's service in such a place of abomination, where he was so disrespectfully treated by a community of adulterers and drunkards, one and all damned, since they believed only in the devil. His Lordship appeared to agree with him and let things slide while he waited for the repentance of the rebellious flock. And so Rognes was without a priest; they had no Mass, no services whatsoever; they reverted to a heathen state. At first some of the villagers were a little surprised, but, good Lord, after all, there wasn't any change for the worse. They all got used to it; the rain didn't fall more often, the wind didn't blow any more strongly, not to mention the fact that the commune saved a lot of money. A priest didn't seem essential after all; their experience proved that the harvest didn't depreciate and no one died any more quickly; and so why not carry on without a priest for ever? Many people reasoned along these lines, not only irresponsibles like Lengaigne, but even common-sense men like Delhomme, who knew which side their bread was buttered. But there were also several who were very much put out at the lack of a priest. Not because they were more pious than the others; they didn't care a rap for a God who had lost the power to scare them, and who could not be taken seriously. But a village without a priest seemed to suggest they were too poor or too mean to pay for one; indeed, it made them look like the lowest of the low, absolute nonentities who wouldn't spend a sou on anything beyond the bare needs of life. The village of Magnolles, with only two hundred and eighty-three inhabitants, ten less than Rognes, had its own priest and threw this fact in its neighbours' faces with such provocative sneers that the inevitable result would be a free-fight. And finally, the women were very set in their ways; not one of them would have consented to be married or buried without a priest. The men themselves went to church at times, during the great festivals when everybody went. In short, there had always been priests, and, though the parishioners clung to the right to damn them, there would have to be one in Rognes.

The municipal council was naturally preoccupied with the question. Mayor Hourdequin, without being a regular churchgoer, upheld religion because of his authoritarian principles; but he made the mistake of not taking sides, in an attempt to be conciliatory. The village was poor, why burden it with the expenses which the repair of the presbytery would entail? Especially as he hoped to get the Abbé Godard to return. Now it so happened that Macqueron, the assessor, who had formerly been a determined enemy of the cloth, put himself at the head of the malcontents who felt humiliated at the lack of their own priest. From that moment Macqueron must have nourished a scheme for deposing the mayor and getting his place; further, it was rumoured that he had become the agent of M. Rochefontaine, the industrialist from Châteaudun, who was standing against M. de Chédeville in the forthcoming elections. As it happened, Hourdequin, tired and worn out by heavy farm worries, missed many of the meetings, leaving his assessor to take charge; and at the latter's persuasion the council voted the funds required for elevating the commune to the level of a parish. Since Macqueron, when the new road was built, had managed to get payment for his expropriated land despite his promise to make a free gift of it, the other councillors described him as a twister but paid him great respect. Only Lengaigne protested against a decision which he said would deliver the village up to the Jesuits. Bécu, too, grumbled when he was thrown out of the presbytery and its garden, and lodged in a miserable hut. For a whole month builders were at work repairing the plaster, putting in window-panes, and replacing the rotten tiles, and so it had come about that on the previous evening a priest had at last installed himself in the little house, newly whitewashed throughout.

As soon as dawn broke, carts started out for the hill-slope, each carrying four or five huge casks of the kind known as *gueulebées* which had one end left open. Women and girls travelled in the carts with their baskets while the men went on foot, whipping up the horses. The carts moved along in single file, with everyone chatting from cart to cart amid a tumult of shouts and laughter.

Lengaigne's cart followed immediately after Macqueron's and, in consequence, Flore and Coelina, who hadn't spoken to each other for six months, became friends again. Flore had La Bécu with her, and Coelina her daughter Berthe. At once the conversation turned to the new priest; and to the beat of horses' hooves the gossip rose noisily into the fresh morning air.

'I caught a glimpse as he was helping to get his luggage down.'
'Did you? What does he look like?'
'O, it was dark, but he seemed very tall and thin, with a long pale face; he looked rather poorly. About thirty perhaps. But with a kind face.'
'They say he comes from the Auvergne, from the mountains where everyone's buried in the snow two-thirds of the year.'

'How dreadful! It'll be a pleasant change here, then!'

'Indeed it will. You know his name is Madeleine?'

'No, Madeline.'

'Madeline, Madeleine . . . but that's not a man's name.'

'He might come and see us in the vineyards. Macqueron promised to bring him along.'

'O, heavens. We'll have to watch out for him!'

The carts stopped at the foot of the hillside, along the bank of the Aigre. And presently, in every little vineyard, the women were at their work between the rows of stakes, moving along bent down with their buttocks in the air, cutting off the bunches of grapes with their pruning-scissors and piling them up in their baskets. The men had all their time taken up with emptying the baskets into their panniers and carrying the grapes down to put them in the *gueule-bées*. As soon as all the casks in a cart were full, they were taken off and discharged into the vat, then brought back to be refilled.

The dew was so heavy that morning that the women's dresses were soon soaked through. Fortunately the weather was so fine that the sun quickly dried them again. There had been no rain for three weeks and the grapes, which everyone had despaired of during the damp summer, had suddenly ripened and sweetened. And that was why the lovely sunshine, unusually warm for the time of year, put everybody in high spirits, laughing and shouting, with bawdy remarks which made the girls giggle together.

'That Coelina!' remarked Flore to La Bécu, as she straightened up and looked over at Mme Macqueron in the neighbouring vineyard. 'She was so stuck-up about her daughter Berthe and her delicate skin, and look at the girl. She's getting all yellow and shrivelled.'

'Well, you know,' exclaimed La Bécu, 'when a girl's left unmarried . . . They made a mistake in not giving her to the wheelwright's son. And anyway from what I hear, the girl's ruined herself by bad habits.'

She bent down again with aching back, to cut more grapes, and then remarked, wriggling her hips, 'That doesn't seem to stop the schoolmaster hanging round her.'

'Good gracious,' cried Flore, 'that Lequeu would stick his nose into a dung-heap for a franc! Look, there he is coming to help them, the big boob.'

They then fell silent again. Victor, returned a fortnight earlier from his military service, was taking their baskets and emptying them into the pannier on Delphin's back. Lengaigne, the cunning snake, had hired Delphin for the vine harvest, pretending that he himself was obliged to stay in his shop. The lad, who had never been outside Rognes and was as firmly rooted in the land as a young oak, gaped with astonishment when he saw how Victor had been transformed into a rollicking swaggerer. Victor indeed took great pleasure in everyone's amazement; they hardly recognised him with his moustache and little beard, his devil-may-care manners and the forage-cap which he still affected. But the jolly fellow was much mistaken if he thought he was making his companion jealous. All his years of barrack-life, his tall stories about sprees, women and wine, went for nothing; the young peasant shook his head, horrified at heart and not in the least attracted. Not on your life! It was too high a price to pay, to leave your home-nook! He had already twice refused to go and make his fortune in Chartres at the restaurant where Nénesse was working.

'But you blasted bonehead, what about when you're called up?'

'Called up? Me? O, I'll draw a lucky number.'

Victor, with all his contempt, couldn't shake the fellow. What a great coward he was, for all his Cossack build! As they chatted, Victor went on emptying the baskets into the pannier without the fool showing any signs of sagging. Then, for fun and braggadocio, he pointed to Berthe.

'Say, has she grown anything since I went away?'

Delphin was shaken by a bellow of laughter; the peculiarity of Macqueron's daughter was still the best joke going among the youngsters.

'Well, I've never had a look. She might have grown something in the spring.'

'Well, she won't get me to water it,' concluded Victor, wrinkling his face in disgust. 'It can't be healthy; you'd surely catch a cold in that place without a wig.'

Delphin laughed so helplessly that the pannier wobbled on his back; but he moved down and emptied the grapes out, still choking with laughter.

In Macqueron's vineyard Berthe continued to act the lady, using tiny scissors instead of the pruning-scissors, in a flutter all the while about thorns and wasps, and expressing much concern because her thin shoes, drenched with dew, wouldn't get dry. She put up with Lequeu's attentions; for though she detested him, she felt flattered at being courted by the only educated man in the village. He even went so far as to take out his handkerchief and wipe her shoes. But an unexpected apparition caught their attention.

'Good God!' whispered Berthe, 'what a frock she's got on! I heard she arrived last night at the same time as the priest.'

It was Suzanne, Lengaigne's daughter, who had ventured on a sudden visit to her native village after three years of wild life in Paris. She had arrived the previous evening and stayed late in bed, letting her mother and brother go off without her to the vintaging. She wanted to join them later and take the peasants unawares as they worked, knocking them speechless with the splendour of her toilette. And she certainly succeeded, for she had put on a dress of so rich a blue that it killed the blue of the sky. Bathed by the brilliant sunshine as she stood against the yellow-green leaves of the vines, she looked a real swell—a tremendous success. She began straight away laughing and talking loudly, taking great bites at the grapes which she held high in the air before dropping them into her mouth. She joked with Delphin and Victor, who seemed very proud of her, and struck her mother and La Bécu dumb with such admiration that their hands were idle and their eyes moist. The peasants in vineyards nearby shared the sensation; they all stopped work and stared, finding it hard to recognise the girl—she had become so much more attractive. Once she had been a very plain girl, but now she looked truly delectable, doubtless because of the way she brought her little fair ringlets down over her face. The conclusion of the long inquisition was a general feeling of deference towards the girl whose plump limbs were so expensively fitted out and whose prosperity was indicated by her carefree demeanour.

Coelina, yellow with envy, bit her lips and burst out in front of her daughter and Lequeu.

'There's a swell for you! Flore keeps on telling anyone who'll listen that her daughter has servants and carriages of her own up in Paris. It's probably true. She'd have to earn plenty to deck herself out like that.'

'O, these idlers and wasters,' said Lequeu, who was trying to wheedle his way into her favour; 'we all know how they get their money.'

'What the hell does it matter how they get it!' Coelina went on bitterly. 'They've got it, that's the thing!'

Just at this moment, Suzanne, who had caught sight of Berthe, recognised her as one of her old friends among the Maids of the Virgin. She tripped over to her.

'Hullo, how are you?' she asked in her most polite tones. She stared straight into Berthe's face and noticed her faded complexion. At once she drew herself up in all her creamy opulence and repeated with a laugh, 'Everything going fine?'

'O yes, thank you,' replied Berthe, embarrassed and crushed.

The day belonged to the Lengaignes and proved a proper smack in the face for the Macquerons. Coelina furiously compared the sallow meagreness of her girl, whose face was already wrinkled, with the blooming looks of the fresh and rosy Lengaigne girl. Where was the justice of it all? Here was a girl who passed from one man to another, morning, noon and night, and still looked unspoiled and bright; and here was a young virtuous maiden, as worn out by her lonely bed as if she had been through three confinements! No, virtue wasn't its own reward; there was no point in staying at home and being a good girl.

The entire crowd of vintage-gatherers did honour to Suzanne. She kissed the children, who had grown ever so much bigger; she touched the old people's hearts by reminding them of the old days. Whatever you are, you are independent of people when you've made your fortune. And this girl was still good-hearted; she didn't spit on her family and she still came to see her old friends, now that she'd become rich.

At eleven o'clock everyone sat down to a meal of bread and cheese. It wasn't that they were hungry. They had been cramming themselves with grapes since dawn; their throats were sticky with sweet juices, their bellies swollen and rounded as barrels; and the juices went on bubbling inside, as good as a purge. Every few moments some girl or other had to run off behind a hedge. And of course, everyone else laughed and the men stood up with a shout to help them on their way. In short, the scene was one of general enjoyment, with a healthy enlivening coarseness.

As they were finishing off the bread and cheese, Macqueron appeared on the lower road with the Abbé Madeline. At once Suzanne was forgotten and all eyes were turned on the priest. Frankly, the first impression was not at all a pleasant one. As thin as a pike-staff, he looked as gloomy as if he'd come from reading the burial service over the Almighty. However, he bowed to every vineyard and murmured a few amiable words to everyone he met, so that the final opinion was that he was a very courteous person, quite amiable, and rather weak. They'd be able to do as they liked with such a person: far better have him than that cantankerous

Abbé Godard. As soon as he had passed, they began to make merry again. He reached the top of the hill and stayed there motionless looking across the flat grey immensity of La Beauce, overcome by a kind of fear and a desperate melancholy. His wide, clear mountaineer's eyes filled with tears as they searched for the narrow skyline of the Auvergne gorges.

As it happened, he was standing close to Buteau's vineyard. Lise and Françoise were cutting the grapes; and Jésus-Christ, who hadn't failed to bring his old father, was already drunk with the grapes he was stuffing down his gullet while making a show of emptying the baskets into the panniers. The grapes inside were fermenting so strenuously and distending him so widely that gas was struggling out of him at every aperture. And the presence of the priest seemed to excite him into unseemly behaviour.

'You ill-bred blighter!' Buteau shouted to him. 'At least wait till Monsieur le Curé has gone.'

But Jésus-Christ wouldn't accept the reprimand. He replied as a man who was quite capable of being polite when he liked: 'I'm not doing it to insult him, it's for my own pleasure.'

Old Fouan had taken his seat on the earth (to use his own phrase), tired but happy in the lovely weather and the excellent grape-harvest. He was chuckling to himself with a touch of malice, because La Grande had come over from her vineyard nearby to wish him good-day; even she had started paying him some respect again since she'd heard that he had an income. But she left him abruptly, noticing from afar that her grandson Hilarion was taking advantage of her absence to stuff himself fast with grapes. She fell on the lad with her stick—greedy pig, swallowing more grapes than he gathered!

'Ah, what an aunt! There's one woman who'll give people pleasure when she turns up her toes,' said Buteau, sitting down beside his father for a moment, ingratiatingly. 'Look at the way she takes advantage of that simpleton because he's as strong and as stupid as a donkey.'

He proceeded to abuse the Delhommes, who were working down below, on the edge of the road. They had the finest vineyard in the district, almost seven acres in a single plot; and it took at least ten workers to get in the crop. The carefully tended vines produced much finer bunches of grapes than did any of their neighbours'; and they were so wrapped up in their high opinion of themselves that they seemed to be gathering all on their own, the only ones who didn't pause to laugh at the sudden colics which sent the girls skipping off. Obviously they were frightened of breaking their legs if they walked up to greet their father, said Buteau; they took care not to notice his presence. That clumsy plodder of a Delhomme, a turnip-headed fool, for all his airs of being a hard worker and a righteous man; and that shrew Fanny who always lost her temper at the slightest thing, expecting everyone to worship her like a holy image—so cocksure that she never even noticed the dirty tricks she played on other people.

'The truth is, father,' Buteau went on, 'I've always been fond of you, while my brother and sister . . . . You know, I'm still sore that we got separated through some damn silly nonsense.'

He blamed everything on Françoise because her head had been turned by Jean. But she was behaving herself now; if she got uppish again, he was determined to cool her off in the pond.

'Come on, father, let bygones be bygones. Why not come back to me?'

Old Fouan remained discreetly silent. He had been waiting for the offer, which his younger son had at last got round to; but he didn't want to say yes or no, because you never know. Buteau went on, making sure that his brother was at the other end of the vineyard.

'Don't you agree? It's hardly proper for you to be in that ruffian's hovel. You might be found murdered there one day or another. Think about it. I'd feed you, lodge you and even pay you your allowance as well.'

The old man blinked with bewilderment. But as he still said nothing at all, his son tried to carry him off his feet.

'And your little luxuries, your coffee and brandy, and your four sous of tobacco, anything you want, in fact!'

The offers were too good and Fouan was scared. No doubt about it, things were getting unpleasant at Jésus-Christ's, but supposing all the old goings-on started again at Buteau's?

'We'll have to wait and see,' was all he said as he rose to his feet and broke off the interview.

The grape-gathering lasted until nightfall. In a continuous line the carts carried off the full barrels and brought them back empty. Among the vines, golden in the light of the setting sun, under the wide rosy sky, the coming-and-going of the baskets and crates became brisker, amid a sort of intoxication induced by the quantity of grapes conveyed to the vats. Suddenly Berthe had an accident.

She was taken so suddenly with colic that she didn't even have time to run off; her mother and Lequeu had to curtain her off with their bodies while she squatted among the stakes. The gatherers in the neighbouring vineyard noticed it all. Victor and Delphin wanted to fetch her some paper; but Flore and La Bécu held them back, declaring that there were limits beyond which only ill-bred people would go.

At last everyone set off for home. The Delhommes led the way. La Grande insisted on Hilarion helping the horse to drag her cart; and Lengaigne and Macqueron hobnobbed in a half-drunken state which blurred away their rivalry. What was most remarked, however, was the polite behaviour of Abbé Madeline and Suzanne to one another. He must have thought her a lady when he saw her wearing clothes so much finer than anyone else's; and so they walked along side by side, the Abbé showing her every attention while she assumed her most sugary manner and asked him what time he celebrated Mass on Sunday. Behind them same Jésus-Christ, who, carried away by his detestation of the cloth, resumed his disgusting tricks with all the playful obstinacy of a drunkard. Every fifth step he eased up his buttock and let off a blast. The trollop in front had to bite her lips to hold back her laughter while the priest affected not to hear; and so, with perfectly grave faces, to the accompaniment of such coarse music, they continued exchanging pious phrases as they followed the long procession of vintage-carts.

When at last they reached Rognes, Buteau and Old Fouan, ashamed, tried to get Jésus-Christ to keep quiet. But he went blithely on, repeating that his reverence would be quite wrong to take offence.

'In God's name! I tell you I'm not doing it for anyone else. It's for myself alone.'

Next week the Buteaus sent out invitations to the tasting of the new wine. The Charleses, Fouan, Jésus-Christ and four or five others were to come at seven in the evening for a leg of mutton, nuts and cheese—a proper spread. During the day, Buteau had barrelled his wine. There were six casks of it, full to the bung. Several of the neighbours were not so far advanced with their processing. One, still vintaging, had been hard at work without a stitch of clothes, treading his grapes; another, using a long bar,. was watching the fermentation and pressing down the layer of skins rising amid the bubbling must; a third, who owned a press, was giving a final squeeze to the grape-skins, then throwing them on to a smoking heap in his yard. Some stage or other of wine-making was to be met in every house; and out of the smoking vats, the streaming presses and overflowing casks, there rose fumes of wine all over Rognes, fumes strong enough by themselves to send the townsfolk reeling with drunkenness.

As Fouan left the Château that day, he had a presentiment which made him take his deeds from the lentil-pot. He deemed it would be as well to hide them on his person; for he thought he had seen Jésus-Christ and La Trouille looking up in the air with a queer glint in their eyes. The trio started off early and arrived at the Buteau house at the same time as the Charleses.

The full moon was so bright and clear that it lit up the earth like the sun itself; and as Fouan walked into the yard he noticed Gédéon the donkey in the outhouse with his head in a bucket. He wasn't in the least surprised to see the donkey loose, for the creature was as crafty as they're made, and knew the trick of lifting a latch with his lips; but the bucket puzzled him. He went up and recognised the bucket as one from the cellar which had been left full of wine out of the press, ready to top up the casks. The damned Gédéon was emptying it.

'Buteau, here, quick! Your donkey's up to mischief!'

Buteau appeared at the kitchen door.

'What's up?'

'Gédéon's cleared the bucket!'

Gédéon, with all the shouting around him, quietly finished sucking the liquid up. He had probably been tippling away for the last fifteen minutes, for the little bucket held at least four to five gallons. The whole lot had gone down his throat; and his belly was tight as a drum, near bursting-point. When at last he lifted his head, his sozzled nose was dripping and a red line ran across it just under his eyes, the high level mark of the wine.

'Oh, the bastard!' bawled Buteau as he ran up. 'Another of his little tricks! There's not another beast that's got half as much wickedness in him.'

Generally when Gédéon was being reprimanded for his vices, he put on a blank don't-care look and spread out his wide slanting ears. But this time, giddily losing all sense of decency, he positively sniggered and swayed his back to show everybody how shamelessly he was enjoying his debauch; and when his master jostled him, he staggered.

Fouan had to prop him up with his shoulder.

'The blasted pig is dead drunk!'

'Drunk as an ass: you can't say the proverb isn't apt,' Jésus-Christ interjected as he watched the creature with an admiring brotherly gaze. 'A whole bucketful: what a gullet!'

Buteau saw nothing to laugh about; and neither did Lise and Françoise, who came running up at the noise. First of all there was the wine lost; next, it wasn't so much the wine as the confusion into which their donkey's bad behaviour threw them in the presence of the Charles family. Both Monsieur and Madame were already somewhat tight-lipped on account of Elodie. And to cap it all, at that moment Suzanne and Berthe, who were strolling around together, happened to meet the Abbé Madeline just in front of the door; and there they stood, the three of them, just waiting to see what it was all about. A proper mess, with all these respectable people around, staring!

'Father, shove him along,' said Buteau in a low voice. 'We must get him into the stable quick.'

Fouan shoved. But Gédéon, quite content and comfortable where he was, refused to budge. There was no malice in his refusal; he was merely a good-humoured drunk, his eyes wet and mischievous, his mouth dribbling and pulled back in a grin. He let his weight hang heavy, reeled about with outspread legs, gathered his resistance afresh after each effort to hustle him on, and seemed to find the whole thing an immense joke. But when Buteau took a hand and pushed beside Fouan, the situation abruptly changed. The donkey went down on his rump, rolled over on his back, and began to bray vociferously as if he wanted to express his low opinion of all the people looking on at him.

'Ah, you filthy brute! You useless lump! I'll teach you to make yourself sick!' howled Buteau, starting to kick the beast hard.

Full of compassion, Jésus-Christ intervened. 'Hey, hey, can't you see he's drunk? How do you expect him to be reasonable? He won't understand a word you say. Better help him back to his stable.'

The Charleses had withdrawn to one side, deeply shocked at the extravagant and mannerless creature; and Elodie, blushing as hotly as if she had been forced to witness some obscene spectacle, turned her head away. The group in the doorway, the priest, Suzanne and Berthe, rebuked the scene by their scandalised silence. Several neighbours came up and made sneering comment at the tops of their voices. Lise and Françoise could have wept with shame.

Buteau, however, swallowed his anger, and endeavoured with the help of Jésus-Christ and Fouan to get the beast back on his feet. The task was by no means easy; for the brute, with the bucketful of wine washing about in his belly, seemed to weigh as much as an elephant. As soon as they pushed him up at one end, he collapsed at the other. The three men were getting exhausted by their efforts to lug him up while they supported him with their knees and elbows. But at last they got him straight up on his four hooves and had even drawn him a couple of steps forward, when, with a kind of backward curtsey, he toppled over again. And there was the whole yard to be crossed before they reached the stable. They'd never manage it. What was to be done?

'All the devils in hell!' swore the three men as they studied him from every angle, quite at a loss to know which end to start on.

Jésus-Christ had the idea of propping the donkey against the out- house wall; thence they could push him along, against the house- wall, till they came round to the stable. The plan succeeded very well at first, although the brute was getting badly chafed and scratched on the plaster. Unhappily the pain of his grazed hide became more than he could bear. All at once, breaking away from the hands which pressed him against the wall, he reared and pranced about.

Old Fouan was almost knocked down and the two brothers yelled: 'Stop him, stop him!'

In the dazzling brightness of the moon Gédéon was seen gallop- ing around the yard in frenzied zigzags, with his two great ears crazily flapping. The men had shaken up his stomach too much and he was feeling bad. A preliminary retch rasped him to a stand- still and he wobbled all over. He tried to get a fresh start, but he stood fixed on his stiffening legs. He stretched out his neck and a horrible quivering movement started deep in his flanks. Then, like a drunkard who strives hard to relieve himself with regular convul- sions, his head jerking forward with each effort, he puked as if he were human.

A huge roar of laughter burst out at the door from the crowd- ing peasants, while the Abbé Madeline, who had a weak stomach, turned pale; and Suzanne and Berthe, protesting indignantly, led him away between them. But the offended attitude of the Charleses was what most emphatically proclaimed that the exhibition of an ass in such a condition was a breach of all decorum, even of the merest politeness due to passers-by. Elodie, weeping in her dismay, flung her arms round her grandmother's neck, asking if the donkey was going to die. In vain M. Charles shouted, 'Stop it, stop it!' in the imperious voice of a master who was once used to obedience. The brute continued spewing, the yard was full of the gushing stream, a red torrent that flowed right down to the pond. Then the donkey slithered and fell wallowing in the mess, with his legs wide apart in such an improper pose that no human drunkard spread out across a roadway could have presented such a revolting sight to passers-by. The wretch seemed almost to be doing it all purposely to disgrace his masters. The scene had become intolerable. Lise and Françoise put their hands over their eyes and fled, taking refuge in the furthest corner of the house.

'That's enough now! Carry him off!'

Indeed there was nothing else to be done. Gédéon, after drowsily becoming as limp as a rag, was going to sleep. Buteau ran to fetch a stretcher and six men helped him to put the donkey on it. Gédéon was carried away with his legs dangling and his head wagging, already snoring with such abandon that he still seemed to be braying and telling the world that he didn't give a damn for it.

Naturally the mishap at first spoiled the feast. But soon the party cheered up. They ended indeed by celebrating the new wine so enthusiastically that by eleven o'clock they all reached the same state as the donkey. Every minute or so, somebody had to retire into the yard to relieve himself.

Old Fouan was in high spirits. Perhaps he had better after all come back and live with his younger son; Buteau's wine would be excellent this year. He had been obliged to leave the room in his turn and was thinking the matter over in the darkness of the night, when he heard Lise and Buteau, who had come out closely after him. They were squatting side by side along the hedge and quarrelling; Buteau was reprimanding his wife for not being affectionate enough to his father. Stupid goose! she ought to be wheedling him into coming back so that they could get their hands on his hoard. The old man, suddenly sober, felt his pocket to make sure that his papers had not been stolen. Then, when the farewell embraces were over and he found himself back in the Château again, he made up his mind not to move at any price. But that very night he saw something which froze his marrow: La Trouille, in her shift, went prowling round the room, fumbling in his trousers, his blouse and even his shoes. Jésus-Christ had obviously instructed his daughter to search and get hold of the hoard after finding that it had gone from the lentil-pot.

Fouan was too profoundly shaken by the sight to stay in bed. He rose and opened the window. The night was still white under the moon and the odour of wine was rising all over Rognes, mingled with the stench of muck all along the walls, which had been trodden down during the previous week—the whole powerful vintage-smell. What would happen to him? Where could he go? His poor money! He'd never let go of it again, he would sew it into his skin. Then as the wind blew the strong smell into his face, he remembered Gédéon. There was a constitution for you! A donkey could take ten times as much as a man and still survive. Well, there was nothing to be done! Robbed at his elder son's house, robbed at his younger's: there was no choice. The best thing was to stay at the Château, keep his eyes open, and wait. Every bone in his old body shuddered at the thought.

V

THE months slipped by. The winter passed, then the spring, and all the while the same old routine went on in Rognes; it took years for any effect of definite change to come about, and every morning the dreary life of toil began afresh. In July, however, under the heavy heat of the blazing sun, the forthcoming elections stirred up the village. This time, under the surface, a particularly weighty matter was at stake. Everyone kept on discussing it while waiting for candidates to turn up on their canvassing visits.

On the very morning when the arrival of M. Rochefontaine, the industrialist from Châteaudun, was announced, a terrible scene took place between Lise and Françoise in Buteau's house—an event that went to show how even under an appearance of quiet things could be deeply at work. The last links which held the two sisters together had been stretched to breaking-point and yet had always been renewed; but they were so weakened by daily quarrels that they finally snapped beyond all possibility of mending—and all because of a bit of foolishness which didn't seem enough to earn a beating for a cat.

That morning, as Françoise was bringing the cows home, she met Jean in front of the church and stopped for a moment to chat. Admittedly she stopped on purpose, standing just in front of the house with the express intention of exasperating the Buteaus. And so, as she entered the house, Lise shouted at her:

'When you want to meet your men, don't make a point of doing it under our window.'

Buteau, repairing his billhook, was there listening.

'My men!' Françoise echoed. 'I see them too often around this place—and you know it! There's one who'd have taken me, if I said the word, not under the window, but in your bed, the swine.'

That allusion to Buteau put Lise into a rage. For a long time she had had only one desire in life—and that was to throw her sister out and get a bit of peace at home, even if it meant the risk of losing half the house and land. This desire of hers had gained her blows from her husband; for he wasn't at all of her opinion. He was determined to carry on his scheming to the end and he still didn't despair of sleeping with the girl, as long as he and she had still got what it took. And Lise, exasperated at being no longer mistress in her own house, had developed a special kind of jealousy. She was still ready to let her husband tumble her younger sister for the sake of getting the thing over; but at the same time she was infuriated at the way he went on panting after the girl, whom she detested for her youth, her small firm breasts, her plump white arms under the rolled-up sleeves. If she could have held the candle for her ravishing, she'd have liked to watch him spoil all this charm, she'd even have banged away from above. She was not worried by the thought of sharing the man, but she suffered from an increasingly bitter rivalry, because her sister was more attractive than she was, and couldn't but provide more satisfaction.

'You bitch,' she screamed, 'it's you who lead him on! If you weren't always hanging round him, he wouldn't go running after your dirty backside. You keep on asking for it.'

Françoise blenched, appalled at this lie. She replied calmly with a cold anger.

'Right, that's enough. Wait two weeks and I won't be in your way any more, if that's what you want. Yes, in two weeks' time I'll be twenty-one and I'll take myself off.'

'So you want to be of age, do you? That's what you're plotting, ah, to make trouble for us! Well, you bitch, there's no two weeks about it, you can get out this instant. Out you go, bugger off!'

'Very well. Macqueron needs a hand. He'll take me on. Good evening.

Françoise went out, just like that. Not another word passed between them. Buteau threw down the billhook which he was sharpening, and ran up to make them friends again by slapping them both.

296

But he was too late; all he could do in his frenzy was to take a swipe at his wife and make her nose bleed. What damned women! The very thing he'd feared, the very thing he'd been struggling against for so long! The girl had run off, and a whole pack of awkward affairs would result! He saw everything slipping through his fingers, girl and land alike.

'I'll go straight over to Macqueron's this afternoon,' he roared. 'She's got to come back, even if I have to bring her back, booting her all the way.'

That Sunday there was great excitement at Macqueron's; for one of the candidates, M. Rochefontaine, the owner of engineering works at Châteaudun, was expected. In the previous session, M. de Chédeville had lost much support—some people blamed his obvious friendship for the Orléanists, while others told of his scandalising the Tuileries by an intrigue with the young wife of one of the ushers of the Chamber of Deputies, who was infatuated with him despite his age. Whatever the reason, the prefectorial patronage had been withdrawn from the retiring deputy and given to M. Rochefontaine, the previous opposition-candidate, whose workshops had been visited by a Minister. M. Rochefontaine had also written a pamphlet on Free Trade which had been favourably noticed by the Emperor. Piqued by the desertion, M. de Chédeville persisted in his candidature. He very much needed the position of deputy for the help it gave him to make a bit on the stock-exchange; the income from La Chamade was no longer sufficient, the farm being heavily mortgaged and half-ruined. And so it happened by a strange chance that the positions were reversed; the landowner had become the independent while the industrialist was the official candidate.

Hourdequin, though Mayor of Rognes, remained faithful to M. de Chédeville. He was determined to disregard any orders from the higher authorities and stood ready to give open battle if pushed into a corner. In the first place he felt it dishonest to veer like a weather-cock at the prefect's faintest breath; further, forced to choose between protectionist and free-trader, he had come to the conclusion that his interest lay with the former at such a time of deep agricultural depression. For some time his irritation over Jacqueline's misbehaviour, added to worries about his farm, had kept him from giving much time to his mayoral duties, and he had left his assessor Macqueron to attend to current affairs. In consequence, when his interest in the elections drew him to preside again over the council, he was completely taken aback at finding it in a state of revolt, of rigid hostility.

The position was the result of Macqueron's behind-the-scenes tactics, carried out with brutish cunning and now reaping their reward. That fellow, a peasant who had grown wealthy and fallen into habits of indolence, now slouched about, slovenly and unkempt, as a gentleman-of-leisure, and bored himself to death; he had gradually acquired an ambition to reach the mayoralty and now made that ambition his sole interest in life. He had begun to undermine Hourdequin's position, making use of the lively hatred imprinted on the hearts of the Rognes villagers against yesterday's lords, against the son of a *bourgeois* who to-day owned the land. Of course he'd got it for nothing, all his land. Got it by robbery, at the time of the Revolution! Not much hope of a poor man having such luck; it was always the scoundrels who saw the chance in time and only gave up filling their pockets when they were too tired to keep it up. Not to mention the nice things going on at La Borderie! La Cognette was a scandal, what with the besotted master always pulling her out of his own labourers' bed-straw. The tales persisted, they travelled round the district in crude forms, arousing indignation even in those peasants who'd have committed incest with their daughters or sold them as whores if they thought there'd be any profit in the deed. And in the end the municipal councillors came to the conclusion that a *bourgeois* ought to stay and commit his thieveries and his lechery among other *bourgeois*, and a peasant community ought to have a peasant as mayor.

The elections provided the clash which startled M. Hourdequin and revealed the Council's antagonism. As he spoke of M. de Chédeville all the faces went wooden. As soon as Macqueron saw the farmer remained faithful to the disgraced candidate, he decided that here was the best ground to fight on, a first-rate chance for knocking his opponent out. So he started supporting the prefect's candidate, M. Rochefontaine, crying out that all loyal citizens ought to come out in support of the Government. Such a profession of faith was sufficient by itself. There was no need to go into details to convince the council members; in their fear of the broom they were always on the side of the broomstick, resolved to support the strongest side, the master's side, so that nothing at all would change and the price of corn would stay high. Delhomme, that honest and upright man, concurred with these views and so won over Clou and the others. What finally compromised Hourdequin was that

Lengaigne, furious at the importance affected by Macqueron, was his only supporter. Abuse entered into the debate and the farmer was accused of being 'a Red', a scoundrel who wanted a Republic so as to liquidate the peasantry. So thoroughly did the calumnies work that the Abbé Madeline took fright, and, believing that he owed his position to the assessor, himself recommended M. Rochefontaine in spite of the underhand support afforded to M. de Chédeville by the bishop.

Then a final blow shattered the mayor's standing. A rumour went the rounds that at the opening of the famous direct road from Rognes to Châteaudun, he had pocketed half the subvention voted. How he had managed such a theft was never explained. The affair simply remained something enigmatic and abominable. When questioned about it, Macqueron assumed a dismayed, sorrowful and discreet air, like a man compelled to maintain silence out of regard for certain proprieties. He it was, in fact, who had invented the tale. In the end the village was thrown into confusion and the council split in half: on one side the assessor and all the councillors except Lengaigne, on the other the mayor, who now at last grasped the seriousness of his position.

A fortnight before, Macqueron had travelled to Châteaudun for the considered purpose of prostrating himself before M. Rochefontaine. He had pleaded with him not to stay in any other house than his, should he deign to visit Rognes. And that was why the innkeeper, on that Sunday after lunch, kept on running into the road on the look-out for his candidate. He had forewarned Delhomme and Clou and other members of the council, and they were emptying a bottle of wine to pass the time. Old Fouan and Bécu were also there, playing cards, as well as Lequeu the schoolmaster, buried in a newspaper that he had brought along, keeping up his pose of being a teetotaller. But two of the customers made Macqueron uneasy: Jésus-Christ and Canon the tramp worker, who sat facing one another over a bottle of brandy. He kept giving them sidelong glances, searching vainly for an excuse to order them out. But for once the scoundrels weren't making a lot of noise; they simply sat there looking as if they didn't give a damn for anyone. Three o'clock struck, and M. Rochefontaine, who had promised to come at two, had still not yet arrived.

'Coelina,' Macqueron nervously asked his wife, 'did you bring up that Bordeaux, so that we can offer him a drink?'

Coelina, behind the bar, made a gesture of grief for her own forgetfulness. At once Macqueron himself rushed down into the cellar. In the neighbouring room, where the haberdashery was sold and the door was always kept open, Berthe, with all the mannerisms of a high-class shop assistant, was showing some pink ribbons to three peasant girls; while Françoise, already at work, was brushing dust from the ledges, in spite of the day being Sunday. The assessor, loath to lose any chance of asserting his authority, had welcomed the girl, flattered that she had come to him for protection. His wife happened to need an assistant, and he agreed to board and lodge Françoise until he could effect a reconciliation with the Buteaus. Françoise swore that she'd kill herself if taken back to their house by force.

Suddenly a landau, drawn by two superb Percherons, stopped outside the door. M. Rochefontaine, the only passenger, stepped out, surprised and offended at finding no one prepared to greet him. He hesitated about entering the inn; and at that moment Macqueron came up from the cellar with a bottle in each hand. He was thrown into confusion, at an agonised loss how to dispose of the bottles.

'Oh, sir, how unfortunate!' he stammered. 'I've been waiting for the last two hours without budging from the doorstep; and then I went down to the cellar for just a minute—all on your account, yes—will you take a glass, M. le Député?'

M. Rochefontaine, who was only a candidate as yet and who ought to have been touched by the poor man's obvious confusion, seemed only more irritated. He was a tall fellow, scarcely thirty-eight years of age, with cropped hair and square-cut beard, quite correctly dressed but without elegance. His manner was chilly and abrupt, his voice clipped and commanding, and everything about him showed a man used to giving orders and exacting obedience from the twelve hundred workers employed in his works. He had made up his mind, it seemed, to crack a whip over these peasants and drive them the way he wanted.

Coelina and Berthe had hastened forward, and the girl's bright eyes glinted boldly under the swollen lids.

'Please do us the honour of coming inside, Monsieur.'

Monsieur gave her a searching glance and summed her up completely. He went inside but refused to sit down.

'Here are some of our friends from the council,' continued Macqueron, beginning to feel more at ease again. 'They're very pleased

300

to make your acquaintance, very pleased indeed. Isn't that so, gentlemen?'

Delhomme, Clou and the others had risen to their feet, much impressed by M. Rochefontaine's unbending manner. In an unbroken silence they listened to the things he had come along to tell them; the theories he held in common with the Emperor, especially the ideas about progress to which he owed the Government's favour, as against the previous candidate, whose opinions were now denounced. Then he began promising roads, railways, canals. Yes, a canal across La Beauce, to slake the thirst which had been burning the plain up for centuries. The peasants gaped in amazement. What was he saying? Water in their fields after all this time? He talked for some time and finished by threatening those who miscast their votes with Government disapproval and with ruinous weather. They all looked at one another. This chap was going to shake them up all right; it'd be as well to keep on his sunny side!

'Of course, of course!' Macqueron repeated after every sentence, though somewhat uneasy at the candidate's harsh tone.

Bécu, however, nodded his head in vigorous approval of such a military approach; and Old Fouan, with staring eyes, seemed to be saying that here was indeed a man. Lequeu himself, usually so impassive, had flushed darkly, though nobody knew for certain whether from pleasure or rage. Only the two scoundrels, Jésus-Christ and Canon, had contempt written all over their faces; but they felt so superior anyway that they merely sneered and shrugged their shoulders.

The moment the speech was concluded, M. Rochefontaine started for the door. The assessor cried out in a voice of misery:

'But, monsieur, won't you honour us by drinking a glass of wine?'

'No, thanks, I'm late enough already. They're waiting for me at Magnolles, Bazoches and a dozen other places. Good evening!'

He went out. Berthe did not even accompany him to the door; and as she returned to the haberdashery, she commented to Françoise:

'Did you ever see such manners? I'd vote for the other one—the old chap!'

M. Rochefontaine had just climbed back into his landau when the crack of a whip made him turn his head. Hourdequin was arriving in his modest gig, driven by Jean. The farmer had chanced to hear of the industrialist's visit to Rognes through one of his wagoners seeing the landau on the road; he had immediately hurried off to confront the enemy. He felt all the more disturbed as he had been pressing M. de Chédeville for the past week to put in an appearance, but had failed: no doubt the candidate found more attraction in some skirt, perhaps the usher's pretty wife.

'So it's you!' he cried out heartily to M. Rochefontaine. 'I didn't know you've already launched your campaign.'

The two vehicles were drawn up wheel to wheel. Neither man got out. But they chatted for a few minutes after bending forward to shake hands. As they had lunched a few times together with the mayor of Châteaudun, they were acquainted.

'You're opposing me then?' asked M. Rochefontaine, in his short way.

Because of his situation as mayor, Hourdequin was anxious not to act too openly; for a moment he failed to hide his perturbation at hearing that this devil of a man had such a well-organised intelligence system. But he had plenty of pluck and replied in a cheerful tone so as to lend his explanation an amiable tone.

'I'm not against anybody. I'm for myself. My man is the one who'll protect my interest. Here's corn fallen to forty-six francs the quarter, exactly what it costs to grow! Might just as well throw the job up and perish.'

At once the other man burst out excitedly. 'Of course, it's Protection you need. That's it, isn't it? An extra tax, a duty prohibiting the import of foreign wheat so that French grain will double its present price! That's what you want—famine in France, a four-pound loaf costing a franc, the poor folk killed off. You're a progressive, how dare you want to bring back such monstrous conditions?'

'A progressive, a progressive,' echoed Hourdequin good-humouredly; 'of course I'm a progressive; but it costs me so much that I soon won't be able to afford the luxury. Machines, chemical fertilisers, all the new techniques—they're marvellous of course, and it's easy to argue their merits. There's only one disadvantage; they ruin you in the name of pure logic.'

'That's because you're impatient, because you demand immediate results from science, everything at once; because you lose heart in the necessary experimental period till you doubt even what's proved a fact and deny the whole thing.'

'Maybe. So all I've been doing is make experiments. Is that it? Well, let them compensate me with a medal and let some other poor beggars get on with the job!'

Hourdequin roared at his own joke and felt he had clinched the argument. M. Rochefontaine took him up sharply.

'So you want the workers to die of hunger?'

'Not at all, I want the peasant to keep alive.'

'But I've twelve hundred workers and I can't raise wages unless I mean to go bankrupt. If wheat went up to thirty francs, I'd have to watch them dying like so many flies.'

'What of it? Don't I employ men? When wheat stands at sixteen francs, we pull in our belts and some poor devils just lie down and die at the bottom of ditches all over the countryside.'

Then he went on, still laughing.

'Damnation! We all stick to our own gods. If I can't sell you my wheat at a high price, French agriculture will be ruined; and if I do sell it to you at a high price, industry will have to stick the key under the door. Your labour-costs will increase and manufactured goods will rise in price—the tools I need, the clothes and all the hundred-and-one things I need. It's a fine mess, and we'll finish by ruining each other all round.'

The two men, the farmer and the manufacturer, the protectionist and the free-trader, stared each other in the face; the former with sly good-humoured raillery, the latter with stern undisguised hostility. Here was the contemporary war, the actual economic struggle, the battle-field of the struggle for life.

'The peasant will be forced to feed the workers,' said M. Rochefontaine.

'Then make sure that the peasant gets something to eat first,' repeated Hourdequin.

At last he jumped out of his gig, while the other man flung the name of some village at his driver. Macqueron was annoyed at noticing that his councillor friends had heard the whole dispute from where they stood in the inn-doorway; he shouted that everyone must have a drink together. But the candidate again refused and omitted to shake hands with anyone; he threw himself back in his landau and the two great Percherons at once went off at a smart trot.

Lengaigne, who stood at his door on the other side of the road, stropping his razor, had watched the scene throughout. He gave a jeering laugh and shouted loudly for his neighbour's benefit, 'Kiss my arse and say thank you!'

Hourdequin meanwhile had gone into the inn, where he accepted a glass of wine. As soon as Jean had tied the horse to one of the

303

shutters, he followed his master inside. Françoise called him over with a little sign and drew him into the haberdashery to recount the whole story of how she had left the house. He was so upset, so much afraid of compromising her before witnesses, that he returned to sit down in the wine-shop after merely whispering to her that they must meet later and work out how to proceed.

'Well, in God's name, you'll be making a rotten choice if you vote for that young sprig!' cried Hourdequin as he put down his glass.

His argument with M. Rochefontaine had decided him on a policy of open struggle, a duel to the death. He dropped all half-measures and compared his opponent with M. de Chédeville, that fine gentleman without any false pride, who was always pleased to be of service, in fact a real French nobleman of the old breed—while that sniffy dog, that jumped-up millionaire, looked down on them from his great height, refusing even to take a glass of the local wine for fear of being poisoned, no doubt! Surely they didn't mean to line up behind him. You didn't change a good horse for a blind one!

'Tell me what you've got against M. de Chédeville? He's been your deputy for years and he's always worked well for you. And now you're deserting him for a rotter that you considered disreputable at the last elections when the Government opposed him. Just remember that, damn it.'

Macqueron, who preferred not to be directly involved, pretended to be occupied in helping his wife. The peasants had all listened with blank faces, without giving the slightest hint of what went on in their minds. At last Delhomme spoke.

'When one doesn't know people——'

'But you know him now, this fine bird! You heard him say that he wanted corn cheap and that he'd vote for foreign wheat to be imported and ruin our crops. I've already explained that it means absolute ruin for us. If you're still stupid enough to trust in his magnificent promises, vote for him then! Yes, vote for him and see how he'll snap his fingers at you afterwards!'

The shadow of a smile flickered on Delhomme's tanned face. All the subtlety latent within the man's direct and narrow intelligence was evident in his slow phrases as he spoke.

'He said what he said; we believe what we believe. He or some-one else, what does it matter? There's only one thing we're concerned about, and that's a stable government that can keep things going as they are. And so, as we see it, there's only one way to be sure we don't make a false step—let the Government have the deputy it wants. We're satisfied as long as this gentleman from Châteaudun is a friend of the Emperor.'

Hourdequin was left bewildered by the last sentence. Why, the year before, M. de Chédeville had been the Emperor's friend! Oh, these abject serfs, always at the beck and call of masters who preyed on them and fed them! Even now they were still bound by inherited self-abasement and self-seeking, seeing nothing, knowing nothing beyond their daily bread.

'Well, by God, I swear that the day Rochefontaine is elected, I'll throw up my position, damn it! D'you take me for a turncoat, black to-day and white to-morrow! If the Republicans were in the Tuileries, you'd be on their side, wouldn't you?'

Macqueron's eyes gleamed. At last he'd brought it off: the mayor had signed his own death warrant. In his unpopular position, the undertaking which he had just given was enough to make the district vote against M. de Chédeville.

But at this moment Jésus-Christ, forgotten in the corner with his friend Canon, laughed out so loudly that every eye turned on him. With his elbows on the table and his chin in his hands he stared round at the assembled peasants and went on shouting, with sneers of contempt:

'You pack of dirty cowards! You pack of dirty cowards!'

As he was shouting, Buteau came in. While he was still crossing the threshold, his quick eyes detected Françoise in the haberdashery and noted Jean seated against the wall, listening and waiting for his master. Good! the girl and her lover were both there; now they'd all see something!

'And here's the biggest dirty coward of the lot, my brother!' bawled Jésus-Christ.

Threatening growls grew sharper. The peasants were about to throw the foul-mouthed scoundrel out, when Leroi, alias Canon, entered the dispute, raising the hoarse voice which had been heard debating at every socialist meeting-place in Paris.

'You shut up, old chap! They aren't as stupid as they look. Listen here, you others, peasants, what would you say if a notice went up on the council office door over the road, printed in big letters: Revolutionary Commune of Paris. First: all taxes abolished; second: military service abolished. Eh, what would you say to that, you clodhoppers?'

The effect was so extraordinary that Delhomme, Fouan, Clou and Bécu sat with mouths hanging open and eyes rounded in astonishment. Lequeu lowered his paper; Hourdequin, on the point of leaving, turned back; Buteau, forgetting Françoise, sat down on a table-corner. They one and all watched the tattered tramp, the terror of the countryside, who lived on extorted alms and thefts. Only the week before, he had been chased out of La Borderie where he had appeared like a ghost at dusk. That was why he was now staying with that scamp of a Jésus-Christ, probably to disappear once more to-morrow.

'Ah, I see that tickles you in the right spot,' he went on gaily.

'God, that's true!' Buteau admitted. 'Only yesterday I had to take some money to the tax-collector! There's no end to it all, they're flaying us alive!'

'Never see our boys marched off again, good God!' cried Delhomme. 'I know what it's costing me to get Nénesse exempted, I can tell you!'

'All the same,' added Fouan, 'if you don't pay, they take the lads and kill them for you.'

Canon nodded his head with a triumphant grin.

'See?' he said to Jésus-Christ. 'They're not such fools as they might be, these clodhoppers.'

Then, turning again to the others, he went on, 'They always complain that you're conservative, that you won't stand for any changes. But what you want to conserve is your own interest, isn't it? You'll let things take their course and you'll help anything that'll help you, eh? There's quite a lot you'd be ready to do, to safeguard your money and your children? If that's not so, you'd be a lot of sheepish idiots!'

No one was drinking now and worried frowns were appearing on the peasants' heavy faces. Canon went on, happily savouring in advance the effect that he'd produce.

'That's why I'm quite satisfied. I know you all pretty well since you've been chasing me away from your doors with stones. As the fat gentleman over there said, you'll side with us, the Reds, the Communists, when we're in the Tuileries.'

'Oh no, we wont!' Buteau, Delhomme and the others shouted in chorus.

Hourdequin, who had been listening attentively, shrugged his shoulders. 'You're wasting your breath, my good fellow!'

But Canon went on smiling, with the unshakeable confidence of a man who has found his faith. Leaning back, he rubbed first one shoulder on the wall, then the other; and went on to explain this thing of the Revolution, which was rumoured from farm to farm, mysterious and not understood, to the terror of both masters and servants. First, the Paris comrades would take over power: it might come about in the normal way of things; then they wouldn't have to shoot as many people as they expected, and the whole bag of tricks would topple over by itself, it was so rotten. When they were absolute masters, they would immediately, on the same day, abolish investment profits and confiscate large fortunes, so that all the wealth as well as all the instruments of production would return to the nation; and a new society would be organised, a society that was one great financial, industrial and commercial enterprise, a reasonable system for sharing-out both labour and comfort. In the countryside the change would be even easier. The first steps would consist of the expropriation of the landlords, the taking-over of the land——'

'You just try!' Hourdequin interrupted again. 'You'd be met with pitchforks. There's not one smallholder who'd let you take over a single handful of his earth.'

'Did I say one word about worrying the poor peasants!' retorted Canon blandly. 'We're not such damn fools as to get on the wrong side of the smallholders. No, no! At first we'll not touch the poor blighters who are scratching a livelihood out of an acre or two. All we'll take over will be the four- or five-hundred-acre farms of the fat gents like yourself, who heap up their pile by making their labourers sweat for them. Good heavens, do you imagine your neighbours will come and defend you with their pitchforks? They'll be laughing too much.'

Macqueron burst into a loud laugh, as if he treated the whole thing as a silly joke, and all the others copied him. The farmer paled, feeling the immemorial hatred in all these men. The scoundrel was right enough; not one of the peasants, not even the most respectable, would miss a chance of plundering La Borderie.

'What about me?' asked Buteau seriously. 'I own about a score of acres. Will I keep them? Will you leave them in my ownership?'

'Of course, comrade. But we're sure that later on, when you see the results attained in the nationalised farms around you, you'll come in without being asked, and add your strips to them. Everything on a large scale, with plenty of capital, lots of machinery, and all sorts of other advantages—all the best things, like science. I my-

307

self don't know much about that side; but you ought to hear the
chaps in Paris talking about it. They explain clearly how agriculture will be completely buggered up unless we organise it the way
I said. Yes, you'll come and offer your land of your own accord.'

Buteau gave a gesture of absolute incredulity. He no longer
understood, but he felt reassured since no one was asking him to
give anything up. But Hourdequin felt his curiosity excited at
the mention of nationalised farming, and he once again listened
patiently. The others were waiting for the dénouement, as if they
were watching a show. Twice Lequeu, with a flush on his pale face,
opened his mouth to join in the argument; but each time, being a
cautious man, he bit his tongue and kept quiet.

'And what about my share?' shouted Jésus-Christ suddenly.
'Everybody must have his share! Liberty, equality, fraternity!'

Canon at once lost his temper and lifted his fist as if he meant to
strike his comrade.

'For God's sake keep your mouth shut about liberty, equality and
fraternity! Do people need to be free! That's all rot. You want the
bourgeoisie to put us all in their pockets again, do you? No, no,
people will be forced to be happy in spite of themselves! Think, do
you want to call a bailiff your brother with equal rights? Why, you
bloody fool, it was because you swallowed all those yarns that your
Republicans in '48 betrayed the cause!'

Jésus-Christ, stupefied, declared that he stood for the great
Revolution.

'You make me sweat, shut up! What? '89, '93! Yes, a pretty
tune, a pretty set of lies always being drummed into our ears! Can
all that ridiculous farce be compared for one moment with the task
we face? You'll see what's what when the people are the masters,
and it won't be long now. Everything is breaking up and I promise
you that our century will end up in a much better way than the
last one did. There'll be a vast clear-out and a clean-up such as has
never been seen before!'

They all shuddered. Even the sodden Jésus-Christ recoiled,
frightened and repelled as soon as he heard that there was no
brotherhood in it. Jean, who had been interested up to that point,
also leaned back with a gesture of revulsion. But Canon stood up,
his eyes flaring and his face transfigured in a prophetic ecstasy.

'It *must* come about. It's fated, just as a stone thrown in the air
has to fall back to earth. And there won't be any more priests'
prattle in it—nothing about the next world, righteousness and

justice that we've never seen, any more than we've ever seen God Almighty! No, nothing beyond the need of every one of us for happiness. And what do you say, comrades, if we fix it so that everybody'll have everything he wants for the least possible work! Machines will toil for us and we'll just supervise them four or five hours a day. We might even get to the stage when all we need do is fold our arms. Enjoyment everywhere, all our needs studied and fulfilled. Yes, there'll be food, wine and women for all—three times as much as we can manage these days, because then we'll be stronger and healthier. No more poverty, no more sickness, no more old age— thanks to better organisation, an easier life, splendid hospitals and fine convalescent homes. It'll be a paradise: every scientific invention will be drawn on to make life run smoothly. At last it'll be real happiness just to be alive!'

Buteau, carried away, smashed his fist down on the table as he shouted, 'Down with taxes! Down with conscription! Down with all our worries! Nothing but a good life! I back you.'

'Of course,' observed Delhomme calmly. 'A man would be his own enemy not to back such a programme.'

Fouan nodded his approval, and so did Macqueron, Clou and the others. Bécu was bewildered. All his ideas about authority were badly shaken up and he stepped over to Hourdequin, with a whispered enquiry whether he shouldn't lock up the rascal who was attacking the Emperor. The farmer soothed him down by shrugging his shoulders. A good life! All very well! People dreamed of its coming through science as they had dreamed of its coming through justice—and perhaps the dream was more reasonable this time, but it wouldn't come true to-morrow. He started once more to leave and gave Jean a call, when Lequeu finally surrendered to his longing to speak up. He had been almost choking for some time, as if struggling to hold back his fury.

'Unless you're all dead by the time these fine things come about,' he burst out in his shrill voice. 'Dead from hunger or dead from police bullets if hunger puts your backs up. . .'

They turned to look at him with uncomprehending faces.

'At any rate it's certain that if wheat goes on coming in from America, in fifty years' time there won't be a single peasant left in France. Can our earth compete with theirs? Just as we begin to try out real farming, we'll be inundated with foreign grain. I've read a book which sets it all out. You fellows are the ones who're doomed.'

Even in his excitement he suddenly became aware of all the frightened faces turned towards him. He didn't even finish the sentence he'd begun, but moved his hand angrily and pretended to bury himself again in his newspaper.

'American wheat will certainly finish you off,' stated Canon, 'unless the people take over control of the big estates.'

'And I,' Hourdequin concluded, 'I tell you again that that wheat musn't be let into the country. Now go and vote for M. Rochefontaine if you want to get rid of me as your mayor and if you want wheat selling at twenty-five francs the quarter.'

He got up into his gig. Jean followed him, after exchanging a significant look with Françoise, and whipped up the horse. He remarked to his master, 'It doesn't do to think too much about these things : they drive a man crazy.' Hourdequin nodded his approval of the sentiment.

In the tavern Matqueron was chatting eagerly to Delhomme in a low voice, while Canon, re-assuming a supercilious air, was finishing off the cognac with the deflated Jésus-Christ, calling him 'Mademoiselle '93'. Buteau, shaking himself out of his day-dream, suddenly noticed that Jean had left, and was astonished to find Françoise still sanding in the doorway, where she had come with Berthe to listen. He felt furious at wasting his time on politics when there were important matters to attend to. Somehow these blasted politics hit a man right in the pit of his stomach. He had a long argument with Coelina in a corner, and she managed to stop him making a scene on the spot: better to persuade Françoise to return of her own free will when she'd calmed down a little. Then he went off, threatening to come back for the girl with a rope and a stick if argument couldn't convince her.

Next Sunday M. Rochefontaine was elected deputy and Hourdequin sent in his resignation to the prefect. So Macqueron at last became mayor, almost bursting out of his skin in his insolent triumph.

That evening the enraged Lengaigne was caught in the act of letting down his trousers at his victorious rival's doorstep. He bawled out in fury, 'I'll do it where I please, now we're governed by swine !'

VI

WEEKS went by and Françoise obstinately refused to return to her sister's house. There was a disgraceful scene on the roadway:

Buteau, who tried to drag her off by the hair, had to let go when she bit deeply into his thumb. Macqueron became so disturbed that he turned the girl out of his house, explaining that as the representative of authority he could not any longer encourage her in her revolt.

La Grande happened to be passing and took Françoise home. She was now eighty-eight; but she still never thought of death except as a trick for involving her heirs in the torment of interminable lawsuits for her estate. She had made an extraordinarily complicated will in which she deliberately muddled everything; under the pretext of being fair to everybody, she made sure that all her heirs would all ruin one another. Since she couldn't take her belongings with her, her scheme was to make certain that she'd at least have the consolation of embroiling all the members of the family. Nothing gave her greater pleasure than to see the pack of them tearing at each other's throats. So she hurried to install her niece in her house, hesitating a moment out of stinginess but quickly deciding that she could get a good deal of work out of the girl in exchange for very little food. And indeed, that very afternoon, she made her wash the stairs and kitchen. Then when Buteau made his appearance, she stood up to receive him, with her evil old bird-of-prey profile; and he who had talked of smashing everything at Macqueron's, trembled and stammered, paralysed by fears of being cut out of her will and not daring to oppose the terrible old woman.

'I need Françoise here, and I'm keeping her because she isn't happy with you. Besides, she's of age now and you must render accounts. That's something we've got to go into.'

Buteau departed in a rage, appalled at the trouble he foresaw.

And a week later, towards the middle of August, Françoise did come of age. She was now her own mistress. But all she had achieved was little more than a change of hardship; for she too was terrified of her aunt. She was killing herself with hard work in the cold miserly house where everything had to shine of its own nature without any expenditure on soap or brushes. Cold water and elbow-grease ought to be able to do the whole job. One day, when she had forgotten herself so far as to give the fowls some grain, she nearly had her head cut open by a blow from her aunt's stick. The saying went that in her anxiety to spare the horses La Grande used to harness her grandson Hilarion to the plough; and even if that was just a yarn, she did in truth treat him like a beast of burden. She beat him, wore him out with work, and took advantage of his

311

animal strength, until he collapsed with exhaustion. And she fed him so poorly, with crusts and leavings, just like the pigs, that he was always dazed with hunger as well as stupefied with terror. When Françoise discovered that she was meant to be the second horse between the shafts, she had only one aim in life : to get out of this house. And as a result, suddenly, she made up her mind to get married.

Her sole motive was to get away from the whole situation. With her rooted ideas of what was just—ideas that even as a child had made havoc of her life—she'd have killed herself rather than return to live at Lise's. Her cause alone was just; and she despised herself for having so long put up with oppression. She never mentioned Buteau; she uttered her complaints only against her sister, blaming her entirely for their failure to live together on good terms. Now that everything was ended between them, ended for ever, she lived only for the recovery of her property, her share of the inheritance. She worried over it day and night, and became so angry at all the formalities that she nearly went crazy. What was it about? This is mine, that is yours: it could all be settled in a few minutes! They were all banding together to do her down, were they? She suspected every member of the family, and finally came to the conclusion that only a husband, a man, could get her out of her troubles. Of course, Jean hadn't a handful of earth to call his own and he was fifteen years older than she was. But no other man had asked for her, perhaps no one dared to on account of the business with Buteau, whom nobody wanted as an adversary, so widely was he feared in Rognes. And then she had been with Jean once; not that it was of much importance as there had been no consequences. But he was kind and gentle and absolutely honest. She might as well take him; for she didn't love anyone else and she was determined to have someone, never mind whom, a man who'd defend her rights and infuriate Buteau. She too would have a man of her own.

Jean still felt a great affection for her. His desire to possess her had quietened considerably during his long wait. Still, the tenderness with which he met her did not lessen and he looked on himself as her man since they had exchanged vows. He had hung on patiently till she was of age, without trying to break down her wish to wait; indeed he had persuaded her not to make things difficult for herself in her sister's house. And now, as a result of her staying she could rightly claim the support of all worthy folk. He had blamed her for the brusque manner of her departure from the

Buteau household; but he assured her that she now had the initiative in her own hands. And he added that whenever she wished to discuss the next step he was ready.

So the marriage was arranged on an evening when he had come to a tryst with her behind La Grande's cow-house. A rotten old gate there opened on to an enclosed yard; and the two of them met to lean against it, he outside and she inside, with the stream of stable manure trickling between their feet.

'Now, Corporal,' she spoke first, looking him straight in the eyes, 'if you still feel the same way, I agree, straight away.'

He steadily returned her gaze and slowly answered, 'I haven't spoken to you before because it'd have looked as if I was after your property. But you're right anyway; now's the time.'

Neither spoke for a while. He had put his hand over the young girl's as it rested on the gate. At last he went on, 'And you mustn't let the thought of La Cognette trouble you, because of any gossip that's got round. It's a good three years since I even touched her.'

'It's just the same with me,' she added. 'I don't want the thought of Buteau to go troubling you. The swine brags everywhere that he's had me. Perhaps you too believe it?'

'Everyone in the district believes it,' he muttered, to avoid answering the question.

But she went on looking at him and he added, 'Yes, I believed it. You see, I understood things, for I know that skunk; you couldn't have helped going through with it.'

'Oh, he tried often enough and he left enough bruises all over me. But if I swear to you that he wasn't ever able to get as far as he wanted, will you believe me?'

'I believe you.'

To show his pleasure, he closed his hand over hers and went on tightly holding her hand with his arm resting on the gate. Then, noticing that the stream dribbling out of the stable was wetting his boots, he straddled his legs out.

'You seemed so willing to stay in his house, it might have been you didn't dislike it, all that mauling.'

She became uneasy and lowered her frank direct gaze.

'Especially as you wouldn't have anything to do with me, remember? Never mind, though I was furious I hadn't got a child on you, it's better that it's happening this way now. It'll be more decent too.'

He paused to tell her she was standing in the puddle.

'Careful, you're getting wet.'

She too set her feet wide apart and remarked, 'We agree then?'

'Yes. Fix any day you like.'

They didn't even kiss, but shook hands like good friends over the top of the gate. Then they went off in opposite directions.

Françoise told her aunt that evening of her decision to marry Jean, explaining that she must have a man to help her recover the property. At first La Grande did not reply. She went on sitting up straight in her chair, with wide eyes; she was calculating the loss and gain, and the pleasure she might get out of the event. Not till next morning did she give her approval to the marriage. She had brooded over the matter all night as she lay on her straw mattress; for she slept little now and always lay with open eyes until dawn, conjuring up all kinds of disagreeable schemes against the family. The proposed marriage seemed to her so pregnant with dire consequences for everyone in the family that she longed with the feverishness of youth to see it come off. She could already foresee the minutest of the troubles liable to arise and set herself to complicate them with fatal effect. She even went so far as to tell her niece that, out of affection, she wished to take charge of the whole proceedings. She stressed the word *affection* with an ominous brandishing of her stick. Since the girl had been cast off, she would take the place of her mother; just let them all wait and see.

First, La Grande called her brother Fouan before her to discuss the accounts of his wardship. But the old man had only one comment to make. It wasn't his fault that he had been appointed guardian; M. Baillehache had arranged everything, so let her apply to M. Baillehache. Moreover, when he realised that a plot was being hatched against the Buteaus, he exaggerated his vacancy. Old age and awareness of weakness left him bewildered and cowardly, at everyone's mercy; so why should he let himself be involved in brawls with the Buteaus? Twice already he had almost gone back to live with them, after the night of terror when he had trembled at seeing Jésus-Christ and La Trouille prowl round his room and push their bare arms under his very pillow in their quest for his papers. He was sure to be murdered sooner or later at the Château if some night he didn't get away. La Grande, who got nothing out of him, sent him off in a terrorised state, shrieking that they'd go to law if a sou of the girl's money had been embezzled. She then proceeded to frighten Delhomme, as a member of the family council, and he went home in a condition of collapse. Fanny came running behind

314

his back to tell the old woman that they would rather pay out of their own pocket than get mixed up in a lawsuit. The game had begun and already was providing a good deal of entertainment.

The problem she now revolved was whether to broach the property claim first or to go ahead with celebrating the marriage. La Grande considered things for two nights, then announced in favour of an immediate marriage. Françoise, married to Jean and assisted by her husband in pressing her claim, would increase the Buteaus' worries. From that moment La Grande hurried the arrangements along. She seemed to regain her youthful strength as she busied herself in dealing with her niece's papers, got Jean's out of him, and arranged the ceremony at the town hall and the church. She went so far in her enthusiasm that she lent them the necessary money, but drew up a receipt form in which the loan was set down at twice its amount, to cover the interest. What wrung her heartstrings more than anything was the amount of wine she was forced to offer people during the preparations; but she had large stocks of her sour vinegar, the 'insect killer', so undrinkable that everyone treated it with distinct respect. She resolved that on account of family dissensions there would be no feast. After the Mass there'd be only a glass of 'insect killer' in which to drink to the health of the newly-married. The Charleses were invited, but excused themselves as too worried over the behaviour of their son-in-law Vaucogne. Fouan felt so uneasy that he went to bed, and sent word that he was ill. Delhomme was the only relation present; he had agreed to act as one of Françoise's witnesses to mark his esteem for Jean, who was such a good steady fellow. Jean himself brought only his witnesses—his master Hourdequin and one of his workmates on the farm. Rognes was all agog. People watched the proceedings from every door, fascinated by the rushed marriage which was likely to beget so many clashes. At the council offices, Macqueron, in the presence of his predecessor, overdid all the formalities, inflated with his importance. At the church a painful incident occurred: the Abbé Madeline fainted as he was conducting the service. He was not feeling well, he sadly missed his native mountains since coming to flat La Beauce, and he was profoundly distressed at the religious indifference of his new parishioners. So borne down was he by the constant gossiping and squabbling of the women that he no longer even dared to try scaring them with the terrors of hell. They had sensed his mild character and took advantage of it to tyrannise over him even in church matters. Still, Coelina, Flore and all the others expressed deep concern when he fell flat on his face at the altar, and exclaimed that his fall was an omen of imminent death for the bridal pair.

It had been decided that Françoise was to go on living with La Grande until she got her share of the property; for with her usual stubbornness she had made up her mind to get the house. So what was the use of taking lodgings for a couple of weeks? For the time being, Jean was to remain as wagoner at the farm and merely come to join her at nightfall. Their wedding-night was saddening and rather stupid, though they were by no means sorry at coming together at last. As he took her, she sobbed so strongly that she almost choked; and yet he hadn't hurt her, in fact he had treated her with the utmost gentleness. The worst of it was that through her sobs she replied to his questions by saying that she had nothing against him, that she couldn't stop herself crying and that she didn't even know why she cried. Obviously such an attitude was not exactly calculated to excite a man. Vainly he took her again and held her fast in his arms; they found no pleasure in the embrace, even less than the first time among the corn. As Jean explained, these things lose their savour when they're over-delayed. And yet, in spite of the constraint and a kind of shame that made them both feel sick at heart, they were happy together. As they couldn't sleep, they spent the night discussing the way that they'd arrange things when they had the house and land.

The very next morning Françoise demanded her share of the property. But La Grande was no longer in a hurry. In the first place she wanted to drag out the pleasure, drawing blood from the family by a series of pin-pricks; and then she was doing too well out of the girl and her husband, who paid for his board with two hours' work every evening, to feel very keen to see them leave her house and live on their own. Still, it was necessary to go and ask the Bateaus how they proposed to divide the property. She herself, on behalf of Françoise, demanded the house, half the arable land and half the pasture, giving up any claim for half of the vineyard, the ground value of which she estimated as equalling the value of the house. It was all fair and reasonable; if a friendly arrangement along these lines had been accepted, there would have been no need for the law courts, where a fat slice of everything in dispute is always left behind. Buteau was bowled over by La Grande's visit; but, obliged as he was to bow down before the old woman because of her wealth, he couldn't stand it any more. He rushed out, fear-

316

ing that he might forget his own interest so far as to bash her over the head. Lise, with burning ears, was left alone with her; she stammered out:

'The house! So she wants the house, does she, the trollop, the worthless slut, getting married without even coming to see me! Well, aunt, you can tell her that the day she gets inside this house will be the day I'm laid out stiff.'

La Grande remained calm. 'All right, all right, my girl, no need to work yourself up so. You want the house too, you're within your rights. We'll see what we'll see.'

For three days she trotted to and fro between the two sisters, telling each one all the abuse uttered by the other, working them up to such a pitch of fury that both almost took to their beds. She untiringly reminded them how much she loved them and how grateful her nieces should be for her undertaking such dog's work. At last it was decided to share out the land, but to hold a sale of house and furniture as well as livestock as no agreement could be reached. Each sister swore that she would buy the house no matter what the cost, ready to part with her last chemise to raise the sum.

Grosbois came to survey the fields and divide them into two lots. There were two and a half acres of meadowland, about the same of vineyard, and about five acres of arable land. It was these last acres at Les Cornailles that Buteau, since his marriage, had set his heart on keeping; they ran alongside the field he himself had inherited from his father, and constituted a field nearly eight acres in size, bigger than any other in the whole of Rognes. Consequently his wrath knew no limits when he saw Grosbois set up his square and stick his poles in the ground. La Grande was there to supervise, as Jean preferred to keep away, fearing that his presence might provoke a fight. An argument sprang up. Buteau wanted the line drawn parallel to the Aigre valley, so that his strip would remain in one piece with his wife's; while the old woman demanded that the line be drawn perpendicular, simply and solely to oppose him. She won the day; and he clenched his fists, choking with suppressed rage.

'But in God's name, if I get the first lot, I'll be cut in two, I'll have that piece on one side and my own field over there.'

'Well, my lad, it's up to you to draw the number that suits you.'

For a whole month Buteau had been in a bad temper. In the first place the girl was escaping him; he had been tormented with baffled desire, ever since he could no longer grasp a handful of

317

her flesh under the skirt, with the obstinate hope of some day getting the whole of her. Since her marriage, he had been fevered at the thought of another man holding her abed, doing as he liked with her. And now this rival was taking the earth out of his grasp, making it his, the earth too. He might just as well cut off a limb. The loss of a girl was nothing that couldn't be retrieved; but the land, a land which he felt was his own and had sworn never to give up! He felt murderous, ransacked his brains for some way out, dreamed confusedly of violent and bloody deeds, which only fear of the police checked him from carrying out.

At last a visit to M. Baillehache was fixed, and then for the first time Buteau and Lise stood face to face with Françoise and Jean. La Grande had accompanied them for amusement, on the excuse of ensuring that nothing went wrong. The five of them passed into the room, stiff and silent. The Buteaus sat down on the right. Jean, on the left, remained standing behind Françoise, as if to say that he was not involved and had come only to support his wife. The aunt, tall and scraggy, took a chair in the middle, turning her round eyes and her vulturine nose first on one party, then on the other, with a pleased air. The two sisters didn't even give any signs of recognition. They sat with hard faces without exchanging a single word or glance. The men however darted one look at each other, a quick glinting look that went deep, like a knife-thrust.

'My friends,' said M. Baillehache, quite unaffected by this show of fiendish hate, 'we'll complete the division of the land, as that is a matter on which you agree.'

This time, he first demanded their signatures. The deed was already prepared, and only the allocation of the strips after the names was left blank. To avoid trouble, he wanted them to sign before the lucky draw, which was to follow at once.

Françoise drew number two, so Lise had to take number one, and Buteau's face darkened as the blood surged furiously through his veins. He never had any luck: his land was now split in two. The trollop of a girl and her man had come shoving in with their piece between his left-hand and his right-hand strip!

'God blast and damn!' he swore between clenched teeth. 'God's cursed swine!'

The notary requested him to keep his oaths till he was outside.

'You see how this cuts us in half up there, on the plain,' remarked Lise without turning towards her sister. 'Perhaps we could

318

exchange. That'd suit us very well and no one would be the worse off.'

'No,' cut in Françoise, drily.

La Grande nodded her approving head. It brought bad luck to try and change what was fated. And the malicious stroke of fate gave her much amusement. Meanwhile Jean, standing behind his wife, had not stirred; he was so determined to hold aloof that his face was quite expressionless.

'Come along now,' the notary continued. 'Do try to get this business finished; we're not playing a game.'

The two sisters, by common consent, had asked him to arrange for the sale of the house, the furniture and the livestock. The sale was advertised to take place on the second Sunday of the month in his office, and the conditions of sale provided that the buyer should have the right to take possession on the same day. Then, after the sale, the lawyer was to proceed to the balancing of accounts between the two heiresses. All this was agreed to without any discussion.

But at that moment Fouan, who should have been there as guardian, was brought in by a clerk, who prevented Jésus-Christ from entering—the scamp was so drunk. Although Françoise had been of age for over a month, the accounts of the guardianship had not yet been rendered, which complicated matters. It was essential for the accounts to be passed so that the old man's responsibility might be ended. He looked at the company, one person after the other, with his small staring eyes; he was trembling with an increasing dread of being somehow compromised and handed over to the law.

The notary read out an abstract of the accounts. Everyone listened with blinking eyelids, afraid of misunderstanding something and terrified that if they let one word pass it might be just that word which would bring them to disaster.

'Have you any objections to raise?' asked M. Baillehache when he had finished.

They sat bewildered. What objections? Were they perhaps forgetting something, were they being done down by that omission?

'Excuse me,' La Grande suddenly broke in, 'but that's certainly not the complete account for Françoise! My brother seems to be shutting his eyes on purpose if he doesn't see how she's being robbed.'

Fouan stammered, 'Eh, what's this? I haven't taken one copper of hers, I swear to God I haven't!'

319

'I'm saying that Françoise has been like a servant in the house since her sister got married, and that's nearly five years. So they owe her wages.'

At this unexpected demand Buteau leaped from his chair. Lise almost choked.

'Wages! To a sister! That's absolutely ridiculous!'

M. Baillehache had to quieten them down, stating that the girl had a perfect right to claim wages if she so wished.

'Yes, I do claim them,' said Françoise. 'I claim everything due to me.'

'But what about her food then?' shouted Buteau dementedly. 'You ought to see her stuff herself with bread and meat. Just feel her. Do you think she got all that fat by licking the walls, the lazy slut.'

'And her linen, and her dresses?' Lise continued angrily. 'And her washing? She sweated so much that she dirtied her clothes every other day!'

Françoise replied with vexation, 'If I sweated as much as all that it was because I worked so hard.'

'Sweat dries up, it doesn't soil things,' added La Grande.

Once again M. Baillehache intervened. He explained that an account must be drawn up, wages on one side, food and upkeep on the other. He took up a pen and tried to work out the indebtedness from the details they provided. But it was a terrible business. Françoise, egged on by La Grande, was very exacting. She set a high price on her work and enumerated all the chores she had done in the house or the cowshed, all the cleaning and dish-washing, and then her work in the fields, where her brother-in-law had made her labour like a man. On their side the exasperated Buteaus piled up the list of expenses, counting up every meal, lying about her clothes, and demanding payment even for the gifts they had given Françoise on fête days. Still, in spite of their sharpness, it worked out that they owed her a hundred and eighty-six francs. They sat with hands trembling and eyes inflamed, trying to think out some other chargeable detail.

The figure was just about to be accepted when Buteau shouted: 'Wait a minute! There's the doctor, when her periods stopped. He came twice, that's six francs.'

La Grande wasn't willing for agreement to be reached after the Buteau victory. She hustled old Fouan to recall how many days the girl had worked on the farm in the past months when he was staying there. Was it five or six days, at thirty sous? Françoise shouted six and Lise five, with as much violence as if they had been hurling stones at one another. And the old man, quite dazed, agreed first with one and then with the other, beating his forehead with both fists. Françoise carried the day and her total climbed to a hundred and eighty-nine francs.

'Now, have we reached the end at last?' asked the lawyer.

Buteau sat looking crushed, beaten by his ever-growing debt; he had given up struggling, sure that nothing worse could happen. In a doleful voice he muttered, 'If you want my shirt, I'll take it off.'

But La Grande held a final blow in reserve, a terrible one: something so huge and simple that everyone had ignored it.

'Listen, what about the five hundred francs indemnity for the road up there?'

Buteau was on his feet in a leap; his eyes were starting out of his head, his mouth wide open. But there was nothing he could say; no possible argument. He had received the money and he'd have to hand over half. For a second he racked his brains; then, finding nothing to help him and unable to restrain the desperation that rose and beat within his head, he suddenly rushed on Jean.

'You damned bastard, you've killed our friendship! If it hadn't been for you, we'd still be a happy family living together in peace and harmony.'

Jean, who had remained silent and restrained, had to put himself on the defensive.

'Don't touch me, or I'll let you have it.'

Françoise and Lise rose hastily to their feet and set themselves in front of their respective men. Their faces were puffed out with their slowly-accumulated hatred; and their nails were outstretched, ready to tear at each other's faces.

Everything was set for a general scrimmage, which neither La Grande or Fouan seemed inclined to check, and which would certainly have sent hats and hair flying. But for once the lawyer discarded his professional apathy.

'Confound it all! At least wait till you're out of here! It's disgusting that we can't reach agreement without brawling.'

As soon as the quivering antagonists had quietened down, he went on.

'You are agreed now, I think, aren't you? Well, I'll have the guardianship accounts drawn up and you'll sign them. Then we'll proceed to the sale of the house and get it completed. Now off with you and behave yourselves. Idiocies sometimes cost a lot of money!'

That phrase succeeded in calming them. But as they were going out, Jésus-Christ, who had been waiting for his father, insulted the entire family. He bawled out that it was a dreadful shame the way they were mixing the poor old man up in their foul doings, only to rob him of course. Then, in his drunken affection, he took his father home as he'd brought him, in a cart bedded with straw which he'd borrowed from a neighbour. The Buteaus made off on one side of the road; while La Grande pushed Jean and Françoise across to the *Jolly Ploughman* where she had herself treated to some black coffee. She was beaming.

'Oh, I've had a good laugh, anyway!' she finished up, putting the unused sugar into her pocket.

That same day La Grande had another idea. When they got back to Rognes, she ran over to talk with old Saucisse, who was said to have been an ancient flame of hers. The Buteaus had threatened to bid against Françoise for the house, till they spent their last franc. So she had the notion that if the old peasant did the bidding for Françoise, they mightn't suspect anything and might let him get away with the house; he was their neighbour and might easily be wanting to enlarge his property. For a consideration he agreed on the spot to do as she asked.

On the second Sunday of the month things went exactly as she had planned at the auction. Once more, in M. Baillehache's office, the Buteaus stood on one side, and Françoise and Jean on the other with La Grande. There was a small crowd, some peasants having come with a vague idea of bidding if the house was going for nothing. But after four or five bids curtly made by Lise and Françoise, the house stood at 3,500 francs, its market value. Françoise stopped at 3,800. Then old Saucisse butted in and pushed the bidding up to four thousand, then 4,500. The Buteaus looked at each other in consternation. They couldn't go any higher, the thought of spending so much money froze their blood. Yet Lise let herself be forced up to five thousand. She was crushed, however, when the old peasant immediately jumped to 5,200. That was the end; the house was knocked down to him for 5,200 francs. The Buteaus sneered. They were ready to gloat over their share of the huge sum as long as Françoise and her filthy blackguard had also failed to get the house.

However, when Lise on her return to Rognes went into the old house where she had been born and lived all her life, she began sobbing. Even Buteau was depressed and felt his throat tighten until he had to relieve himself by blaming his wife. He swore that he'd have given the last hair on his head for the house; but women were heartless, they only opened their purses or their legs if they wanted some pleasure for themselves. He was lying, he himself had checked her; and so they began fighting. Ah, the poor old Fouan house, built by their ancestors three centuries ago and now tottering, cracked, sunken, patched all over, leaning forward under the buffets of La Beauce's tempestuous winds! To think that the family had lived there for three hundred years and they'd come to love and honour it like a holy relic, rating it as a weighty item in the family inheritance! With a single blow Buteau knocked Lise down; and when she struggled up, she nearly broke his leg with a hefty kick.

But worse was to come on the morrow's evening. Then it was that the thunderbolt fell. Old Saucisse had gone to complete the sale in the morning, and by noon the whole of Rognes knew that he'd acted as proxy for Françoise, with Jean's authorisation; buying not only the house, but also the furniture, with Gédéon and La Coliche as well. A howl of anguish and distress rose from the Buteau house, as if the place had been struck by lightning. Man and woman had thrown themselves on the ground, moaning and roaring out their despair at being beaten, at being outwitted by that bitch of a girl. What above all made them crazy was to know the village must be laughing at them for their lack of cunning. God in Heaven! To be cheated like that, thrown out of their own house by a mere sleight of hand. It couldn't be done! Wait and see!

When La Grande presented herself that same evening, on Françoise's behalf, for a polite discussion with Buteau as to the day on which he intended to move, he lost all caution and flung her out, answering her with one word:

'Shit!'

She went off very happily, simply shouting back that the bailiff would be calling. And indeed the next day Vimeux, pallid and uneasy, looking scruffier than ever, climbed the hill and gave a mild knock under the scrutiny of all the gossips from the neighbouring houses. There was no reply. He had to knock more loudly and he plucked up courage to cry out that he was there to serve a notice to quit. At that the attic-window was opened and a voice bawled out the word used against La Grande, the very same word, the one and only word:

'Shit!'

A pot full of the mentioned substance was emptied over his head. Soaked from head to foot, he had to depart with the notice still unserved. Rognes is still chuckling loudly over it all.

La Grande immediately took Jean over to Châteaudun, to see the lawyer. The latter explained that it would need at least five days before the Buteaus could be evicted. Complaint would have to be formally laid, an order obtained from the president of the court, then the order would have to be registered, and finally the eviction would be effected by the bailiff, with police aid if necessary. La Grande argued hard to gain a day; and when on this Tuesday she got back to Rognes, she told everyone that on Saturday the Buteaus would be driven into the street with sabre blows like robbers, if they hadn't already left of their own accord.

When Buteau was informed, he made a fearful threatening gesture. He went on shouting to anyone ready to listen, that he wouldn't come out alive and the soldiers would have to break down the walls before they'd drag him out. His fury was so extravagant that the villagers couldn't make out whether he was acting the madman or whether he had really gone out of his mind. He drove wildly along the roads, standing up in the forepart of his cart with his horses in full gallop, took no heed whatever of greetings and gave no shouts of warning to pedestrians. He was even met at night, sometimes in one place, sometimes in another, returning from no one knew where, probably from a call on the devil. One man, who went up to him, received a cut from the whip. He spread terror abroad and the village was soon in a continual state of alarm. One morning it was seen that he had barricaded the house. Dreadful screams arose behind the closed doors, howls in which the neighbours thought they recognised the voices of Lise and her two children. The whole neighbourhood was badly upset; a discussion was held and an old peasant finally took the risk of putting a ladder against a window to climb up and look in. But the window opened and Buteau pushed the ladder over, so that the old fellow nearly had his legs broken. Couldn't a man do what he liked in his own house? He brandished his fists and yelled that he'd skin them all alive if they disturbed him any more. The worst of it was that Lise showed herself too with the two children, shouting abuse and accusing them all of poking their noses where they had no right. No one dared intervene any more. But alarm increased at each new outburst. People came along to listen to the terrible noises that could be heard right out in the road. The cynics thought that Buteau was acting a part. Others swore that he had lost his wits and that it would all end in some dreadful mishap. The truth was never known.

On the Friday, the day before the eviction was expected, there was a particularly astonishing scene. Buteau met his father near the church and began to bellow like a calf, kneeling in front of the old man and asking his forgiveness for all the wrongs he had done him in the past. Perhaps they were what had brought him down. He besought Fouan to come back and live with him, and seemed to believe that only his father's return could restore his good luck. Fouan, irritated at the things he was bellowing out, and astonished at his apparent repentance, promised to accept the invitation later, when all the family conflicts were settled.

At last Saturday arrived. Buteau's agitation had been mounting up. All day, from morning to night, he senselessly harnessed and unharnessed his horses; and people rushed out of the way of this furious driving that was frightening in its aimlessness. At about eight o'clock he harnessed up once again, but didn't go out. Instead, he planted himself in the doorway, calling to the neighbours as they passed, sneering and sobbing and yelling out the story of his troubles in vile language. Just think! Wasn't it a funny thing after all to be all buggered up by a young slut who'd been his bit of stuff for five years! You, a whore! And so was his wife! A couple of fine whores they were, fighting for the first turn! He revived this lie and invented all sorts of foul details out of spite. Then Lise came out and a fierce quarrel began. He thrashed her in full view of everyone, sending her back indoors deflated and quietened, while he himself felt eased at the whacking he'd administered. He kept on standing at the door, mocking at the Law with jeers and insults. The Law was a whore too, being prostituted somewhere on the open road, no doubt. He felt that the danger was past, and began crowing.

Vimeux didn't show up until nearly four o'clock. Then he arrived, accompanied by two policemen. Buteau turned pale and hastily shut the yard-door. Perhaps he had never really believed that things would be carried to the bitter end. A dead silence fell over the house while Vimeux, insolent now with the protection of armed force, beat on the door with both fists. There was no response. The policemen joined in and made the old door shake with blows from the butts of their guns. A crowd of men, women and children had come up behind them; the whole of Rognes was there, waiting to see the siege. Then suddenly the door opened again and Buteau appeared standing in the forepart of his cart, whipping up his horse and coming out at a gallop straight at the crowd.

'I'm going to drown myself! I'm going to drown myself!' he bawled amid the cries of alarm.

The end had come: he was going to finish with the whole business, hurl himself into the Aigre with cart, horse, everything!

'Out of my way, I'm going to drown myself!'

The scared watchers dispersed before the lash of the whip and the wild charge of the cart. But as Buteau started down the slope at a speed liable to smash the wheels, several men ran along to stop him. The obstinate fool was quite capable of plunging into the river in order to make trouble for other people. They caught him up and had to fight him to a standstill, jump at the horse's head and climb into the cart. When they brought him back, he stood without uttering a word; his teeth were clenched and his whole body stiffened as he let fate take its course, with no protest left him but a dumb impotent fury.

La Grande now arrived, escorting Françoise and Jean along to take possession of the house. Buteau was content to stare at them with the dark looks with which he now followed the concluding stage of his misfortune. It was Lise's turn to shout and fight like mad-woman. The police were inside, telling her to pack up and get out. She had no choice but to obey since her husband was coward enough to leave her defenceless. With her hands on her hips she began abusing him.

'You sissy, to let us be thrown into the street! Haven't you any guts? Can't you even hit these swine? Get out of my sight, you coward! You're no man!'

Exasperated by his immobility, she went on yelling into his face, till he stopped her with a shove that made her howl. But he didn't break his silence; he only glared at her with his dark look.

'Now, come on, ma, hurry up,' said Vimeux in triumph. 'We're not leaving till you've handed over the keys to the new owners.'

Lise began to get her things out in a rush of fury. For three days she and Buteau had already been transfering a large quantity of things, tools and implements and large household utensils, to La Frimat's house next door. It was clear that they had really expected the eviction; for they had made an arrangement with the old woman, hiring her house till they had time to look around. The place was too big for La Frimat, who now merely retained the bedroom where her paralysed husband lay. As the furniture had been sold with the house as well as the beasts, Lise had only to take away her linen, the mattresses and other small objects. Everything was tossed out of the door and windows into the middle of the yard, while the two children screamed as if their last day had come. Laure clung to her mother's skirts and Jules had fallen down, sprawling amid the scattered goods. As Buteau gave no help, the gendarmes kindly started to pile the bundles into the cart.

However, everything went wrong again when Lise caught sight of Françoise and Jean waiting behind La Grande. She rushed up at them and let out the accumulated flood of her bitterness.

'Ah, you cat, so you've come to look on with your tom, eh? Well, now you've seen our misery. It's as if you were lapping up our blood! You thief! You thief! You thief!'

She choked on the word, which she screamed afresh at her sister every time she carried some fresh object into the yard. Françoise had gone pale but made no reply; she kept her lips tightly closed while her eyes blazed. She seemed absorbed in an insulting scrutiny and followed every object with her eyes to make sure nothing was taken from her. Presently she caught sight of a kitchen stool which had been included in the sale.

'That's mine, that,' she cried out roughly.

'Yours? Go and fetch it then,' retorted Lise, throwing the stool into the pond.

The house was cleared. Buteau took the horse by the bridle. Lise picked up the two children, her two last bundles, Jules on her right arm and Laure on her left; then, as she finally left the old home, she went up to Françoise and spat in her face.

'There! that's for you.'

Her sister immediately spat back.

'And that's for you!'

After these venomously embittered farewells, Lise and Françoise slowly wiped their faces without taking their eyes away from one another. They were cut apart for ever now; there was nothing between them any longer except the blood which they shared and which seethed with hatred.

At last Buteau opened his mouth again and bawled out the order to go, with a threatening gesture towards the house.

'It won't be long before we're back!'

La Grande followed them to see things through to the end.

Now that the Buteaus were hopelessly down-and-out, she decided to turn against the winning pair; they had left her in too much of a hurry and she already found them too happy together. For long, groups of people stood around chatting in low voices. Françoise and Jean had gone into the empty house.

While the Buteaus were unpacking their bundles in La Frimat's house, they were surprised to see Old Fouan make his appearance. He threw a frightened glance over his shoulder, as if some evil-doer were chasing him, and asked in a stifled voice, 'Is there a corner for me? I've come to sleep here.'

He had just fled in terror from the Château. For a long time past whenever he awoke at night he saw the bony and boyish form of La Trouille prowling round his room in her shift, searching for the papers. He had hidden them outside, deep in a rock-hole, and covered the hole over with earth. Jésus-Christ used to put the girl on the job because she was so light-footed, so lithe in her bare feet; she could glide everywhere, in and out of the chairs, under the bed, supple as a snake. She put all her energy into the search, convinced that the old man hid the papers somewhere on himself when he dressed, and exasperated at not being able to find where he had stuck them before going to bed. She knew for certain there was nothing in the bed; for she had felt it all over with her thin arm and her touch was so light that her grandfather hardly felt her fingers. But on that particular day he turned giddy after breakfast and fell down in a faint against the table. When he came to himself again, still so weak that his eyes remained closed, he realised he was lying on the ground in the same place, and he felt Jésus-Christ and La Trouille at work undressing him. Instead of helping him, the devils thought only of taking advantage of his condition to search him. The girl in particular was pulling him about angrily, no longer using her gentle touch but wrenching off his jacket and trousers, and even poking into every aperture of his body to make sure he hadn't stuffed his hoard there. She turned him over callously, pushed his legs apart and rummaged about as if he were an empty old purse. Nothing! Where then was his hiding-place? They'd have to cut him open and look inside! He was so terrified of being murdered if he moved, that he went on pretending to be unconscious, keeping his eyes closed and his arms and legs limp. But as soon as he found himself left alone and free again, he fled, determined never to sleep another night at the Château.

'Well, have you a corner for me?' he repeated.

328

Buteau seemed revived by this unexpected return of his father. It was money coming back.

'But of course, old man! We'll squeeze together somehow! It'll bring us luck. By God, I'd be rich if all I needed was a good heart!'

Françoise and Jean had gone slowly into the empty house. Night was falling and a last sad glow filled the silent rooms. It was all so old, an old family-roof which had sheltered the toil and hardship of three centuries; a solemn atmosphere pervaded the place, like that felt in old village churches.

The doors were still open and it seemed as if a storm-wind had blown under the rafters; chairs were overturned on the floors in the general chaos of the removal. It might have been a house of death.

Françoise walked slowly round, looking into every corner. Bewildering sensations and cloudy memories stirred in her mind. Here she had played as a child. There, in the kitchen, her father had died. In the bedroom, standing by the bed stripped of its mattress, she remembered the evenings when Lise and Buteau had embraced so fiercely that she'd heard their panting breath through the ceiling. Were they going to torment her even now? She felt in her bones that Buteau was still in the house. Here he had taken hold of her one evening and she had bitten him. And there, and there. In every corner she found a memory which filled her mind with turmoil.

Then as she turned, she stood stricken with surprise at seeing Jean. What was this stranger doing there in their house? He looked uncomfortable as though he were on a visit and didn't dare to touch anything. A feeling of loneliness swept over her and she was bitterly unhappy not to feel the tang of victory any more. She had thought that she'd enter the house crying out with joy, in triumph, after her sister's retreat. And now the house yielded her no pleasure; her heart was weighed down and uneasy. Perhaps her mood came from the gloomy dusk which was falling. But when night had come, she and her man were still wandering from room to room without having the heart even to light a candle.

A noise brought them back to the kitchen and they burst out laughing when they saw Gédéon there. He had come in in his usual way and had stuck his head inside the open cupboard. The old cow, La Coliche, was lowing in her stable.

Then Jean took Françoise in his arms and kissed her gently, as if to tell her that they were going to be happy in spite of everything

FIFTH PART

I

BEFORE the winter ploughing, La Beauce, as far as eye could reach under the wan September skies, lay spread with manure. From morning till night a slow procession of carts rattled along the country roads, with overflowing loads of old straw-litter, which smoked thickly as if warmth itself were being carried to the earth. On all sides the fields were studded with little heaps, like the waves of a mounting and surging sea of stable and cowshed dung; while in some places the piles had been levelled out and the soil for miles around was darkened with a flood of blackish mud. The new life that in time would be spring lay hidden inside this fermenting manure; the decomposed matter was returning to the common womb and death would once more breed life. From one end of the immense plain to the other a smell rose up, the strong stink of the dung which nourished what would one day be the bread of men.

One afternoon Jean was driving a heavy load of manure to his field at Les Cornailles. It was a month since he and Françoise had settled down, and their life had already fallen into the busy monotonous routine of the countryside. As he reached the field, he saw Buteau on the neighbouring plot, his fork busy spreading out the manure heaps which had been brought up the week before. The two men glanced sideways at one another. Being neighbours, they often met and found themselves forced to work side by side. Buteau suffered a great deal; for Françoise's field, torn out of his seven-acre plot, left him with one strip on the left and another on the right, so that he was obliged to make many detours in his work. The two never spoke to one another. Probably, on the day when they clashed and quarrelled, murder would be done.

Meanwhile Jean began unloading the manure from his cart. He had climbed on top of it, and, buried up to his hips, was forking it out, when Hourdequin came up on one of his morning rounds of inspection. The farmer preserved a warm liking for his former labourer, and stopped for a chat. He seemed to have aged; his face was worn with worries about his farm and about other things.

'Jean, why haven't you tried phosphates?'

Without waiting for a reply, he went on talking for some time, as if trying to crush down his thoughts. The only solution of the agricultural question, he said, lay in the proper use of manures and fertilisers. He himself had tried everything; he had just got over the craze for manures which sometimes seizes a farmer. He had experimented with all sorts of things, grasses, leaves, grape-dregs, rape and colza; and after these, crushed bones, cooked and pounded flesh, dried and powdered blood. He was much disappointed at not being able to try liquid blood, since there was no slaughter-house in the district. He was now using road-scrapings, ditch-scourings, cinders and ashes from furnaces, and, above all, waste wool, having bought up the sweepings of a cloth factory at Châteaudun. His theory was that anything coming out of the earth was good to give back to her. He had made huge compost pits behind his farm where he heaped the whole district's refuse—anything he could get hold of, carrion and putrefying matter picked out of stagnant ponds or any odd corner. It was all pure gold.

'I've had very good results sometimes with phosphates,' he repeated.

'It's so easy to get cheated,' replied Jean.

'That's true, if you buy from casual agents who haunt the small country markets. There ought to be an expert chemist at every market with the job of analysing the chemical fertilisers which it's so hard to obtain unadulterated. The future lies in them, beyond a doubt; but before that future comes along we'll all be dead. Still, we ought to have courage to suffer for those to come.'

The stink of the dung which Jean was forking seemed to enliven him a little. He loved it and breathed it in with a virile delight as if it were the very odour of the earth's coitus.

'No doubt at all,' he went on after a moment's silence, 'there's nothing to touch farmyard manure. Only, there's never enough of it. And the men spoil it. They don't understand how to prepare it or how to use it. Look, even yours has been dried up in the sun. You don't keep it covered.'

He inveighed against the old rut of habit when Jean admitted that he still used the old manure-pit made by the Buteaus in front of the stable. For many years the farmer himself had had various layers of earth and grass introduced into his pits. He had built up a whole system of pipes to carry off into a pit the kitchen-slops, animal and human urine, all the farm refuse; and twice a week the

332

dunghill was watered with this liquid manure. Finally he had come to collect all the latrine deposits.

'Heavens, yes, it's ridiculous to throw away the goodness that God gives us. For a long time I shrank from the practice, just as fastidiously as our peasants. But old Mother Caca converted me. You know her, don't you? She's your neighbour. Well, she set about things the right way and she was the only one. The cabbages whose roots she empties her pots over are royal cabbages, both in size and flavour; and there's no possible doubt—the results all come from what she did.'

Jean began laughing as he jumped down from his empty cart and went on to divide the manure into small heaps. Hourdequin followed after him through the warm steam which floated all around.

'The yearly sewerage of Paris alone could fertilise some seventy thousand acres. It's been fully worked out. And yet it's all wasted except for a small amount used in the form of dried night-soil. Just think of it, seventy thousand acres! Can you imagine it here: La Beauce covered with it and the grain swelling up!'

With a sweeping gesture he embraced the whole flat and immense expanse of La Beauce. In his enthusiasm he saw Paris, all Paris, opening the flood-gates of its sewers and loosing the fertilising river of human manure. Streams went winding in all directions, every field was richly spread, as the sea of sewage mounted higher and higher under the cloudless sun, under the great winds which wafted the odour far and wide. The great town was giving back to the fields the life she had drawn from them. Slowly the earth drank in the fertilising tide; and out of the gorged, enriched soil the wheat for the white bread would grow until it burst forth in giant harvests.

'Sounds as if we'd have to have boats, then!' said Jean, vastly amused and disgusted by this new scheme for submerging the plain-lands under sewer-waters.

But at that moment a cry made him turn his head. He was surprised to see Lise standing in her gig, which she had pulled up at the side of the road, and shouting to Buteau at the top of her voice.

'Hey, I'm off to Cloyes to get M. Finet. Father's fallen down in a fit in his room. I think he's dying. You go home and attend to him.'

Without waiting for a reply, she whipped up the horse and went off again, her bobbing figure dwindling into the distance along the straight road.

Buteau took his time, fully spreading out the last heaps. He was grumbling to himself. What a nuisance if the old man was ill. Perhaps he was putting on a show, hoping to get himself pampered a bit. Then he realised that things must be serious before his wife would take on herself a doctor's expense. He decided to put on his coat and see for himself.

'That chap weighs out his precious manure!' muttered Hourdequin, scrutinising the dung on the next field with interest. 'But the mean peasant finds the earth is mean. He's a wretched fellow and you'd better be on your guard against him, after all the trouble he gave you. How can things go right when there are so many scoundrels and bitches on the earth? She's had enough of us, for sure.'

He went off towards La Borderie, once more plunged in gloom, at the same moment as Buteau, slouching heavily, got back to Rognes. Jean, left alone, completed his work, forking out the manure every ten yards or so, while ever stronger ammoniacal fumes kept rising up. Other heaps, smoking in the distance, smudged out the horizon with a fine bluish mist. The whole Beauce plain would now lie warm and odorous until the days of frost.

The Buteaus were still living with La Frimat. They occupied the entire house except the ground-floor room at the back, which she reserved for herself and her paralysed husband. They found the place very crowded and particularly missed a vegetable garden; for of course La Frimat herself kept the small garden-plot which enabled her to maintain her husband and provide him with a few luxuries. They would therefore have looked round for a larger place and moved into it had they not noticed that their nearness got on Françoise's nerves. Only a party-wall separated the two properties. And they made a point of remarking in raised voices, intended to be overheard, that they were only camping at La Frimat's and would soon be back again to their own house next door—yes, in no time. So what would be the point of going through all the nuisance of a new move? They never gave the least explanation of why and how they'd get back into the house; and indeed it was this cool assurance, this crazy certainty, based on something unknown, which put Françoise beside herself and spoiled her joy in having remained the house's mistress. In addition Lise would sometimes lean a ladder against the wall in order to shout insults at her. Since the final accounts had been settled in M. Baillehache's office, she insisted that she'd been robbed, and she never grew tired of screeching her foul charges from one yard to the other.

When Buteau at last reached the house, he found Old Fouan stretched out on his bed in the little closet where he lived behind the kitchen, under the loft-staircase. The two children were keeping watch over him. Jules was eight already and Laure three; and they were playing about on the floor at a game of rivers, pouring out the water from their grandfather's jug.

'Well, what's up then?' asked Buteau, standing at the foot of the bed.

Fouan had regained consciousness. His wide staring eyes turned slowly towards his son, but he did not move his head and seemed turned to stone.

'I say, dad, there's too much work on my hands, no nonsense now. You mustn't lay yourself out to-day.'

Laure and Jules now managed to smash the jug and he gave them a couple of smacks which sent them howling. The old man's eyes were still wide open, staring with his dilated, fixed pupils. There was nothing to be done then, since he hadn't any more kick in him. They must wait and see what the doctor had to say. Buteau was sorry he had left the field and started chopping wood in the yard, so as not to stand there idling.

But Lise returned almost the next moment with M. Finet, who made a long examination of the stricken man. Buteau and his wife waited uneasily. The old man's death would have taken a burden off them if the stroke had only killed him at once; but his present condition might last a long time and perhaps cost a lot of money. Then again, if he died before they had their hands on his hoard, Fanny and Jésus-Christ would certainly give them a lot of bother. The doctor's silence deepened their anxiety; and when he sat down in the kitchen to draw up his prescriptions, they decided to question him.

'Is it serious then? Might go on for a week, eh? God, what a long list! What's all that you're writing down there for him?'

M. Finet made no reply. He was used to questions of this sort being put to him by the peasants, who were always thrown off their balance by illness. He had taken the line of treating them like a pack of horses and never let himself be drawn into a discussion. He had wide experience of common ailments and usually cured his patients with more ease than a man of greater theoretical knowledge would have done. But he accused them of having reduced him to a level of mediocrity and was consequently harsh towards them, which increased their deference in spite of continual doubts about the efficaciousness of his draughts. Would they do as much good as the money they cost?

'So you think,' Buteau persisted, scared at the page of prescriptions, 'you think that all that stuff'll make him better?'

The doctor merely shrugged his shoulders. He had gone back to the sick man's bedside, interested and surprised at noting some signs of fever after the mild attack of cerebral congestion. With his eyes on his watch, he took the old man's pulse again, and made no effort to draw any information from Fouan, who went on blankly staring. Then, as he was leaving, he merely stated, 'It'll take about three weeks, I'll call again to-morrow. Don't be surprised if he's got bats in his belfry to-night.'

Three weeks! That was all the Buteaus heard. They were struck dumb. What money they'd have to pay out if there was a whole pageful of medicines every night! The worst of it all was that Buteau had now to get into the cart and drive off to the chemist at Cloyes. It was Saturday, and when La Frimat came back from selling her vegetables she found Lise alone and so depressed that she was roaming aimlessly about. The old woman broke into lamentations too, when she heard the story. She never had any luck; if the trouble had happened on any other day, she could at least have taken advantage of the doctor's visit by asking him to have a look at her husband into the bargain.

The news had already made the rounds of Rognes. People had seen the impudent La Trouille run to the house, where she had refused to leave without touching the old man's hand. She then ran back to Jésus-Christ with the tidings that he certainly wasn't yet dead.

Close behind the slut came La Grande, evidently despatched by Fanny. The old woman set herself in front of her brother's bed and decided on his condition by considering the clearness of his eyes, just as she did with eels from the Aigre; then she went off with a twitch of the nose that seemed to express her regret that the present stroke wouldn't be the last. After that the family stopped worrying. Why worry, since the odds were that the old man would get over the attack?

The house was in chaos until midnight. Buteau had come home in a foul temper. Mustard-plasters had to be made for Fouan's legs, a draught had to be administered every hour, and a purge next

336

morning if the symptoms bettered. La Frimat offered her help; but about ten o'clock, dropping with drowsiness and not very interested in the situation, she went off to bed. Buteau, who wanted to do the same, tried to hustle Lise away. What were they messing about there for? They were certainly not soothing the old man by standing there looking at him.

For he was rambling in his talk now, chattering inconsequentially; he must have been dreaming that he was out in the fields, working hard, as in the remote days of his youth and strength. Lise was upset by these memories, stammered out in a lowered voice, as if the old man was already buried and his ghost had come back. She was about to follow her husband, who was already undressing, when she paused to put away the old man's clothes which had been thrown on a chair. She shook them carefully, after going minutely through every pocket and finding nothing but a broken knife and some string. Then, as she hung the things up at the end of the cupboard, she saw, just in the middle of a shelf, staring her in the face, a little bundle of papers. Her heart missed a beat. The hoard! Here was the hoard that they'd sought for so many months and rummaged for in so many out-of-the-way places: now it had turned up, not hidden at all, practically put into her hand. Presumably the old man had been knocked out by the stroke while about to change the hiding-place.

'Buteau! Buteau!' she called, in such a constricted voice that he ran out in his shirt, thinking that his father must be on the point of death.

At first he too stood transfixed. Then a mad joy took hold of them both; they grasped hands and jumped about together like a pair of goats, completely forgetting the sick man who now lay with closed eyes, his head seemingly nailed to the pillow. Ceaselessly he went on muttering the broken phrases of his delirium. At the moment he was ploughing.

'Hey, there, you brute, get along there! What's holding things up? A big bit of flint, by God! It's breaking the handles. I'll have to buy some more. Hey up! you brute!'

'Hush!' murmured Lise, turning round with a shudder.

'Nonsense!' replied Buteau, 'do you think he's listening? Can't you hear the drivel he's talking?'

They sat down near the bed; for their legs had given way in the violent shock of exultation.

'Anyway,' she went on, 'no one can say we hunted for it. As

337

God's my witness, I wasn't thinking about it at all. It jumped right into my hand. Let's have a look.'

He was already opening the paper and counting out loud.

'Two hundred and thirty, plus seventy, exactly three hundred. That's it: I worked it all out according to the quarter's interest after I saw the fifteen five-franc pieces that day at the tax-collector's office. At five per cent interest. Isn't it funny these dirty bits of paper are worth money all the same, just as good as real cash.'

Lise again hushed him, frightened by a sudden cackle from the old man, who now seemed to be helping to gather the huge harvest in the reign of Charles X, when there was too much grain for the granaries and storehouses.

'Heaps, what heaps! It's enough to make you laugh, there's so much! Ah, by Heaven, when there's heaps, there's heaps.'

His choking laugh sounded like a death-rattle. His delight must have been deep buried within; for no sign of it appeared on his motionless features.

'He's only babbling a lot of childish things,' said Buteau, with a shrug.

There was a hush as they both stared at the papers, thinking hard.

'What'll we do now?' whispered Lise at last. 'We'll have to put them back, I suppose.'

He made a vigorous gesture of denial.

'Yes, we must put them back. He'll look for them and he'll shout and scream. It'll make a lot of trouble for us with the other swine of the family.'

She paused for the third time, startled at hearing his father's sob. The sound was one of misery and hopeless despair; the sobs seemed growing out of his whole life, for no definite reason. He muttered a single phrase in a voice that grew more and more hollow, 'It's all up—it's all up—it's all up.'

'What,' Buteau replied vehemently to Lise, 'd'you think I'm going to leave the papers about for an old man who's cracked? So he can tear them up or burn them, eh? Never!'

'Yes, that's very true,' she whispered.

'Come on, that's enough, let's go to bed. If he asks for the papers, I'll tell him that they're in my charge. And no one had better try to interfere!'

They went to bed after hiding the papers in their turn under the marble slab of an old wash-stand, which seemed safer than the bottom of a locked drawer. The old man, left alone without a candle for fear of fire, went on babbling and sobbing all night long in his delirium.

Next day M. Finet found him calmer, much better than he had expected. These old plough-horses have got their souls well rivetted to their bodies! The ominous fever seemed to have been avoided. The doctor ordered iron, quinine and other costly drugs which again upset the household with their price. Then, as he was leaving, he had a tussle with La Frimat, who had been watching out for him.

'But, my good woman, I've already told you that your husband and this block of stone here are exactly the same. I can't make stones move, can I? You know how it will end, don't you, and the sooner the better—for you and for your husband alike.'

He whipped up his horse, and she collapsed in tears on the block of stone. She had been looking after her man for twelve years now, a long hard time; her strength was failing her with age and she was terrified that she'd soon be incapable of cultivating their patch of garden. But no matter, her heart sank at the thought of losing the old invalid who had become like her child as she moved him about, dressed and undressed him, and spoiled him with little treats. The one good arm which he could still use was beginning to get stiff like the other; she now had to put his pipe in his mouth.

In a week's time M. Finet was amazed to see Old Fouan on his feet again, very shaky but determined to get about, because, he said, what stops a man dying is his refusal to die. Buteau chuckled behind the doctor's back; for he had ignored all the prescriptions after the second one, saying that the best cure was to leave the illness to consume itself. However, on market-day, Lise had been weak enough to bring back a draught prescribed the day before; and when the doctor came on Monday for his final visit, Buteau told him that the old man had almost had a relapse.

'I don't know what they put in the bottle you ordered, but it made him bloody sick.'

That evening Fouan made up his mind to speak. Since he had been on his feet, he had roamed uneasily round the house, unable to recall where he could have stowed his papers away. He rummaged and ferreted everywhere, making desperate efforts to remember. Then a shred of memory returned: perhaps he hadn't hidden them at all, but had just left them on the shelf. But then, supposing he was mistaken, supposing they hadn't been stolen, could he risk raising an alarm and confessing that the money, painfully saved over long years and then assiduously hidden, did exist after all? For two days more he struggled, torn between his wrath at the papers' sudden disappearance and the dire need he felt to keep his mouth closed about them at all costs. But his mind gradually became clearer and he recalled that on the morning of his attack he had put the papers on the shelf while waiting for a chance to slip them into a crack in the ceiling rafters which he had just noticed as he lay on his bed gazing upwards. So, despoiled and desperate, he blurted everything out.

The family had just finished the evening meal and Lise was putting the dishes away. Buteau had closely watched his father from the moment he left his bed; and he was now leaning back in his chair with his sly look, expecting something. The moment had come, he told himself; the old chap seemed so miserable and worked-up. And in fact the old man, who had been stubbornly shambling round the room on his feeble legs, suddenly planted himself before his son.

'Where are the papers?' he asked in a harsh choked voice.

Buteau blinked with a show of extreme surprise, as if he didn't understand.

'Eh? what did you say? Papers, what papers?'

'My money!' roared the old man, menacing, drawing himself up, stiff and tall.

'Your money! So you've still got some money? You swore blind we'd bled you until you didn't have a sou left. You cunning old fellow, so you've got some money!'

He was still leaning back in his chair, sneering and highly amused, proud of his instinct as he remembered that he'd been the first to suspect the existence of a hoard.

Fouan was trembling all over.

'Give it back!'

'Give it back? Have I got it? Do I even know where it is, this money of yours?'

'You've stolen it, give it back, by God! or I'll force you to cough it up.'

Old as he was, he seized Buteau by the shoulders and shook him. But his son then stood up and grasped him in turn, not to push him over but just to yell straight into his face:

'Yes, I've got it and I'm going to keep it. I'm going to keep it for you, you old fool, because you're going crazy. Yes, we only just

340

got those papers away from you in time. You were going to tear them up. Isn't that so, Lise, wasn't he tearing them up?'

'Yes, true as I'm here. When a man doesn't know what he's doing, well. . . !'

Fouan gasped in terror, overwhelmed at what he heard. Was he really out of his wits, as he couldn't remember doing any such things? If he'd really been trying to destroy the deeds, like a child tearing up pictures or bits of paper, then he was good for nothing and only fit for his coffin. Heart-broken, he felt his last strength and courage ebb away, as he stammered out tearfully, 'Give them back, won't you?'

'No.'

'Give them back, I'm better now.'

'No, I won't. So you can wipe yourself with them or use them to light your pipe? Not likely!'

After that the Buteaus obstinately refused to hand over the deeds. They talked about them quite openly and fabricated an exciting account of how they had arrived in the nick of time to snatch them from the sick man's hands as he began ripping them up. One evening they even showed La Frimat the little notch of the tear. Who could blame them for preventing such a misfortune? The money would have been torn to tatters and lost to everyone. The villagers approved their action in public, but privately suspected them of lying. Jésus-Christ in particular was furious. To think that the hoard which it had been impossible to track down in his own house, had been so easily winkled out in someone else's! Worse than that, one day he had actually had the papers in his hands and had been fool enough to put them back! What was the use of being thought a bad lot if you didn't act like one? He swore that he'd settle accounts with his brother when the old man gave up the ghost. Fanny also said that a division would have to be made. The Buteaus never disputed that; but, of course, the old man might regain his money or dispose of it by deed.

As for Fouan, he trailed about from door to door telling his version of the story. Every time he managed to stop someone on the road, he poured out the tale of his unhappy lot. One morning he even went into his niece's yard next door.

Françoise was helping Jean to load the cart with manure. Jean was in the ditch throwing the dung up on his fork, while she stood in the cart, spread the muck and pressed it down with her feet to

341

pack it tighter. The old man leaned on his stick before them and began the recital of his woes.

'You know how bothered I am about my money. They took it away and they won't give it back. What would you two do?'

Françoise let him repeat the question three times. She was very annoyed at his intruding on them with his wrongs and she treated him coldly in her anxiety to avoid giving the Buteaus any excuse for a grievance.

'You see, uncle,' she replied at last, 'it's nothing to do with us. We're only too pleased to be out of it all—out of that hell.'

Turning her back, she continued her work, buried in dung to the thighs and almost submerged as her husband flung up one forkful after another. She was lost to sight there in the warm steam that rose from the turned-over manure, and yet she felt at ease and self-confident, amid the asphyxiating fumes.

'I'm not mad, you can see that, can't you?' Fouan insisted, seeming not to have heard her. 'They ought to give me back my money. What do you two think? Do you think I'm capable of destroying it?'

Neither Françoise nor Jean spoke a word.

'I'd be mad to do such a thing and I'm not mad. You could both bear witness to that, couldn't you?'

Françoise straightened herself abruptly on top of the loaded cart. She looked very tall, healthy and strong, as if she'd grown there and as if the smell of fecund life was coming out of her own body. As she stood there, arms akimbo, with her well-rounded breasts, she was a proper woman at last.

'Now, uncle, that's enough, I say. I've told you that we don't want to get mixed up with all this backbiting. And while we're on the matter, it might be best if you didn't come to see us any more.'

'So you're sending me away?' asked the old man, trembling.

Jean thought it was time to intervene.

'No, but we don't want any rows. There'd be a three day fight if you were seen in here. Everyone has a right to peace and quiet, hasn't he?'

Fouan stayed motionless, turning his poor weak eyes from one to the other. Then he went away.

'Right, if I need help, I'll have to go somewhere else.'

They were troubled at heart as they watched him go; for they were not yet lost to decent feeling. But what could they do? Any interference by them wouldn't have helped him and they'd only have spoiled their own sleep and appetite. As her husband went to fetch his whip, Françoise carefully collected the fallen bits of dung with a shovel and threw them back into the cart.

Next day a violent scene broke out between Buteau and Fouan. Every day the same old arguments about the deeds had gone on— the old man repeating his eternal 'Give them back to me!' with monomaniac persistence, while the son replied with his invariable refusal, 'Hold your row and leave me alone!' But gradually matters grew tenser, particularly since the old man had started trying to find the place where his son had hidden the hoard. He was now the one who pried about the whole house, examining drawers and cupboards, tapping the walls for a hollow spot. A single thought held his mind and his eyes never ceased peering into one corner or another. As soon as he was left alone, he pushed the children out and renewed his rummaging with the obsession of a randy lad who leaps at the servant-girl the moment his parents are out of the way. That day, however, Buteau returned unexpectedly and found Fouan stretched out flat on his stomach, with his nose under the chest-of-drawers, trying to make out if the hiding-place was located there. Buteau was enraged; for his father was now hot on the trail. What the old man was looking for underneath was actually hidden above, sealed fast, so to say, by the weight of the marble top.

'You damned old crack-pot! Playing snakes, are you? Get up with you!'

He pulled him out by the legs and set him on his feet with a rough shaking.

'Now that's enough sticking your nose in every hole! I'm fed up with your poking about into every crack and cranny in the house!'

Fouan, furious at being caught in the act, stared back at his son and shouted in a sudden access of wrath, 'Give them back!'

'You bloody well leave me alone!' Buteau bawled in his face.

'Well, I'm too miserable here. I'm going away.'

'Right you are! Get out and good riddance! And if you come back, by God, it'll show you've got no guts!'

He seized the old man by the arm and shoved him out of the house.

II

Fouan went down the slope. His anger had suddenly faded away; and when he came to the highway at the foot of the hill, he halted, bewildered at finding himself out of doors with nowhere to go. The church-clock struck three and the damp wind of the grey autumn afternoon blew bitterly cold. He shivered. Everything had happened so quickly that he hadn't even picked up his hat. But luckily he had his stick. For a while he went on up the opposite slope towards Cloyes; but then he asked himself why he was going that way, and turned back to Rognes with the dragging step that had now become normal to him. As he came up to Macqueron's, he had an impulse to go in and drink a glass; but he searched his pockets and found he hadn't even a copper. He felt suddenly ashamed of being seen, wondering whether everyone already knew about his homelessness. He was sure that Lengaigne, standing in his doorway, was watching him with the sidelong look that people give to highway-beggars. Lequeu, gazing out of one of the school windows, did not even nod. That he should once more rouse everybody's contempt was understandable; for he was penniless a second time, stripped afresh of everything—this time down to the bare skin.

When he reached the Aigre, he leaned his back a moment on the bridge parapet. The thought of the oncoming night harrassed him. Where was he to sleep? Without even a roof over his head! The Bécu dog, which passed him at that moment, stirred his envy; for at least the creature knew a snug straw-lair where he could sleep. The old man racked his muddled brains, but he felt drowsy now that his rush of anger had worn itself out. His eyelids would not stay open as he tried to recall some sheltered nook, protected from the cold. The strain had an effect of nightmare; he saw the whole countryside wheeling past, bare and swept by gusts of wind. He shook himself and broke through his drowsiness in a sudden access of energy. He mustn't lose heart like that. A man of his age would never be left to freeze in the ditch.

Without thinking, he crossed the bridge and found himself in front of the Delhommes' little farm. As soon as he noticed where he was, he turned aside and went behind the house to avoid being seen. Again he stopped, right up against the stable wall. Now he could hear his daughter Fanny talking inside. Had he thought of going back to live with her? He couldn't have answered the question; his feet had led him there of their own accord. He saw the interior of the house just as if he had gone back inside: the kitchen on the left, his own room on the first floor at the end of the hay-loft. A yearning tenderness weakened his legs; he would have fallen, had not the wall been there to support him. For a long time he stood unmoving, with his old back pressed against the house. Fanny went on talking inside the shed, but he could not make out the words. Perhaps it was that loud muffled sound which moved him so deeply. She must have been scolding a servant, for her voice grew shriller and he could distinguish her stern, harsh tone. He knew that without using coarse language, she was saying such hurtful things that the unfortunate girl was sobbing aloud. The old man suffered with the girl. His tender feelings disappeared and he stiffened in the certainty that if he had pushed open the door, his daughter would greet him in the same ugly voice. Once more he heard her saying: 'Oh, dad'll come back on his knees asking us to take him in again!'—the phrase which had severed all bonds between them for ever, as if it had been an axe-blow. No, no, he'd rather die of starvation, rather sleep under a hedge, than see her triumph with that smug expression of a woman beyond reproach. He detached himself from the wall and painfully went on his way.

To avoid going back on to the road, Fouan, who felt that everyone was staring at him, climbed up the right bank of the Aigre past the bridge, and soon found himself in the vineyards. His plan was to get out to the plain by this route, skirting the village. However, he was thus obliged to pass near the Château. His legs seemed again to have taken control and brought him back to a familiar spot with the instinct of an old beast of burden that finds its way back to the stable where it used to munch its oats. The climb made him short of breath; he sat down panting beside the path and brooded. He knew that he had only to say to Jésus-Christ 'I'm taking Buteau to court, I want your help', and the rascal would receive him with a welcoming blurt; and then they'd spend a riotous evening together. From the corner where he was hiding he could make out a feast in progress, a drinking-party which had been going on since morning. Fascinated and famished, he went nearer. He recognised Canon's voice and sniffed the lentil stew which La Trouille cooked to perfection when her father wanted to celebrate one of his comrade's sudden appearances. Why shouldn't he go in and make merry with the two scamps? He could hear them yelling at one another through the smoke from their pipes, pleasantly warm, and so sozzled that he envied them. A sudden explosion from Jésus-Christ drew the old man so strongly that his hand was reaching for the door-knob when the shrill laugh of La Trouille paralysed him. The girl was the one who frightened him now; he kept seeing her, slim in her shift, writhing up to him in her adder's nakedness, feeling him all over, preying on him. What use would it be if the father helped him to regain his documents? The daughter would sneak them away from him again. All of a sudden the door opened and the ragamuffin came out to look around, scenting the presence of a stranger. He barely had time to drop behind some bushes; and as he slipped away, he made out her green eyes shining through the thickening dusk.

When he reached the open plain, he felt a kind of relief; here he was safe from attack, glad at being away from others, free to die alone. For hours he went on wandering anywhere. Night came on and the icy wind lashed him. He had to turn his back, his breath snatched from him by the fierce gusts, and his white hair blown up over his bare head. Six o'clock struck: everyone in Rognes was now at dinner. His limbs were failing him and he had to slow down his pace. Between two wind-squalls the rain came pouring over him, fiercely stinging. Soaked to the skin, he walked on through two more downpours. Then, without knowing how he got there, he found himself near the church, in front of the old family-house of the Fouans where Françoise and Jean now lived. No, he couldn't seek refuge there, they too had chased him away. The rain came down more heavily still and he began to lose heart. He went over to the door of the Buteau house and peered into the kitchen, attracted by the smell of cabbage soup. Every inch of his poor body yearned to give in; a physical need for food and warmth urged him on. But, amid the champing of busy jaws, some fragments of conversation halted him.

'What about father? What if he doesn't come back?'

'Don't worry! He thinks too much of his belly not to come back as soon as he's hungry!'

Fouan hurried away again, afraid that he might have been seen at the door like a thrashed dog that crawls back for a bone. Choking with shame, he resolved wildly to die in some corner. They'd see if he only thought of his belly! Again he went down the hill and then collapsed on the end of a log in front of Clou's forge. His legs wouldn't support him any further and he gave way completely in the black solitude of the road. The winter evenings had come round again and the houses were so closely shuttered against the bad weather that not a living soul seemed left in the village. The downpour had quietened down the wind, the showers grew worse, falling straight down, steadily, in torrents. He couldn't summon the

346

strength to rise and look for shelter. With his stick between his knees and water streaming from his head, he sat there stone-still, stupefied by his hopelessness. He didn't even think. What had happened was what always happened; when a man lost children, house, everything, he had to pull in his belt and sleep in the open. Nine struck, then ten. The rain was still falling, soaking him right through to his old bones. But some lantern-light now appeared, flitting rapidly about. The even-calls were ending. He was brought back to himself by recognising La Grande, who had spent the evening with the Delhommes to save lighting her own candles and was now leaving. He got up with an effort which made his limbs creak, and followed her at a distance, failing to catch her up in time on the doorstep. Faced by the closed door, he hesitated and his heart sank. But at last, he knocked in a blind impulse of abject misery.

He had chosen a most unfortunate moment; La Grande was in a ferocious mood because of a disaster which had upset her last week. One evening when she was alone with her grandson Hilarion, she had had the idea of making him chop wood, to extract some more work out of him before packing him off to sleep in the straw; and as he was working half-heartedly, she stayed at the end of the woodshed to heap insults on him. Till this moment the brutish creature with the twisted body and bull-sinews had felt such a grovelling fear of his grandmother that he'd let her take advantage of his strength without so much as daring to raise his eyes. But for several days past he had been quivering under the burden of excessive toil and his limbs had stiffened with the rush of blood. She should have been more cautious; but she made the mistake of trying to hurry him up with a welt of her stick across the back. He dropped the cleaver and looked straight at her. Furious at his revolt, she beat him about the legs, the thighs, all over the body, till suddenly he threw himself on her. She expected to be thrown down, kicked, strangled. But no, he had known too much abstinence since the death of his sister, Palmyre, and his anger turned into a different kind of fury which recognised neither kinship nor age, hardly even the sex of the old woman. The creature violated her, his eighty-nine-year old grandmother, with her flesh as dry as a stick and nothing of a woman left in her but her cloven body. The old woman, still tough and able to defend herself, put up a hard fight. She managed to get hold of the cleaver and split Hilarion's skull with one blow. The neighbours ran up at her outcry and she told them the story in all its details. An inch further and she'd have been done for; the blackguard was about there. Hilarion did not die till morning. Then the magistrate came to investigate. Next there was the funeral, after that all sorts of vexations, which she had now fortunately put behind her. She was restored to peace of mind, though still stung by the world's ingratitude and swearing that she'd never again do anything for a member of her family.

Fouan had to knock three times; but he did it so timidly that La Grande failed to hear him. At last she came back to the door and asked:

'Who's there?'

'Me.'

'Who's that?'

'Me, your brother.'

She had certainly recognised his voice at once; but she wasn't in a hurry. She enjoyed forcing him to talk. She said nothing for a while, then she spoke again:

'What do you want?'

He shivered and dared not reply. She roughly flung the door open; but as he tried to enter, she barred the way with her thin arms and kept him out in the road under the dismal rain which never ceased for a moment.

'Yes, I know what you want. They came over and told me to-night. Ah, you've been fool enough to let them do you down again. You haven't even been able to keep the money you hid away, and now you want me to take you in, eh?'

He tried to find excuses for himself and stammered out explanations; but she angrily cut him short.

'It isn't as if I didn't warn you! I told you time and time again that a man must be a fool and a coward to give up his land! Well, you see I was right and you've ended just as I said you would, thrown out by your scoundrelly children, roaming in the night like a beggar who hasn't even a stone to lay his head on.'

With outstretched hands he went on sobbing, trying to push past her. But she refused to give way and finished pouring out her thoughts.

'Never, never! You can go and ask shelter from the ones who've robbed you. I don't owe you anything. They'd all accuse me of meddling again. Not that that's the point anyway. You gave up your property and I'll never forgive you for it.'

Drawing herself up to her full height, with her withered neck and round vulturine eyes, she slammed the door violently in his face.

348

'Serves you right, go and die on the road!'

Fouan stood there, stiff and motionless, staring at the pitiless door while the rain went on pattering monotonously down behind him. At last he turned round and went off into the inky night which was being drowned in the slow, icy flood falling from the skies.

Where did he go? He could never properly remember. His feet stumbled in puddles, his hands groped ahead to save him from bumping into walls and trees. He couldn't think, his mind was a blank. The section of the village where he knew every stone had turned into an unknown faraway land, a dreadful place where he felt himself a stranger, lost and unable to find his way. He strayed to the left, drew back in fear of deep holes, moved again to the right, halted in tremulous uncertainty, feeling dangers all around. When his hand touched a fence, he followed it till he reached a small door which opened to his touch. The ground fell away from under his feet and he rolled into a pit. Here at last he was comfortable. The rain could not reach him and the place was warm; but a grunt startled him and he realised that he was in a pigsty. The pig was disturbed, thinking that food had been tossed in, and began poking its snout into Fouan's ribs. He tried to beat it off; but he felt so weak that he grew afraid of being eaten and crawled into the open again. Then, unable to walk any further, he lay down against the door, curled up into a ball so that the eaves might shelter him from the wet. But the drips still soaked his legs and the gusts of wind began freezing the damp clothes on his body. He envied the pig and would have gone back into the sty if he hadn't heard the creature in his rear gnawing at the door with greedy snorts.

At dawn he awoke from the painful drowse into which he had sunk. Again he was filled with shame—the shame of knowing that his story was running all over the countryside, and everyone knew he'd been turned out on the road like a beggar. A man who's stripped of everything needn't expect any justice or mercy. He slipped along the hedgerows, scared that a window would open and some early-rising woman would recognise him. It was still raining as he reached the plain and hid himself under a rick. All the long day he spent in fleeing from one shelter to another, so overcome with the fear of discovery that every couple of hours he changed his lair. The one question which now throbbed in his brain was the length of time it took to die. He wasn't feeling the cold so much; it was hunger which now tortured him; he would die of hunger for sure. One more night, one more day, perhaps. As long as it was light he did not waver; he would rather die out there than return to the Buteaus.

But a ghastly despair seized him when twilight fell and he foretasted the horror of another night under the ceaseless rain. The cold pierced him again to the marrow; hunger past bearing gnawed at his stomach. When the sky was completely overcast, he felt as though he were drowning, washed away by the flowing dark. His mind had no longer any control of his movements; his legs carried him along of their own accord and animal instinct guided him. And so it was that without any conscious intention he found himself back in the Buteau kitchen the moment after pushing the door open.

Buteau and Lise were just finishing their meal of yesterday's cabbage soup. Buteau turned his head at the noise and stared at Fouan, who stood there without a word, with the steam from his soaked garments rising round him. There was a long pause. Then Buteau remarked with a sneer, 'I knew you wouldn't have the guts.'

The old man, rooted in a frozen stupor, did not open his lips, did not utter a word.

'Come on then, woman, give him his fodder. He's hungry—that's why he came back.'

Lise, who had already risen to her feet, fetched a plateful of soup. But Fouan took the plate and went to sit by himself on a stool, as if refusing to join his children at the table. He began swallowing the soup greedily in huge mouthfuls. His whole body went on shuddering with the violence of his hunger. Buteau himself finished his meal without haste, tipping up his chair and stabbing pieces of cheese which he ate from his knife-point. The old man's ravenous appetite fascinated him and he sneered as his eyes followed the busy spoon.

'Well, well, your walk in the fresh air seems to have given you a good appetite. You'd better not do it every day or you'll cost too much to feed.'

The father went on gulping, gulping, with noisily-working throat, but he said nothing. So the son continued, 'The old joker's been sleeping out! Perhaps he's been after the wenches. That's what's cleaned you out, eh?' Still there was no reply. Only the same obstinate silence, the same low noise of swallowing as the old man stuffed himself.

'Hey, I'm talking to you,' shouted Buteau in irritation, 'you might be polite enough to reply.'

Fouan did not even lift his filmy eyes from the soup that engrossed him. He seemed deaf and blind, completely alone, miles distant, as if he were explaining that he had come back only to eat—that his stomach was there, but his heart had gone far away for ever. Now he was scraping the bottom of the bowl with the spoon, roughly, so as not to lose even a speck of nourishment.

Lise, touched by his enormous hunger, dared to put in a word. 'Leave him alone if he wants to pretend he's a corpse.'

'I'm not going to have him play me up again!' furiously retorted Buteau. 'It's all right for once. But, d'you hear, you damned old mule, let to-day be a lesson to you! If you give me any more trouble, I'll let you starve on the highway.'

When Fouan had finished, he rose stiffly from his chair; and still without a word, in a silence which seemed to grow more and more sepulchral, he turned away, dragged himself under the staircase till he reached his bed, and threw himself down fully-clothed. Sleep came on him like a thunderbolt and he was instantly asleep, hardly breathing, shut in a leaden slumber. Lise went to look at him and came back to tell her husband that perhaps he was dead. But Buteau, after going to have a look, shrugged his shoulders. Bah, dead! a man didn't die like that! All the same he must have wandered a bit to get into such a state. Next morning, when they peeped in, the old man had not stirred. He slept right through that day and only woke up on the second morning, after thirty-six hours of oblivion.

'So, here you are again!' said Buteau with a snigger. 'I thought it would go on and on, so you wouldn't need any more food.'

The old man didn't look at him or reply. He went out and sat by the roadside for a breath of fresh air.

Henceforward Fouan stuck to his own ways. He seemed to have forgotten the deeds that they refused to return him; at least he never mentioned them, he never searched for them. Maybe he was indifferent now; in any case he was resigned. But his rupture with the Buteaus was complete and he stayed enclosed in his silence as though he were cut off and buried. Never, under any circumstance whatsoever, did he speak directly to them. The family life went on as before: he slept in the house, he ate there, he saw the others and lived shoulder to shoulder with them; but never a look was exchanged, never a word. He might have been blind and dumb, dragging himself about like a ghostly shadow among the living. At last Buteau and even Lise grew tired of bothering about him with-

351

out even the response of a sigh; they left him alone in his dogged self-isolation. They stopped talking to him; they treated him as a piece of furniture which changed its place now and again; and in the end they became quite unaware of his presence. The horse and the two cows were much more important creatures.

In the entire household Fouan had only one friend left, young Jules, who was now in his ninth year. Laure, four years old, stared at him as coldly as her parents and used to wriggle out of his arms with an indignant scowl as if already bitter against someone who ate but did no work. But Jules delighted in playing about with the old man. The boy remained his last link with the living, and carried his messages when he could not avoid replying to some question. His mother sent him to ask and he brought back the answer; for to him, and him alone, his grandfather opened his mouth. The old man was so neglected that the boy also became a sort of little servant-maid, helped him to make his bed in the morning and took him the plateful of soup which he ate sitting near the window; for he had refused to resume his place at table. And they used to play together. Fouan's greatest pleasure was to take Jules by the hand and go off on a long ramble in any direction. On these occasions he made up for his long silences; he chattered on and on until the boy was almost dazed—though he spoke now with considerable difficulty, his powers of speech seeming to grow rusty through disuse. But the pair got on well together—the old man who stammered away and the small boy with no interests beyond birds' nests and blackberries. Somehow they chatted away for hours. Fouan taught the boy how to set limed twigs and made him a little cage to keep crickets in. Clasping the child's frail hand, he wandered over the deserted roads of the countryside where he no longer possessed either land or family; and these excursions were the only thing that sustained the old man and gave him the wish to keep alive a little longer.

In everything else Fouan might have been crossed off the list of the living. Buteau acted for him in everything, received and signed for all moneys, on the plea that the poor old chap was weak in the head. The interest of a hundred and fifty francs coming from the house sale was paid direct to him by M. Baillehache. His only trouble was with Delhomme, who refused to hand over the two hundred francs allowance and insisted on paying it direct to his father-in-law. Delhomme insisted on the old man's presence, but Buteau hardly waited for his back to be turned before pocketing it. He thus got

in three hundred and fifty francs a year, but moaned that he had
to spend more than twice that sum to feed and keep the old man.
Nowadays he never spoke of the deeds; they stayed hidden and
could be dealt with later. As for the interest in the investments, he
alleged that they all went to pay the agreed sums to old Saucisse,
fifteen sous a morning, for the purchase of the acre and a quarter
of land. He complained loudly that he couldn't let the contract
lapse, there was too much money involved. However, the rumour
got round that old Saucisse had been threatened and browbeaten
into cancelling the agreement and had given back half the money
already paid over: that is, some thousand francs out of the two
thousand. The reason that the old twister kept his mouth shut was
his overweening vanity. He didn't want people to learn that he had
been beaten at his own game. Buteau felt in his bones that Fouan
would die first; for the old man was obviously so weak that a strong
push would send him over and he wouldn't be able to get up again.

A year went by in this way. Fouan grew daily more enfeebled, yet
somehow managed to go on living. No longer was he the neat old
peasant with clean-shaven face, trimmed side-whiskers, new blouse
with black trousers. His great bony nose, curving more and more
downwards, seemed the only feature intact in his thin, ravaged face.
He had yearly grown a little more bent, till now he moved about
bent almost double. All he had left to make was the last tumble,
which would land him in the grave. He dragged himself about on
two thick sticks with a long dirty white beard straggling over his
face; he wore the torn old clothes cast off by his son and was so
neglected that he stank in the sunlight, like one of those old ragged
tramps that people avoid on the roads. In his general breakdown
all that persisted was the human animal whose only instinct is to
keep alive. In his voracity he threw himself on his soup; he was
never satisfied, even stealing Jules' bread-and-butter if the boy
didn't hang on to it. As a retort to these predatory tricks, the Buteaus
reduced his food and took advantage of his position to underfeed
him, pretending that he'd kill himself with overeating. Buteau
accused him of being demoralised while he lived in the Château
with Jésus-Christ; and the charge was true. The man who had been
a sober peasant, harshly self-disciplined on a diet of bread and
water, had picked up a taste for dissipation, an appetite for meat
and brandy. Vicious ways quickly eat into a man, even when it's
a son who debauches his father. Lise found the wine disappearing
and had to lock it up. The days when there was a stew on the fire,

little Laure had to stay and keep watch over it. Since the old man had fallen into debt at Lengaigne's over a cup of coffee, the grocer and Macqueron had been told that they would not be paid if they gave him drinks on credit. Fouan still kept his mouth shut; but sometimes, when his plate wasn't full, when the wine was put away without his glass being filled, he stared at Buteau with his aged eyes flaring in impotent ravenous anger.

'Go on, go on, stare away!' Buteau used to say. 'D'you think I'd waste food on a man who does no work? If you want meat, you must work for it, you old greedy-guts! Aren't you ashamed of starting to be dissipated at your time of life?'

Fouan had refused to return to the Delhommes' house because his obstinate pride resented his daughter's insult; but he reached the stage of enduring all indignities from the Buteaus, sharp words and even blows. He never thought of his other children now; he resigned himself to living where he was, so completely worn-out that the thought of getting away from it all never occurred to him. Things were no better anywhere else, so what was the use? When Fanny met him, she passed by stiffly, having sworn that she would not be the first to speak. Jésus-Christ was more good-natured, despite his grievance against his father for the mean way he'd run off from the Château. One evening he amused himself by getting the old man horribly drunk at Lengaigne's; he then carried him back and laid him on the Buteaus' doorstep. There was a dreadful row and the house was in an uproar. Lise had to wash out the kitchen and Buteau swore that next time he'd throw his father out to sleep on the dung-heap. As a result, the old man was so frightened that he took to avoiding his eldest son, even plucking up enough courage to refuse an invitation to drink. He often saw La Trouille with her geese when he sat down at the road-side on his rambles. She stopped, stared piercingly at him out of her narrow eyes, and chatted for a moment, while her geese waited behind her, standing on one leg and thrusting out their necks. But one morning he discovered that she had stolen his handkerchief, and after that, as soon as he saw her approaching, he threatened her with his sticks. She was highly entertained, and set her geese on him, only running off when some passer-by gave her a slap over the ear for pestering her grandfather.

So far, however, Fouan had been able to walk, and in wandering about he found his one consolation. He was still interested in the land and often climbed towards his old fields like a decrepit rake who haunts his one-time mistress. He would move slowly along the roads with the painful steps of old age, stopping at the edge of a field and spending hours leaning on his sticks. Then he would drag himself along to another field and fall into another trance, standing motionless like a gnarled and rooted tree. His dim eyes could no longer distinguish between wheat, oats and barley. Everything was blurred; confused memories of past days reigned in his mind: in the year so-and-so a particular field had produced so many bushels. But even dates and figures became mixed up. Only one keen image persisted undiminished. The earth, the earth he had deeply desired and fiercely possessed, the earth to which for more than sixty years he had given everything, his body, his heart, his life; the ungrateful earth that, passing into the arms of another lover, went on producing its yield without a share for him. A deep melancholy gripped him when he thought that the earth knew him no longer, that he had kept nothing of the things which came out of her, not a copper coin or a crust of bread, and that he would have to die and turn to dust in her, while she, in her indifference, would make herself new life out of his old bones. Had it been worth the while killing himself with work if he must end up thus, infirm and naked? Then, after his long wanderings through the land that had once been his, he would drop on to his bed in such exhaustion that not even the sound of breathing could be heard.

He lost his last interest in life when his legs failed him. Soon he found walking so painful that he hardly stirred beyond the village. On good days he had three favourite places, the logs outside Clou's forge, the bridge over the Aigre, and a stone bench near the school. He tottered slowly from one to the other, taking an hour to cover a couple of hundred yards, dragging his wooden shoes as though they were heavy carts, waddling and twisted, with a shambling lurch of the hips. He often spent a whole afternoon of oblivion seated on a log, huddled up, just soaking in the sunshine. He sat inert in a state of torpor, though his eyes remained open. Passers-by did not greet him; nowadays he was merely a thing, not a man. Even his pipe was too much for him; he had stopped smoking because it weighed so heavily on his gums, apart from the labour of filling and lighting it. His one desire was never to move; for as soon as he stirred, he shivered with a chill even in the hot midday sun. His will and his authority had gone, and he was now in the last stages of decrepitude, an aged animal, completely abandoned, and miserable because of having once lived the life of a man. Yet he made no complaint, reared as he was on the understanding that a foundered horse, however well it has worked, must go to the slaughterer's as soon as it cannot earn its oats. An old man is quite useless and he costs money. He himself had longed for his own father's death. If in turn his children wanted him to die, he felt neither astonishment nor resentment. That was how things were.

Sometimes a neighbour exclaimed, 'Well, well, so you're still alive?'

'Ah,' he groaned in reply, 'it's a damned long business, dying, and yet it isn't the will that's lacking.'

He spoke truly, out of that stoicism of the peasant who accepts death and wishes for it as soon as he has no land and the earth is calling him back.

One final grief awaited him. Jules turned against him, prompted by little Laure. The girl seemed jealous every time she saw her brother with his grandfather. The nasty old man kept getting in the way. It was so much more fun for Jules and herself to play together. So if Jules didn't follow her immediately, she hung round his neck and pulled him away. Then she made herself so pleasant that the boy forgot the little kindly services he used to do his grandfather. Gradually she won him over completely, just like a grown woman who has set herself to make a conquest.

One evening Old Fouan had gone to wait for Jules by the school and was so tired that he wanted the boy's help to get back up the hill. But Laure came out with her brother; and as the old man felt for the boy's hand with his trembling fingers, she gave a cruel laugh.

'There he is, the old nuisance! Let him look after himself!' And, turning to the other kids, she went on, 'Isn't he a sissy to put up with it!'

Jules, surrounded by yelling children, blushed and felt the need to assert himself. So he jumped away, echoing his sister's taunt to his old walking companion:

'You're an old nuisance!'

Bewildered, with tears blinding his eyes, Fouan staggered as if the earth gave way beneath him when the little hand was withdrawn. The laughter swelled and Laure forced Jules to dance with her round the old man, singing to the tune of a play-song:

> 'Tumble down, tumble down,
> Pick your dry bread off the ground.'

Fouan, almost fainting, took nearly two hours reaching home by himself, so weakly did his feet drag. The end had come. The child

356

no longer brought him his meals or helped him make his bed; and his straw mattress wasn't turned once a month. Now that he hadn't even the boy left to talk to, he sank into complete silence. His solitude had spread till it was complete. Never a word about anything to anyone.

III

THE winter ploughing was almost finished. On a cold and overcast February afternoon Jean had just come up to his big field at Les Cornailles with the cart. He had still a good two hours' work ahead. He wanted to sow a strip at the edge of the field with a Scottish variety of wheat, an experiment advised by his old master Hourdequin, who himself had put a few bushels of seed-corn at his disposal.

Jean at once got to work, starting where he had finished the evening before. He put the blade into its cutting position, grasped the handles, and gave the raucous cry that started the horse off, 'Gee up! Hup!'

Plentiful rain, falling after weeks of full sunshine, had hardened the clayey soil so thoroughly that the ploughshare and coulter had difficulty in getting rid of the lengths of earth through which they cut with their steel edges. The thick clods could be heard scraping along the moulding-board as it turned them over and buried the manure that lay in a thick layer over the field. Now and again a stone or some other obstacle suddenly jarred the plough.

'Gee up! Hup!'

Jean, with arms outstretched, took care to trace a furrow so precise and straight that it might have been marked out by string; and the horse, with lowered head and feet sinking into the soil, drew the plough along in a steady regular rhythm. When the ploughshare got clogged, Jean shook off the mud and grass with a jerk of both arms, then the plough slid forward again, while the up-turned earth in its rear seemed moving and quivering richly with life, exposed down to its very entrails.

When he reached the furrow's end, he turned and started afresh. Soon he became almost drunken with the strong odour released by the stirred earth, an odour of moist warm recesses where seeds are germinating. His slow heavy tread and the fixed line of his gaze served to doze him into abstraction. He would never become a true peasant. He had not been born to the earth; he was still a town

357

worker, a soldier who had gone through the Italian campaign; he could see and feel what the peasants never saw or felt, the vast melancholy calm of the plain, the powerful breathing of the earth under sunshine and rain. He had always dreamed of taking refuge in the country. But how foolish he had been to imagine that as soon as he dropped his gun and his carpenter's plane, the plough would bring him all the peace he desired! If the earth was peaceful and gracious to those who loved her, yet the villages that clung to her like nests of vermin and the human insects preying on her flesh were enough to dishonour her and pollute all contact. He could not remember having suffered so deeply in the period before he turned up many years ago at La Borderie.

Jean had to raise the handles a little to ease the passage of the plough. A slight bend in the furrow bothered him. Turning, he concentrated even more intently, urging the horse forward, 'Gee up! Gee up!'

Yes, what misery he had been through in those ten years! First, his long wait for Françoise; then the war with the Buteaus. Not one single day had passed without something unpleasant happening. And now that he had Françoise, now that they had been married two years, could he say he was really happy? Even if he still loved her, he had soon guessed that she didn't love him and that she never would love him as he wanted, with open arms and open heart. They lived together as good friends and their household was prospering with their hard work and thrift. But that was not what mattered. He felt her remote, cold, thinking of something else even when they were in bed together and he held her close. She was five months gone now, carrying a child conceived without pleasure; and such a child is never anything but a source of pain to a mother. Her pregnancy had not even brought them closer to one another. He was particularly hurt by a feeling which had been growing clearer and clearer ever since they had taken possession of the house, the feeling that in his wife's eyes he was still a stranger, a man from another country, a man who'd grown up elsewhere, no one knew where, a man who didn't think like the people of Rognes, who seemed to her to be differently made, and who could have no real link with her, even though he had got her with child. On the Saturday after their marriage, in her bitterness against the Buteaus she had brought a sheet of stamped paper back from Cloyes, intending to will all her property away to her husband. She had been informed that house and land would go back to her sister if she died before having a child; only money and furniture were included in the common property of man and wife. Then, without giving any explanation, she seemed to change her mind and the paper remained in the drawer, untouched. Jean felt a deep but undivulged pain, not for mercenary reasons, but because he scented a lack of affection. Anyway, now that there was to be a child, why bother to draw up a will? Still, he was oppressed every time he opened the drawer and caught sight of the unused sheet of stamped paper.

He halted to give his horse a breather. The frosty air helped him to shake off his stupor. He looked slowly round the empty horizon and over the immense plain, where other ploughmen were at work in the distance, smudged under the grey sky. He gave a start on noticing that Old Fouan was plodding along the new road from Rognes, urged on by some remembrance, some need to gaze yet again on one or other of the fields. Then he lowered his head and stared for a moment at the open furrow, the gaping earth at his feet. The soil was yellow and firm underneath, exposed to the light by the upturned clods like rejuvenated flesh; while the buried manure made a bed of rich fertility. His thoughts became confused. What a strange thing it was that men had thought of delving about in the earth in order to get bread. And how depressed he was because he couldn't feel that Françoise loved him. Other thoughts, even vaguer, floated through his mind: the growth of crops, the approaching birth of his child, all the labour of men that so often brought no happiness. He grasped the plough-handles again and shouted his guttural cry, 'Gee up! Hup!'

He was just finishing his ploughing when Delhomme, returning on foot from a neighbouring farm, stopped at the edge of the field.

'I say, Corporal, heard the news? Seems there's going to be war.'

Jean let go of the plough and stood upright, surprised and startled at this shattering news.

'War? What's happened?'

'It's the Prussians, they say. It's all in the newspapers.'

Jean, with a fixed glance, was looking back on Italy and the battles there, the slaughter through which he had passed without so much as a wound. How frantically he had longed in those days to live at peace, in some quiet corner. And now at a single word, called out by a chance passer on the road, the thought of war had sent the blood pulsing through his whole body.

'Well, damn it, if the Prussians are mucking us about, we can't let them treat us like dirt!'

Delhomme had a different view of the matter. He shook his head and remarked that it would be the finish of the countryside if the Cossacks came in again, as they did after Napoleon. Fighting did nobody any good; much better to come to some agreement.

'When I say that, I'm thinking of other folks' interests. I myself have put the money down with M. Baillehache. Whatever happens, Nénesse, who has to draw for conscription to-morrow, won't go into the army.'

'Yes, of course,' agreed Jean, calming down. 'It's the same with me. I've served my time and now I'm married, so I don't give a damn if they fight or don't. So it's the Prussians, is it? Well, they'll get a hiding, and that'll fix 'em.'

'Good evening, Corporal!'

'Good evening!'

Delhomme went off. A little further on, he stopped to shout the news to someone else. Then, still further off, he stopped again. The threat of the coming war echoed all over La Beauce, through the mournful ashen-grey air.

When Jean had finished, he decided to go straight away to La Borderie and get the promised seed-corn. He unharnessed, left the plough at the end of the field, and jumped on his horse. But as he rode off, he remembered Old Fouan, looked around, but failed to see him. The old man must have taken shelter from the cold behind a strawrick which still stood in the Buteau field.

At La Borderie, after tying up his horse, Jean called but got no answer; everyone must have gone out to work in the fields. He had entered the empty kitchen and stood hammering on the table, when he at last heard Jacqueline's voice coming up from the cellar where the dairy was. It was reached through a trap-door opening immediately below the staircase, and was so dangerous that an accident was always being expected.

'Hullo, who's there?'

He squatted down on the top step of the steep little stairway and she recognised him from below.

'So it's you, Corporal!'

He in turn made her out in the semi-dark of the dairy, which was lighted only by a grating in the wall. She was working down there among the bowls and pans, while the whey was running slowly, drop by drop, into a stone trough. Her sleeves were rolled up to her arm-pits and her bare arms were white with cream.

'Come down. Are you frightened of me?'

360

She talked to him as familiarly as in the old days and laughed in the same enticing way. But he felt awkward and stayed where he was.

'I've come for the seed-corn that the master promised.'

'Oh yes, I know. Wait a minute and I'll come up.'

When she emerged into the full light of day, he saw that she looked fresh and glowing, with a pleasant smell of milk about her and her bare arms very white. She gazed at him with her pretty, lascivious eyes and finally asked him, with a playful air, 'Aren't you going to kiss me? Even if you're married that's no excuse for being impolite.'

He kissed her, doing his best to give her such a smacking salute on each cheek that the whole thing could only be construed as a token of friendship. But she disturbed him. Memories of past embraces made the blood tingle all over his body, and he shuddered. He had never felt like that with his wife, though he loved her so deeply.

'Come along then,' Jacqueline went on. 'I'll show you the seed-corn. Just think, even the servant-girl's out at the market.'

She crossed the yard and went into the barn, stepping behind a pile of sacks. There lay the seed, against the wall, held in place by boards. He had come along after her and felt rather disturbed at finding himself alone with her in this out-of-the-way spot. So he immediately began to show a great interest in the grain, a fine variety of Scottish wheat.

'Look, how big the grains are!'

She gurgled softly in her throat and brought him back to the subject which interested her.

'I hear your wife's pregnant; you've been at work on her, eh? Tell me, what's it like with her? As good as with me?'

He flushed hotly and she smiled with amusement, charmed at seeing him so put out. Then a sudden thought cast a shadow over her face.

'I've had plenty of trouble, you know. Luckily it's over now and it's all turned out to my advantage.'

The fact was that one evening Hourdequin's son Léon, the captain, had turned up at La Borderie after not having shown his face there for years; and from the first day the fellow, who had come to find out the state of things, had tumbled to everything when he found that Jacqueline occupied his mother's room. For a little while Jacqueline was frightened; for her ambition was to

361

marry Hourdequin and inherit the farm. But the captain made the mistake of playing the old game; he tried to get her away from his father by being found in bed with her. It was all too simple. Jacqueline put on a severely virtuous act, screamed and sobbed, told Hourdequin that she'd leave the house where she was no longer treated with respect. There was a violent scene between the two men, the son trying to open his father's eyes, and only making matters worse. Two hours later the captain departed, shouting from the threshold that he'd rather lose everything and that if he ever returned it would only be to kick the slut out of the place.

Jacqueline's mistake, in her triumph, was to believe that she could now hazard her final throw. She announced to Hourdequin that after such persecutions, which were the talk of the countryside, she'd have to leave him if he didn't marry her. She even began to pack her things. But the farmer, still heartbroken at the rupture with his son, had reacted with a rage that was all the more uncontrollable because in his heart he knew himself in the wrong and felt desperately sorry for the whole affair. He almost ended her career with a couple of blows and she didn't mention leaving again. She realised that she had played her cards in too much of a hurry. All the same she was now absolute mistress, sleeping openly in the marriage-bed, eating alone with the master, giving orders, keeping the accounts, holding the keys of the safe, and behaving so autocratically that the farmer never did anything without taking her advice. He was failing, ageing quickly, and she hoped to overcome his last revulsions and make him marry her when she had quite worn him out. In the meantime, as he had sworn in his transport of rage to cut off his son, she worked hard to make him draw up a will in her favour; and she already felt herself the owner of the farm — for she had dragged a promise out of Hourdequin one night in bed.

'I've been wearing myself out to keep him amused for years past,' she told Jean, 'and you can well understand that I haven't done it for love of his good looks.'

Jean couldn't help laughing. While she talked, she had mechanically plunged her bare arms into the corn. She drew them out, then plunged them in again, covering her skin with a fine soft powder. He watched her movements and then suddenly spoke aloud a thought which he immediately regretted.

'Still keeping on with Tron?'

She didn't seem offended, but talked freely, as if to an old friend. 'Oh, I like him a lot, the big simpleton, but he acts very unreasonably, I can tell you. He's terribly jealous. We have dreadful scenes and he won't stand for anyone else except the master—and hardly him! I believe he comes at night to listen at the door and find out if we're asleep.'

Once again Jean was highly amused. But she herself didn't laugh, being secretly afraid of the giant. She considered him sullen and treacherous, like all people from Le Perche. He had threatened to strangle her if she was unfaithful; and she never went to him without fear, despite the excitement he still roused in her with his big body. She was so slender that the fellow could have crushed her with one hand.

She shrugged her shoulders prettily as if to say that she dealt successfully with others as difficult. Then she went on with a smile, 'Y'know, Corporal, we used to get on better than that, we were so well matched!'

Without taking her enticing eyes away, she again began to dip into the corn. Jean was once more her slave. He forgot all about his departure from the farm, his marriage, the child that was on the way. He seized her wrists where they lay deep within the pile of corn; then he moved his hands up her arms, velvety with flour, till he reached her white childlike bosom, which seemed only to grow firmer with all the handling it got. This was just what she had desired from the moment she caught sight of Jean at the top of the cellar-steps. She had felt an uprush of her former warm feelings for him, intensified by the malicious pleasure she'd find in drawing him away from another woman, his lawful wife. He was already fumbling at her body and had thrown her down on the heap of grain, where she lay panting and making throat-noises, when a tall thin figure rose up from behind the sacks. It was Soulas the shepherd, coughing noisily and spitting. Jacqueline was on her feet in one bound, while Jean, breathing hard, stammered out, 'Right you are, I'll come back and fetch fifteen bushels. Oh, what big grains! What big grains!'

The woman fumed, staring at the back of the shepherd, who showed no signs of departure. She murmured with gritted teeth, 'It's too much, by God! Whenever I think I'm alone he's somewhere around to rile me. I'll find a way of having him thrown out!'

Jean, who had now calmed down, hastened to leave the barn and untie his horse in the yard, ignoring Jacqueline's gestures. She would have hidden him in the family-bedroom rather than be cheated of her will. But he was anxious to escape and repeated that

363

he'd return next day. He was going off on foot, leading his horse by the reins, when Soulas, who had come out to catch him, spoke to him in the gateway.

'So it's good-bye to all decency: she's even got you back into her clutches? You'd better advise her to keep her trap shut unless she wants me to open mine. Ah, there's going to be some ugly squabbles here soon, you see!'

Jean went on his way with a coarse gesture, refusing to get himself mixed up any further. He was full of shame, furious at what he had almost done. He had thought that he loved Françoise deeply, yet nowadays he never felt such a wild surge of desire for her. Was it that he loved Jacqueline better? Had the bitch got right under his skin? His memories of her revived and he grew angrier still when he felt that he'd go back to her in spite of his revulsion. With a shudder he jumped on his horse and galloped as fast as possible back into Rognes.

That afternoon Françoise happened to have the idea of going to cut a bundle of lucerne for her cows. She usually did this sort of job and she decided to go now, thinking that her man was still up there in the field; for she hardly ever risked going there alone in her fear of coming too close to the Buteaus. They were always trying to pick a quarrel in their anger at not having the whole field to themselves. She took a scythe, relying on the horse to carry the bundle of lucerne back. But when she reached Les Cornailles, she was surprised to see that Jean wasn't there, though she hadn't warned him of her coming. The plough was still there, but where could he have gone? She felt worried as soon as she recognised Buteau and Lise standing at the edge of the field, waving their arms and looking infuriated. They had obviously stopped there on the way back from a neighbouring village, for they were in their best clothes, at leisure. For a moment she thought of turning back. Then she felt angry at her fear. After all she was the landowner on her own land; so on she walked with the scythe over her shoulder.

The truth was that whenever Françoise met Buteau, particularly when he was alone, she was deeply perturbed. For two years she had not spoken a single word to him. But she couldn't see him without a shock running through her whole body. The sensation might well be one of anger, but might as easily be something else. Several times on this same road, as she had been going to her patch of lucerne she had seen him in front of her; he turned his head two or three times to glance at her with his grey yellow-flecked eyes. Every time a little thrill passed over her body and she couldn't stop herself from hastening her steps. He in turn slowed down; she had to pass by him and their eyes met for a flash. Then she was disturbed by feeling him close behind her back; she tightened herself up and could scarcely go on walking. The last time they met she had been so confused that she had tripped full length as she tried to jump from the roadway on to her patch of lucerne; and he had burst out laughing.

That evening, when Buteau maliciously told Lise of her sister's fall, they had the same thought as they exchanged glances. If the damned bitch had been killed with the child in her womb, the husband would have been left with nothing; the house and the land would revert to them. They had heard from La Grande about the postponed will, which had become unnecessary since the pregnancy. But they never had any luck; it wasn't likely that chance would get rid of both mother and child for them. They returned to the subject as they were going to bed, simply for something to talk about. Talking can't kill people, not even talk about their death. Just think, if Françoise died without issue, everything would be fine, and what a God-sent retribution! Lise, venomous in her hatred, went so far as to swear that her sister was no longer her sister and that she'd gladly hold her head on the block, if that was the only thing needed for the restoration of their home, their home which that trollop had so foully stolen from them. Buteau himself didn't ask so much; he merely remarked what a fine thing it would be if the baby was born dead. The pregnancy was what angered him. A child would mean the death of his obstinate hope, the final loss of the property. And later, as they were getting into bed and Lise was putting out the candle, she laughed in a peculiar way and said that as long as an infant was not in the world it could easily be stopped from coming. There was a hush in the darkness and then he asked her why she had said such a thing. She pressed up against him and made a confession. Last month she had been horrified to find that she had been caught again, and, without warning him, she had gone off to see La Sapin, an old woman in Magnolles who was a witch. Pregnant, again: no, thanks! She'd have got a loving reception from her husband with this news. La Sapin had very simply fixed things with a needle. Buteau listened without expressing either approval or disapproval, and his satisfaction was only manifested in the chuckle he gave in telling her that she should have got hold of the needle for Françoise. She laughed too, and catching him tightly in her

365

arms, she whispered that La Sapin told her of another way—such a funny way! What? What way? Well, a man could undo what a man had done. He simply had to take the woman and at the same time trace a sign of the cross three times across her belly, say an *Ave* backwards. If there was a baby inside, it would disappear into thin air. Buteau stopped laughing and they pretended not to believe such a prescription; but there was still so much of their race's ancient beliefs in their bones that they shivered. Everyone knew that the old woman of Magnolles had changed a cow into a weasel and brought a dead man back to life. The spell must be effective if she said so. Finally Lise, wheedlingly, suggested that he should try on her the *Ave* backwards and the three signs of the cross, to see if she felt anything. No, nothing: the needle had done its job. But with Françoise the trick would have worked. How could he do that, he said laughing. Well, why not? He'd had her already, hadn't he? No, never! He now denied it as his wife, suddenly jealous, began to pinch him. They went to sleep in each other's arms.

From this day they were haunted by the thought of the growing child, which would take the house and land from them for ever; and they never met the younger sister without their eyes immediately going to her belly. When they saw her coming along the road, they measured her with a glance and were startled to realise that the pregnancy was well advanced and that there soon wouldn't be any time left.

'By God,' roared Buteau, coming back from an examination of the furrows, 'the thief has bitten a good foot out of our land. There's no argument about it, you can see the boundary-stone.'

Françoise was approaching calmly, without haste, hiding her fear. She now grasped the reason for their angry gestures: Jean's plough must have cut into their strip of land. There were continual disputes on this score; not a month went by without a boundary-dispute setting them by the ears. The arguments were bound to finish with blows and litigation one day.

'D'you hear?' he went on, raising his voice, 'you're trespassing and I'll prosecute you!'

The young woman, without even turning her head, walked on towards the lucerne patch.

'We're talking to you,' screamed Lise, beside herself. 'Come and look at the boundary-line, if you think we're lying. You'll have to pay for the damage.'

In the face of her sister's assumption of silent contempt, she lost all control and rushed towards her with clenched fists.

'Look here, are you making fun of us? I'm your elder sister, you owe me some respect. I'll force you on to your knees to ask pardon for all the stinking things you've done to me.'

She was confronting Françoise, seething with spite, unable to see with the rush of blood to her head. 'Down on your knees, down on your knees, you bitch.'

Still without a word, Françoise spat in her face, exactly as she had done when the Buteaus were put out of the house. Lise began screaming, but Buteau intervened and shoved her roughly aside.

'Get away, this is my business!'

Ah yes, she'd leave it to him. He could strangle the girl or break her back like a rotten tree; he could trample her into dog's-meat or use her as his slut. No question of her trying to stop him, rather she'd help! From that moment she drew herself up and kept watch so that no one should come and disturb him. Around them the immense grey plain stretched out under the brooding sky, deserted.

'Get on with it, there's no one about.'

Buteau walked towards Françoise. The girl saw him come up with stony face, holding out his arms, and believed he was going to hit her. She still held her scythe, but she was trembling. Buteau quickly grasped the scythe-handle, tore it out of her hands and threw it into the lucerne. Her only way to escape was to turn back. She did so, crossing into the next field and making for the rick there, as if she hoped to find shelter in it. He was in no hurry and seemed to be driving her towards the rick on purpose. His arms were held slightly away from his body; his face was widened with a silent grin which exposed his gums. Suddenly she realised that he wasn't going to hit her. No, he wanted something else, the thing that she had so long withheld from him. She trembled even more, feeling her strength ebb away—she who had been so brave in past days, who had struggled so hard and sworn that he'd never get what he wanted. Yet she was no longer a girl, she'd be twenty-three on Saint Martin's Day. She was a grown woman now, with her lips still red and her eyes as large as crown-pieces. She felt within her such a warm soft sensation that her limbs grew heavy and languid.

Buteau, still forcing her to go backwards, spoke at last in a deep passionate voice.

'You know that things aren't finished between us. I want you and I'll have you.'

He had managed to bring her up against the rick. Seizing her by the shoulder, he threw her on her back. But at that moment she began to struggle, distracted, returning without thought to her old ways of resistance. He held on and tried to avoid her kicks.

'You're pregnant already, you damned fool, what difference can it make? I won't give you another one, you can be sure of that!'

She burst out weeping and had a sort of fit. She made no further attempt to defend herself, but her arms twisted about and her legs jerked in nervous convulsions. Buteau found it impossible to take her; he was continually thrown to one side or other whenever he tried. His anger made him callous and he turned towards his wife.

'You damned lazy slut, what are you standing there for? Come and help me, hold her legs if you want me to do it.'

Lise had remained standing motionless about ten yards away, scanning the countryside, then looking back at the other two, without the least change of expression. At her husband's call she didn't hesitate a moment, but went forward, grasped her sister's left leg, pulled it to one side and sat on it as if she wanted to crush it. Françoise, pinned to the ground, went suddenly limp, with deadened nerves and closed eyelids. But she remained conscious all the while; and when Buteau took her, she was carried away by such a spasm of keen ecstasy that she clung smotheringly to him with both arms and let out a long cry. The crows flying above were frightened. Behind the rick Old Fouan's white face appeared; he had been sheltering there from the cold. He had seen everything and was doubtless terror-stricken, for he immediately dropped down in the straw again.

Buteau rose to his feet and Lise stared sharply at him. She had had only one interest: to see that everything was done properly. But in his excitement he had forgotten their whole plan, the signs of the cross and the *Ave* repeated backwards. She was struck dumb with fury. So it was for his own pleasure that he had done it!

Françoise gave her no time for explanations. For an instant she remained lying on the ground, as if she had fainted under the stress of a rapture which she had never before experienced. She had suddenly learned the truth: she loved Buteau, she never had and never would love anyone else. The discovery filled her with shame; and she was infuriated with herself, as her sense of justice flared up. A man who didn't belong to her, a man belonging to a sister whom she loathed, the one man whom she could never have without being a whore! She had just now let herself be fully possessed; she had embraced him so madly that he must know!

She leaped to her feet, tousled and disarranged, and spat out all her fury and suffering in stammered words.

'Swine! Bastards! Yes, you're both bastards and swine. You've ruined me. People are hung for less than what you've done. I'll tell Jean, you filthy swine! He'll settle with you.'

Buteau complacently shrugged his shoulders and leered, satisfied at having got at last what he wanted.

'Rot, you were dying for it. I felt you bucking all right. We'll have another go one day.'

His mocking words completed Lise's exasperation. All the anger which had been rising within her against her husband, now broke over her younger sister.

'It's true, you whore! I saw you. You hugged him, you forced him. I always said all my bad luck came from you. And now you won't dare say that you haven't seduced my husband from me! Yes, ever since the day after our wedding, when I was still wiping your nose for you.'

Her jealousy burst out, contradicted by her complicity in the deed, a jealousy based less on the act itself than on the way this sister of hers had always stolen half her life away. If this sister of her own blood had never been born, she wouldn't have had to divide everything with her. She cursed her for being younger, more desirable.

'You're a liar!' shouted Françoise. 'You know you're lying!'

'So I'm lying, am I? So it wasn't you who wanted him, you who kept on following him right down into the cellar?'

'Me? Me? What about just now, was that my doing too? You held me down, you cow! Yes, you almost broke my leg! I just can't understand it, you must be something abominable, or else you wanted to kill me, you slut!'

Lise replied with a swinging blow. This brutal act sent Françoise crazy and she threw herself at her sister. With hands in pockets, Buteau stood chuckling and made no attempt to intervene, like a strutting cock who watches two hens pecking each other for his favours. The scrimmage went on, vilely, desperately, with caps torn off and faces bleeding, as each woman felt with her cruel fingers for a vital spot. In their furious tussle they went staggering back into the lucerne. Lise screamed as Françoise's nails drove into her throat; then she saw red and her brain was filled with a single sharp clear thought—to kill her sister. To the left of Françoise she had glimpsed the scythe, with its handle fallen across a clump of thistles and its blade sticking up into the air. In a flash she pushed Françoise over with all the strength she could muster. Stumbling, the unfortunate woman turned and fell leftwards, giving a terrible scream. The scythe had pierced her side.

'Good God! Good God!' stammered Buteau.

Everything was over. One second had sufficed; the irreparable was done. Lise, agape at the sudden realisation of the thing she had so much longed to see, stared at the torn dress reddening with a gush of blood. Had the blade pierced right through to the child, for such an abundance of blood to flow? Behind the rick the white face of Old Fouan re-appeared. He had seen the struggle and he blinked with frightened eyes.

Françoise lay unstirring, and Buteau approached but dared not touch her. A gust of wind came up and its chill bit through to his bone. His hair stood on end as he shuddered with fear.

'She's dead! Let's run, for God's sake!'

He grabbed Lise's hand and they rushed along the deserted road as if they were possessed. The low gloomy sky seemed falling on their heads; the echoes of their scampering footsteps sounded like the clatter of a crowd in hot pursuit. They fled over the empty cropped plain, Buteau's blouse ballooning out in the wind, Lise's hair streaming back and her cap held in her hand. Both fugitives went on repeating the same words, panting like hunted animals.

'She's dead! God! Run, run, good God!'

Their strides grew longer and they couldn't articulate any more words. But they moaned out meaningless sounds which followed the rhythm of their flight; a sort of gasping in which a few words could still be distinguished.

'Dead, in God's name! Dead! Dead! in God's name!'

They disappeared from view.

A few minutes later Jean trotted up on his horse. He was struck to the heart with what he found.

'What is it? What's happened?'

Françoise, who had opened her eyes, still lay motionless. She stared at him for a long time with her huge grieving eyes; but she made no reply, as if she was already far away and thinking of other things.

'You're wounded, there's blood on you, tell me, tell me!'

He turned towards Old Fouan who had come near.

370

'You were here, what happened?'

Then Françoise spoke in a slow voice.

'I came to cut some grass. I fell on the scythe. Oh, it's all over!'

Her eyes sought out Old Fouan's. She was telling him, and him alone, other things—things which only the family should know about. The old man, despite his daze, seemed to understand. He repeated what she had said.

'That's right, she fell, she hurt herself. I was there, I saw it.'

Jean had to gallop to Rognes for a stretcher. As she was being carried home, she fainted again. No one thought they would get her back alive.

IV

IT was on the following day, Sunday, that the lads of Rognes were to go to Cloyes for the conscription ballot; and as La Grande and La Frimat, who had rushed to the house through the dusk, were undressing Françoise and putting her to bed with extreme care, the drum-beats were heard in the road below, sounding like a knell for the poor folk in the depths of the mournful twilight.

Jean, who had lost his head, was hurrying to get Doctor Finet when beside the church he met the vct Patoir, who had been called to see old Saucisse's horse. Jean ignored his demurs and dragged him into the house to attend to the wounded woman. But when Patoir saw the ghastly wound, he absolutely refused to touch the case. What was the use? Nothing could be done. Two hours later Jean brought M. Finet, who said the same thing. Nothing could be done. The only course was to give narcotics to deaden the pain. Françoise's five months' pregnancy complicated the case; the child could be felt moving in the wounded womb, dying with its mother's death. Before leaving, the doctor did his best to put on a bandage, and, though promising to return next day, he declared that the poor woman couldn't last the night. But she was alive the next morning and lingered on till almost nine o'clock, when the drum started beating once more to call the conscripts together in front of the school.

The whole night long, rain had been flooding down from the sky, and Jean had listened to the streaming deluge as he sat at the end of the bedroom, stupefied, his eyes filled with big tears. And now he heard the drum, muffled as if with crêpe, and the morning was damp and close. The rain had stopped but the sky was still leaden-grey.

The drum-beating went on for a long time. The drummer was a new one, a nephew of Macqueron's who had just come back from army service, and went on beating as if he were leading a regiment into battle. All Rognes was in a state of great tension. This year the rumours that had been going round for several days about the threat of a new war had sharpened the anxiety, always keen enough, that accompanied the conscription ballot. What, go and have your head broken by the Prussians? There were nine local lads to take part in the ballot, probably the largest number ever known at Rognes. Among them were Nénesse and Delphin, who at one time had been inseparables but who had been parted recently since Nénesse had taken a job in a restaurant at Chartres. The day before, Nénesse had come home to stay with his parents and Delphin had hardly recognised him, so great was the change. He looked a real gentleman, with a walking-stick, a silk hat and a sky-blue cravat pulled through a ring. His clothes were made by a tailor and he now jeered at Lambourdieu's ready-mades. Delphin, on the contrary, had thickened and grown heavier; his face was tanned a dark red by the sun and he had sprouted up like some vigorous plant in the good earth. The two lads had, however, renewed their friendship on the spot. After spending part of the night together, they arrived arm in arm before the school at the call of the drum with its persistent beat, heady and importunate.

The parents stood around. Delhomme and Fanny, proud of Nénesse's distinction, wanted to see him off; as they had assured his exemption, they were quite without anxiety. Bécu, wearing his badge of office, well-polished, was threatening to hit his wife because she was crying. What, wasn't Delphin ready to serve his country? The lad himself appeared indifferent, saying he was sure to draw a lucky number. When the nine were ready—and it took a good hour for them all to turn up—Lequeu delivered the flag to them. A discussion ensued as to who should have the honour of carrying it. As a rule, the tallest and strongest was chosen, so that in the end everyone agreed on Delphin. He appeared rather worried, being shy at heart in spite of his big fists, uneasy about anything unfamiliar. Look how long the pole was and what a strain the thing was on the arms! Providing it didn't bring bad luck!

At the two corners of the street Flore and Coelina were giving a final sweep to their respective inn-parlours in readiness for the evening. Macqueron was gloomily staring from his threshold when Lengaigne appeared in his own doorway, sneering. The latter was undeniably in a position to crow; for two days previously the excise officers had seized four barrels of wine hidden under one of his rival's wood-stacks. After such a damned misfortune, what choice had he but to send in his resignation as mayor? Everyone was convinced that the anonymous letter of denunciation had come from Lengaigne. The final straw for Macqueron was that his daughter Berthe had become so compromised with the wheelwright's son, whom he had long refused as son-in-law, that he had been obliged after all to bless the pair. For the past week the women at the fountain had gossiped of nothing but the daughter's wedding and the father's prosecution. He was sure to be fined and he might even get sent to prison. And so, faced with his neighbour's insulting smile, Macqueron preferred to retreat indoors, unpleasantly aware that all the other people were also beginning to laugh.

But Delphin had taken tight hold of the flag and the drum resumed its thudding; Nénesse fell into step and the other seven followed. They made quite a little troop as they marched in file along the flat road. Several urchins ran beside them, while the Delhommes, Bécu and others accompanied them to the village end. Freed from her husband, La Bécu hurried up and slipped furtively into the church. Finding herself alone there, she knelt down in tears, though not a pious woman, and prayed God to give her son a lucky number. For more than an hour she mumbled out this heart-felt prayer. In the distance towards Cloyes the silhouette of the flag was gradually lost and the drum-beats faded away into the vast open space.

It was nearly ten o'clock when Doctor Finet came back. He seemed very surprised to find Françoise still alive; for he had thought he would only have to write out the death certificate. He examined her and shook his head, preoccupied by the tale he had been told and having no suspicion of any other facts. He wanted to hear the whole account again. How the devil had the unfortunate woman managed to fall on the point of a scythe? He went off again, indignant at such clumsiness and irritated that he would have to come back yet once more to sign the death certificate. But Jean remained gravely scrutinising Françoise, who closed her eyelids and remained speechless as soon as she felt her husband's questioning eyes on her. He guessed at a lie, something she was hiding from him. With the first light he had left her for a short time and rushed up to the lucerne field up on the hill to look at the place; but he could make nothing out clearly. The footsteps had been washed out by the night's rain and the trampled grass showed no doubt where she had fallen. After the doctor had gone, he sat down again at the dying woman's bedside and stayed alone with her. La Frimat had gone off to breakfast and La Grande had had to return home for a quick glance to make sure everything was in order.

'Are you in pain, tell me?'

She closed her eyes tightly but made no reply.

'Tell me, are you hiding something from me?'

She lay there like a corpse except for the weak and painful movement of the breath in her throat. All the while she had lain on her back as if stricken into immobility and silence. She was in a burning fever, but her innermost will seemed to gather itself to resist delirium, so acute was her fear of blurting out the truth. She had always had a very strong personality, with the typical Fouan obstinacy. She never did anything just because other people did it, and had ideas which shocked everyone. Perhaps she was reacting to a deep feeling of family-kinship, a feeling stronger than either hatred or the desire for vengeance. What was the good anyway, since she was going to die? There were things that must be buried with her in the corner of the land where they had all been born and bred, things which must never at any price be exposed to a stranger; and Jean was the stranger, the man she had never been able to love with a real love, whose child she was taking away with her unborn as if she were being punished for having conceived it.

Meanwhile Jean, ever since he brought back the dying woman, had been thinking about the will. All night he had thought that if she died like this, he would only get half the furniture and half the money, one hundred and twenty-seven francs kept in the drawer. He loved Françoise very much and would have given his own body to save her; but that made his distress all the greater, the thought that he would lose the land and the house as well as Françoise. Up to that moment, however, he had not dared mention it to her. It would be so callous; and besides there had always been people about. But at last, seeing that he would never learn any more about the way the accident happened, he made up his mind to broach the other question.

'Are there any matters you'd like to put in order?'

Françoise lay stiffly and did not seem to have heard. Her eyes stayed shut and her face remained quite without expression.

374

'You see, I'm thinking of your sister, in case anything happens to you. The paper is here, in the drawer.'

He brought out the blank document, and went on in an increasingly embarrassed voice.

'Well, would you like me to help you? Let's see if you still have strength to write. I'm not thinking of myself. It's only the idea that you can't want to leave anything to people who've been so cruel to you.'

Her eyelids trembled slightly and he knew that she could hear him. So she was still refusing to make the will. He was shattered, completely at a loss. Perhaps she herself could not have explained why she was shamming death in this way before being nailed down in her coffin. The land and the house could not go to this man, who had crossed her path quite by chance, like a mere passer-by. She owed him nothing; the child was dying with her. By what right should the property go out of the family? Her childish and obstinate conception of justice protested: this is mine, that is yours, we are quits, good-bye! Yes, all those things were in her mind, and other things too, vaguer and more confused. Her sister Lise receded, was lost in the distance, and only Buteau was left, her beloved in spite of all his roughness, desired and forgiven.

Jean grew irritated, himself now caught and embittered by a passion for the earth. He raised her, tried to set her upright and put a pen in her hand.

'Is it possible? You really like them better than me? Do you want those devils to have everything?'

Then Françoise opened her eyes at last, and the look she turned on him cut him right to the heart. She knew she was dying and her great wide eyes revealed an unfathomable grief. Why did he torture her? She couldn't do it, she wouldn't. A thin cry of pain was all that escaped her lips. Then she fell back and her eyes closed again and her head lay unmoving on the pillow.

Jean was so sick at heart, so ashamed of his unkindness, that he was still standing there with the stamped paper in his hand when La Grande came back. She understood what was happening, and took him to one side to ask if there was a will. Stammering out a lie, he said he had been about to hide the paper away for fear of someone worrying Françoise with it. The old woman seemed to approve; for she was on the side of the Buteaus, forseeing all kinds of shocking scenes if they inherited the property. Then, as she seated herself at the table again and began to knit, she added aloud

'As for me, I'm doing the right thing by everybody. My will has been drawn up for a long time. Everybody has his share; for I'd be dishonest if I favoured one above the others. You're all in it, my children. You'll see, you'll see, one day!'

She said this daily to members of the family, and she repeated it, without thinking, at this death-bed. Each time she was tickled inwardly at the thought of the famous will which would set the whole pack at one another's throats when she was dead. There wasn't a clause in it which hadn't been carefully inserted so as to ensure litigation.

'Ah, if only we could take our property with us!' she finished up. 'But as we can't, other people might as well have some enjoyment from it.'

Then La Frimat returned to sit at the other side of the table opposite La Grande. She was knitting too. The afternoon drifted by while the two old women chatted quietly away. Jean couldn't sit still. He walked up and down, went out, came in again, painfully restless. The doctor had said there was nothing to be done, so they did nothing.

At first La Frimat lamented that no one had called in Maître Sourdeau, the bone-setter from Bazoches, who could also cure wounds. He used to recite a few words and then breathe over the sufferers, and their wounds closed up immediately.

'He's a wonderful fellow!' declared La Grande, full of respect. 'He was the one who put Lorillon's breast-bone back into place. You remember how old Lorillon's breast-bone dropped. It stuck down and pressed on his stomach till he nearly died of exhaustion. The worst of it was that his wife got the same wretched trouble, it's catching, you know. In the end they all had it, his daughter, son-in-law and the three children. They were all at death's door when they called Maître Sourdeau in, and he put them right just by rubbing their stomachs with a tortoise-shell comb.'

The other old woman confirmed every detail with a wag of her head. It was well known, you couldn't argue about it. She herself brought out another example.

'It was Maître Sourdeau, too, who cured Budin's daughter when she had the fever, just by cutting a pigeon in two and putting it on her head.'

She turned to Jean, who stood in a trance by the bed.

'If I were you, I'd call him in. It may not be too late even now.

He answered with an angry gesture. He, with the intellectual

376

pride of the townsman, didn't believe in such cures. But the two women chatted on for a long time and exchanged various remedies, such as putting parsley under the mattress to cure pains in the back, or keeping three acorns in your pocket to cure inflammation, or drinking on an empty stomach a glass of water whitened by the moon to get rid of wind.

'I say,' La Frimat suddenly turned to Jean, 'if you aren't going to fetch Maître Sourdeau, at any rate you'd better get the priest.'

Jean repeated his angry gesture and La Grande pursed her lips.

'Why on earth? What the devil could he do, that priest!'

'What would he do? He would bring the good God along, and that's not a bad thing, sometimes.'

La Grande shrugged her shoulders as if to say that nobody believed that sort of thing nowadays. Let everyone keep in his proper place: God up aloft and people in their own homes.

'In any case,' she remarked after a short silence, 'the priest wouldn't come, he's ill. La Bécu told me just now that he's going away in a carriage on Wednesday, because the doctor told him he'd be sure to die if he stays in Rognes.'

As a matter of fact, during the two and a half years he had served the parish, the Abbé Madeline had gradually faded away. Homesickness, a desperate longing for his Auvergne mountains had daily broken him down in the flat Beauce land where the sight of the endlessly flat rolling plain weighed him down with melancholy. Not a single tree or rock, stagnant pools instead of the rushing streams which, in the mountains, cascade over the rocks. His eyes dimmed and he grew thinner and thinner, till people said he was going into a consumption. If he had only received some comfort from his parishioners! But, after his previous pious parish, his timid and uneasy soul was profoundly shocked by this new district, infected with irreligion and respecting nothing but outward forms. The women deafened him with their clamour and quarrelling. They took advantage of his weakness to such a point that they practically snatched the religious control out of his hands. As a result he was reduced to consternation, full of scruples as he was and perpetually afraid of some involuntary sin. A final blow had been reserved for him; on Christmas Day one of the Handmaidens of the Virgin was taken in labour in the church. After such a scandal the priest had been rapidly failing, and now he was to be carried back to Auvergne, a dying man.

'Without a priest again!' said La Frimat. 'I wonder if Abbé Godard would be willing to come back.'

'That cross-grained brute!' exclaimed La Grande, 'Why, he'd burst with spleen!'

The entrance of Fanny made them fall silent. She was the only member of the family who had called on the previous evening. And now she had come back to hear the news. Jean simply pointed to Françoise with a trembling hand. There was a softened hush full of pity. Then Fanny enquired in a lowered voice if the stricken woman had asked for her sister. No, she hadn't opened her mouth on the subject, as if Lise had never existed. It was very surprising; for even if they'd quarrelled, death is death after all. When would they make things up if not before the last parting?

La Grande was of the opinion that the matter ought to be referred to Françoise. She rose and leaned over the dying woman.

'Tell me, my dear, what about Lise?'

The dying woman made no sign. Only a scarcely perceptible shiver passed across her eyelids.

'Perhaps she's expecting us to bring her. I'll go.'

But then, still keeping her eyes closed, Françoise said no by rolling her head gently from side to side on the pillow. Jean insisted that her wishes be respected. The three women sat down again. They were astonished that Lise didn't come of her own accord at such a moment. But there was often a great deal of obstinacy in families.

'Troubles never come singly,' Fanny remarked with a sigh. 'Ever since this morning I've been worried to death about the balloting. Yet I've no reason to worry. I know very well that Nénesse won't be picked to go.'

'Yes, indeed,' murmured La Frimat, 'it's upsetting all the same.'

The dying woman was once again forgotten. They went on discussing the luck of the draw, the boys who would be called up, the boys who wouldn't be. It was three o'clock now; and although the balloters were not expected back before five o'clock at the earliest, reports from Cloyes were already flying about. Nobody could tell how, but they'd come by that sort of aerial telegraphy which flies from village to village. The Briquet boy had drawn number thirteen; his luck was out. The Couillot lad had drawn two hundred and six; he'd be all right. But there was no agreement about the others;

378

the reports were contradictory and produced a mounting excitement. Nothing was known about Delphin or Nénesse.

'Oh, my heart keeps jumping, isn't it stupid?' Fanny repeated.

They called to La Bécu who was passing. She had gone back to the church and now was wandering about like a lost soul. Her anxiety was so extreme that she did not even stop to chat.

'I can't stand it any longer, I'm going to meet them.'

Jean, standing by the window, had not heard a word; he went on staring vaguely at the outer world. Since morning he had several times noticed Old Fouan dragging himself round the house on his two sticks. Now he suddenly saw the old man again. Fouan's face pressed against the window pane and he was trying to make out what was happening inside the room. Jean opened the window, and the old man, with a startled look, asked stammeringly how things were going. Very badly, the end was near. Fouan thrust his head into the room and stared across at Françoise with such a prolonged intensity that it seemed he couldn't tear himself away.

When Fanny and La Grande noticed him, they returned to the idea of sending for Lise. Things couldn't end like this, folk had to get together around their own. But when they asked the old man to fetch her, he hurried away shivering with terror. As he went, he growled and spluttered some words out through lips that were stiff from his long silence. 'No, no. . . Impossible, impossible. . .'

Jean was impressed by the man's fear, but the women merely made a gesture of resignation. After all, the matter lay between the two sisters; you couldn't force them to make peace. At that moment a sound was heard, feeble at first as the buzzing of a big fly, then louder and louder, rolling along like a gust of wind through the trees. Fanny started.

'Listen, the drum! Here they come! Good-bye!'

She rushed out without pausing to kiss her cousin for the last time. La Grande and La Frimat went out to the doorway for a look. Françoise and Jean were left alone. She lay in her tenacious stillness and silence, probably hearing every word that was said and wanting to die like an animal gone to earth at the bottom of its hole; he stood facing the open window, restless with uncertainty, overwhelmed by a grief which seemed to him to come from people and things alike, from the whole immense plain. Oh, that drum! how it echoed and vibrated through his heart. The drum with its persistent roll confused his present sorrow with his memories of past

days, the barracks, the battles, the dog's life of those poor devils
with neither wife nor child to comfort them.

As soon as the flag appeared far away down the flat road, darkened
by the twilight, a crowd of children began running out to meet the
conscripts and a group of parents gathered at the village entrance.
The nine lads and the drummer were already very drunk, bellowing out a song into the melancholy night air. They were decorated
with tricolour ribbons and most of them had stuck the number of
their ballot in their hats, fastening it with pins. When they came in
sight of the village they roared yet more vociferously and entered at
a quick march, full of bravado.

Delphin still bore the flag; but he now carried it slung over his
shoulder like a troublesome rag for which he could find no possible
use. He looked weary, with his face set hard; he was not singing and
he hadn't pinned his number to his cap. As soon as she saw him
La Bécu rushed forward trembling, at the risk of being trampled
by the marching band.

'Well?'

Delphin furiously pushed her aside without slackening his pace.

'Bugger off out of my way!'

Bécu too had come forward, suffering as deeply as his wife. When
he heard his son's remark, he put no further question. The mother
was sobbing and he found the greatest difficulty in holding back his
own tears in spite of all the patriotic bluster.

'What d'you think you can do about it? He's conscripted!'

They lagged behind on the deserted road and went home miser-
ably together: the man recalling his hard life as a soldier and the
woman turning her anger against the good God to whom she had
twice gone with her prayers and who had not listened.

Nénesse had stuck in his hat a splendid 214, daubed in red and
blue. It was one of the highest numbers and he was celebrating his
luck, brandishing his cane as leader of the wild chorus and beating
out the rhythm. When Fanny saw the number, instead of rejoicing
she gave a cry of deep regret. Ah, if only they'd known, they need
not have thrown away a thousand francs in M. Baillehache's lottery.
But all the same she and her husband embraced their son as if he
had just escaped from some great danger.

'Oh, leave me alone!' he shouted. 'You're a bloody nuisance!'

The band continued their riotous march across the seething
village. No parents now approached it, knowing that they'd be told
to go to hell. All the young devils seemed to have come back home

in a foul-mouthed mood, both those who'd been conscripted and those who'd escaped. Anyway they couldn't have talked sensibly if they'd tried. Their eyes were starting out of their heads and they were all as drunk with their long yelling out of songs as with liquor. One little chap, who'd been unlucky in the draw, came along playing the trumpet with his nose; but two others, who were certainly among the lucky, marched with white faces and downcast eyes. The crazy drummer in the van could have led them all into the Aigre and they'd have gone splashing in after him.

At last, outside the municipal offices, Delphin handed back the flag.

'By God, I've had enough of this bloody piece of stuff! It's only brought me bad luck!'

He grasped Nénesse's arm and took him off, while the others invaded Lengaigne's wine-shop, surrounded by parents and friends, who at long last learnt what had happened. Macqueron came to his door heart-broken at seeing his rival get all the business.

'Come with me,' said Delphin curtly. 'I'm going to show you a good joke.'

Nénesse followed him. There was plenty of time to get back for drinks. The blasted drum was no longer beating in their ears and it was a relief to roam along the deserted road together as the night slowly darkened. As his comrade was silent, sunk in meditations which didn't seem at all pleasant, Nénesse began to discuss a very important matter. A few days before, he had gone to the Rue aux Juifs in Chartres for some entertainment and had learned that Vaucogne, the Charleses' son-in-law, wanted to sell the house. The place was going to rack and ruin under such a ne'er-do-well, who was diddled right and left by the women. But what a success it could be turned into, what pickings it could produce, if it were in the hands of a sensible hard-working chap with good arm-muscles and a head for business! He felt sure it'd suit him, all the more as in his present restaurant job, he was in charge of the dance room, where he had to superintend the behaviour of the girls—and did he have to keep his eyes skinned! So the plan was to frighten the Charles family into believing that No. 19 was within an ace of being closed by the police on account of the disreputable goings-on there; then to get the place from them for a mere song. Much better than having to mess about with farming, eh? He'd be a gentleman overnight.

Delphin was only half listening, absorbed in his own thoughts; he started when his companion gave him a sly dig in the ribs.

'Some fellows are born lucky,' he muttered. 'You were begotten to be a pride to your mother.'

Then he relapsed into silence again, while Nénesse, who had everything worked out, went on detailing the improvements he'd make at No. 19 if his parents advanced enough money. He was a bit young, but he felt he was made for the job. At that moment he caught sight of La Trouille, skipping nearby along the shadowy road on her way to meet some lad or other; and to show his experience with women, he gave her a hard smack as she went past. La Trouille at once hit back, then recognised the pair of lads.

'It's you two! How you've grown!'

She laughed as she remembered their pranks in the old days. She was the one who had least changed; she was still a slip of a girl despite her twenty-one years, as slender and supple as a poplar shoot, with breasts still childishly hard. The encounter delighted her and she kissed the two lads one after the other.

'We're still good friends, aren't we?'

In her pleasure at meeting them she would easily have gone further if they had shown any inclination, just as men take a drink together to celebrate a meeting.

'Listen,' said Nénesse jokingly. 'I might be taking over the Charleses' house. Would you come and work there?'

Abruptly she stopped laughing, choked and burst into tears. She seemed to fade back into the shadows of the road and disappeared, sobbing out like a broken-hearted child, 'Oh, how beastly, how beastly! I shan't love you any more.'

Delphin hadn't spoken a word. He now started walking on with a determined look on his face.

'Come along and I'll show you something funny.'

He quickened his pace and turned off the road across the vineyards, towards the house where the parish had lodged the constable after the presbytery was handed over to the priest. He lived there with his father. Taking his comrade into the kitchen, he lit a candle, glad to find his parents still away from home.

'We'll have a glass,' he said, putting a bottle and two glasses on the table.

Then after drinking, he clicked his tongue and added, 'I wanted to tell you that if they think they've caught me because I drew an unlucky number, they're very much mistaken. When I had to stay in Orleans for three days for Uncle Michel's funeral it almost killed me being away from home. I know you think I'm stupid, but there it is. I can't help it. I'm like a tree that withers away if it's up-rooted. And now they want to take me off and send me to the devil in some place I've never even heard of. Well, they won't, they won't!'

Nénesse had often heard him talk in that vein and merely shrugged.

'Talk's cheap. You'll go just the same. Don't forget the police.'

Without replying, Delphin turn round. With his left hand he took down a small hatchet which was used to split wood. Then he calmly set his right index finger on the edge of the table and with a clean blow sliced the finger off.

'That's what I wanted to show you. I wanted you to tell every-body that a coward wouldn't do that.'

'God, you damned idiot!' exclaimed Nénesse in agitation. 'You can't go about crippling yourself. You're no use now.'

'I don't give a damn. Let them come, police and all. Now I'm sure of being exempted.'

He picked up the severed finger and threw it into the wood fire. Then, after shaking his bloody hand, he wrapped it roughly in his handkerchief and tied it up with a piece of string to stop the gush of blood.

'Won't stop us finishing off the bottle before we go and join the others. Here's to you.'

'And to you.'

Lengaigne's wine-shop was so full of smoke and shouting that nothing could be seen or heard. In addition to the lads who had been to Cloyes, a big crowd had gathered. Jésus-Christ and his friend Canon were busy making Old Fouan drunk, the three of them encircling a bottle of brandy. Bécu, hard hit by his son's bad luck, was dead to the world with his drunken head on a table. Delhomme and Clou were playing a game of piquet. And of course Lequeu was there with his nose in a book, pretending to read through all the uproar. A skirmish among the women had heightened everyone's excitement. Flore had gone to the well for a jug of fresh water; Coelina had gone for her there with her nails, accusing her of being paid by the excise officers to betray her neighbours. Mac-queron and Lengaigne both ran up and were almost drawn into the fight themselves; the former swore to get the other pinched for adulterating his tobacco while the latter sneered and chaffed him about his resignation. The onlookers joined in for the pleasure of shaking their fists and raising their voices till it almost looked as if there would be slaughter all round. The row blew over, but a feeling of frustrated anger was left and a longing for a downright brawl.

First, there was almost a flare-up between Victor, son of the house, and the conscripts. The young man, who had served his time in the army, was showing off before the lads, yelling louder than the lot of them put together and egging them on with all kinds of idiotic wagers; such as holding a bottle up in the air and pouring all its contents down your throat or sucking a full glass through your nose without a drop passing between the lips. Suddenly, as some reference was made to Macqueron and his daughter's nearing marriage, young Couillot began tittering about Baldy, clownishly reviving all the old cracks. Hey, we'll get the husband's opinion the day after! Has she got any, or hasn't she? They drew the joke out so long that it became tediously stupid.

Then everyone was startled by Victor's sudden outburst of anger —Victor, who had been the most implacable insister on the girl's lack.

'That's enough, she's all right.'

His statement was greeted with a loud shout. So he'd seen; he'd slept with her! But he vigorously denied the second half of the charge. You can see a thing without touching it. He had satisfied himself one day when the need of settling the fact of the matter had been nagging at him. How? That was his own business.

'She's all right, I swear she is.'

A dreadful scene resulted when young Couillot, extremely drunk, went on yelling that she hadn't got any. He knew nothing about it, but just didn't want to give in. Victor roared that he used to say the same once upon a time, but he didn't say it now, not because he wanted to butter up the blasted Macquerons, but because facts were facts. He attacked the conscript who had to be rescued from the mauling he was giving him.

'Say she's all right, by God, or I'll do for you!'

Lots of people, however, were still doubtful on the subject. Nobody could make out why Lengaigne's son was so worked up about it; he was usually very severe on women and he had publicly repudiated his sister, whose promiscuous embraces, the rumour ran, had brought her into hospital. That foul Suzanne! Just as well she kept her infected carcass away from the village.

Flore brought up more wine; but no matter how much they now

384

clinked glasses, there was still a threat of blows and insults in the air. No one thought of going off to eat. When a man drinks, he ceases to feel hunger. The conscripts, thundering out a patriotic song, beat time with such hammerings on the table that the paraffin lamps flickered and belched out a bitter black smoke. The room was so stifling that Delhomme and Clou decided to open the window behind them. At that moment, Buteau came in and slipped into a corner. He lacked his usual provocative air and looked around from one person to another with an uneasy glint in his small eyes. Obviously he had come to find out what the others were talking about; he had found it impossible to stay at home, where he had shut himself in since the previous evening. The presence of Jésus-Christ and Canon seemed to strike him so strongly that he made no attempt to object to the way they were making Old Fouan drunk. For some time he scrutinised Delhomme. But it was Bécu, sleeping solidly through all the racket, who most preoccupied him. Was he really sleeping or was he pretending? He nudged him with his elbow and was somewhat relieved to find him slobbering all over his own sleeve. He turned all his attention to the schoolmaster, whose face suddenly struck him as showing a most peculiar expression. Why didn't he look as he usually did?

Indeed, though Lequeu was pretending to bury himself in his book, he kept starting violently. The conscripts with their singing and their imbecile merriment were reducing him to a state of fury.

'Bloody fools,' he muttered, still restraining himself.

For the last few months his position in the village had been becoming rather difficult. He had always been rough and strict with the children, sending them back to their paternal dung-heaps with a clip over the ear. But he had recently grown much more harsh and had got into a difficult situation over a little girl, whose ear he had split open with a blow from his ruler. Her relatives had sent in a petition for his replacement. And in addition Berthe Macqueron's marriage had just destroyed a long-nourished hope, a carefully-laid scheme which he had thought to be nearing consummation. Oh, this filthy breed of peasants! They refused him their daughters, and now were going to steal the bread out of his mouth because of a little girl's split ear!

Suddenly, as if he were in his classroom, he dropped his book against his open hand and shouted at the conscripts.

'For God's sake, be quiet! Do you really think it's funny to go and get yourselves killed off by the Prussians!'

Greatly astonished, everyone turned eyes on him. Of course it wasn't funny. They were all agreed about that. Delhomme repeated the statement about the need for every man to defend his own piece of earth. If the Prussians invaded La Beauce, they'd soon find that the Beaucerons were no cowards! But as for going to fight for other people's land, well, that was no joke at all, agreed.

At that moment Delphin came in followed by Nénesse. He was very flushed and his eyes glittered with fever. He had heard what Delhomme said, and sat down among his comrades, shouting, 'That's it, if they come, these Prussians, we'll mince them up properly.'

Some of the drinkers had noticed the handkerchief tied round his hand and asked him about it. Nothing serious, just a cut. He brought his other fist violently down on the creaking table and ordered a bottle of wine.

Canon and Jésus-Christ watched the boys without anger, with an air of pitying superiority. You certainly had to be young and daft to fall for that sort of thing. Canon himself ended up by getting sentimental, lost in his plan for organising future happiness. He spoke out loud with his chin in his hands.

'War! By God, it's time we took things over. You all know my scheme: no more military service, no more taxes. Every man to get everything he wants, for the least possible amount of work. And it'll come. The day is coming when you'll be able to keep your money and your sons, if you're on our side.'

Jésus-Christ nodded in approval; but Lequeu lost all self-control and burst out, 'Oh yes, you damned buffoon, with your earthly paradise, forcing everybody to be happy whether they want to or not. It's all a bad joke. Could it possibly happen in such a world? Aren't we too rotten already to have a different life? First of all, we'd have to be well cleaned out by some horde of Cossacks or Chinese!'

This time the shock was so profound that complete silence fell. What next! At last he'd spoken up—this sullen fellow, cold as a fish, who had never let anyone know what he really thought, and who, in mortal fear of his superiors, always retreated when he should have stood up for himself. Everybody was listening, especially Buteau, who waited uneasily for what he'd say next, as if the argument might have some connection with the matter obsessing his own mind. The open window had cleared away the smoke and the sweet wet air of the night came in, bringing with it the quiet dark peace of the great sleeping countryside. The schoolmaster, breaking out

386

at last after his ten years of reserve, went on jeering at everything; faced with the wreck of his career, he let go and relieved himself of the rankling hatred which had become intolerable.

'You seem to think these people are stupider than their own calves, the way you come telling them that larks will drop ready roasted into their mouths. But before you organise your system, the land'll be worn out and everything buggered up.'

At this violent attack Canon, who had never yet met his match, visibly quailed. He tried to repeat his stories about the lads in Paris, the nationalisation of the land and large-scale scientific farming His adversary cut him short.

'I know, a lot of rubbish! By the time you come to try it out, this large-scale farming of yours, all the fields of France will have disappeared under a deluge of corn from America. Listen! this little book I'm reading tells you all about it. God's truth, our peasants might just as well lie down and die. The game's up!'

In the same voice he used to address his children in school, he talked about the corn-lands across the ocean. Plains vast as kingdoms, in which La Beauce would be lost like a single clod of dry clay; earth so fertile that instead of manuring it, you had to skim off something of its energies with a preliminary crop, which still didn't prevent it yielding two harvests a year; farms of seventy thousand acres, divided into sections, sub-divided into lots—each section under a director, each lot under a foreman, provided with accommodation for men, animals, tools, kitchens; whole battalions of farm-labourers hired in springtime and organised just like an army in the field, living out in the open, boarded, lodged, numbered, doctored, and paid off in the autumn; furrows to be ploughed and sown several miles long; oceans of wheat-ears to be levelled, spreading out of sight; men acting merely as supervisors with all the work done by machines, double ploughs with deep cutting disks, sowers and weeders, combined reapers and binders, steam-threshers with stacking attachments; peasant mechanics, squads of workmen on horseback following the machines, ready at any moment to dismount and tighten a screw, change a bolt or hammer a bar; the land, in short, turned into a bank, exploited by financiers, given an annual cut, shorn naked, yielding to the material impersonal power of science ten times as much as was wrung from her by the love and strong arms of a man.

'And you hope to fight all that with your tuppenny tools,' he went on, 'you that know nothing and want nothing: your highest aim is to stay squatting in your old ruts. Heavens, you're already buried knee-deep in the wheat from over there. And the boats will bring over more and more of it. Just wait a few years, and you'll be sunk up to your bellies, your shoulders, your mouths—then over your heads! You're up against a river, a torrent, a flood that'll drown you one and all.'

The peasants stared wide-eyed and panic-stricken at the picture of their inundation by overseas corn. They were already pinched enough by the competition: were they going to be drowned and swept away as this bugger said? His words had a very concrete significance for them. Rognes, their fields, the whole of La Beauce was being swamped.

'No, no, never!' came Delhomme's strangled voice. 'The Government will protect us!'

'A lot of good the Government is!' retorted Lequeu with contempt. 'Can't protect itself! The funniest thing of all is that you elected M. Rochefontaine. The landlord of La Borderie at least acted consistently in supporting M. de Chédeville. But in any case it's six of one and half a dozen of the other: they're both like putting a plaster on a wooden leg. No Chamber of Deputies would dare vote a big enough duty. Protection can't save you. You're all finished. You might as well say good night!'

An uproar broke out, with everyone trying to talk at once. Wasn't it possible to stop this ruinous grain coming in? They could go and sink the boats in the ports: they could welcome them with gunshot. All their voices shook. They were on the verge of stretching out their hands, wailing and praying for salvation from the abundant grain, the cheap bread which threatened the country with disaster. The schoolmaster mocked at them, exclaiming that here indeed was something new. In the old days, the one great fear was the fear of starvation; men were always afraid there wouldn't be enough corn. Things had come to a pretty pass if they were now afraid of having too much. Intoxicated with his own eloquence, he bore down every angry interruption.

'You're a finished race! You're used up by your idiotic devotion to the land, to those little patches of earth that keep you enslaved and stunt your minds, and for which you'd do murder. You've been wedded to the earth for centuries and she keeps on deceiving you. Look at America: there the farmer is master of the earth. He isn't bound to it by anything, neither by family ties nor traditions. As soon as his piece of land is exhausted, he moves on. If he hears that three hundred leagues away they've found more fertile plains, he strikes his tent and moves over. Thanks to his machines, he's the one that's master; he's the one whose will matters. He's free and he makes money, but you're prisoners, you're dying of hardship!'

Buteau grew pale: Lequeu had glanced his way when he spoke of murder. He tried to put a good face on it.

'That's how we're made. What's the good of getting worked-up? You said yourself that it all won't change anything.'

Delhomme nodded approval and everyone broke into laughter— Lengaigne, Clou, Fouan, even Delphin and the conscripts, who were much tickled at the whole scene, hoping it would finish in a free fight. Canon and Jésus-Christ, angry at finding themselves shouted down by a fellow whom they styled the ink-pisser, also pretended to be amused. They were driven into the position of siding with the peasants.

'It's ridiculous to shout at one another,' declared Canon, with a shrug of his shoulders. 'What's needed is organisation.'

Lequeu annihilated him with a gesture. 'Now I'll tell you what I really think at last! I'm for destroying every bloody thing on earth!'

His face was livid and he spat the words at them as if he wanted to grind them to shreds.

'You cursed cowards, yes, I mean the peasants, all the peasants. Look how you outnumber them and yet you let the *bourgeois* and the town workers bleed you dry. By God, I've only one regret and that is that my parents were peasants. Perhaps that makes me despise you all the more. For there's no doubt about it, you could be the masters. Only, there you are, you can never agree among yourselves. You're always secretive, suspicious, ignorant. All your cunning is wasted in fighting among yourselves. Tell me, what goes on deep down in your still waters? Are you just stagnant pools that look deep but where you couldn't drown a cat? You're the hidden undeveloped power; the force out of which the future ought to come; and yet you've got no more go in you than logs of wood. The most exasperating thing of all is that you've lost your faith in your priests. Think, if there isn't a God, what's holding you back? As long as you were held down by fear of hell-fire, it was quite understandable you should grovel on your bellies. But nowadays, what holds you back? Loot and burn everything! And as a start, you can do something simpler and more amusing—you can go on strike. You've all got a bit of money put away: you could stick

389

things out as long as you needed. Only grow what you need, take nothing to market, not even one sack of corn or one bushel of potatoes. Then Paris would starve! What a clean sweep it would make, by God!'

They all felt as if a cold blast had swept in through the open window from the distant black spaces. The lamp flames were wildly flickering. No one now interrupted the crazy fellow despite the insults he was heaping on every man there.

He banged his book down on a table and made the glasses ring; then he yelled his concluding remarks.

'I tell you all this; but I'm not worried myself. You may be as cowardly as you like; yet you'll be the ones to smash everything down when the time comes. It's often happened before and it'll happen again. Just wait until misery and hunger unloose you on the towns like a pack of wolves. Perhaps the corn that's coming in will be your opportunity. When there's too much, then there won't be enough and we'll see scarcity again. Corn is always the motive for revolts and massacres. Yes, there'll be towns burned to the ground, deserted villages, earth left untilled and thick with weeds, and blood, rivers of blood. Then maybe she'll produce bread again for those who come after us!'

Lequeu flung the door violently open and slipped out. Behind him a roar rose from the dazed peasants. The blackguard; he needed a lot of blood-letting himself. A fellow who'd always been so reserved he must surely be going mad. Delhomme lost his normal phlegm and exclaimed that he'd write to the prefect; and the others urged him on. In particular Jésus-Christ and his friend Canon were infuriated: the former with his '89, his humanitarian slogans of liberty, equality, fraternity; the latter with his scheme for an authoritarian and scientific organisation of society. Both men were pale and exasperated at not having found a word in reply, growing angrier than the peasants and shouting that an individual of that kind ought to be guillotined. Buteau, on hearing the wild man call for a flood of blood over the earth, stood up shuddering; his head jerked in nervous involuntary movements as if he were nodding approval. Then he slithered along by the wall and disappeared in his turn.

At once the conscripts started their celebrations afresh. They were shouting and calling Flore to cook them some sausages when Nénesse pushed them aside and pointed to Delphin, who had fainted across the table. The poor chap was as white as a sheet. The handkerchief which had slipped from his wounded hand was stained with red. Men shouted into the ear of Bécu, who had been asleep throughout everything. At last he woke up and stared at his son's mutilated hand. He must have understood what had happened; for he grabbed a bottle and bawled that he'd finish the lad off. Then, when he had staggered out with his son in his charge, he was heard out in the street, in the middle of his curses, bursting into tears.

That evening Hourdequin heard of Françoise's accident while he was having his dinner. He came to Rognes to get the latest news out of friendship for Jean. He had walked over, smoking his pipe in the dark night and brooding on his troubles in the deep silence. Before calling on his former labourer, he went down the hill, feeling something of calm restored to his spirit and wanting to delay a short while longer. But down in the village, Lequeu's voice, echoing into the dusky countryside through the open window, brought him to a standstill and he halted unmoving in the shadows. Then, as he decided to go back up the hill, the voice followed him; and even when he reached Jean's house, he could still hear it, thin and sharpened by distance, as clear as ever and cutting like a knife.

Jean was leaning against the wall just outside the door. He had found it impossible to stay any longer by Françoise's bed; he felt suffocated there, anguished.

'My poor fellow,' asked Hourdequin, 'how are things going?'

The mourner made a despairing gesture. 'Oh sir, she's dying.'

Neither of them spoke another word. The vast silence reasserted itself, though Lequeu's voice still carried all the way from the tavern with its vibrant persistence.

After a few moments the farmer, who was listening in spite of himself, muttered angrily, 'D'you hear that chap bawling? What nonsense such stuff sounds when a man is unhappy.'

All his troubles came crowding back on him as he listened to the terrifying voice, with a dying woman so close at hand. The earth he had loved so much, with such strong emotion, almost with an intellectual passion, had finished him off after the last harvest. His fortune was exhausted and soon La Borderie wouldn't yield him enough to live on. Nothing had been any good: hard work, new methods, fertilisers, machines. He explained his ruin by lack of capital; yet his own arguments did not convince him. So many others were failing. The Robiquets had been turned out of La Chamade for not paying the rent and the Coquarts had been forced to sell up their farm at Saint Juste. Yet there seemed no way by which he could escape his fetters; he had never felt so much a prisoner to his earth; every day the money he put into the farm, the labour he spent, riveted him there more tightly and closely. A deep crisis was approaching, which would bring to an end the age-old antagonism between small and large-scale farming by killing them both off. The foretold hour of doom was at hand, when wheat would fall below sixteen francs and be sold at a loss, and the earth would fail; a crisis brought about by social causes outside the will of men.

Suddenly Hourdequin, tortured by the conviction of failure, nodded approval of Lequeu.

'By God, he's right! Let everything go, let us all die, let the brambles cover the earth. The race is finished and the earth is done for!'

He added, alluding to Jacqueline, 'Luckily I've got another burden on my back which will break me down before that happens.'

They heard La Grande and La Frimat moving about and whispering inside the house. Jean shivered at the slight noises. He went in, but too late. Françoise was dead; perhaps she had been dead for some time. Her eyes had not opened, nor had her mouth relented. La Grande, on touching her, had simply noticed she was no longer alive. Her face was very white, drawn and tense; and she seemed to be sleeping. Jean looked at her as he stood at the foot of the bed. His confused ideas bewildered him. His grief at the loss mingled with his surprise that she had not wanted to make a will; and he felt as though something had broken and died in his own life.

At the moment when Hourdequin waved him a silent greeting and moved away, still brooding, Jean saw a shadow on the road move away from the window and hurry into the shadows. He thought it might be a prowling dog. It was Buteau who had come to watch for Françoise's death and who had gone running to tell Lise.

V

NEXT morning, as Françoise's body was being laid out in the coffin which rested on two chairs in the middle of the room, Jean was surprised and indignant to see Lise and Buteau enter, one behind the other. His first reaction was to throw them out—heartless relations who hadn't come to give a dying woman the last kiss, but who walked in, as soon as the lid was nailed over her, as if they now were relieved of the fear of seeing her again face to face. However, the members of the family who were there, Fanny and La Grande, stopped him. Bad luck was sure to come from quarrels round a corpse. Besides, what was the use? No one could stop Lise making amends for her bitterness by coming to join the vigil over her sister's remains.

The Buteaus, who had counted on the respect due to the coffin, settled themselves down. They said nothing about resuming possession of the house; they simply took over, as a matter of course, as if the situation automatically righted itself now that Françoise was no longer there. She was in fact still in the house, but packed up for her final journey, hardly more in the way than a piece of furniture. After sitting for a while with the others, Lise so far forgot herself as to open the cupboards to make sure that nothing had moved from its place in her absence. Buteau was already prowling about the stable and the cowshed like the accepted master on his round of inspection. By evening they both appeared quite settled in and the only inconvenience was the coffin, which still took up the centre of the bedroom. However, they had only to wait one night: the room would be clear early on the following morning.

Jean walked relentlessly up and down among the members of the family, looking lost and not knowing what to do with his hands and feet. At first it had seemed that the house and furniture, with Françoise's body, belonged to him. But as the hours went by, everything appeared to detach itself from him and pass over to the others. When night fell, all the others had ceased to speak to him and he became merely a tolerated intruder. He had never felt so painfully a stranger before, with not one relative of his own among these people who were all related and who all agreed on his exclusion. Even his poor dead wife ceased to belong to him; indeed Fanny wanted to get rid of him when he talked of watching by the coffin, saying that there was already too much of a crowd. Still, he persisted, and even had the idea of taking the money from the drawer to make sure that the hundred and twenty-seven francs did not fly away. Lise must have seen the francs as well as the stamped paper when she opened the drawer soon after her arrival; for she had immediately begun a lively whispered conversation with La Grande. It was after that that she settled down in comfort, assured that there was no will. Well, at least she wouldn't have the money. Jean, with considerable misgivings about the morrow, promised himself that he would at least hang on to that. Then he spent the night sitting in a chair.

The funeral took place early next morning. The Abbé Madeline, who was due to leave Rognes that very night, managed to conduct the service and walk as far as the graveside; but there he fainted and had to be carried away. The Charleses' were present as well as Delhomme and Nénesse. The funeral was respectable, with nothing special about it. Jean wept. Buteau wiped his eyes. At the last moment Lise had declared that her legs were giving way beneath her and that she'd never have the strength to follow her poor sister's body to the grave. So she had remained alone in the house, while La Grande, Fanny, La Frimat, La Bécu and other neighbours joined the procession. On their return all the villagers waited about on the Place de l'Eglise, to see the row which had been expected since the previous evening.

Up to that moment the two men, Jean and Buteau, had avoided looking at one another, afraid that a fight would break out over the scarcely-cold body of Françoise. And now both of them were walking towards the house with the same resolute step and watching each other out of the corners of their eyes. At the first glance Jean realised why Lise had not attended the funeral. She had wanted to be left alone so as to move her furniture over, or as much of it as possible. An hour had been sufficient. She had thrown her bundles over the wall from La Frimat's and wheeled round the things that were breakable. She had brought Jules and Laure round to the yard with a clip over the ear, and they were already wrestling there, while Old Fouan, also hustled across, was panting on the stone bench. The house had been regained.

'Where're you off to?' Buteau asked sharply, stopping Jean on the doorstep.

'I'm going home.'

'Home? where's that? Not here, anyway. This is our home.'

Lise had rushed up and with arms akimbo she started screaming in tones even louder and coarser than her husband's.

'What's that? What does that rotter want? He's been poisoning my poor sister long enough, he must have, or she wouldn't have died from her accident. She's shown her opinion of things by not leaving him anything. Give him what-for, Buteau! Don't let him come in or he'll give us all some awful disease!'

Jean was furious at this crude attack, but he tried to argue.

'I know that the house and the land revert to you. But I get half the furniture and live-stock. . . .'

'Half! You've got a cheek!' Lise interrupted. 'You filthy pimp, you just dare take half of anything! You didn't even bring a comb into the place, you came with only a shirt on your back. So you batten on women, eh! That's a swinish trade!'

Buteau backed her up with a sweeping gesture across the threshold.

'She's right,' he cried, 'get off with you! You came with your shirt and trousers, and you can go off with them, we'll leave you that much.'

The other members of the family, particularly the women, Fanny and La Grande, who had halted some thirty yards away, seemed to give their approval by keeping silent. So Jean, paling at the outrage and cut to the heart by the charge of base calculations, grew angry and began to shout as loud as the others.

'So you're looking for trouble. All right, you can have it! First of all, I'm coming in. This is my house until the division takes place. Then I shall go to M. Baillehache, who'll seal the place up and put me in charge of it. It's my home, so you can bugger off!'

He advanced so threateningly that Lise let go of the doorpost. But Buteau leapt at him and a fight started. The two men went swinging round in the middle of the kitchen and a violent dispute continued indoors as to who was to be thrown out, the husband or the sister and brother-in-law.

'Show me the paper which gives you the house!'

'The paper—wipe your bum on it! We're within our rights, and that's enough.'

'All right, bring the bailiff and the police, as we did before.'

'The bailiff and the police can go and shit. Only swindlers need them. When a man is honest, he can settle his affairs without them.'

Jean had barricaded himself behind the table. He wanted desperately to prove himself the stronger and he was anxious not to leave the house which had seen his wife's death-throes and which seemed to enclose all the happiness he had ever known. The enraged Buteau was also determined never to relinquish the reconquered house; he realised that now was the testing moment.

'That's not all either,' he shouted, 'the long and the short of it is that we're bloody well fed up with you.'

He leapt over the table to come to grips with Jean. But Jean swung up a chair and sent him flying with a cut across his shins;

he then dodged into the next room to barricade himself in. Lise suddenly remembered the hundred and twenty-seven francs she had seen in the drawer. She thought he was running to get the money; she rushed ahead of him and opened the drawer. Then she howled with bitter rage.

'The money, the scoundrel has stolen the money during the night.'

From that moment Jean was lost; for he had to protect his pocket. He shouted that the money belonged to him, that he was quite ready to account for everything and that he was sure they must owe him much more than the sum in question. But the man and woman did not listen. Lise threw herself at Jean, hitting out even harder than Buteau. He was dislodged from the room by the furious onslaught and hustled back into the kitchen, where they all three whirled round in a confused tangle, crashing into the edges of the furniture. He got rid of Lise by kicking out at her. She came back again and sank her nails in his neck, while Buteau gathered himself together and using his head like a battering ram, sent him flat on his back outside in the road.

The Buteaus stood blocking up the doorway and screaming:

'Thief, stealing our money! Thief, thief, thief!'

Jean struggled to his feet and stammered out a retort of pain and fury, 'All right. I'll go to the magistrate at Châteaudun and he'll get me back into my house. I'll take you to law and get damages. You'll see me again.'

He gave a last menacing gesture and went off up the hill towards the plain. When the rest of the family saw the blows begin, they had all prudently vanished, to keep out of possible lawsuits.

The Buteaus burst out in a wild cry of victory. At last they had thrown out the stranger, the usurper, into the gutter. They had returned to the house, just as they'd said they would. The house! The house! When they realised that they were back, in the old family house built long ago by one of their ancestors, they were overcome with such a shock of mad joy that they rushed from room to room, yelling themselves hoarse for the sheer pleasure of making a noise in their own house. The children, Laure and Jules, ran in and started beating on an old saucepan like a drum. Only Old Fouan watched them all with his uneasy old eyes, never smiling.

Suddenly Buteau stopped in his tracks.

'God, he went by the upper road! What if he's gone to damage the fields!'

His fear was absurd; but with his passionate cry he became

396

frantic. The thought of the land came back to him in a whirl of joyous perturbation. His feeling for the land went far deeper than his delight in the house. That strip of earth up there which filled in the gap between his own two strips! Now he had his seven acre field again, that beautiful field; even Delhomme had nothing to compare with it. His whole body began trembling with joy just as a man trembles at the return of a desired woman whom he has thought lost for ever. He needed to see the ground at once; his demented fear that the other man might somehow take it away made him lose his head. He set off running, muttering that he couldn't feel at ease until he knew for sure.

Jean had indeed gone up to the plain so as to avoid the village. Without thought he followed the road to La Borderie. When Buteau caught sight of him, he was just passing the field at Les Cornailles; but he didn't stop, he merely glanced at the hotly-disputed piece of earth with an air of hostility and sadness as if accusing it of having brought him bad luck. A memory brought tears to his eyes, the thought of the day when he had first spoken to Françoise. Wasn't it at Les Cornailles that La Coliche had dragged her along through the lucerne when she was still a child? He went on his way, walking more slowly and with his head bent low. Buteau, who had been closely watching him, ill at ease and suspecting him of some evil design, approached the field in his turn. He stood staring for a long time. The field was still there, with every appearance of being in good trim; no one had done it any harm. His heart swelled and yearned towards it in the realisation that he now possessed it again —for ever. He bent down, took a lump of earth in his two hands, crushed it, sniffed it, then let it run through his fingers. It was indeed his own earth, and he went back home singing, as if he were drunk with the smell of it.

Meanwhile Jean walked on with distracted gaze, not knowing where his feet were leading him. At first he had meant to hurry to Cloyes to see Baillehache and ask for steps to be taken about his return to the house. Then his anger cooled. If he went back in to-day, he'd have to leave to-morrow. Why not swallow his bitter chagrin straight away and resign himself to the inevitable? The scoundrels had been right in one point: poor he had come, poor he was going away. But what broke his heart more than anything and made him take the decision of renunciation was his inability to deny that Françoise at the moment of death must have wished things to fall out as they had, since she had not willed her property

397

to him. So he abandoned his scheme of taking immediate action; and then his anger rose again, summoned up by the rhythm of his walking; it now merely took the form of an oath to exact vengeance from the Buteaus, to drag them into the courts and make them give up his full share, the half of the personal estate which fell to him as the dead woman's husband. They'd see if he'd let them fleece him like a lamb.

When he raised his eyes, he was astonished to find himself at La Borderie. Some inner instinct, of which he was only half aware, had led him to the farm as to a refuge. And indeed, if he wanted to stay in the district, here was the one place where he was sure to find lodging and work. Hourdequin had always thought well of him and he felt quite certain of a good welcome.

But from a distance he grew worried at seeing La Cognette rushing madly across the yard. It was eleven o'clock when he arrived and he was met by the news of a frightful catastrophe. That morning, going downstairs before the servant girl, La Cognette had found the cellar trap-door, which was so dangerously placed below the stairs, left open. Hourdequin lay at the bottom, dead, with his back broken on the steps. The young woman had screamed, the farm servants came running up, and the whole place was thrown into a terrified uproar. Now the farmer's body was lying on a mattress in the dining-room while Jacqueline was going frantic in the kitchen, her face twisted and tearless.

As soon as Jean entered she began talking in order to relieve her feelings.

'I told him so often, I always wanted him to change the place of that trap-door. But who on earth could have left it open? I am sure it was shut last night when I went to bed. I've been puzzling my brains about it all this morning.'

'Did the master go downstairs ahead of you?' asked Jean, who was horrified by the accident.

'Yes, just as dawn was breaking. I was asleep. I think I heard someone calling him from downstairs. I must have dreamt it. He often got up like this and went down in the dark to catch the servants as soon as they got out of bed. He must have missed seeing the trap-door and have fallen in. But who, who could have left it open? Oh, this will be the death of me!'

Jean had felt a passing suspicion, but he at once thrust it out of his mind. Jacqueline had no interest in Hourdequin's death and her grief was obviously genuine.

'It's a great tragedy,' he murmured.

'Indeed it is, a great tragedy, a great tragedy for me!'

She collapsed into a chair, overwhelmed, as though the house was falling round her ears. The man she had at last hoped to marry! The master who had sworn to leave her everything in his will! And now he was dead, before he'd had time to sign anything. She would not even get any wages, the son would come home and would kick her out as he had threatened. She'd get nothing. A few jewels and clothes: what she stood up in. It was ruination, the end of everything.

What Jacqueline did not mention, in fact what she had forgotten, was the dismissal of Soulas the shepherd, which she had succeeded in effecting the previous night. In her anger at finding him always at her elbow to spy on her, she insisted that he was too old for his work; and Hourdequin, although he did not agree with her, had given in. He was now completely under her domination, conquered and ready to purchase his nights of pleasure by slavish submission. When he gave Soulas his dismissal with kindly words and promises, the old shepherd looked his master straight in the face with his pale eyes. Then he slowly began to pour out all he knew about the slut who had brought about his sacking. He detailed the long file of her lovers, with Tron completing the list; he set out the story of this last affair, the shameless abandon of the pair under everyone's nose; the whole countryside whispered that the master seemed to enjoy his servant's leavings. The distracted farmer tried vainly to stop the old man; for he clung to his ignorance and didn't want to know what was going on, in terror of being forced to throw the woman out. But Soulas doggedly persisted and refused to leave out a single one of the occasions on which he had found them together. Then he felt that he had relieved his heart and mind of some of his years-old bitterness. Jacqueline was unaware of what had happened; for Hourdequin had at once escaped into the fields, afraid of throttling her if they met at that moment. On his return he simply sacked Tron on the excuse that he left the yard in a foul condition. Jacqueline then had a definite suspicion; but she dared not defend the cow-herd. She merely begged permission for him to sleep at the farm that night, trusting that she'd be able to smooth things over in the morning and get the dismissal cancelled. But now the whole episode was forgotten in the blow of fate which had struck down the whole edifice built up in ten years of laborious planning.

Jean was alone with her in the kitchen when Tron came in. She had not seen him since the previous evening and the other servants were wandering uneasily around the farm, doing nothing. When she caught sight of the huge Percheron fellow with his milky skin and stupid face, she cried out with an insight born from the sneaking manner of his entry.

'You opened the trap.'

Suddenly everything was clear to her. He paled, with staring eyes and trembling lips.

'You opened the trap-door and you called him down, so that he'd fall and break his neck!'

Aghast at the scene, Jean started back. Neither one nor the other of them, however, seemed to notice his presence in the violence of the emotions that agitated them. With head hanging, Tron sullenly confessed.

'Yes, I did it. He'd given me the sack and I'd never have seen you again. It was too much. I couldn't bear it. And then I thought that if he was dead we'd be free to get married.'

She listened to him, stiffening, with her whole body in acute nervous tension. The man went on smugly rumbling and poured out everything that had been mulling round in his thick head, his humble bitter jealousy against the master he obeyed, his secret murderous scheming to get hold of the woman he wanted for himself alone.

'I thought you'd be pleased when it was done. I didn't tell you as I didn't want to worry you. But now that he isn't in the way any longer, I've come to take you off to be married.'

Jacqueline burst out in a grating voice.

'But I don't love you and I don't want you. You killed him to get me, did you? You must be more of a fool than I thought you were! What blind stupidity—before he'd married me and made his will. You've ruined me, you've taken the bread out of my mouth. It's my back you've broken, d'you hear? And you think I'm going to go off with you! Listen here, look straight at me, do you take me for an absolute fool?'

He listened in stupefaction at his unexpected reception.

'Just because I played with you and we had some fun together, do you imagine I'm going to be bothered with you all my life? Get married! Never, never. If I wanted a husband, I'd choose one who wasn't such a fool. Get away with you, you make me sick. I don't love you and I don't want you. Get away.'

He was shaken with rage. What? he'd done murder for nothing? She was his, he'd drag her off by the hair.

'You're a proud bitch,' he growled. 'That won't prevent you coming with me. Otherwise I'll settle your hash as I settled his!'

La Cognette marched up to him with her fists clenched.

'Try it and see!'

He was powerfully built, heavy and tall, while she had little strength in her small stature, her girlish slightness. But he was the one to retreat, she scared him so, with her teeth bared to bite, her sharp eyes flashing like daggers.

'It's all over, get out. Rather than go off with you I'd never see a man again. Get out—get out—get out!'

Tron went out backwards like a wild beast in cowardly retreat, surrendering to fear and sullenly deferring vengeance. As he went, he glared at her and added, 'Dead or alive, I'll get you.'

When he had left the farmhouse, Jacqueline heaved a sigh of relief. Then she turned round, shivering all over, and seemed not in the least surprised at seeing Jean there. She cried out in an access of frankness, 'The brute, how I'd love to get him pinched by the police, but I'm afraid of getting myself involved!'

Jean was horror-struck. Then a nervous reaction set in with the young woman. She almost choked with the sobs and fell into his arms, stammering out that she was miserable, so miserable! Her tears fell unceasingly; she wanted to be soothed and loved, and she clung to him as though she wanted him to carry her off and protect her. He was beginning to feel an extreme discomfort when the dead man's brother-in-law, Maître Baillehache, who had been summoned by one of the farm servants, jumped out of his gig in the yard. Jacqueline ran out to him and paraded her despair.

Jean made his escape from the kitchen and soon found himself on the bare plain again, walking under the rainy March skies. But he took notice of nothing around him; he was too deeply upset by the whole affair, which had piled its horror on top of the suffering inflicted by his own misfortune. He had had enough bad luck and the instinct of self-preservation made him hasten his steps despite his sorrow for his old master's fate. It was hardly his business to betray La Cognette and her lover; the police only had to use half an eye. He turned round twice under the delusion that someone was calling him, and felt something of an accomplice. Only when he reached the first houses in Rognes did he breathe more freely; he told himself now that the farmer's death was the result of his

401

own sin, and pondered on the great truth that men would be much happier without women. Then the memory of Françoise returned, bringing with it a shattering anguish.

When he found himself back in the village, Jean remembered that he had gone to the farm to ask for work. All at once he began worrying and wondered which door he could knock on at that time of day; then it struck him that for some days the Charleses had been looking for a gardener. Why not go and offer his services? He was still in some small way a member of the family and that might be a recommendation. Straight away he went off to Roseblanche.

It was one o'clock and the Charleses were just finishing their morning meal when the servant announced him. Elodie was serving the coffee, and M. Charles, giving him a chair, offered him a cup. Jean accepted, though he had eaten nothing since the day before and his stomach felt very empty. The coffee would shake him up a bit. But when he found himself sitting at a table with these *bourgeois* folk he no longer dared ask for the gardener's job. He'd do it later when an opening turned up. Mme Charles began to sympathise with him and cry over poor Françoise's death, and he was much moved. The family obviously thought he had come to say good-bye.

When the servant announced the Delhommes, father and son, Jean was forgotten. 'Bring them in and set two more cups.'

All that morning the Charleses had felt themselves caught in a whirl of important events. When they left the cemetery, Nénesse had accompanied them to Roseblanche; and while Mme Charles and Elodie went inside, he had detained M. Charles with a blunt proposal of himself as a purchaser for No. 19, if only they could come to an agreement. According to him, the house, with which he was familiar, would fetch a miserable price. After letting it depreciate so lamentably, Vaucogne wouldn't get five thousand for it. Everything needed replacement; the furniture was shabby and the personnel so ill-chosen and incompetent that even the soldiers were going elsewhere. For nearly twenty minutes he ran down the establishment, bewildering his uncle and impressing him with his understanding of the profession, his bargaining methods and the extraordinary talents he showed for one so young. What a fine young chap: he certainly had a sharp eye and a ready hand. Nénesse ended with the remark that he would come back with his father after lunch for a serious discussion.

On going indoors, M. Charles had a talk with his wife, who was also astonished to hear of such capabilities in the boy. If only their

402

son-in-law Vaucogne had had half his ability! They'd have to play their cards carefully or the young chap would do them down. The main problem was to save Elodie's dowry from the debacle; and yet at the heart of their fear there lurked an irrepressible sympathy with Nénesse, a strong wish to see No. 19 back in the astute vigorous hands of a master who'd restore its glory, even if they personally lost by the change. And so, when the Delhommes came in, they were very warmly greeted.

'You'll have some coffee, won't you? Elodie, pass the sugar round.'

Jean had pushed back his chair and they were all seated round the table. Freshly-shaved, with tanned and expressionless face, Delhomme sat without a word, preserving a diplomatic silence; but Nénesse, dressed in his smartest clothes, patent leather shoes, gold-flowered waistcoat, mauve cravat, seemed very much at his ease and smiled charmingly. When the blushing Elodie handed him the sugar basin, he looked at her and searched for some compliment.

'Your lumps of sugar are very big, cousin.'

She blushed even more deeply, at a loss for words: in her innocence she felt quite overcome by the comment of such an amiable young man.

Nénesse, with his artful way, had disclosed only a half of his scheme in the morning. On catching sight of Elodie at the funeral, he had in a flash seen how to expand his plans. No. 19 was not enough; he wanted the girl as well. The idea was quite simple. First, he'd have nothing to pay for the premises as he'd insist on the house being included in her dowry; secondly, even if she only brought him that rather shabby business at marriage, she would later inherit a proper fortune from the Charleses. And so he had brought his father along, determined to put his proposal straight away.

For a few moments they talked about the weather, which was really mild for the time of the year. The pear trees had flowered wonderfully, but would the bloom set? But as they finished their coffee, conversation flagged.

'My darling,' M. Charles suddenly said to Elodie, 'suppose you go out into the garden for a walk?'

He was sending her away in his anxiety to strike a bargain with the Delhommes.

'Excuse me, uncle,' Nénesse interrupted, 'I'd be very obliged if you'd allow my cousin to stay. I want to talk about something

403

which affects her; and I'm sure you agree it's always better to finish a thing off at one stroke than to have to go over it twice?'

He rose to his feet and made his proposal like a well-bred young man.

'What I wish to say is that I would be very happy to take my cousin in marriage if you consent and if she herself consents.'

There was general astonishment. But Elodie in particular seemed so overwhelmed that she left her seat and threw herself on Mme Charleses bosom, in such a state of bashfulness that she reddened to her ears. Her grandmother exerted herself to calm the girl.

'Come, come, my little puss, this is too much, have some sense. No one's going to eat you. He's only asking for your hand in marriage. Your cousin has said nothing improper. Look at him, don't be foolish!'

But no coaxing words would induce her to show her face.

'Good heavens,' M. Charles said at last, 'your request has taken me completely by surprise, my boy. Perhaps it would have been better to talk it over with me first. You see how sensitive our darling is. But whatever comes of it, be assured that I have a great respect for you, as you seem to me to be a good and hard-working young man.'

Delhomme, whose face had so far remained utterly expressionless, now allowed three words to pass his lips:

'Indeed, he is!'

Jean, feeling it was time to say something polite, added, 'Ah yes, indeed he is!'

M. Charles had regained his composure and was already considering that Nénesse wasn't a bad match; he was young, energetic and the only son of rich peasants. His granddaughter wouldn't find a better mate. And so, after exchanging a look with Mme Charles, he continued the discussion.

'It's for the child to decide. We would never interfere with her in such a matter and so we leave things in her hands.'

Nénesse gallantly renewed his request.

'My cousin, if you would give me the honour and pleasure. . . .

She still kept her face buried in her grandmother's bosom; but she did not give him time to finish the sentence. She accepted him at once with three energetic nods of the head, while hiding her face even more deeply. She seemed to muster up courage by not looking at anybody. The company sat dumbfounded, amazed at her hasty consent. Could it be that she was in love with the boy, though she had seen him so infrequently? Or was it that she wanted a man, no matter who, as long as he was a handsome fellow?

Mme Charles kissed her hair and smiled. 'My poor darling, my poor darling.'

'Very well,' exclaimed M. Charles, 'if she agrees, then we agree too.'

But a sudden thought shadowed his face. His heavy eyelids drooped and he made a gesture of regret.

'Of course, my dear fellow, we shall have to give up the other thing, the matter you brought up with me this morning.'

Nénesse was astonished. 'But why?'

'Why? Because—look here—surely you can see why! We haven't kept her for twenty years at school with the Sisters of the Visitation for her to—well, obviously the idea is out of the question!'

He winked his eye, contorted his lips and tried to make himself understood, though he was afraid to say too much. To think of the girl down there in the Rue aux Juifs! A young lady of such good education, who was perfectly innocent, brought up to know nothing about anything.

'Pardon me,' Nénesse declared bluntly, 'but that won't suit me at all. I want to marry and settle down, I want my cousin and the house.'

'The confectionery business!' exclaimed Mme Charles.

As soon as this word was introduced, the arguers seized on it and brought it into the conversation at every possible opportunity.

Now really, was it reasonable to give up the confectionery shop?

The young man and his father persisted in claiming it for the dowry; they insisted that it was impossible to let it go when it held the key to a prosperous future; and they called on Jean for support. He agreed with a wag of his chin. In the end they all began shouting simultaneously, were quite carried away, and went into every detail with the crudest precision until they were reduced to silence by an unexpected incident.

Elodie had at last slowly raised her head. She stood up looking like some tall lily that had grown in the darkness, with her thin, pale, chlorotic face, her vacant eyes, and her colourless hair. She looked round at them all and then spoke quietly.

'My cousin is right, the business mustn't be given up.'

Mme Charles stammered out in her confusion, 'But my puss, if you only knew. . .'

'I do know. Victorine told me about it long ago, our maid

405

Victorine that you dismissed because of the men. I know all about it and I've thought things over. I am quite sure it must not be given up.'

M. and Mme Charles were petrified. Wide-eyed, they watched the girl in a state of blank amazement. What, she knew of No. 19, she knew what went on there, what the place earned, even what the profession was; and she talked about it in this serene way! O, how innocence could touch anything at all without defilement!

'It'd be impossible to give it up,' she went on. 'It's too good and profitable a business. And then you yourselves built up the house, you worked there so hard. How could we let such a business go out of the family?'

M. Charles was quite overwhelmed. Bewildered as he was, he felt an indescribable thrill spring up from his heart and constrict his throat. He rose from his chair, staggered, and supported himself by catching hold of Mme Charles, who was also on her feet, choking and trembling. They both treated the offer as a sacrifice and tried to refuse in distracted tones.

'O, darling, darling, no! No, darling. . . . !'

But Elodie's eyes filled with tears and she kissed her mother's old wedding ring which she was wearing, the wedding ring which had worn so thin with the hard work down there.

'Yes, yes, let me carry out my plan. I want to be like mamma. What she did, I can do. There's nothing wrong in it, for you did it yourselves. I'd love it, I assure you. And you'll see what a help I shall be to my cousin and how quickly the pair of us will raise the establishment up again. It's got to be done, and I'll prove to you that I can do it. Really, I can.'

This outburst carried everyone away and the Charleses dissolved into tears. Emotion flooded them and they sobbed like a pair of children. Of course, they hadn't brought the girl up for the work, but what could you do against the call of the blood? In her demand they recognised the clear accents of a vocation: exactly the same thing had happened with Estelle; she too had been shut up with the Sisters of the Visitation, kept ignorant, and instructed in the most rigid rules of morality; and she had nevertheless become an outstanding house-manager. Education went for nothing; it was intelligence which counted. But the deep emotion stirring the Charleses, the tears which irresistibly poured down their cheeks, came even more directly from the glorious thought that No. 19, their creation, flesh of their flesh, would now be saved from ruin.

Elodie and Nénesse, with the lively energy of youth, would carry on the tradition. They could already see the place restored, re-established in public favour with the brilliant reputation it had enjoyed in the most prosperous days of their own reign.

As soon as M. Charles was able to speak, he drew his granddaughter into his arms.

'Your father has given us a great deal of worry; but you, my angel, you console us for everything.'

Mme Charles also warmly embraced her, so that all three of them were entwined together, mingling their tears.

'The matter's settled then?' asked Nénesse, who wanted a definite statement of the position.

'Yes, everything's settled!'

Delhomme beamed: a father delighted at setting up his son in an unhoped-for way. Cautiously, with much fidgeting, he expressed his opinion.

'Well, by heaven, if there's no regrets on your side I'm sure there'll never be any on ours. No need to wish the children good luck. When you're making money, nothing goes wrong.'

At this point they all sat down again to talk the details over quietly.

Jean felt that he was in the way. He himself had been greatly embarrassed by his presence at the effusive scene; he'd have slipped away much sooner if he had been able to find a way of departing. Now, he at last managed to take M. Charles aside and speak to him about the gardener's job. M. Charles' dignified face became severe. He could never give a job to a relative. You can never get useful service out of a relative; you can't knock him about. In any case, the situation had been filled the day before. So Jean went away as Elodie's thin girlish voice was heard remarking that if her father tried to be disagreeable she'd undertake to bring him to his senses.

Outside, he walked slowly along, not knowing where to turn for work. Out of his hundred and twenty-seven francs he had already paid for his wife's funeral, the cross and the railings around it in the cemetery. He had barely half left; but that would easily keep him some three weeks, and then he'd have to see how things were going. He was not afraid of hard work; his only worry came from his reluctance to leave Rognes because of his projected law-suit. Three o'clock struck, then four, then five. For a long time he wandered over the countryside, his head whirling with confused daydreams of going back to La Borderie or to the Charleses' house.

It was the same everywhere: money and women, they meant either death or life. There was nothing strange in the fact that all his bad luck came from the same cause. He began to feel weak in the legs and realised that he hadn't eaten all day, so he turned back to the village, meaning to go to Lengaigne, who let rooms. But as he crossed the Place de l'Eglise, the sight of the house out of which he had been chased that morning stirred him afresh to anger. Why should he leave his two pairs of trousers and his frock-coat to those blackguards? They were his and he wanted them, even at the risk of coming to blows again.

Dusk was approaching and Jean could hardly make out Old Fouan as he sat on the stone bench. He reached the kitchen door and saw the candle burning inside when Buteau recognised him and rushed forward to bar his entrance.

'By God, you again! What do you want?'

'I want my two pairs of trousers and my frock-coat.'

A fearful quarrel broke out. Jean persisted and demanded the right to go and look in the cupboard; Buteau, who had picked up a billhook, swore to slit his throat if he took one step over the threshold. At last Lise shouted from inside the house.

'Get on with you—give him his rags back. You'll never wear them, he's infected!'

The two men fell silent. Jean waited. But just behind him, on the stone bench, Old Fouan was muttering out of some crazy dream, stammering out in his thickened voice:

'Get out quick! They'll get your blood just like they got the girl's.'

In a flash Jean understood everything, Françoise's death and her obstinate silence. He had already had a suspicion and now he no longer doubted that she had wanted to save her family from the guillotine. His hair stood on end at the shock and he could neither cry out nor move, when full in the face came the trousers and frock-coat which Lise had thrown at him through the open door.

'There! Take your filthy things! They stink so bad that they'd have given us the plague!'

He picked them up and went away. It was only when he got safely out of the yard on to the road that he shook his fist at the house and shouted a single word which rent the silence.

'Murderers!'

Then he disappeared into the black night.

Buteau stood frozen with fear; for he had heard Fouan's nightmare mutterings and Jean's shouted word struck him to the heart like a rifle bullet. God, would the police get on his track, now when he had thought the whole affair buried with Françoise? Since he had seen her body going down into the earth that morning, he had been breathing more freely; and now here was the old man who knew everything! Was he pretending to be imbecile, in order to spy on them? The idea completed Buteau's demoralisation and he went inside, feeling so upset that he left half his meal uneaten. When Lise was told his fears, she began to shiver and could not eat either.

The pair of them had been looking forward to their first night in the reconquered house; but the night was ghastly, a night of horror. They had put Laure and Jules down on a mattress in front of the chest of drawers until better arrangements could be made; and the children were still awake when they themselves went to bed after blowing out the candle. They couldn't sleep a wink and they kept turning over as though the bed was scorching them, till in the end they talked together in hushed voices. O, what a burden the old man had become since he had gone into his second childhood. He was a real expense and cost so much that they were almost ruined. You couldn't believe how much bread he guzzled, and he was such a pig, mauling the meat with his fingers and pouring the wine into his beard, getting himself so filthy that it made you sick just to look at him. Nowadays he always had his trousers undone and he'd been caught exposing himself to little girls. He'd fallen into the filthy ways of an old dodderer; it was a disgusting end for a man who, in his day, had never been any dirtier than his fellows. Really, as he didn't seem inclined to die of his own accord, he ought to be finished off with a pick-axe!

'When you think that one breath of wind would blow him over!' whispered Buteau. 'And yet he hangs on and enjoys being a nuisance to us. These damned old men, the less they do the more they cling to life. He'll never die, not he.'

Lise spoke as she lay on her back. 'It's a pity he came back. He'll be too comfortable and get a new lease of life. If I'd had a prayer to make to God, I'd have prayed that he wouldn't let the old man sleep a single night in this house.'

They both ignored their real source of anxiety, which was that Fouan knew everything and he might betray them, even without meaning it. That was the last straw. He might go on being an expense, getting in their way, preventing them from properly enjoying the stolen dividends: all that they'd already put up with for a good while. But when one word from him could get their heads cut off, that was going too far. Something would have to be done.

'I'm going to see if he's asleep,' said Lise suddenly.

She re-lit the candle, made sure the children were sleeping fast, then slipped in her nightshift into the beet room where the old man's iron bed had been replaced. When she returned, she was shivering and her feet were icy from the tiles. She hurried back under the coverlets and pressed against her husband, who took her in his arms to warm her up again.

'Well?'

'He's sleeping. His mouth is open like a fish's because he can hardly breathe.'

They fell silent, and yet as they lay entwined they could feel the thoughts throbbing under their skins. This old man who was always at the point of choking, it would be so easy to finish him off. Any obstruction in his throat, a handkerchief or even a finger, and they'd be free of him. It would even be a kindness. Wouldn't it be better for him to be quietly asleep in the cemetery than to remain a burden to others and himself?

Buteau was still holding Lise close in his arms. Both of them were now afire, as if some desire was making the blood course through their veins. He loosened his arms abruptly and jumped out on to the tiled floor in his bare feet.

'I'm going to look too.'

He disappeared with the candle in his hand while she held her breath and listened with eyes wide open in the darkness. But the minutes ticked away and not a sound reached her from the neighbouring room. At last she heard her husband returning without the light. His feet pattered gently and he was so worked-up that he could not restrain his panting breath. He crept to the bed and felt about for her, then whispered in her ear.

'You come too, I don't dare do it alone.'

Lise followed him. They went along stretching out their arms for fear of bumping into things. They no longer felt the cold; their shifts were merely a nuisance. The candle stood on the floor in a corner of the old man's room; but it gave enough light for them to make him out as he lay on his back with his head slipped off the pillow. He was so rigid, so emaciated with age, that he might have been dead except for the painful breathing rattling out of his wide-open mouth. He had no teeth left and it was into a black hole that

410

his lips seemed to be falling. The pair leaned over this hole as if they wanted to find out how much life remained at its bottom. For a long time they stared, side by side, their hips touching. But their arms went limp; it was so easy and yet so difficult to put something in the mouth and block it up. They moved away, then came back. Their dry tongues could not shape a single word; only their eyes spoke. With a glance Lise indicated the pillow. Go on! What was Buteau waiting for? He blinked, pushed her forward in his stead. Suddenly Lise snatched up the pillow in exasperation and clapped it down on the old man's face.

'You bloody coward, women have to do everything!'

Buteau threw himself forward and pressed down with the whole weight of his body, while she climbed on to the bed and sat there, adding the weight of her naked bottom, as broad as a dropsical mare. It was a mad attack. The pair of them drove down with their hands, their shoulders, their buttocks. The old man had given a violent jerk and his legs stretched out with a sound of snapping springs. He slithered about like a fish thrown on dry land. But the struggle did not last long. They were holding him down too strongly; they felt him flattening out beneath them and pouring out his life. There was a long shudder, a last tremor, then nothing at all. His body was limp as a dish-cloth.

'I think it's over,' panted Buteau in a growl.

Lise, still squatting all of a heap, stopped bumping up and down and waited to see if the least quiver of life was left.

'Yes, it's over, there's not a sign of life in him.'

She slid off the bed with her shift rolled up over her hips, and removed the pillow. Then they groaned with terror.

'God in heaven, he's all black, we're done for.'

It was out of the question to say that he had got himself into such a condition. In their furious desire to crush him, they had jammed his nose right into his mouth; and he was dark purple in the face, almost like a negro. For a moment they felt the earth quake under their feet; they heard the rush of the police, the prison chains, the swish of the guillotine blade. Their blotched work filled them with a terrified regret. But how could they mend matters now? No use giving him a scrub with soap; he'd never be white again. But the very horror of his sooty appearance gave them an idea.

'Suppose we burn him?' whispered Lise.

Buteau fetched a deep breath of relief.

'Good idea, we'll say he set fire to himself.'

Then, as the thought of the documents flashed into his mind, he clapped his hands and his whole face lit up with a triumphant grin.

'Good God, we'll tell them he burned the papers as well as himself. Then there can't be any rendering of accounts.'

At once he ran to fetch the candle. But she, afraid of setting fire to the place, wouldn't let him approach the bed. There were some straw-bands in a corner, behind the beets. She took one, lighted it, and started singeing her father-in-law's long white hair and beard. There was a smell of melting grease and a sputter of small yellow flames. Suddenly they started back staring as though an icy hand had yanked them back by the hair. Under the dreadful pain of the scorching flames the old man, not quite suffocated, had opened his eyes; and the ghastly mask, black and broken-nosed, with its burning beard, glared out at them. A frightful expression of pain and hate twisted the face; then the features all came apart and the man died.

Wild with fear, Buteau let out a yell of fury, when he heard a noise of sobs in the doorway. It was the two children, Laure and Jules, in their nightshirts. They had been woken by the noise and attracted by the bright light streaming through the open door. They had seen everything and they screamed with terror.

'You damned little vermin,' shouted Buteau, rushing towards them. 'If you say a word about this I'll throttle you both. And take that to remind you.'

He gave them each a blow which sent them sprawling to the ground. They picked themselves up without a tear and rushed to bury themselves in their bed, where they lay too terrified to stir.

Wanting to get the whole thing over, he set fire to the bed, in spite of his wife. Luckily the room was so damp that the straw burned slowly. Thick smoke rose up and they had to open the shutter so as not to stifle. Then the flames caught hold and almost licked at the ceiling. The old man began to crackle in the fire and the unbearable smell grew stronger, the smell of burning flesh. The whole ancient building would have gone up in flames like a haystack if the straw had not begun to smoke again as the body bubbled and melted. There was nothing left on the cross-ribs of the iron bedstead except the half-calcined, disfigured, unrecognisable corpse. One corner of the palliasse remained intact, and a scrap of sheeting still hung over the bed.

'Let's get away from here,' said Lise, who was shivering again in spite of the great heat.

'Wait a minute,' replied Buteau. 'I must fix things properly.'

He placed a chair by the bedside and upset the old man's candle to make it look as though it had fallen on the palliasse. He even had the cunning to burn some bits of paper on the ground. The cinders would be found and he would say that the old man had discovered his papers the night before and had kept them.

'That's done now. Get to bed.'

Buteau and Lise rushed away, jostling each other and plunged back into bed. The sheets were icy and they seized each other tightly in a violent embrace as they struggled for warmth. Dawn came before they slept. They said not a word, shivering and listening to the heavy thump of their hearts. The open door of the neighbouring room was what kept them on edge; but the thought of closing it made them even more uneasy. At last they dozed off, still clinging to one another.

Next morning the neighbours came running up when they heard the Buteaus' frenzied shouts. La Frimat and the other women took note of the overturned candle, the half-burned palliasse, the ashes of paper. They all exclaimed how it was bound to happen sooner or later and that they had prophesied it a hundred times since the old man had reached his dotage. It was good luck the whole house hadn't been burned down with him!

VI

Two days later, on the morning when Old Fouan was to be buried, Jean awoke late after a restless night in the small room he had hired at Lengaigne's. He had not yet been to Châteaudun to start his law-suit, though that was the only thing which kept him in Rognes; each evening he put the matter off till the morrow and went on hesitating as his anger cooled down. His inability to sleep had come from a last struggle with himself, and he was in a fever, unable to decide what course to take.

What beasts the Buteaus were, murderous brutes and killers; some honest men ought to have got their heads chopped off. As soon as he heard of the old man's death, he guessed what had occurred. The scoundrels must have just burned him alive to stop him talking. First Françoise, then Fouan. The murder of one had necessitated the murder of another. Whose turn next? He felt it would be his, for they knew that he had read their secret. They

413

would certainly shoot him down in some wooded corner if he stayed in the district. Why not then denounce them straight away? He made up his mind to go and tell the whole story to the police as soon as he was out of bed. But then he began to hesitate again; he shrank from involving himself as witness in such a business which might bring on his own head as much suffering as on the criminals themselves. Why make fresh trouble for himself? He admitted that he was hardly showing much pluck, but he argued that by keeping quiet he was obeying Françoise's dying wish. Scores of times during the night he decided to act, then changed his mind, sick at heart at the thought of this duty that he could not face.

When he jumped out of bed at nine o'clock, he plunged his head into a basin of cold water. Suddenly he reached a decision. He would say nothing; he wouldn't even start a law-suit for the recovery of his half of the furniture. The game wasn't worth the candle. A sense of pride restored his calm of mind; he felt happy at not being one of the swindlers, at being the stranger amongst them. They could damn well go ahead and devour each other; it'd be a good riddance if they all swallowed each other up. The sufferings and horror of the ten years he had lived in Rognes rose in a surge of anger from his heart. To think that he had been so overjoyed the day he had left the army after the Italian war, never again to drag a sword around, never again to be a killer of men! Yet since that time he had met nothing but foulness; he had been living among savages. From the moment of his marriage he had had plenty to bear; but now these people had taken to robbery and murder. They were nothing but rabid wolves let loose on the huge calm plain. No, he'd had enough. These rapacious wolves spoiled the countryside for him. Why should he set the hunt on a couple of them, one female and one male, when the whole troop of them ought to be wiped out? He'd rather get away from it all.

At that moment Jean's eyes fell on a newspaper he had brought up from the wine-shop the previous evening. He had been interested in an article on the approaching war; for rumours had been circulating and terrifying everyone for the last few days. Something unconscious in him, something that lurked unknown in the depths of his being was aroused by the news; a smothered but smouldering flame sprang up again and gave a sudden flare. His last hesitation about departure, his feeling that he didn't know where to go, were caught up and swept away as if by a storm-wind. Yes, he'd join up again and go to fight. He had done his army service; but what of

414

it? When a man has no trade left, when life has become a burden and anger rises against an enemy's persecution, the best thing still is to advance and attack. He felt relieved, thoroughly relieved, thrilled with a sombre joy. As he dressed, he whistled the trumpet-calls which had led him into battle in Italy. People were too horrible; the hope of killing some Prussians soothed him. Since he had failed to find peace in this corner of the country where families drank one another's blood, he might just as well go back to the slaughter. Men had made his life intolerable; so the more men he killed, the redder the earth was stained with their blood, the better his revenge would be.

On going downstairs, he ate the two eggs and slice of bacon which Flore put before him. He then called for Lengaigne and paid his account.

'Going away, Corporal?'

'Yes.'

'But you'll be coming back, won't you?'

'No.'

The innkeeper looked at him in astonishment but kept his thoughts to himself. So the big lout was giving up his rights?

'What are you going to do now? Thinking of becoming a carpenter again?'

'No, a soldier.'

Lengaigne, startled, opened his eyes wide in amazement and failed to suppress a contemptuous laugh. What an idiot!

Jean had already started on the Cloyes road when a last access of tenderness made him stop and go back up the hill. He couldn't say good-bye to Rognes without a final good-bye to Françoise's grave. There was something else too, a longing to see once more the vast plain stretching out into the distance, the melancholy La Beauce which he had come to love after his long hours of lonely labour.

Behind the church, the cemetery lay enclosed by a low wall half in ruins; so low indeed that a man standing among the graves could let his eyes travel without let or hindrance from one horizon to the other. A pale March sun whitened the sky which was veiled in a mist as fine as the finest white silk, with scarcely a fleck of blue to liven it; and under this soft light La Beauce, numbed by the winter frosts, seemed to cling to its slumbers like a woman who is not deeply asleep but who avoids stirring in order to enjoy to the full her lazy doze. The distance was hazy and made the plain seem even wider as the fields stretched out, already green with wheat, oats and rye of the autumn sowing; in the bare plough-land the spring sowing had begun. Everywhere men were walking over the rich soil with the scattering gesture of seed-sowing. Jean could clearly see the golden grain, like a living dust, as it escaped from the fingers of the nearest sowers. The forms of the men dwindled, were lost in the endless vista; and the grain enveloped them in a wave which seemed, from afar, nothing more than the vibration of light itself. For leagues around, from every point of the limitless expanse, the life of the summer to come rained through the sunny air.

Jean stood in front of Françoise's tomb. It lay in the middle of a row and the grave of Old Fouan waited gaping beside it. Rank weeds overran the cemetery; for the municipal council could never reach the point of voting fifty francs to the rural constable to keep them down. Crosses and railings had rotted as they stood; a few mouldering stones still stood in position; but the attraction of this lonely corner was in its very wildness, its profound quiet, disturbed only by the cawing of the ancient crows flying round the top of the bell-tower. Here, at the world's end, the dead lay sleeping, in humility and oblivion. And Jean, succumbing to the peace of death, went on gazing out over the great plain of La Beauce shivering into life with the grain-sowing, when the bell began to toll slowly—three strokes, then two more, then a full peal. The coffin of Old Fouan was being lifted up, it was on its way to the grave.

The bandy-legged gravedigger came limping along to take a look at the grave.

'It's too small,' remarked Jean, who felt deeply stirred and who wanted to stay and watch.

'Ah, well, you see,' replied the lame digger, 'it shrinks a man to roast him.'

The Buteaus, two days earlier, had been in a panic until the doctor had called; but Doctor Finet's only preoccupation had been to get the signing of the burial certificate over as quickly as possible, so that he wouldn't have to make another journey. He came in, took a look, swore at the stupidity of relations who leave a candle near old people gone soft in the head; and even if he felt any suspicions, he was too cautious to mention them. Good God, what if the old man with his obstinate clinging to life had been grilled? He had seen so much that he was quite unmoved. In his indifference, born of bitterness and contempt, he merely shrugged his shoulders. A filthy lot, these peasants!

416

The Buteaus, relieved of their main worry, had now only to
sustain the family assault, which they knew was coming and which
they met with resolution. As soon as La Grande appeared, they
burst into tears, thinking to put a good face on things. She stared
at them in some surprise and decided that they didn't show much
cunning by crying so much; anyway, she had only come along for
amusement as she had nothing to claim by way of inheritance. The
real danger began when Fanny and Delhomme entered. Delhomme
had been appointed mayor in Macqueron's place and his wife was
so inordinately proud that she almost burst through her skin. She
had held to her vow and her father had died without a reconciliation between them; her susceptibility to offence remained so alive
that she stood dry-eyed in front of the body. But there was uproar
and sobbing when Jésus-Christ arrived in a state of complete intoxication. He spilt his tears all over the corpse and bawled that the
death was a blow from which he would never recover.

Meanwhile Lise had got out wine and glasses in the kitchen; and
everyone began to chat. It was immediately agreed that the hundred
and fifty francs rent coming from the sale of the house should be
left out of the reckoning, for it had been agreed that this would go
to the children who had looked after the old man in his last days.
But there was the question of the hoard. Buteau started telling his
story, how the old man had found the documents under the marble
top of the chest of drawers, and how it must have been while he
was gloating over them during the night that he had set fire to his
beard and hair; they had even found the ashes of the papers, as
several people had witnessed, La Frimat, La Bécu and others.
During the recital everybody watched him closely, but he did not
flinch as he beat his chest and called on the light of day to bear
him out. The family obviously guessed the truth; but he didn't give
a damn as long as they made no attempt to get at him and left him
with the money. Fanny, however, let herself go with all the out-
spoken energy of a proud woman, and accused the Buteaus of being
thieves and murderers. Yes, they had set their father on fire, they
had robbed him, it was all quite obvious! The Buteaus retorted
with a flood of insults and frightful counter-accusations. So she
wanted to get them into trouble, did she? What about the poisoned
soup which had nearly killed off the old man when he was living
with his daughter? And they had plenty of things to bring up about
all the others, if the latter wanted to butt in. Jésus-Christ began to
weep again and howled with grief when he learned that such terrible

o

crimes were possible. God in heaven, O poor father! Were there children really vile enough to roast a father alive? La Grande let fall a few words to keep the fires well-stoked as soon as they seemed to be sinking for lack of breath. Delhomme finally became uneasy about the noise and went to shut the doors and windows. He had to keep up his position, and anyway he was always for a reasonable solution of problems. He brought things to a close by saying that no one should speak of such matters. They'd all be in a pretty kettle if the neighbours heard. They'd have to go to law and maybe the innocent parties would lose more than the guilty in the long run. The group fell silent. He was right; it never did any good to wash one's dirty linen in public court. And Buteau frightened them; he was ruffian enough to bring them all down in ruin. Besides, underlying their acceptance of the crime, their voluntary silence about murder and theft, was the deep-seated complicity of peasants with the rebels of the countryside, the poachers, the killers of game-keepers, the men of whom they are afraid and whom they never betray.

La Grande stayed to drink coffee during the vigil, but the others went off discourteously, in the way that people leave a household held in contempt. The Buteaus laughed in their sleeves; they had the money and the certainty that from that time forth they would meet no further worries. Lise regained her hectoring tone and Buteau resolved to do things in style, ordering the coffin and going to the churchyard to supervise the position where the grave was to be dug. The peasants of Rognes who have been at loggerheads in their lifetime, it must be admitted, dislike sleeping side by side when they are dead. But as the graves were dug in rows the positions became a question of luck. So, when fate decreed that two enemies should die in succession, there was always a great deal of bother for the authorities. The family of the second would often talk quite seriously of holding fast to the body rather than giving it up to be laid beside the dead enemy. And it so happened that Macqueron, during his term of office as mayor, had taken advantage of his position to buy a piece of ground instead of waiting for his turn. Unfortunately this strip ran alongside the place where Lengaigne's father was buried, and Lengaigne had reserved a place for himself in the same grave; since then Lengaigne could never get over his indignation. He was burning with rage still from his long feud; and the thought that his corpse would lie rotting beside the corpse of his scoundrelly enemy spoiled the rest of his days. A similar anger

418

flooded Buteau when he examined the place chosen for his father. The old man would have Françoise on his right hand, which was as it should be; but ill-luck had it that in the row of graves higher up, immediately opposite, stood the grave of old Saucisse's dead wife, in which Saucisse himself would be buried. This would mean that when the old scamp died at long last he would lie with his feet on Fouan's head. Could such a thing be tolerated for a single minute? Two old men who hated each other, particularly since the shady affair of the life-annuity, placed in such a way that the greater rascal of the two—the one who had tricked the other— would dance on his victim's head for all eternity? No, in God's name. If the family were so callous as to tolerate it, then Old Fouan's bones would turn round in their box and do battle with old Saucisse. Seething with rage, Buteau went down to kick up a row at the Town Hall. There he attacked Delhomme, trying to force him, now that he was in charge of things, to assign another piece of ground. Then, when his brother-in-law refused to swerve from the usual procedure and pointed to the unfortunate example of Macqueron and Lengaigne, Buteau called him coward and traitor. He stood in the middle of the road and roared out that he was the only good son; the other men of the family didn't care a straw whether or not their father lay at rest in the earth. He disturbed the whole village, then went home in a fury.

Delhomme had just come up against a much more serious difficulty. The Abbé Madeline had left two days before and Rognes once again found itself without a priest. The experiment of owning and paying for their own priest, a costly luxury for a parish, had on the whole succeeded so badly that the town council decided to withdraw the allocated money and return to the old method of having the services performed by the priest from Bazoches-le-Doyen. But the Abbé Godard, though the bishop argued hard with him, swore that he would never celebrate the sacrament in the place again. He was furious when his colleague left Rognes, and accused the villagers of having half-murdered the poor man with the sole aim of forcing himself to go back there. He had already declared in public that Bécu could ring the bell for Mass until it was time for vespers on the following Sunday, when the situation suddenly became very serious with the unexpected death of Old Fouan. A burial is a different matter from a Mass; it can't be indefinitely put off. In his heart Delhomme was glad of the accident; as his common-sense had a touch of malice, he took the opportunity of calling personally on the priest at Bazoches. As soon as the latter saw him, his temples started throbbing, his face darkened and he waved the visitor away without letting him open his mouth. No, no, no! He'd rather lose his parish. When he heard that he was being asked to deal with a funeral, he became speechless with fury. These heathen villagers died on purpose; they thought that would force him to give way. Well, they could just bury themselves; he certainly wasn't going to give them a helping hand into heaven! Delhomme calmly waited until the first paroxysm of fury was passed; then he spoke his own thoughts. After all you refused holy water only to dogs, and a dead man couldn't stay for ever in the family bosom; then he brought out his personal plea. The dead man was his father-in-law, the mayor's father-in-law. Come now, the funeral would take place at ten the next morning. No, no, no! the Abbé Godard chokingly protested, and the peasant had to go away without having made him change his mind, though he hoped that a night's sleep would set matters right.

'I tell you I won't come!' the priest shouted after him in a final refusal on the doorstep. 'You needn't ring the bells. No, a thousand times no!'

Next morning Bécu was ordered by the mayor to ring the bells at ten o'clock. They would see. In the Buteaus' house everything was ready. The corpse had been laid in the coffin the previous night under the practised eyes of La Grande; the room had already been washed down and no trace of the fire was left, except the body of the old man screwed down between his four planks. The bell was tolling when the family, which had gathered outside the house waiting for the coffin's removal, saw the Abbé Godard hurrying up the street past Macqueron's, panting from his run. He was so flushed with anger that he was swinging his three-cornered hat in one hand and walking bare-headed, as though afraid of having a fit. He looked at nobody but plunged straight into the church, promptly reappearing in his surplice with two children from the choir in front, one holding the cross and the other the holy water. He muttered some rapid words over the corpse, then, without bothering to ensure that the bearers were following him with the coffin, he turned back into the church and started the service at a furious pace. Clou with his trombone and the two choir-boys worked hard to keep up. The family sat in the front row—Buteau and Lise, Fanny and Delhomme, Jésus-Christ and La Grande. M. Charles honoured the funeral with his presence but brought excuses from

Mme Charles, who had left for Chartres two days before with Elodie and Nénesse. As for La Trouille, just as she was preparing to start off for the church, she had noticed that three of her geese were missing, and rushed off in search of them. Behind Lise sat the children, Laure and Jules, motionless, very well-behaved, keeping their arms crossed and their dark eyes wide open. The other benches were crowded with acquaintances, women for the most part, including La Frimat, La Bécu, Coelina, Flore, making up such a gathering as the family might well be proud of. Before the exordium, as the priest turned towards the congregation, he flung out his arms with a fiercely threatening gesture as though he was going to slap them all in the face. Bécu, completely drunk, went on tolling the bell all the while.

Altogether it was quite a respectable Mass, although it was rushed through too fast. Nobody was angry; in fact they were all smiling at the Abbé's fury, which was very understandable. It was quite natural that he should be upset by his defeat, just as that they should be pleased at the victory won by Rognes. A sly satisfaction glowed on all the faces because they had had the last word with God Almighty. They had forced the Abbé to bring back his God, whom they weren't really at all concerned about.

At the end of the Mass the sprinkler was passed from hand to hand and then the procession formed up again—the cross first, then the choir-boys and Clou and his trombone, then the priest puffing from his exertions, the coffin borne by four peasants, the family, and the general crowd at the tail. Bécu started ringing the bell again so furiously that the steeple crows flew out and squawked their distress. The procession went at once to the cemetery, which lay only a few paces away round the corner of the church. The singing and the music burst out more resonantly in the deep silence, under the misty sunshine which gave warmth to the shivering peace of rank weeds. Out there in the open air the coffin suddenly seemed so incredibly tiny that everybody was struck by it. Jean, still standing near, was quite startled. The poor old man, he had been so ravaged by age, so shrunken away by the misery of his life, that he fitted easily into what looked like a box of toys, a mere pretence of a coffin. He wouldn't take up much room or overburden the earth, the vast earth which had been his sole passion and which had sucked out the marrow of his bones. The corpse reached the edge of the gaping grave and Jean's eyes followed it and went beyond, over the wall, from one end of La Beauce to the other; and as he looked he saw the sowers in the ploughed fields, their ceaseless movement producing an infinite living wave of fertility, the seeds falling in a rain over the open furrows.

When the Buteaus caught sight of Jean, they glanced uneasily at one another. Had the blackguard come to wait for them there and to make a scandal? As long as they felt his presence in Rognes, they would never rest easy. The choir-boy who was holding the cross had just placed it at the foot of the grave, while the Abbé Godard was hurrying through the last prayers, standing before the coffin set on the grass. But the congregation found its attention distracted by noticing that Macqueron and Lengaigne, who arrived late, were staring towards the plain. They all turned to look and were surprised to see a column of smoke billowing into the sky. It seemed certainly to come from La Borderie; probably some ricks were burning behind the farm.

'*Ego sum. . .*' exclaimed the priest angrily.

The faces turned back to him and all the eyes fixed themselves once more on the body. But M. Charles continued conversing with Delhomme in a low voice. He had received a letter that morning from Mme Charles and was absolutely enchanted with the news. Elodie, from the minute she arrived in Chartres, had begun to show the most astonishing talents, the same energy and shrewdness as Nénesse. She had certainly taken in her father; she was now running the house. She had the right sort of gifts: a sharp eye and a ready hand. M. Charles went into raptures on his now-assured happiness in old age; he could go on living in peace at Roseblanche, where his roses and carnations had never bloomed more richly and where the birds in his aviary, fully recovered, were singing again with a sweetness that brought tears to his eyes.

'Amen!' the boy carrying the holy water ejaculated in a loud voice.

Then Abbé Godard immediately went on to the psalm, still in tones of fury.

'*De profundis clamavi ad te, Domine. . .*'

As he went on, Jésus-Christ took Fanny aside and started abusing the Buteaus again.

'If only I hadn't been so drunk the other day. We mustn't be such fools as to let ourselves be robbed like this.'

'If anyone's ever been robbed, we have,' agreed Fanny.

'The scoundrels have got the deed for sure,' he went on. 'They've been drawing the dividends for a long time; they came to an agreement with old Saucisse, I know that for certain. Good God, surely we'll take out an injunction against them?'

She started back and vigorously shook her head.

'No, no, I won't do that. I've got enough on my hands. You go ahead if you like.'

Jésus-Christ in his turn made a gesture of fear and resignation. As soon as he saw he couldn't push his sister to take action, he drew back; he didn't feel any too secure about his own past relations with the law.

'O no, not me, everyone thinks the worst about me. No matter, if a man's honest, at least he has the consolation of holding his head high.'

La Grande, who was listening, watched him draw himself up with an air of dignity and self-respect. She had always thought him a bit simple, for all he was such a scamp. She felt a deep regret that such a big chap didn't go and smash everything up at his brother's place and demand his share. Then, just to tease him and his sister Fanny, she repeated her usual promises without any preliminaries, as if she had just thought of them out of the blue.

'Ah, you may be sure that I shan't do wrong by anybody. My will is all in order and has been for a long time; everyone has a share, I wouldn't die easy if I thought I was showing any favouritism. Hyacinthe is in it, and you too, Fanny. I'm ninety now. The day will come, yes, it'll come.'

But she didn't believe a word of it. She had resolved she would never die, such was her obstinate determination to stick to her property. She would bury them all. And now here was one more, her brother, for her to watch going underground. All the paraphernalia, the carrying of the corpse, the open grave, the last ceremony, seemed to be something which concerned the neighbours and not herself. Tall and thin, with her stick tucked under her arm, she stood there among the tombs without the slightest emotion, merely intrigued at the fear of dying which seemed to affect these other people.

The priest was spluttering out the last verse of the psalm.

'*Et ipse redimet Israel ex omnibus iniquitatibus ejus.*'

He took the sprinkler out of the vessel, shook it over the coffin and raised his voice. '*Requiescat in pace.*'

'Amen!' came the response from the two choir-boys.

Then the coffin was let down into the grave. The gravedigger had attached the ropes and two men were able to handle the thin

423

coffin alone, for Fouan's corpse was as light as a child's. Then the movement began afresh, as the sprinkler passed from hand to hand again and every mourner shook it in a sign of the cross over the grave.

Jean had come near and found the sprinkler pushed into his hand by M. Charles. He stared down to the bottom of the grave. He was dazzled after looking out over the immense plain for so long, watching the sowers sowing the bread of the future from one end of the plain to the other till their shadows disappeared into the luminous mists of the horizon. However, he made out the coffin lying in the earth, looking still smaller than ever, with its narrow pinewood lid the golden colour of corn. Clods of rich earth were falling over it and half covering it so that he could only see one pale patch like a handful of the wheat which his comrades out on the plain were scattering into the furrows. He shook the sprinkler and handed it to Jésus-Christ.

'Your reverence! Your reverence!' Delhomme was calling discreetly.

He had to run after Abbé Godard who, at the last word of the service, had rushed off at a furious pace, forgetting all about his two choir-boys.

'What is it now?' asked the priest.

'I wanted to thank you for your kindness. And now I suppose we may ring the bell for Mass on Sunday at nine o'clock, mayn't we?'

The priest looked keenly at him without replying, and Delhomme hastened to add, 'We have a poor sick woman here, she's quite alone and she hasn't a penny. You know her, Rosalie, the chair-mender. I've sent her some soup, but I can't do everything.'

Abbé Godard's face softened and a sweet emotion of charity swept away his violent anger. He searched his pockets in despair, finding only seven sous.

'Lend me five francs, I'll repay you on Sunday. Until Sunday then.'

Off he went in a fresh burst of haste. Without a shadow of doubt the good God would send all the damned souls of Rognes to hell in spite of the fact that he was being forced once more to come and preach His word amongst them; but what of it? It was no reason for letting them suffer too greatly in this life on earth.

When Delhomme returned to the others, he fell into the midst of a raging quarrel. At first the congregation had been content to

424

watch the shovelfuls of earth which the gravedigger was throwing over the coffin. But, as chance had put Macqueron shoulder to shoulder with Lengaigne at the edge of the hole, the latter began to abuse the former roundly on the question of the burial plots. The family, who were preparing to leave, stayed behind and became fascinated with the struggle, which was accompanied by the low, regular thuds of the falling clods of earth.

'You had no right!' shouted Lengaigne. 'Even though you were the mayor, you should have taken your turn; it was just to annoy me that you pushed yourself next to my father. But, by God, you're not there yet.'

'Leave me in peace!' retorted Macqueron. 'I've paid for it and it's mine. I'll be buried there and no dirty swine like you will stop me.'

They had been pushing one another; and now each man stood before his own plot, the few feet of earth in which he would finally rest.

'But look here, you dirty coward, doesn't it make you sick to think that we'll be lying there, neighbours in death, as if we were a couple of bosom friends? It makes my blood boil. After hating each other all our lives, d'you think we'll make peace down there and lie quiet side by side? Never, no, never! I'll never shake your hand.'

'What the hell do I care? You're too much on top of me now, for me to worry about where you'll be when you rot.'

This disdainful reply brought out all Lengaigne's hatred. He stuttered that if he survived he'd dig up Macqueron's bones one dark night. His adversary sneered that he'd like to see him try, and then the women joined in. Coelina, lean and dark, argued wildly against her husband.

'You're all wrong, I've told you before, you haven't got any feelings when it comes to such a matter. If you stick to that plot, you'll stay there all alone in your hole. I'll go somewhere else. I don't mean to be infected by this filthy drab here.'

She jerked her chin towards Flore, who for all her softness whined back in resolute retort.

'Don't be so sure which one'd infect the other. Don't get so worked-up, my dear. I've got no wish to have your carcass passing its disease over to mine.'

La Bécu and La Frimat had to intervene and separate them.

'Now, now,' urged the former, 'you've both agreed that you're not to be laid together. Everybody's free to choose his or her own company.'

La Frimat nodded approval.

'Of course, it's only right. My own old man who's dying, well, I'd rather keep him in the house than let him be put near old Couillot—they used to quarrel such a lot years ago.'

Tears flooded into her eyes at the thought that her paralytic husband would probably not last out the week. When trying to get him into bed the previous night, she had fallen over with him; and if he died she would certainly not be long following him.

But suddenly Lengaigne started attacking Delhomme, who had just come back.

'I say, you, you're supposed to be a just man, you'll have to make him give up that plot of ground and send him back to wait in the queue, like other people.'

Macqueron shrugged his shoulders and Delhomme confirmed that as he had paid for the ground it definitely belonged to him. Nothing could be done about it, and that was that. Then Buteau, who had been trying to restrain himself, burst out. The bereaved family had been trying to behave fairly circumspectly while the clods of earth were falling with heavy thuds on the old man's coffin; but his anger proved too strong for him. He shouted out to Lengaigne as he pointed at Delhomme.

'Damn it, if you're counting on that fellow for any feeling of decency, don't expect much. He buried his father at a thief's side.'

An uproar began and the whole family joined in. Fanny supported her husband, saying that the real mistake was made when they buried their mother Rose; they should have then bought the next plot for the old man. Jésus-Christ and La Grande fell upon Delhomme, expressing much disgust at Old Fouan's nearness to Saucisse. It was inhuman and quite inexcusable. M. Charles was of the same opinion, but in more moderate tones.

They finished up with everybody shouting at once; but Buteau dominated the tumult as he yelled, 'Yes, their very bones will turn over under the earth and fight!'

Now relatives, friends and acquaintances all joined in. That was just it; he had hit the nail on the head: their bones would turn over in the earth. The Fouans would still pursue each other after death; Lengaigne and Macqueron would bicker until they rotted; the women, Coelina, Flore, La Bécu would scream and scratch each other. You could not rest in company, even under the ground,

426

when you hated one another. In the ancient cemetery, bathed in sunlight, from coffin to coffin under the tranquil wild flowers, there went on a furious battle between the dead, with no quarter given— the same battle that was now being fought out by the living as they stood among the tombs.

But a cry from Jean separated the brawlers and made all the heads turn.

'La Borderie is on fire!'

Doubt was no longer possible. Flames were leaping up through the rooftops, quivering whitishly in the full light of day. A huge cloud of smoke was slowly floating away to the north. And just then La Trouille came rushing and galloping from the direction of the farm. While searching for her geese, she had noticed the first sparks and had thoroughly enjoyed the spectacle until the idea of telling all about it to the others had sent her running off. She jumped astride the low wall and shouted in her sharp childish voice, 'Oh, look how it's burning! It was started by that big scoundrel Tron. He came back to do it. It's in three places, the barn, the stable and the kitchen. They nabbed him as he was setting the straw alight, and the wagoners half killed him. The horses and cows and the sheep are all roasting. Oh, you should hear them screeching out. You never heard such a row.'

Her green eyes glittered and she burst out laughing.

'And then there's La Cognette. You see, she's been ill since the master died. So they forgot she was in bed. She was almost singed, she only had time to rush out in her shift. Oh, she looked such a funny sight skipping about with her shanks all bare. She hopped about and showed herself back and front till everybody shouted "Gee up! Gee up!" to keep her going, because they don't like her much. There was an old man who said, "There she goes with only a shift on her back, just like she came!".'

A new burst of laughter doubled her up.

'Come over and see, it's such a funny sight. I'm going back.'

She jumped down and rushed madly off towards the flaming farm.

M. Charles, Delhomme, Macqueron and nearly all the other peasants followed her; while the women, with La Grande at the head, also left the cemetery and walked up to the road to get a better view. Buteau and Lise stayed behind, and Lise stopped Lengaigne to question him about Jean, quite casually of course. Had he found a job as he was lodging in the neighbourhood? When the

427

tavern keeper replied that he was going away to join the army again, Lise and Buteau, feeling hugely relieved, broke into the same exclamation.

'Well, what a fool!'

Their troubles were over and they could begin to live merrily again. They gave a last glance at Fouan's grave, which the sexton had now almost filled up. The two children lingered to watch, but their mother called them over.

'Come along, you two! Be good, now, and do as you're told, or that man will come and bury you underground too.'

The Buteaus then went off, pushing the children before them. The two infants, who knew everything, walked along very sensibly with their big dark eyes quite expressionless.

Only Jean and Jésus-Christ remained in the cemetery. The latter disdained the spectacle and was quite content to watch it from a distance. He stood motionless between two tombstones, his eyes vacantly dreaming, while his drunken saintly face expressed the profound melancholy that lies at the end of all philosophy. Perhaps he was thinking how all existence goes up in smoke. And as all serious thinking always affected him strongly, he unconsciously lifted his leg as he stood there in a trance. He let off a blast, then a second, then a third.

'Good God,' exclaimed Bécu as he drunkenly crossed the cemetery on his way to have a look at the fire.

A fourth explosion blew out at him as he passed, and he nearly felt the vibration on his face. As he moved on, he shouted to his old pal, 'If that wind continues, there'll be a fall of dung.'

Jésus-Christ quickly felt at himself.

'I say, you're right. I want to shit.'

Off he hurried around the wall, waddling with his legs stiffly apart.

Jean was left alone. Away in the distance only great reddish clouds of smoke were rising from the ruins of La Borderie, whirling about and throwing cloud-shadows across the ploughed fields and the scattered sowers. His eyes travelled slowly back to the ground at his feet, and he stared at the fresh mounds of earth under which Françoise and Old Fouan now rested. His anger of the morning his revulsion against men and things, was dissipated, and he felt a profound peace. In spite of himself a sense of gentleness and hope flooded into his heart, perhaps because of the warm sunshine.

His master Hourdequin had made a lot of trouble for him-

428

self with new inventions and hadn't had much to gain from his machines, his fertilisers and all the other scientific things which were still so inefficiently applied. Then La Cognette had arrived to finish him off; he too was sleeping in this cemetery; and nothing remained of the farm—the wind was carrying even the ashes away. But what did it matter? Buildings might be burned down, you couldn't burn the earth. The earth, the sustainer, would always remain, and she would go on nourishing those who sowed seed in her. She contained space and time; she would always give corn and was content to wait until men knew how to make her yield even more.

It was just the same with the prophecies of revolution, the political upheavals which were foretold. The soil, they said, would pass into other hands; the harvests of foreign lands would come in and swamp our own; there would be nothing but brambles in our fields. Well, what of it? Have we the power to destroy the earth? Whatever happens, she'll belong to someone, and that someone will be forced to cultivate her so as not to die of hunger. If weeds grow over her for years, she'll be rested, she'll regain her youth and her fertility. The earth takes no part in our maddened insect-struggles; she is the eternal worker, ceaselessly toiling and taking no more notice of us than of a nest of ants.

There was grief too, and blood, and tears, all the things which make men suffer and rebel. Françoise was killed, Fouan killed, the wicked triumphant, the bloodthirsty stinking vermin of the villages polluting and preying upon the earth. But who can tell? Just as the frost that sears the crops, the hail that slashes them to shreds, the lightning that smashes them down, are all, maybe, necessary things, so it might be that blood and tears were needed to make the world move on. What does our happiness count in the great system of the stars and the sun? God cares precious little about us! We only gain our bread through a terrible struggle renewed day after day. Only the earth remains immortal, our mother from whom we come and to whom we return, the earth that we love enough to do murder for her. She uses even our crimes and our miseries to make life and more life for her hidden ends.

For a long time this confused daydream whirled cloudily through his brain. But a trumpet sounded in the distance, the trumpet announcing the arrival of the Bazoches fire-engine galloping up too late. When he heard it, he suddenly straightened himself. It seemed like war passing amid clouds of smoke, with its horses and cannons and bloodthirsty cries. His heart beat loudly. Well, as he no longer had the heart to till the soil of France, he'd defend it in battle!

He turned to go, but looked for one last time at the two bare earth-mounds of the graves, and then beyond them to the endless plough-lands of La Beauce, filled with the unceasing gesture of sowing. Death and the sowing of seeds: and the life of bread growing up out of the earth.